HOW IT ALL ENDS

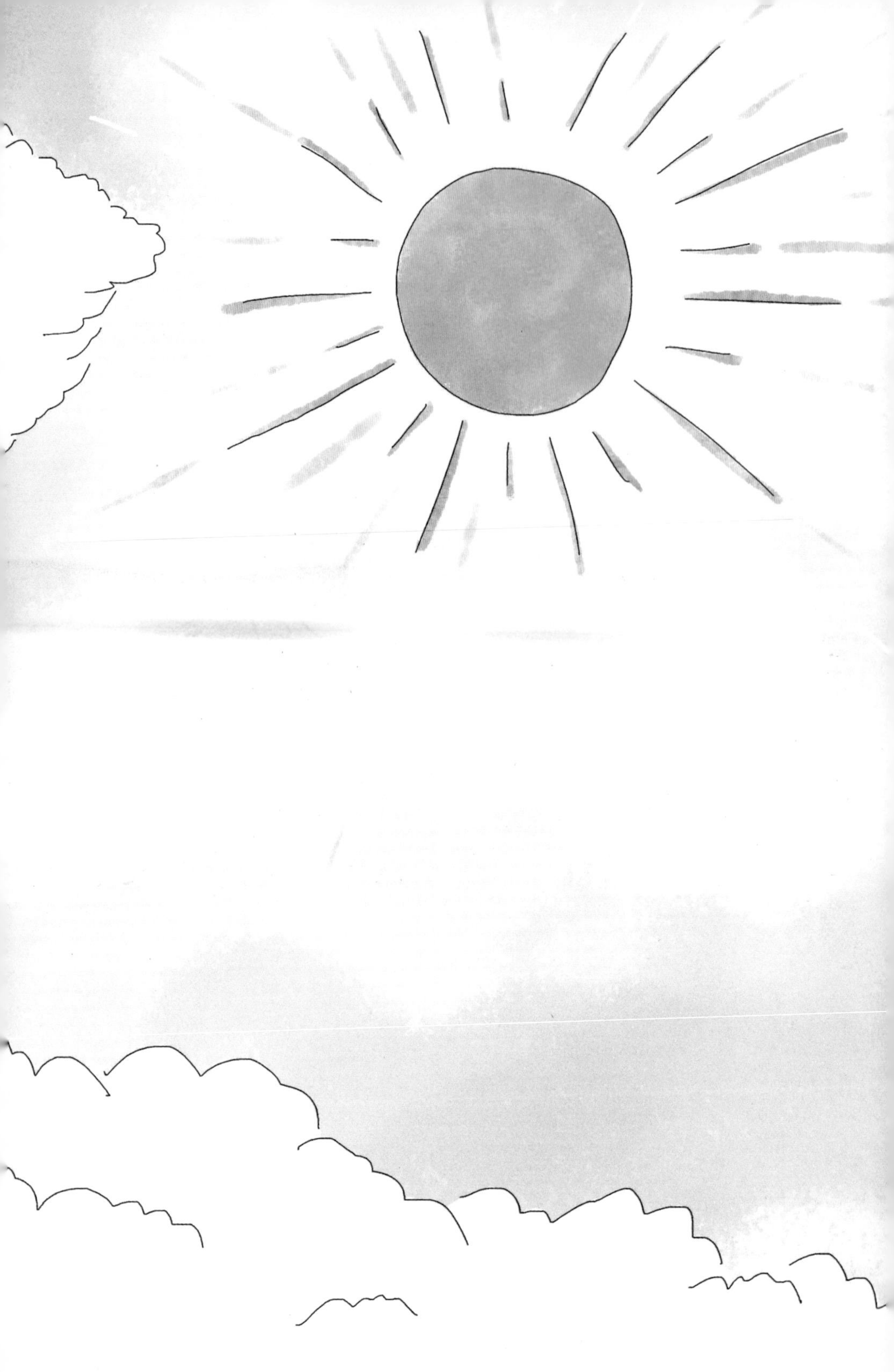

HOW IT ALL ENDS

EMMA HUNSINGER

GREENWILLOW BOOKS
Imprints of HarperCollinsPublishers

Manufactured in Malaysia. For information address HarperCollins Children's Books, a division of HarperCollins Publishers, 195 Broadway, New York, NY 10007.
www.harperalley.com

The text of this book is set in 12-point Emma Hunsinger. Colors by Tillie Walden. Book design by Paul Zakris.

Library of Congress Cataloging-in-Publication Data

Names: Hunsinger, Emma, author, illustrator.
Title: How it all ends / Emma Hunsinger.
Description: First edition. | New York, NY : Greenwillow Books, an Imprint of HarperCollins Publishers, 2024. |
Audience: Ages 8 up |
Summary: "Thirteen-year-old Tara skips eighth grade to go directly to high school
and struggles with adjusting, until she meets her classmate Libby"—Provided by publisher.
Identifiers: LCCN 2023053521 (print) | LCCN 2023053522 (ebook) |
ISBN 9780063158153 (hardcover) | ISBN 9780063158146 (paperback) |
ISBN 9780063158160 (ebook)
Subjects: CYAC: Graphic novels. | Schools—Fiction. | Adjustment—Fiction. | Friendship—Fiction. | LCGFT: Graphic novels.
Classification: LCC PZ7.1.H86326 Ho 2024 (print) |
LCC PZ7.1.H86326 (ebook) | DDC 741.5/973—dc23/eng/20231220
LC record available at https://lccn.loc.gov/2023053521
LC ebook record available at https://lccn.loc.gov/2023053522

24 25 26 27 28 COS 10 9 8 7 6 5 4 3 2 1
First Edition

GREENWILLOW BOOKS
Imprints of HarperCollins*Publishers*

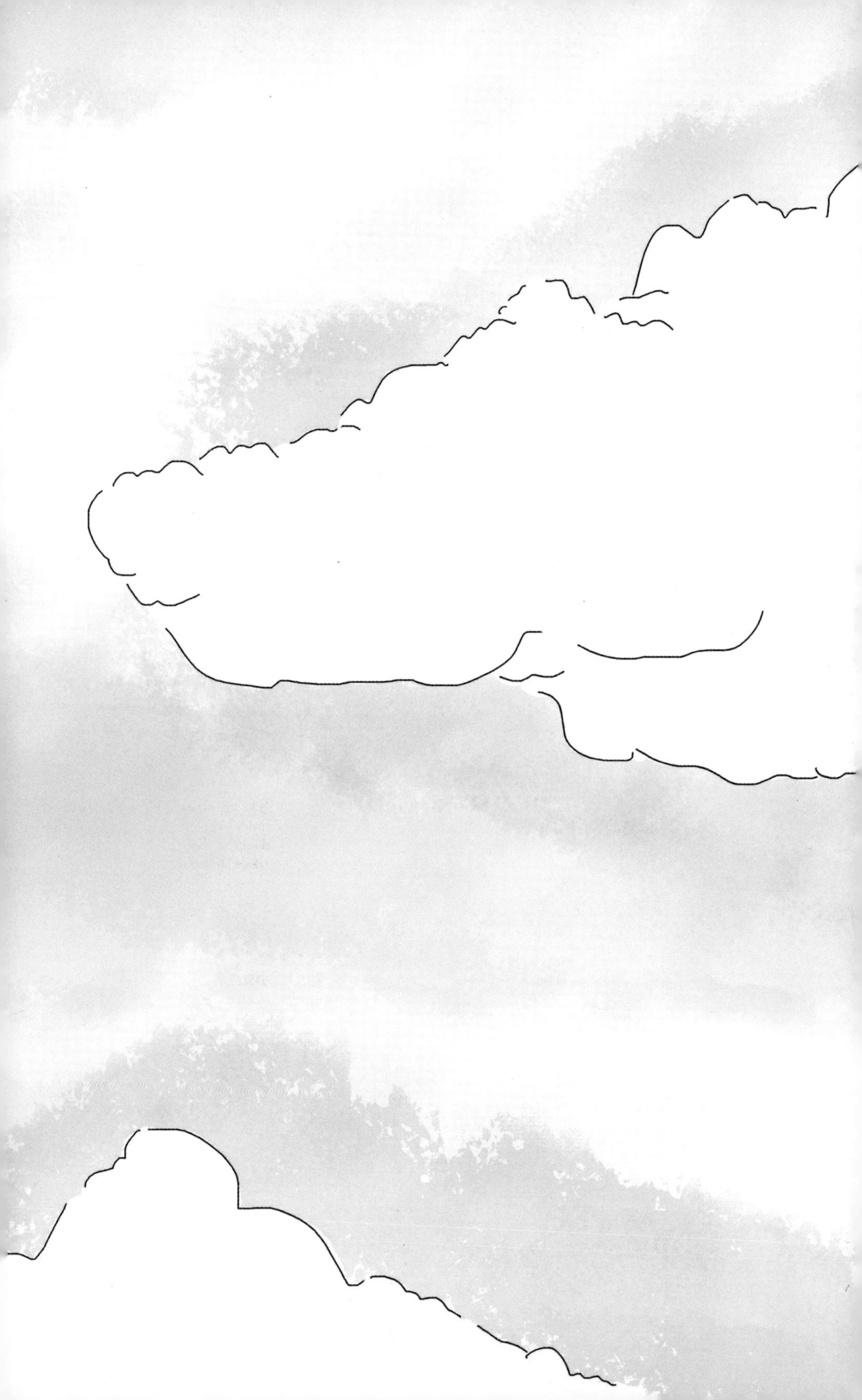

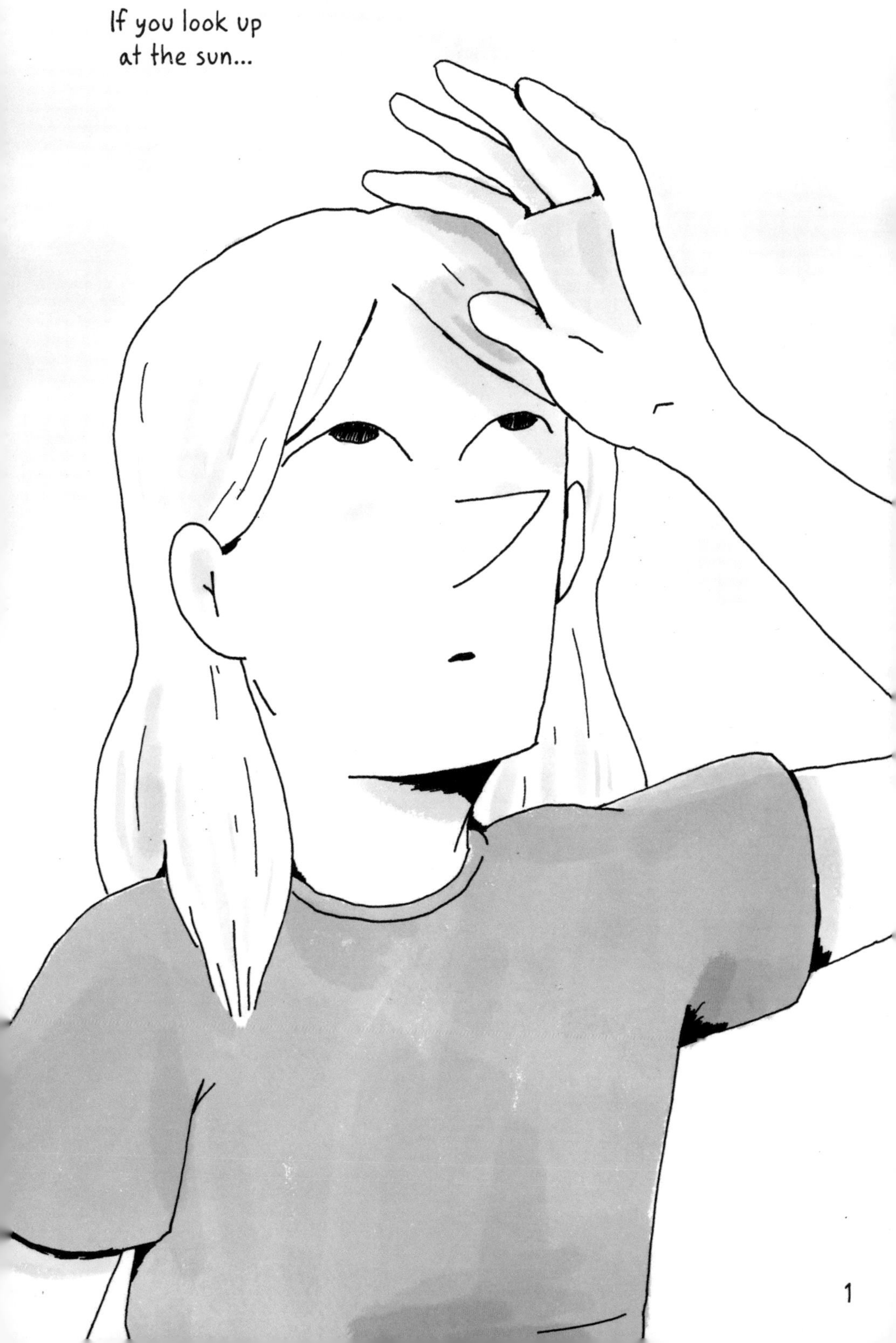
If you look up
at the sun...

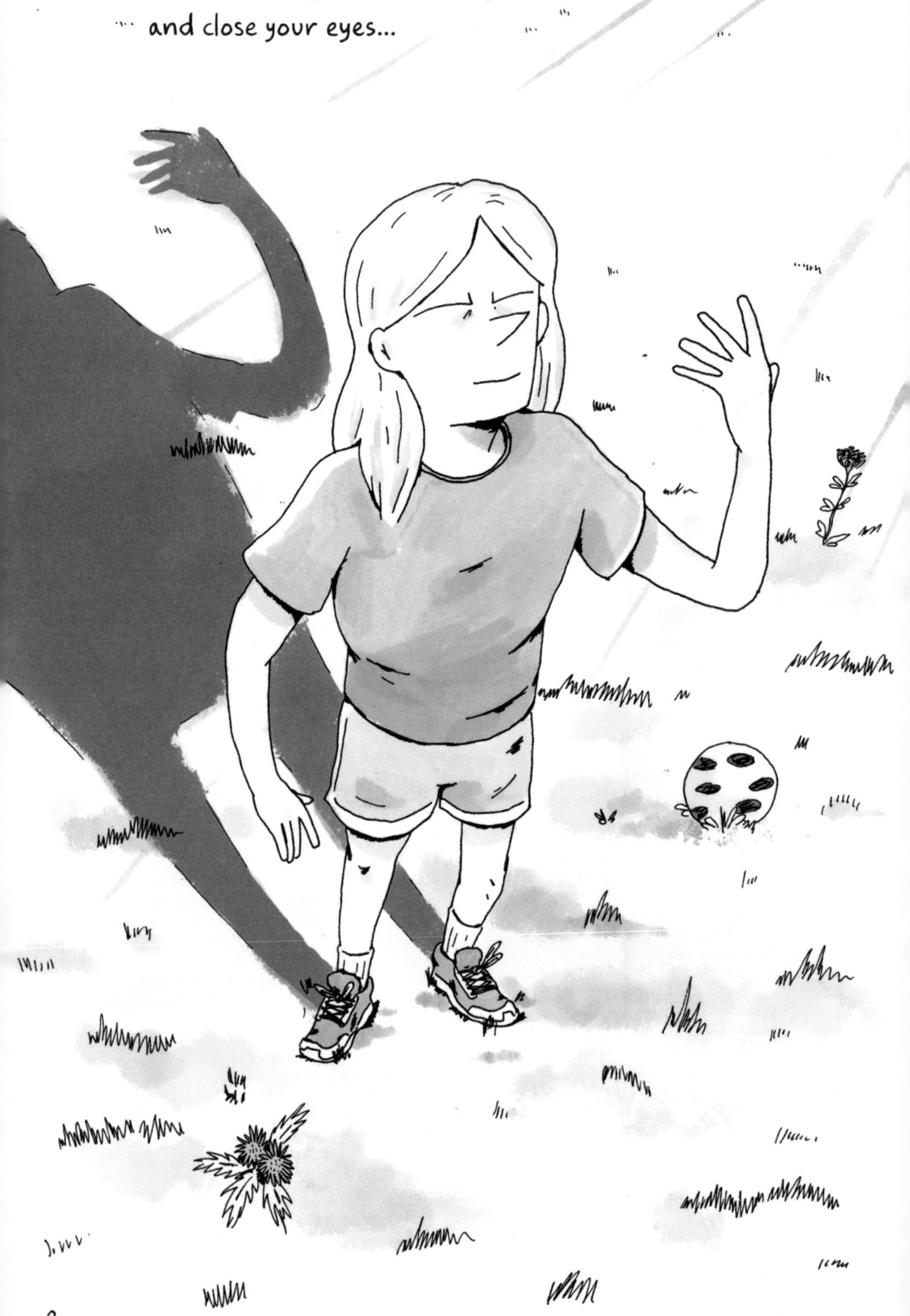
... and close your eyes...

you see the color red.

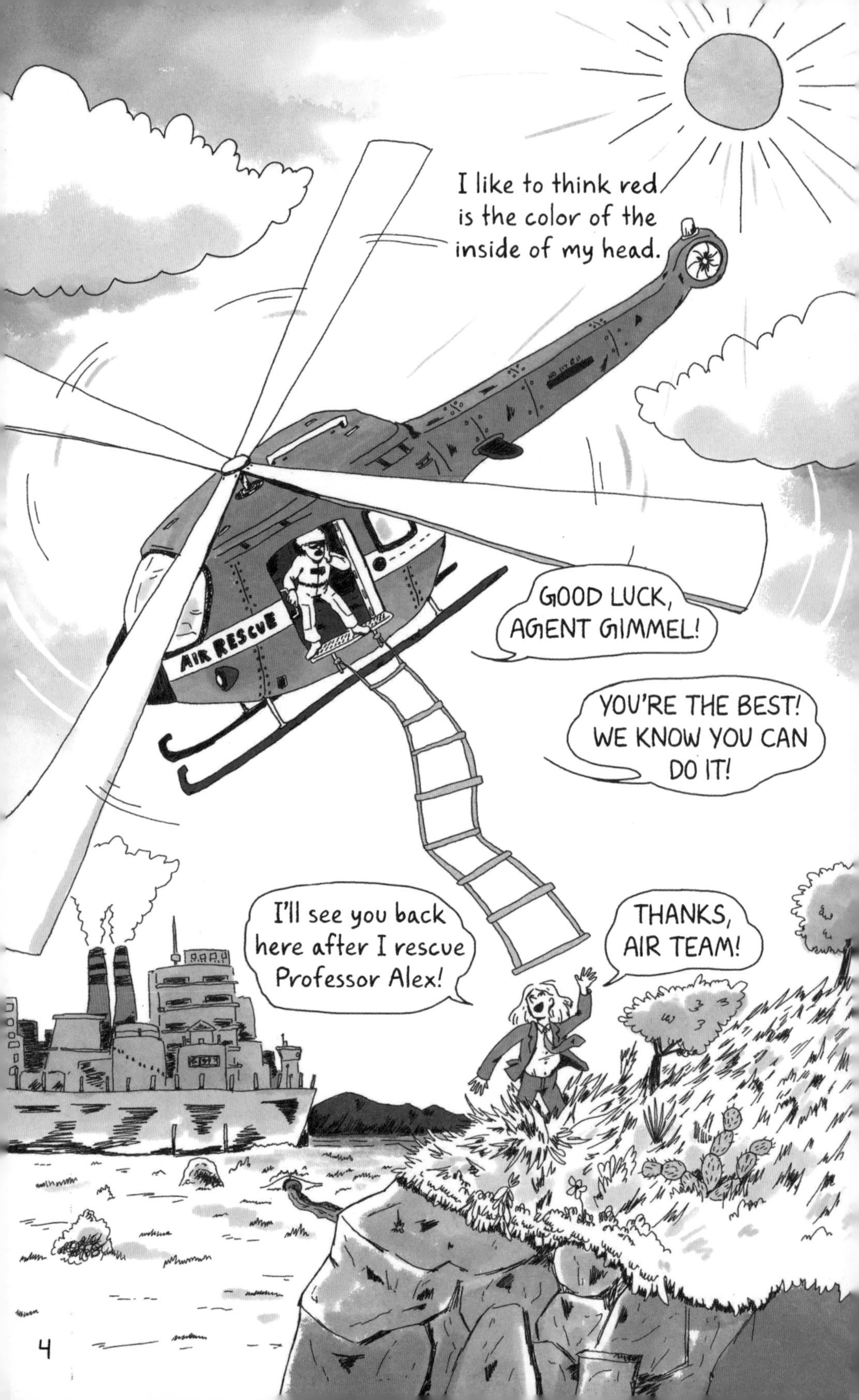
I like to think red is the color of the inside of my head.
AIR RESCUE
GOOD LUCK, AGENT GIMMEL!
YOU'RE THE BEST! WE KNOW YOU CAN DO IT!
I'll see you back here after I rescue Professor Alex!
THANKS, AIR TEAM!

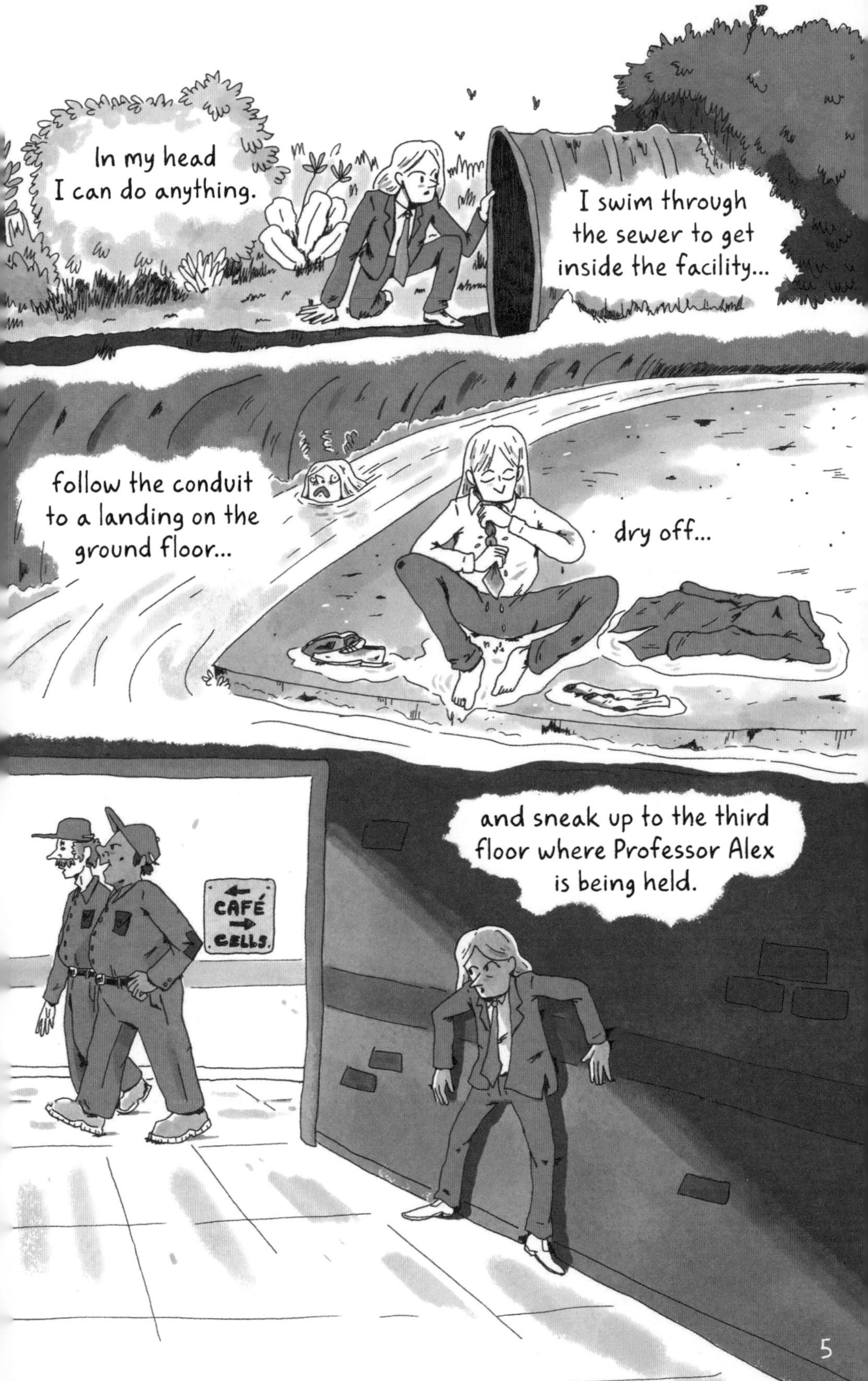
In my head I can do anything.
I swim through the sewer to get inside the facility...
follow the conduit to a landing on the ground floor...
dry off...
CAFÉ
CELLS
and sneak up to the third floor where Professor Alex is being held.

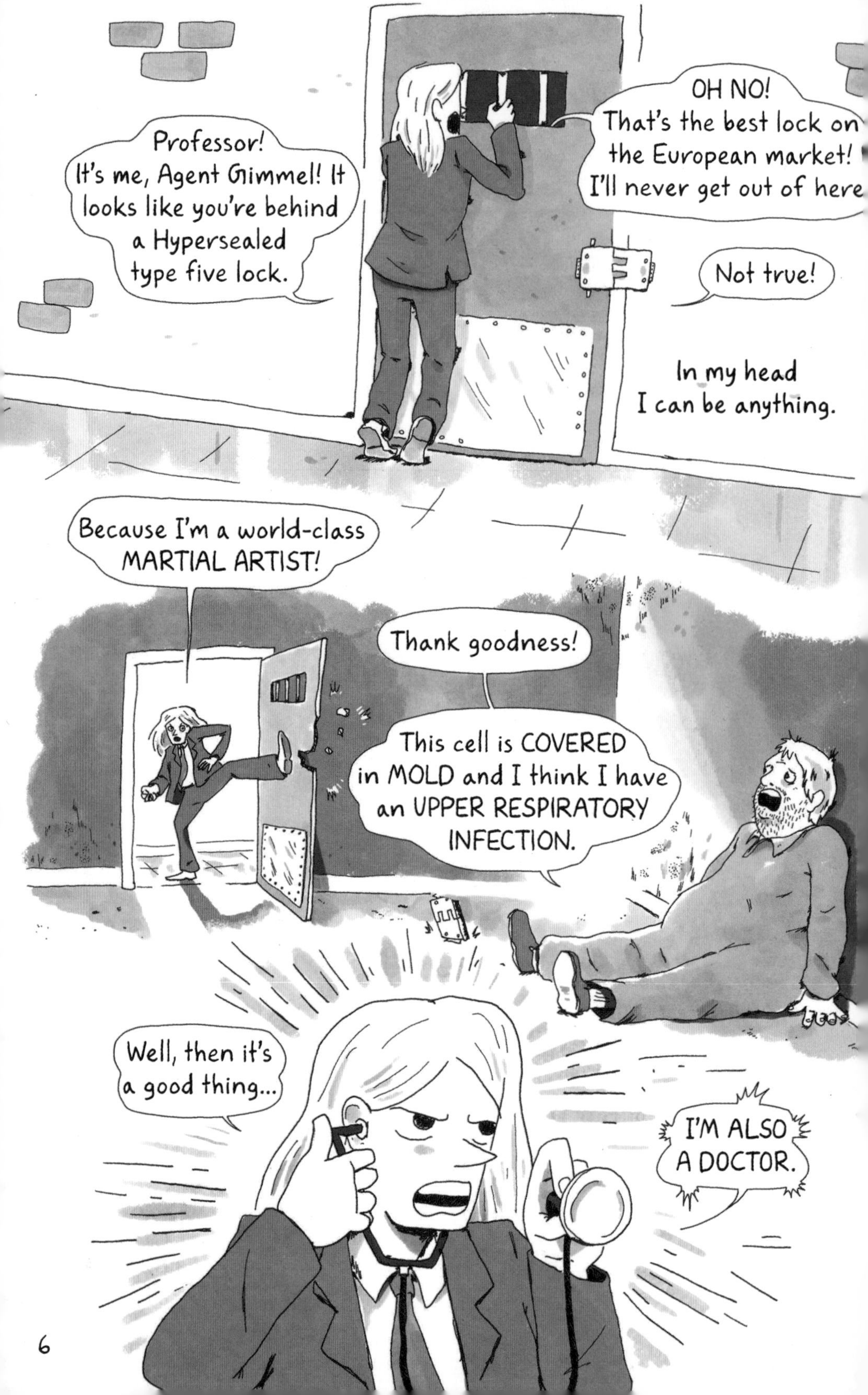

Professor! It's me, Agent Gimmel! It looks like you're behind a Hypersealed type five lock.
OH NO! That's the best lock on the European market! I'll never get out of here
Not true!
In my head I can be anything.
Because I'm a world-class MARTIAL ARTIST!
Thank goodness!
This cell is COVERED in MOLD and I think I have an UPPER RESPIRATORY INFECTION.
Well, then it's a good thing...
I'M ALSO A DOCTOR.

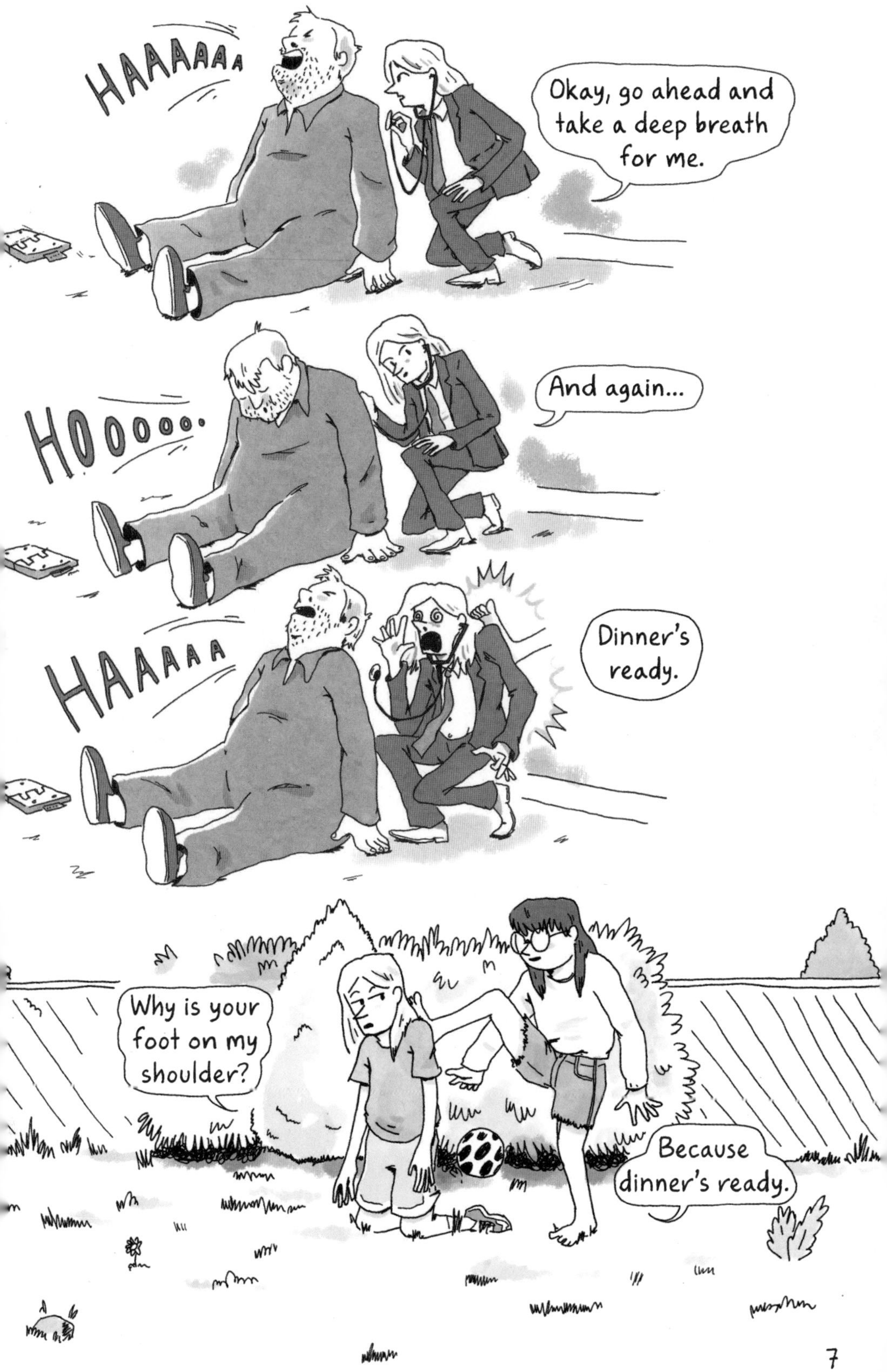
HAAAAAA
Okay, go ahead and take a deep breath for me.
HOOOOO.
And again...
HAAAAA
Dinner's ready.
Why is your foot on my shoulder?
Because dinner's ready.

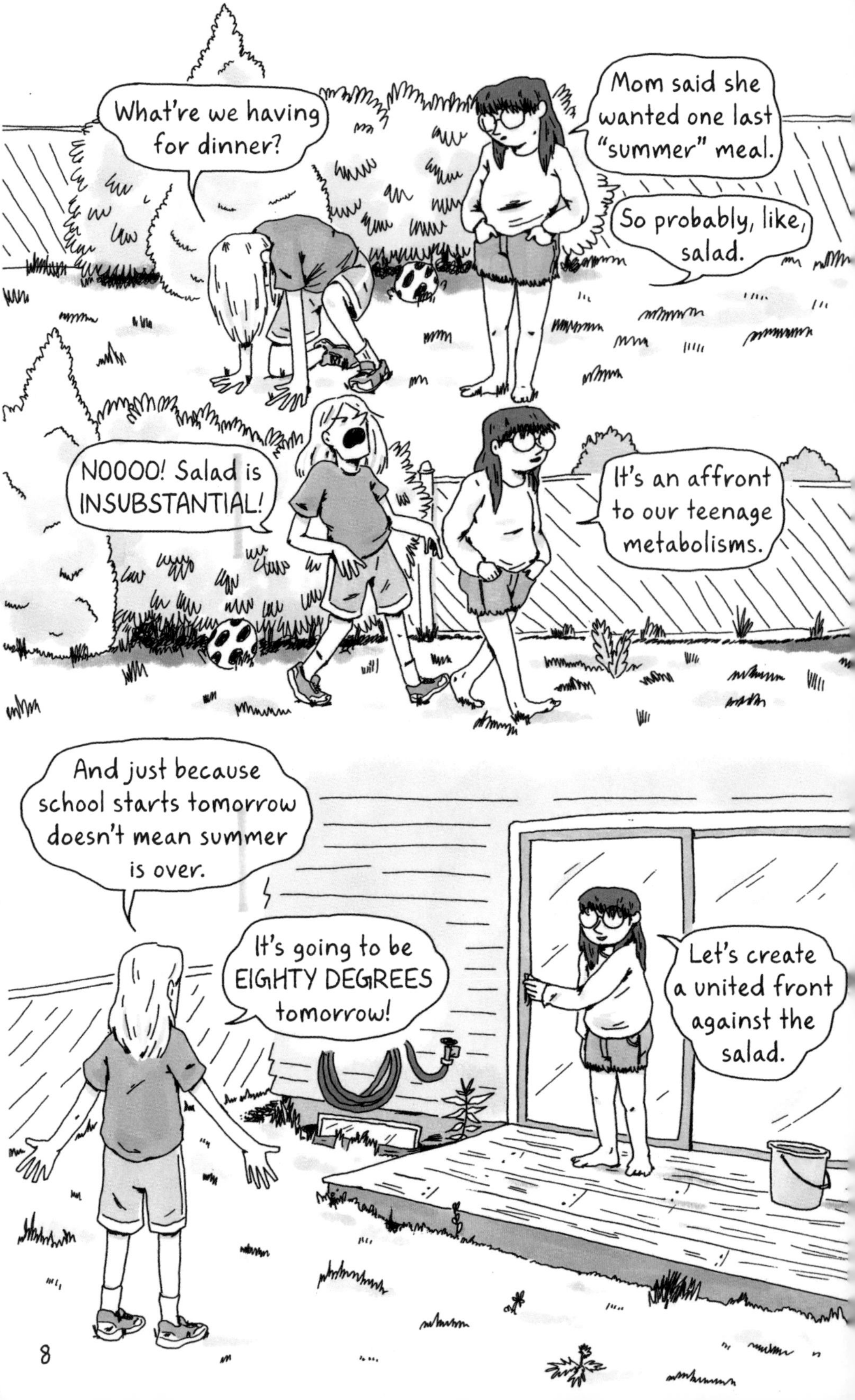
What're we having for dinner?
Mom said she wanted one last "summer" meal.
So probably, like, salad.
NOOOO! Salad is INSUBSTANTIAL!
It's an affront to our teenage metabolisms.
And just because school starts tomorrow doesn't mean summer is over.
It's going to be EIGHTY DEGREES tomorrow!
Let's create a united front against the salad.

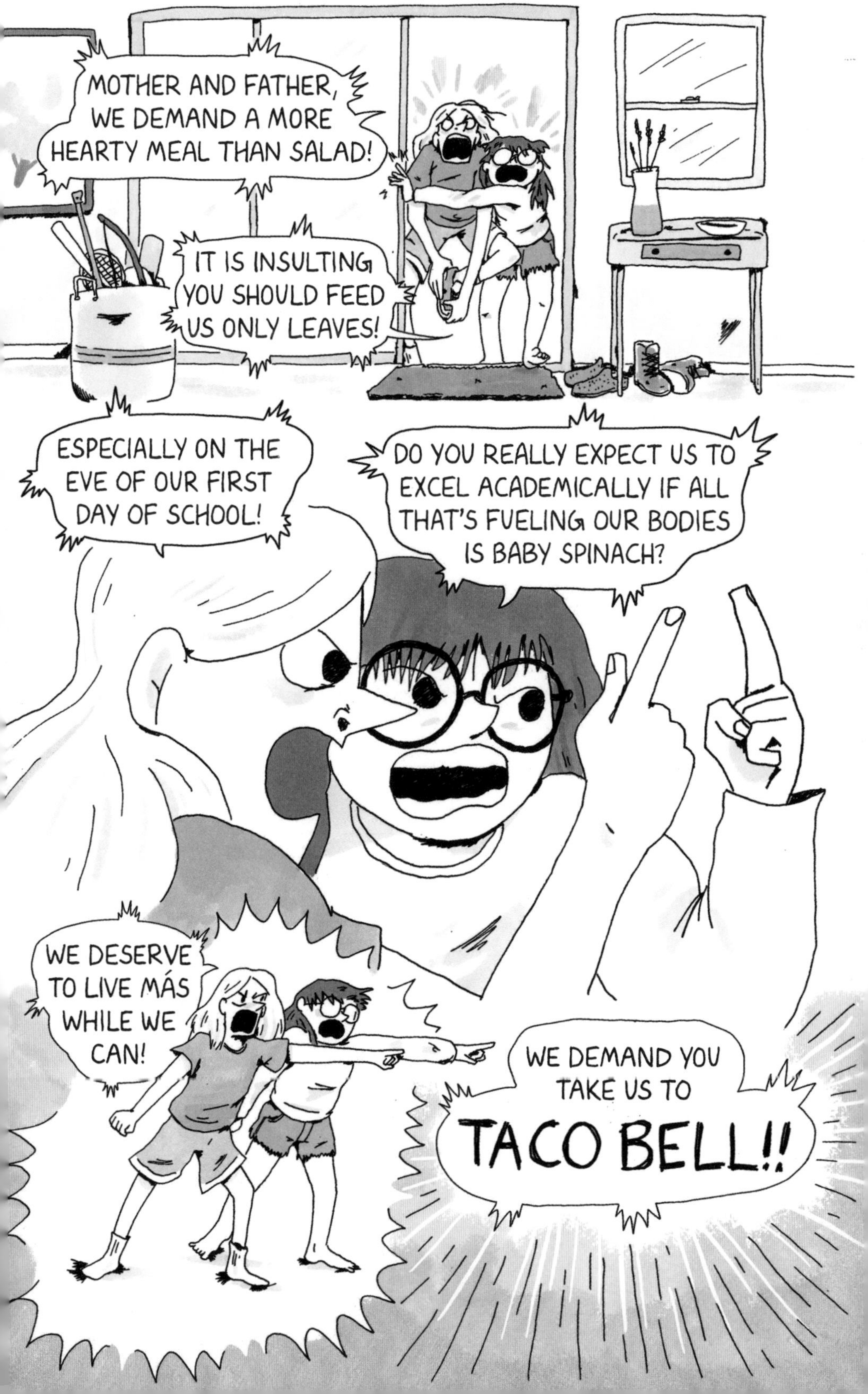

MOTHER AND FATHER, WE DEMAND A MORE HEARTY MEAL THAN SALAD!
IT IS INSULTING YOU SHOULD FEED US ONLY LEAVES!
ESPECIALLY ON THE EVE OF OUR FIRST DAY OF SCHOOL!
DO YOU REALLY EXPECT US TO EXCEL ACADEMICALLY IF ALL THAT'S FUELING OUR BODIES IS BABY SPINACH?
WE DESERVE TO LIVE MÁS WHILE WE CAN!
WE DEMAND YOU TAKE US TO TACO BELL!!

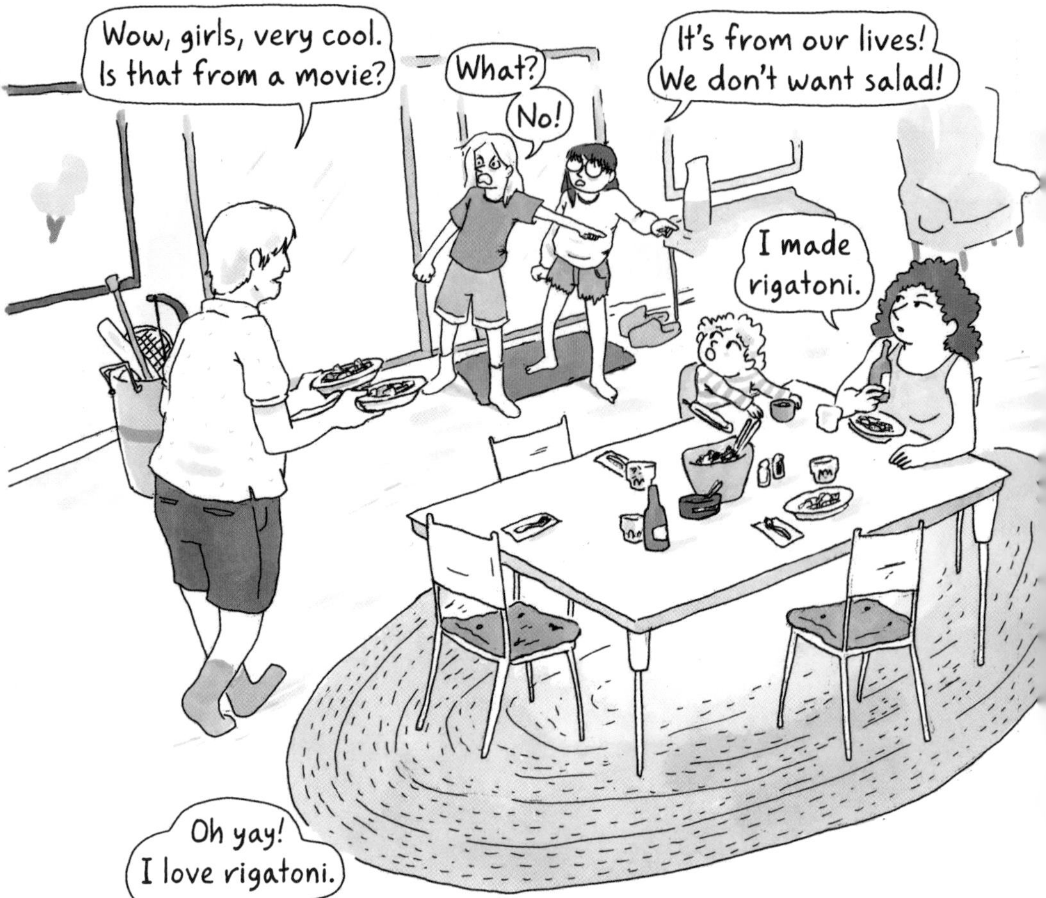
Wow, girls, very cool. Is that from a movie?
What?
No!
It's from our lives! We don't want salad!
I made rigatoni.

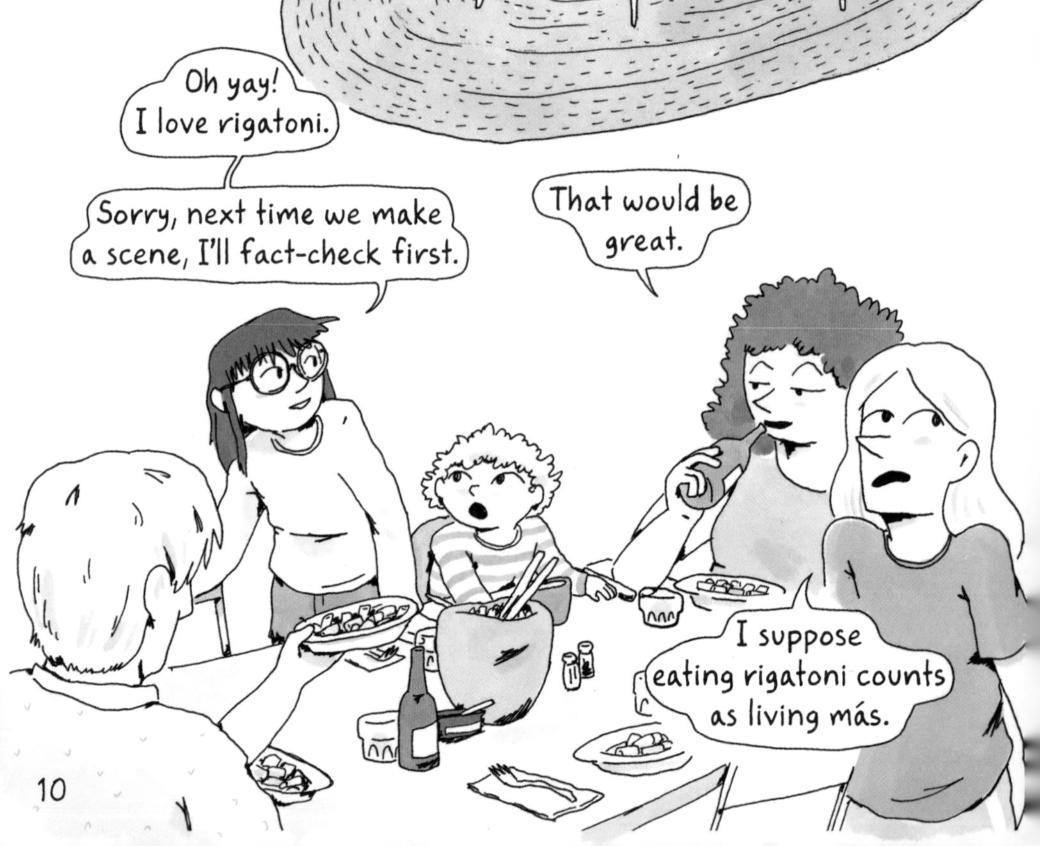
Oh yay! I love rigatoni.
Sorry, next time we make a scene, I'll fact-check first.
That would be great.
I suppose eating rigatoni counts as living más.

This is my family:

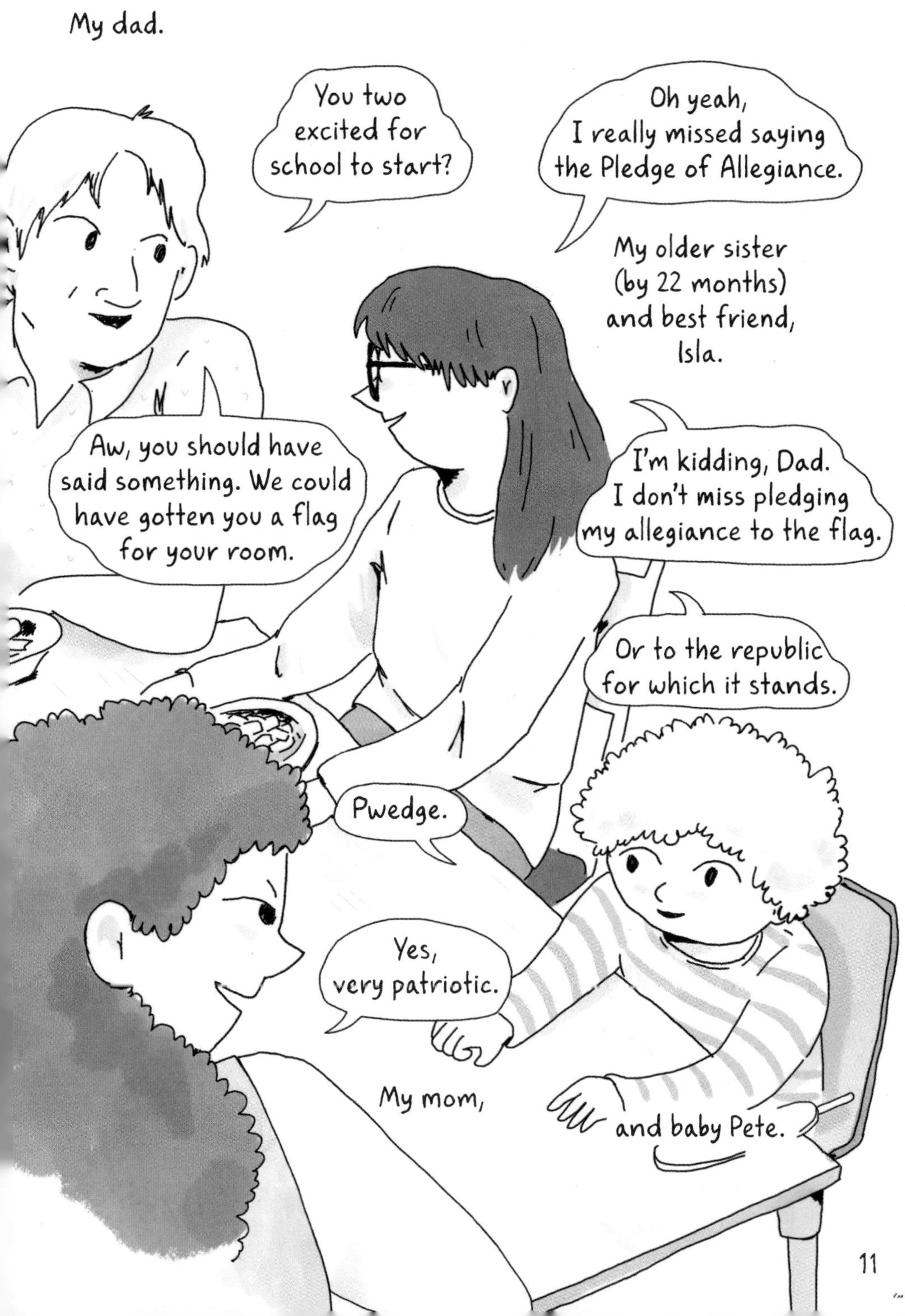
My dad.
You two excited for school to start?
Oh yeah, I really missed saying the Pledge of Allegiance.
My older sister (by 22 months) and best friend, Isla.
Aw, you should have said something. We could have gotten you a flag for your room.
I'm kidding, Dad. I don't miss pledging my allegiance to the flag.
Or to the republic for which it stands.
Pwedge.
Yes, very patriotic.
My mom,
and baby Pete.

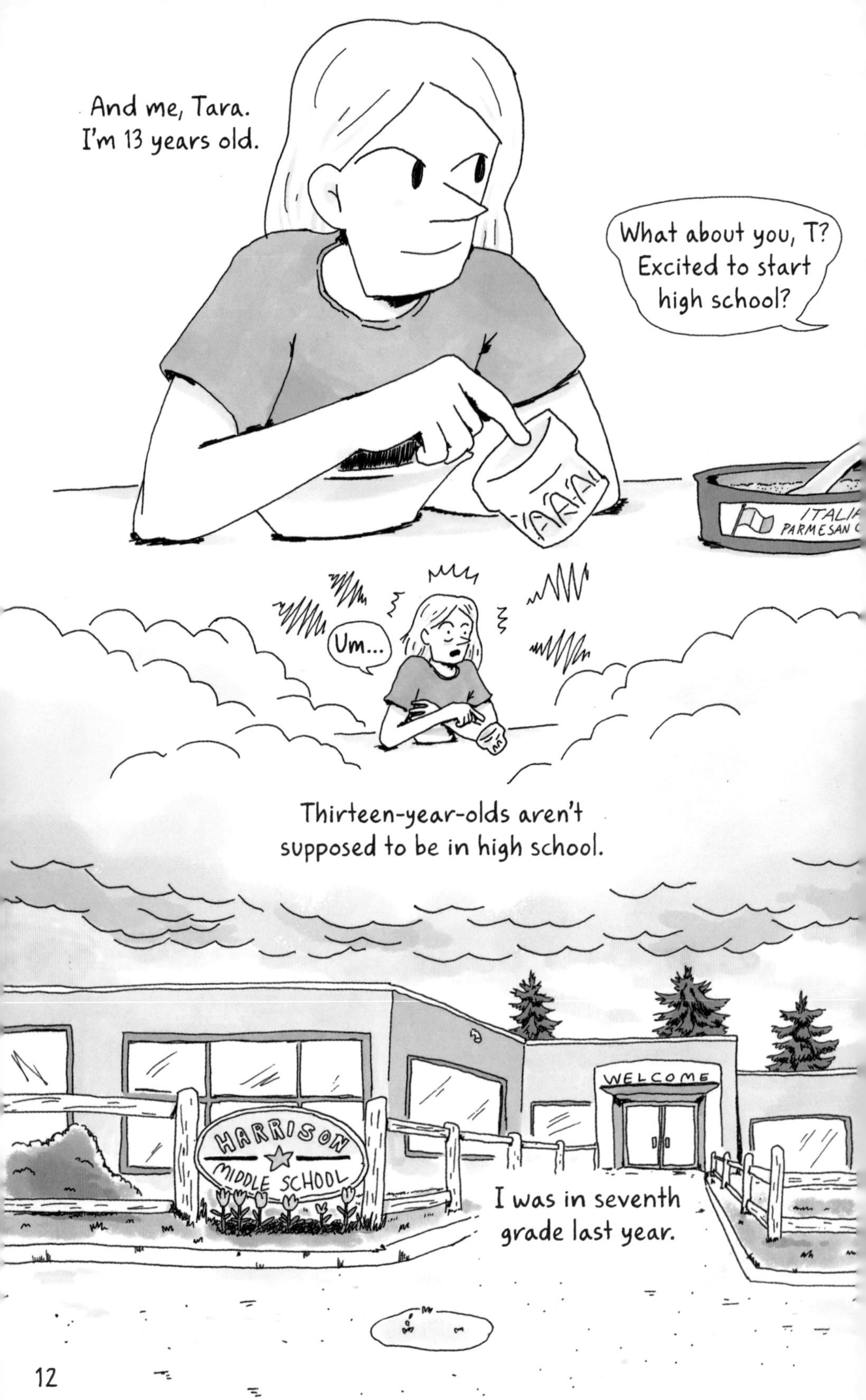
And me, Tara.
I'm 13 years old.
What about you, T? Excited to start high school?
Um...
Thirteen-year-olds aren't supposed to be in high school.
HARRISON MIDDLE SCHOOL
WELCOME
I was in seventh grade last year.

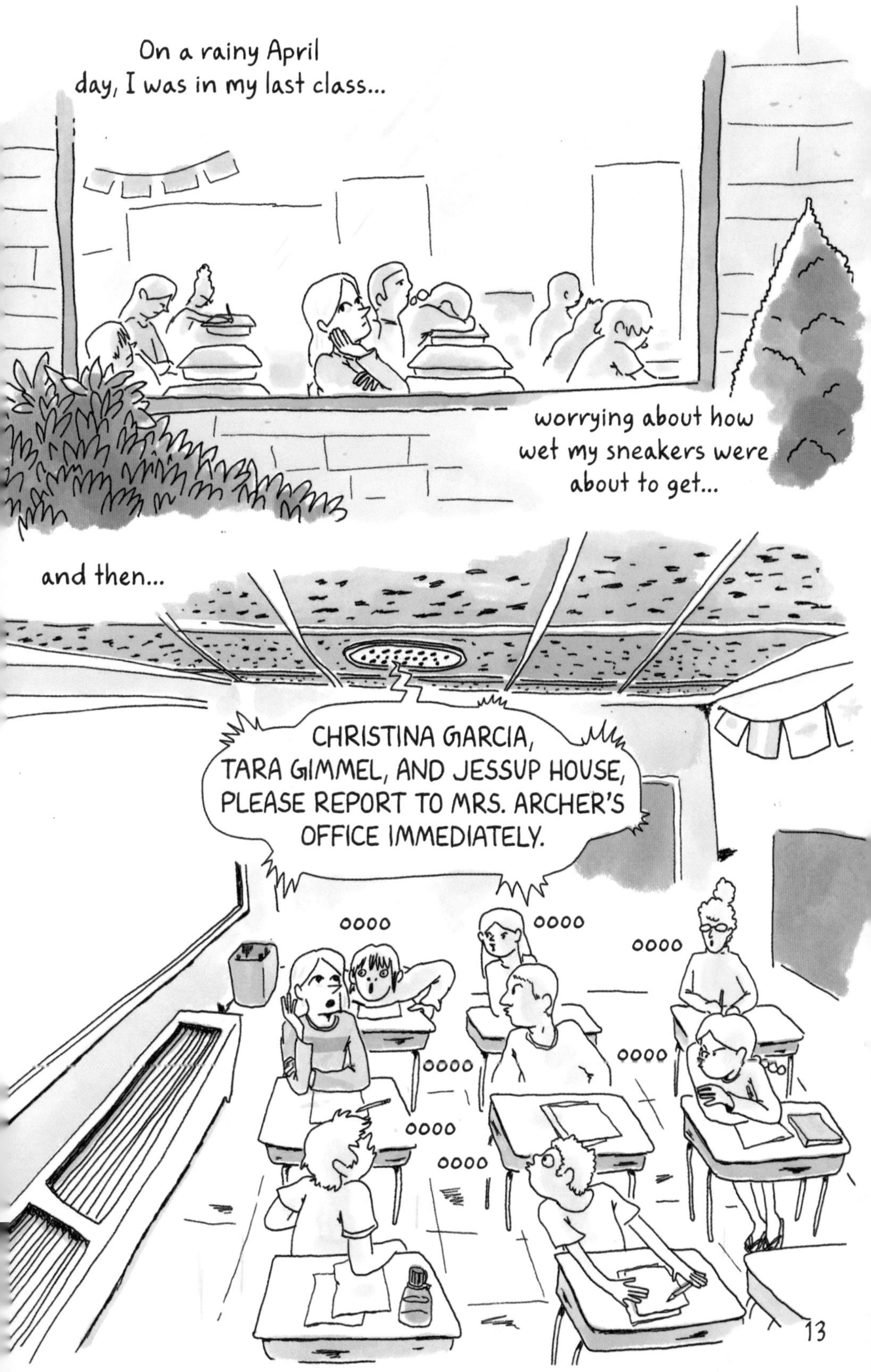
On a rainy April day, I was in my last class...
worrying about how wet my sneakers were about to get...
and then...
CHRISTINA GARCIA, TARA GIMMEL, AND JESSUP HOUSE, PLEASE REPORT TO MRS. ARCHER'S OFFICE IMMEDIATELY.
oooo
oooo
oooo
oooo
oooo
oooo
oooo

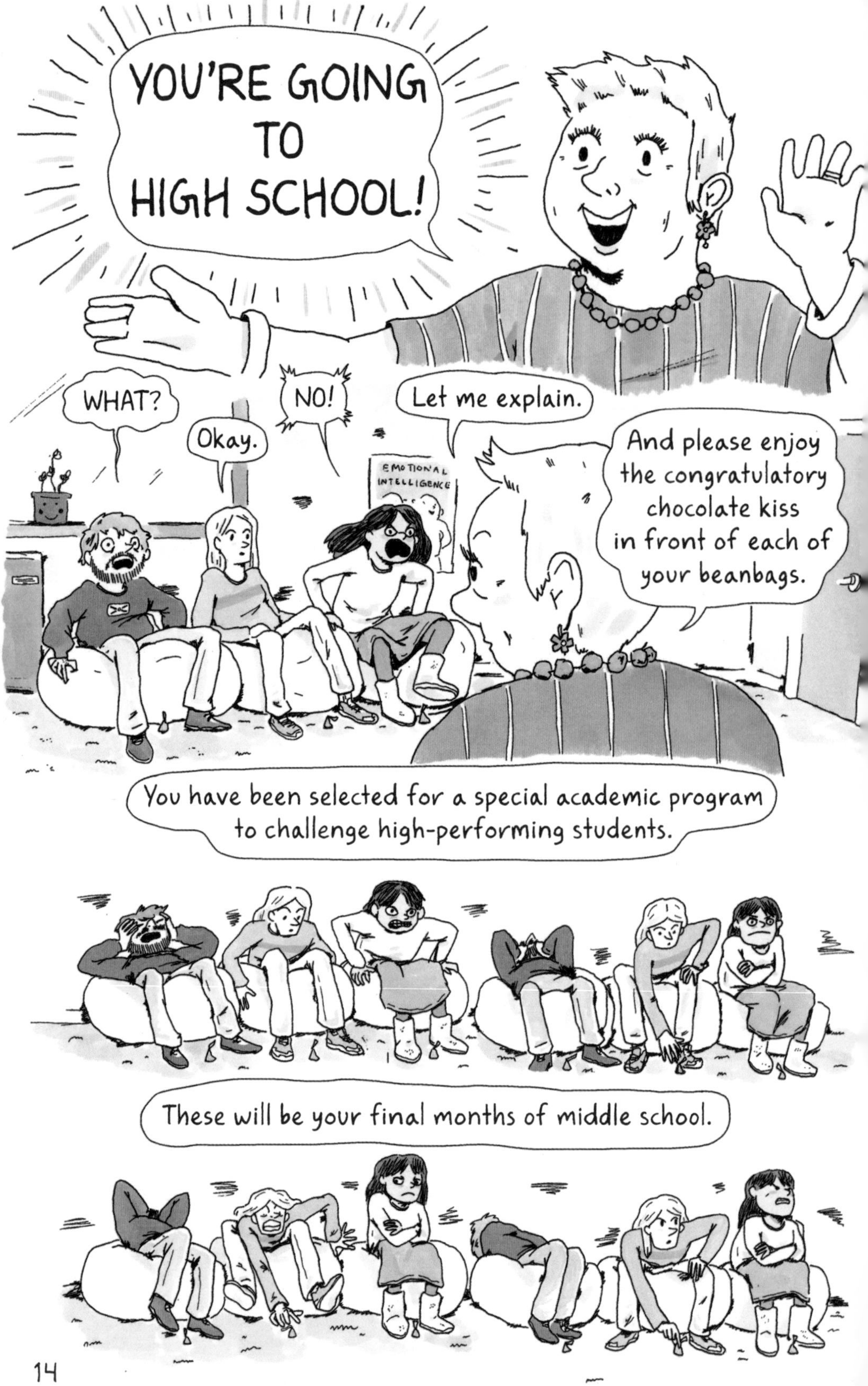

YOU'RE GOING TO HIGH SCHOOL!
WHAT?
Okay.
NO!
Let me explain.
EMOTIONAL INTELLIGENCE
And please enjoy the congratulatory chocolate kiss in front of each of your beanbags.
You have been selected for a special academic program to challenge high-performing students.
These will be your final months of middle school.

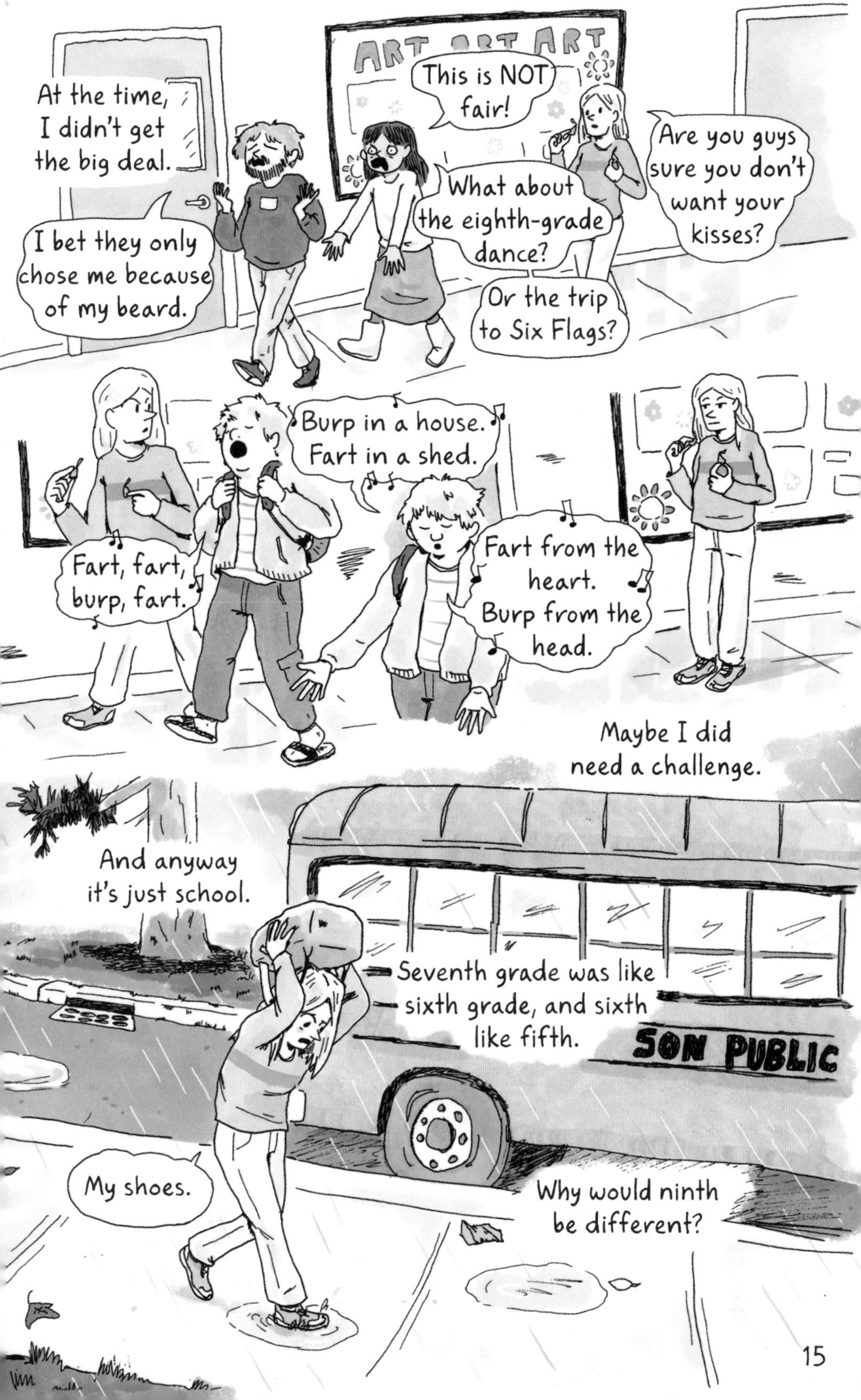
ART ART ART
At the time, I didn't get the big deal.
I bet they only chose me because of my beard.
This is NOT fair!
What about the eighth-grade dance?
Or the trip to Six Flags?
Are you guys sure you don't want your kisses?
Burp in a house. Fart in a shed.
Fart, fart, burp, fart.
Fart from the heart. Burp from the head.
Maybe I did need a challenge.
And anyway it's just school.
Seventh grade was like sixth grade, and sixth like fifth.
SON PUBLIC
My shoes.
Why would ninth be different?

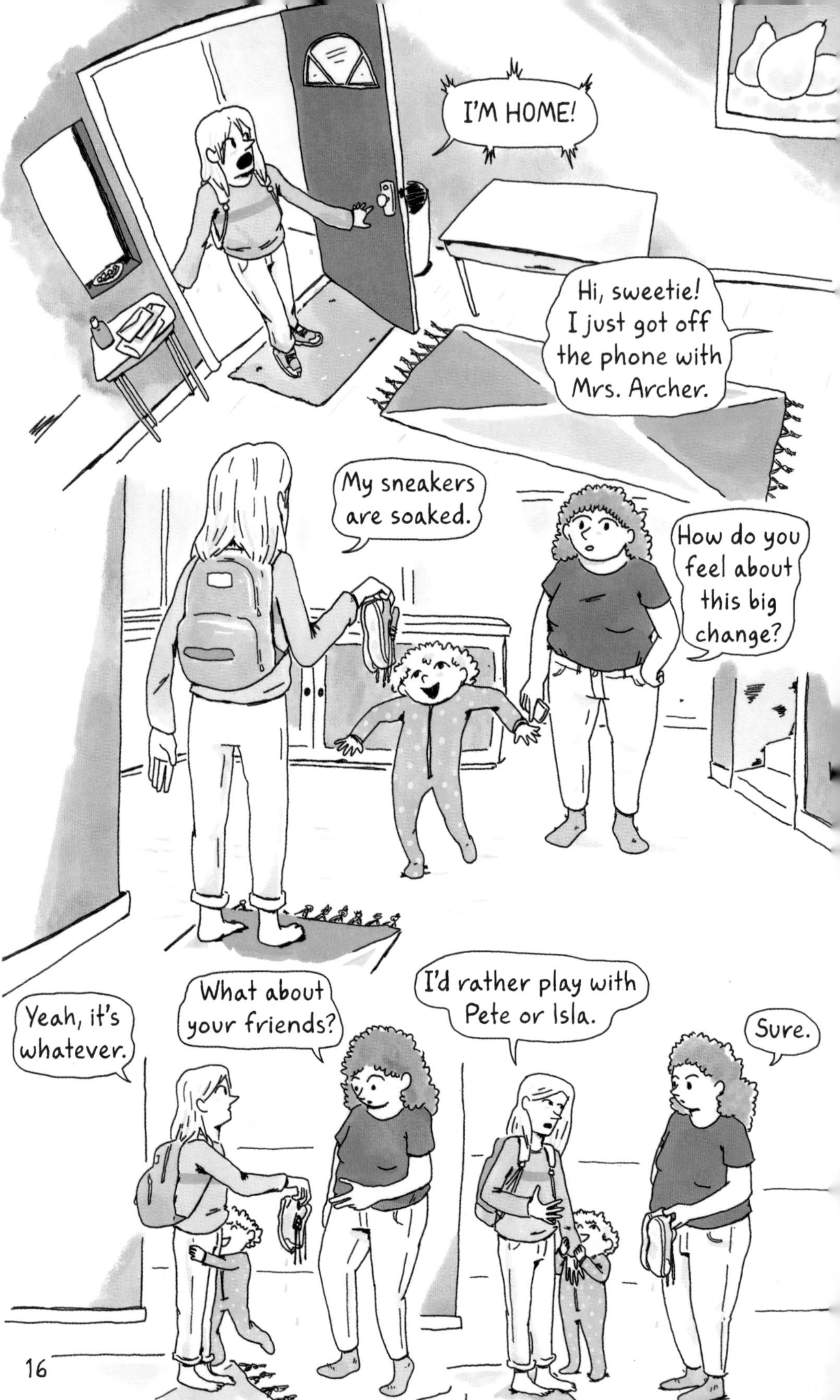
I'M HOME!
Hi, sweetie! I just got off the phone with Mrs. Archer.
My sneakers are soaked.
How do you feel about this big change?
Yeah, it's whatever.
What about your friends?
I'd rather play with Pete or Isla.
Sure.

I stopped thinking it was "whatever" after I talked to Isla.

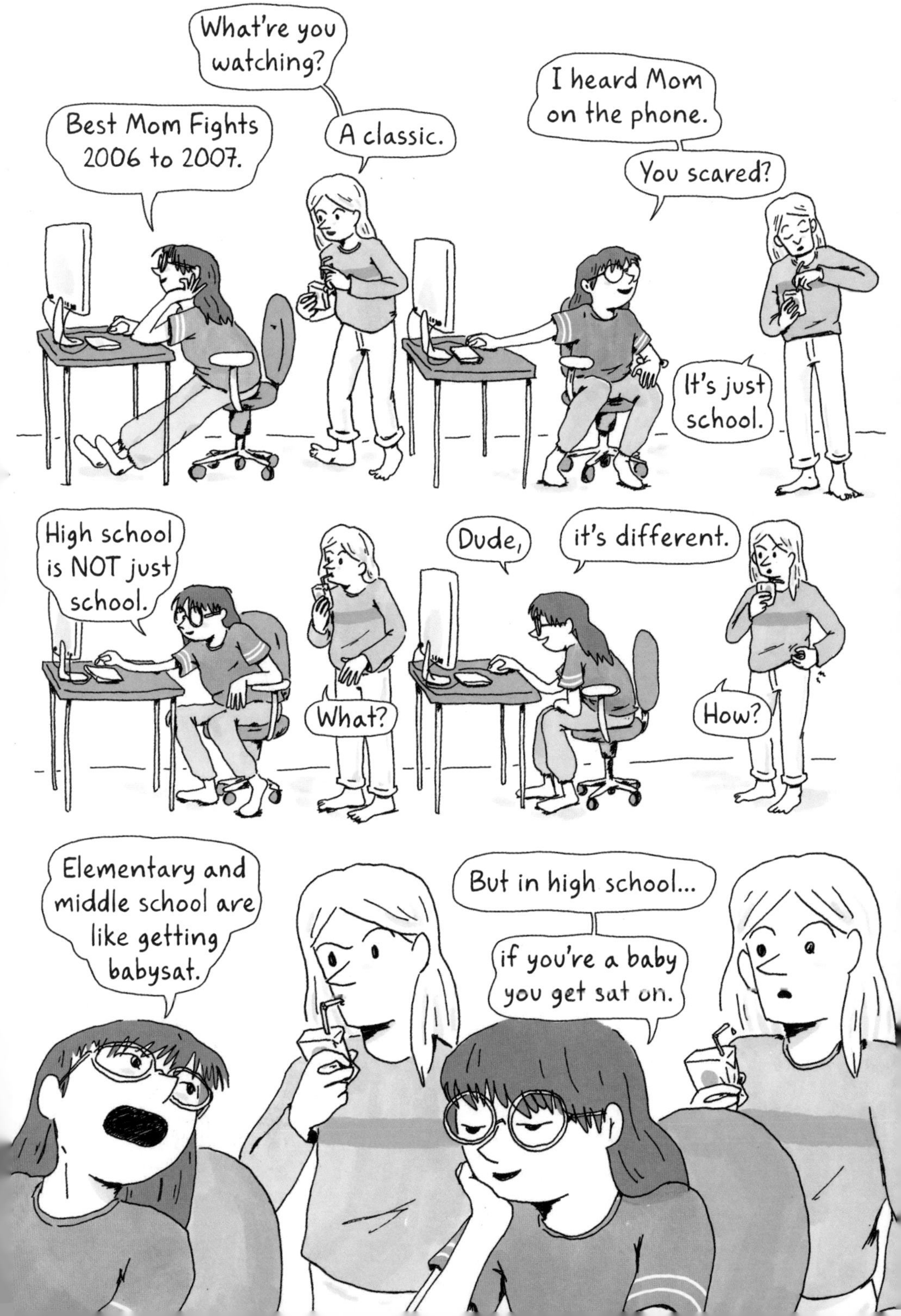
What're you watching?
Best Mom Fights 2006 to 2007.
A classic.
I heard Mom on the phone.
You scared?
It's just school.
High school is NOT just school.
What?
Dude,
it's different.
How?
Elementary and middle school are like getting babysat.
But in high school...
if you're a baby you get sat on.

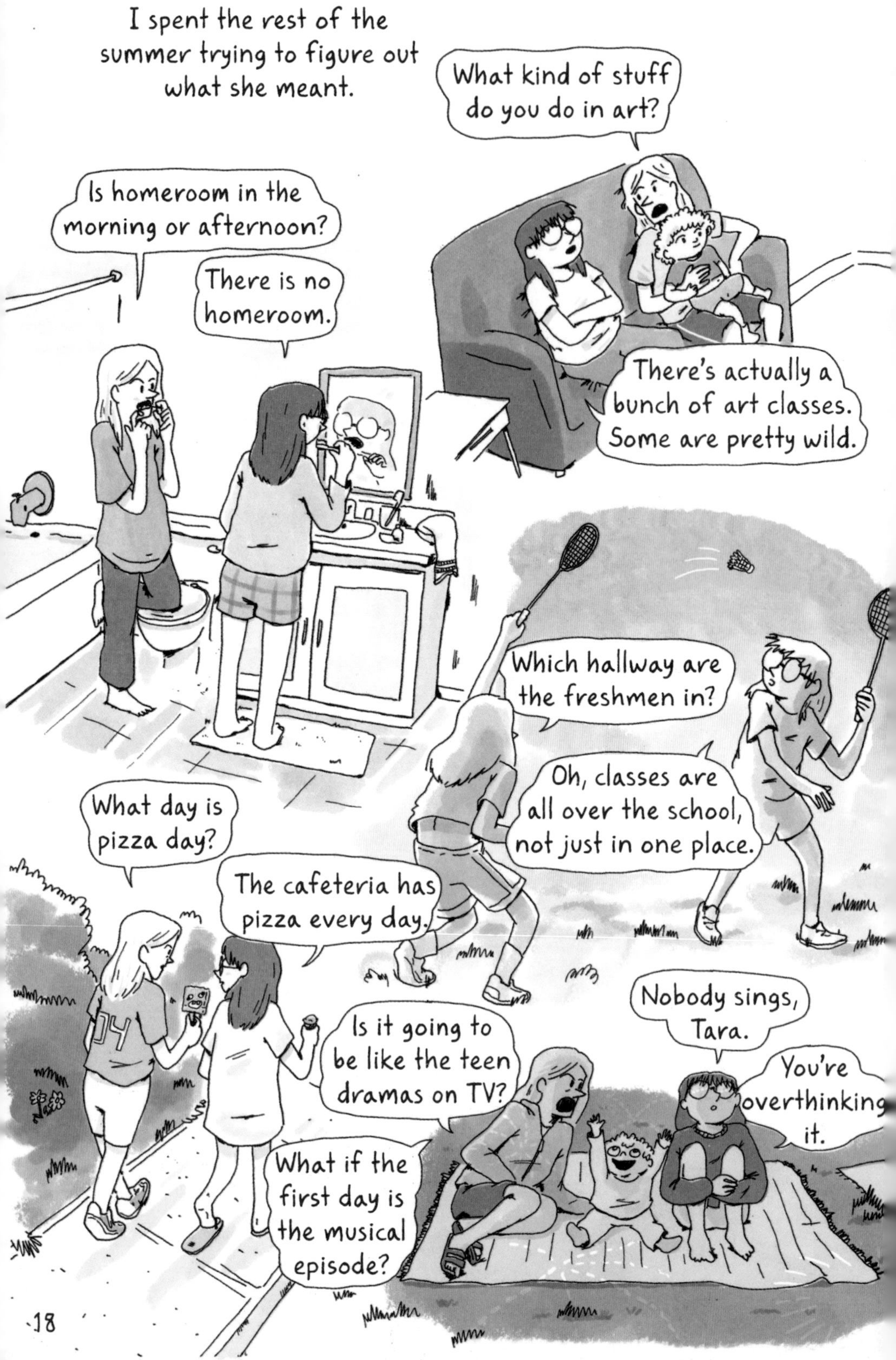
I spent the rest of the summer trying to figure out what she meant.
What kind of stuff do you do in art?
Is homeroom in the morning or afternoon?
There is no homeroom.
There's actually a bunch of art classes. Some are pretty wild.
Which hallway are the freshmen in?
Oh, classes are all over the school, not just in one place.
What day is pizza day?
The cafeteria has pizza every day.
Is it going to be like the teen dramas on TV?
What if the first day is the musical episode?
Nobody sings, Tara.
You're overthinking it.

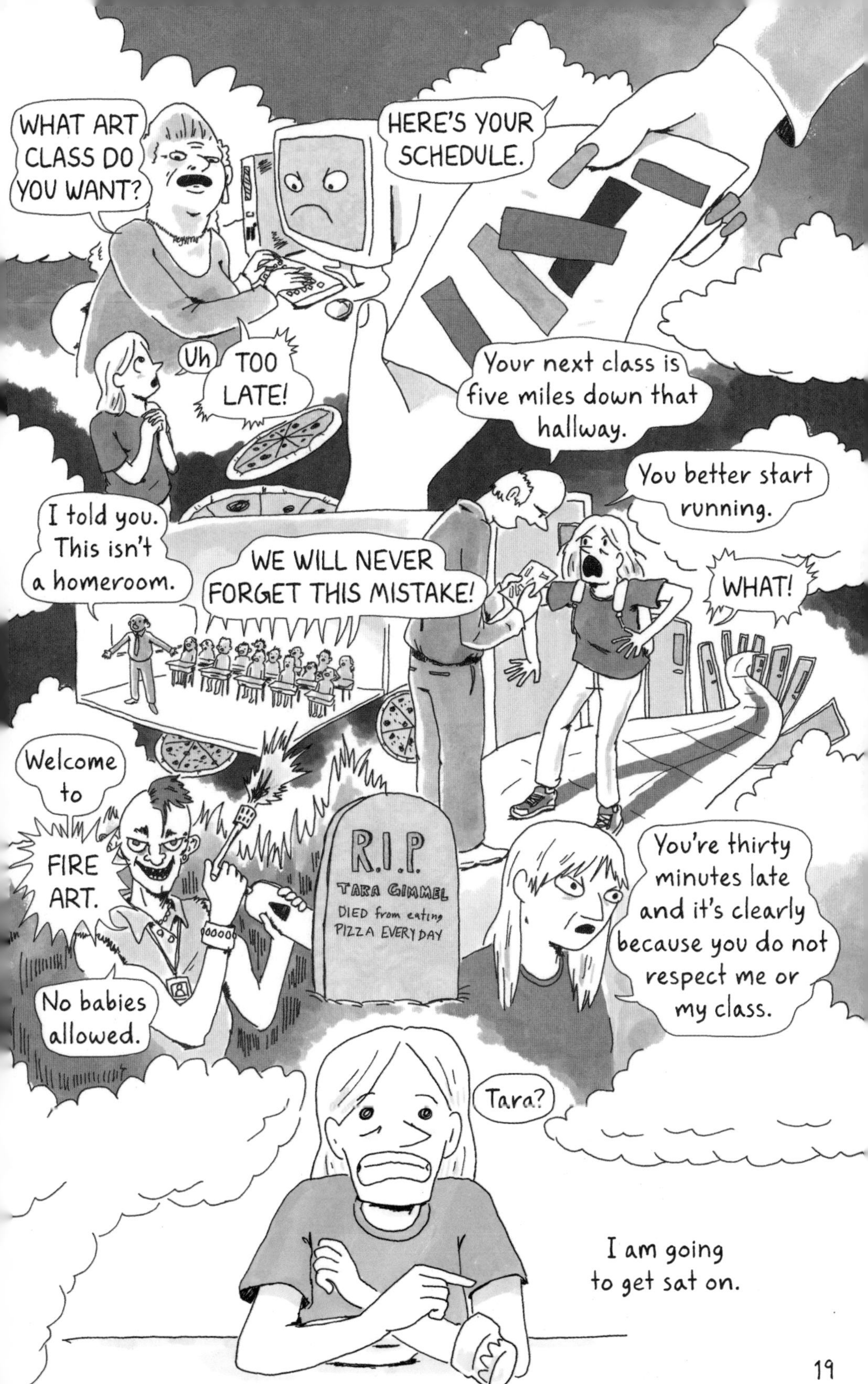
WHAT ART CLASS DO YOU WANT?
HERE'S YOUR SCHEDULE.
Uh
TOO LATE!
Your next class is five miles down that hallway.
You better start running.
I told you. This isn't a homeroom.
WE WILL NEVER FORGET THIS MISTAKE!
WHAT!
Welcome to
FIRE ART.
R.I.P.
TARA GIMMEL
DIED from eating PIZZA EVERY DAY
No babies allowed.
You're thirty minutes late and it's clearly because you do not respect me or my class.
Tara?
I am going to get sat on.

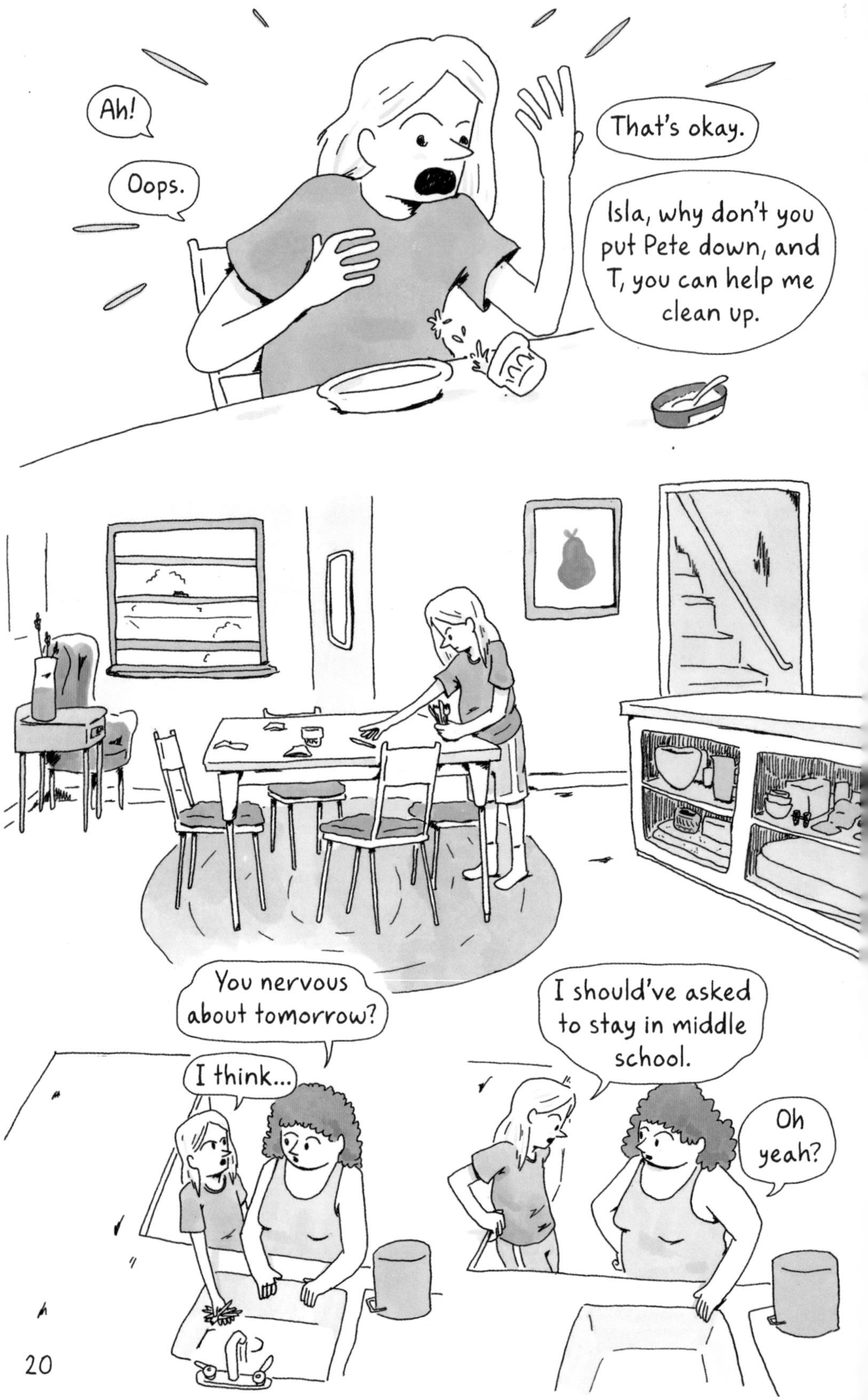
Ah!
Oops.
That's okay.
Isla, why don't you put Pete down, and T, you can help me clean up.
You nervous about tomorrow?
I think...
I should've asked to stay in middle school.
Oh yeah?

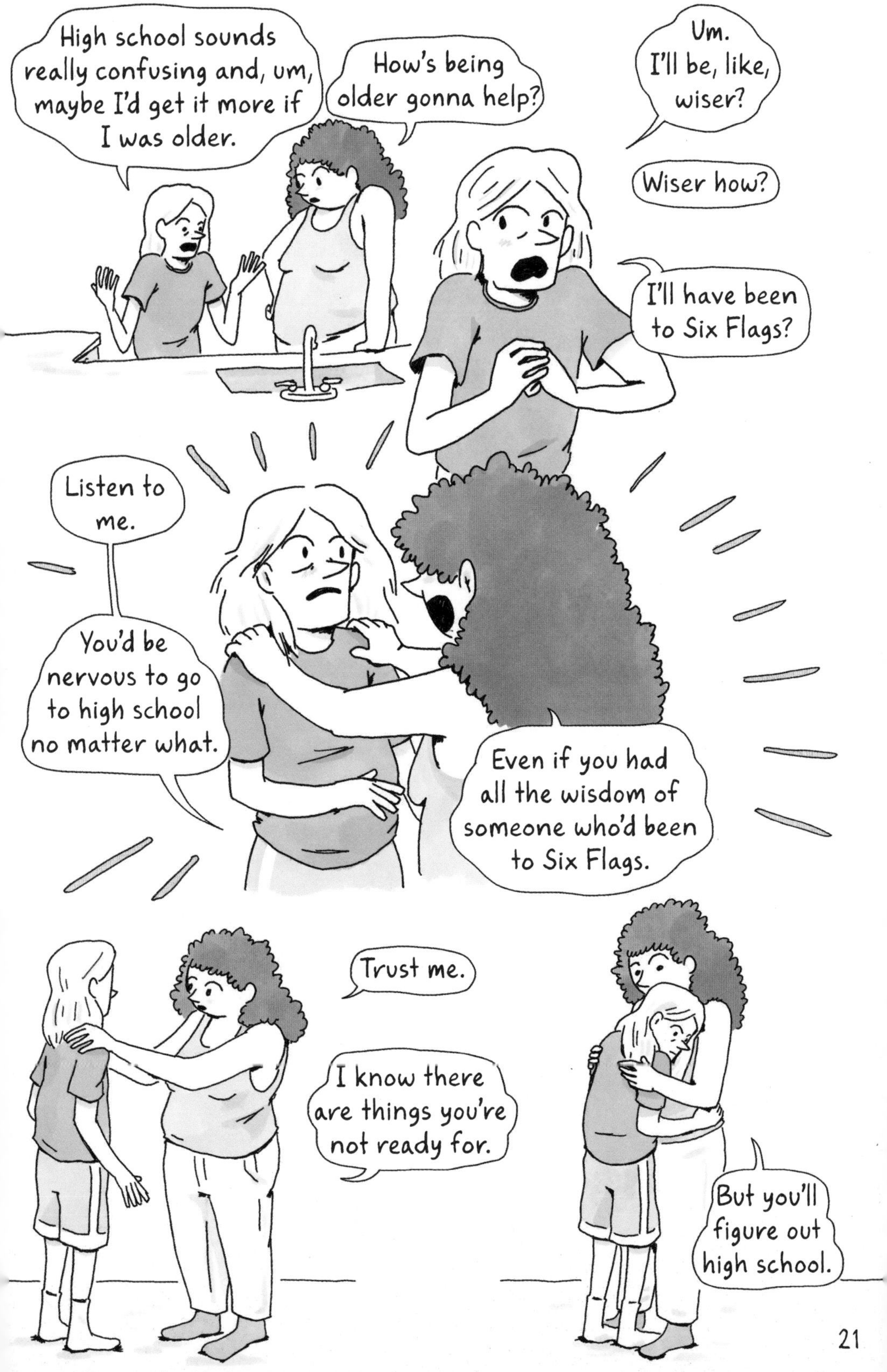
High school sounds really confusing and, um, maybe I'd get it more if I was older.
How's being older gonna help?
Um. I'll be, like, wiser?
Wiser how?
I'll have been to Six Flags?
Listen to me.
You'd be nervous to go to high school no matter what.
Even if you had all the wisdom of someone who'd been to Six Flags.
Trust me.
I know there are things you're not ready for.
But you'll figure out high school.

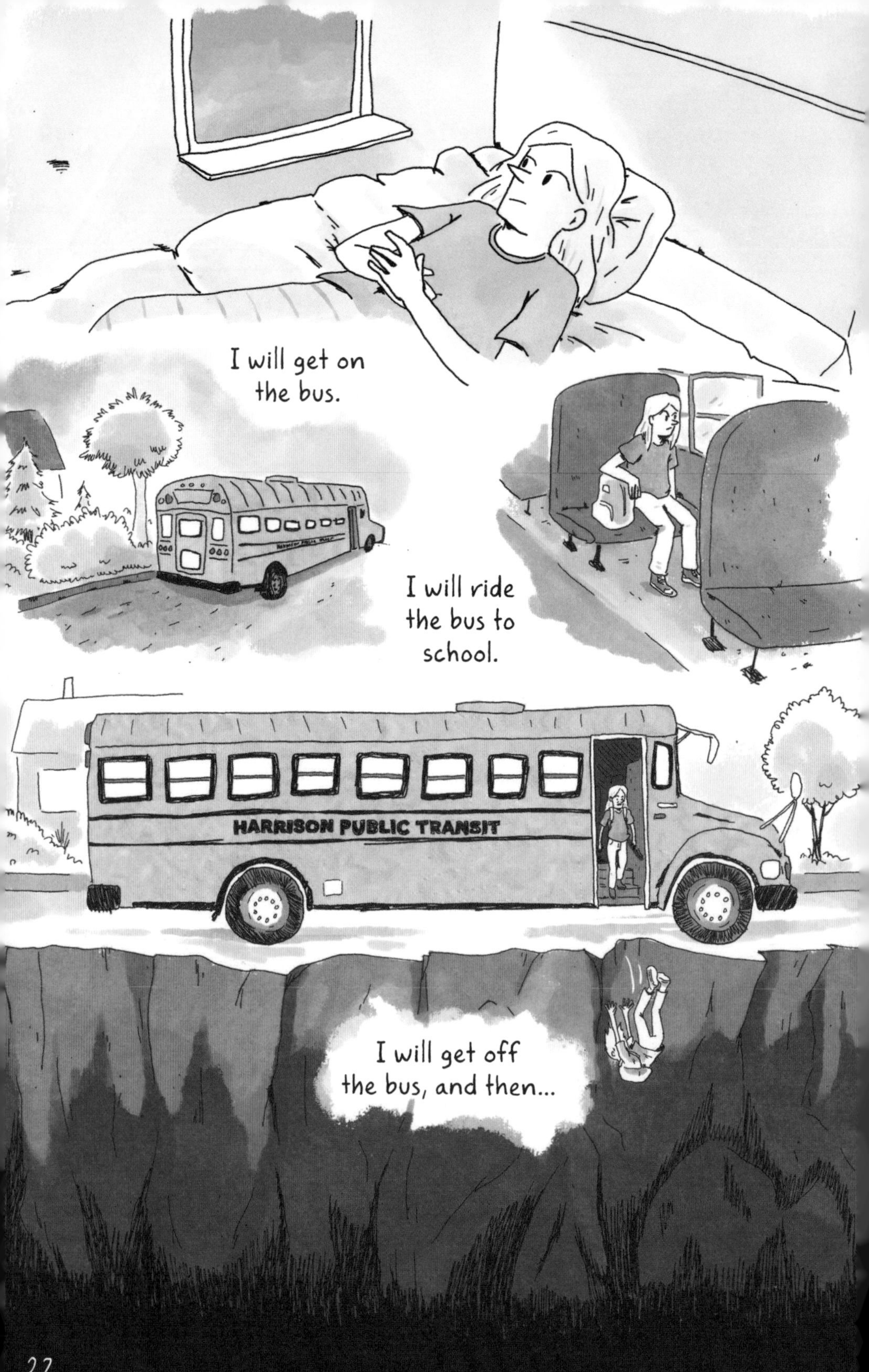
I will get on the bus.
I will ride the bus to school.
HARRISON PUBLIC TRANSIT
I will get off the bus, and then...

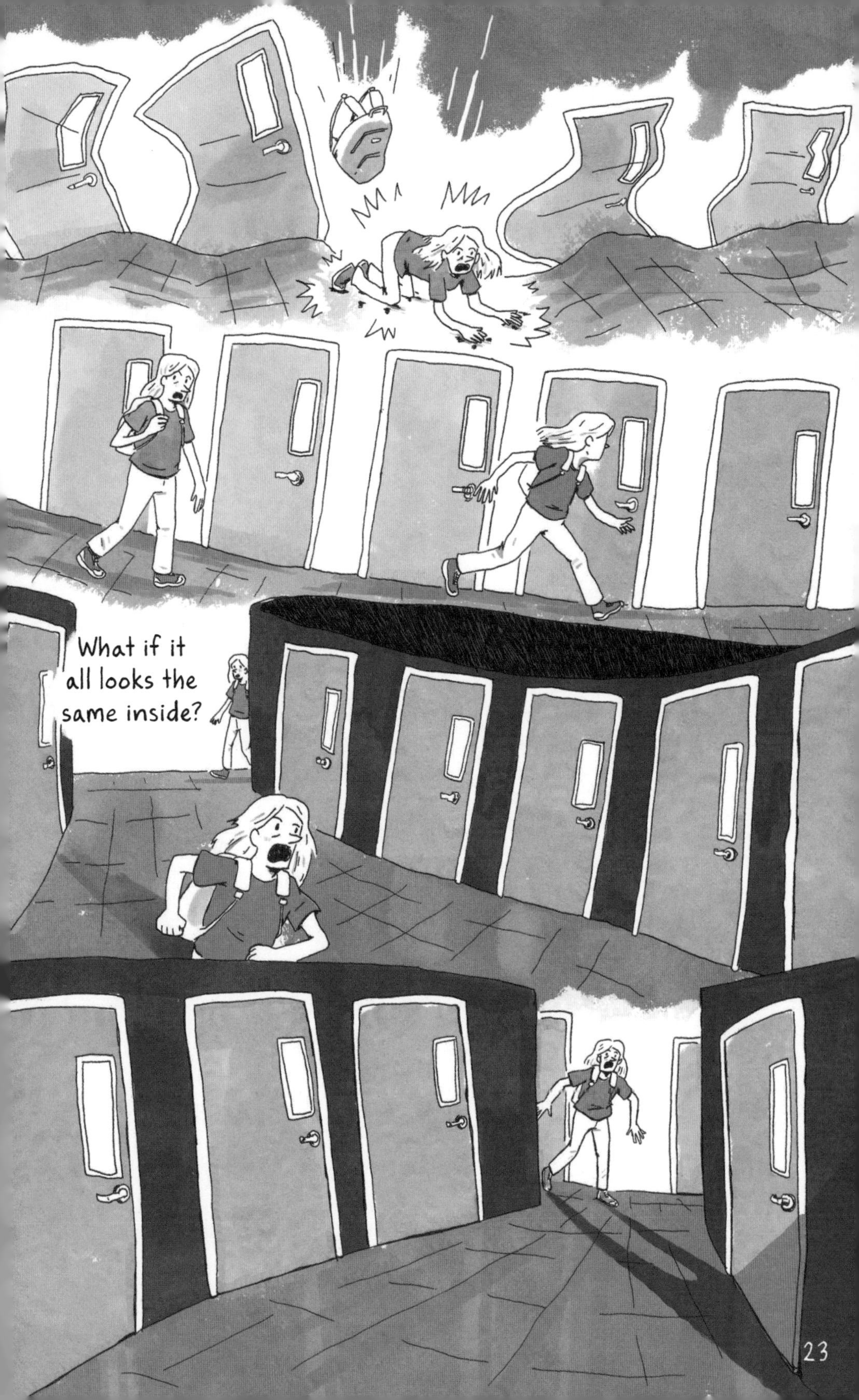
What if it all looks the same inside?

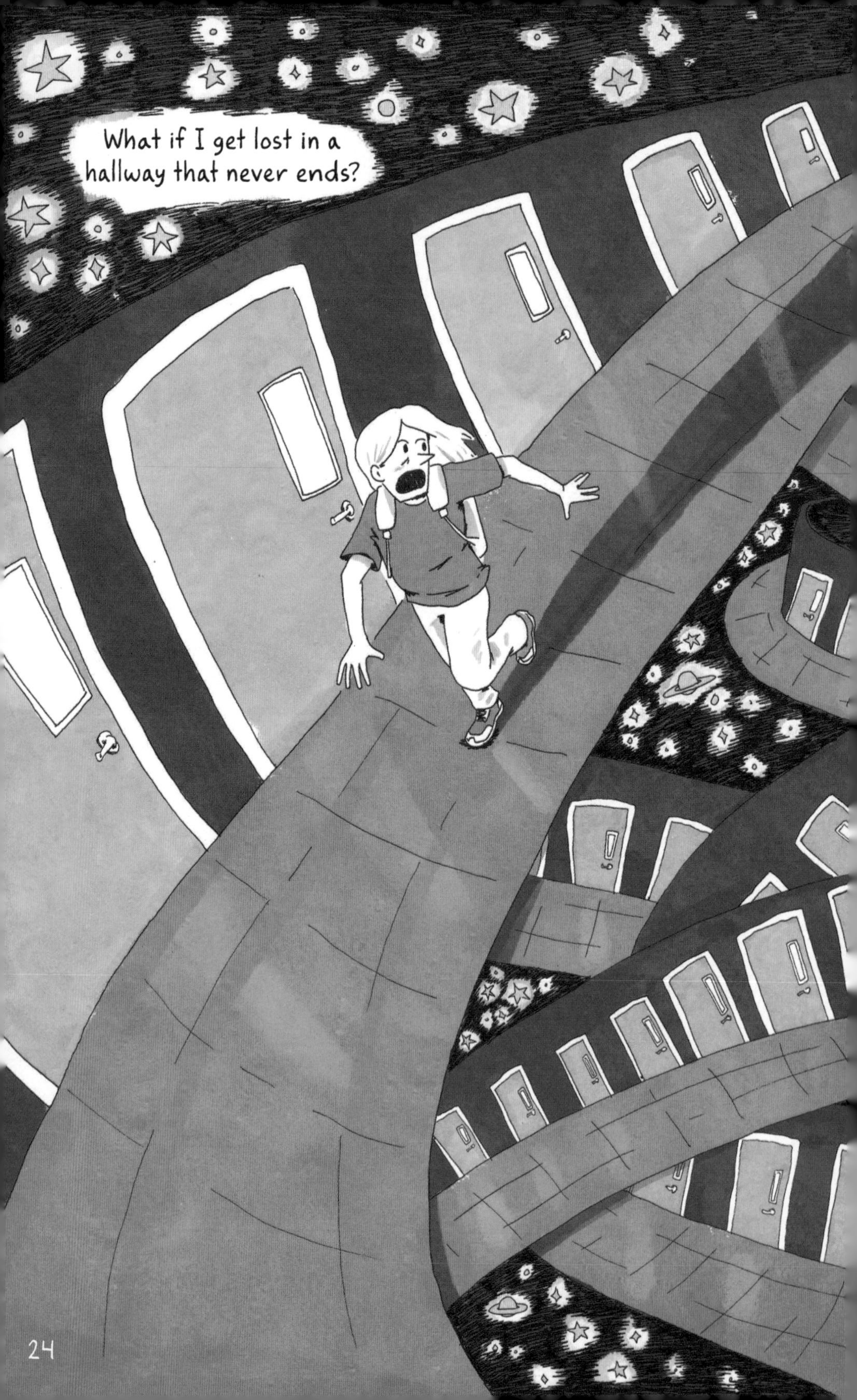
What if I get lost in a hallway that never ends?

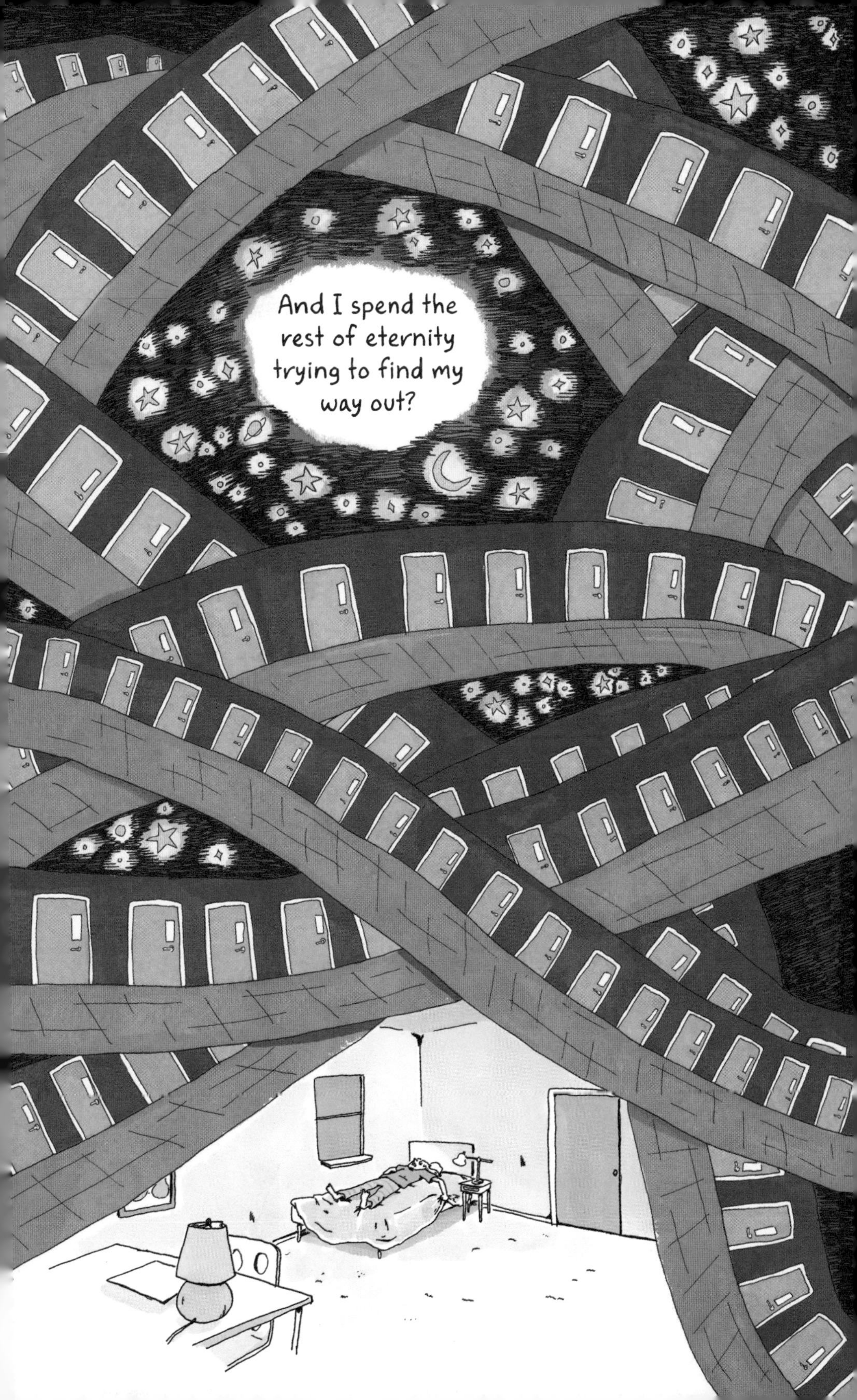
And I spend the rest of eternity trying to find my way out?

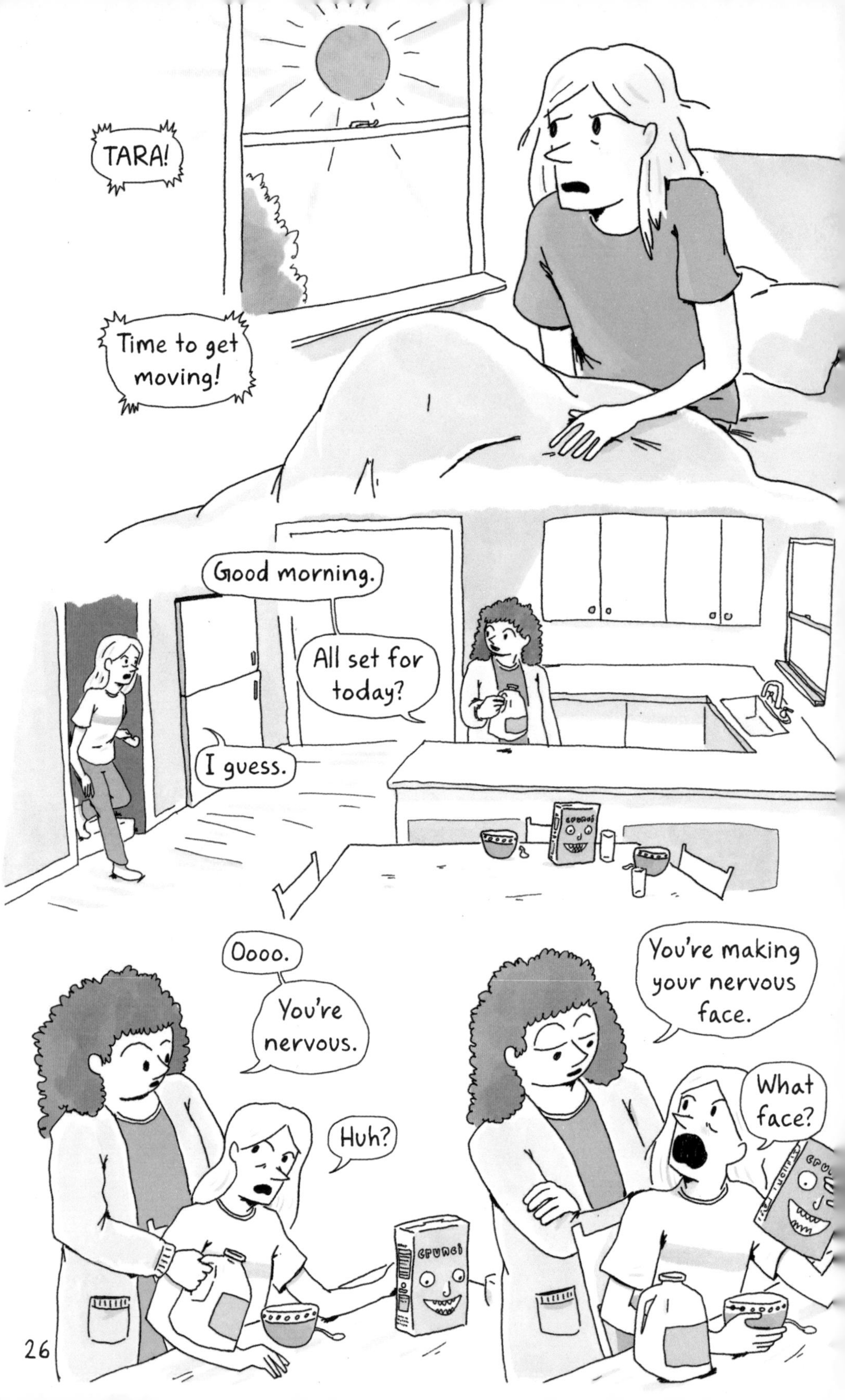
TARA!
Time to get moving!
Good morning.
All set for today?
I guess.
CRUNCH
Oooo.
You're nervous.
Huh?
CRUNCH
You're making your nervous face.
What face?

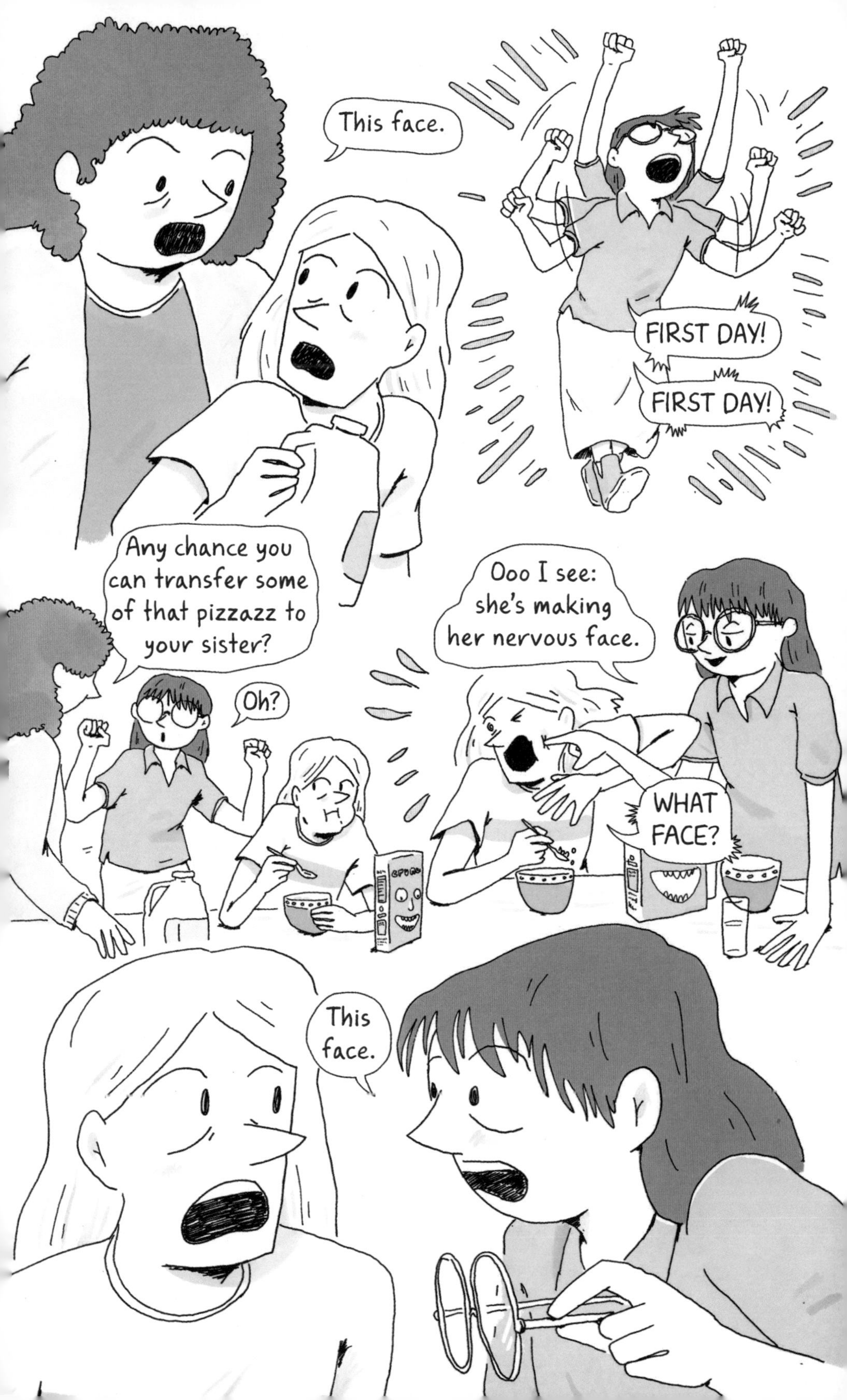
This face.
FIRST DAY!
FIRST DAY!
Any chance you can transfer some of that pizzazz to your sister?
Oh?
Ooo I see: she's making her nervous face.
WHAT FACE?
This face.

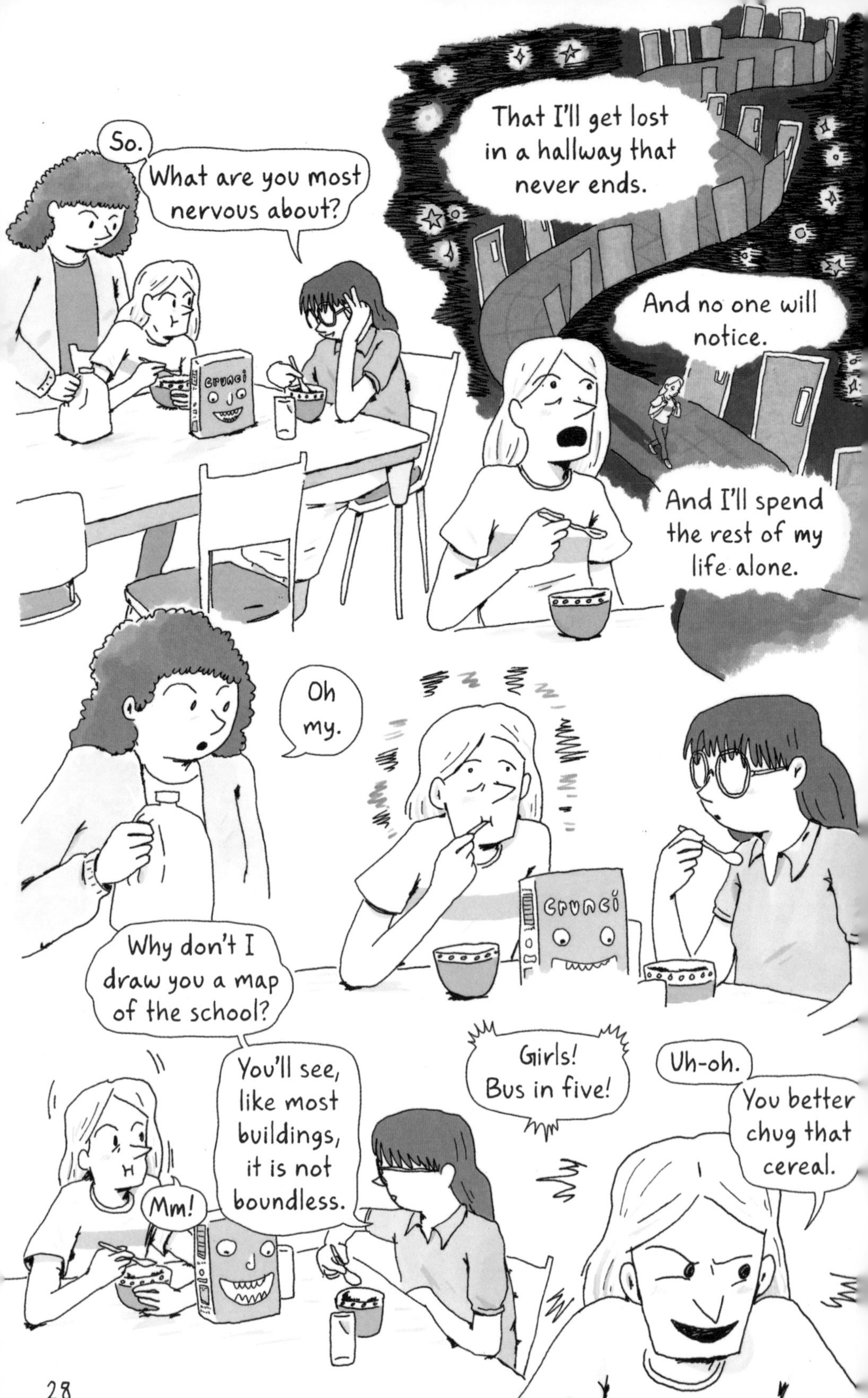
So.
What are you most nervous about?
That I'll get lost in a hallway that never ends.
And no one will notice.
And I'll spend the rest of my life alone.
Oh my.
Why don't I draw you a map of the school?
You'll see, like most buildings, it is not boundless.
Mm!
Girls! Bus in five!
Uh-oh.
You better chug that cereal.

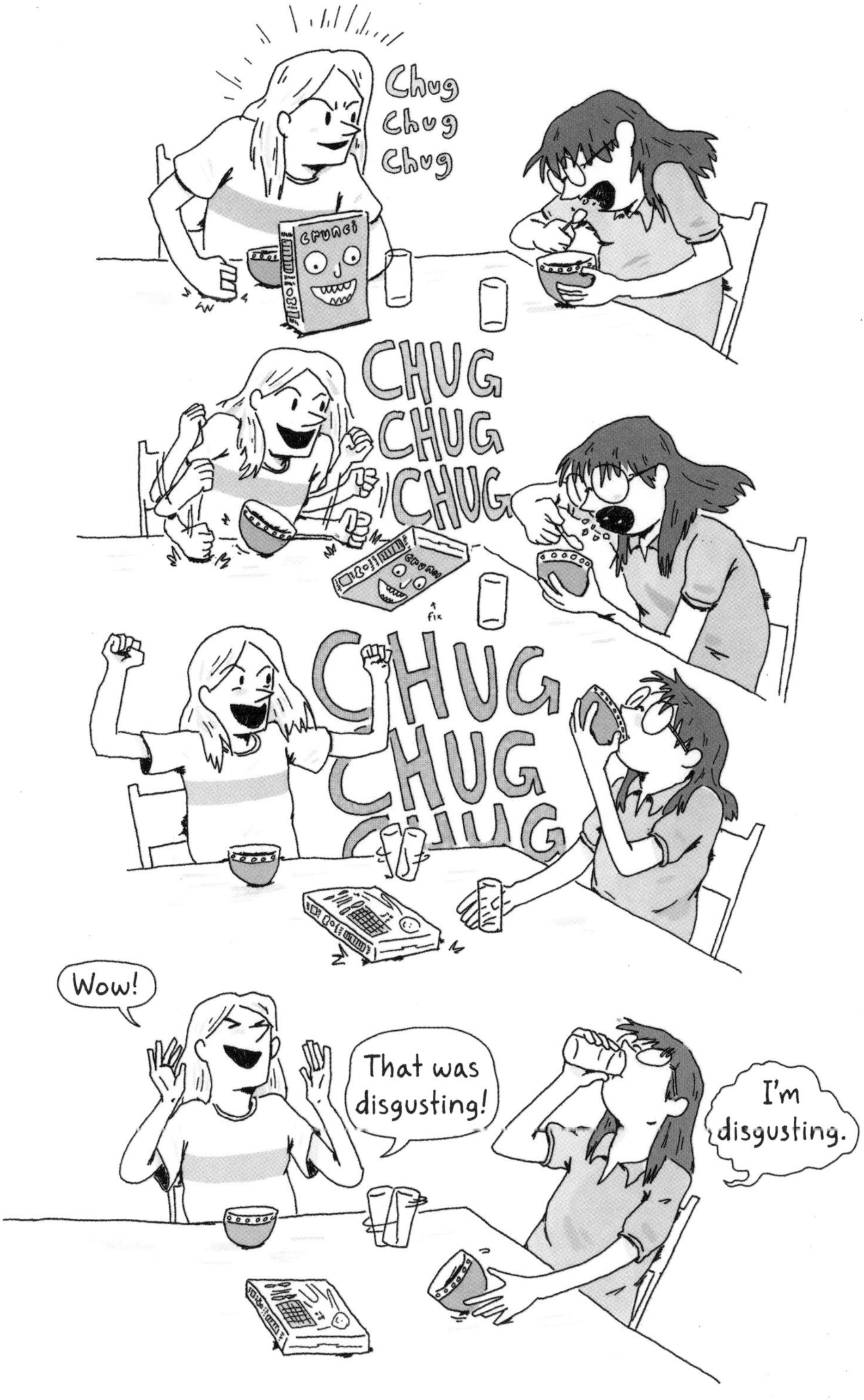
Chug
Chug
Chug
crunci
CHUG
CHUG
CHUG
crunci
CHUG
CHUG
Wow!
That was disgusting!
I'm disgusting.

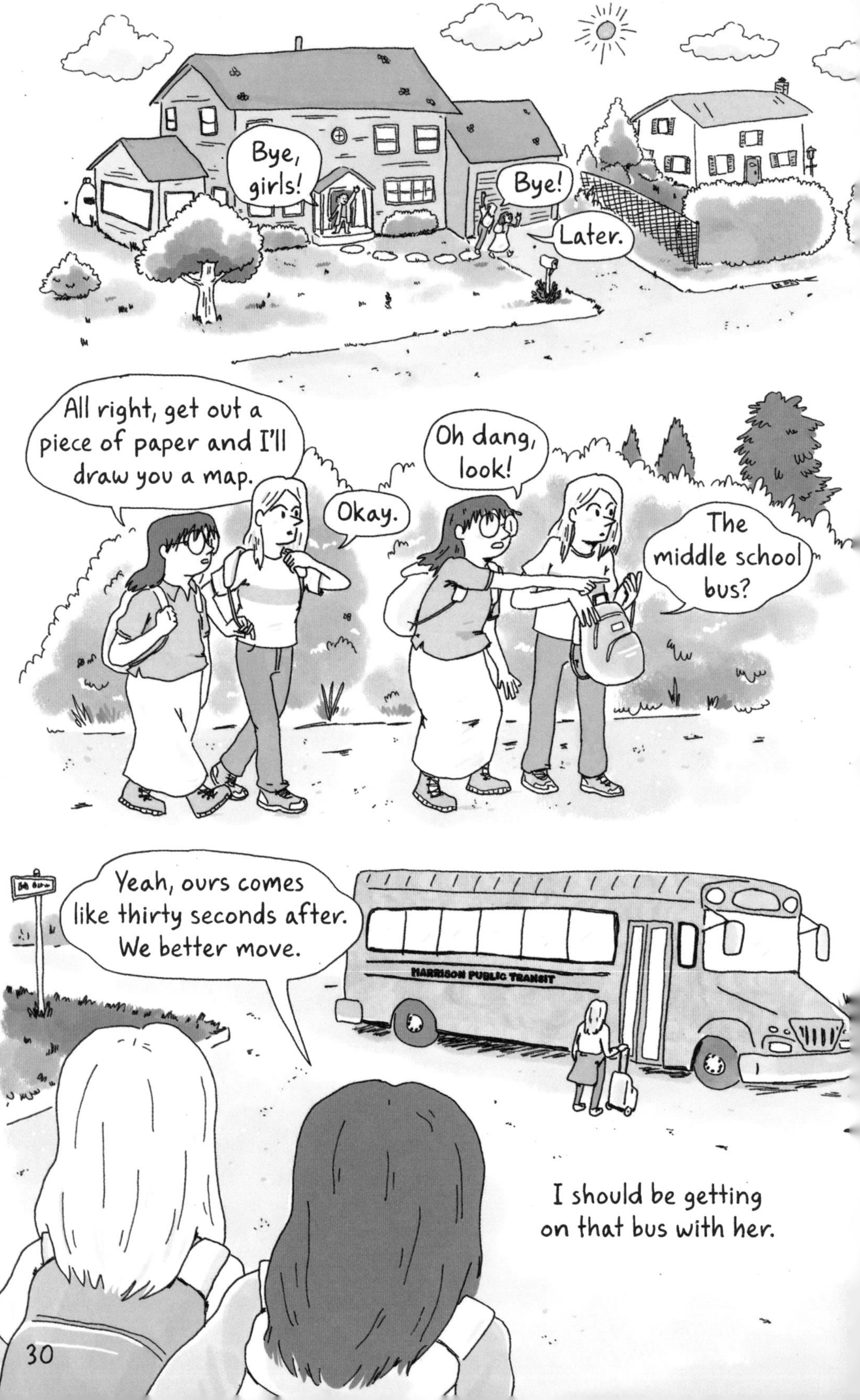
Bye, girls!
Bye!
Later.
All right, get out a piece of paper and I'll draw you a map.
Okay.
Oh dang, look!
The middle school bus?
Yeah, ours comes like thirty seconds after. We better move.
HARRISON PUBLIC TRANSIT
I should be getting on that bus with her.

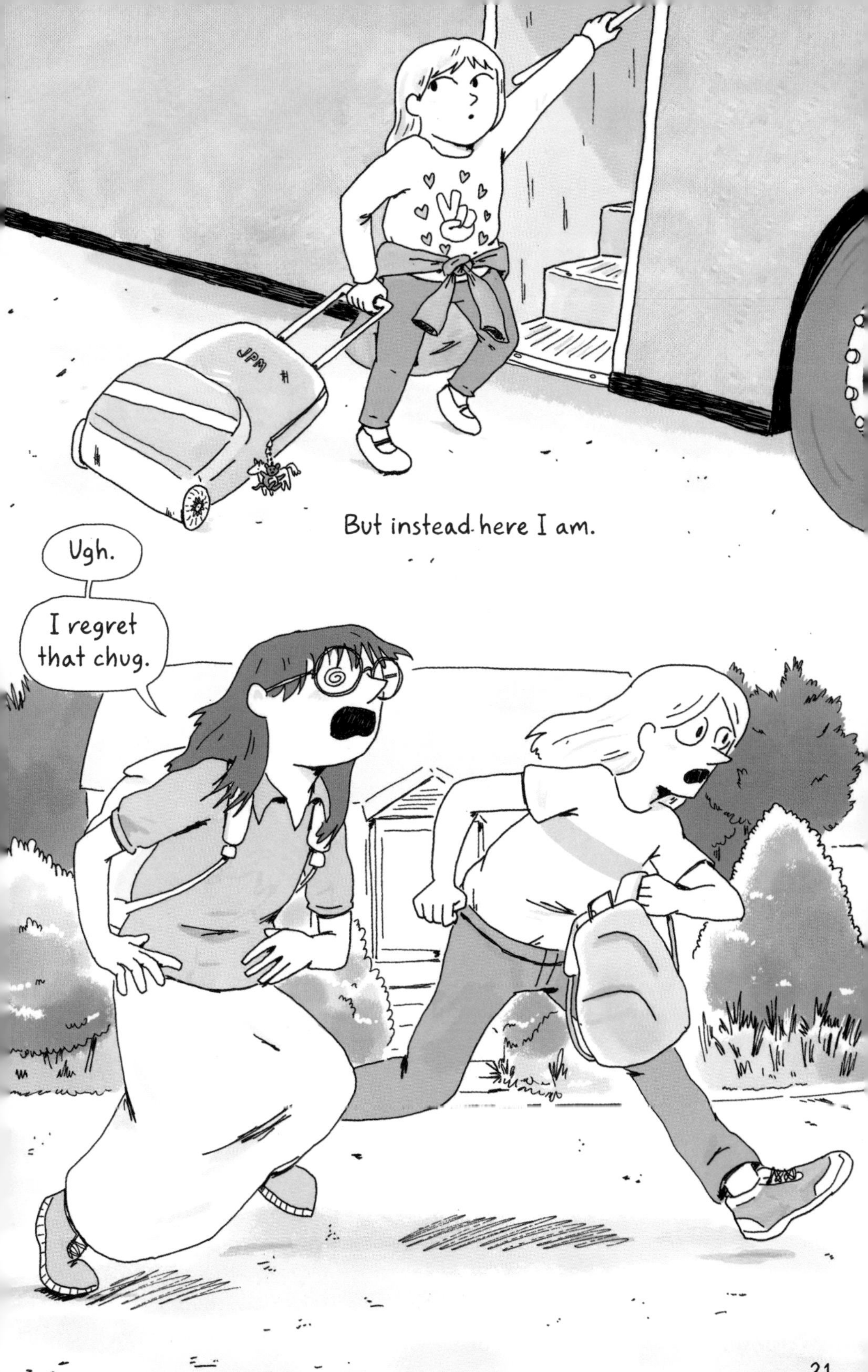
JPM
But instead here I am.
Ugh.
I regret that chug.

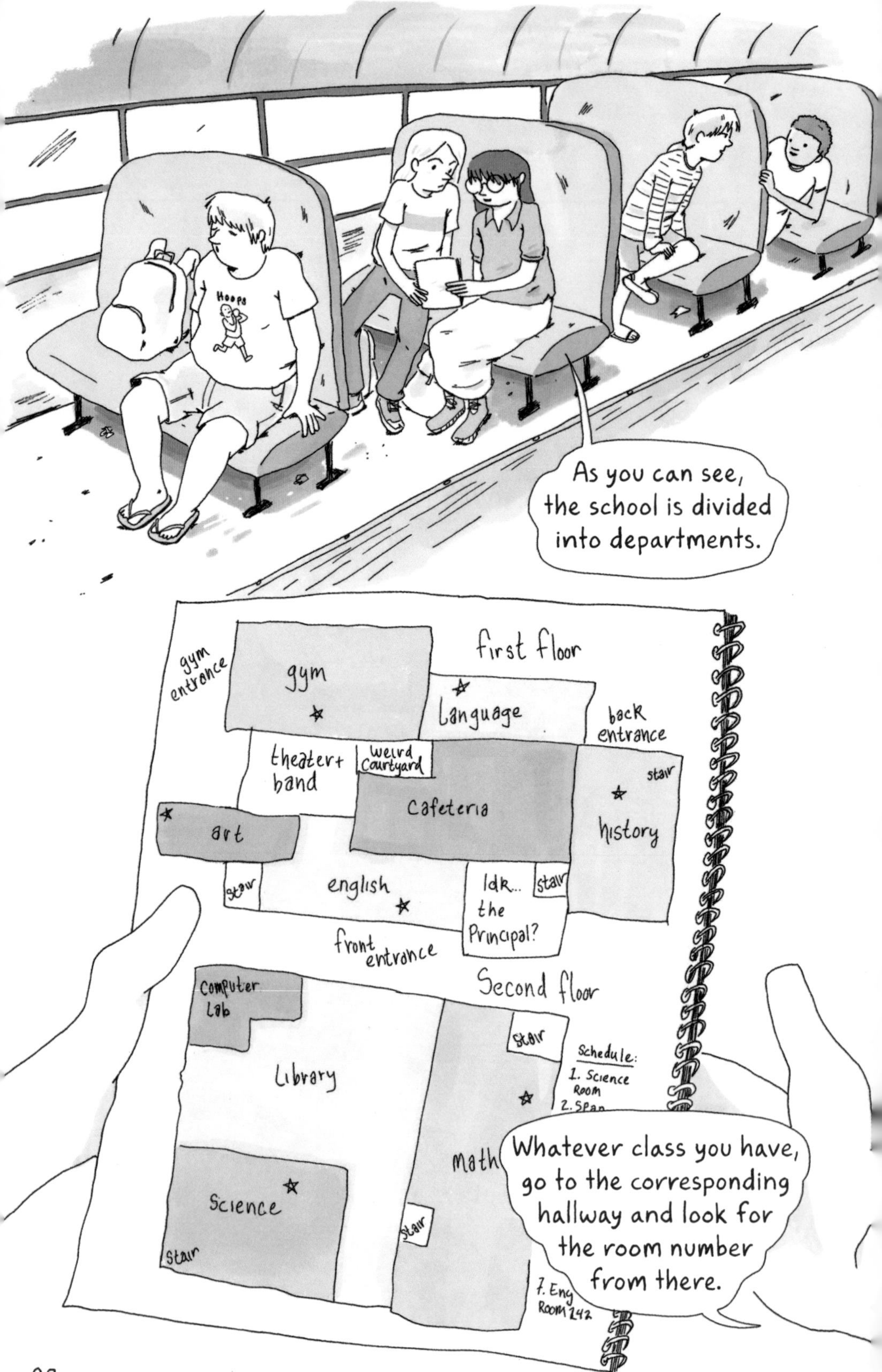
HOOPS
As you can see, the school is divided into departments.
first floor
gym entrance
gym
Language
back entrance
theater+ band
weird courtyard
Cafeteria
stair
history
art
stair
english
Idk... the Principal?
stair
front entrance
Second floor
Computer Lab
Library
stair
Schedule:
1. Science Room
Math
Science
stair
stair
Whatever class you have, go to the corresponding hallway and look for the room number from there.

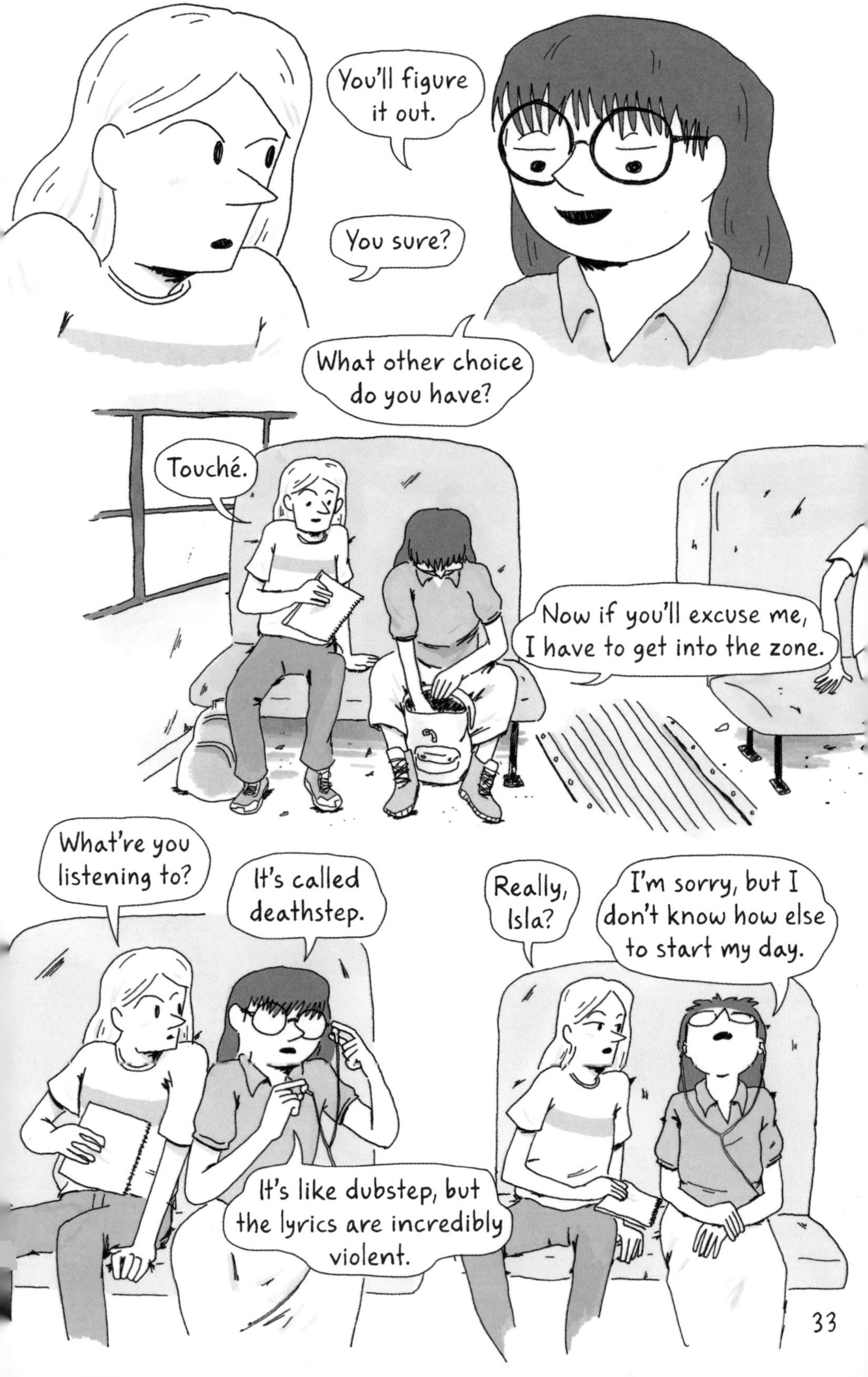
You'll figure it out.
You sure?
What other choice do you have?
Touché.
Now if you'll excuse me, I have to get into the zone.
What're you listening to?
It's called deathstep.
It's like dubstep, but the lyrics are incredibly violent.
Really, Isla?
I'm sorry, but I don't know how else to start my day.

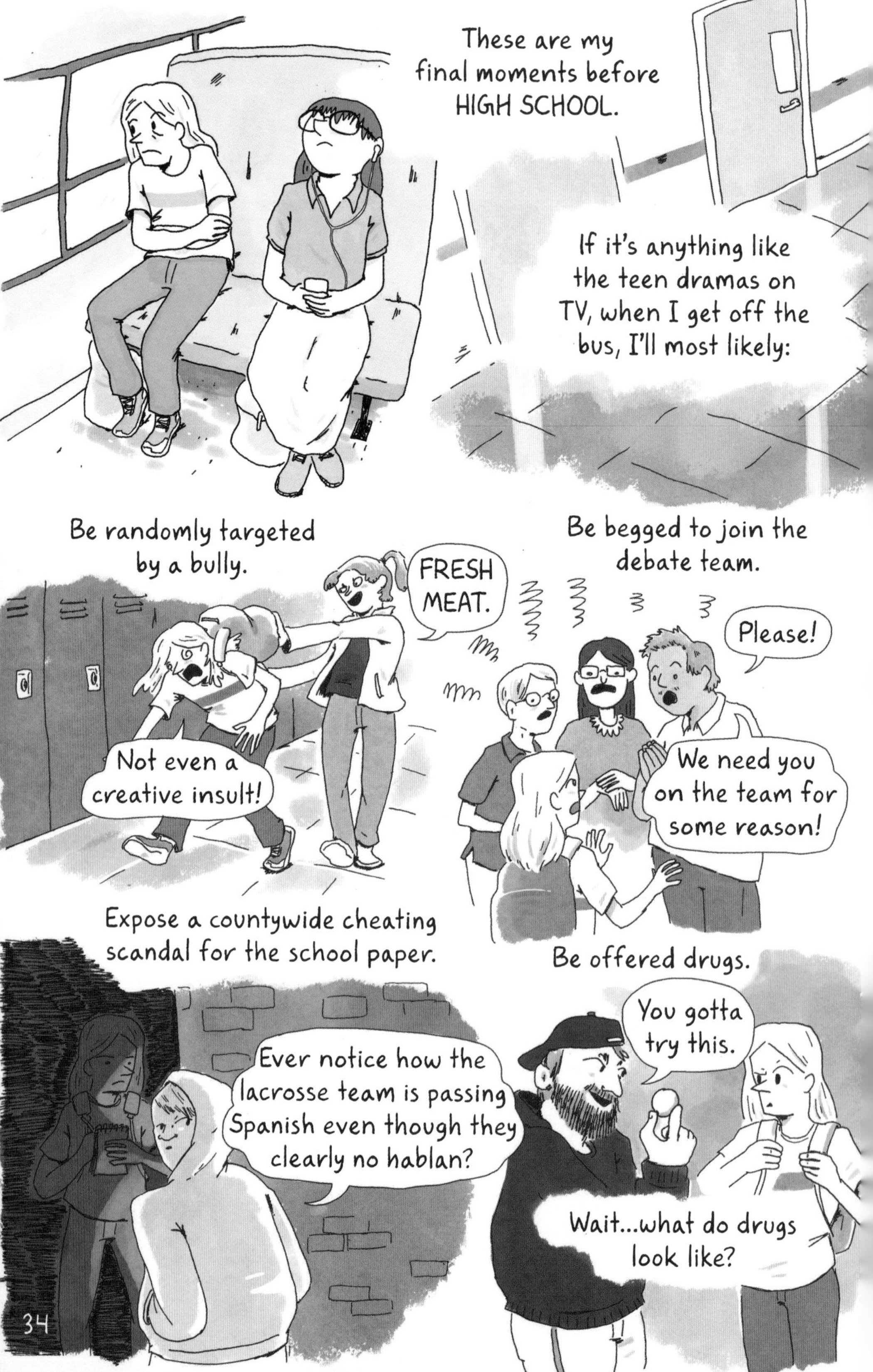
These are my final moments before HIGH SCHOOL.
If it's anything like the teen dramas on TV, when I get off the bus, I'll most likely:
Be randomly targeted by a bully.
FRESH MEAT.
Not even a creative insult!
Be begged to join the debate team.
Please!
We need you on the team for some reason!
Expose a countywide cheating scandal for the school paper.
Ever notice how the lacrosse team is passing Spanish even though they clearly no hablan?
Be offered drugs.
You gotta try this.
Wait...what do drugs look like?

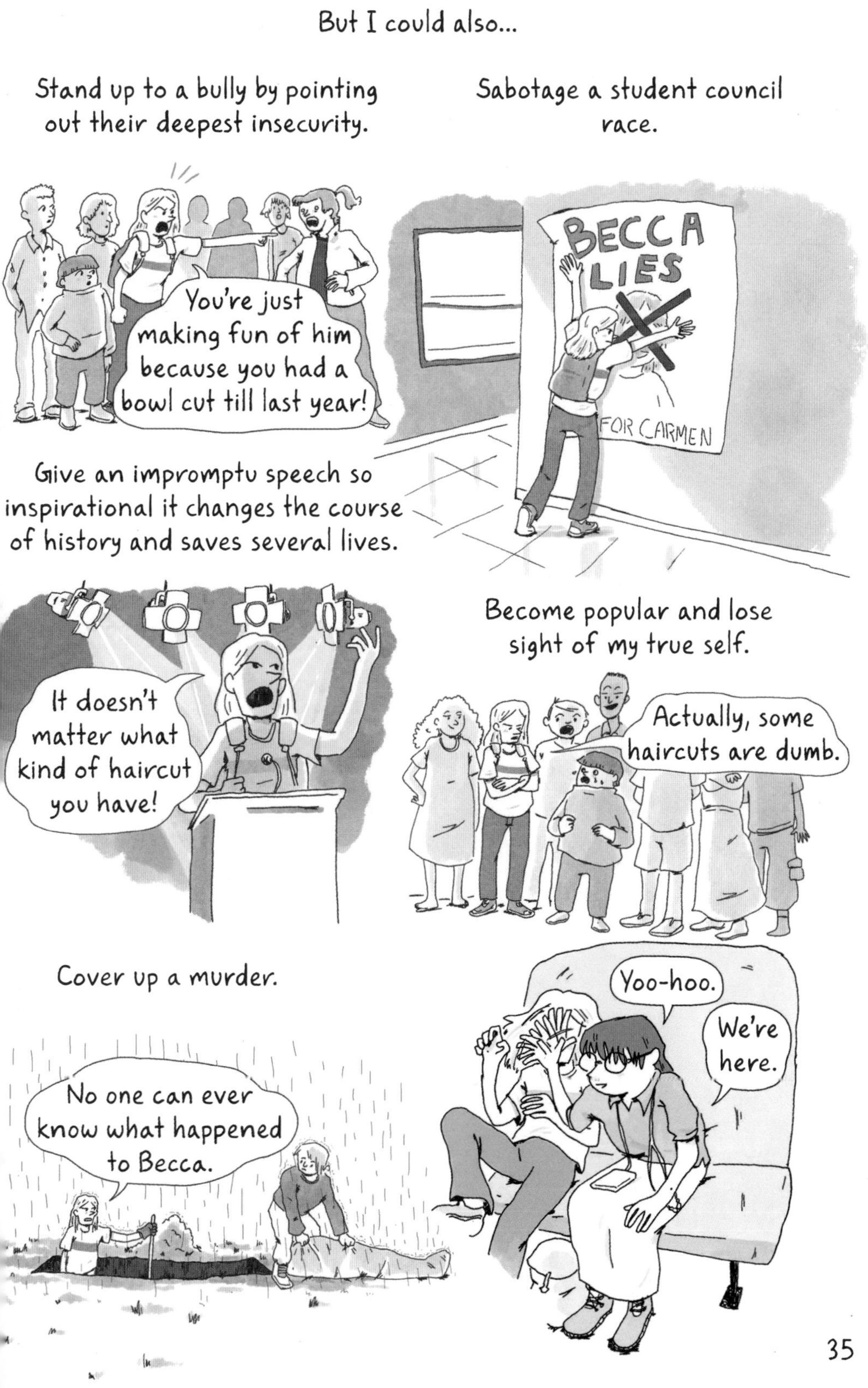
But I could also...
Stand up to a bully by pointing out their deepest insecurity.
You're just making fun of him because you had a bowl cut till last year!
Sabotage a student council race.
BECCA LIES
FOR CARMEN
Give an impromptu speech so inspirational it changes the course of history and saves several lives.
It doesn't matter what kind of haircut you have!
Become popular and lose sight of my true self.
Actually, some haircuts are dumb.
Cover up a murder.
No one can ever know what happened to Becca.
Yoo-hoo.
We're here.

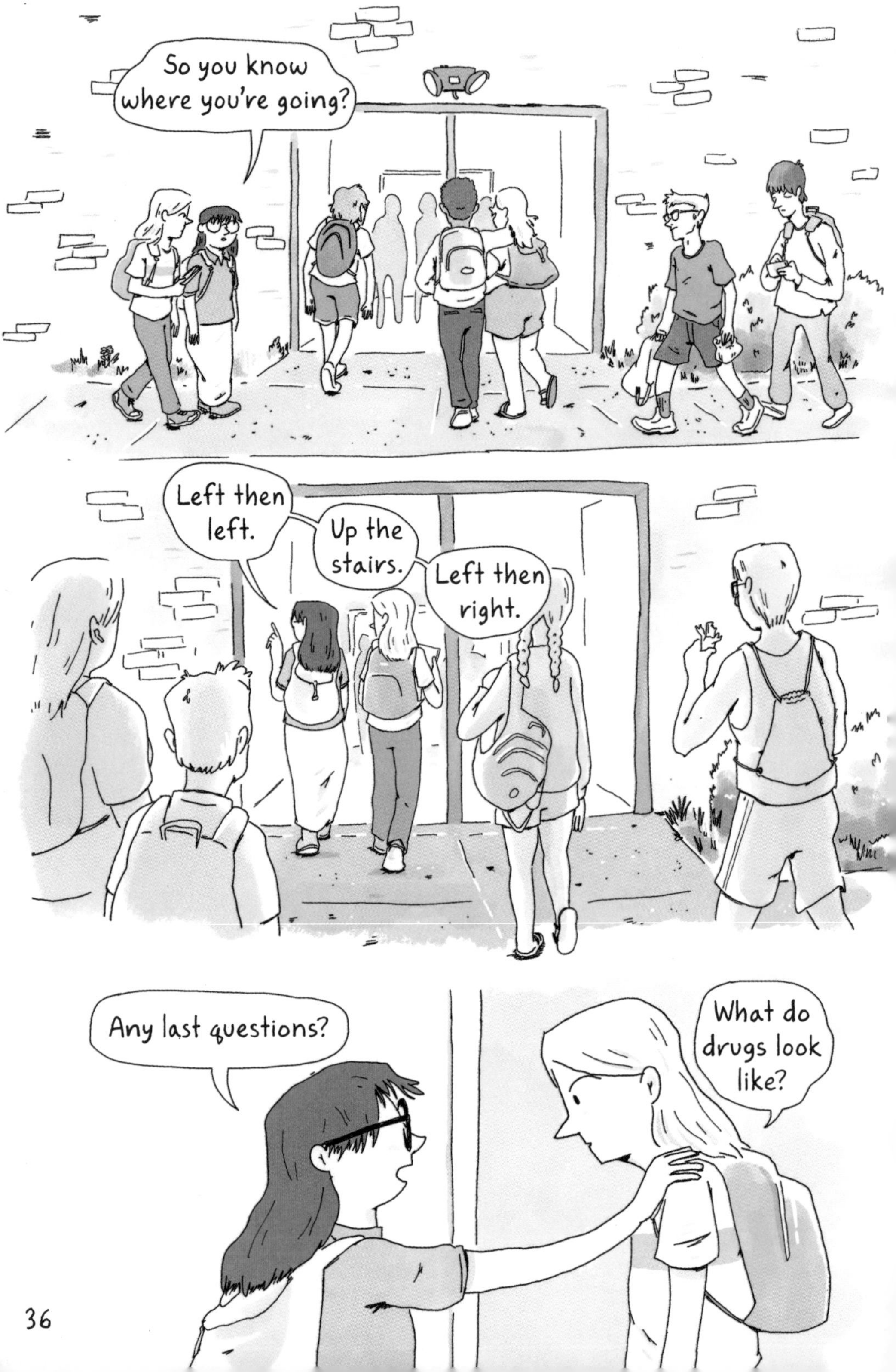
So you know where you're going?
Left then left.
Up the stairs.
Left then right.
Any last questions?
What do drugs look like?

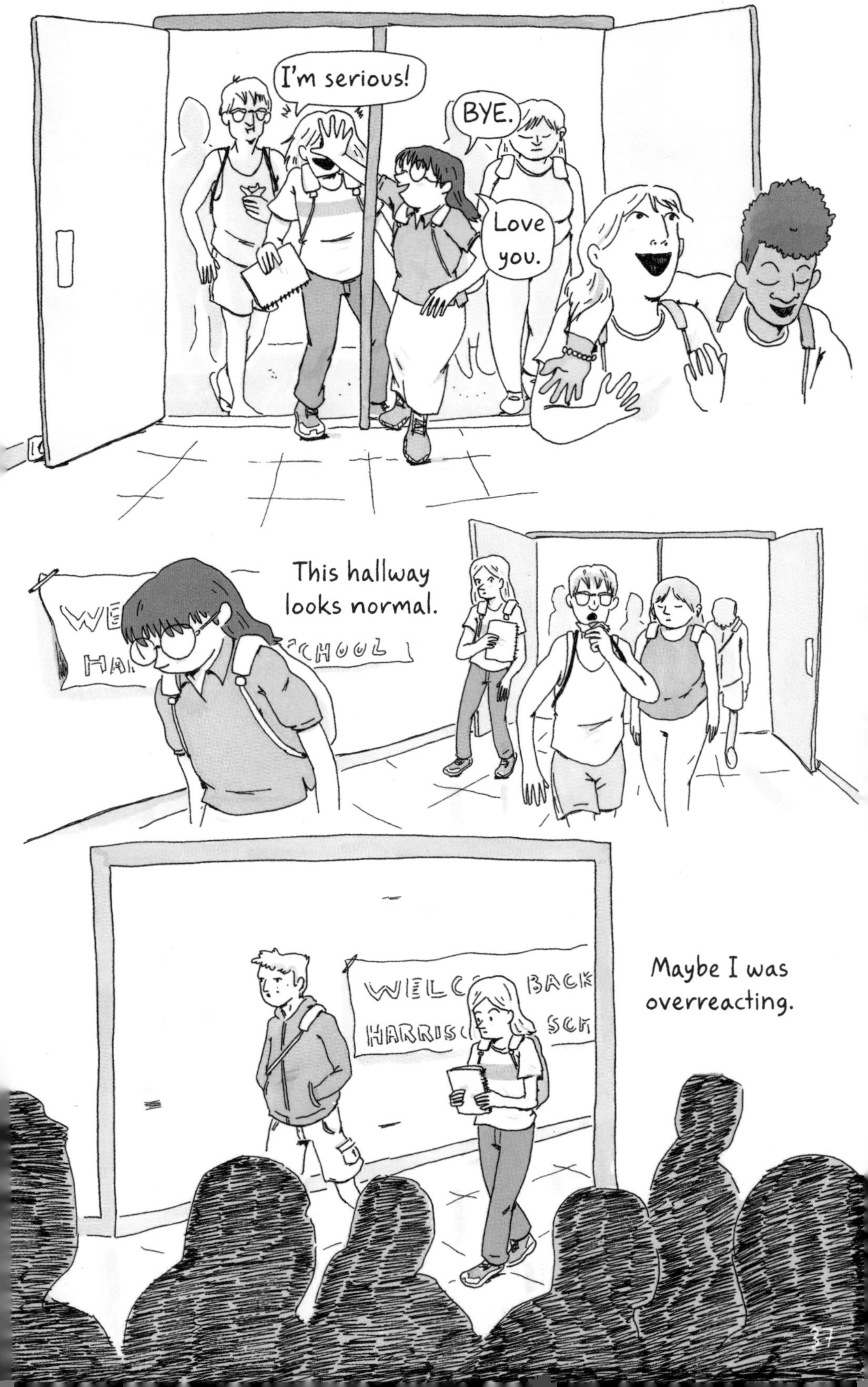
I'm serious!
BYE.
Love you.
This hallway looks normal.
Maybe I was overreacting.

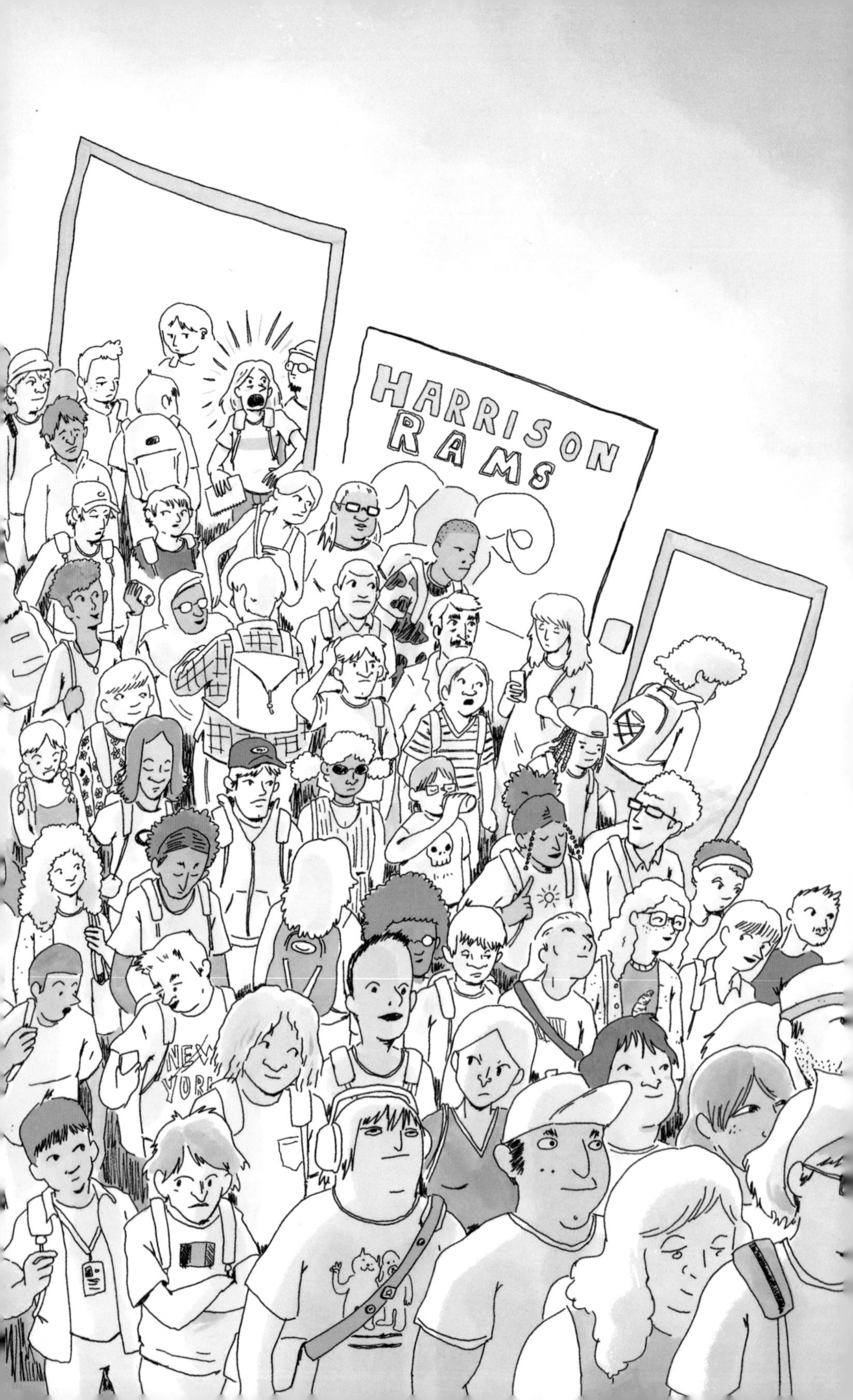
HARRISON
RAMS
NEW
YORK

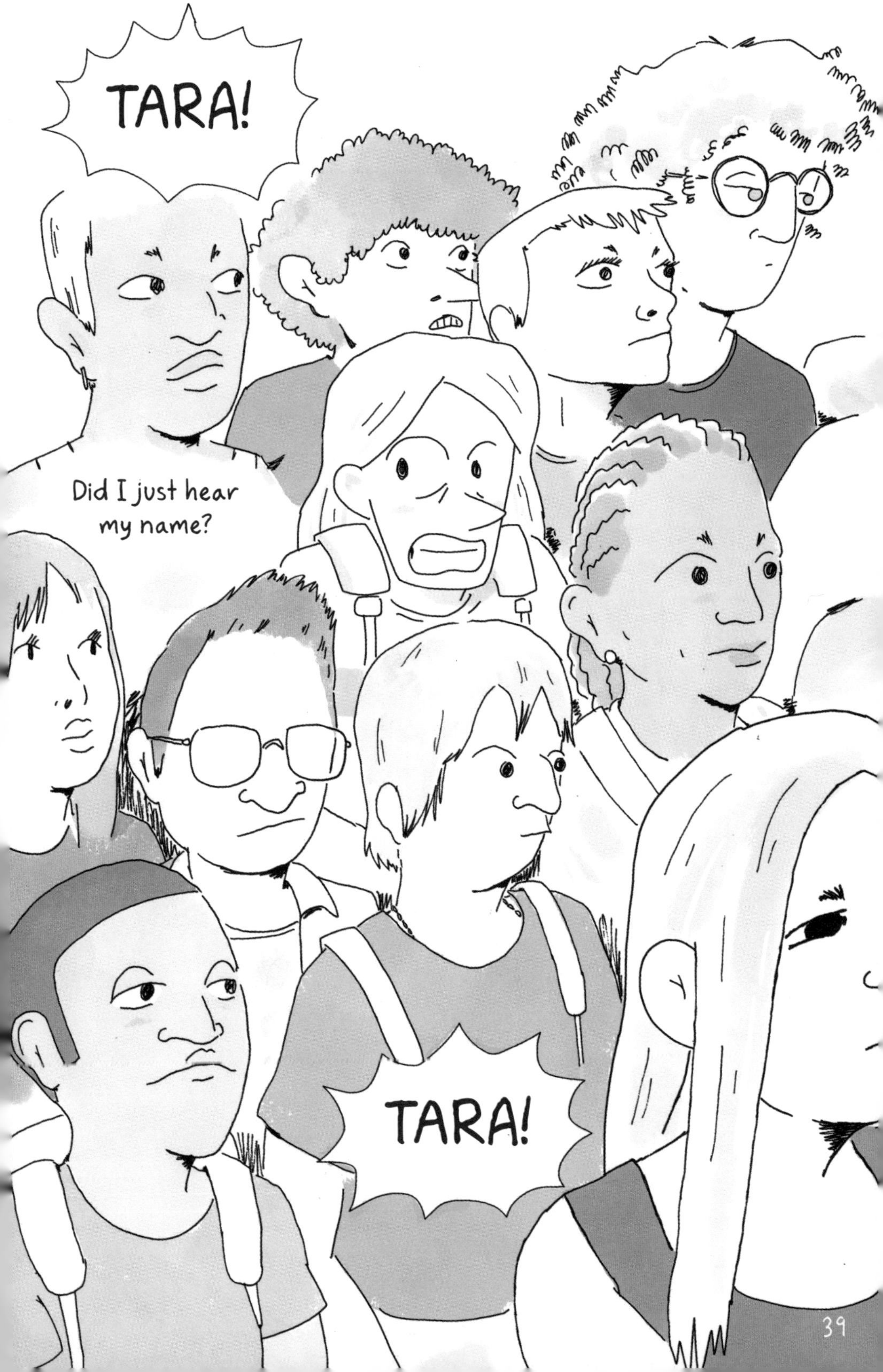
TARA!
Did I just hear my name?
TARA!

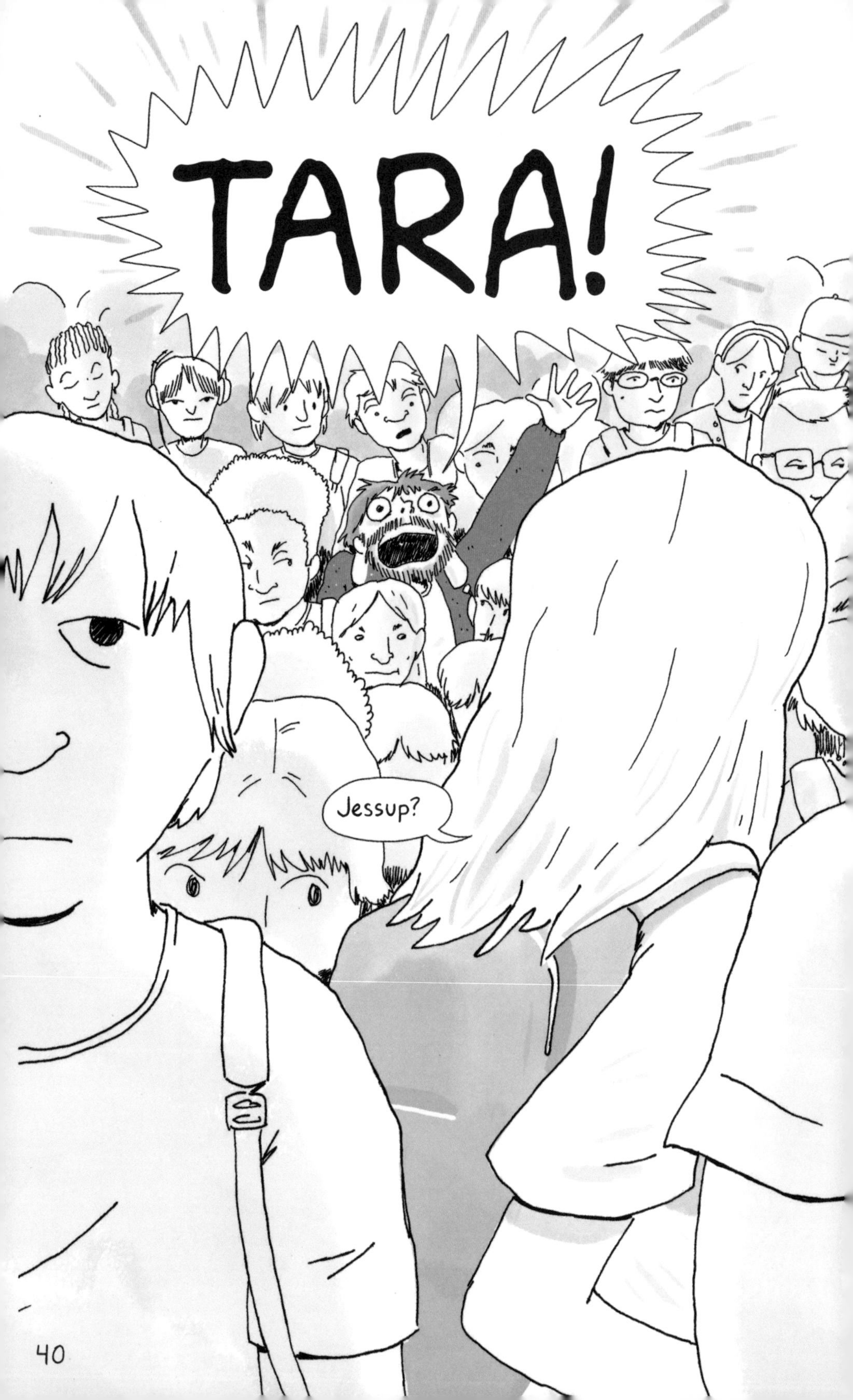
TARA!
Jessup?

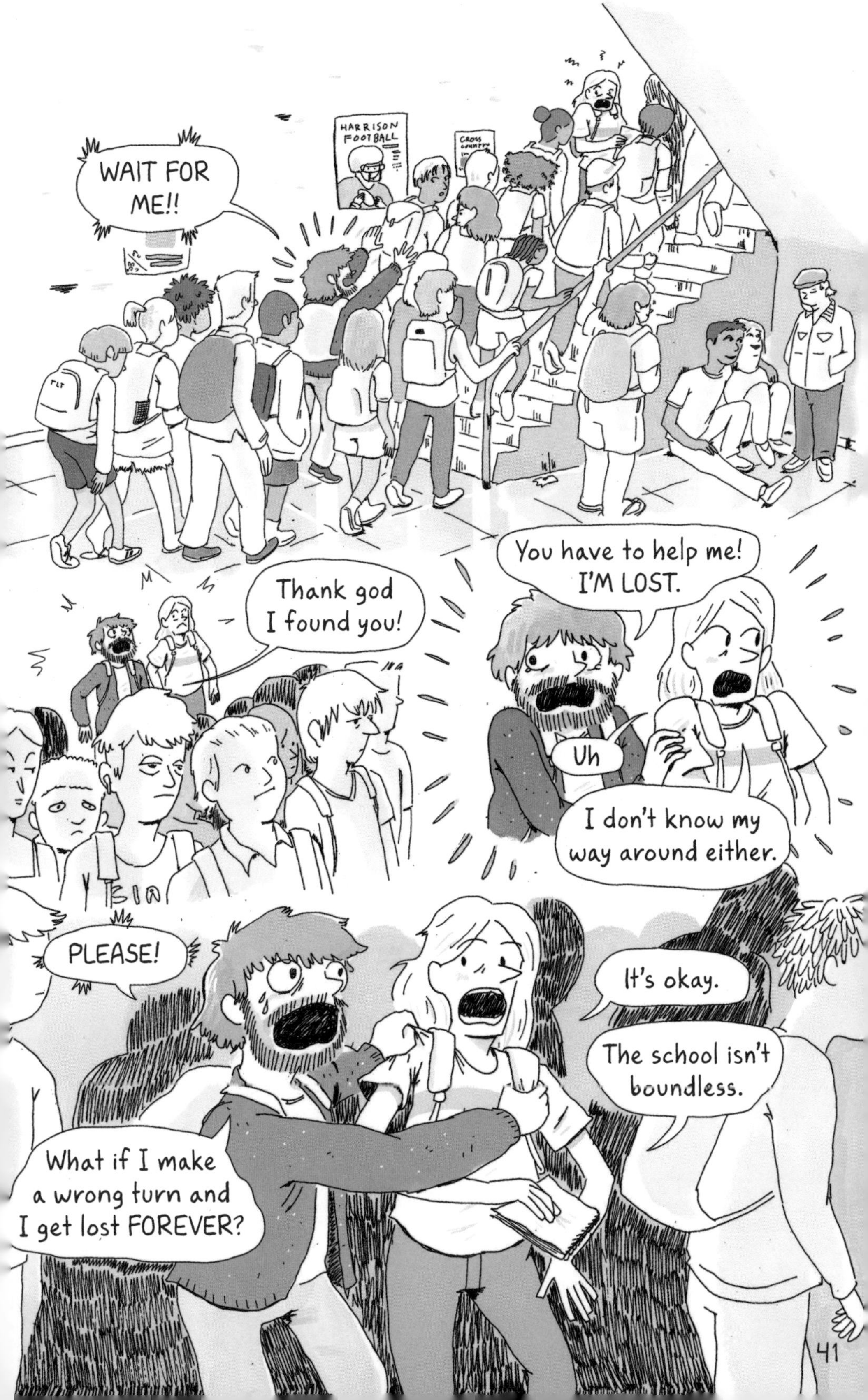
HARRISON FOOTBALL
WAIT FOR ME!!
Thank god I found you!
You have to help me! I'M LOST.
Uh
I don't know my way around either.
PLEASE!
It's okay.
The school isn't boundless.
What if I make a wrong turn and I get lost FOREVER?

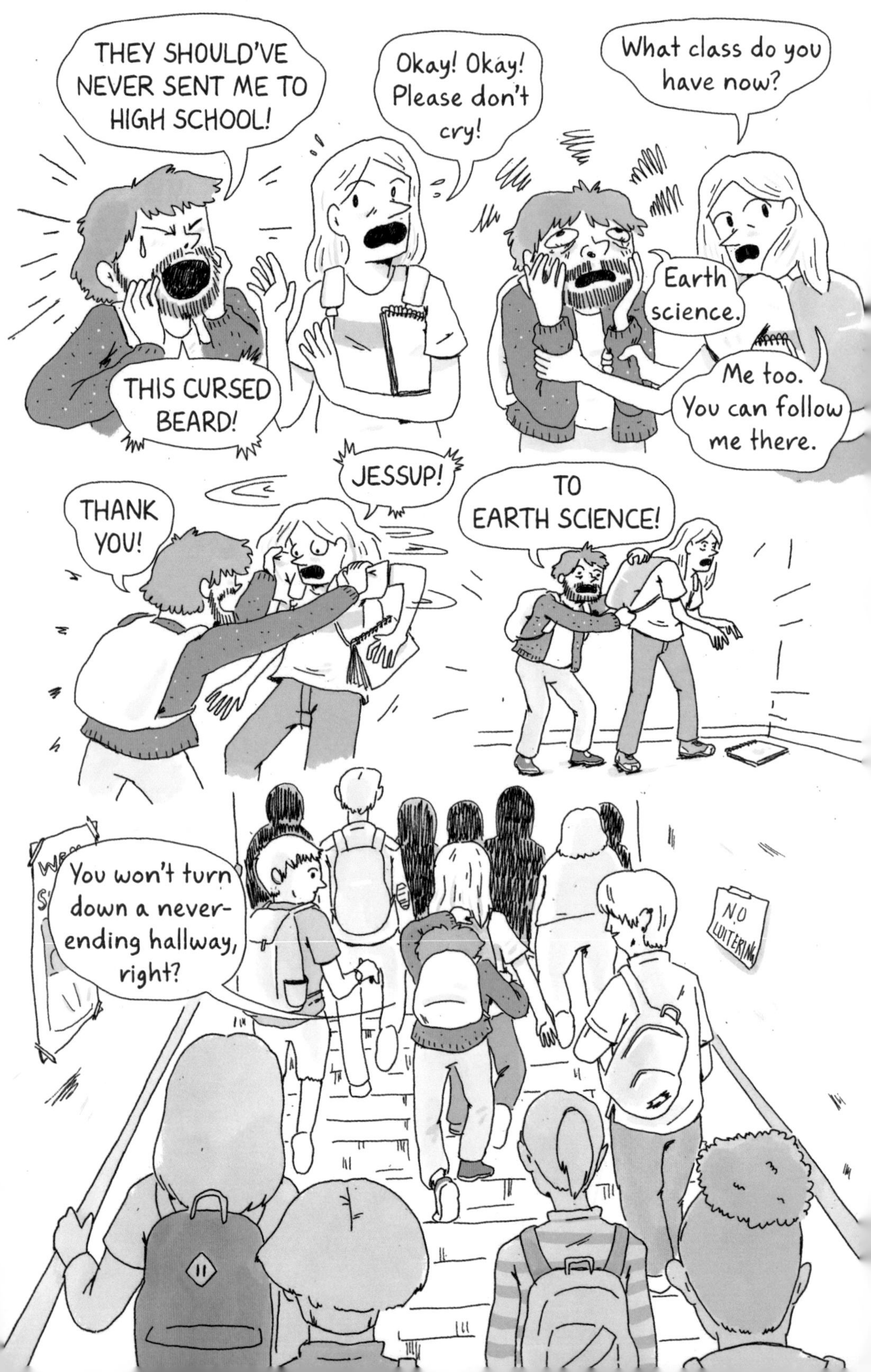
THEY SHOULD'VE NEVER SENT ME TO HIGH SCHOOL!
THIS CURSED BEARD!
Okay! Okay! Please don't cry!
What class do you have now?
Earth science.
Me too. You can follow me there.
THANK YOU!
JESSUP!
TO EARTH SCIENCE!
You won't turn down a never-ending hallway, right?
NO LOITERING

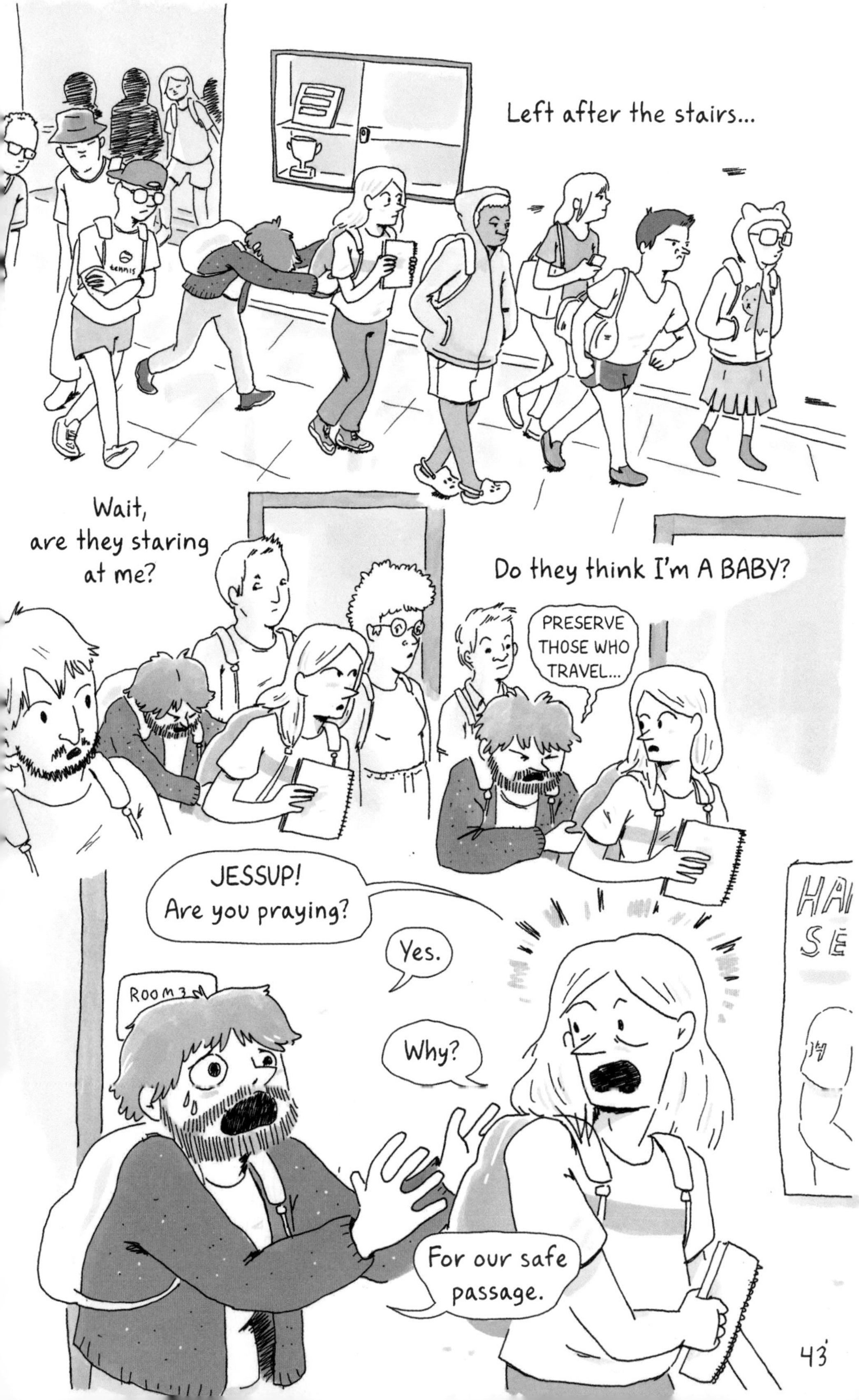
Left after the stairs...
Wait, are they staring at me?
Do they think I'm A BABY?
PRESERVE THOSE WHO TRAVEL...
JESSUP! Are you praying?
Yes.
Why?
For our safe passage.

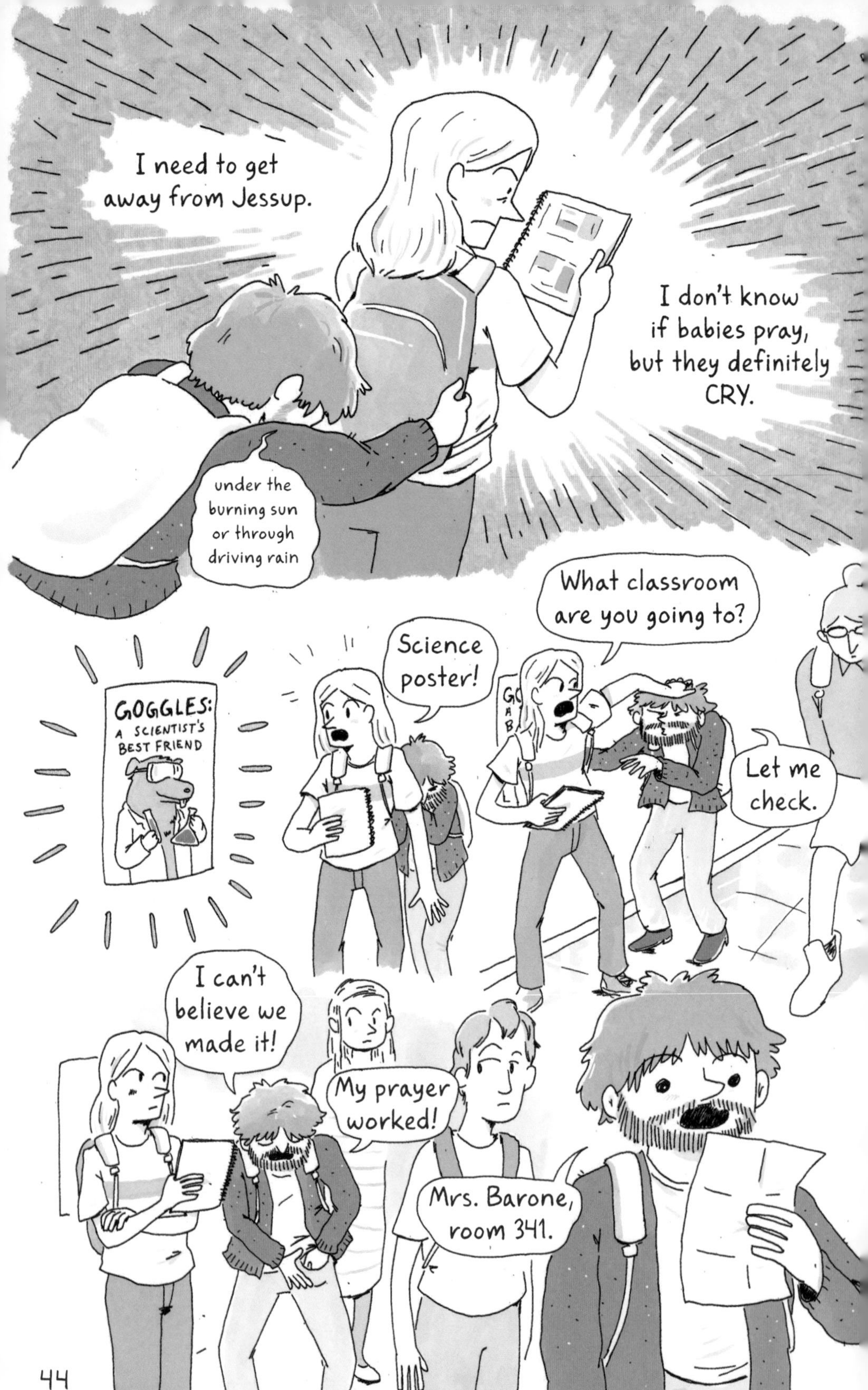
I need to get away from Jessup.
I don't know if babies pray, but they definitely CRY.
under the burning sun or through driving rain
GOGGLES: A SCIENTIST'S BEST FRIEND
Science poster!
What classroom are you going to?
Let me check.
I can't believe we made it!
My prayer worked!
Mrs. Barone, room 341.

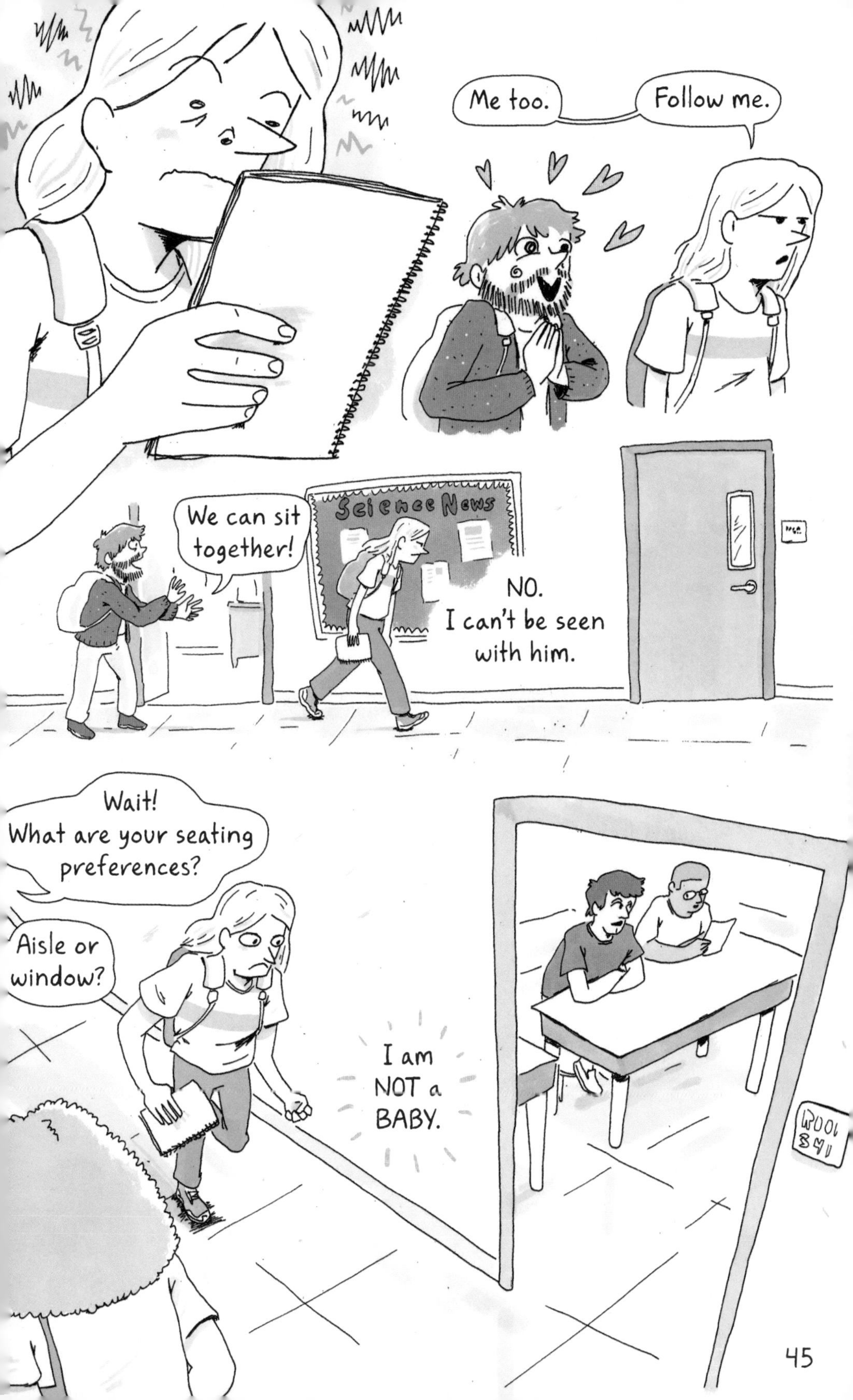
Me too.
Follow me.
Science News
We can sit together!
NO.
I can't be seen with him.
Wait!
What are your seating preferences?
Aisle or window?
I am NOT a BABY.

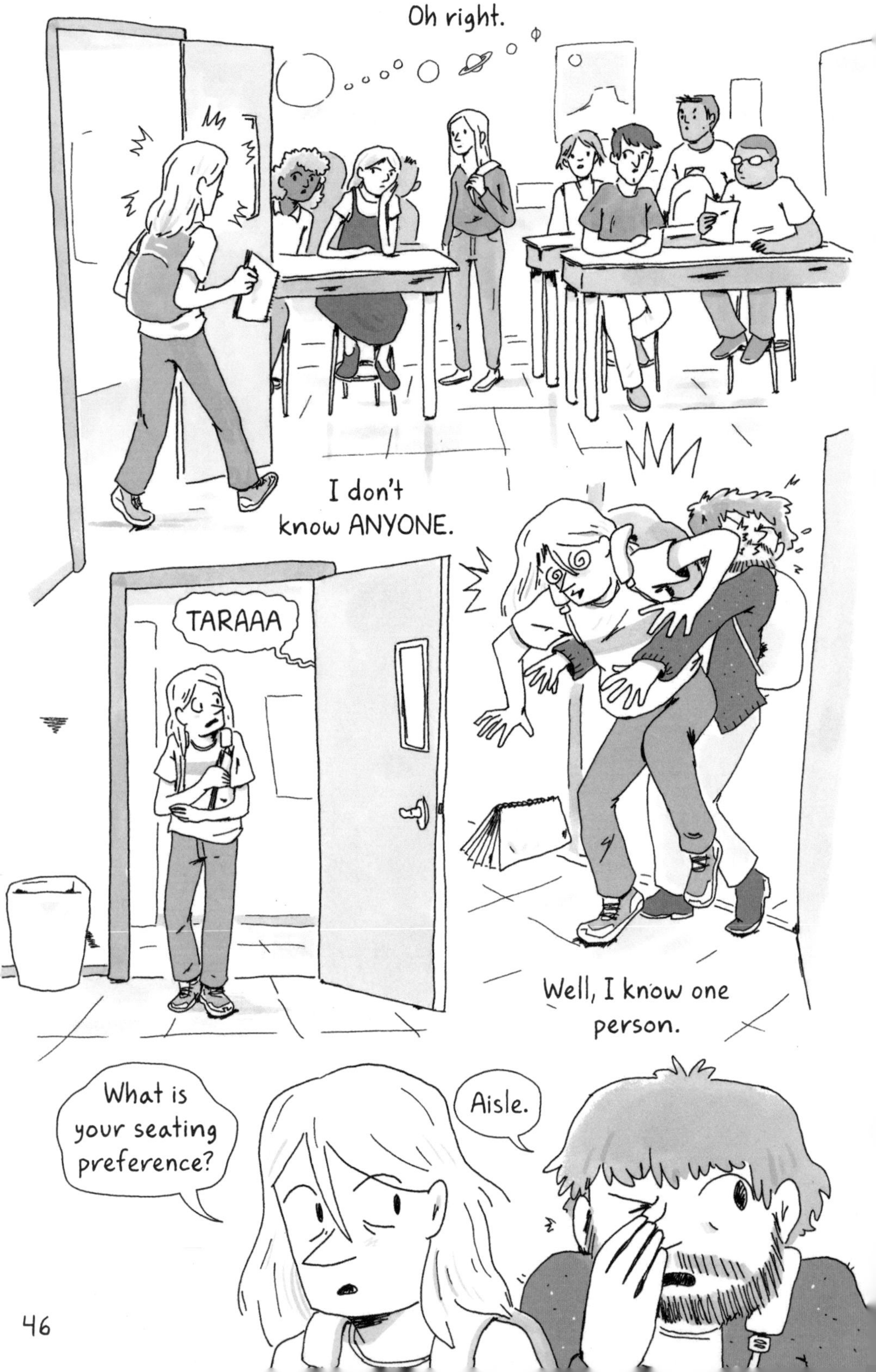
Oh right.
I don't know ANYONE.
TARAAA
Well, I know one person.
What is your seating preference?
Aisle.

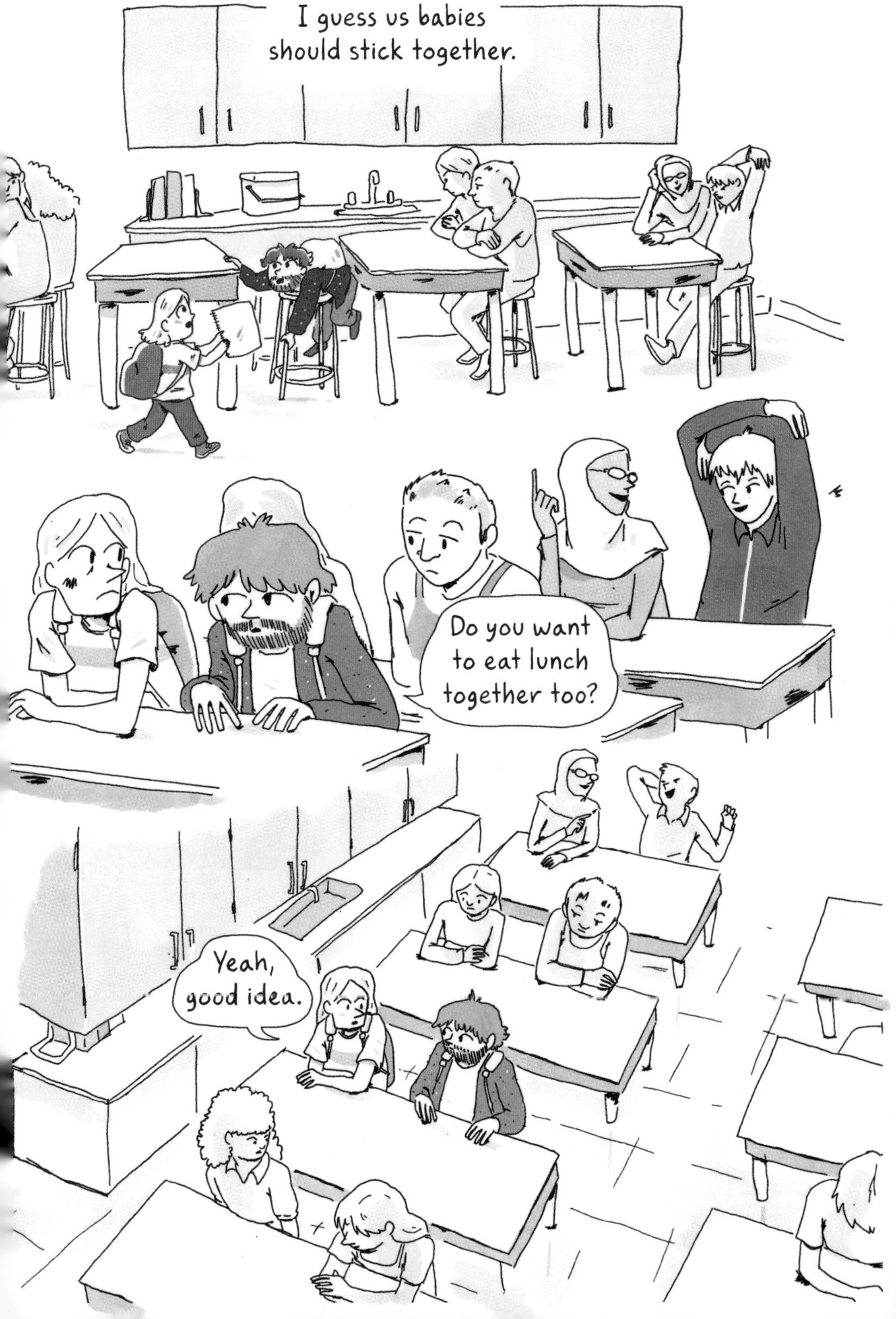
I guess us babies should stick together.
Do you want to eat lunch together too?
Yeah, good idea.

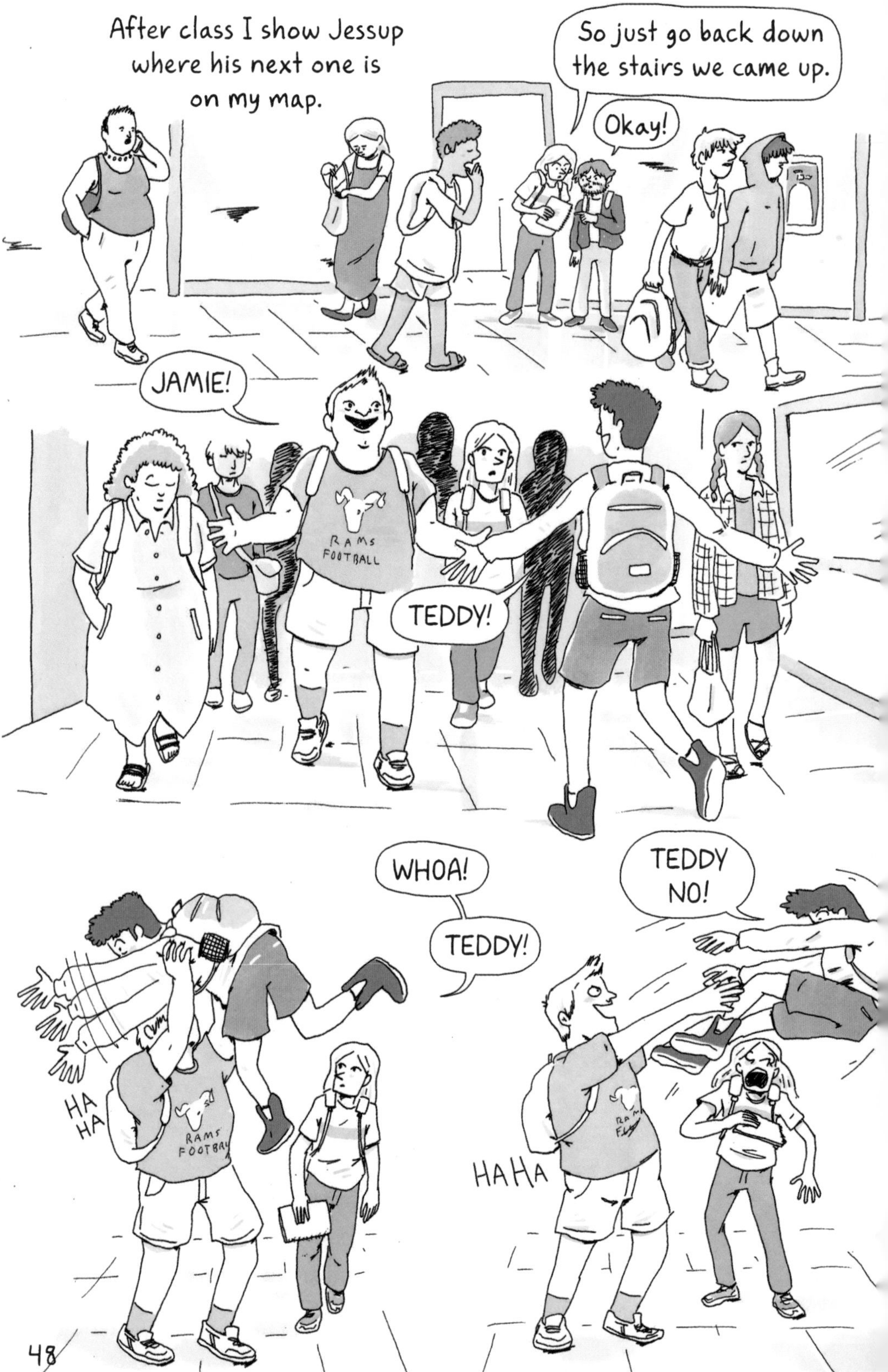
After class I show Jessup where his next one is on my map.
So just go back down the stairs we came up.
Okay!
JAMIE!
TEDDY!
WHOA!
TEDDY!
HA HA
TEDDY NO!
HAHA

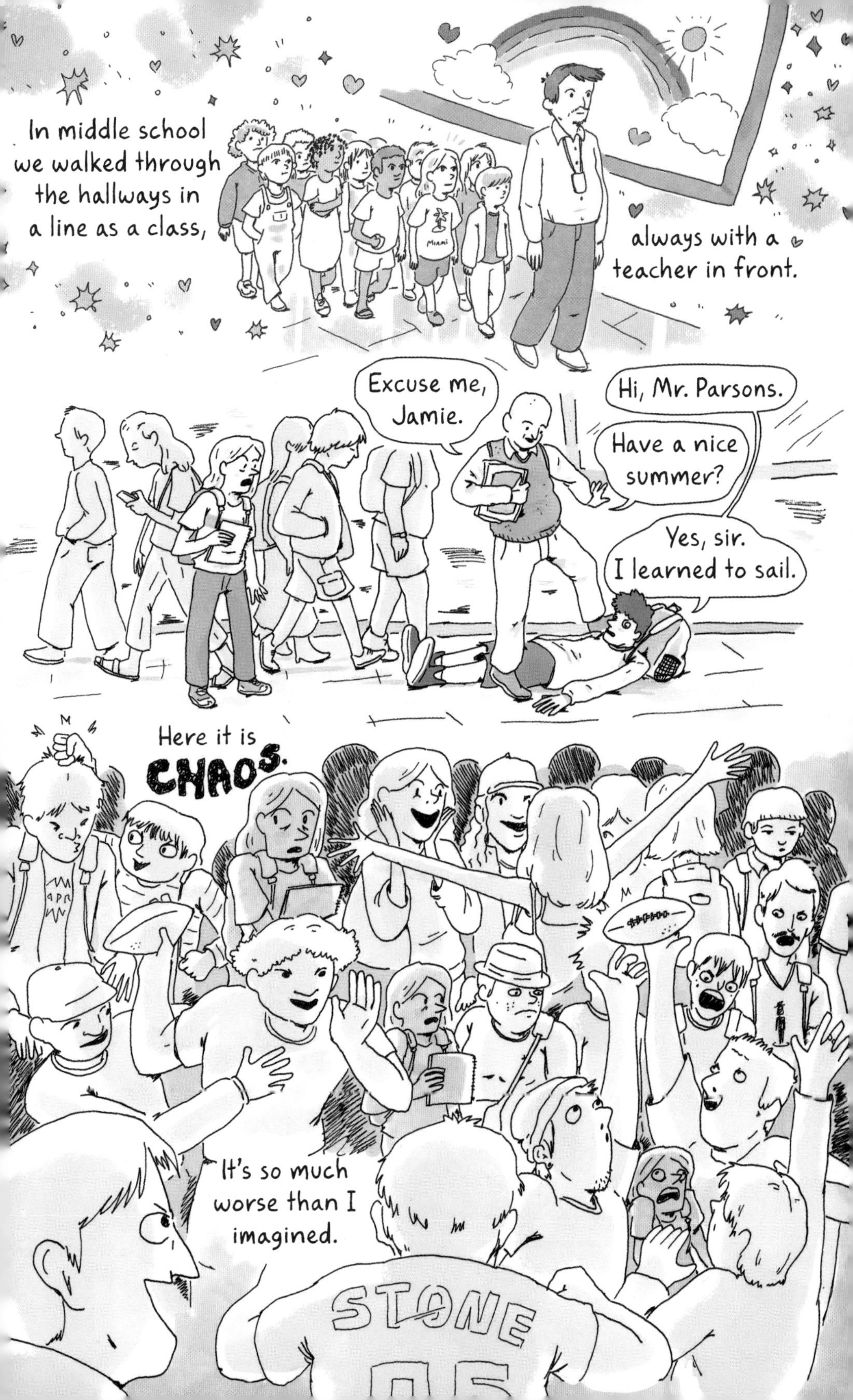
In middle school we walked through the hallways in a line as a class,
always with a teacher in front.
Miami
Excuse me, Jamie.
Hi, Mr. Parsons.
Have a nice summer?
Yes, sir. I learned to sail.
Here it is CHAOS.
It's so much worse than I imagined.
STONE

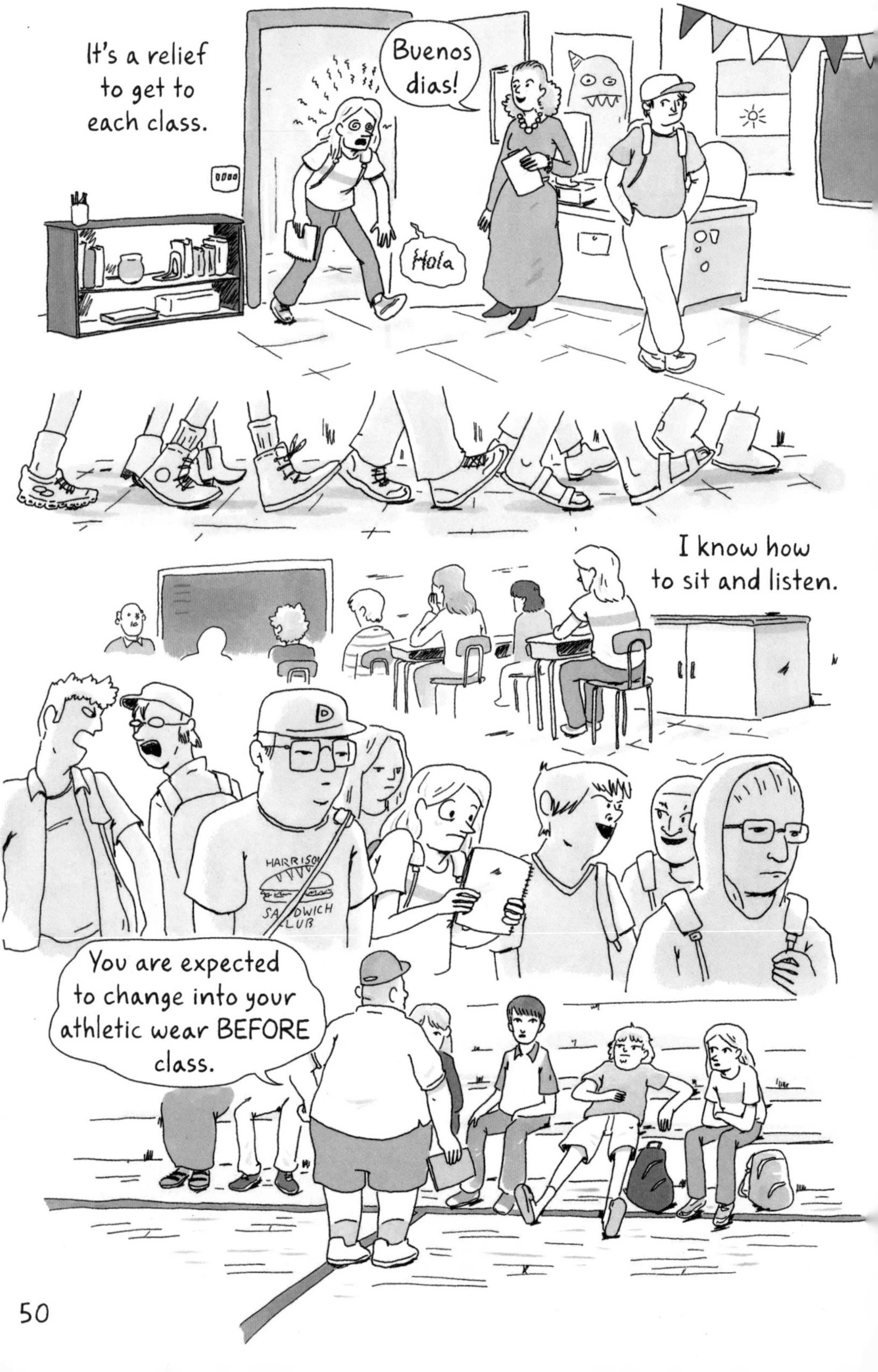
It's a relief to get to each class.
Buenos dias!
Hola
I know how to sit and listen.
HARRISON SANDWICH CLUB
You are expected to change into your athletic wear BEFORE class.

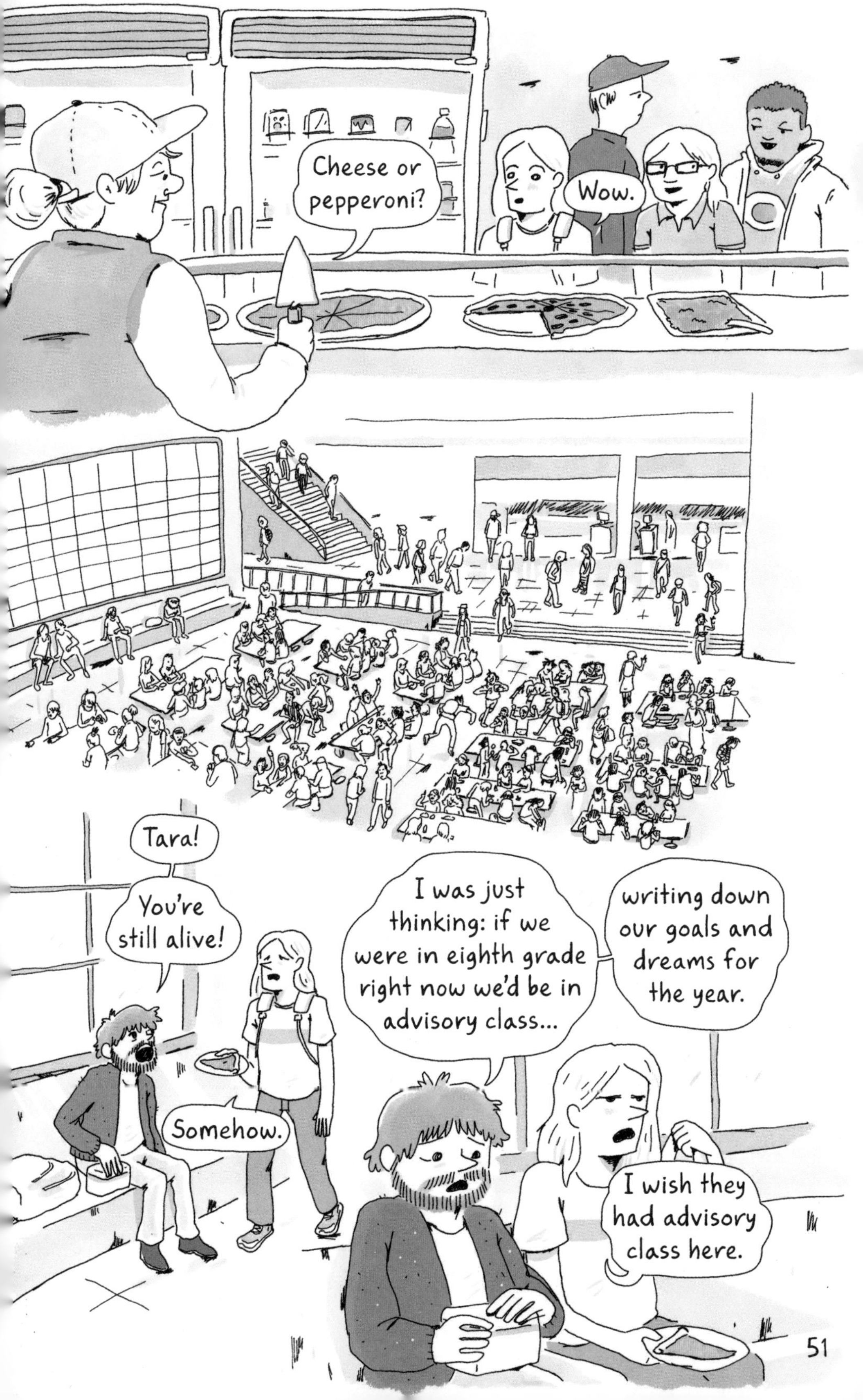
Cheese or pepperoni?
Wow.
Tara!
You're still alive!
Somehow.
I was just thinking: if we were in eighth grade right now we'd be in advisory class...
writing down our goals and dreams for the year.
I wish they had advisory class here.

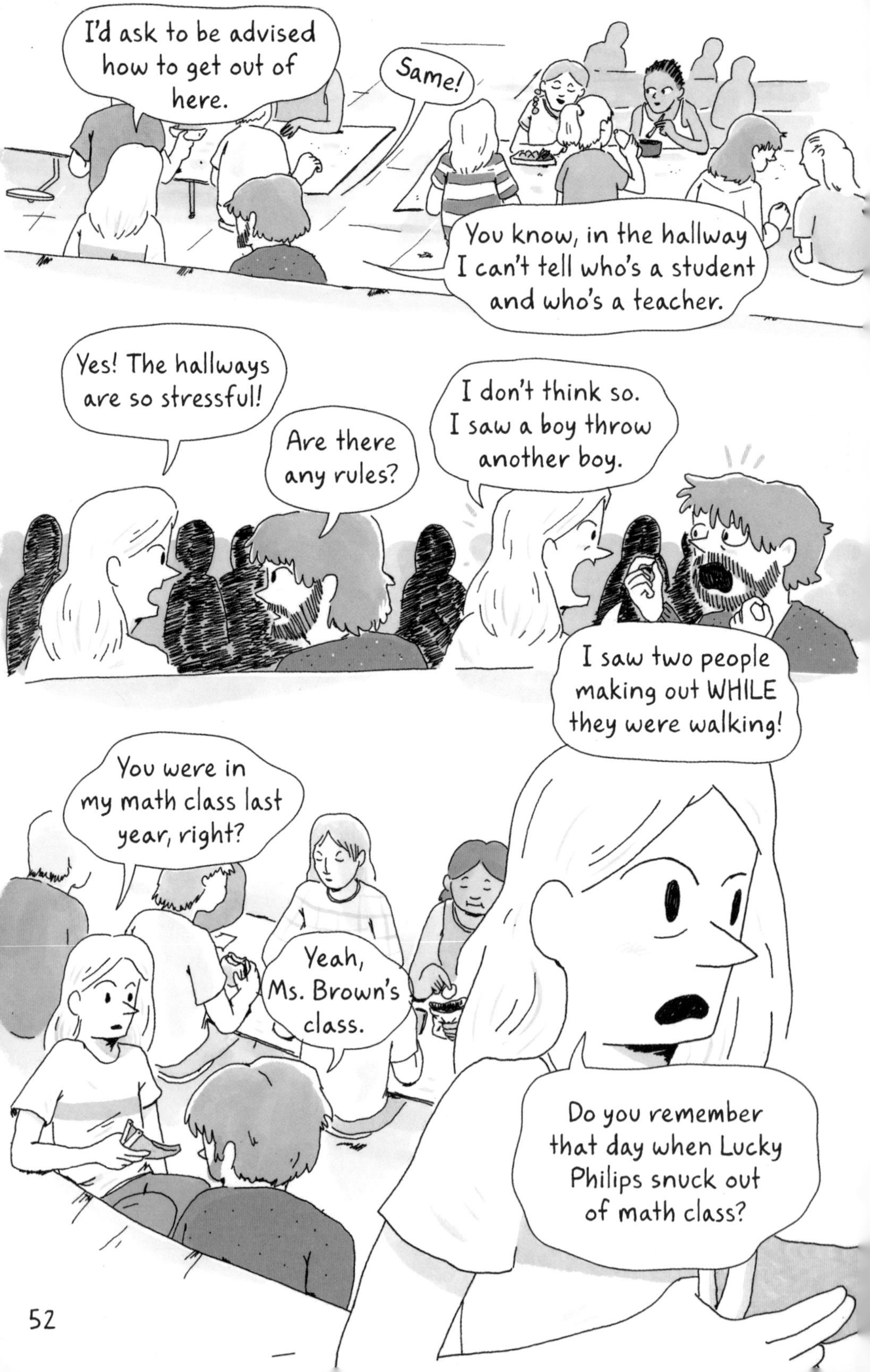
I'd ask to be advised how to get out of here.
Same!
You know, in the hallway I can't tell who's a student and who's a teacher.
Yes! The hallways are so stressful!
Are there any rules?
I don't think so. I saw a boy throw another boy.
I saw two people making out WHILE they were walking!
You were in my math class last year, right?
Yeah, Ms. Brown's class.
Do you remember that day when Lucky Philips snuck out of math class?

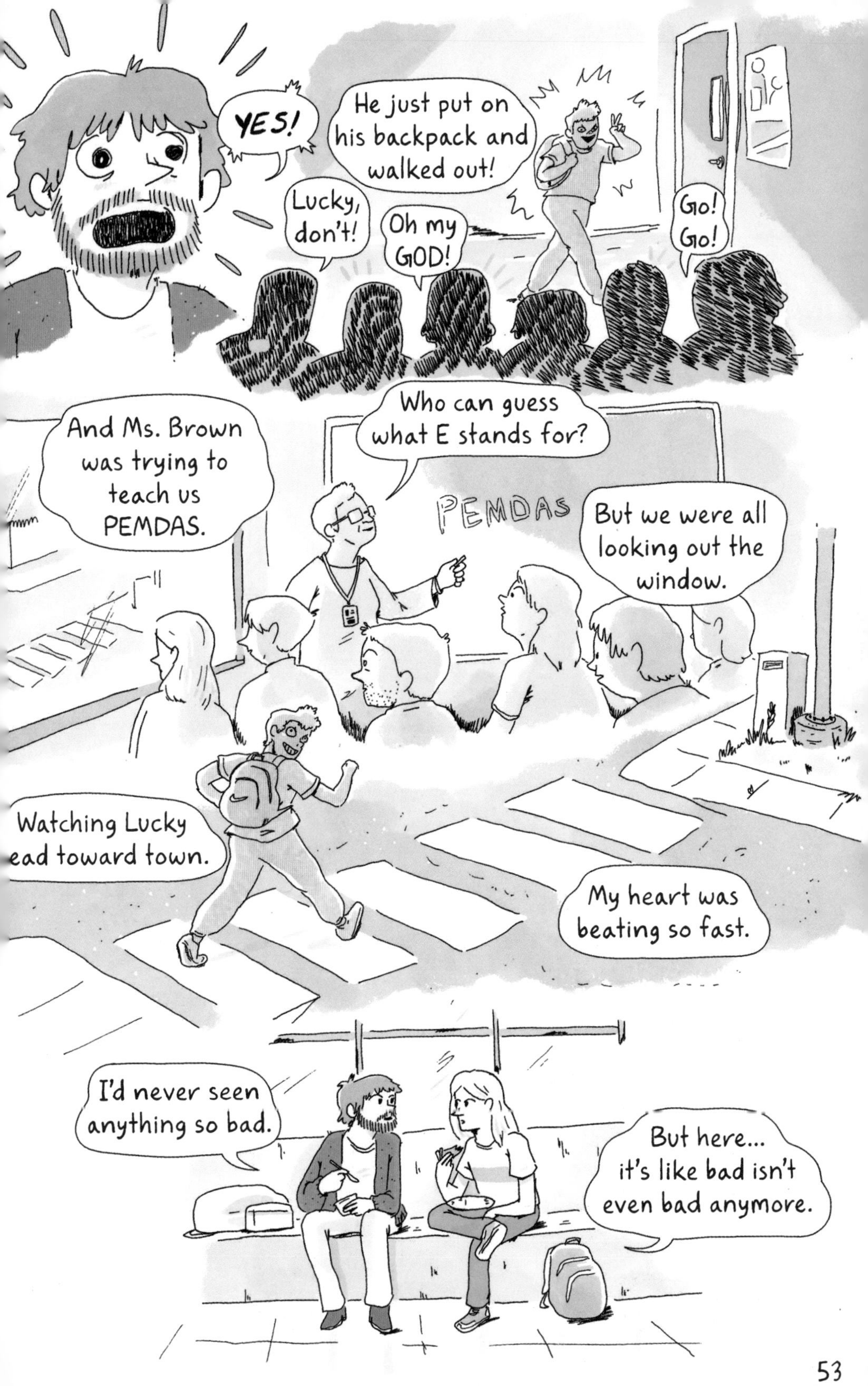
YES!
He just put on his backpack and walked out!
Lucky, don't!
Oh my GOD!
Go! Go!
And Ms. Brown was trying to teach us PEMDAS.
Who can guess what E stands for?
PEMDAS
But we were all looking out the window.
Watching Lucky ead toward town.
My heart was beating so fast.
I'd never seen anything so bad.
But here... it's like bad isn't even bad anymore.

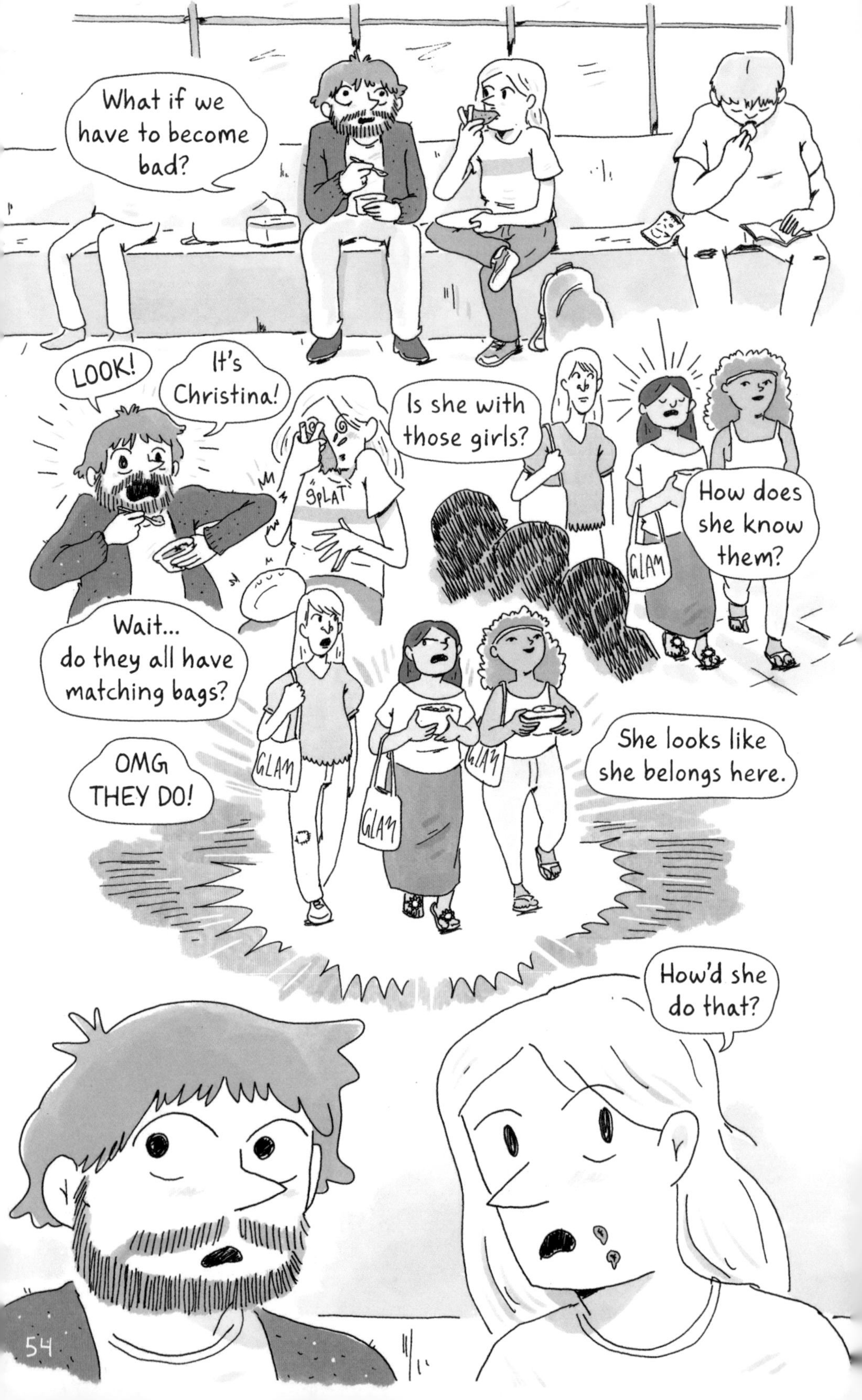
What if we have to become bad?
LOOK!
It's Christina!
SPLAT
Is she with those girls?
How does she know them?
Wait... do they all have matching bags?
GLAM
GLAM
GLAM
GLAM
OMG THEY DO!
She looks like she belongs here.
How'd she do that?

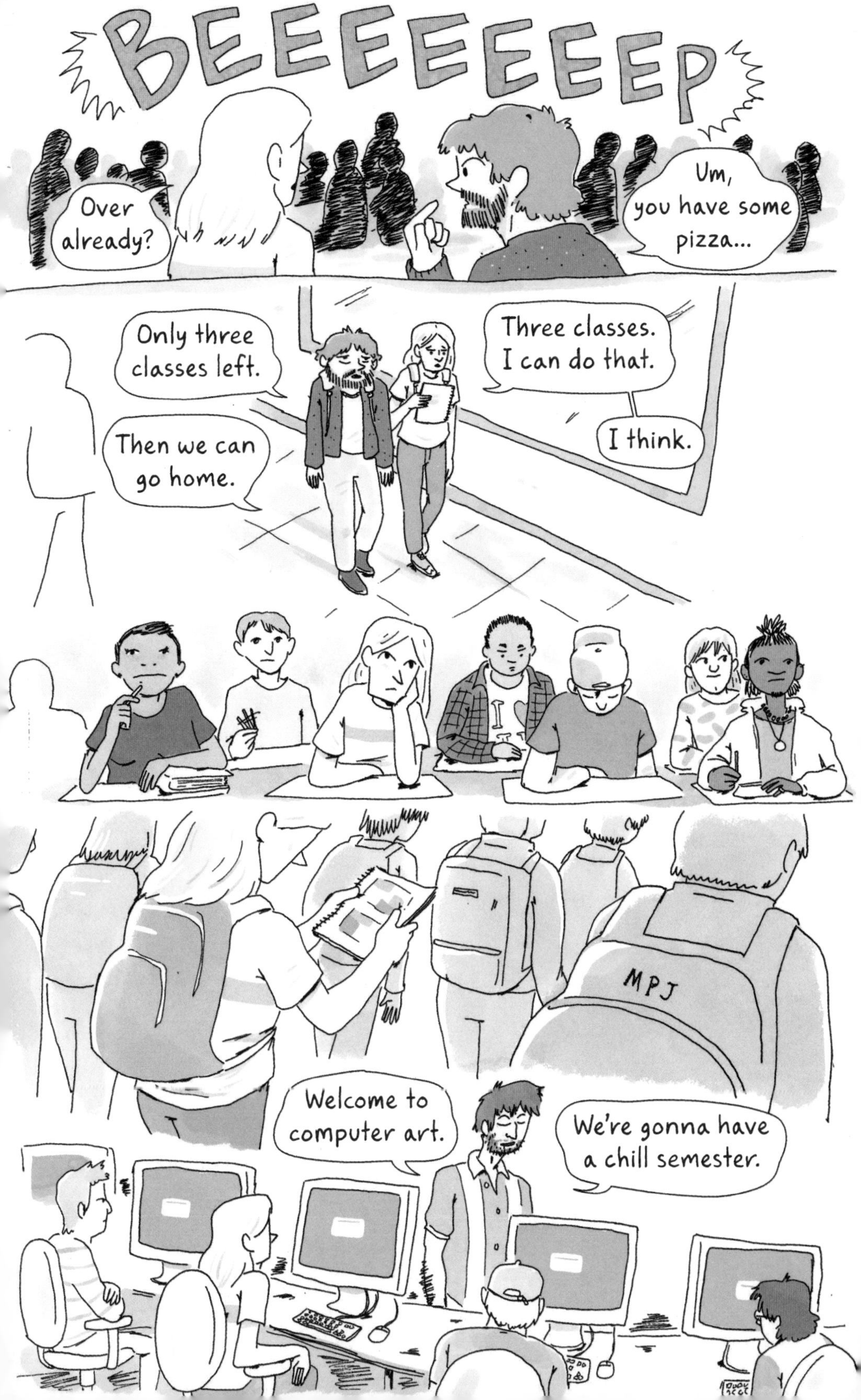
BEEEEEEEP
Over already?
Um, you have some pizza...
Only three classes left.
Then we can go home.
Three classes. I can do that.
I think.
MPJ
Welcome to computer art.
We're gonna have a chill semester.

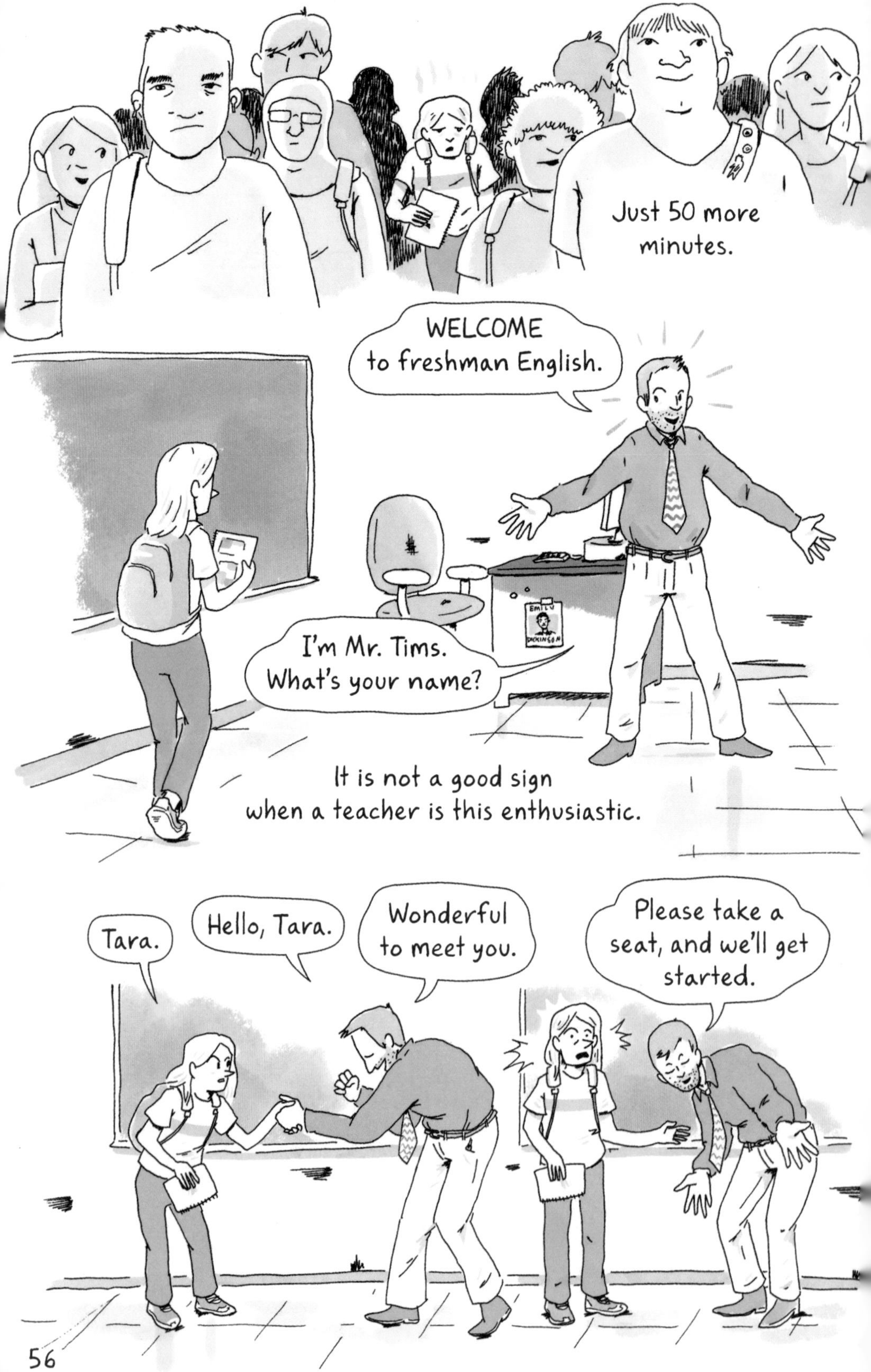
Just 50 more minutes.
WELCOME to freshman English.
I'm Mr. Tims. What's your name?
It is not a good sign when a teacher is this enthusiastic.
Tara.
Hello, Tara.
Wonderful to meet you.
Please take a seat, and we'll get started.

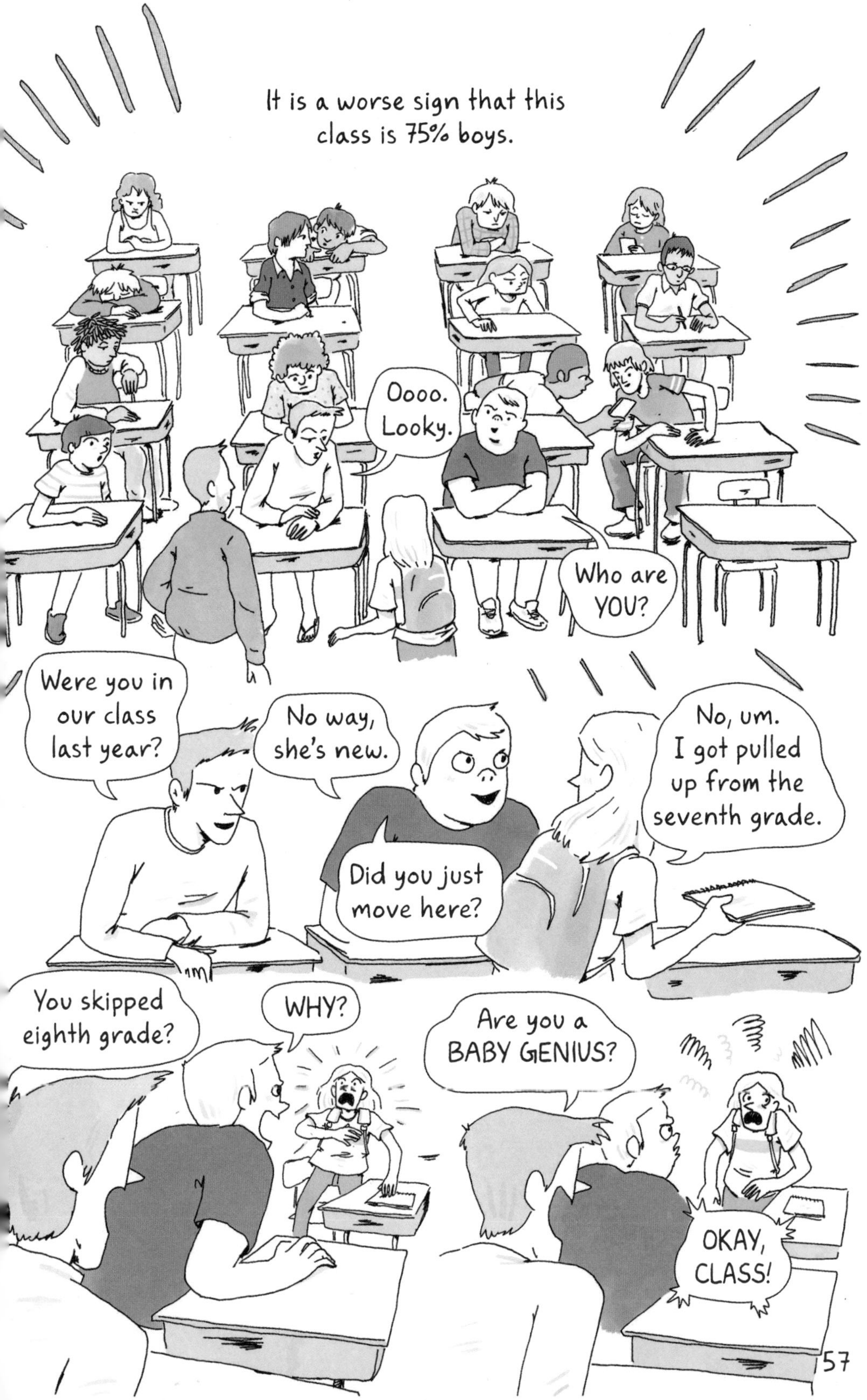

It is a worse sign that this class is 75% boys.
Oooo. Looky.
Who are YOU?
Were you in our class last year?
No way, she's new.
No, um. I got pulled up from the seventh grade.
Did you just move here?
You skipped eighth grade?
WHY?
Are you a BABY GENIUS?
OKAY, CLASS!

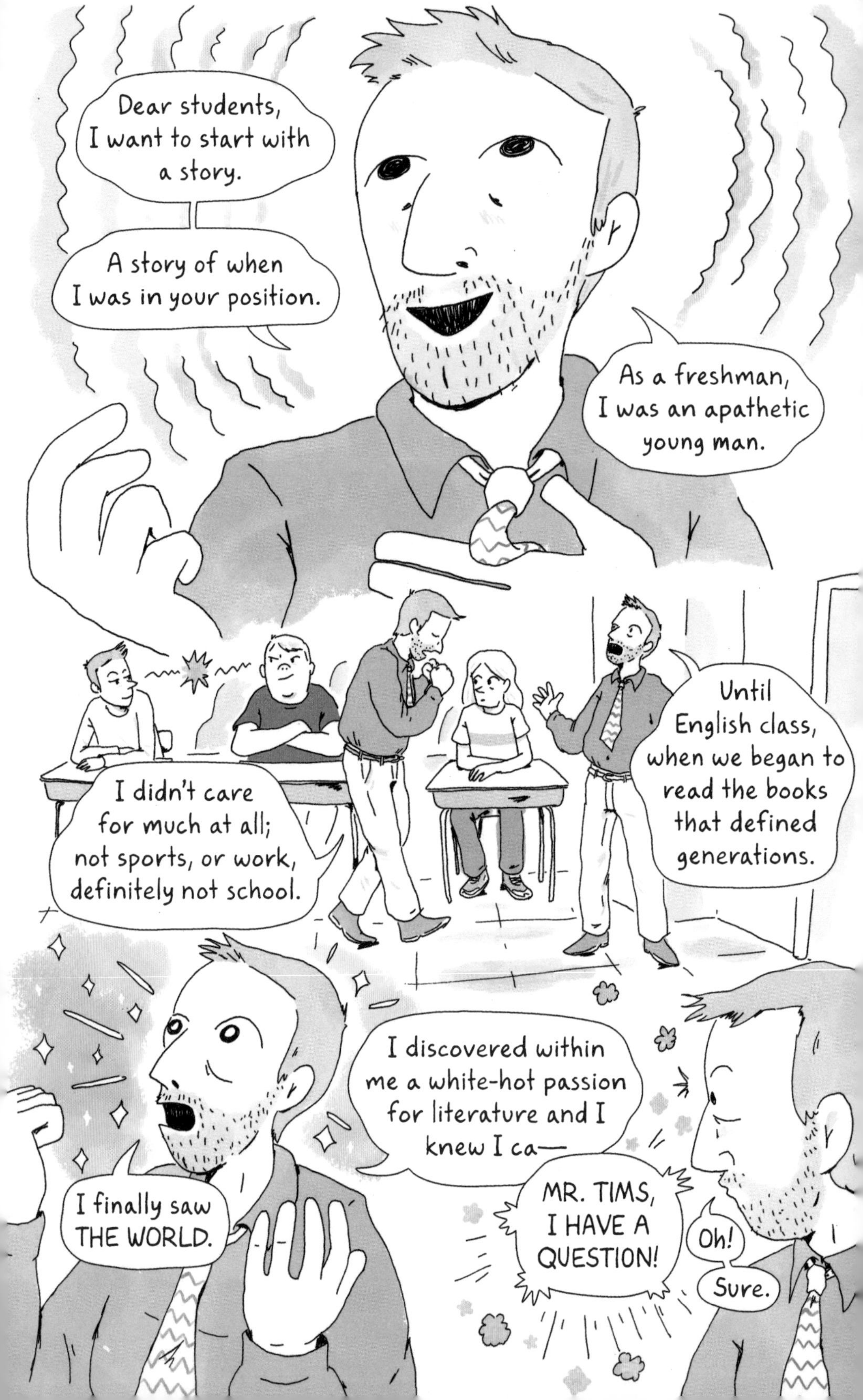
Dear students, I want to start with a story.
A story of when I was in your position.
As a freshman, I was an apathetic young man.
I didn't care for much at all; not sports, or work, definitely not school.
Until English class, when we began to read the books that defined generations.
I finally saw THE WORLD.
I discovered within me a white-hot passion for literature and I knew I ca—
MR. TIMS, I HAVE A QUESTION!
Oh!
Sure.

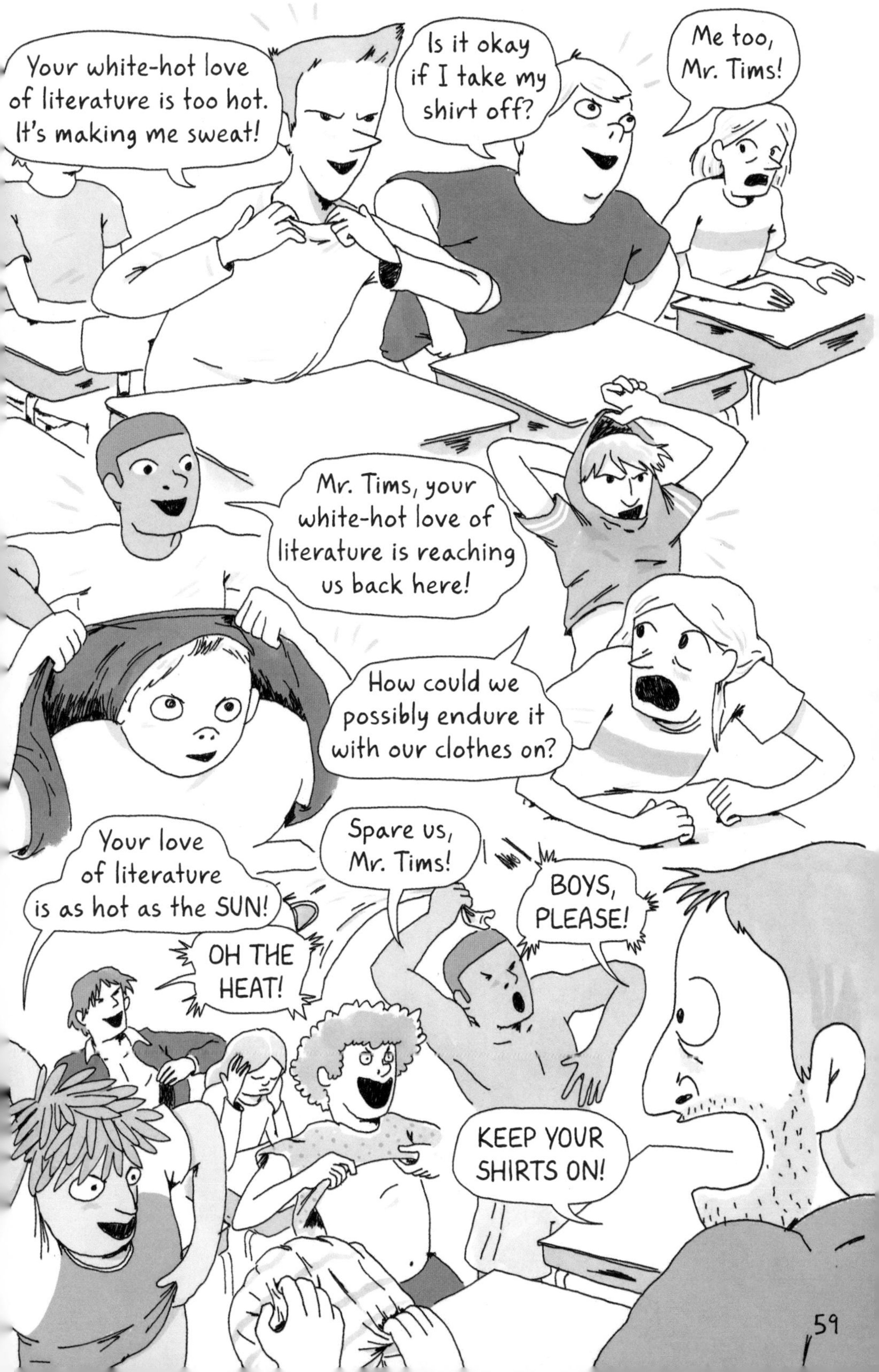
Your white-hot love of literature is too hot. It's making me sweat!
Is it okay if I take my shirt off?
Me too, Mr. Tims!
Mr. Tims, your white-hot love of literature is reaching us back here!
How could we possibly endure it with our clothes on?
Your love of literature is as hot as the SUN!
Spare us, Mr. Tims!
BOYS, PLEASE!
OH THE HEAT!
KEEP YOUR SHIRTS ON!

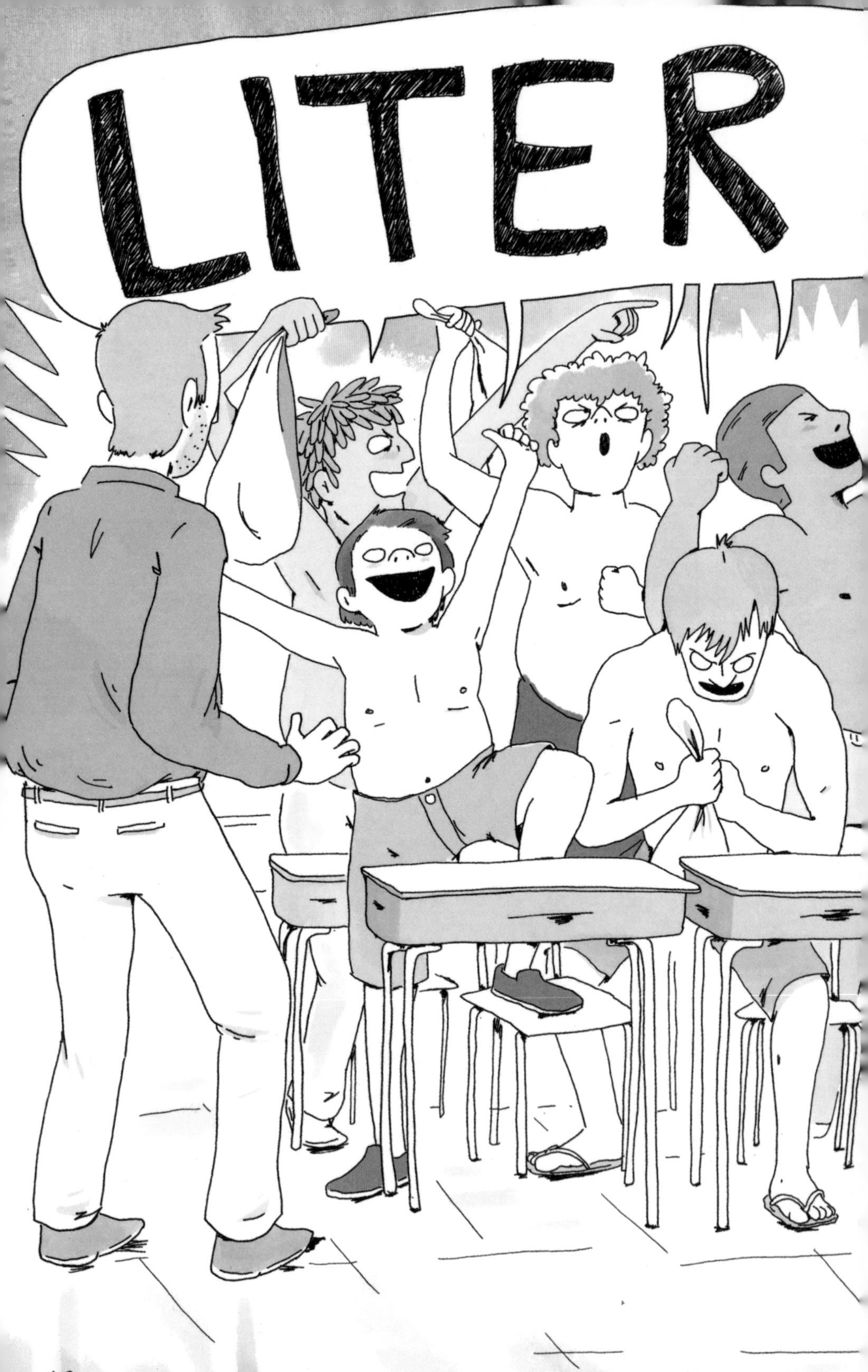
LITER

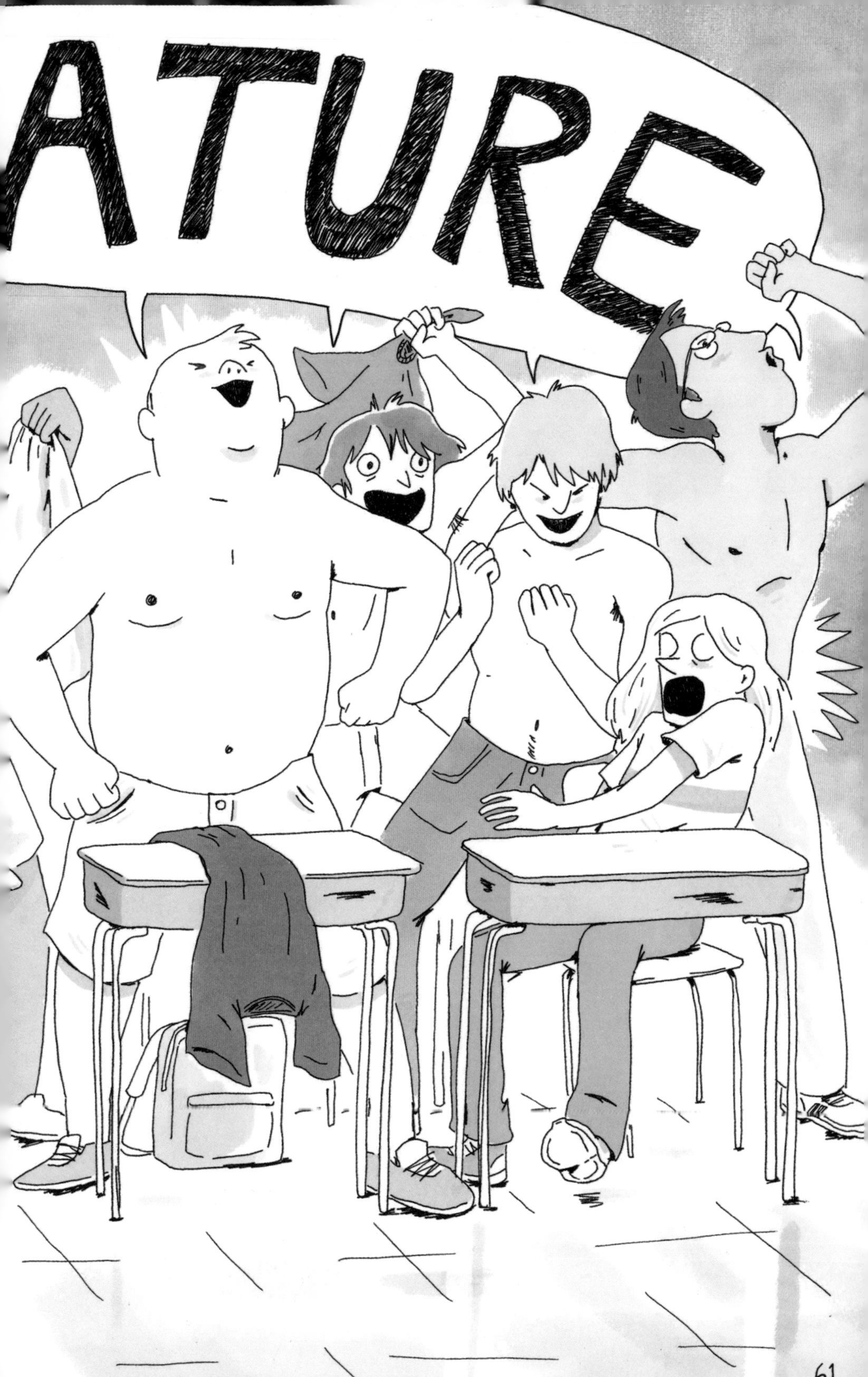
ATURE

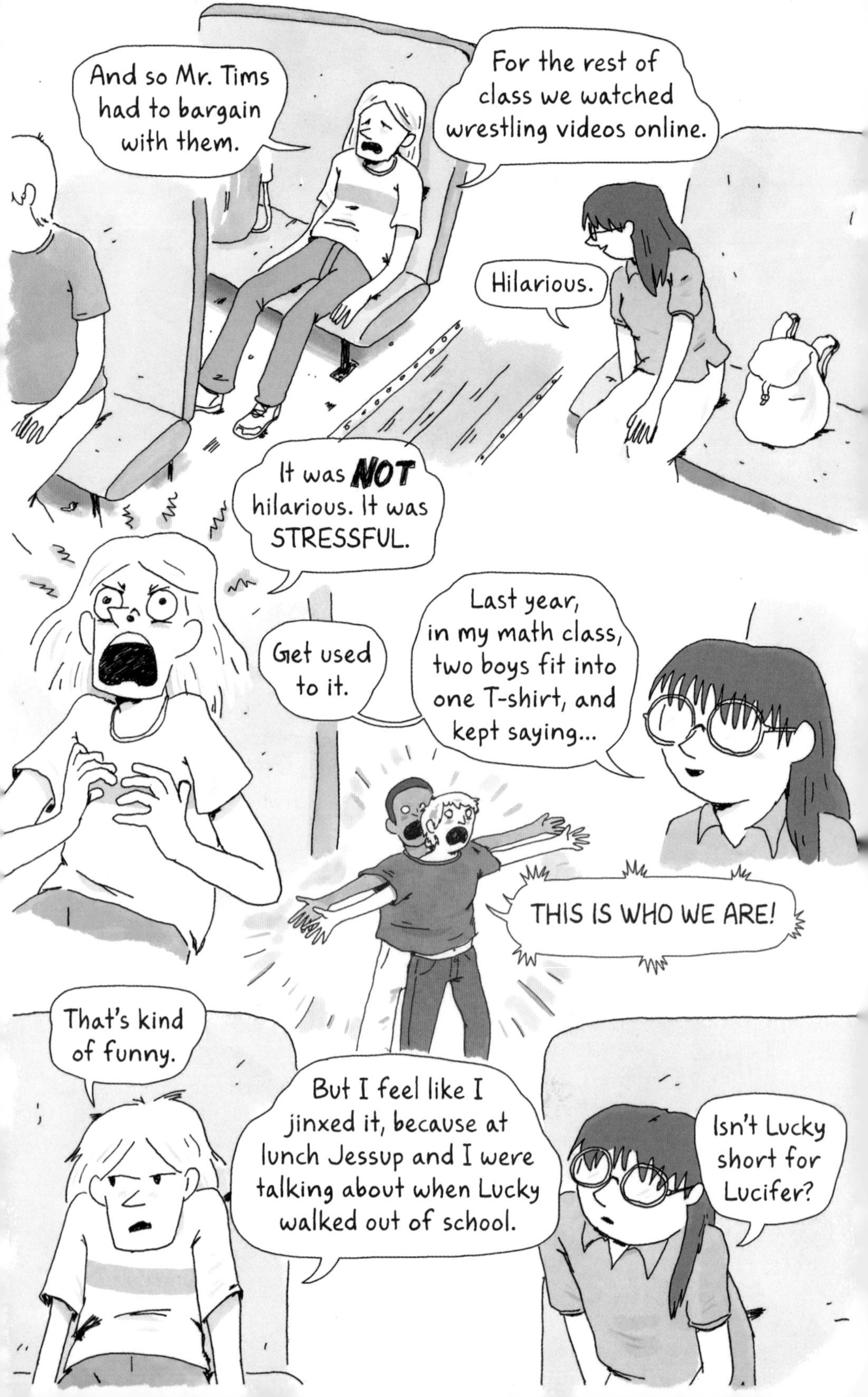
And so Mr. Tims had to bargain with them.
For the rest of class we watched wrestling videos online.
Hilarious.
It was NOT hilarious. It was STRESSFUL.
Get used to it.
Last year, in my math class, two boys fit into one T-shirt, and kept saying...
THIS IS WHO WE ARE!
That's kind of funny.
But I feel like I jinxed it, because at lunch Jessup and I were talking about when Lucky walked out of school.
Isn't Lucky short for Lucifer?

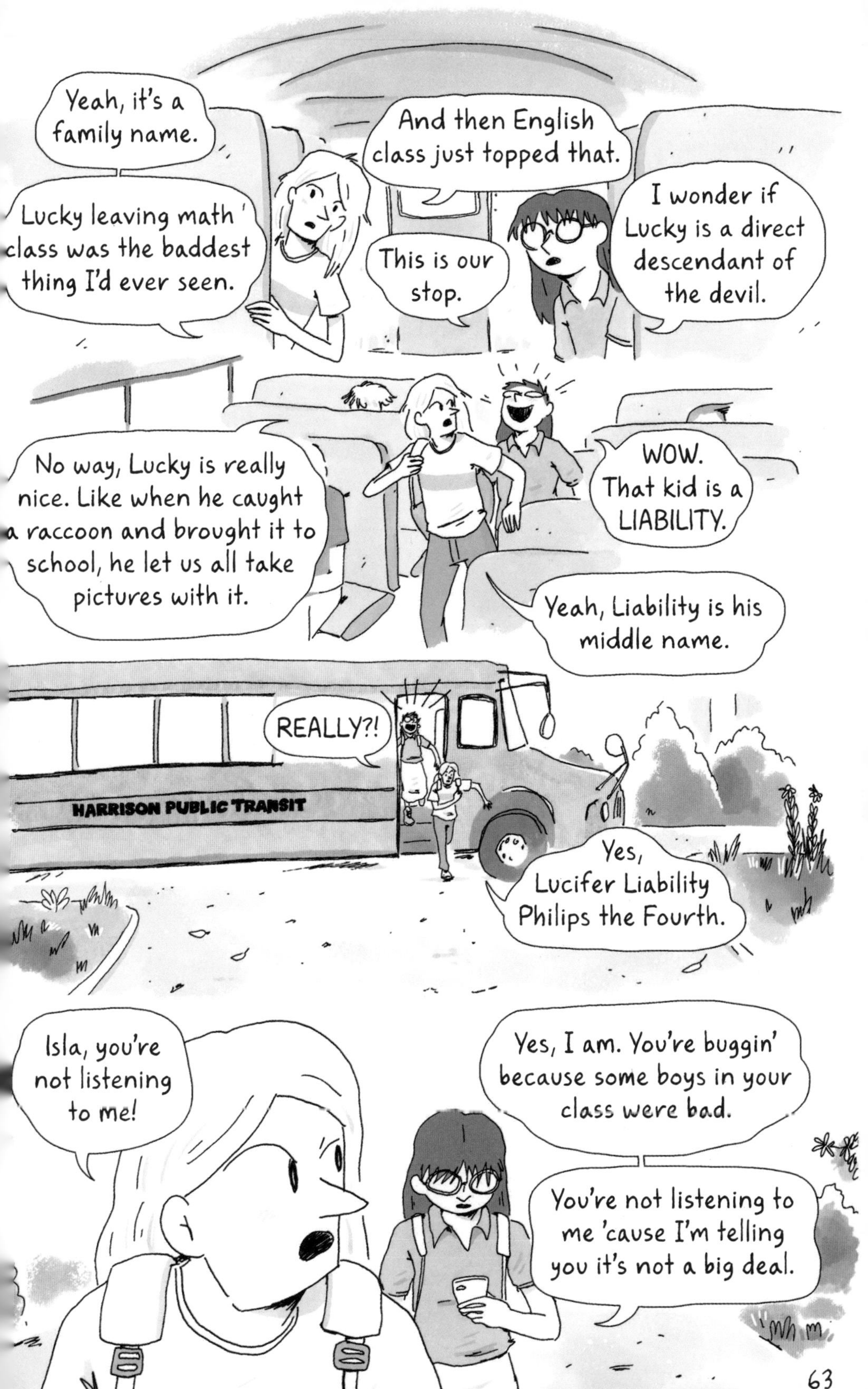
Yeah, it's a family name.
Lucky leaving math class was the baddest thing I'd ever seen.
And then English class just topped that.
This is our stop.
I wonder if Lucky is a direct descendant of the devil.
No way, Lucky is really nice. Like when he caught a raccoon and brought it to school, he let us all take pictures with it.
WOW. That kid is a LIABILITY.
Yeah, Liability is his middle name.
REALLY?!
HARRISON PUBLIC TRANSIT
Yes, Lucifer Liability Philips the Fourth.
Isla, you're not listening to me!
Yes, I am. You're buggin' because some boys in your class were bad.
You're not listening to me 'cause I'm telling you it's not a big deal.

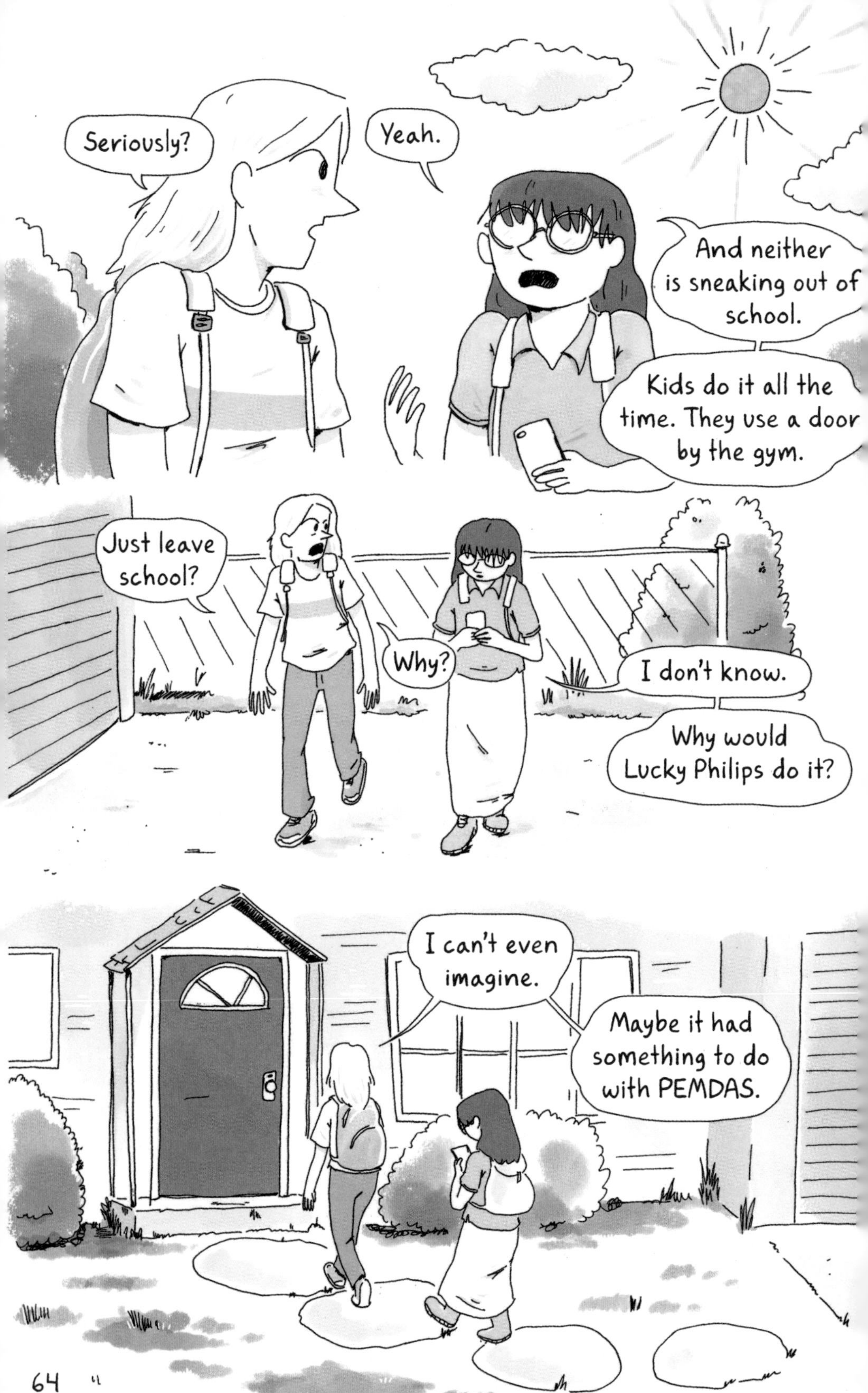
Seriously?
Yeah.
And neither is sneaking out of school.
Kids do it all the time. They use a door by the gym.
Just leave school?
Why?
I don't know.
Why would Lucky Philips do it?
I can't even imagine.
Maybe it had something to do with PEMDAS.

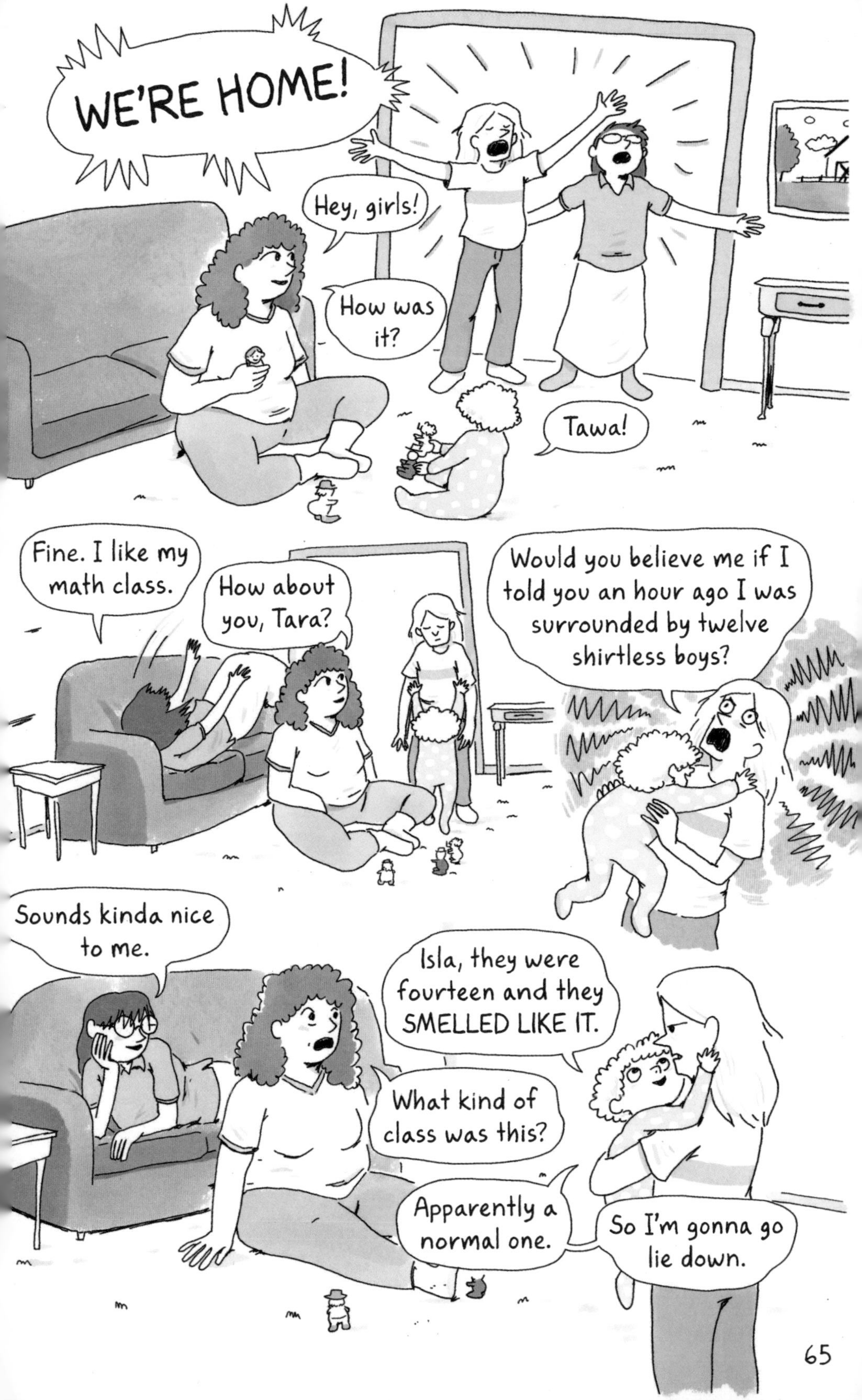
WE'RE HOME!
Hey, girls!
How was it?
Tawa!
Fine. I like my math class.
How about you, Tara?
Would you believe me if I told you an hour ago I was surrounded by twelve shirtless boys?
Sounds kinda nice to me.
Isla, they were fourteen and they SMELLED LIKE IT.
What kind of class was this?
Apparently a normal one.
So I'm gonna go lie down.

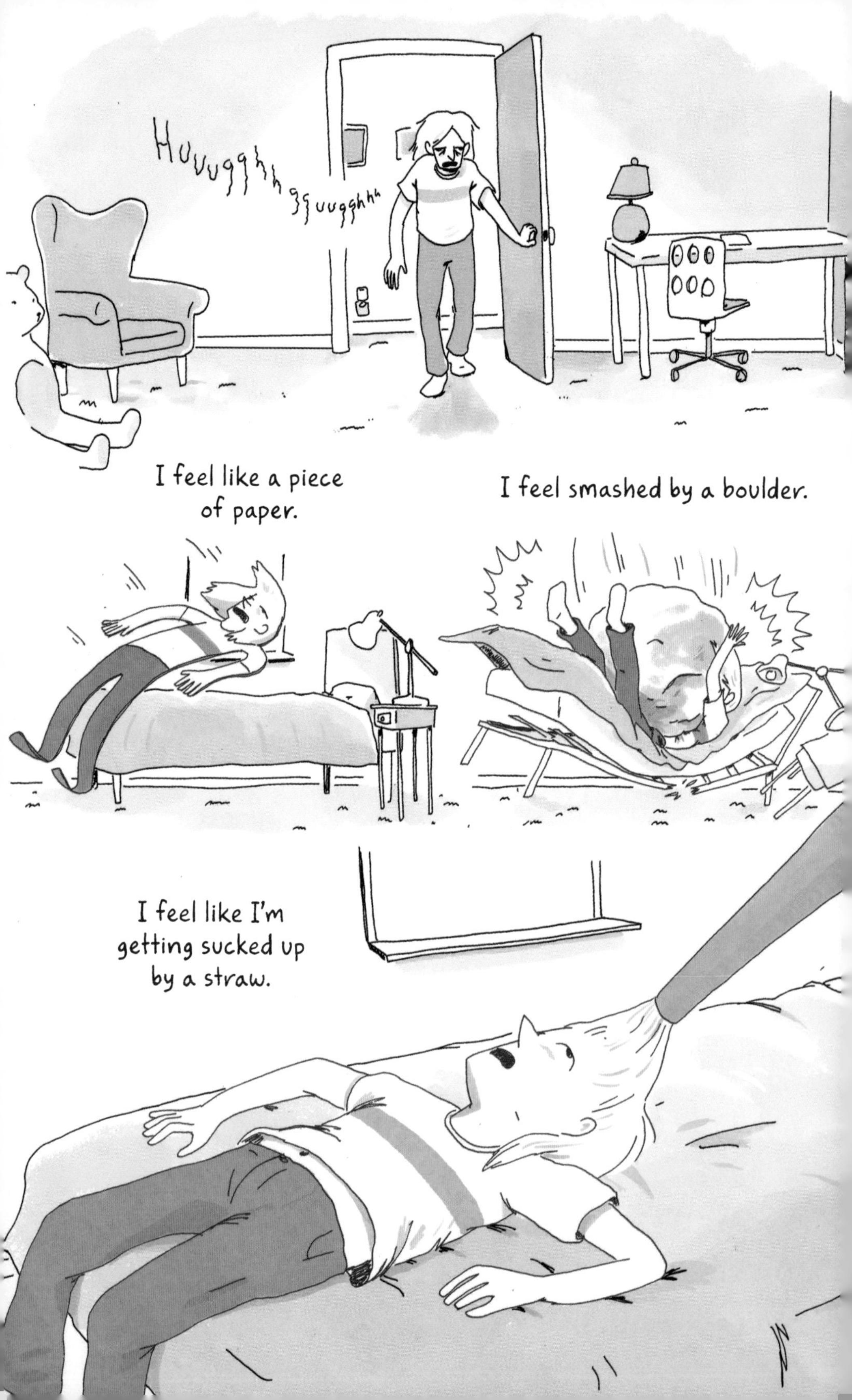
Huuugghhhggguugghhh
I feel like a piece of paper.
I feel smashed by a boulder.
I feel like I'm getting sucked up by a straw.

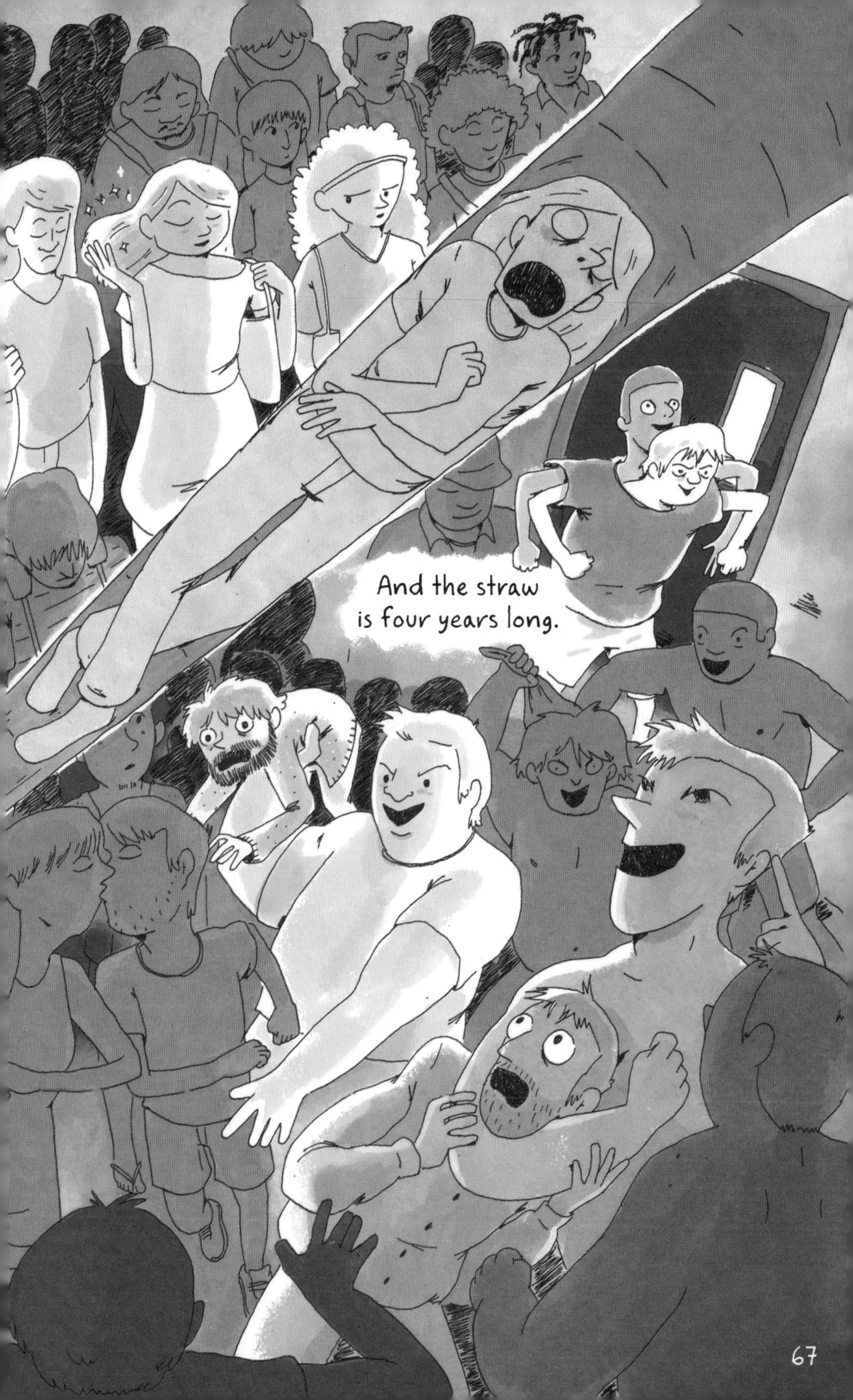
And the straw
is four years long.

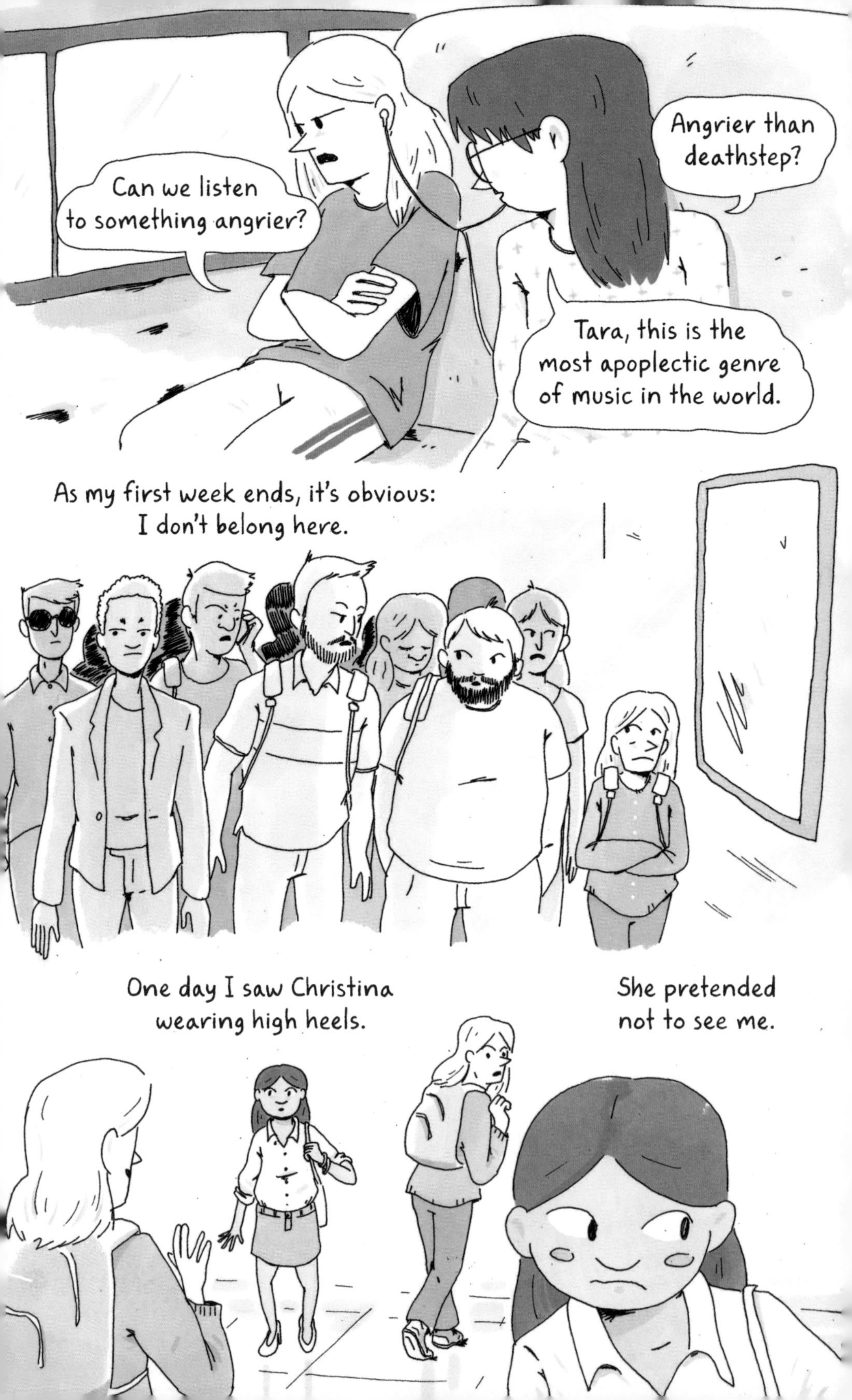
Can we listen to something angrier?
Angrier than deathstep?
Tara, this is the most apoplectic genre of music in the world.
As my first week ends, it's obvious: I don't belong here.
One day I saw Christina wearing high heels.
She pretended not to see me.

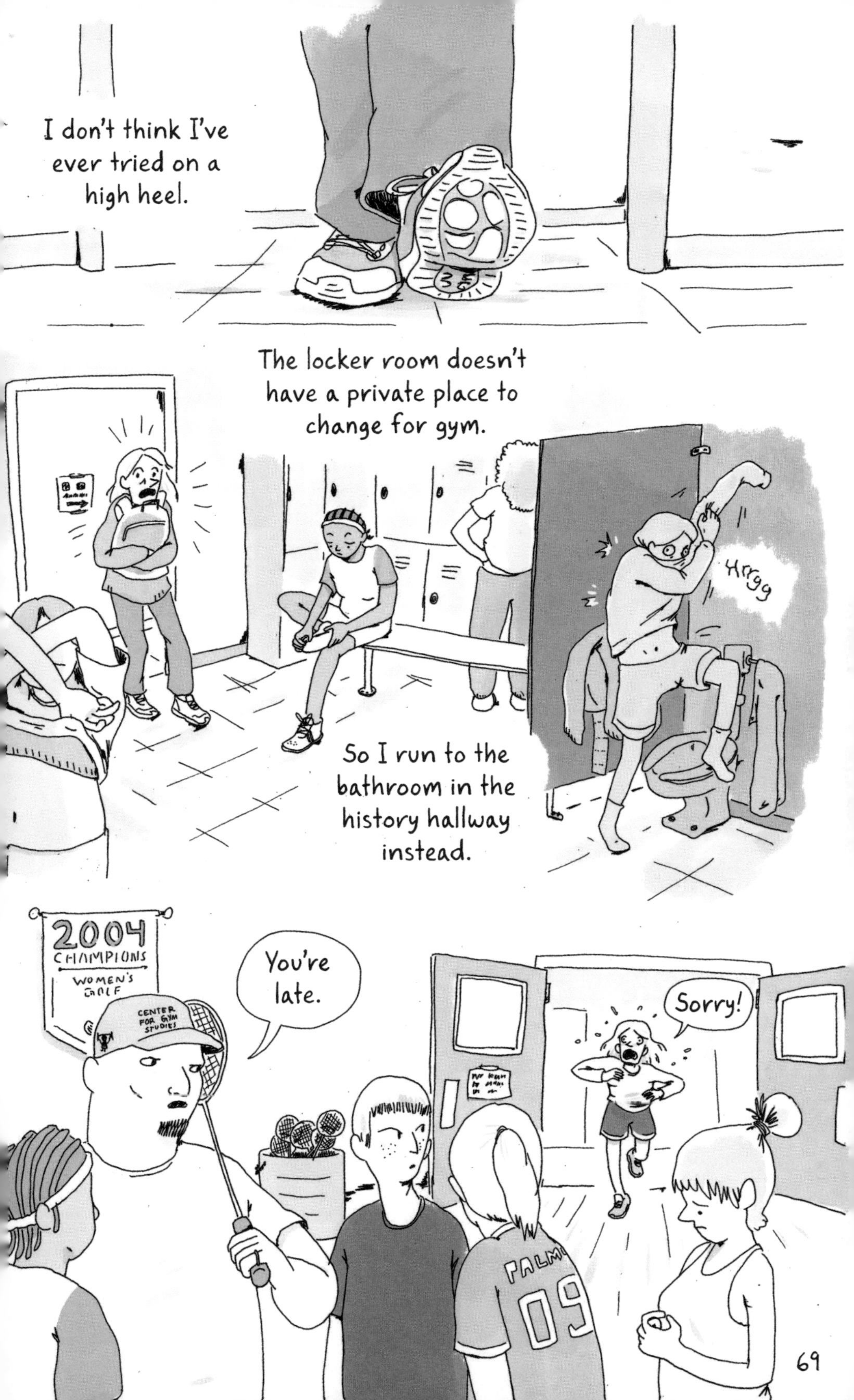
I don't think I've ever tried on a high heel.
The locker room doesn't have a private place to change for gym.
Hrrgg
So I run to the bathroom in the history hallway instead.
2004 CHAMPIONS WOMEN'S GOLF
CENTER FOR GYM STUDIES
You're late.
Sorry!

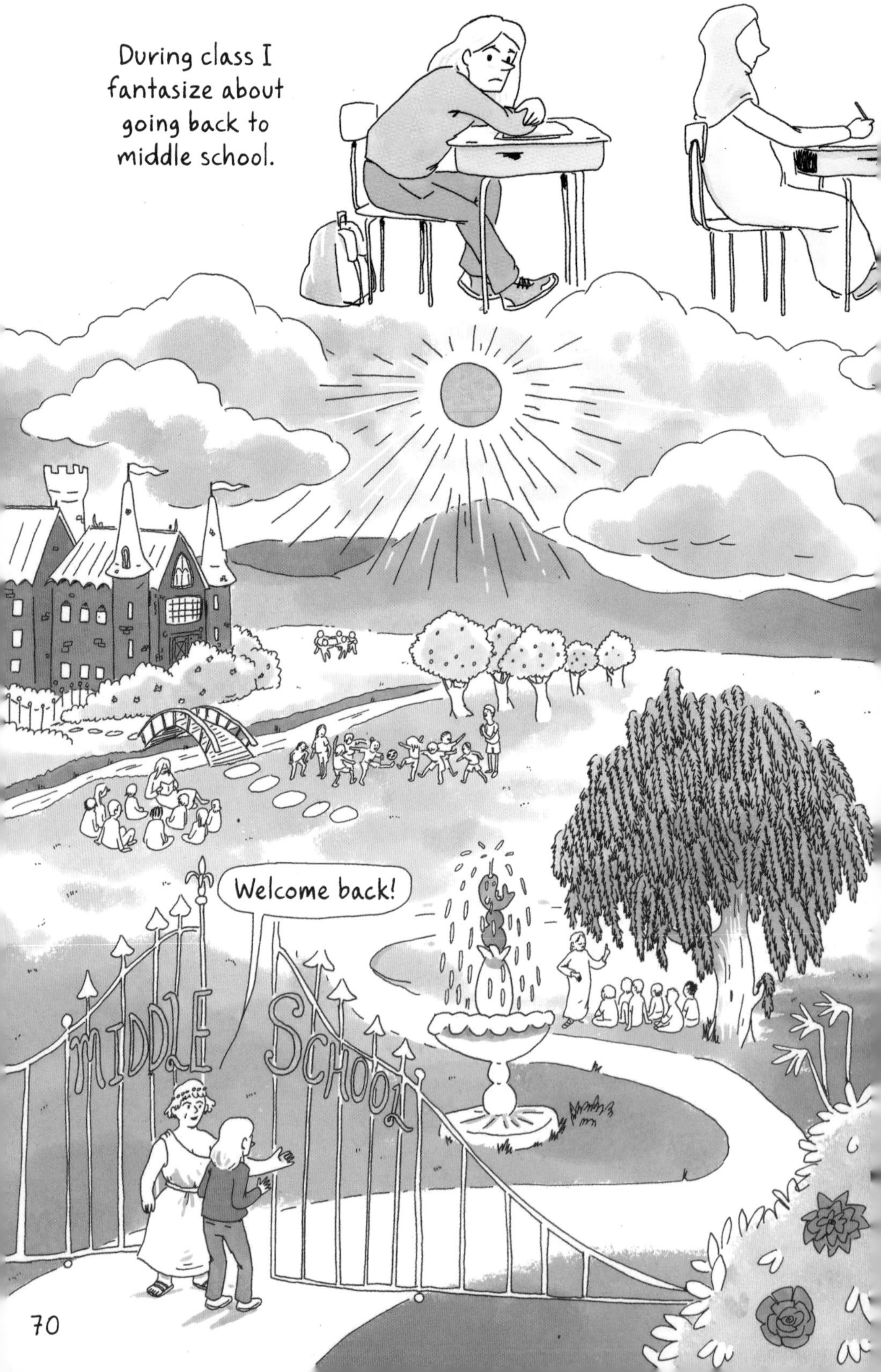
During class I fantasize about going back to middle school.
Welcome back!
MIDDLE SCHOOL

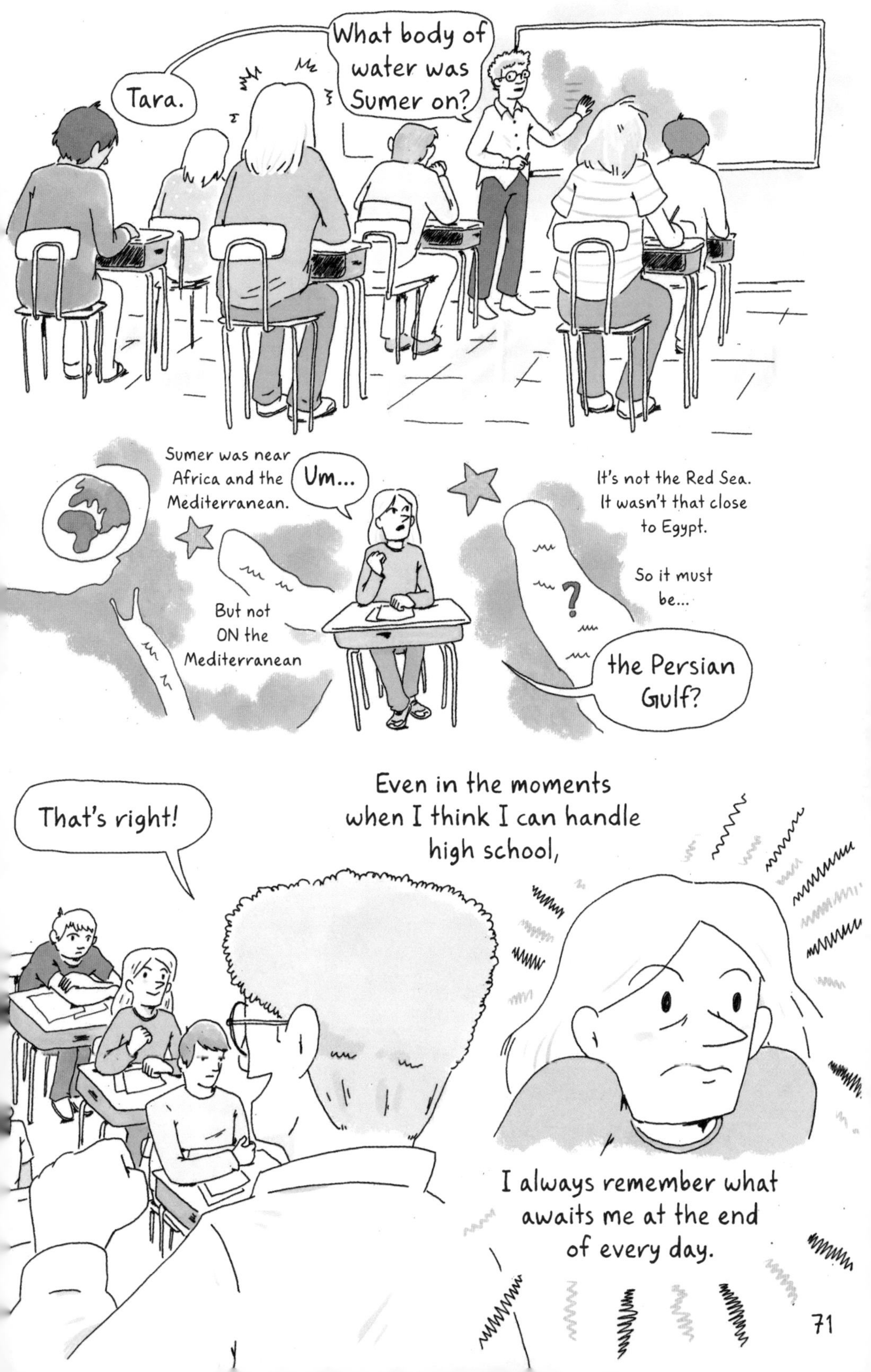
What body of water was Sumer on?
Tara.
Sumer was near Africa and the Mediterranean.
Um...
It's not the Red Sea. It wasn't that close to Egypt.
But not ON the Mediterranean
So it must be...
the Persian Gulf?
That's right!
Even in the moments when I think I can handle high school,
I always remember what awaits me at the end of every day.

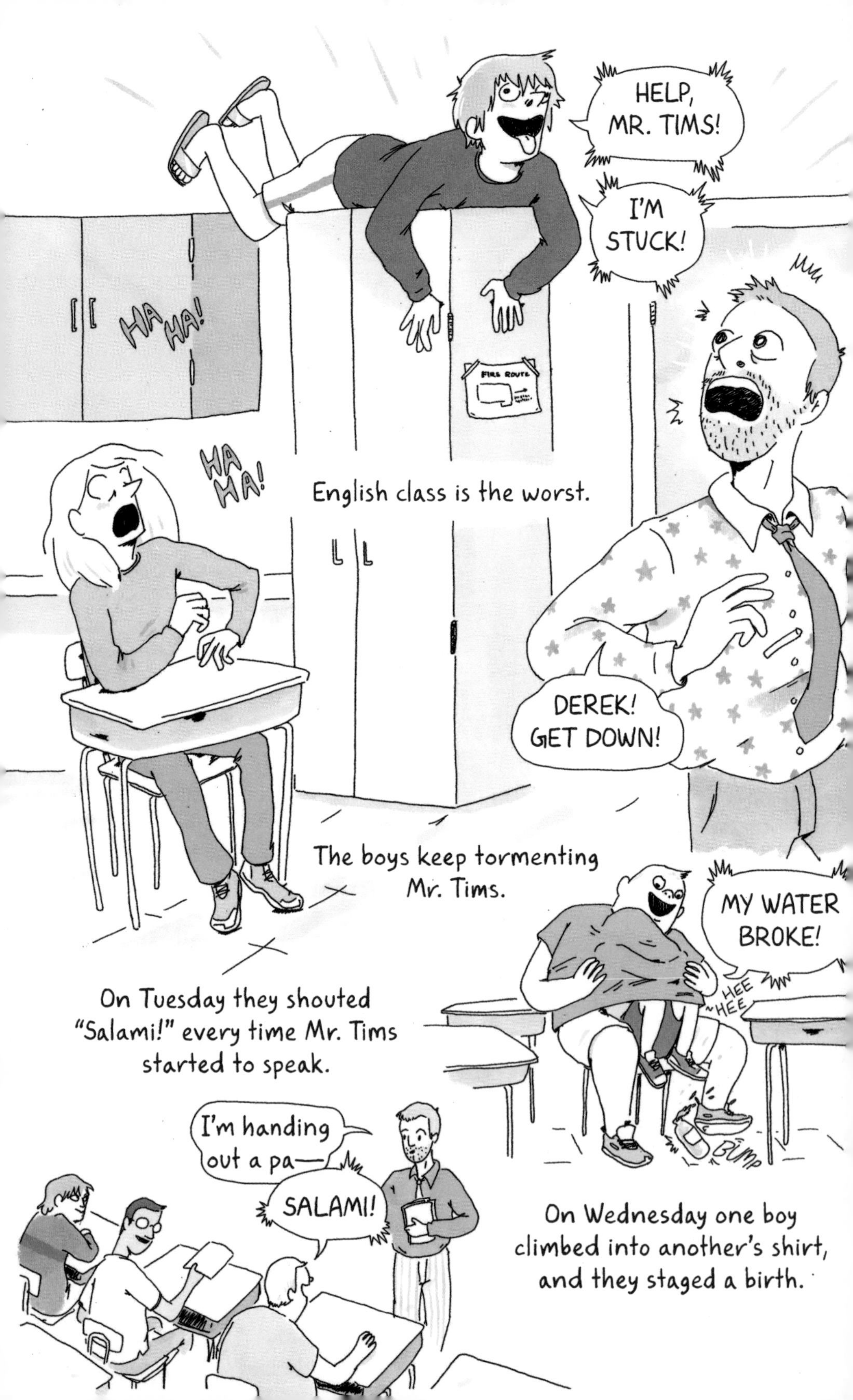
HELP, MR. TIMS!
I'M STUCK!
HA HA!
HA HA!
English class is the worst.
DEREK! GET DOWN!
The boys keep tormenting Mr. Tims.
MY WATER BROKE!
HEE HEE
BUMP
On Tuesday they shouted "Salami!" every time Mr. Tims started to speak.
I'm handing out a pa—
SALAMI!
On Wednesday one boy climbed into another's shirt, and they staged a birth.

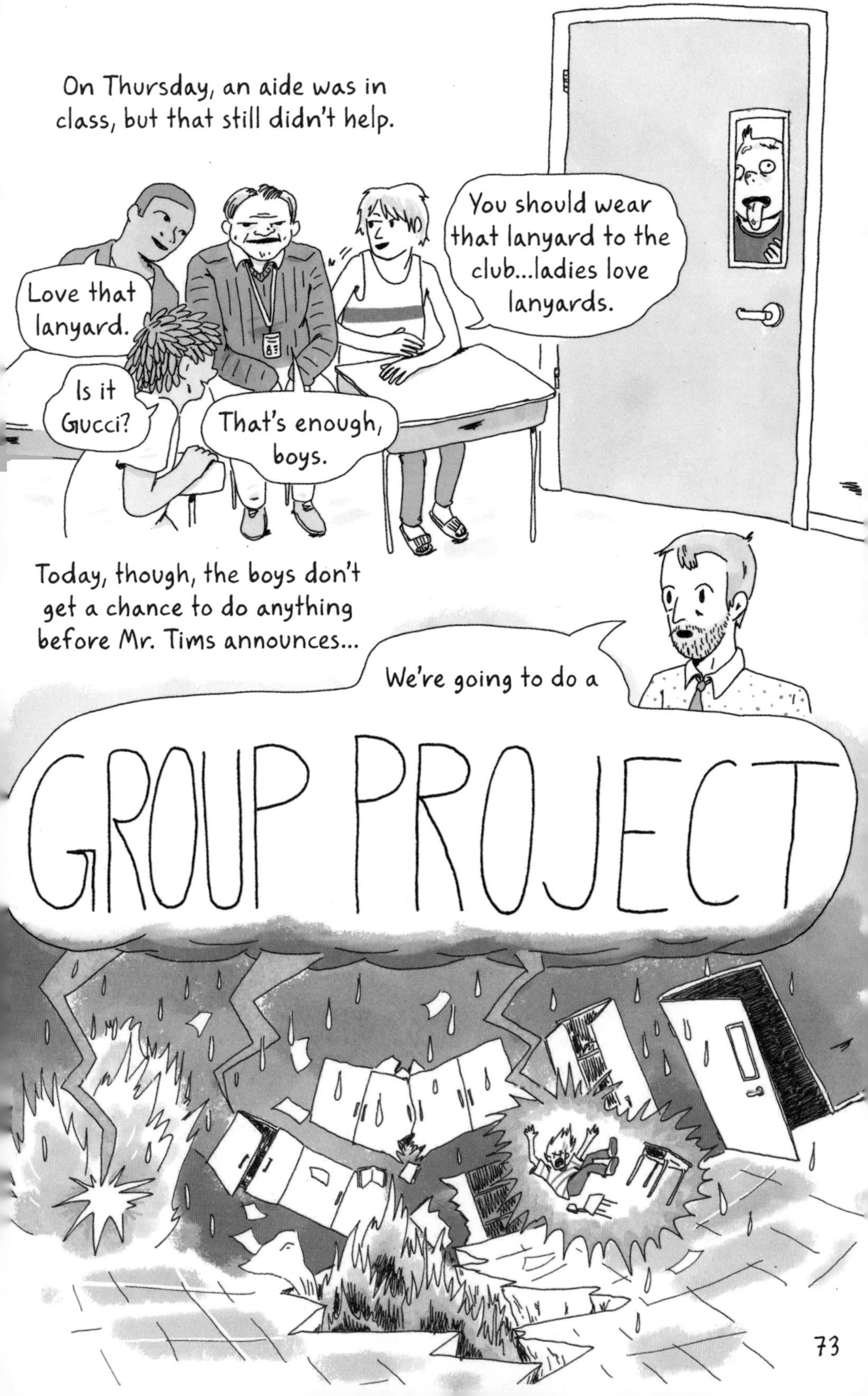

On Thursday, an aide was in class, but that still didn't help.
Love that lanyard.
You should wear that lanyard to the club...ladies love lanyards.
Is it Gucci?
That's enough, boys.
Today, though, the boys don't get a chance to do anything before Mr. Tims announces...
We're going to do a
GROUP PROJECT

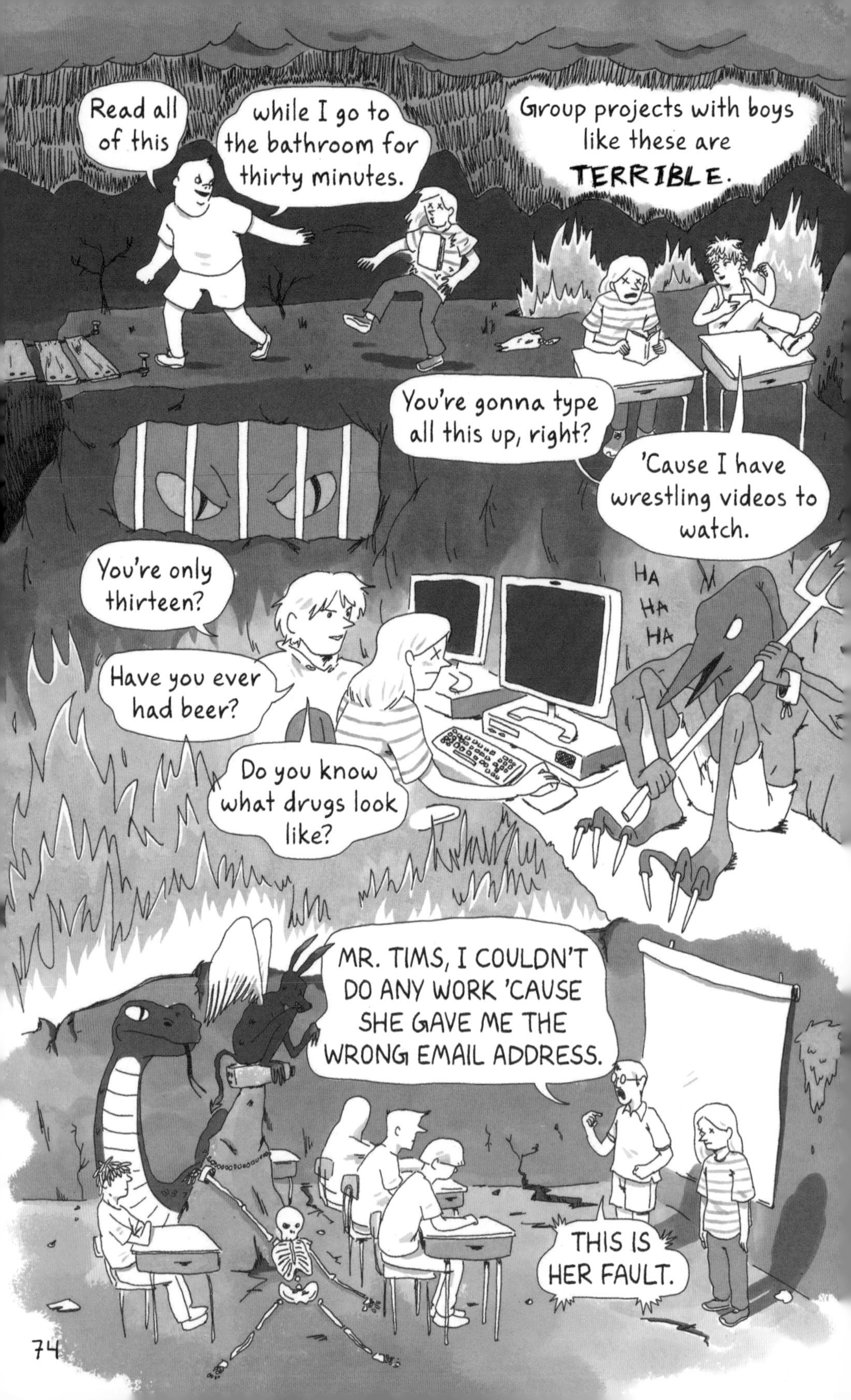
Read all of this
while I go to the bathroom for thirty minutes.
Group projects with boys like these are TERRIBLE.
You're gonna type all this up, right?
'Cause I have wrestling videos to watch.
HA HA HA
You're only thirteen?
Have you ever had beer?
Do you know what drugs look like?
MR. TIMS, I COULDN'T DO ANY WORK 'CAUSE SHE GAVE ME THE WRONG EMAIL ADDRESS.
THIS IS HER FAULT.

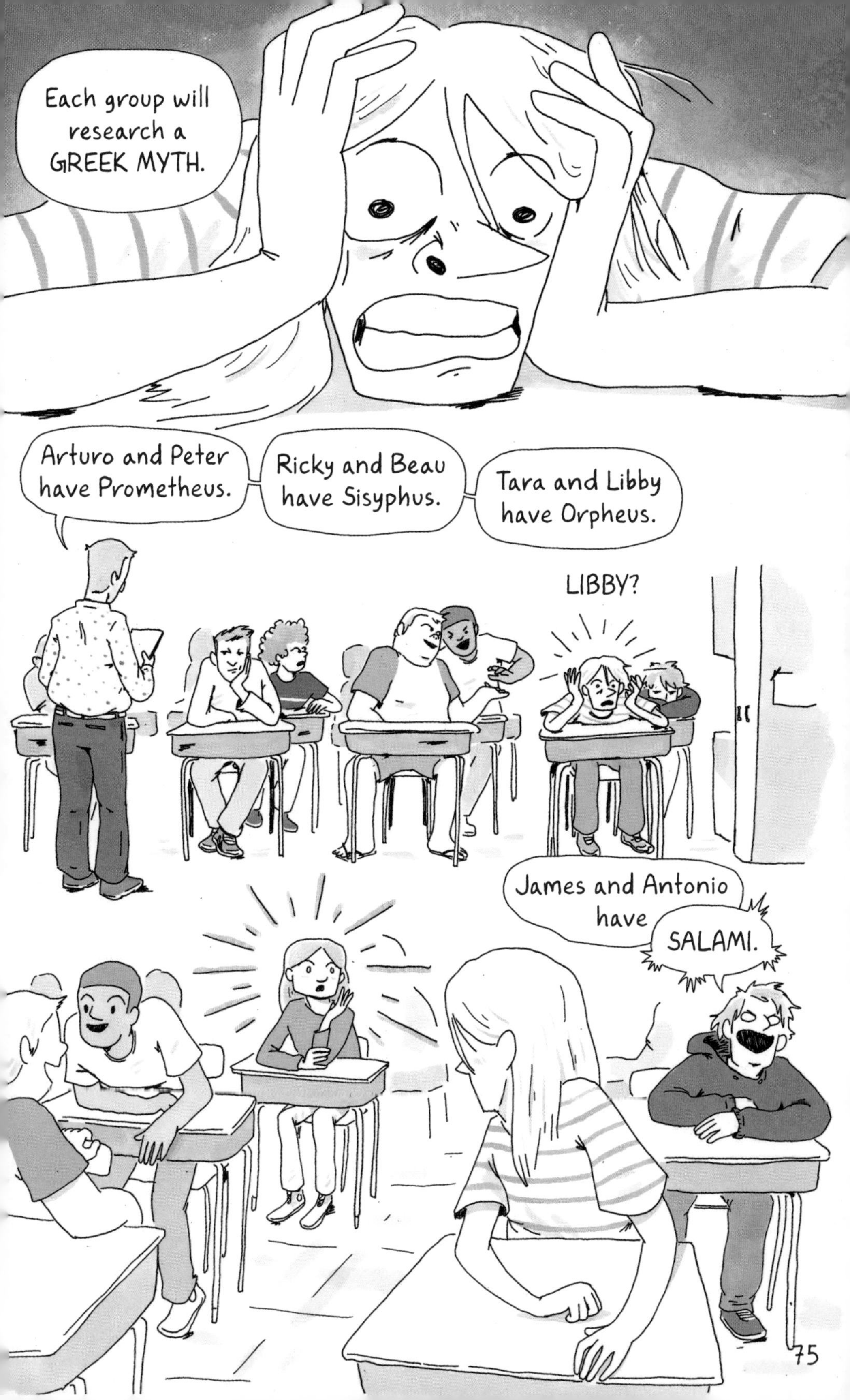

Each group will research a GREEK MYTH.
Arturo and Peter have Prometheus.
Ricky and Beau have Sisyphus.
Tara and Libby have Orpheus.
LIBBY?
James and Antonio have
SALAMI.

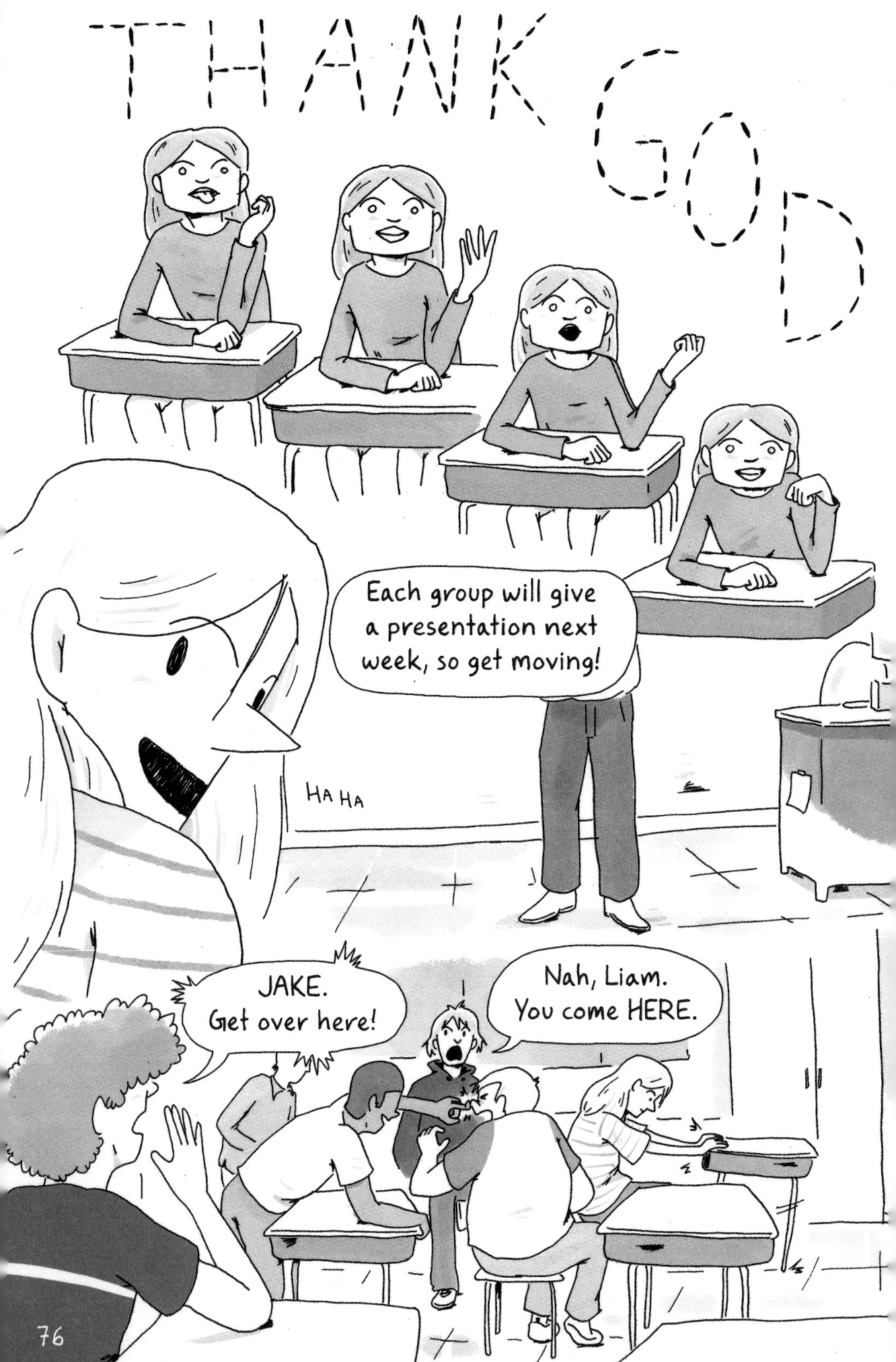
THANK GOD
Each group will give a presentation next week, so get moving!
HA HA
JAKE. Get over here!
Nah, Liam. You come HERE.

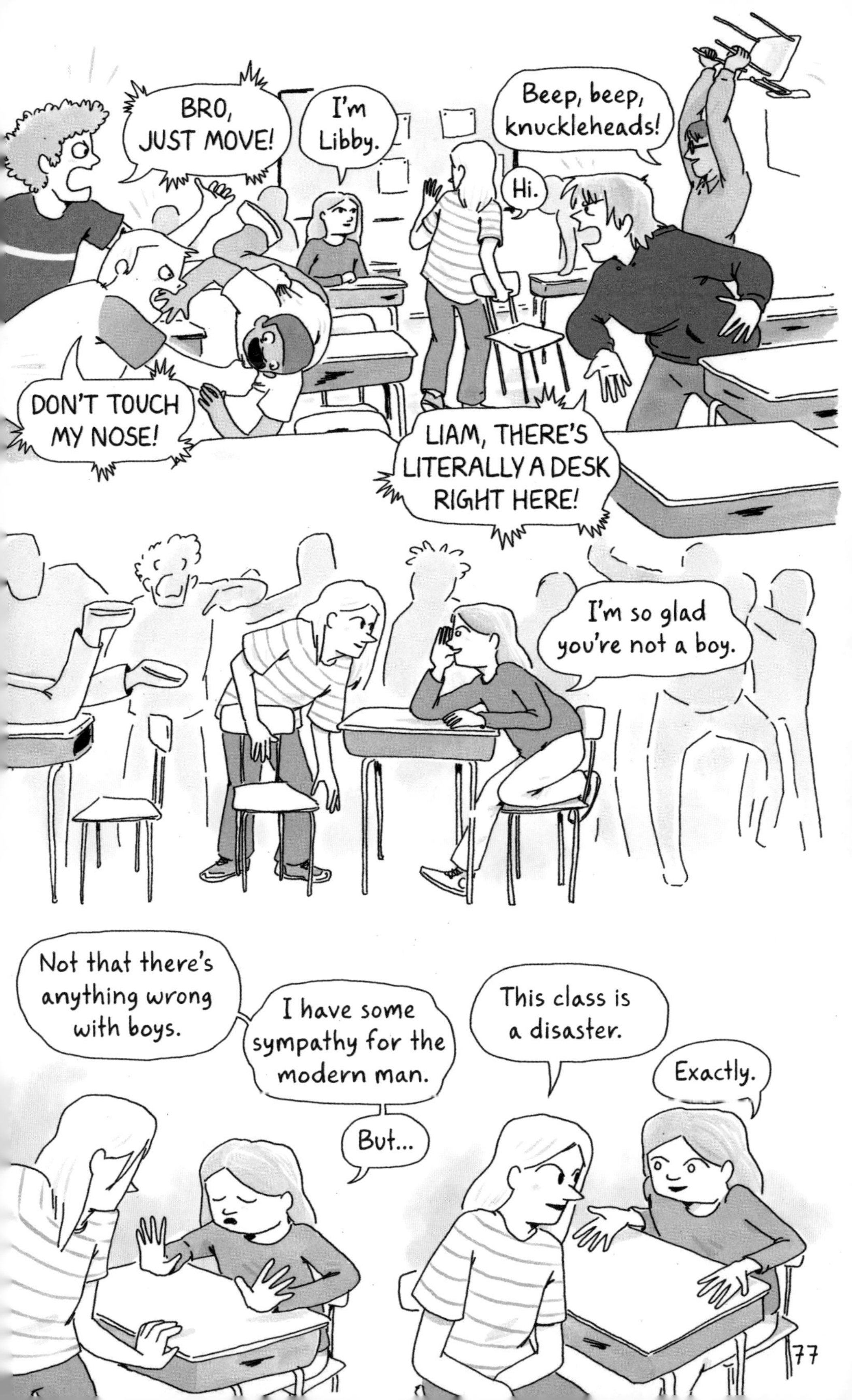
BRO, JUST MOVE!
I'm Libby.
Beep, beep, knuckleheads!
Hi.
DON'T TOUCH MY NOSE!
LIAM, THERE'S LITERALLY A DESK RIGHT HERE!
I'm so glad you're not a boy.
Not that there's anything wrong with boys.
I have some sympathy for the modern man.
But...
This class is a disaster.
Exactly.

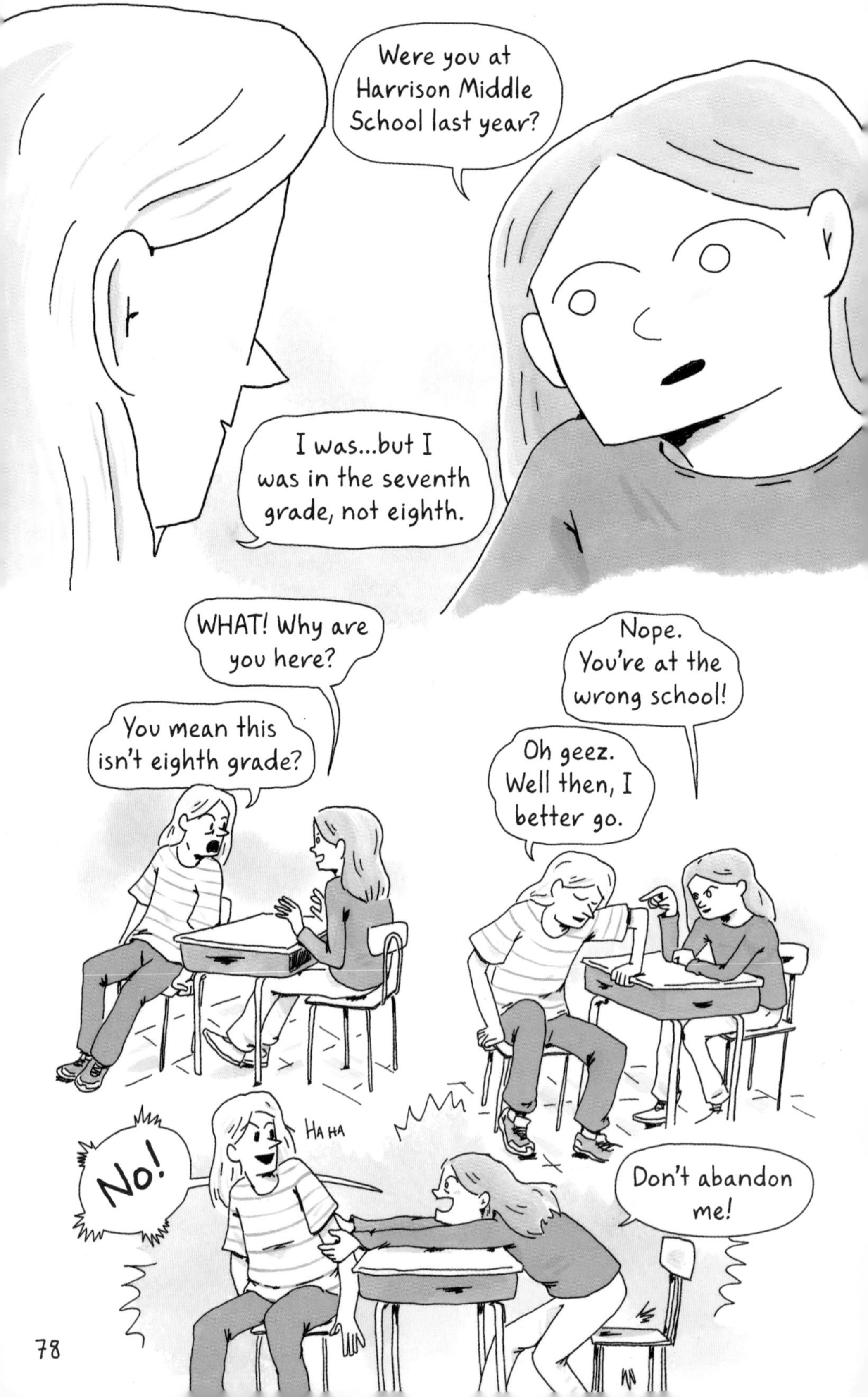
Were you at Harrison Middle School last year?
I was...but I was in the seventh grade, not eighth.
WHAT! Why are you here?
You mean this isn't eighth grade?
Nope. You're at the wrong school!
Oh geez. Well then, I better go.
No!
HA HA
Don't abandon me!

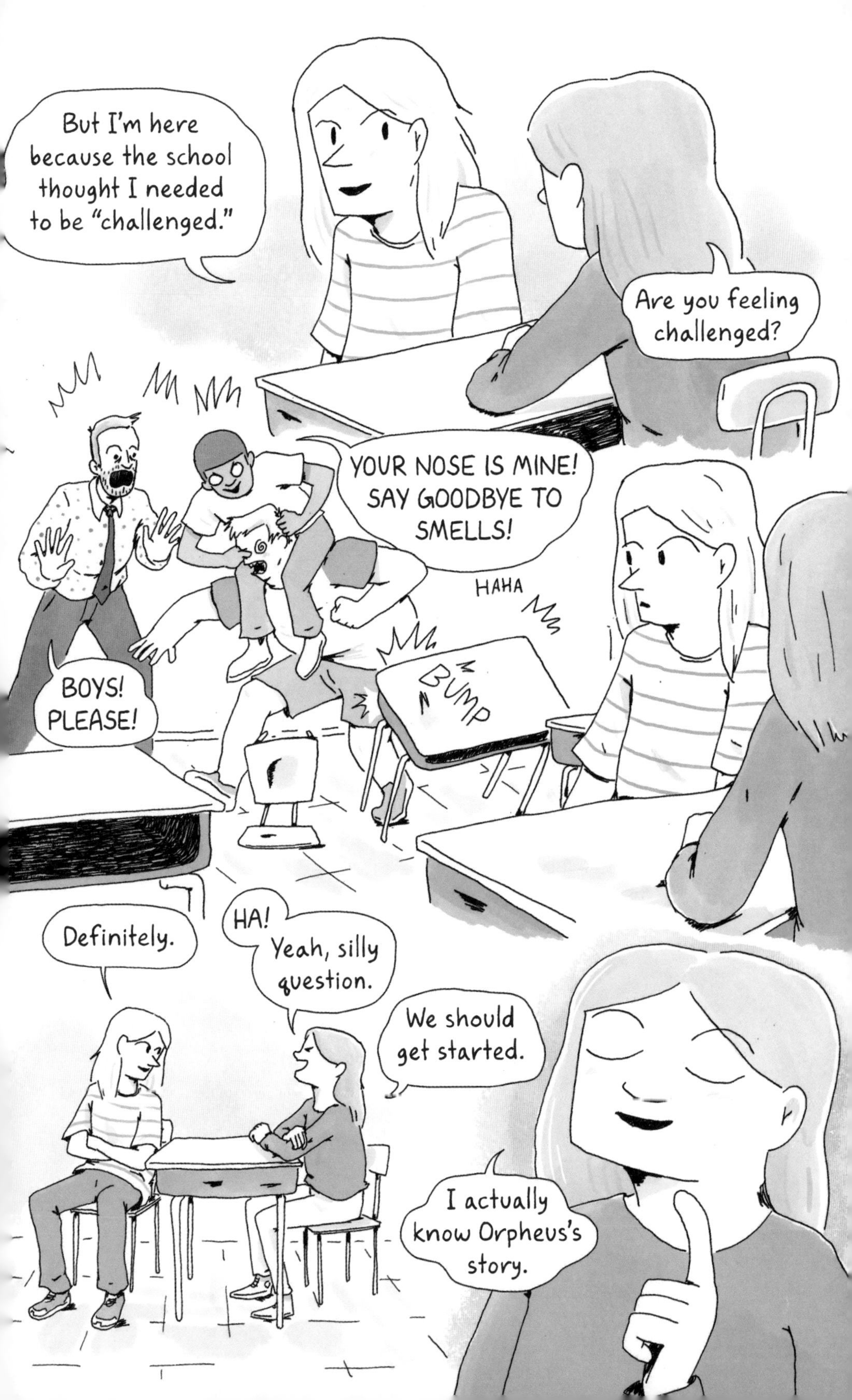
But I'm here because the school thought I needed to be "challenged."
Are you feeling challenged?
YOUR NOSE IS MINE! SAY GOODBYE TO SMELLS!
BOYS! PLEASE!
HAHA
BUMP
Definitely.
HA! Yeah, silly question.
We should get started.
I actually know Orpheus's story.

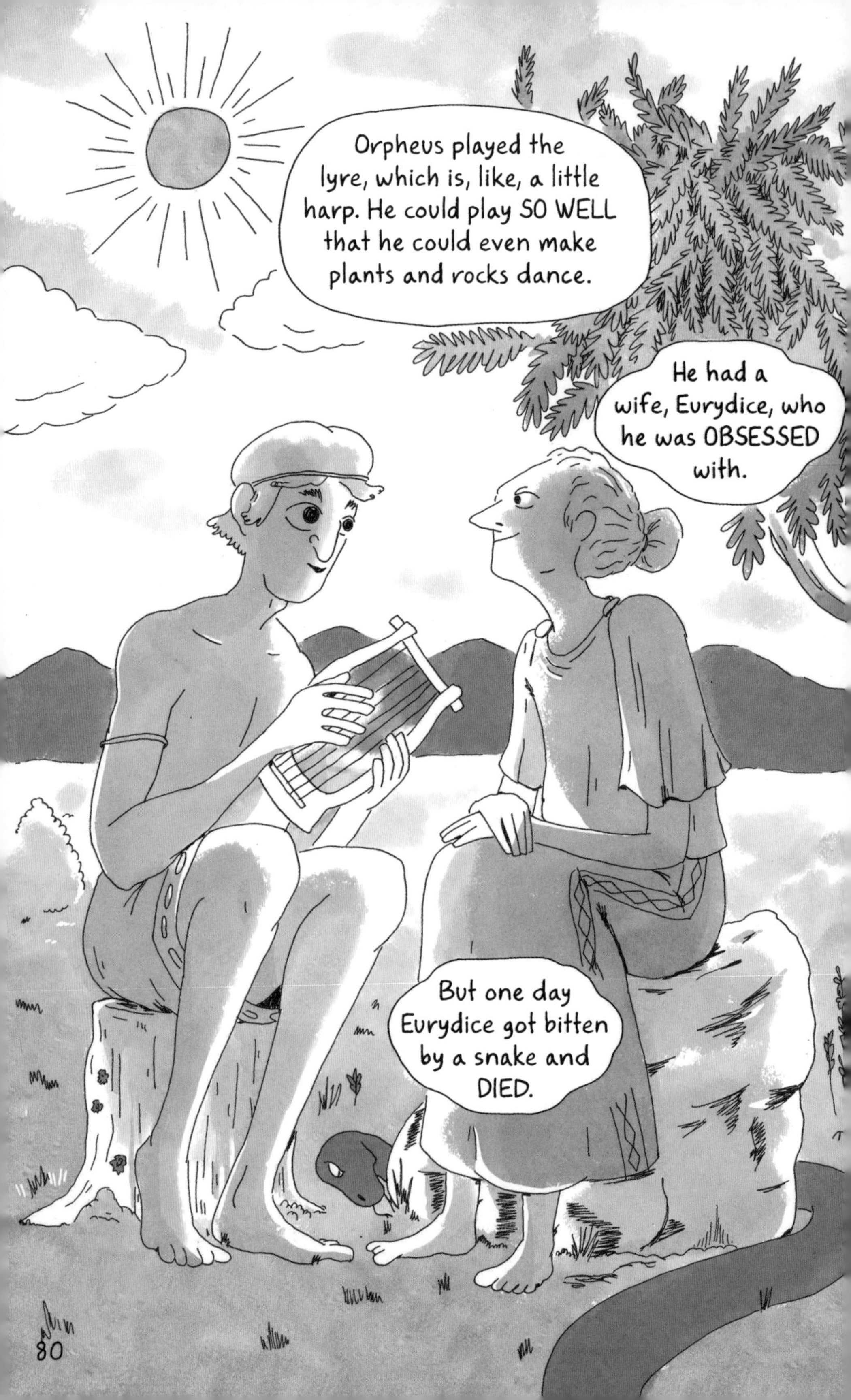
Orpheus played the lyre, which is, like, a little harp. He could play SO WELL that he could even make plants and rocks dance.
He had a wife, Eurydice, who he was OBSESSED with.
But one day Eurydice got bitten by a snake and DIED.

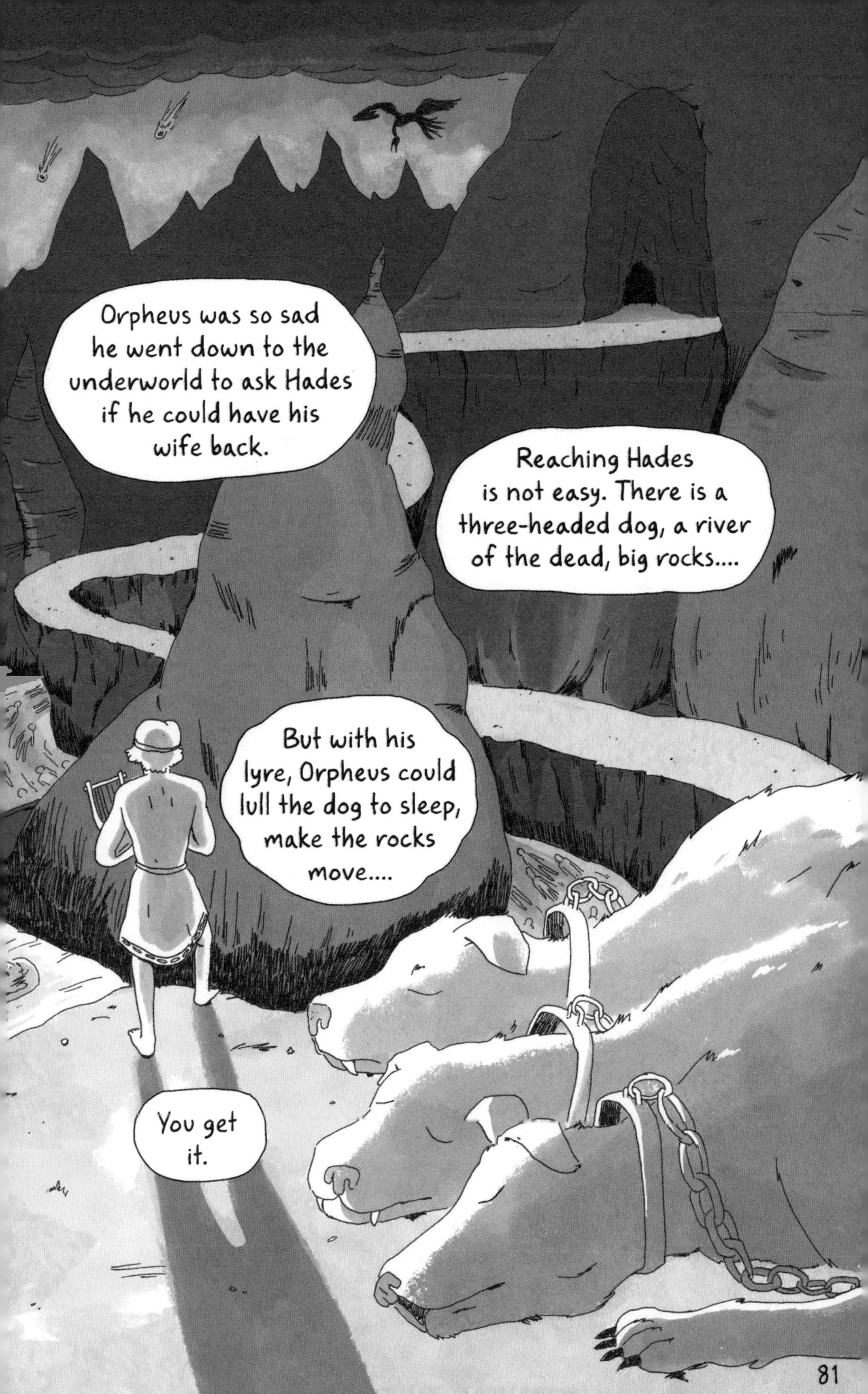
Orpheus was so sad he went down to the underworld to ask Hades if he could have his wife back.
Reaching Hades is not easy. There is a three-headed dog, a river of the dead, big rocks....
But with his lyre, Orpheus could lull the dog to sleep, make the rocks move....
You get it.

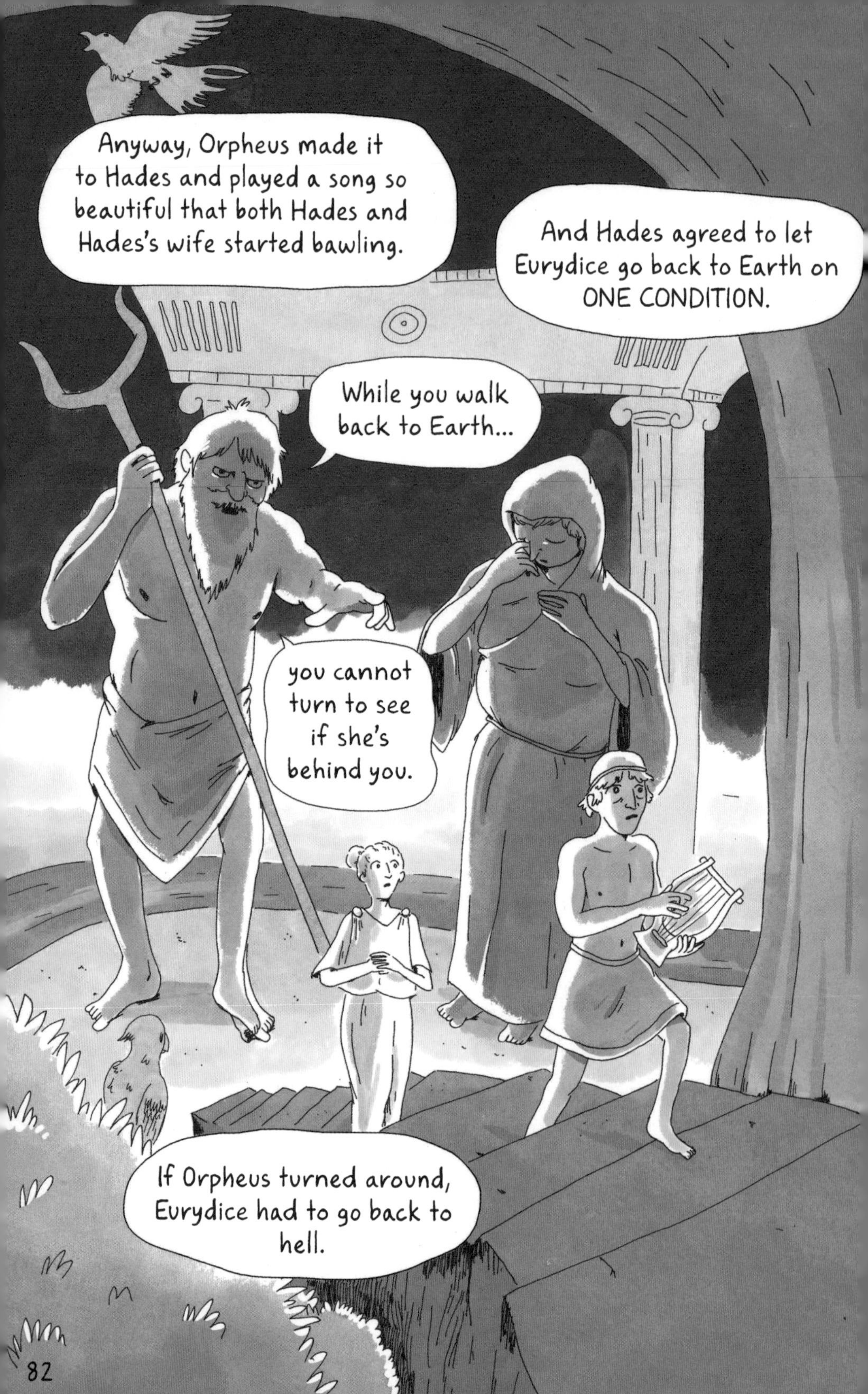
Anyway, Orpheus made it to Hades and played a song so beautiful that both Hades and Hades's wife started bawling.
And Hades agreed to let Eurydice go back to Earth on ONE CONDITION.
While you walk back to Earth...
you cannot turn to see if she's behind you.
If Orpheus turned around, Eurydice had to go back to hell.

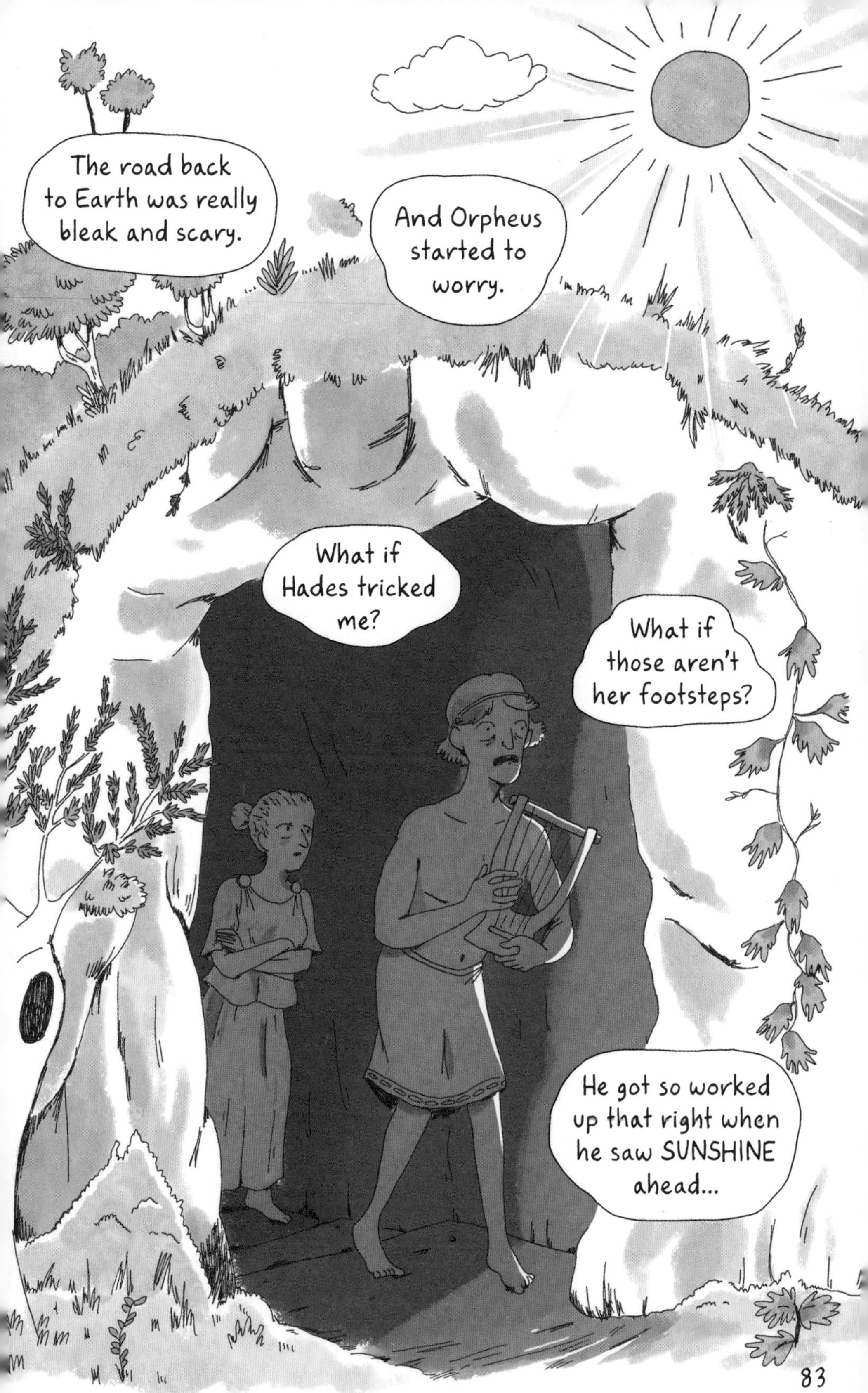
The road back to Earth was really bleak and scary.
And Orpheus started to worry.
What if Hades tricked me?
What if those aren't her footsteps?
He got so worked up that right when he saw SUNSHINE ahead...

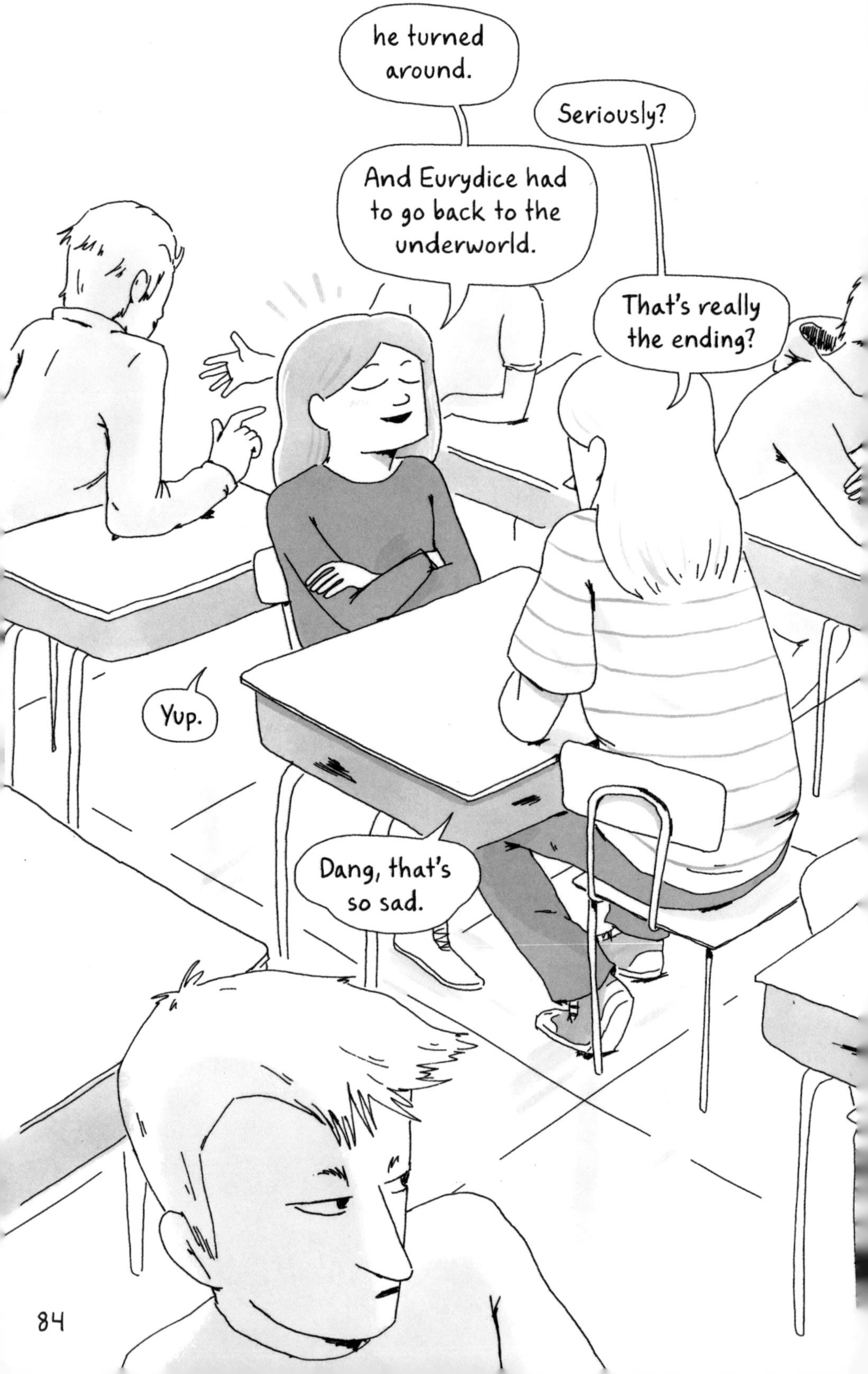
he turned around.
And Eurydice had to go back to the underworld.
Seriously?
That's really the ending?
Yup.
Dang, that's so sad.

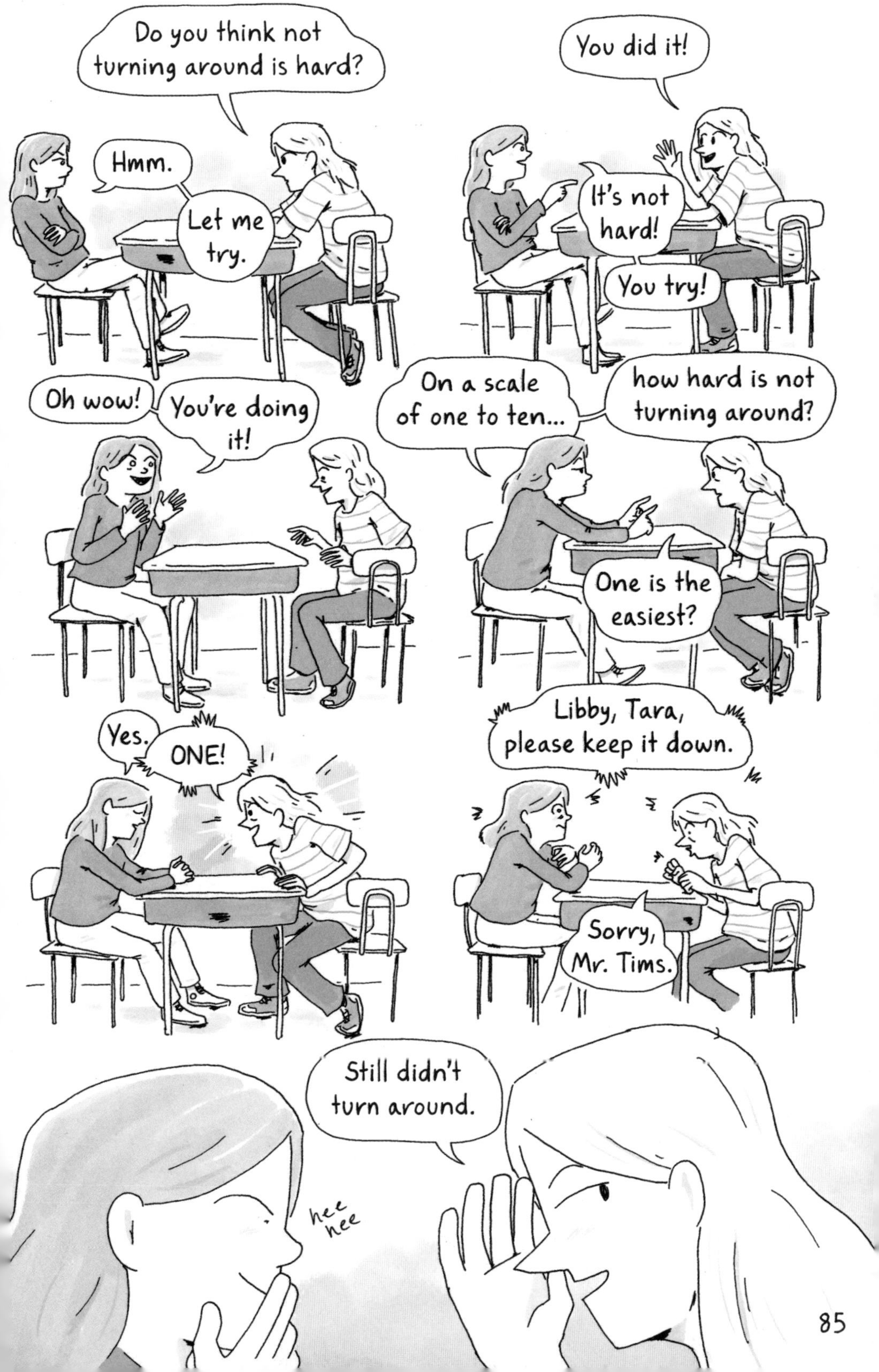

Do you think not turning around is hard?
Hmm.
Let me try.
You did it!
It's not hard!
You try!
Oh wow!
You're doing it!
On a scale of one to ten...
how hard is not turning around?
One is the easiest?
Yes.
ONE!
Libby, Tara, please keep it down.
Sorry, Mr. Tims.
Still didn't turn around.
hee hee

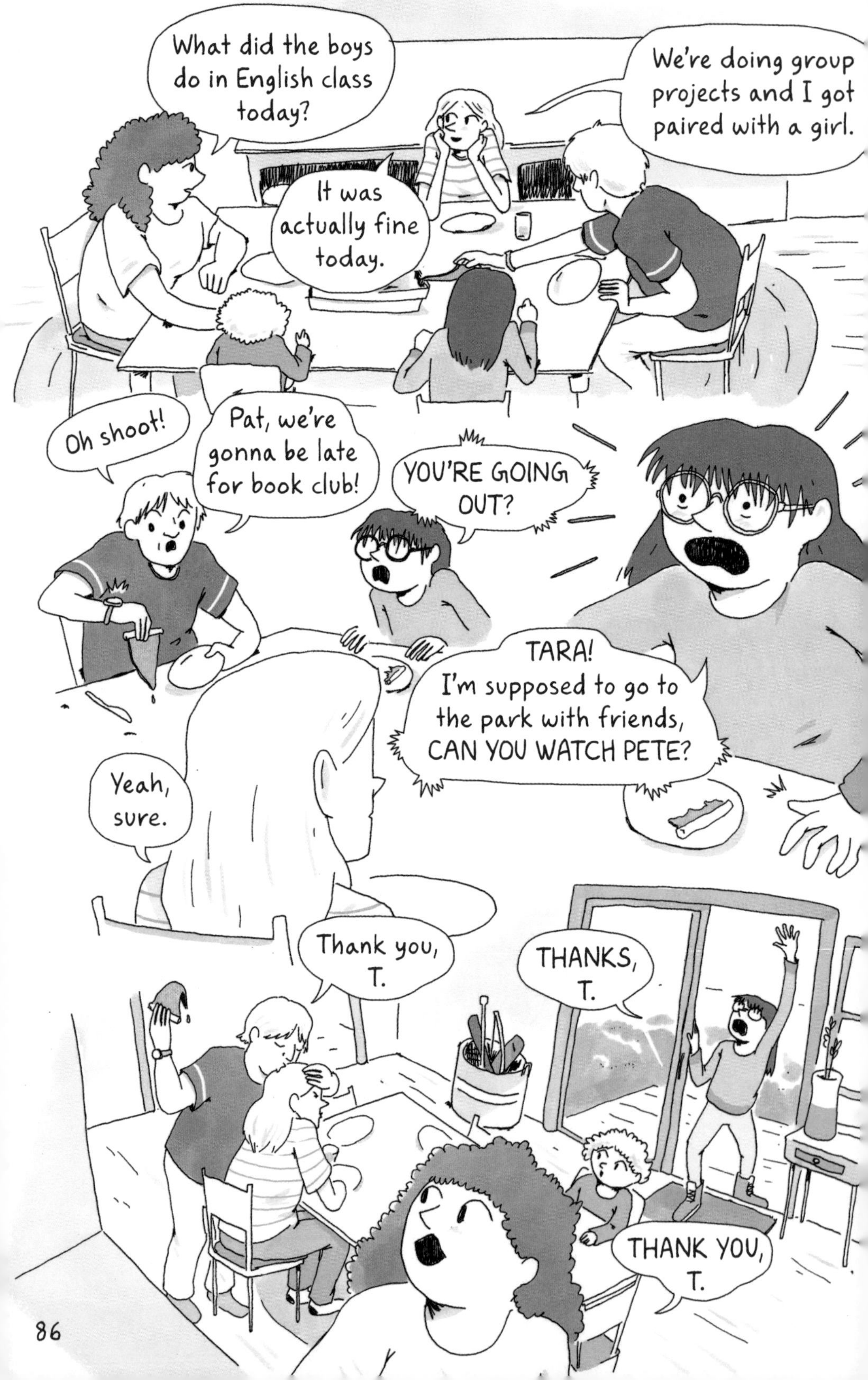
What did the boys do in English class today?
We're doing group projects and I got paired with a girl.
It was actually fine today.
Oh shoot!
Pat, we're gonna be late for book club!
YOU'RE GOING OUT?
TARA! I'm supposed to go to the park with friends, CAN YOU WATCH PETE?
Yeah, sure.
Thank you, T.
THANKS, T.
THANK YOU, T.

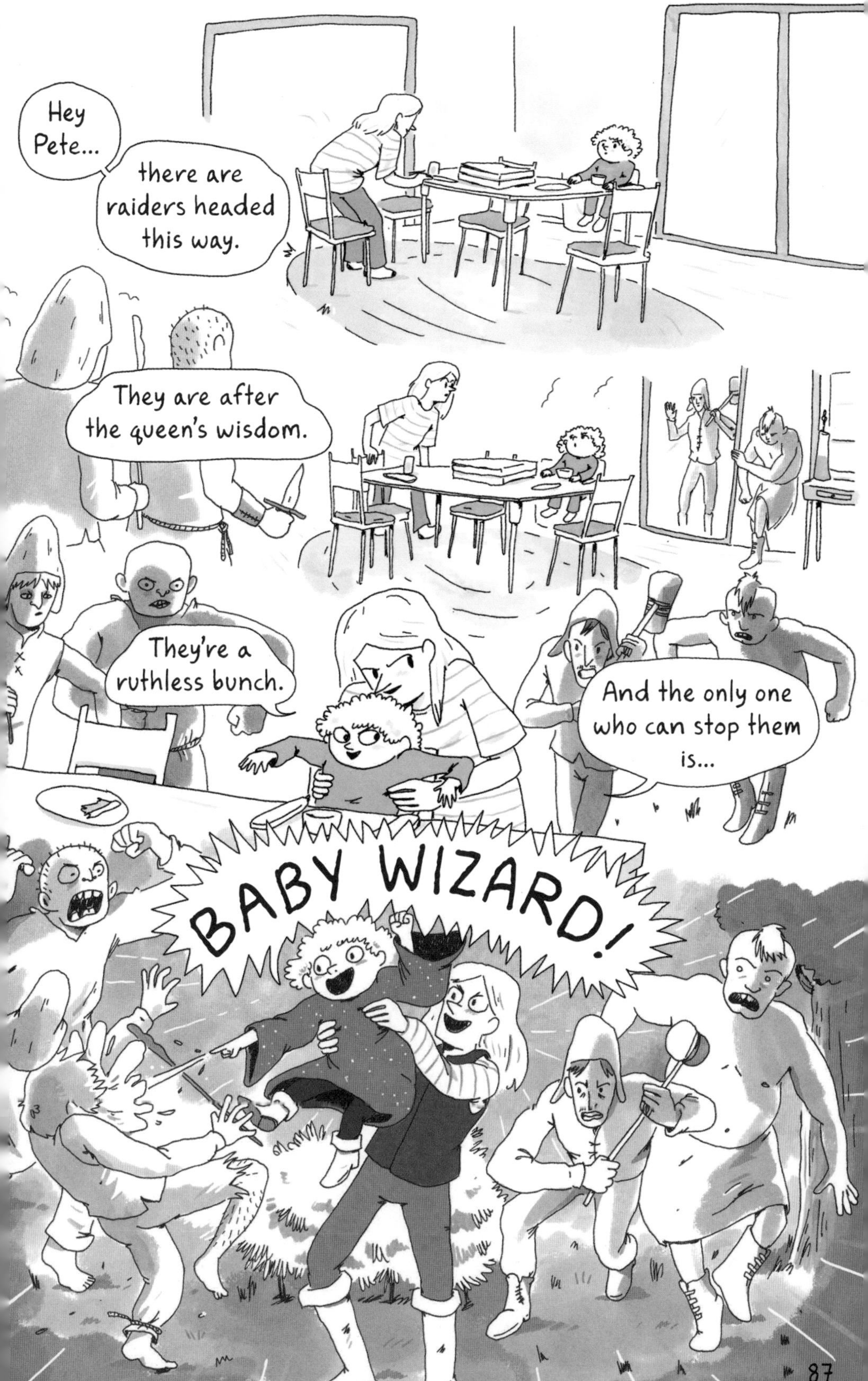
Hey Pete...
there are raiders headed this way.
They are after the queen's wisdom.
They're a ruthless bunch.
And the only one who can stop them is...
BABY WIZARD!

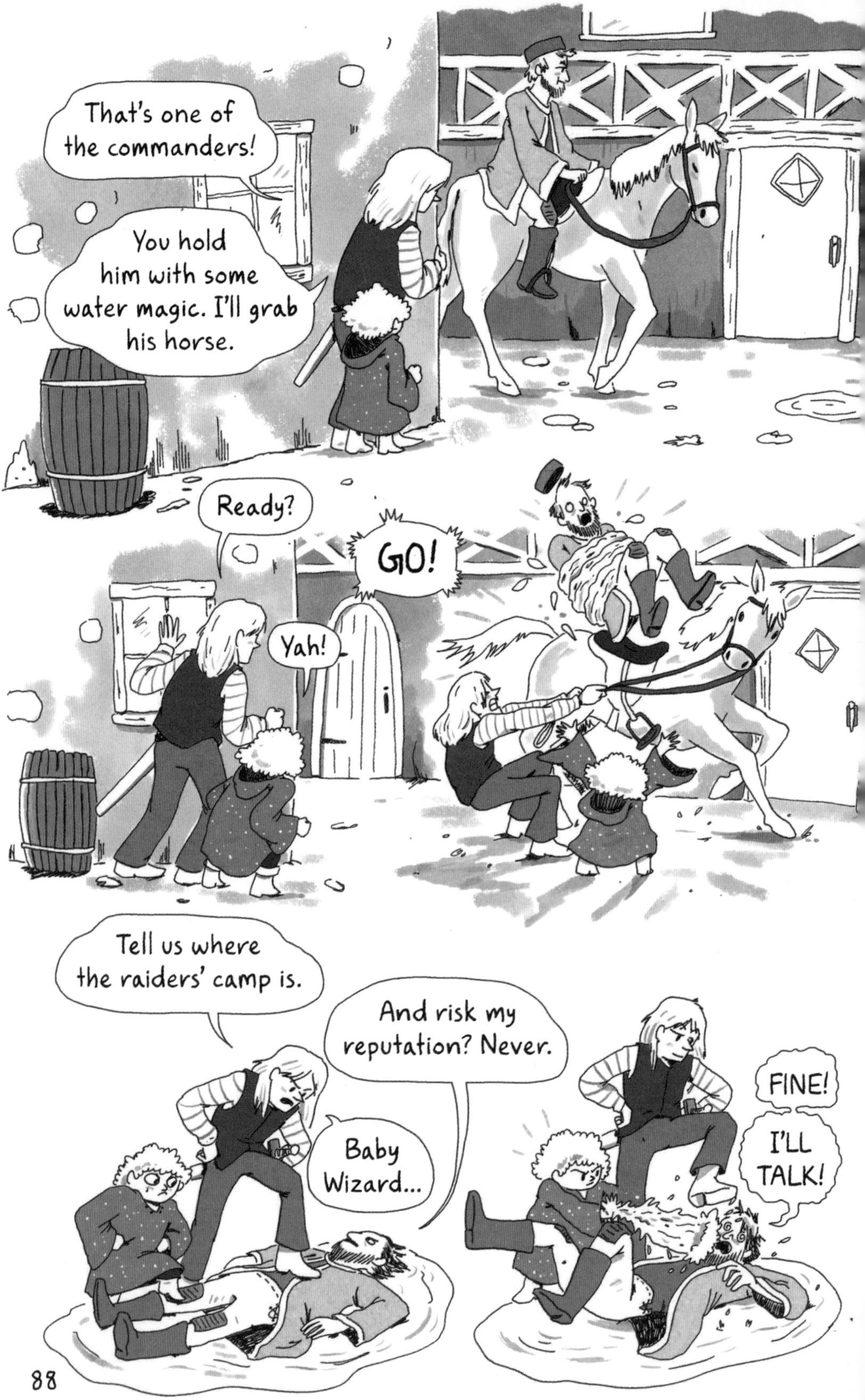
That's one of the commanders!
You hold him with some water magic. I'll grab his horse.
Ready?
GO!
Yah!
Tell us where the raiders' camp is.
And risk my reputation? Never.
Baby Wizard...
FINE!
I'LL TALK!

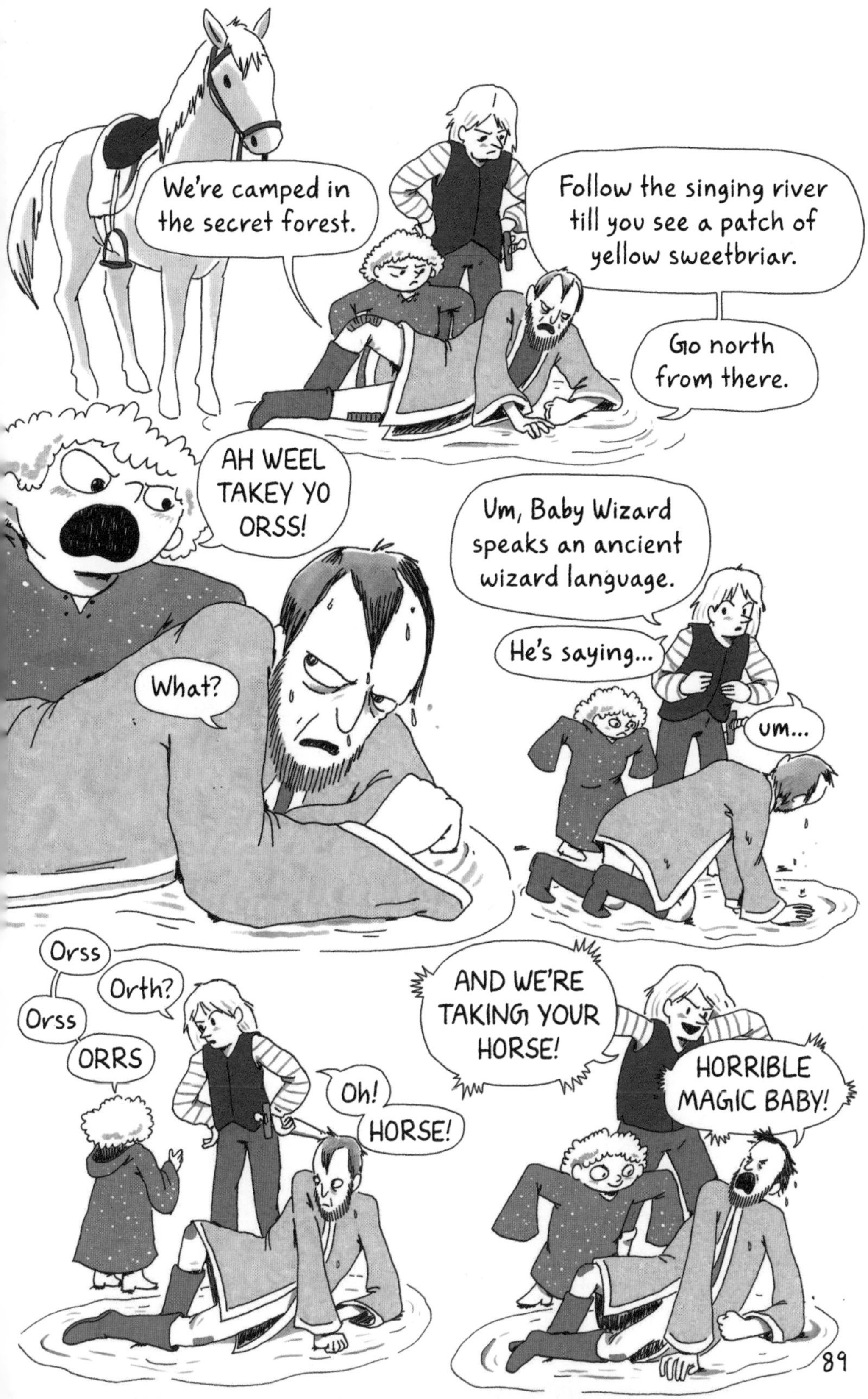
We're camped in the secret forest.
Follow the singing river till you see a patch of yellow sweetbriar.
Go north from there.
AH WEEL TAKEY YO ORSS!
Um, Baby Wizard speaks an ancient wizard language.
What?
He's saying...
um...
Orss
Orth?
Orss
ORRS
Oh! HORSE!
AND WE'RE TAKING YOUR HORSE!
HORRIBLE MAGIC BABY!

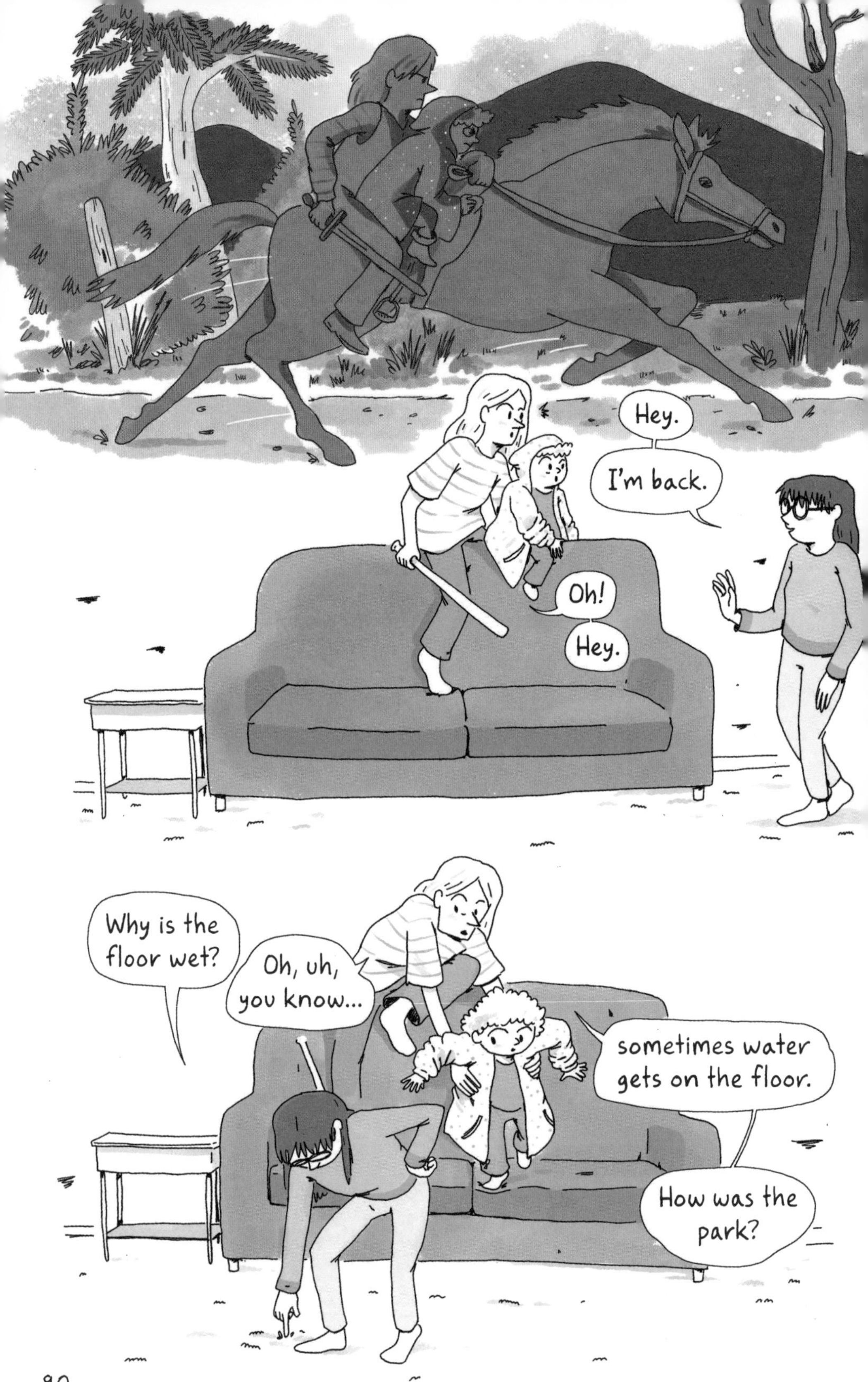
Hey.
I'm back.
Oh!
Hey.
Why is the floor wet?
Oh, uh, you know...
sometimes water gets on the floor.
How was the park?

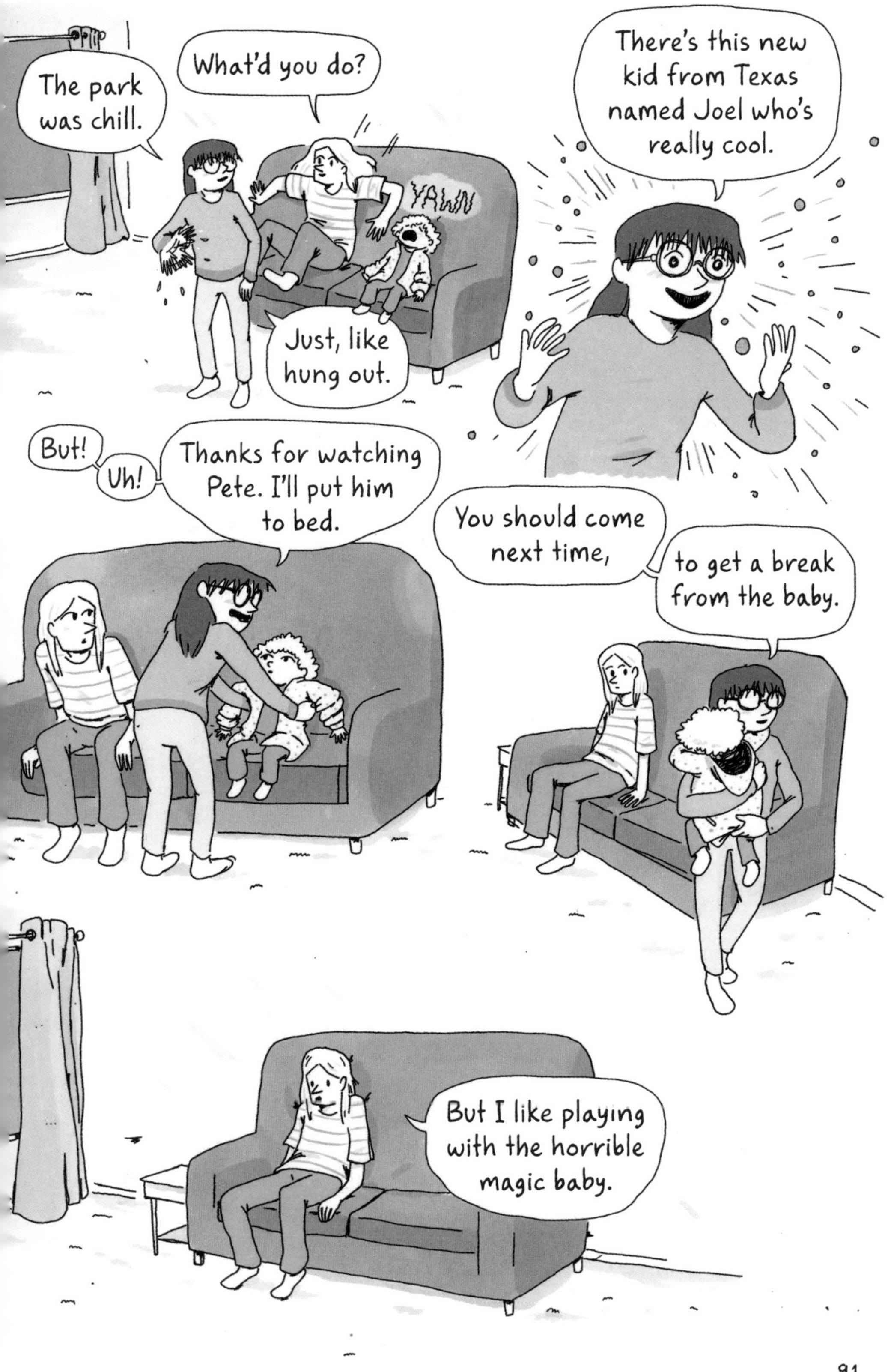
plip
The park was chill.
What'd you do?
YAWN
Just, like hung out.
There's this new kid from Texas named Joel who's really cool.
But!
Uh!
Thanks for watching Pete. I'll put him to bed.
You should come next time,
to get a break from the baby.
But I like playing with the horrible magic baby.

For some reason, on Monday, I'm not dreading going to school.

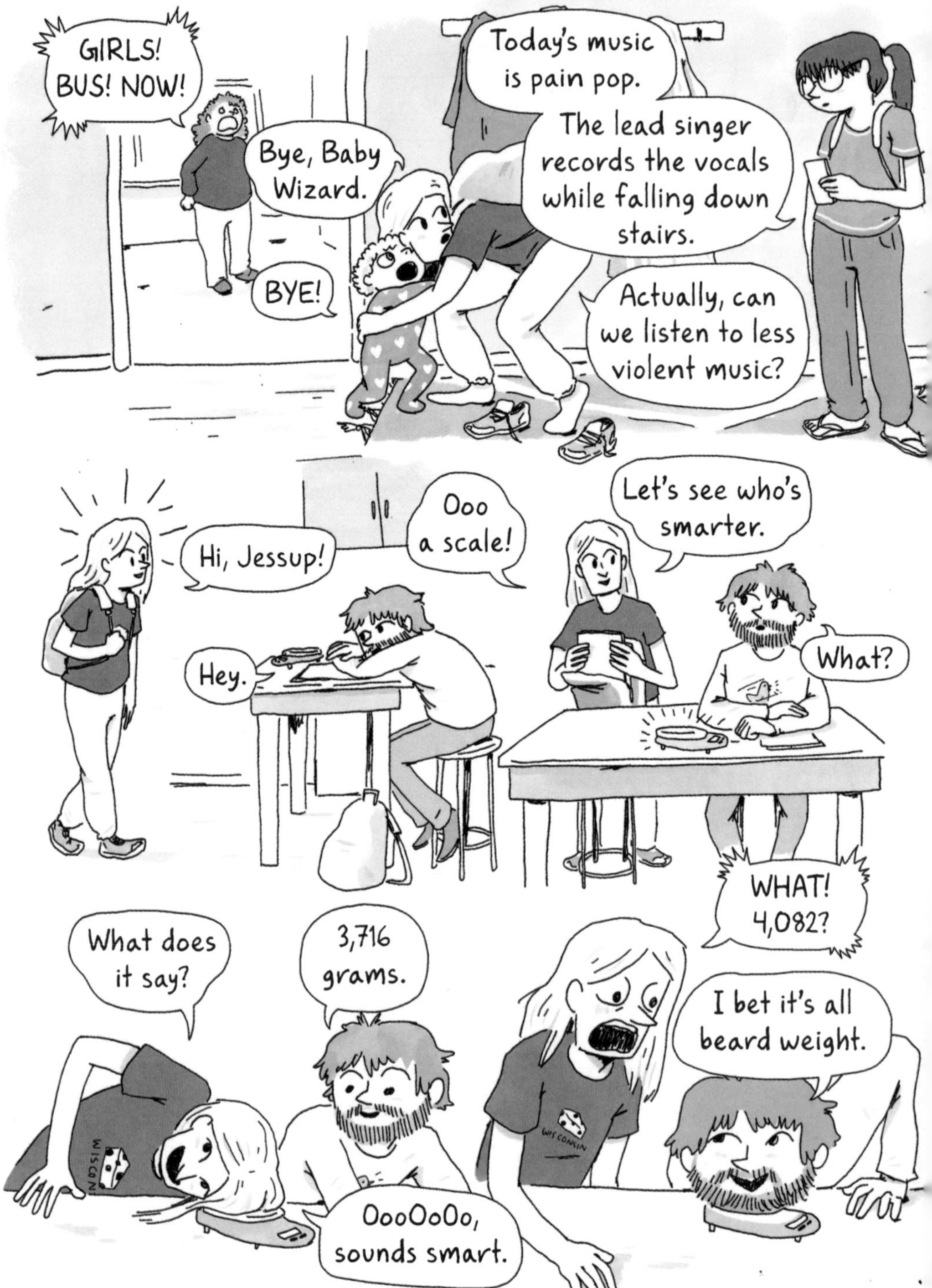
GIRLS! BUS! NOW!
Bye, Baby Wizard.
BYE!
Today's music is pain pop.
The lead singer records the vocals while falling down stairs.
Actually, can we listen to less violent music?
Hi, Jessup!
Hey.
Ooo a scale!
Let's see who's smarter.
What?
What does it say?
3,716 grams.
WHAT! 4,082?
I bet it's all beard weight.
OooOoOo, sounds smart.

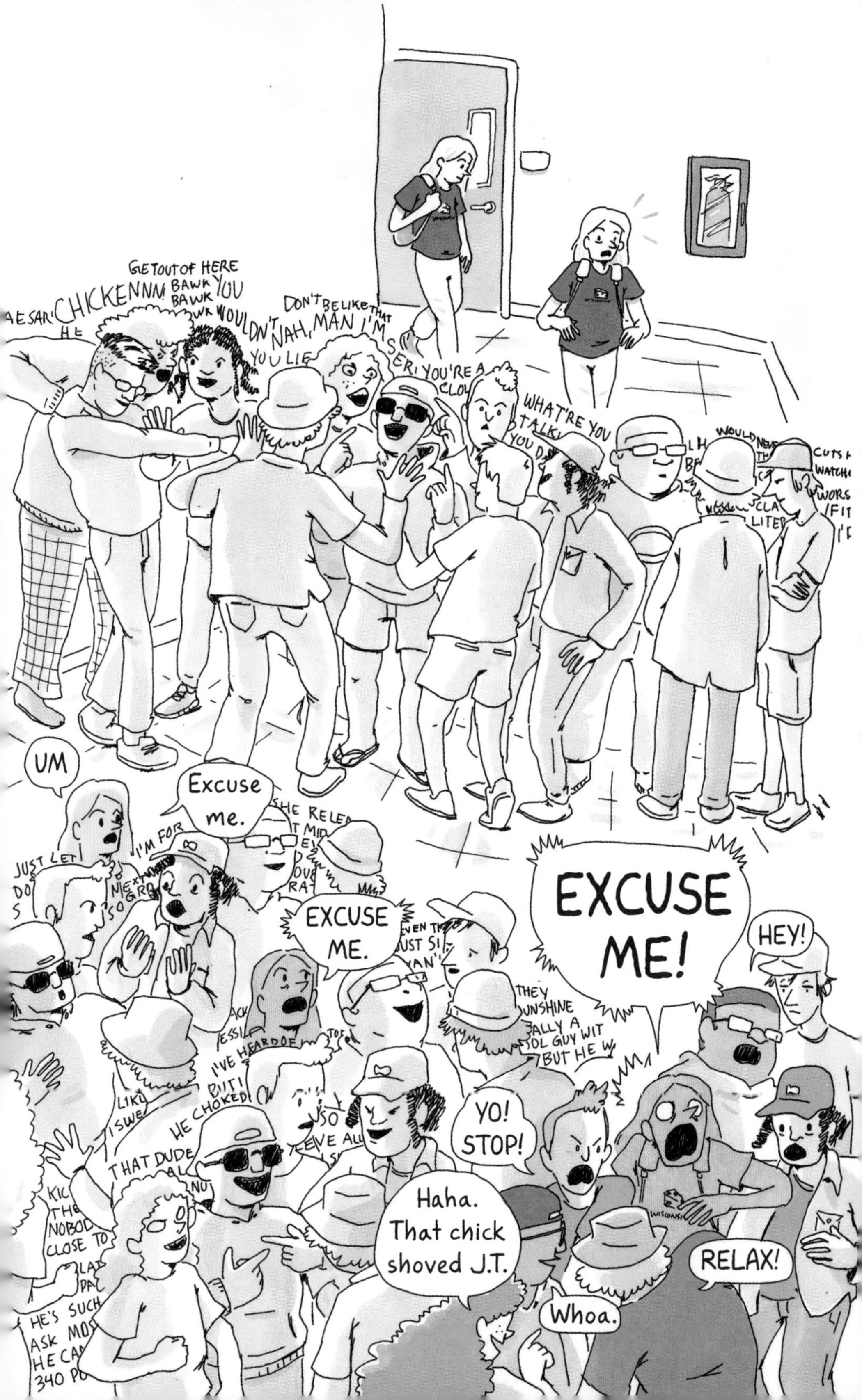
GET OUT OF HERE
CHICKENNN! BAWK BAWK
YOU WOULDN'T
DON'T BE LIKE THAT
NAH, MAN I'M SER
YOU LIE
YOU'RE A CLO
WHAT'RE YOU TALK
UM
Excuse me.
EXCUSE ME.
EXCUSE ME!
HEY!
THEY
I'VE HEARD OF
HE CHOKED!
THAT DUDE
YO! STOP!
Haha. That chick shoved J.T.
Whoa.
RELAX!
HE'S SUCH
340 P

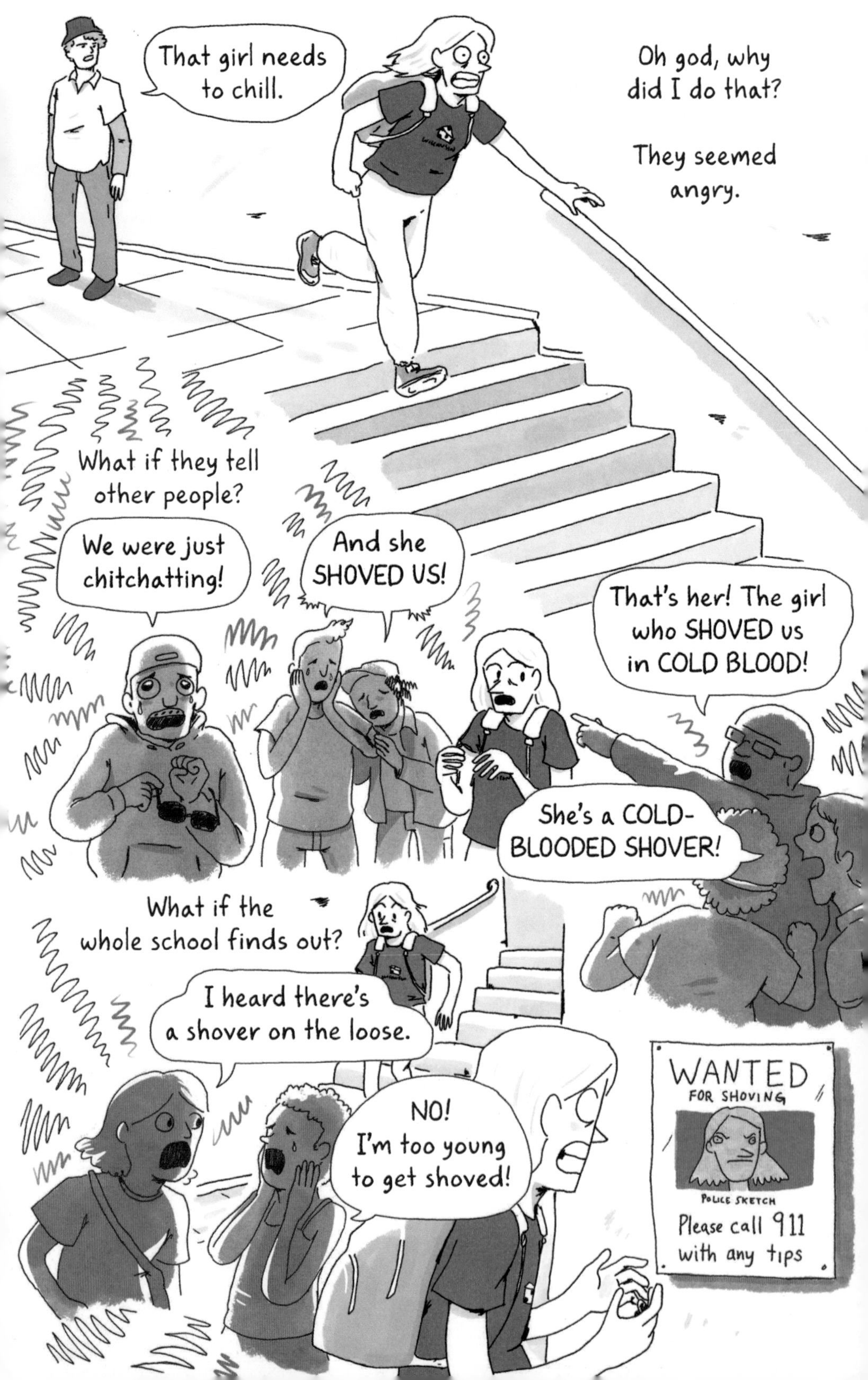
That girl needs to chill.
Oh god, why did I do that?
They seemed angry.
What if they tell other people?
We were just chitchatting!
And she SHOVED US!
That's her! The girl who SHOVED us in COLD BLOOD!
She's a COLD-BLOODED SHOVER!
What if the whole school finds out?
I heard there's a shover on the loose.
NO! I'm too young to get shoved!
WANTED
FOR SHOVING
POLICE SKETCH
Please call 911 with any tips

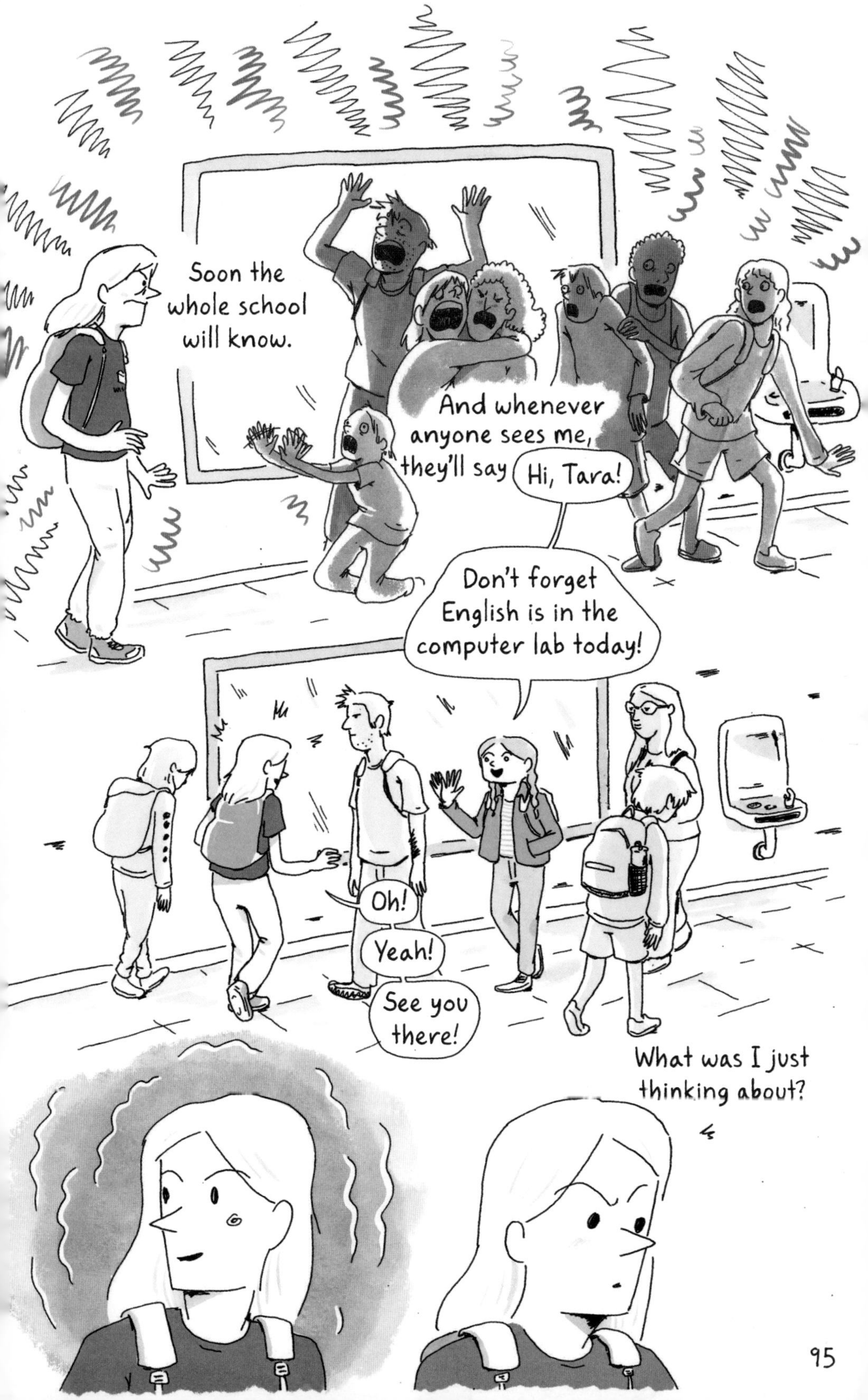
Soon the whole school will know.
And whenever anyone sees me, they'll say
Hi, Tara!
Don't forget English is in the computer lab today!
Oh!
Yeah!
See you there!
What was I just thinking about?

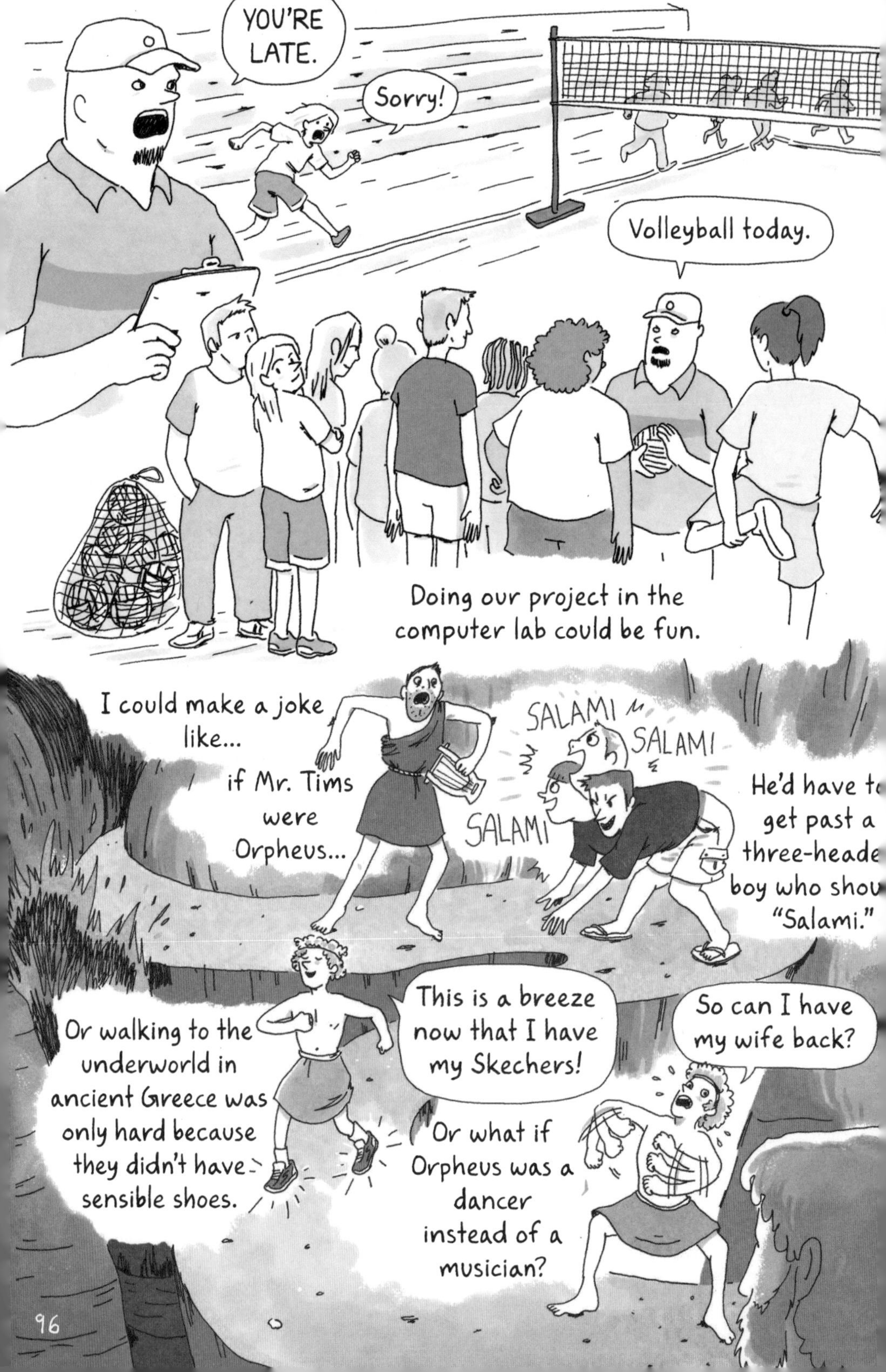
YOU'RE LATE.
Sorry!
Volleyball today.
Doing our project in the computer lab could be fun.
I could make a joke like...
if Mr. Tims were Orpheus...
SALAMI
SALAMI
SALAMI
He'd have t
get past a
three-heade
boy who shou
"Salami."
Or walking to the underworld in ancient Greece was only hard because they didn't have sensible shoes.
This is a breeze now that I have my Skechers!
So can I have my wife back?
Or what if Orpheus was a dancer instead of a musician?

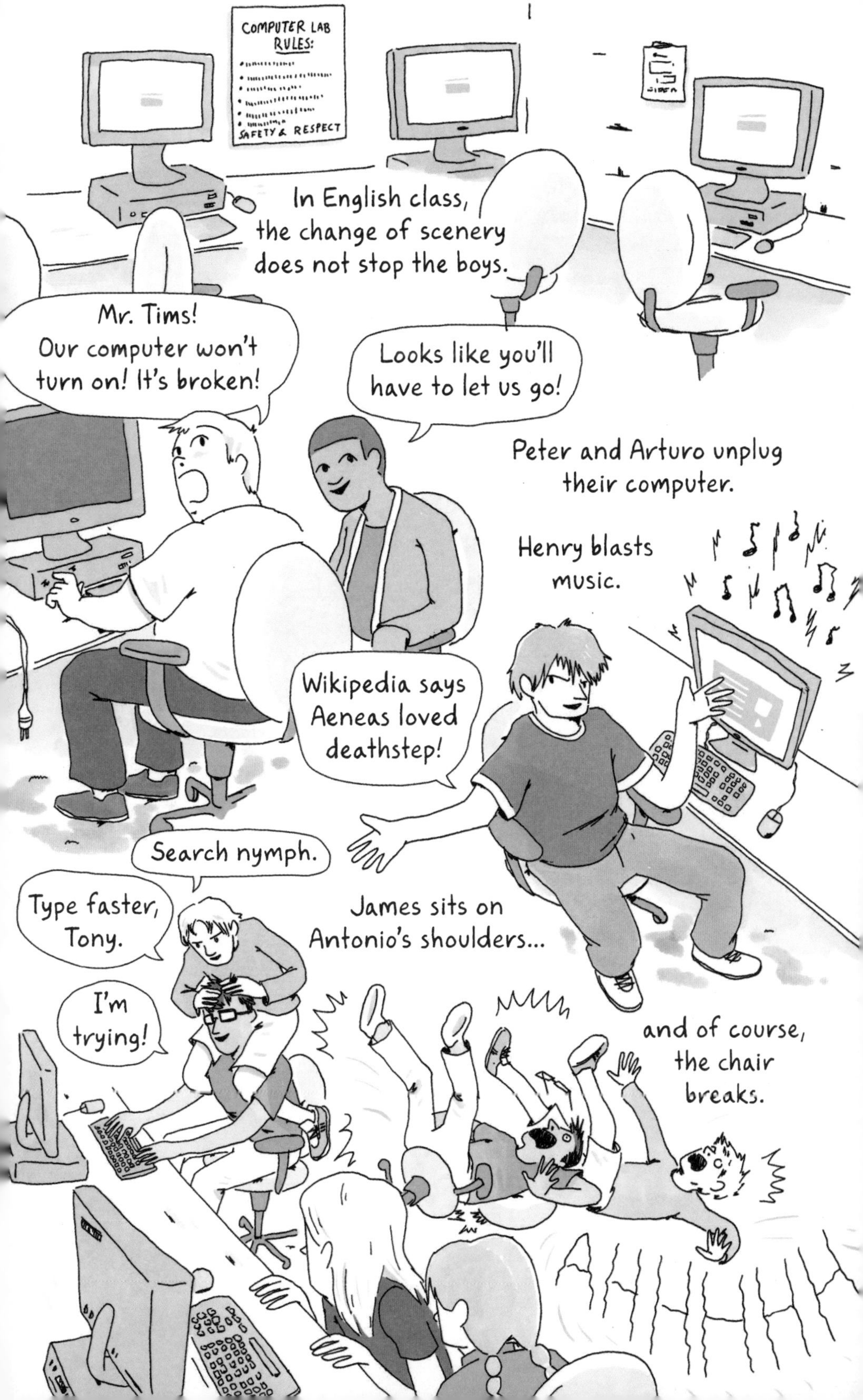
COMPUTER LAB RULES:
SAFETY & RESPECT
In English class, the change of scenery does not stop the boys.
Mr. Tims! Our computer won't turn on! It's broken!
Looks like you'll have to let us go!
Peter and Arturo unplug their computer.
Henry blasts music.
Wikipedia says Aeneas loved deathstep!
Search nymph.
Type faster, Tony.
I'm trying!
James sits on Antonio's shoulders...
and of course, the chair breaks.

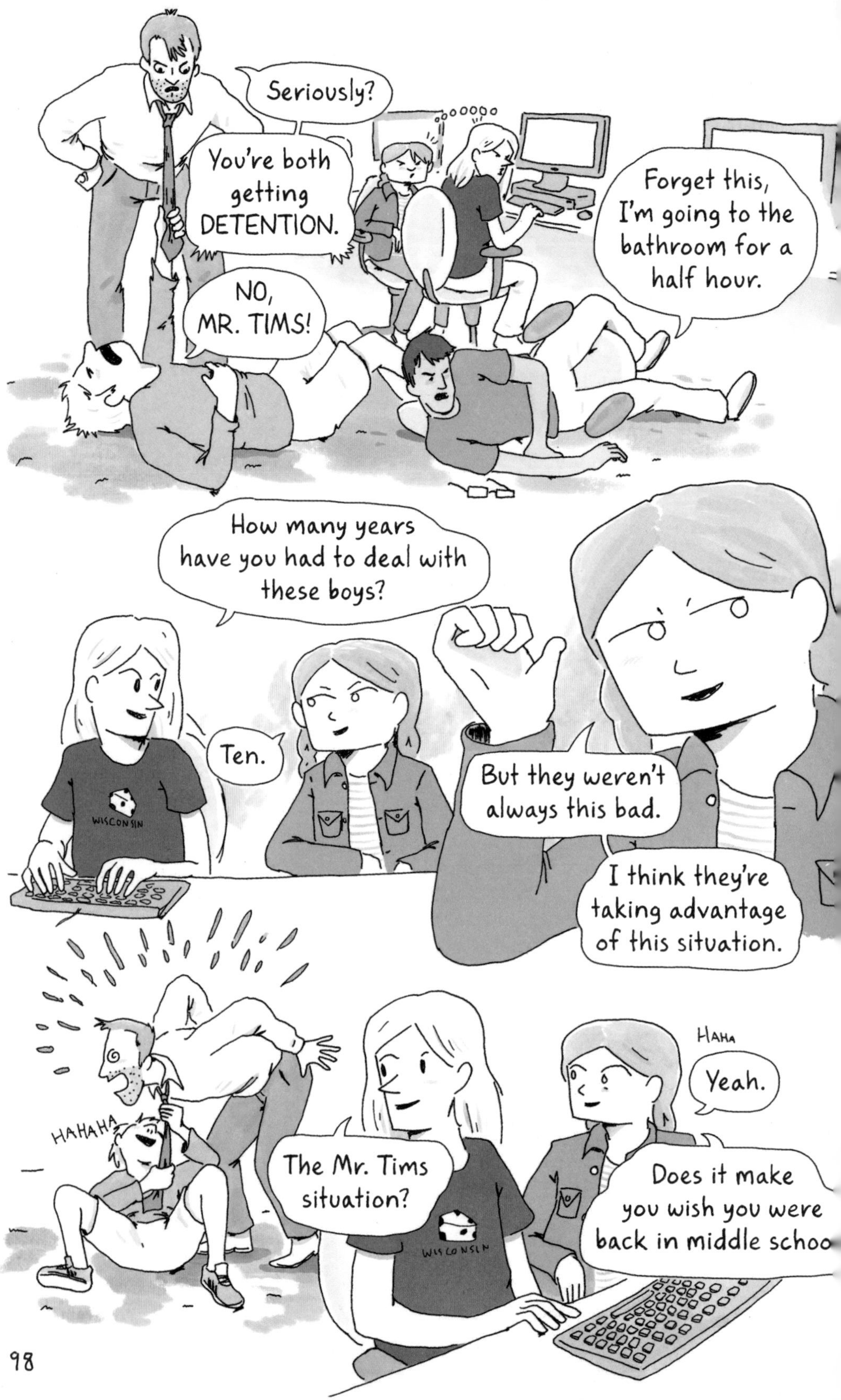
Seriously?
You're both getting DETENTION.
NO, MR. TIMS!
Forget this, I'm going to the bathroom for a half hour.
How many years have you had to deal with these boys?
Ten.
WISCONSIN
But they weren't always this bad.
I think they're taking advantage of this situation.
HAHAHA
The Mr. Tims situation?
HAHA
Yeah.
Does it make you wish you were back in middle schoo
WISCONSIN

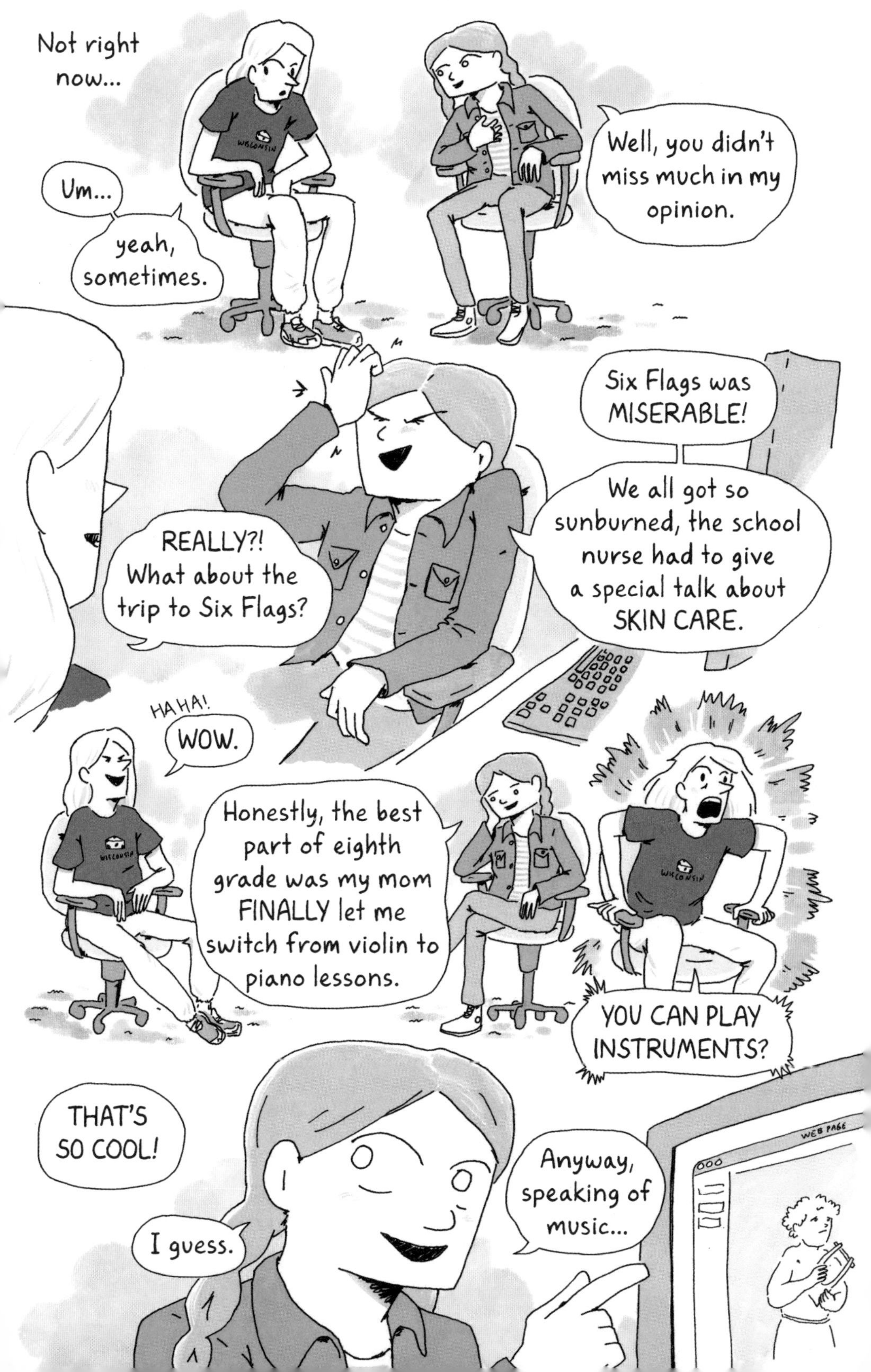

Not right now...
Um...
yeah, sometimes.
Well, you didn't miss much in my opinion.
REALLY?! What about the trip to Six Flags?
Six Flags was MISERABLE!
We all got so sunburned, the school nurse had to give a special talk about SKIN CARE.
HA HA!
WOW.
Honestly, the best part of eighth grade was my mom FINALLY let me switch from violin to piano lessons.
YOU CAN PLAY INSTRUMENTS?
THAT'S SO COOL!
I guess.
Anyway, speaking of music...

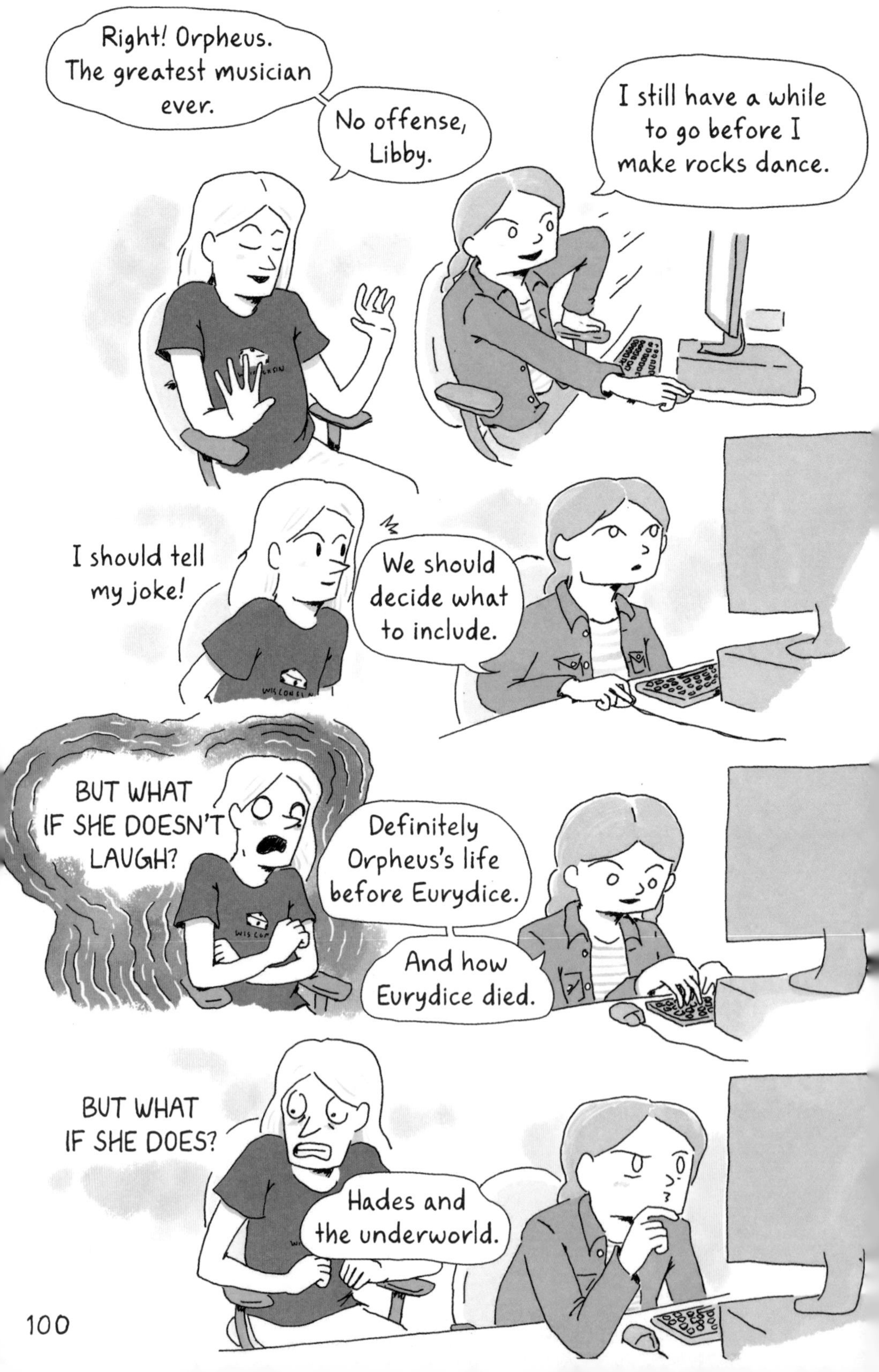
Right! Orpheus. The greatest musician ever.
No offense, Libby.
I still have a while to go before I make rocks dance.
WISCONSIN
I should tell my joke!
We should decide what to include.
BUT WHAT IF SHE DOESN'T LAUGH?
Definitely Orpheus's life before Eurydice.
And how Eurydice died.
BUT WHAT IF SHE DOES?
Hades and the underworld.

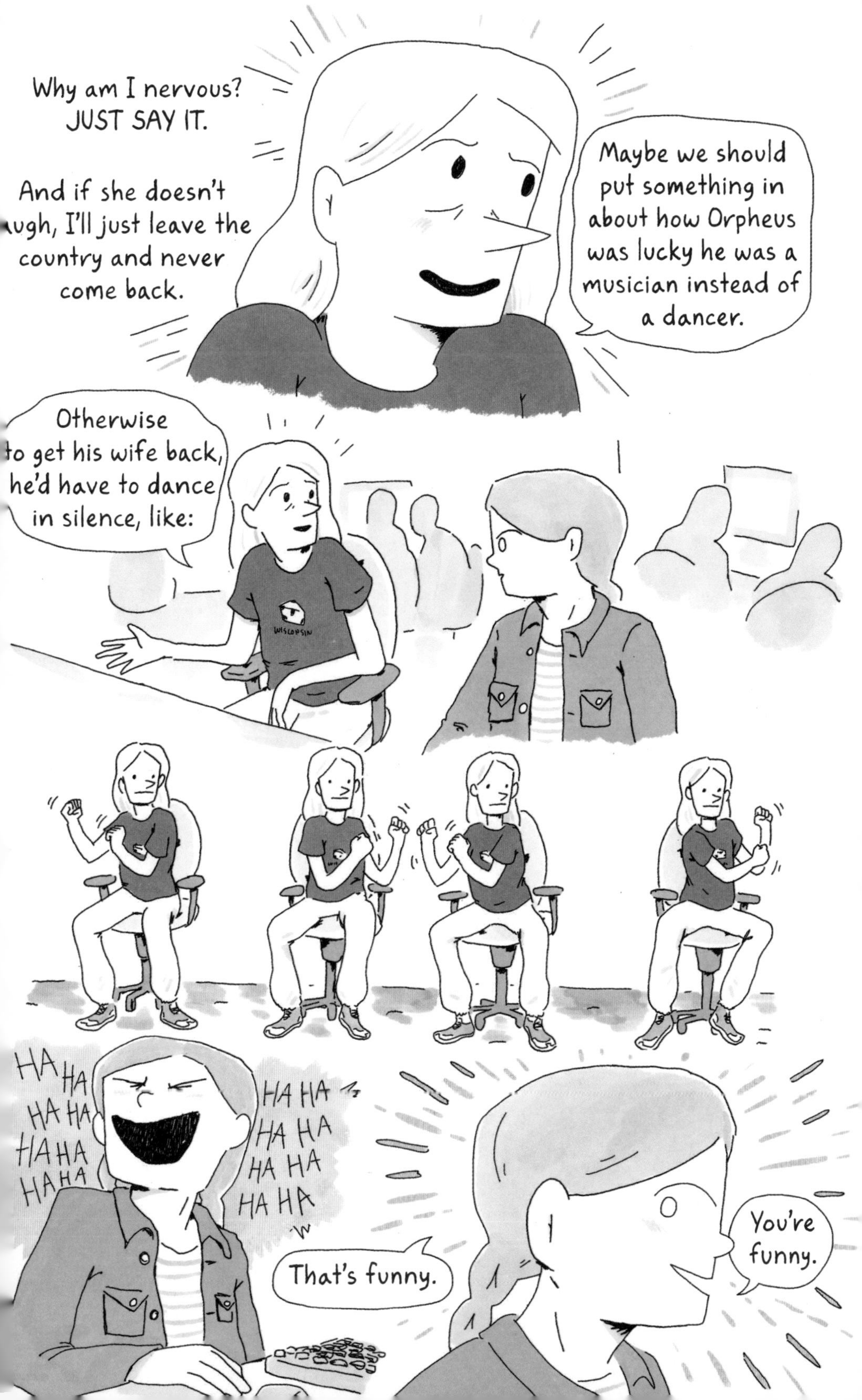
Why am I nervous? JUST SAY IT.
And if she doesn't ugh, I'll just leave the country and never come back.
Maybe we should put something in about how Orpheus was lucky he was a musician instead of a dancer.
Otherwise to get his wife back, he'd have to dance in silence, like:
WISCONSIN
HA HA HA HA HA HA HA HA
HA HA HA HA HA HA HA HA
That's funny.
You're funny.

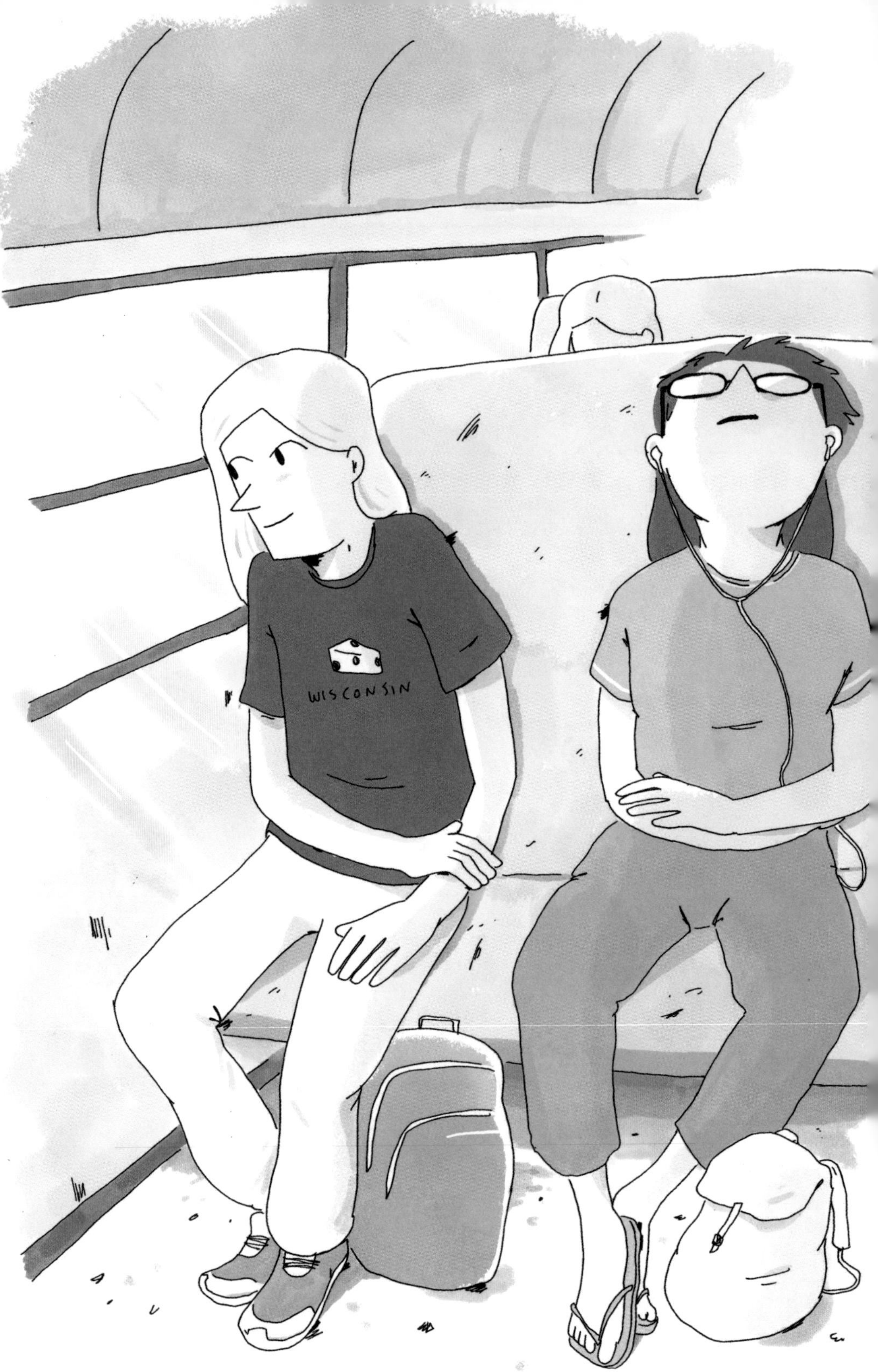
WISCONSIN

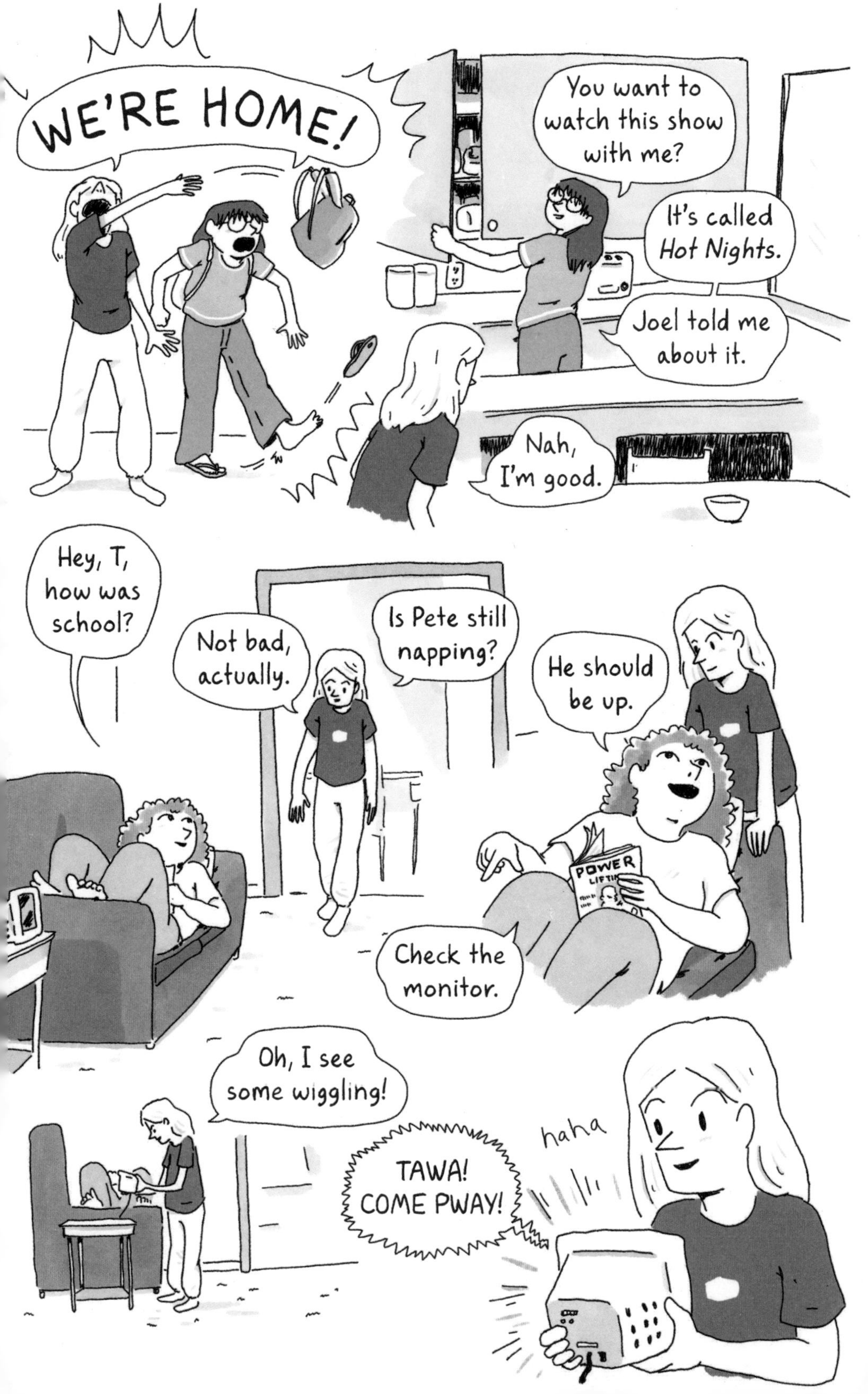
WE'RE HOME!
You want to watch this show with me?
It's called Hot Nights.
Joel told me about it.
Nah, I'm good.
Hey, T, how was school?
Not bad, actually.
Is Pete still napping?
He should be up.
Check the monitor.
POWER LIFTI
Oh, I see some wiggling!
TAWA! COME PWAY!
haha

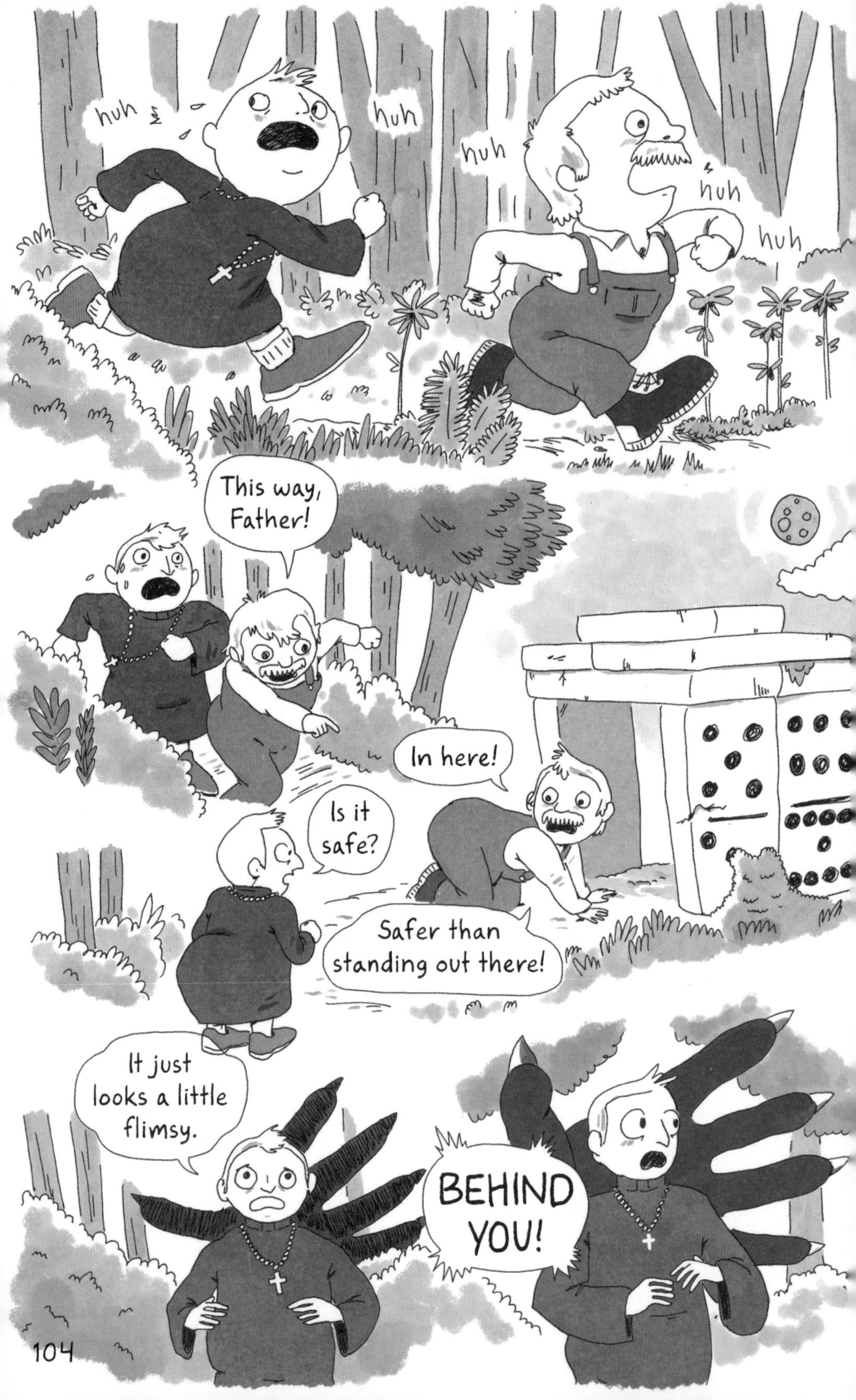
huh
huh
huh
huh
huh
This way, Father!
In here!
Is it safe?
Safer than standing out there!
It just looks a little flimsy.
BEHIND YOU!

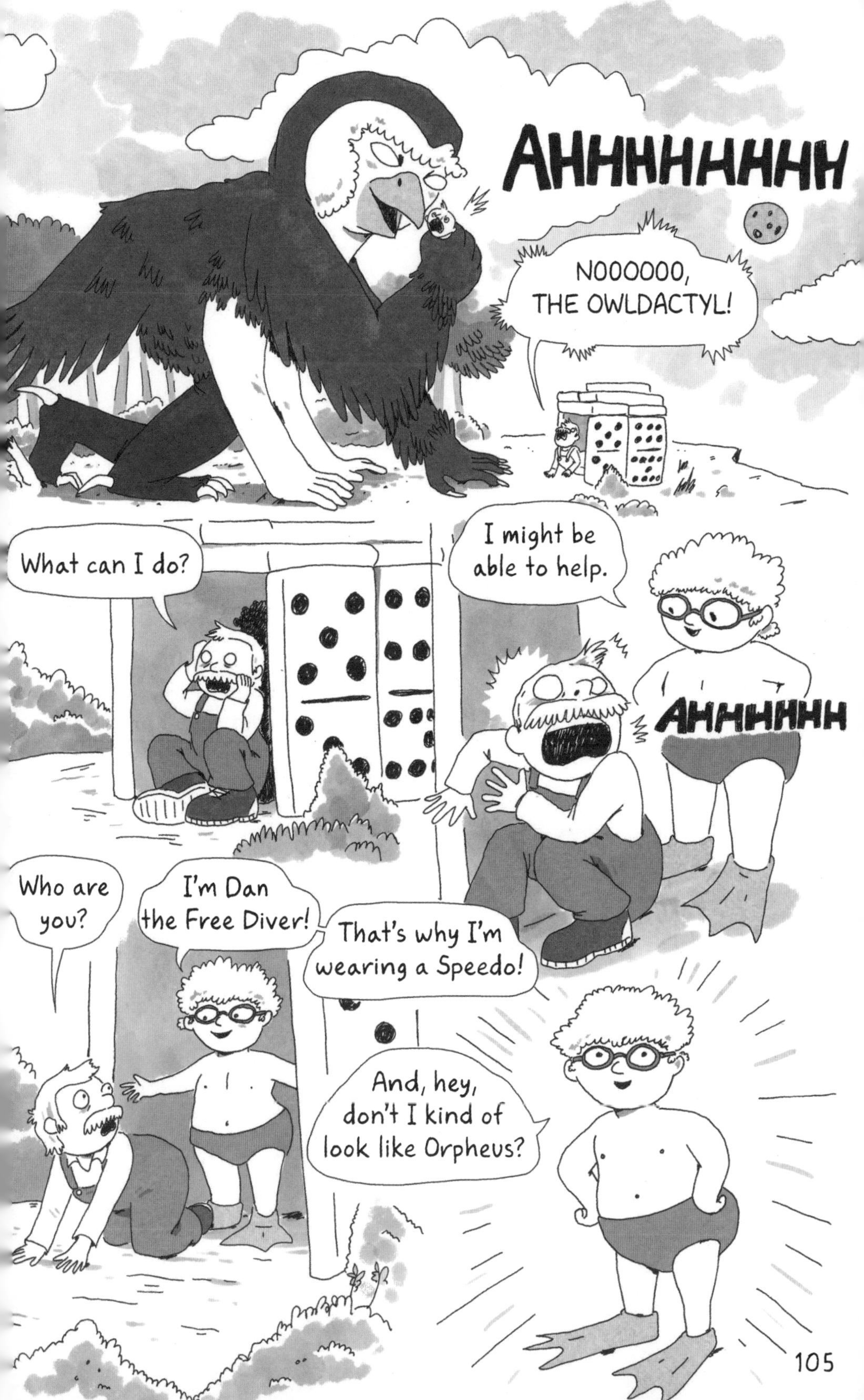
AHHHHHHHH
NOOOOOO,
THE OWLDACTYL!
What can I do?
I might be
able to help.
AHHHHHH
Who are
you?
I'm Dan
the Free Diver!
That's why I'm
wearing a Speedo!
And, hey,
don't I kind of
look like Orpheus?

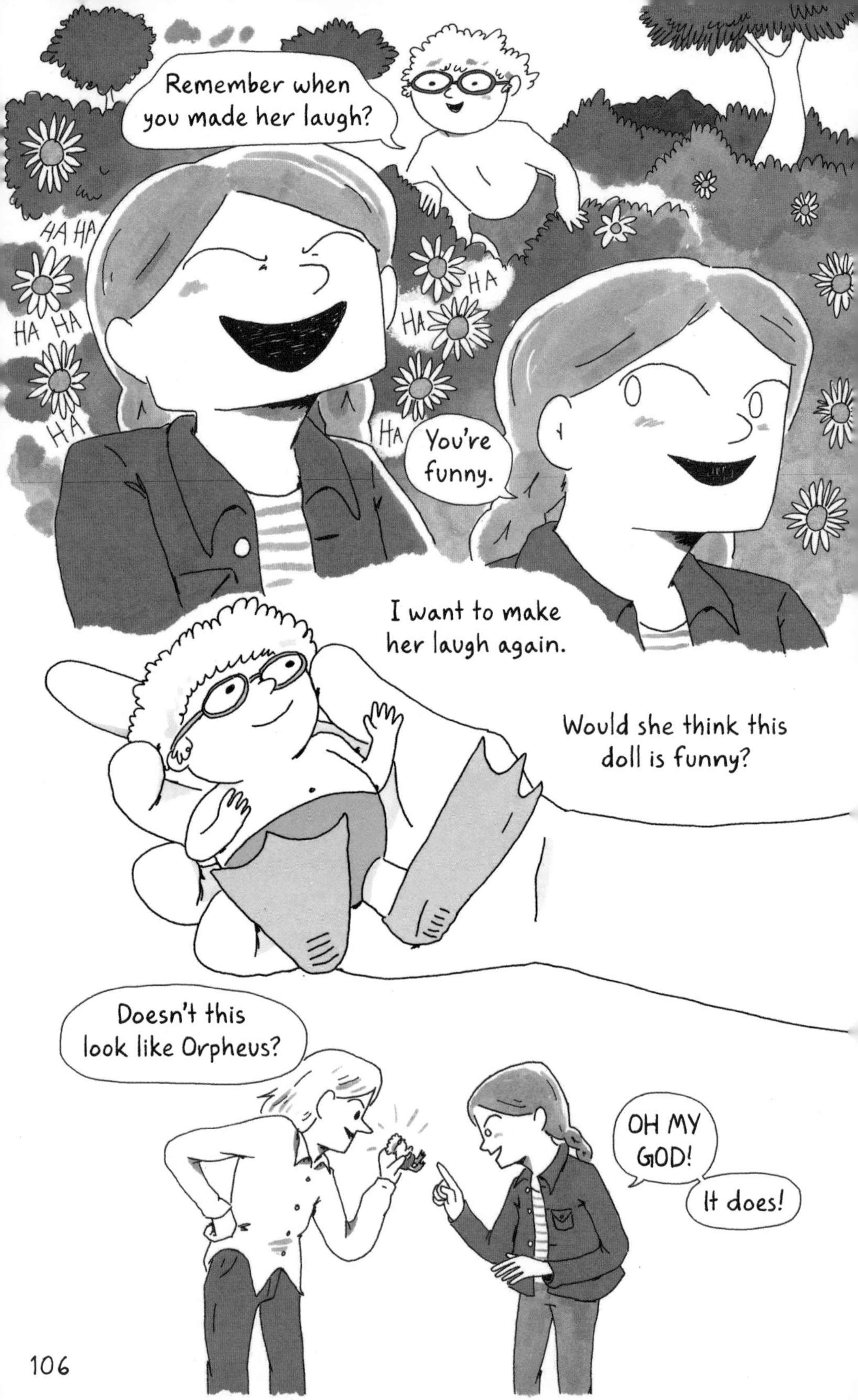
Remember when you made her laugh?
HA HA
HA HA
HA
HA
HA
HA
HA
You're funny.
I want to make her laugh again.
Would she think this doll is funny?
Doesn't this look like Orpheus?
OH MY GOD!
It does!

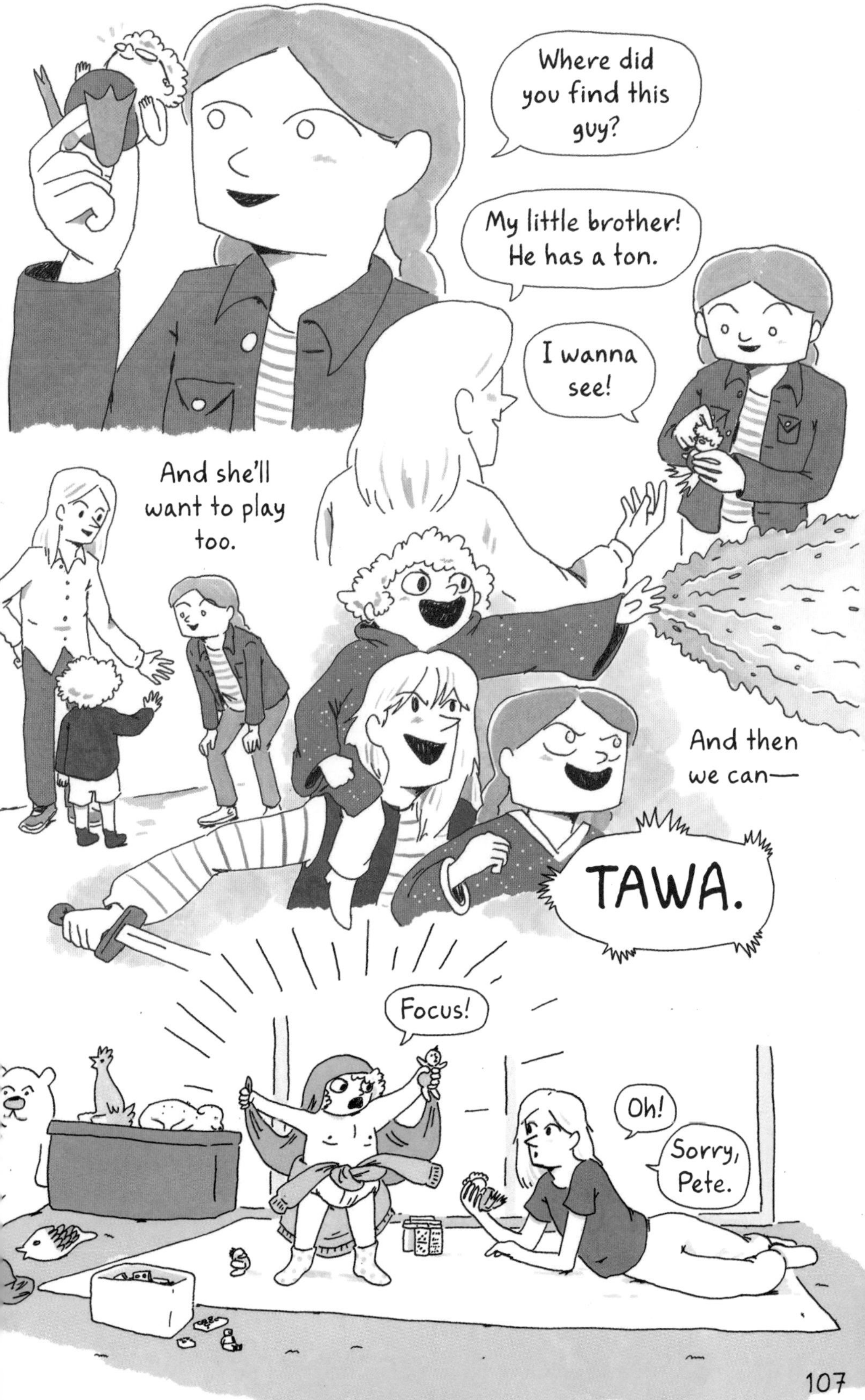
Where did you find this guy?
My little brother! He has a ton.
I wanna see!
And she'll want to play too.
And then we can—
TAWA.
Focus!
Oh!
Sorry, Pete.

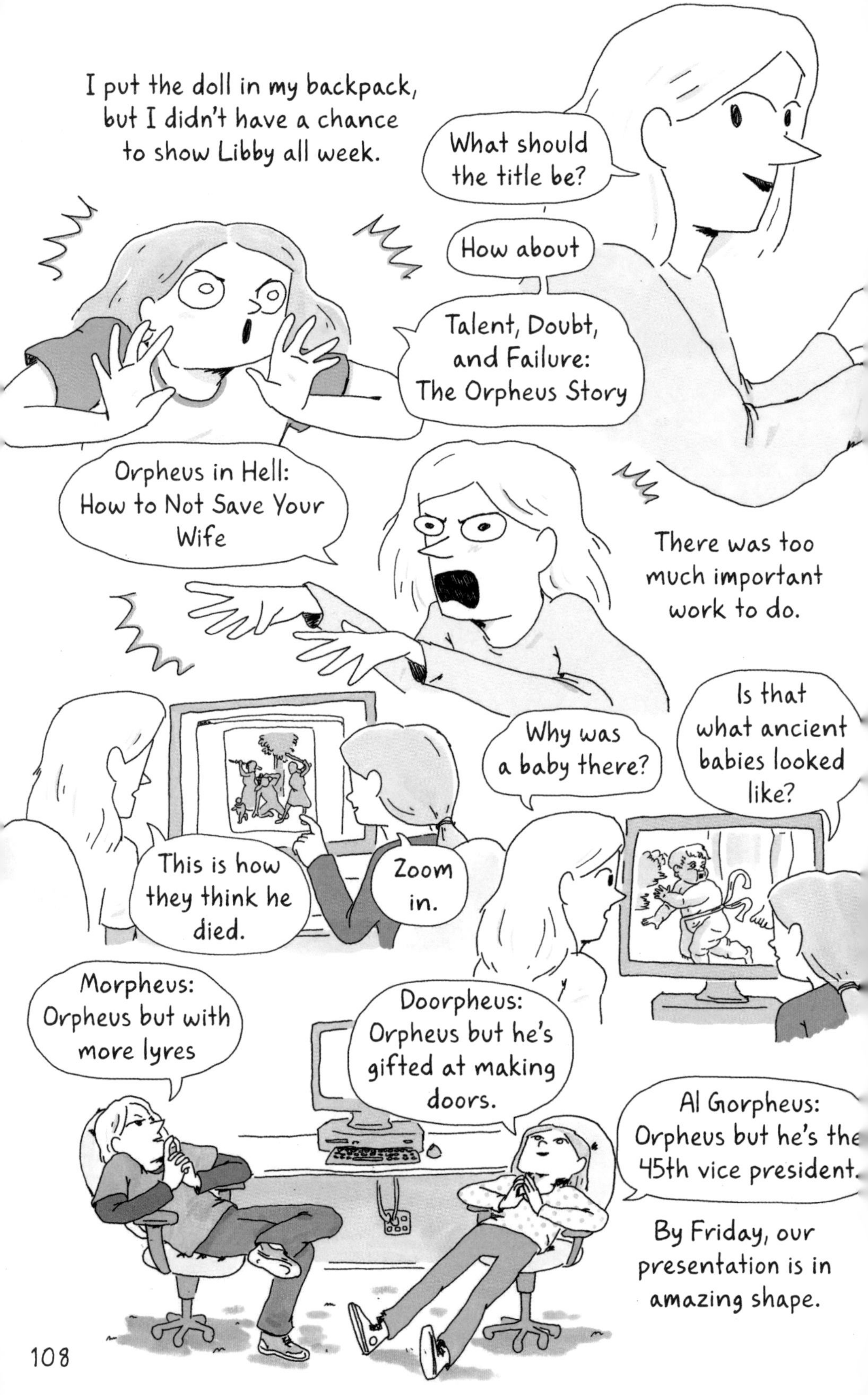

I put the doll in my backpack, but I didn't have a chance to show Libby all week.
What should the title be?
How about
Talent, Doubt, and Failure: The Orpheus Story
Orpheus in Hell: How to Not Save Your Wife
There was too much important work to do.
This is how they think he died.
Zoom in.
Why was a baby there?
Is that what ancient babies looked like?
Morpheus: Orpheus but with more lyres
Doorpheus: Orpheus but he's gifted at making doors.
Al Gorpheus: Orpheus but he's the 45th vice president.
By Friday, our presentation is in amazing shape.

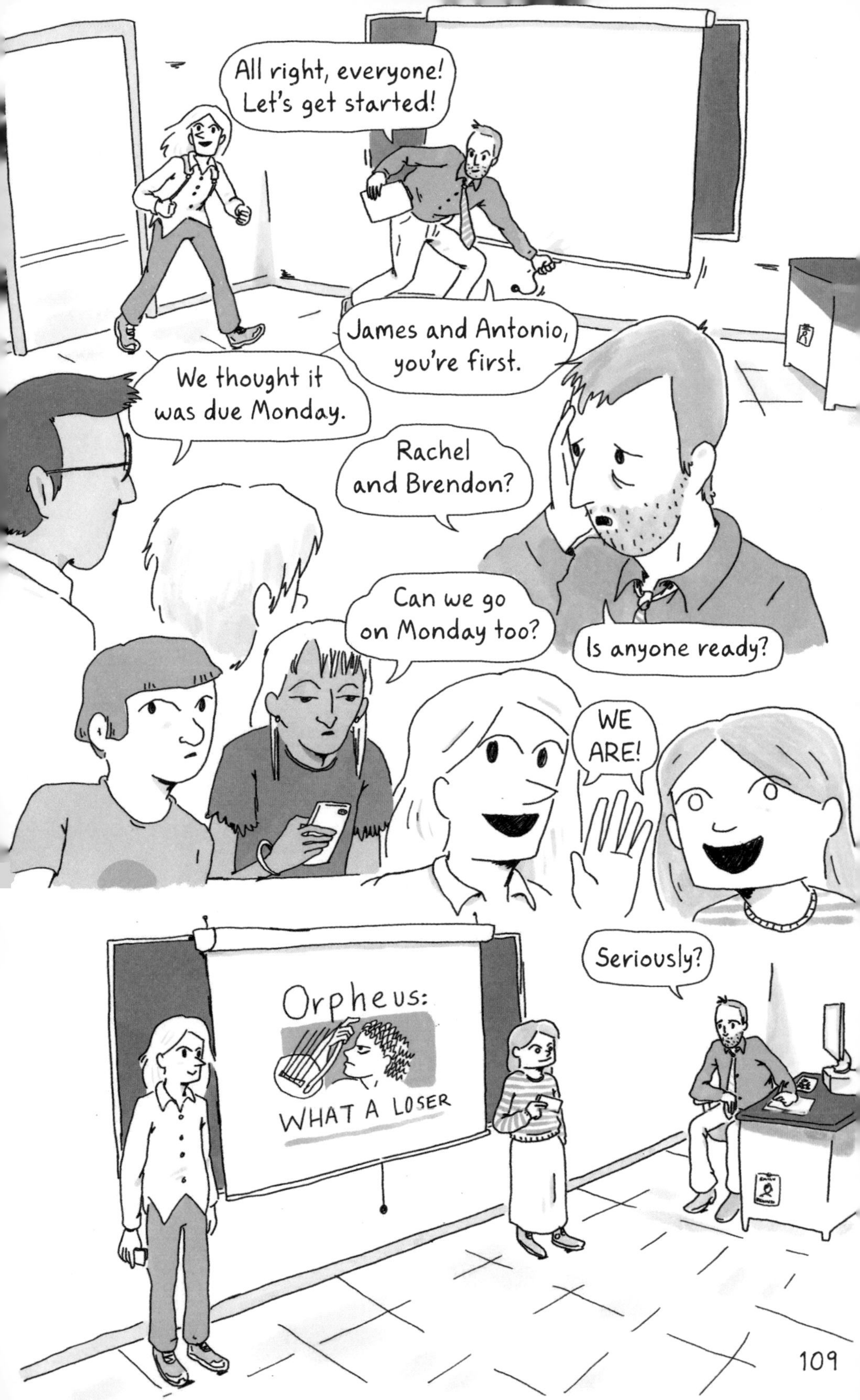
All right, everyone! Let's get started!
James and Antonio, you're first.
We thought it was due Monday.
Rachel and Brendon?
Can we go on Monday too?
Is anyone ready?
WE ARE!
Seriously?
Orpheus:
WHAT A LOSER

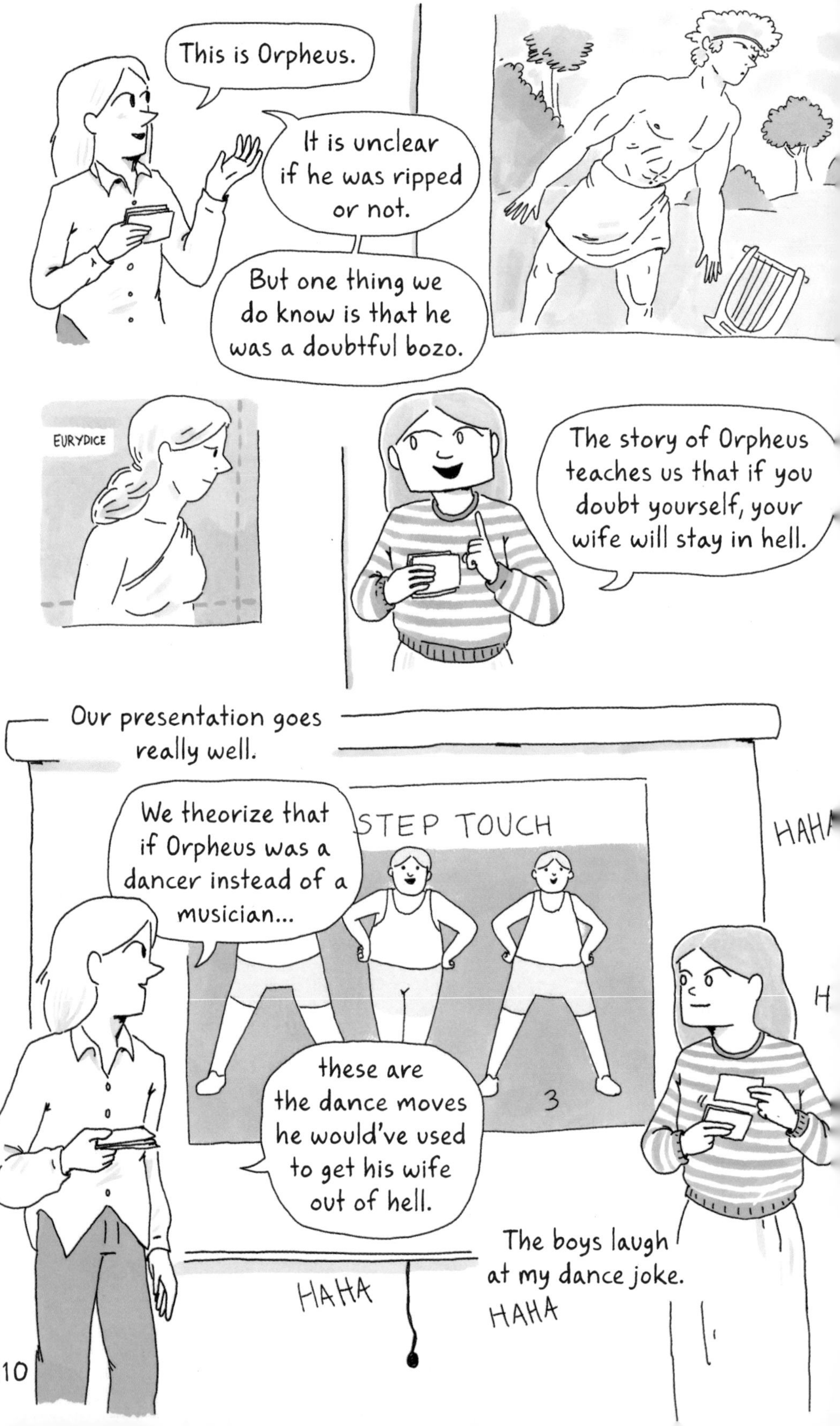
This is Orpheus.
It is unclear if he was ripped or not.
But one thing we do know is that he was a doubtful bozo.
EURYDICE
The story of Orpheus teaches us that if you doubt yourself, your wife will stay in hell.
Our presentation goes really well.
STEP TOUCH
We theorize that if Orpheus was a dancer instead of a musician...
3
these are the dance moves he would've used to get his wife out of hell.
HAHA
The boys laugh at my dance joke.
HAHA

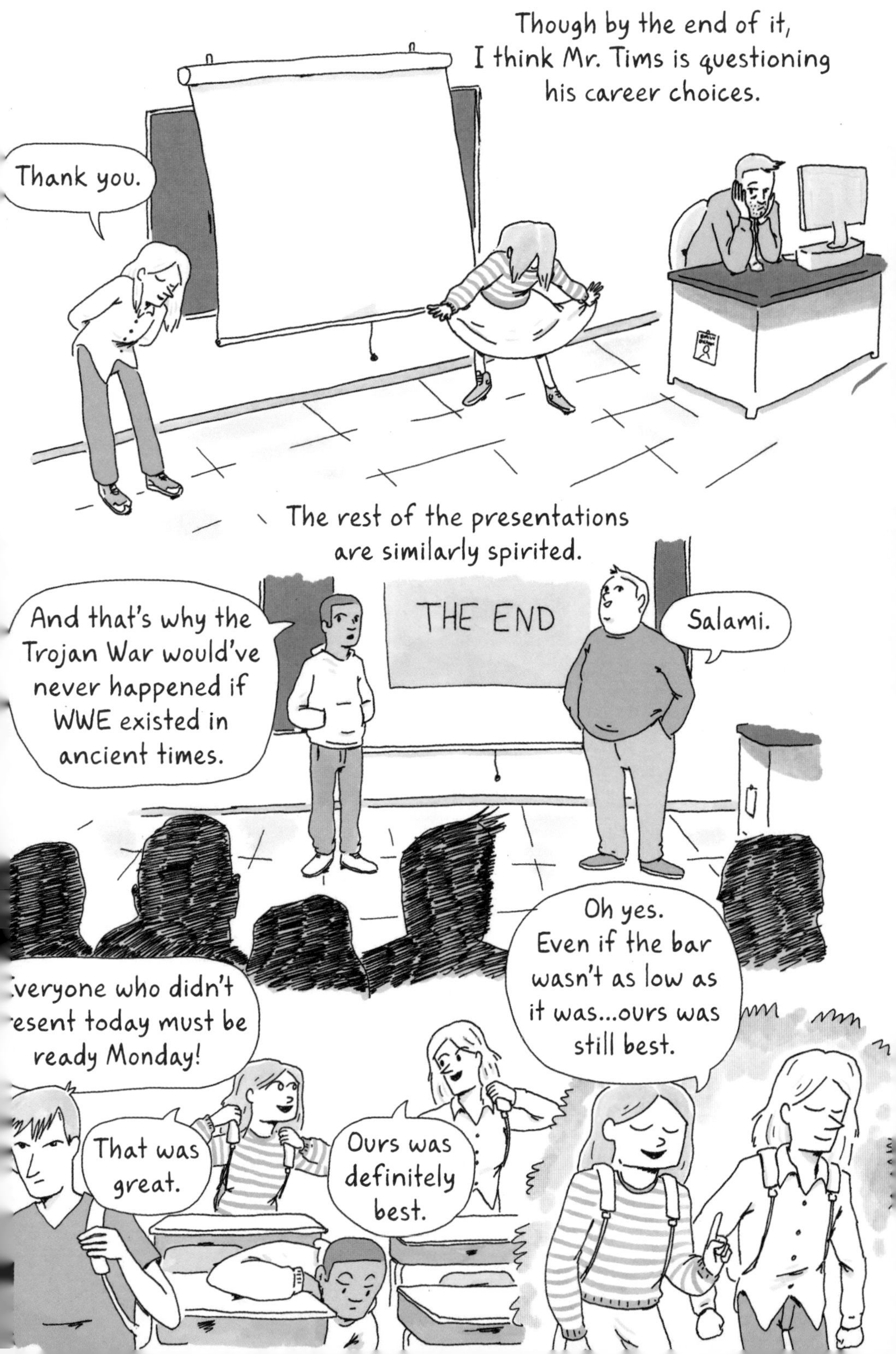
Though by the end of it, I think Mr. Tims is questioning his career choices.
Thank you.
The rest of the presentations are similarly spirited.
And that's why the Trojan War would've never happened if WWE existed in ancient times.
THE END
Salami.
veryone who didn't
esent today must be
ready Monday!
That was great.
Ours was definitely best.
Oh yes. Even if the bar wasn't as low as it was...ours was still best.

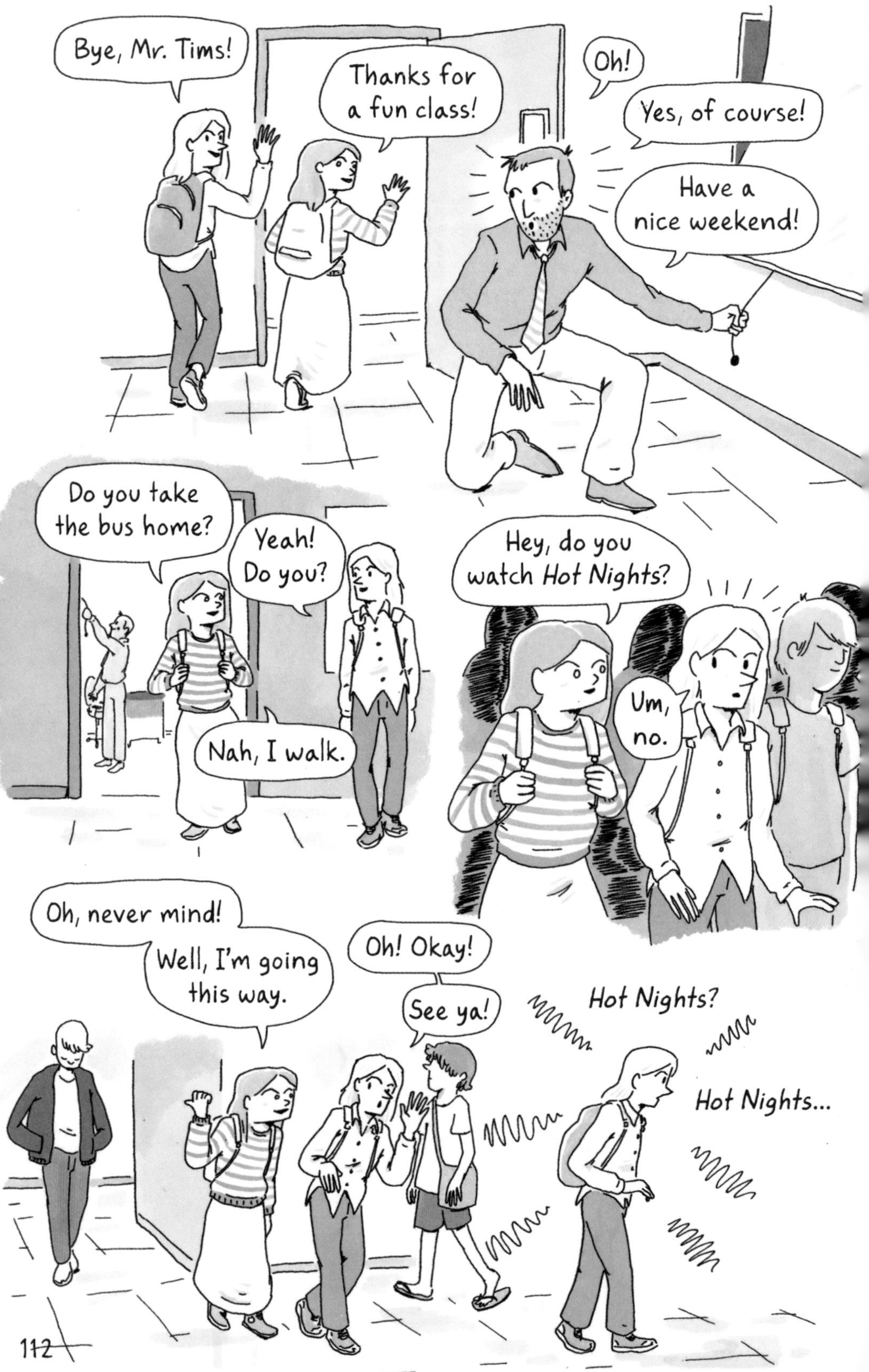
Bye, Mr. Tims!
Thanks for a fun class!
Oh!
Yes, of course!
Have a nice weekend!
Do you take the bus home?
Yeah! Do you?
Nah, I walk.
Hey, do you watch Hot Nights?
Um, no.
Oh, never mind!
Well, I'm going this way.
Oh! Okay!
See ya!
Hot Nights?
Hot Nights...

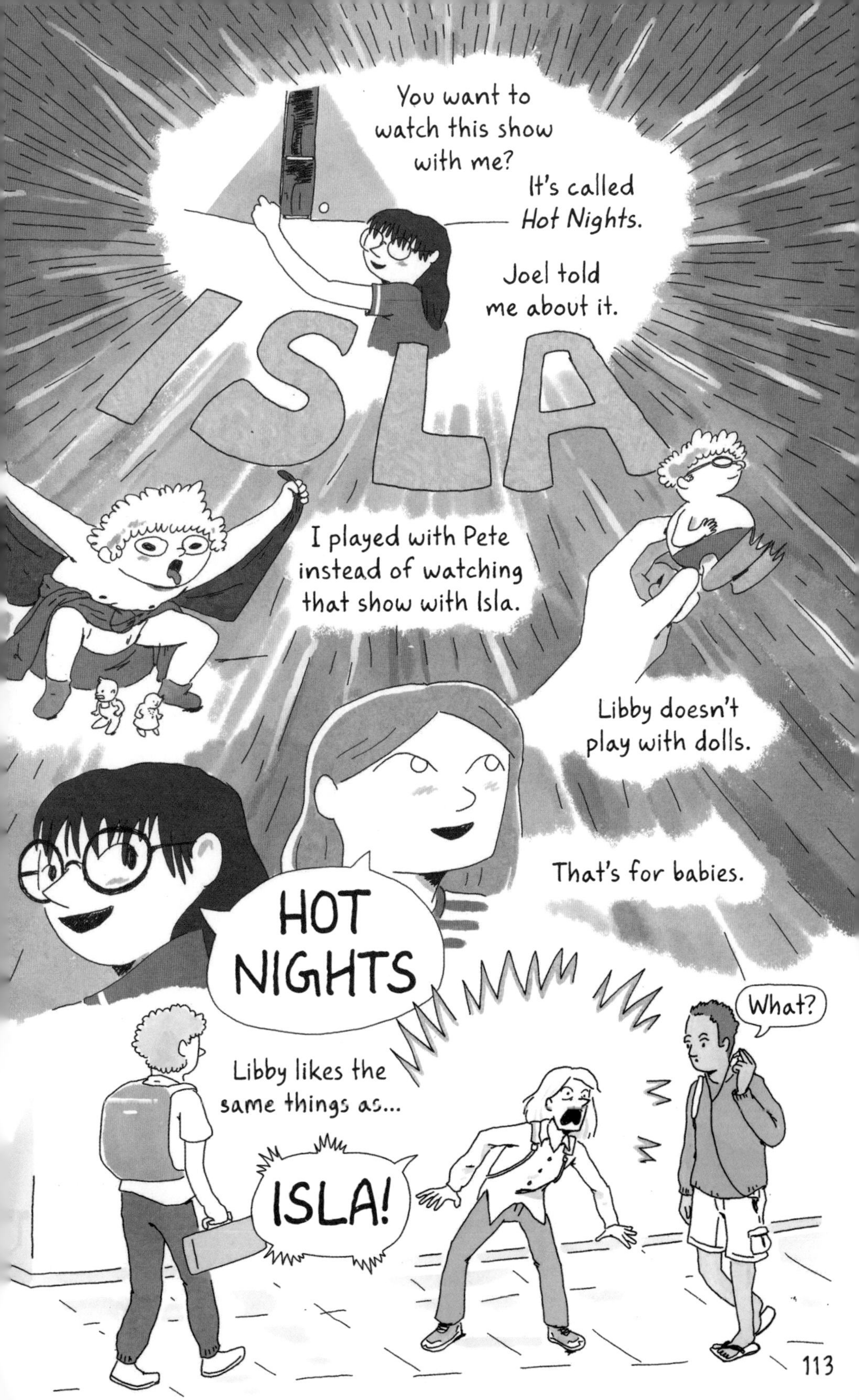
You want to watch this show with me?
It's called *Hot Nights*.
Joel told me about it.
ISLA
I played with Pete instead of watching that show with Isla.
Libby doesn't play with dolls.
That's for babies.
HOT NIGHTS
Libby likes the same things as...
ISLA!
What?

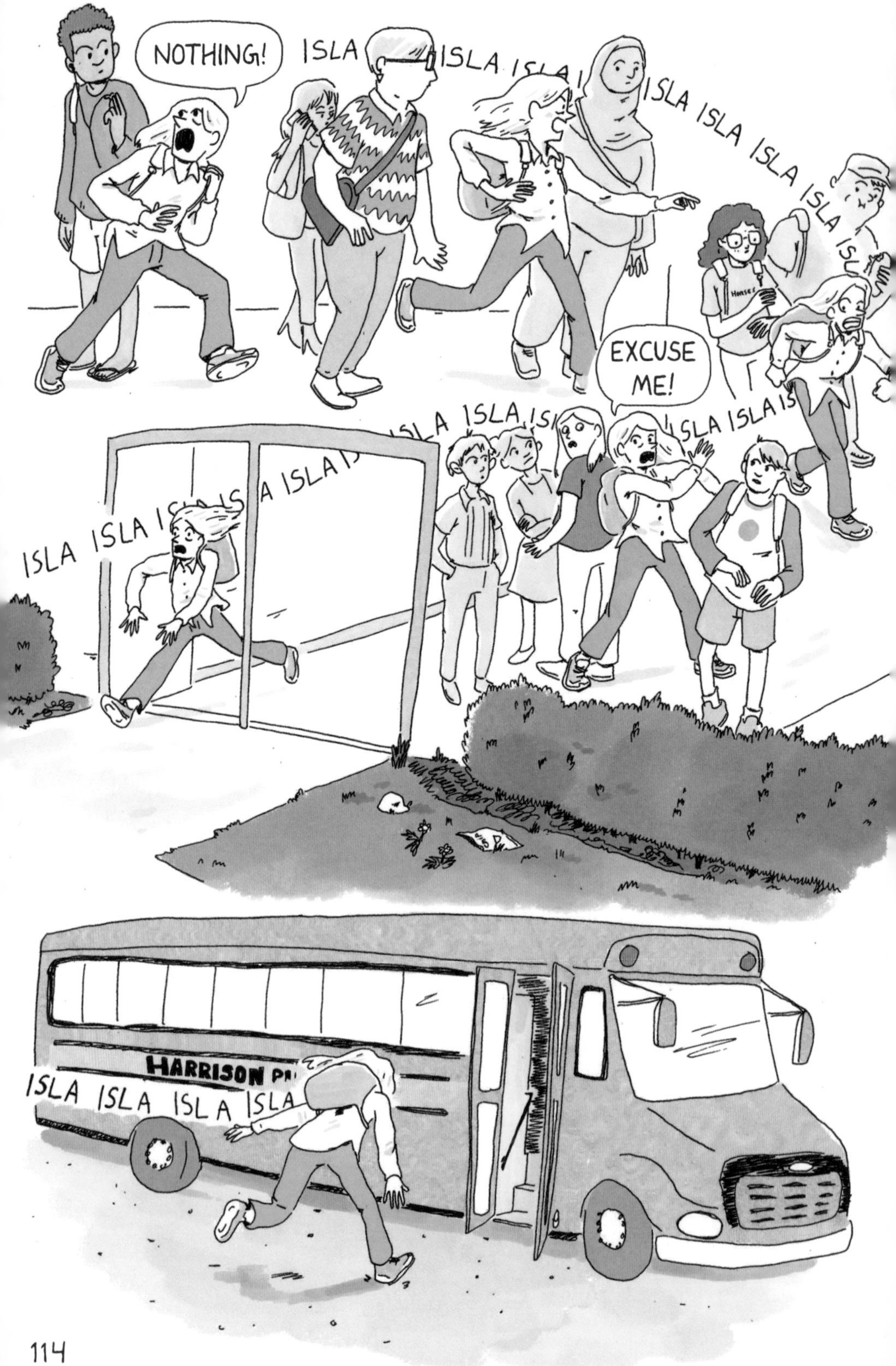
NOTHING!
ISLA
ISLA ISLA
ISLA ISLA ISLA ISLA ISLA
EXCUSE ME!
ISLA ISLA
ISLA ISLA
ISLA ISLA ISLA ISLA
ISLA ISLA ISLA ISLA
HARRISON

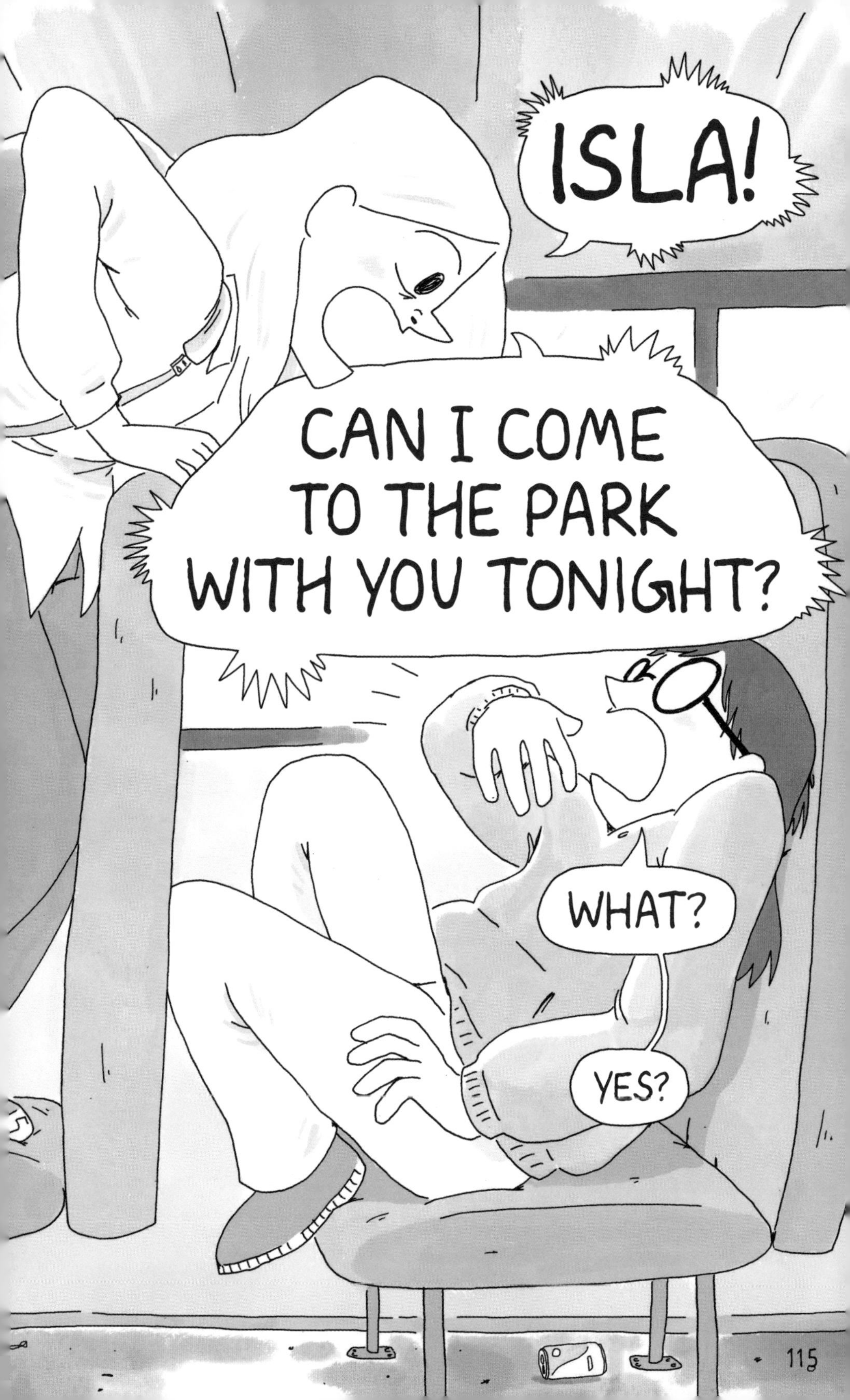
ISLA!
CAN I COME TO THE PARK WITH YOU TONIGHT?
WHAT?
YES?

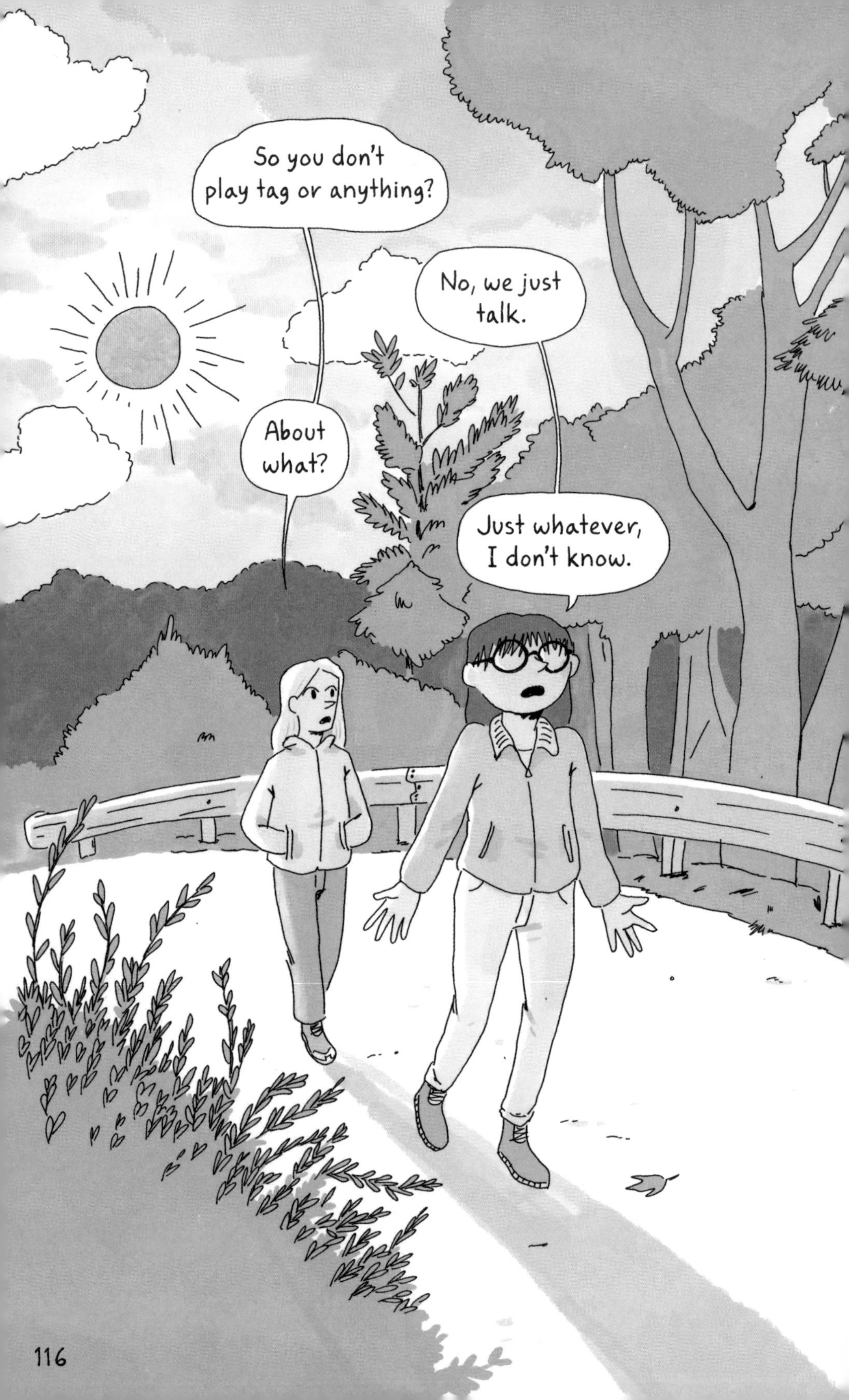
So you don't play tag or anything?
No, we just talk.
About what?
Just whatever, I don't know.

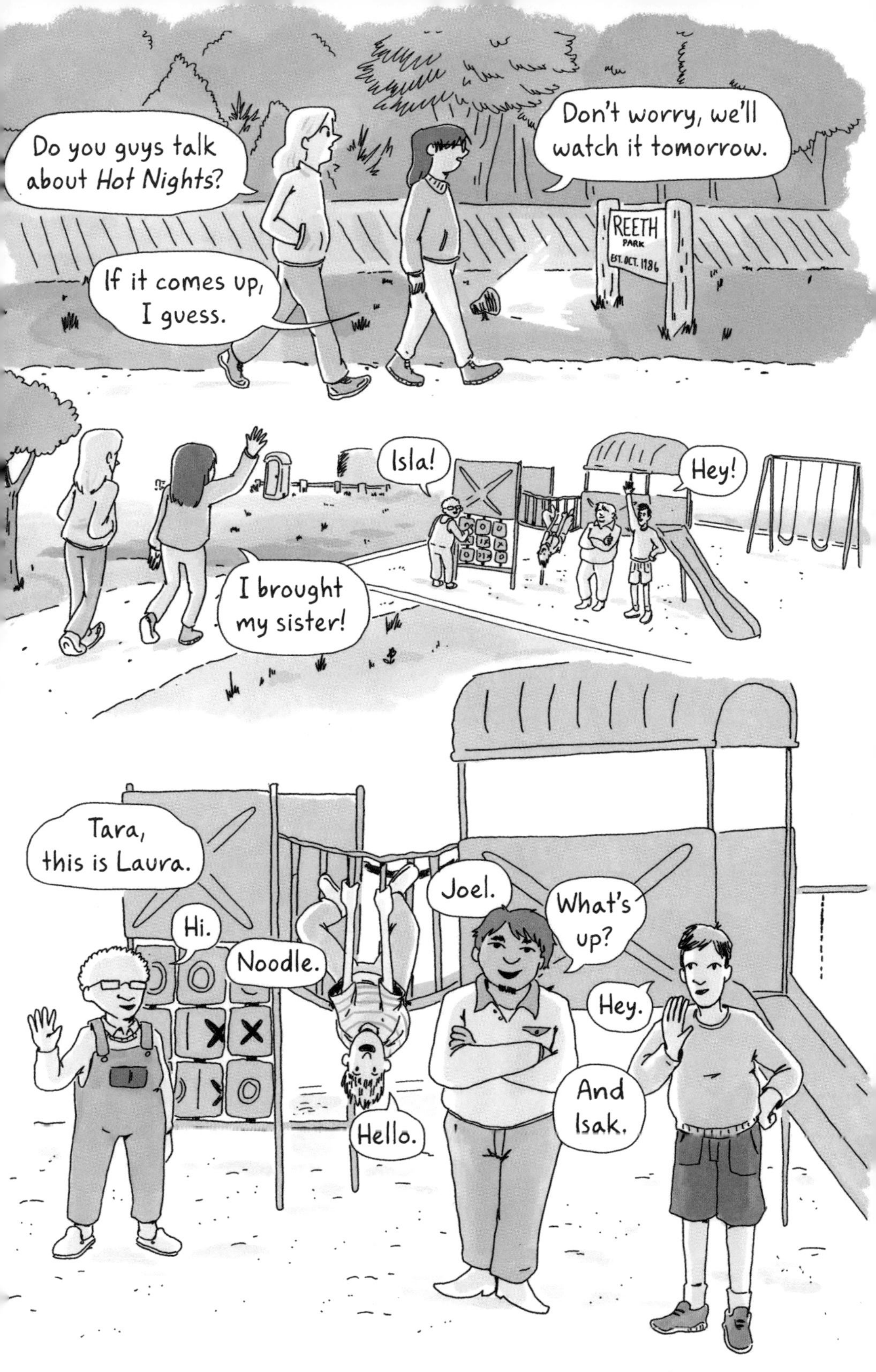
Do you guys talk about Hot Nights?
If it comes up, I guess.
Don't worry, we'll watch it tomorrow.
REETH PARK EST. OCT. 1986
I brought my sister!
Isla!
Hey!
Tara, this is Laura.
Hi.
Noodle.
Hello.
Joel.
What's up?
Hey.
And Isak.

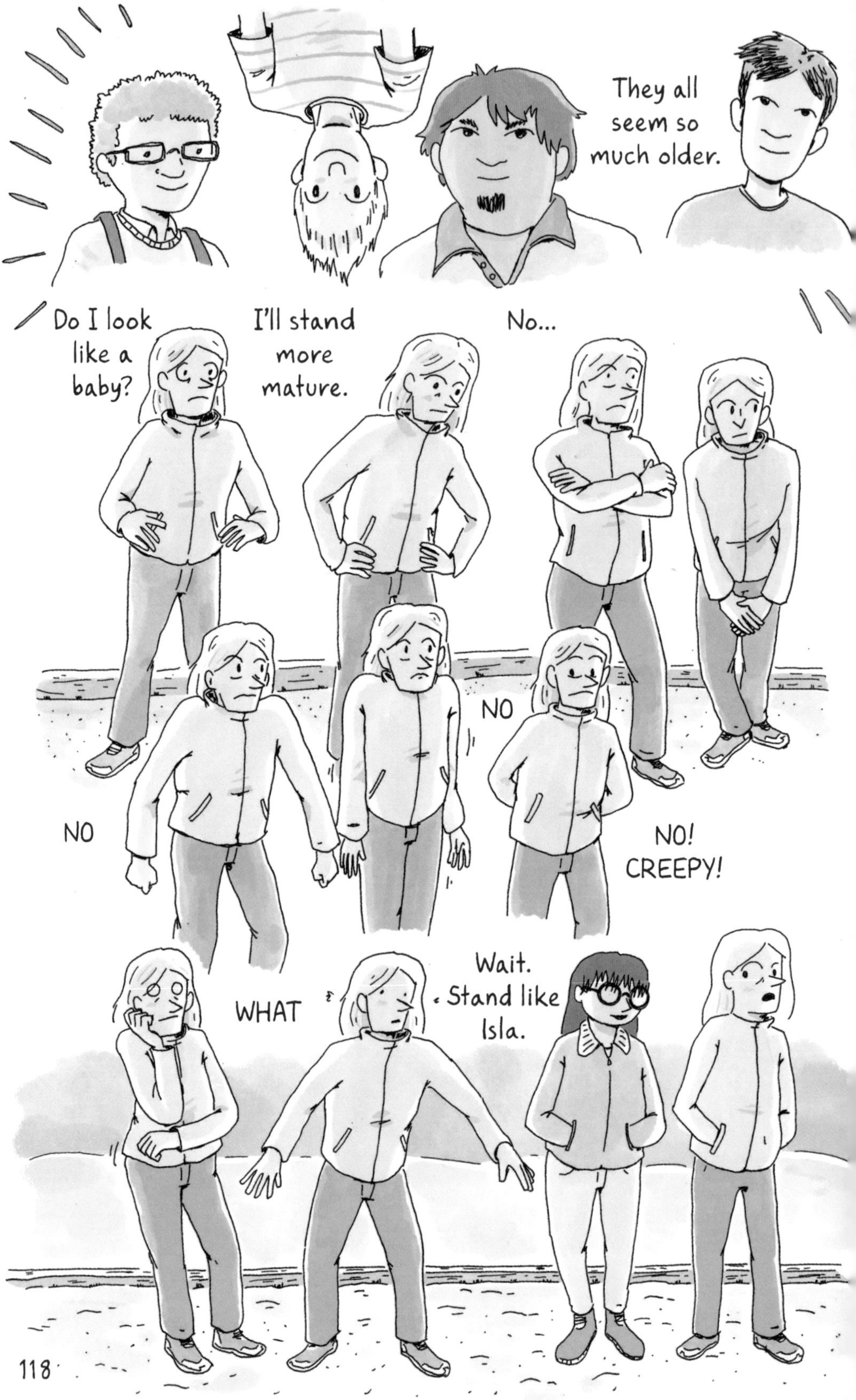
They all seem so much older.
Do I look like a baby?
I'll stand more mature.
No...
NO
NO
NO! CREEPY!
WHAT
Wait. Stand like Isla.

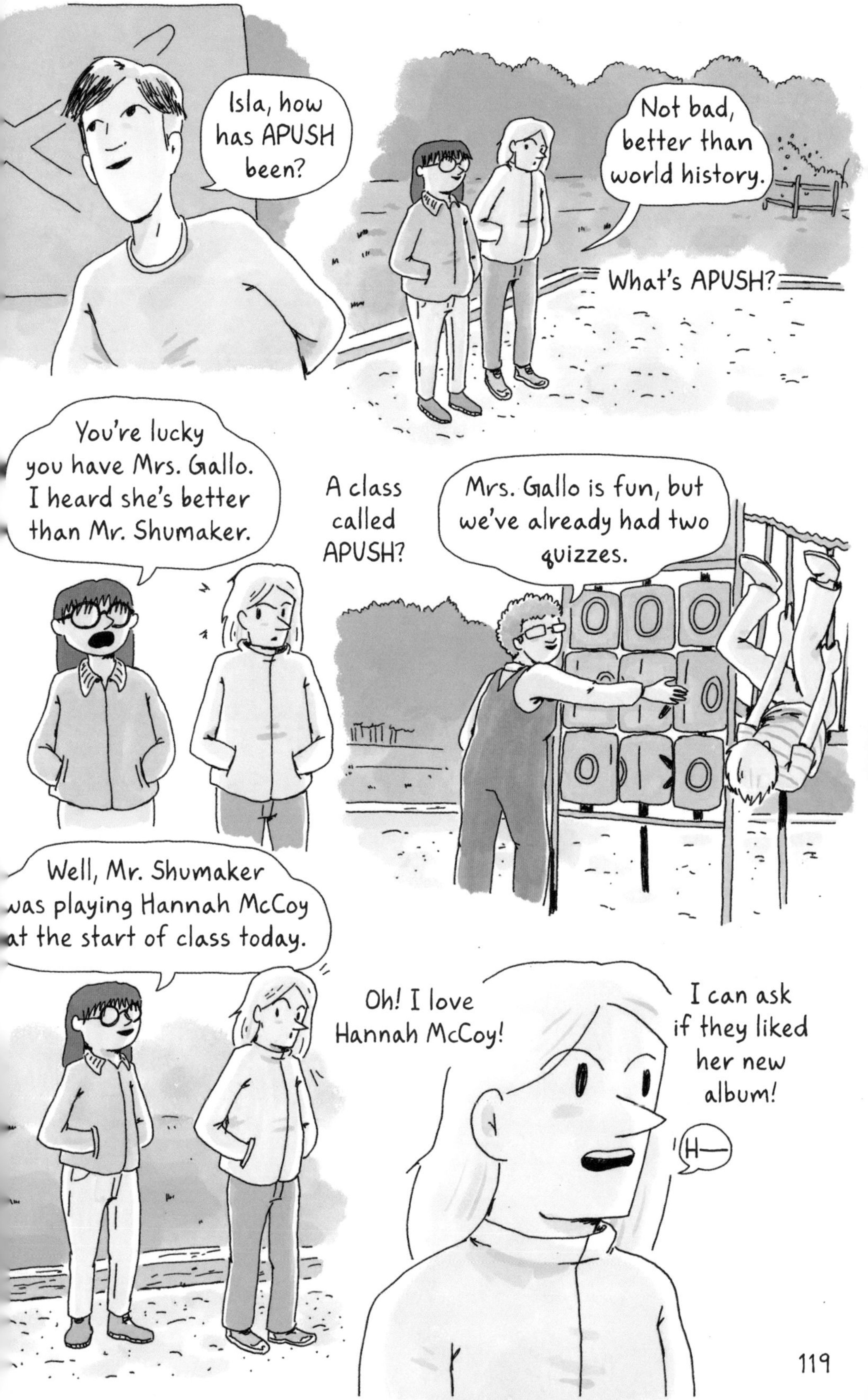
Isla, how has APUSH been?
Not bad, better than world history.
What's APUSH?
You're lucky you have Mrs. Gallo. I heard she's better than Mr. Shumaker.
A class called APUSH?
Mrs. Gallo is fun, but we've already had two quizzes.
Well, Mr. Shumaker was playing Hannah McCoy at the start of class today.
Oh! I love Hannah McCoy!
I can ask if they liked her new album!
H—

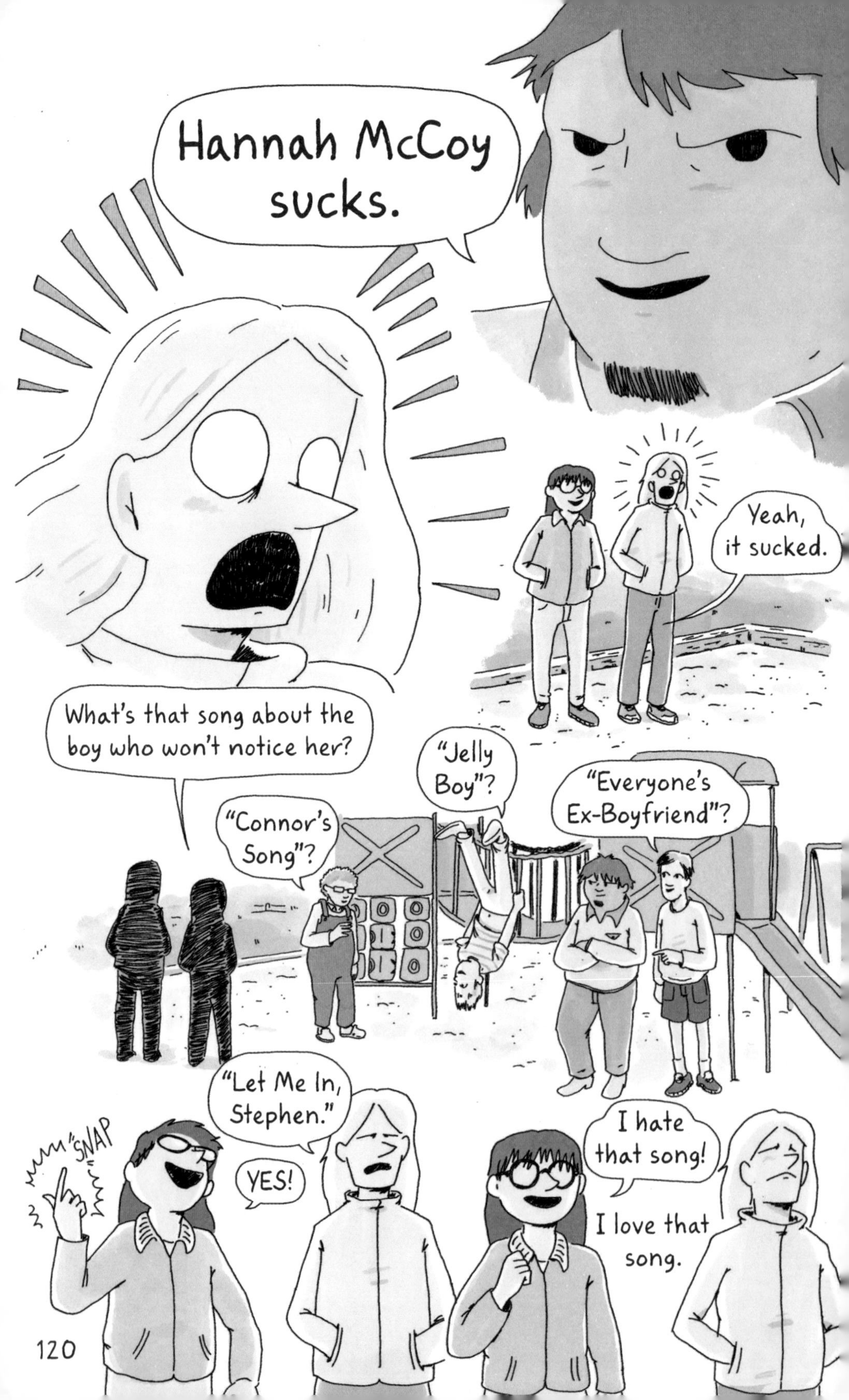
Hannah McCoy sucks.
Yeah, it sucked.
What's that song about the boy who won't notice her?
"Connor's Song"?
"Jelly Boy"?
"Everyone's Ex-Boyfriend"?
SNAP
"Let Me In, Stephen."
YES!
I hate that song!
I love that song.

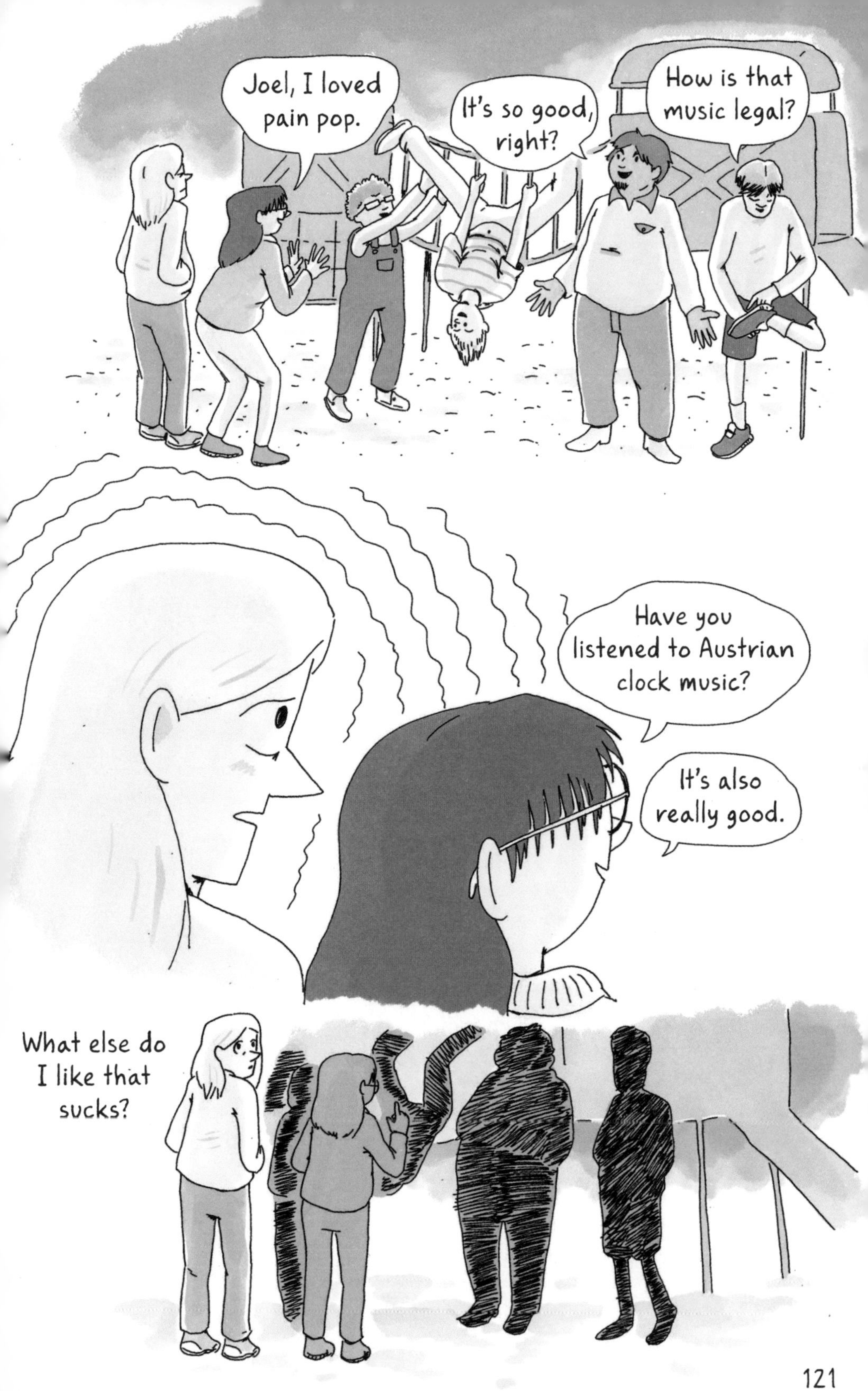
Joel, I loved pain pop.
It's so good, right?
How is that music legal?
Have you listened to Austrian clock music?
It's also really good.
What else do I like that sucks?

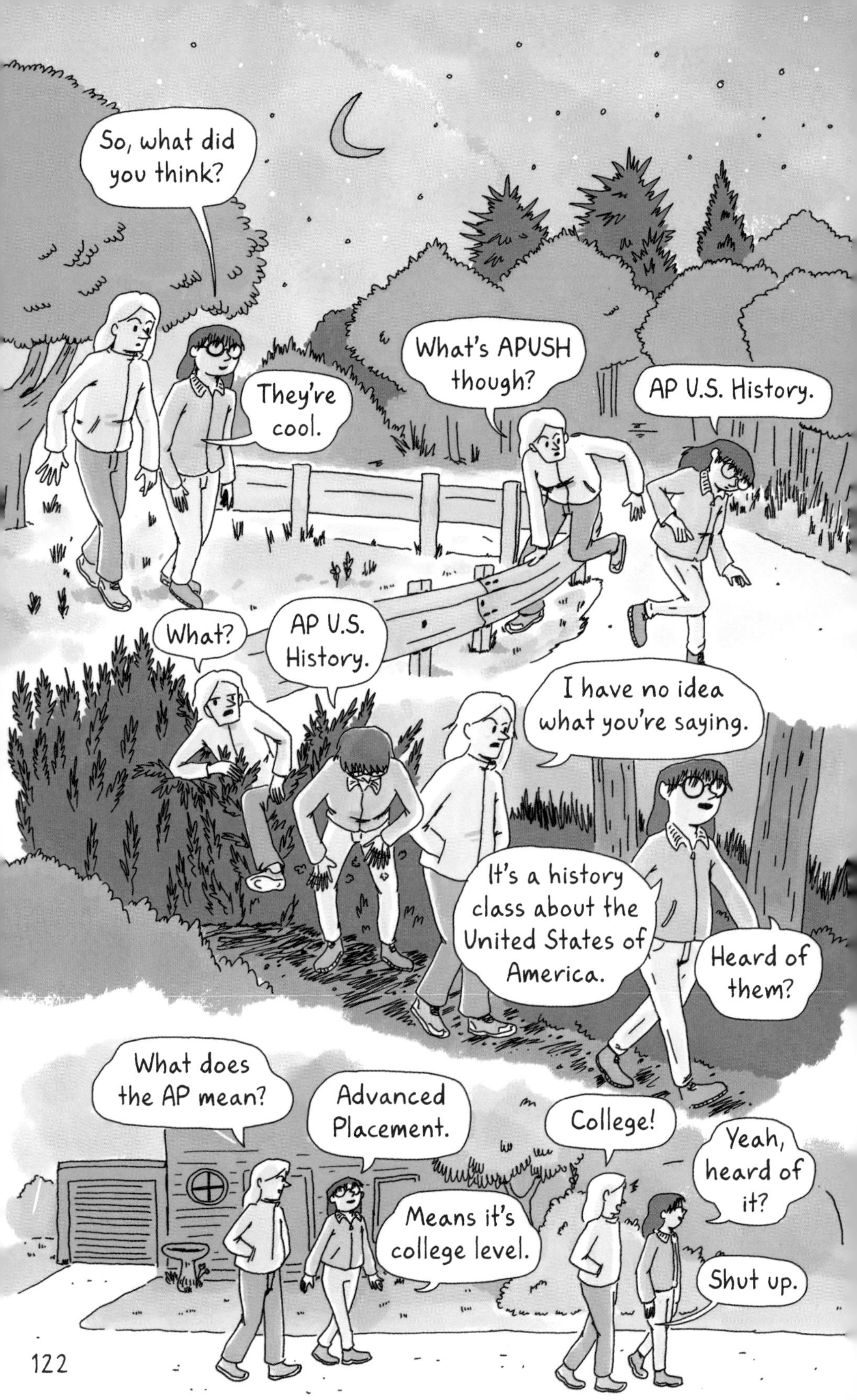

So, what did you think?
They're cool.
What's APUSH though?
AP U.S. History.
What?
AP U.S. History.
I have no idea what you're saying.
It's a history class about the United States of America.
Heard of them?
What does the AP mean?
Advanced Placement.
Means it's college level.
College!
Yeah, heard of it?
Shut up.

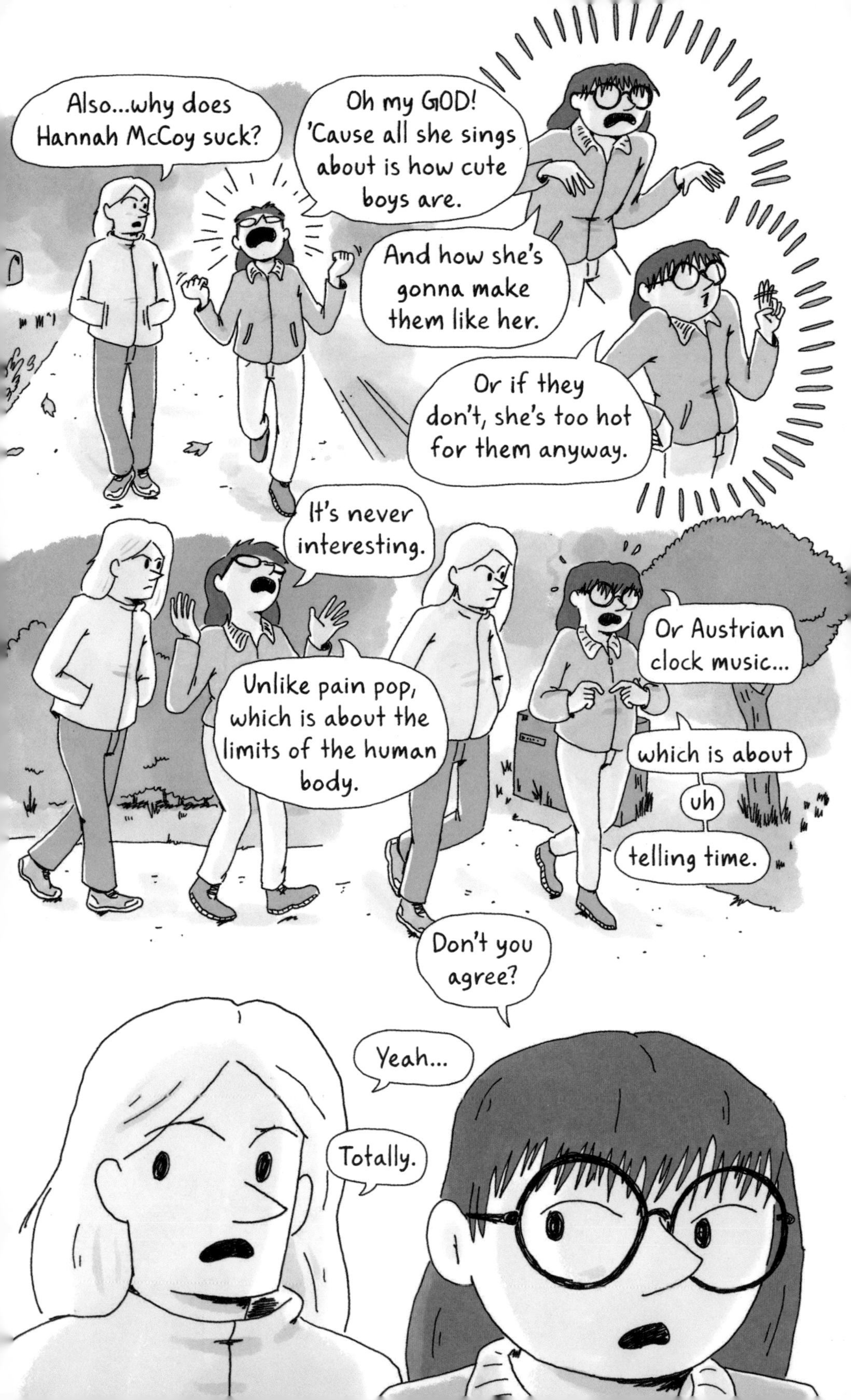

Also...why does Hannah McCoy suck?
Oh my GOD! 'Cause all she sings about is how cute boys are.
And how she's gonna make them like her.
Or if they don't, she's too hot for them anyway.
It's never interesting.
Unlike pain pop, which is about the limits of the human body.
Or Austrian clock music...
which is about
uh
telling time.
Don't you agree?
Yeah...
Totally.

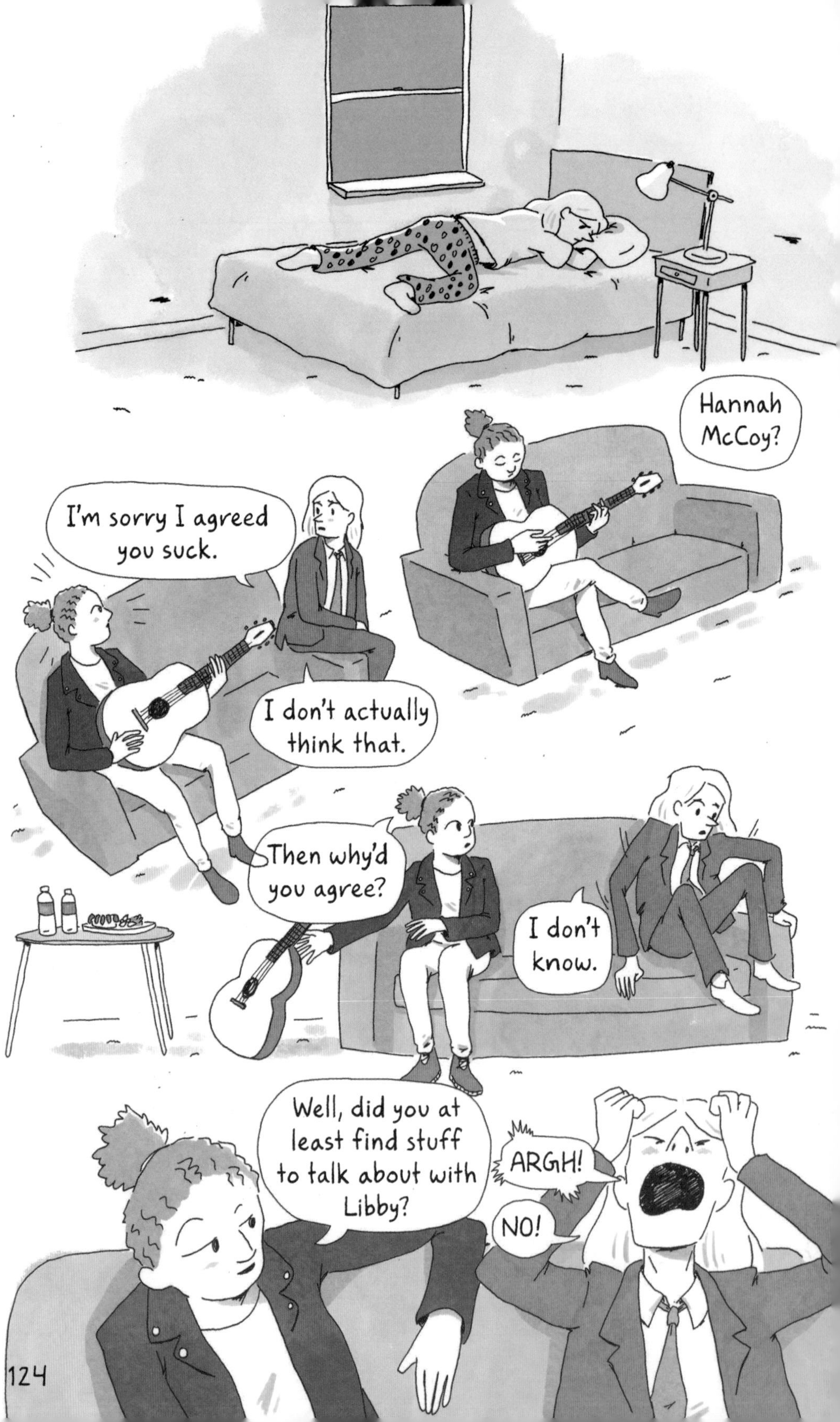
Hannah McCoy?
I'm sorry I agreed you suck.
I don't actually think that.
Then why'd you agree?
I don't know.
Well, did you at least find stuff to talk about with Libby?
ARGH!
NO!

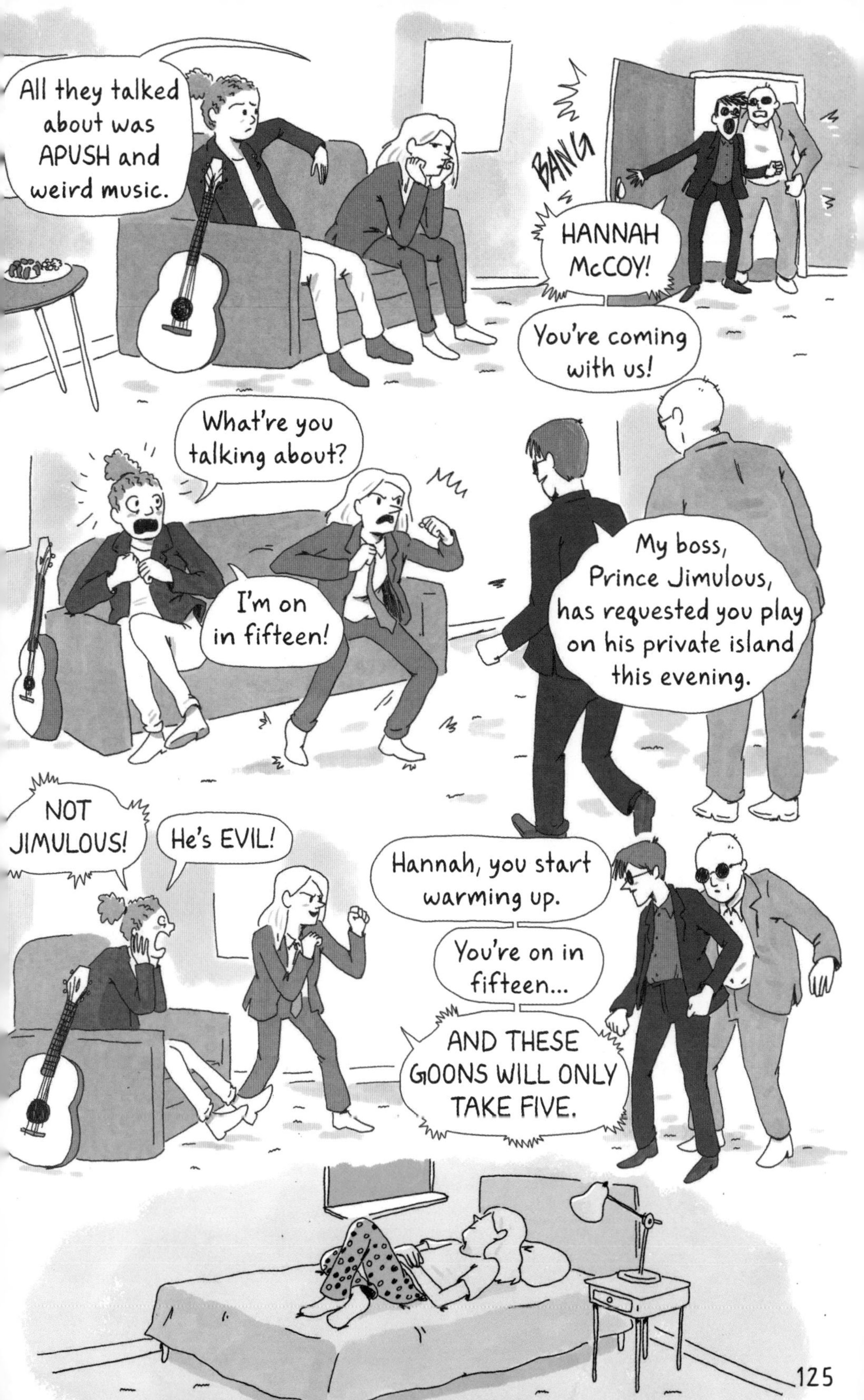
All they talked about was APUSH and weird music.
BANG
HANNAH McCOY!
You're coming with us!
What're you talking about?
I'm on in fifteen!
My boss, Prince Jimulous, has requested you play on his private island this evening.
NOT JIMULOUS!
He's EVIL!
Hannah, you start warming up.
You're on in fifteen...
AND THESE GOONS WILL ONLY TAKE FIVE.

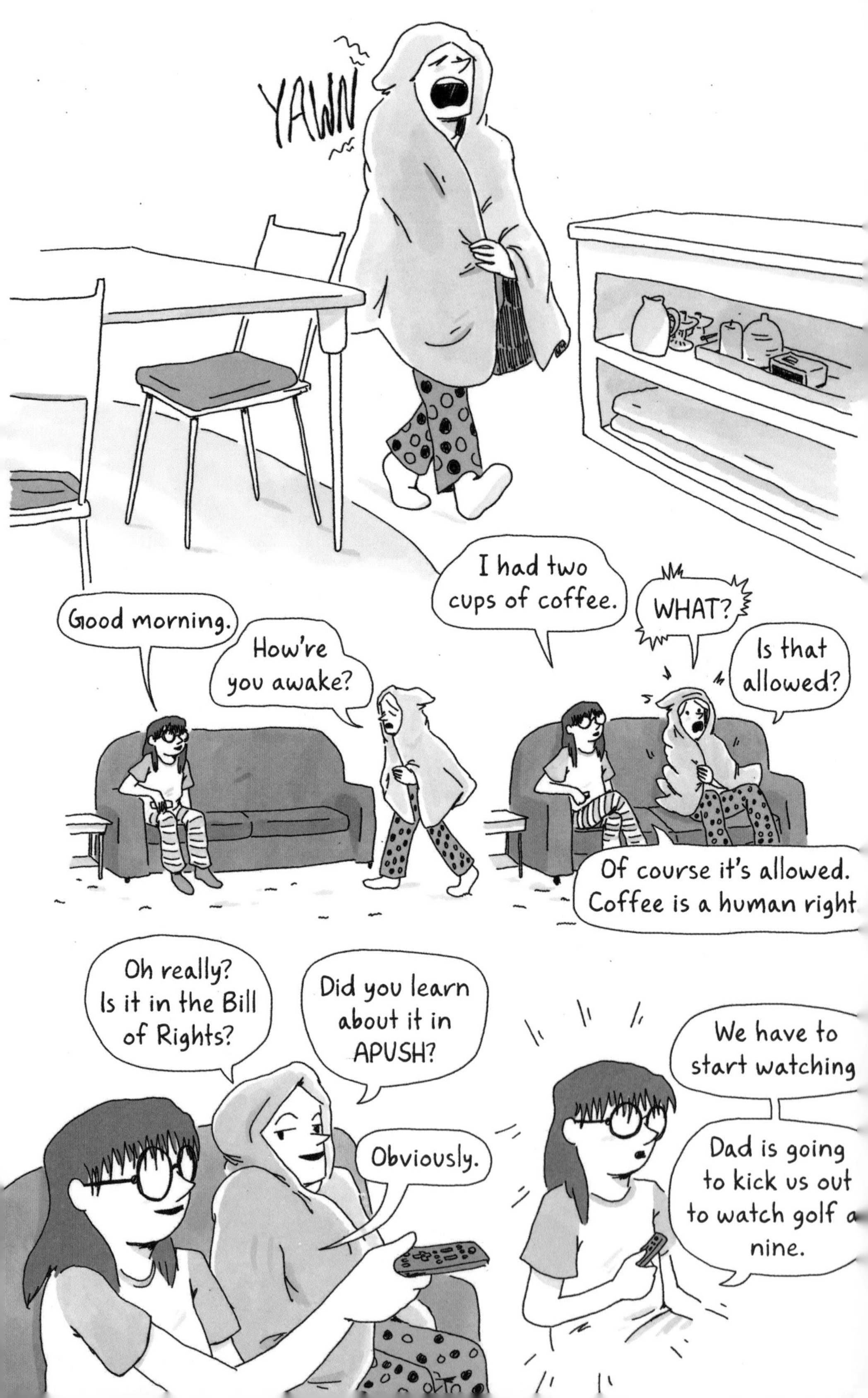
YAWN
Good morning.
How're you awake?
I had two cups of coffee.
WHAT?
Is that allowed?
Of course it's allowed. Coffee is a human right
Oh really? Is it in the Bill of Rights?
Did you learn about it in APUSH?
Obviously.
We have to start watching
Dad is going to kick us out to watch golf a nine.

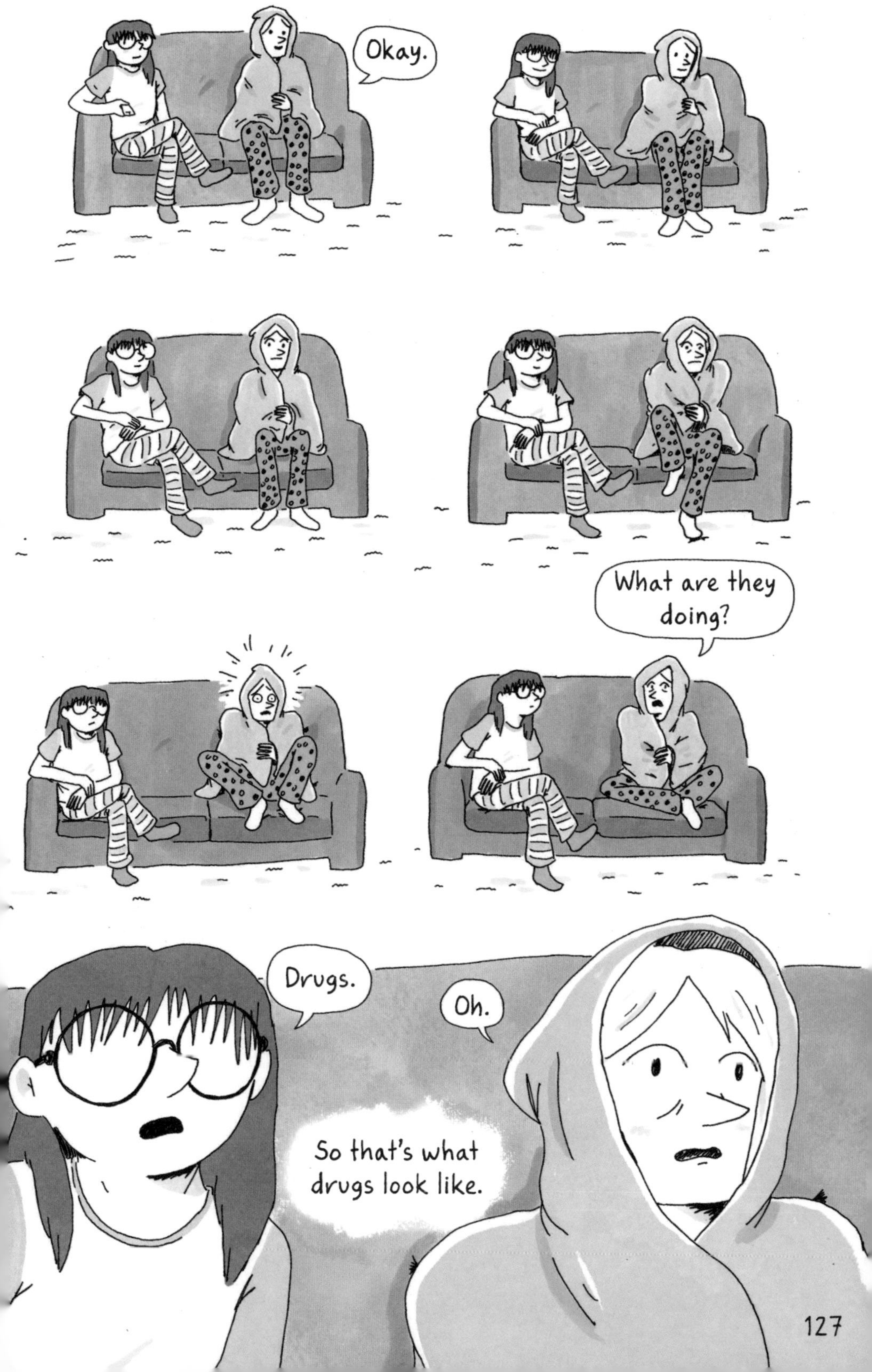
Okay.
What are they doing?
Drugs.
Oh.
So that's what drugs look like.

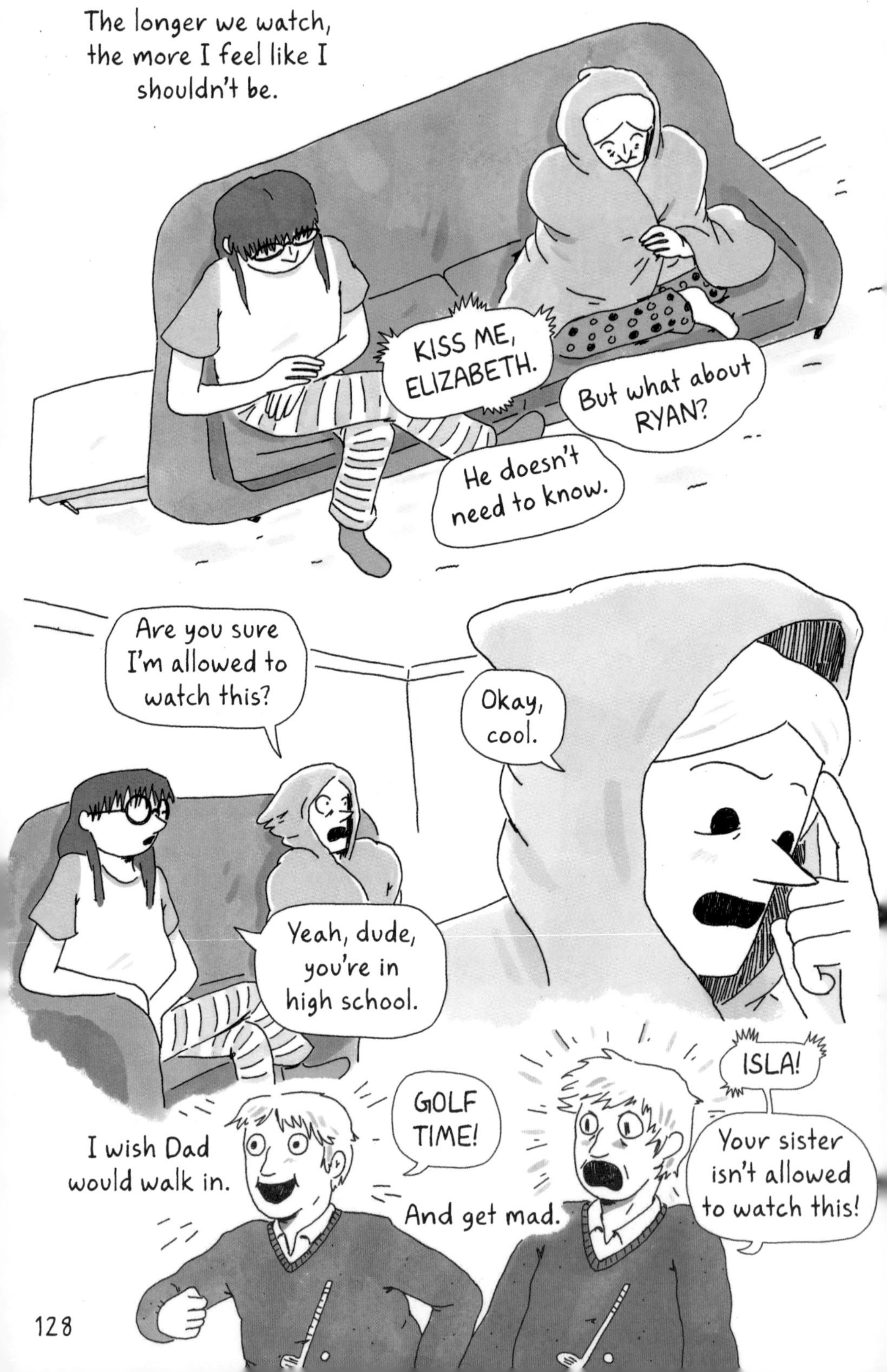
The longer we watch, the more I feel like I shouldn't be.
KISS ME, ELIZABETH.
But what about RYAN?
He doesn't need to know.
Are you sure I'm allowed to watch this?
Okay, cool.
Yeah, dude, you're in high school.
I wish Dad would walk in.
GOLF TIME!
And get mad.
ISLA!
Your sister isn't allowed to watch this!

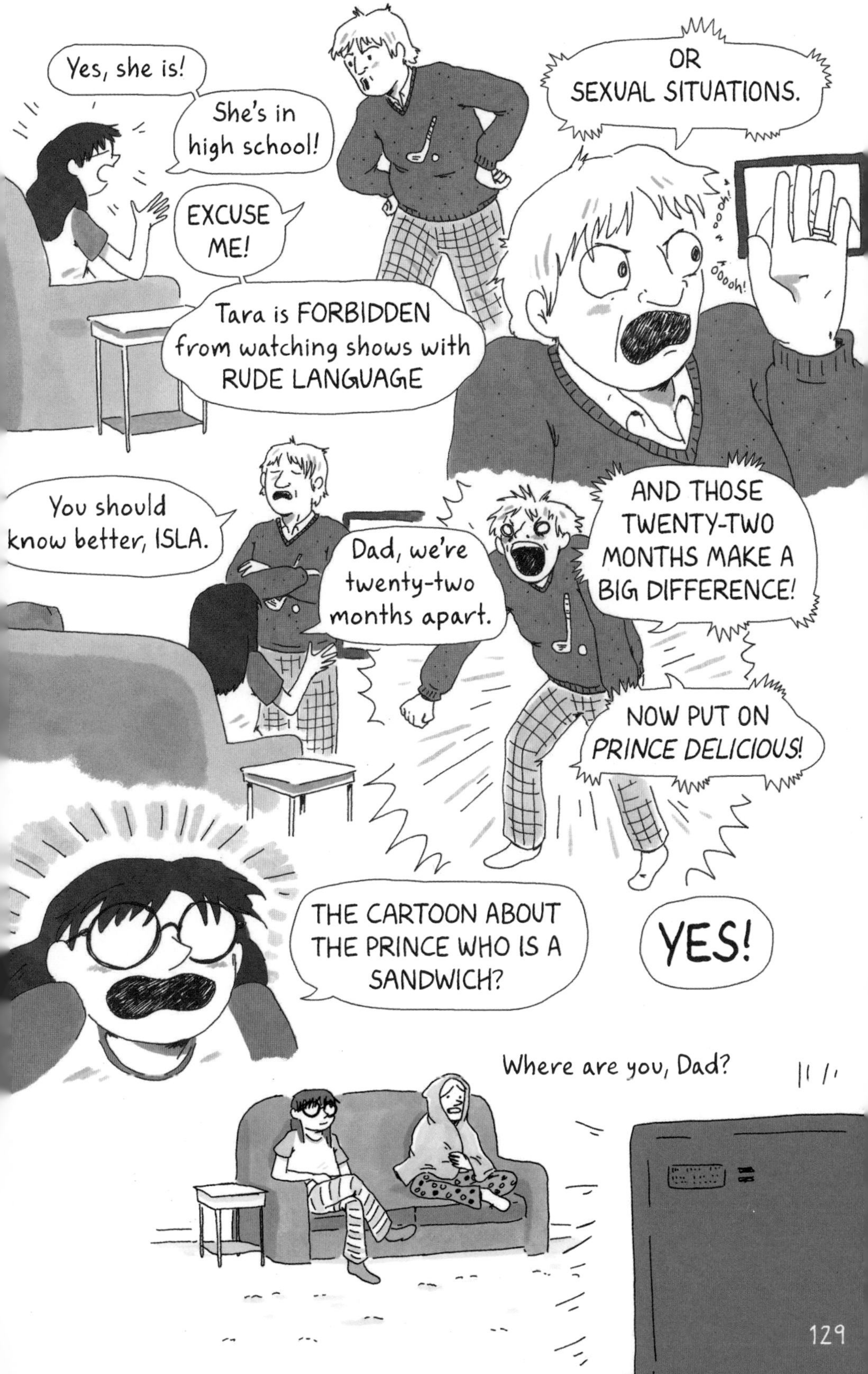
Yes, she is!
She's in high school!
EXCUSE ME!
Tara is FORBIDDEN from watching shows with RUDE LANGUAGE
OR SEXUAL SITUATIONS.
Ooooh!
Ooooh!
You should know better, ISLA.
Dad, we're twenty-two months apart.
AND THOSE TWENTY-TWO MONTHS MAKE A BIG DIFFERENCE!
NOW PUT ON PRINCE DELICIOUS!
THE CARTOON ABOUT THE PRINCE WHO IS A SANDWICH?
YES!
Where are you, Dad?

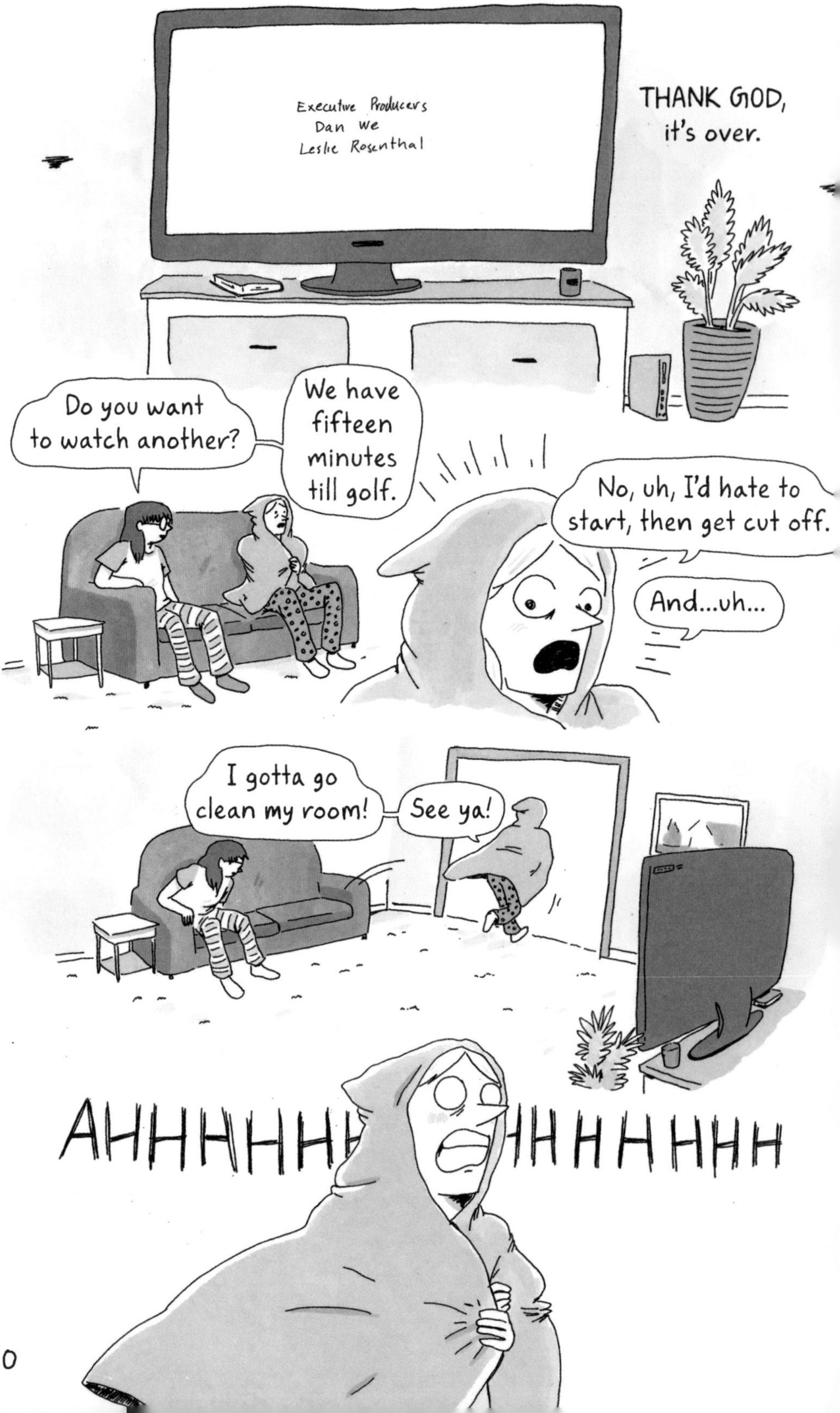
Executive Producers
Dan We
Leslie Rosenthal
THANK GOD, it's over.
Do you want to watch another?
We have fifteen minutes till golf.
No, uh, I'd hate to start, then get cut off.
And...uh...
I gotta go clean my room!
See ya!
AHHHHHHHHHHHHHHH

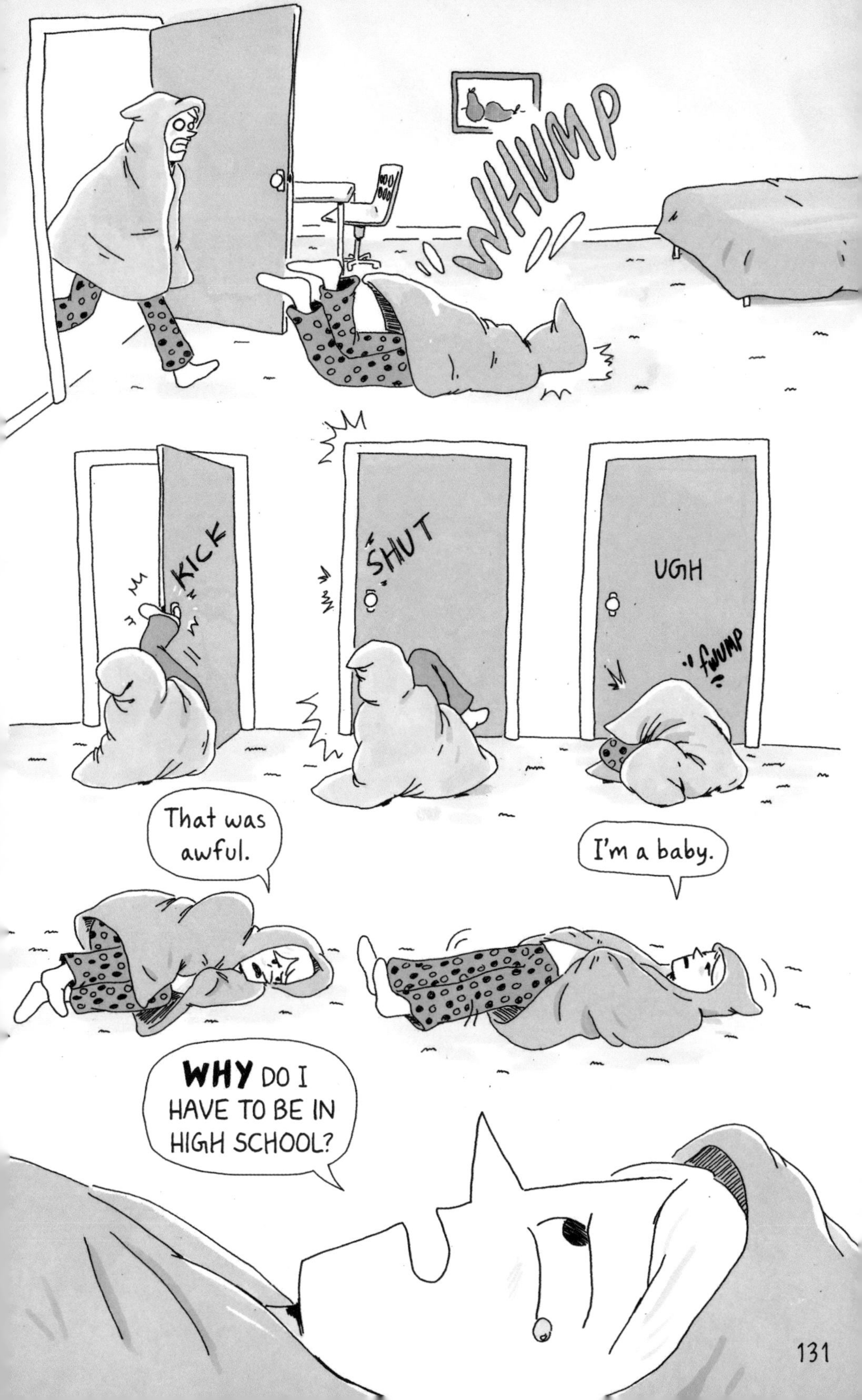
WHUMP
KICK
SHUT
UGH
fwump
That was awful.
I'm a baby.
WHY DO I HAVE TO BE IN HIGH SCHOOL?

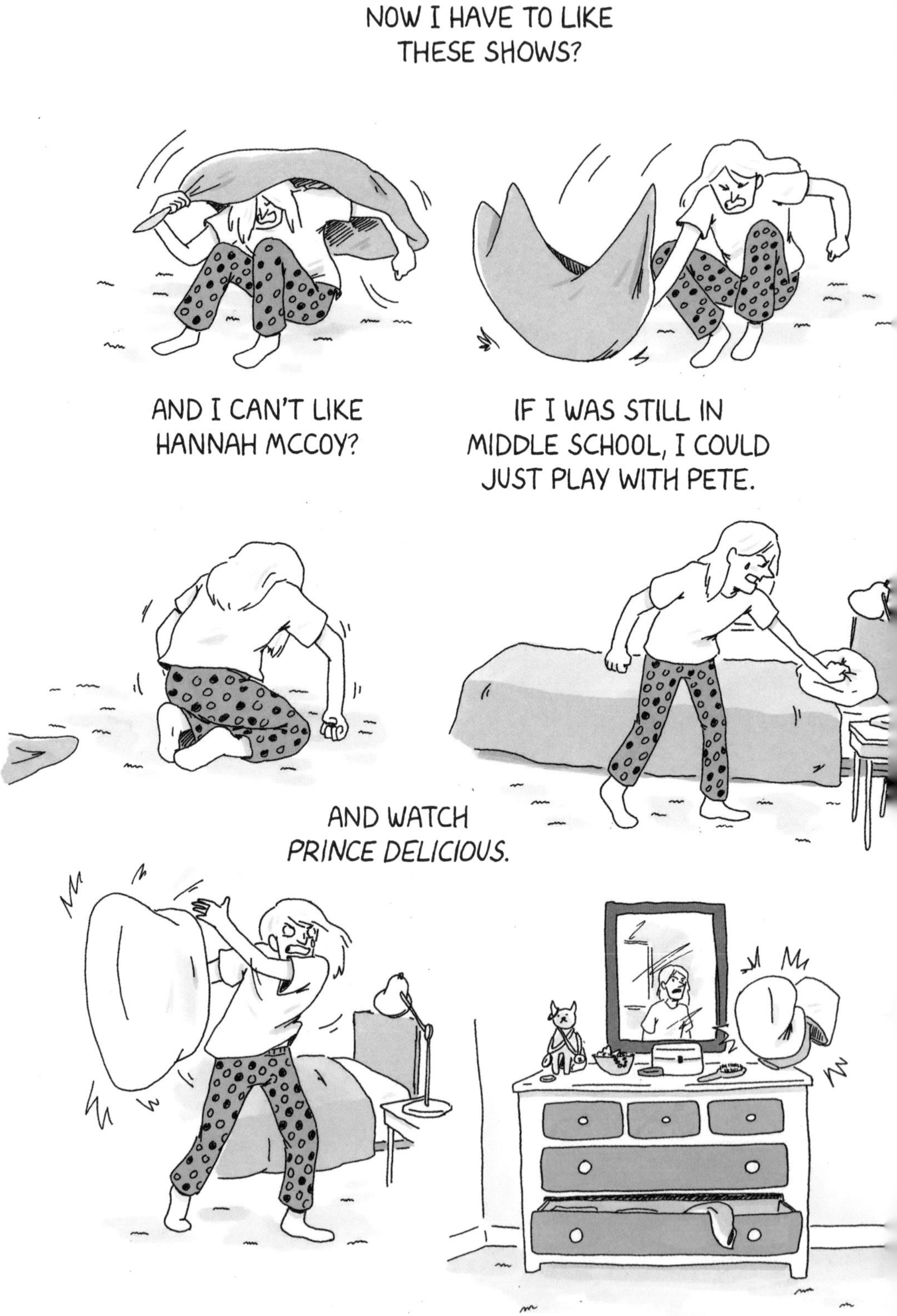
NOW I HAVE TO LIKE THESE SHOWS?
AND I CAN'T LIKE HANNAH MCCOY?
IF I WAS STILL IN MIDDLE SCHOOL, I COULD JUST PLAY WITH PETE.
AND WATCH PRINCE DELICIOUS.

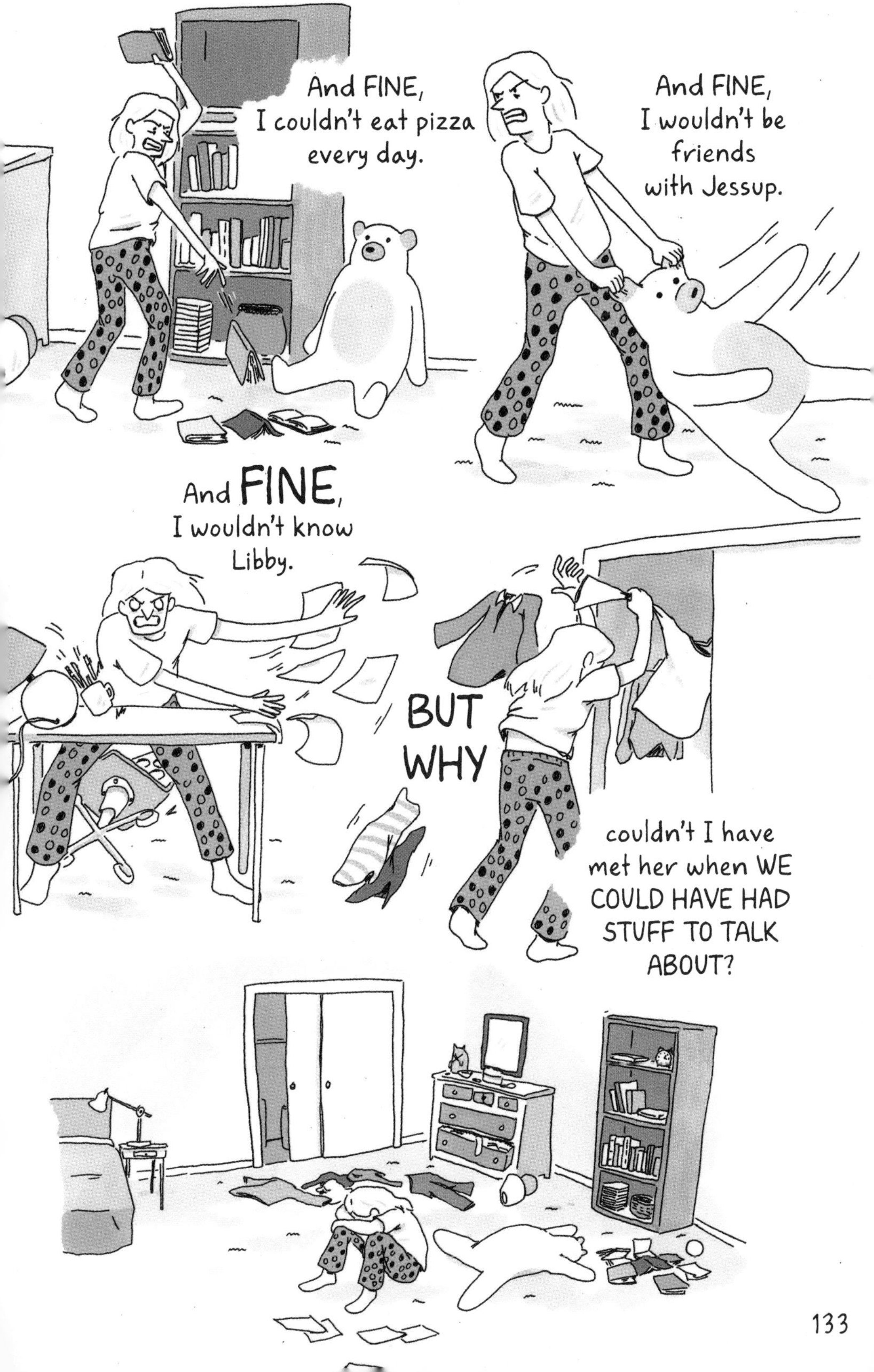
And FINE, I couldn't eat pizza every day.
And FINE, I wouldn't be friends with Jessup.
And FINE, I wouldn't know Libby.
BUT WHY
couldn't I have met her when WE COULD HAVE HAD STUFF TO TALK ABOUT?

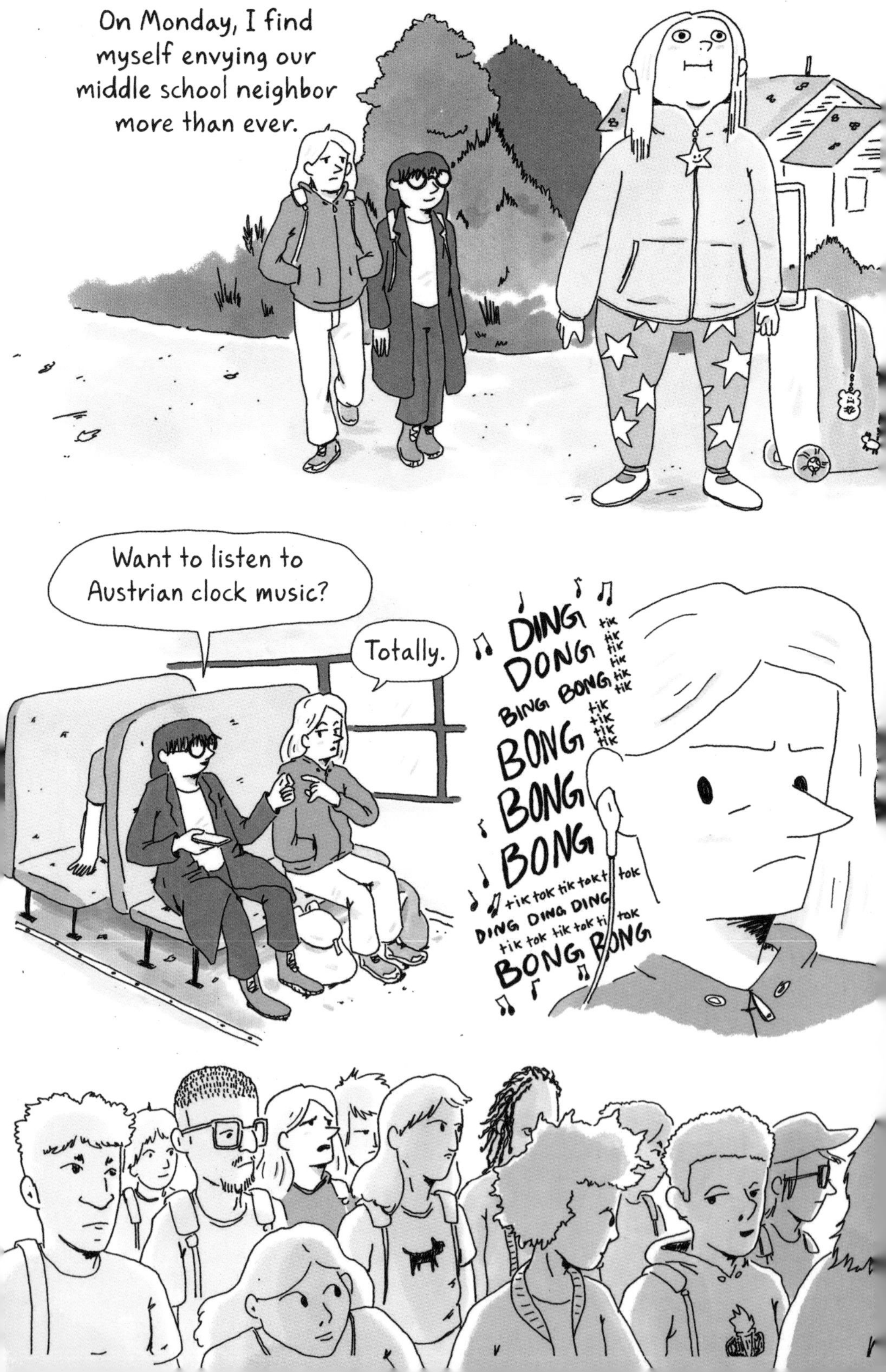
On Monday, I find myself envying our middle school neighbor more than ever.
Want to listen to Austrian clock music?
Totally.
DING DONG
BING BONG
BONG
BONG
BONG
tik tok tik tok tik tok
DING DING DING
tik tok tik tok tik tok
BONG BONG

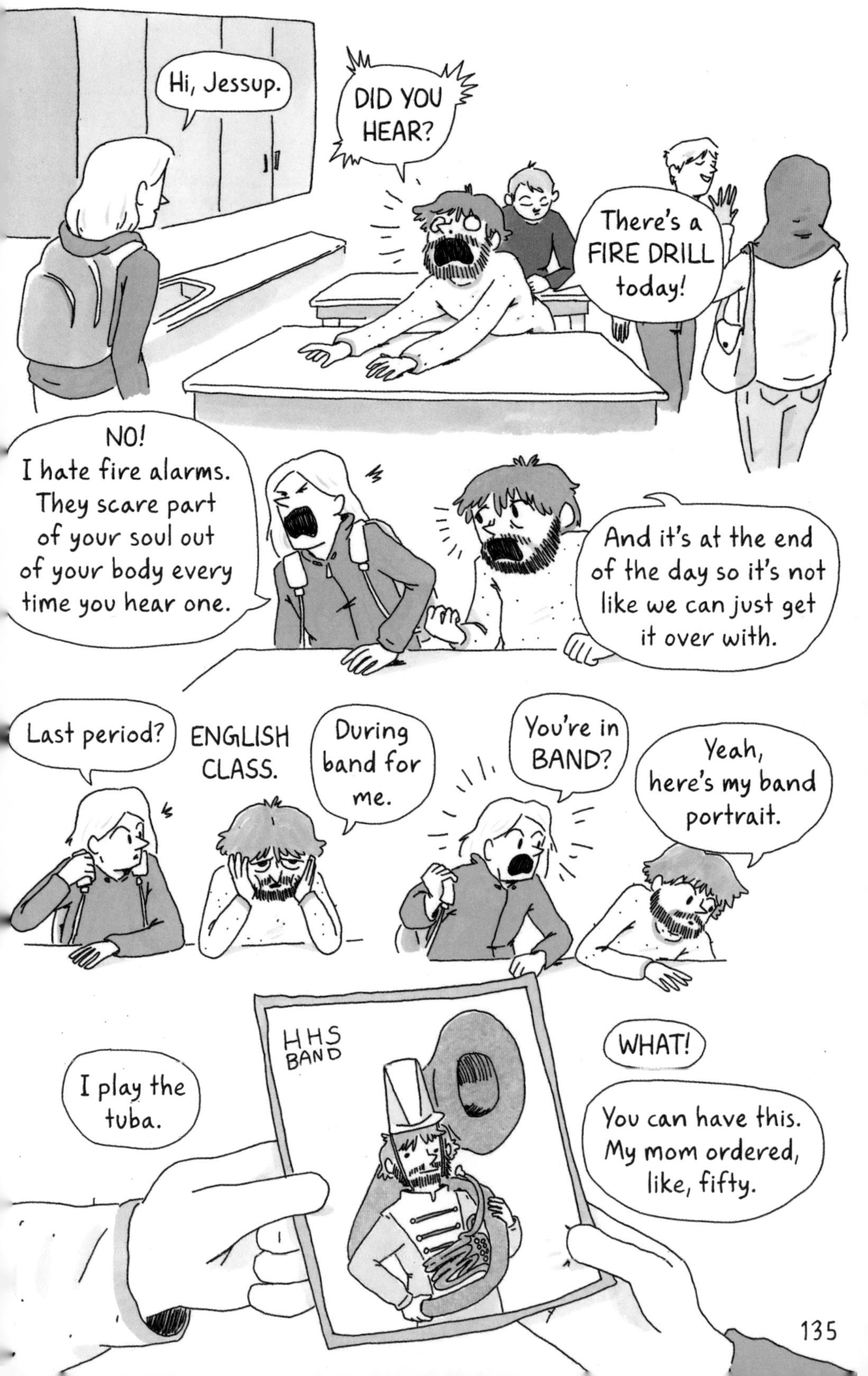
Hi, Jessup.
DID YOU HEAR?
There's a FIRE DRILL today!
NO! I hate fire alarms. They scare part of your soul out of your body every time you hear one.
And it's at the end of the day so it's not like we can just get it over with.
Last period?
ENGLISH CLASS.
During band for me.
You're in BAND?
Yeah, here's my band portrait.
I play the tuba.
HHS BAND
WHAT!
You can have this. My mom ordered, like, fifty.

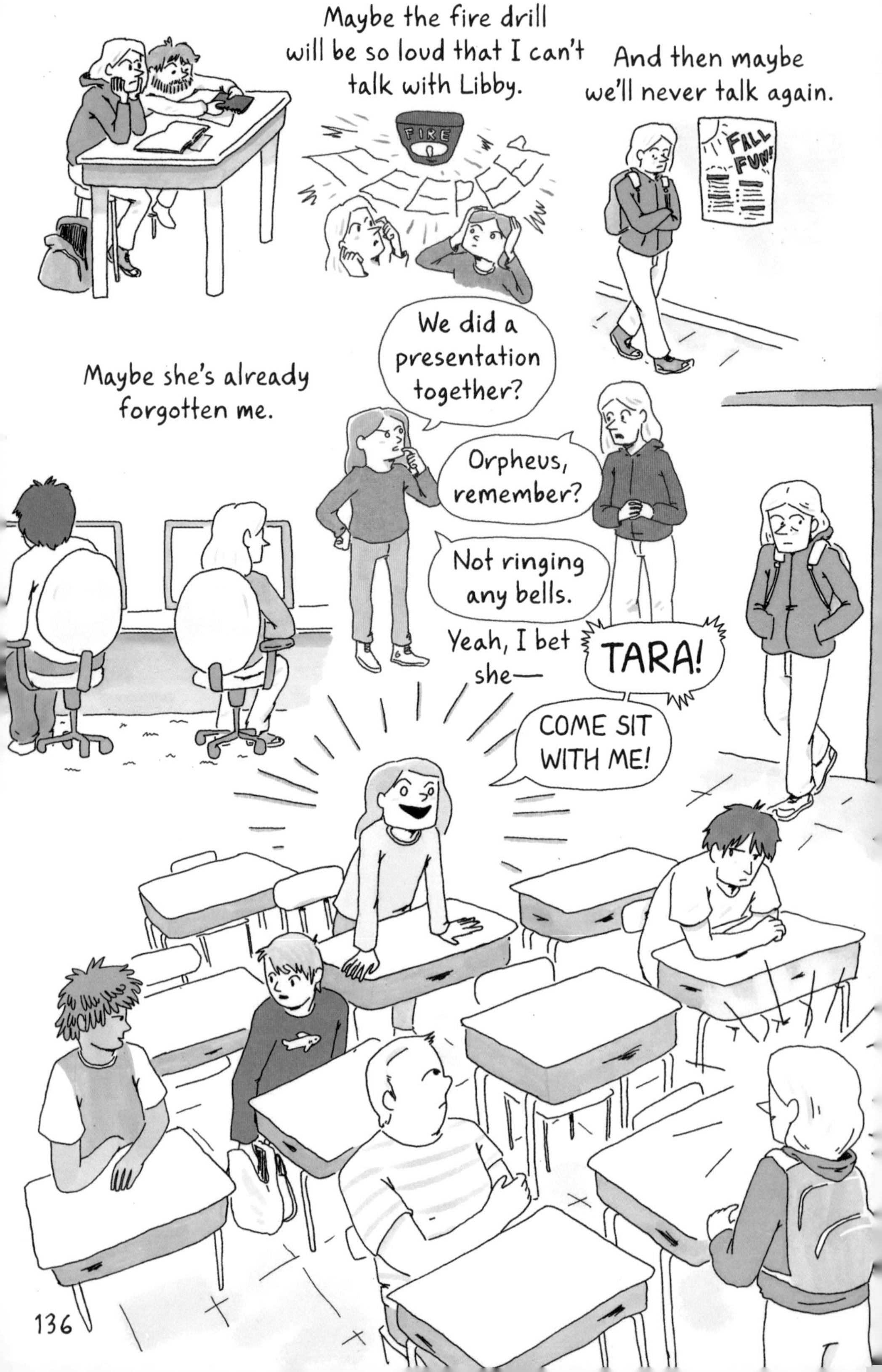
Maybe the fire drill will be so loud that I can't talk with Libby.
FIRE
And then maybe we'll never talk again.
FALL FUN!
Maybe she's already forgotten me.
We did a presentation together?
Orpheus, remember?
Not ringing any bells.
Yeah, I bet she—
TARA!
COME SIT WITH ME!

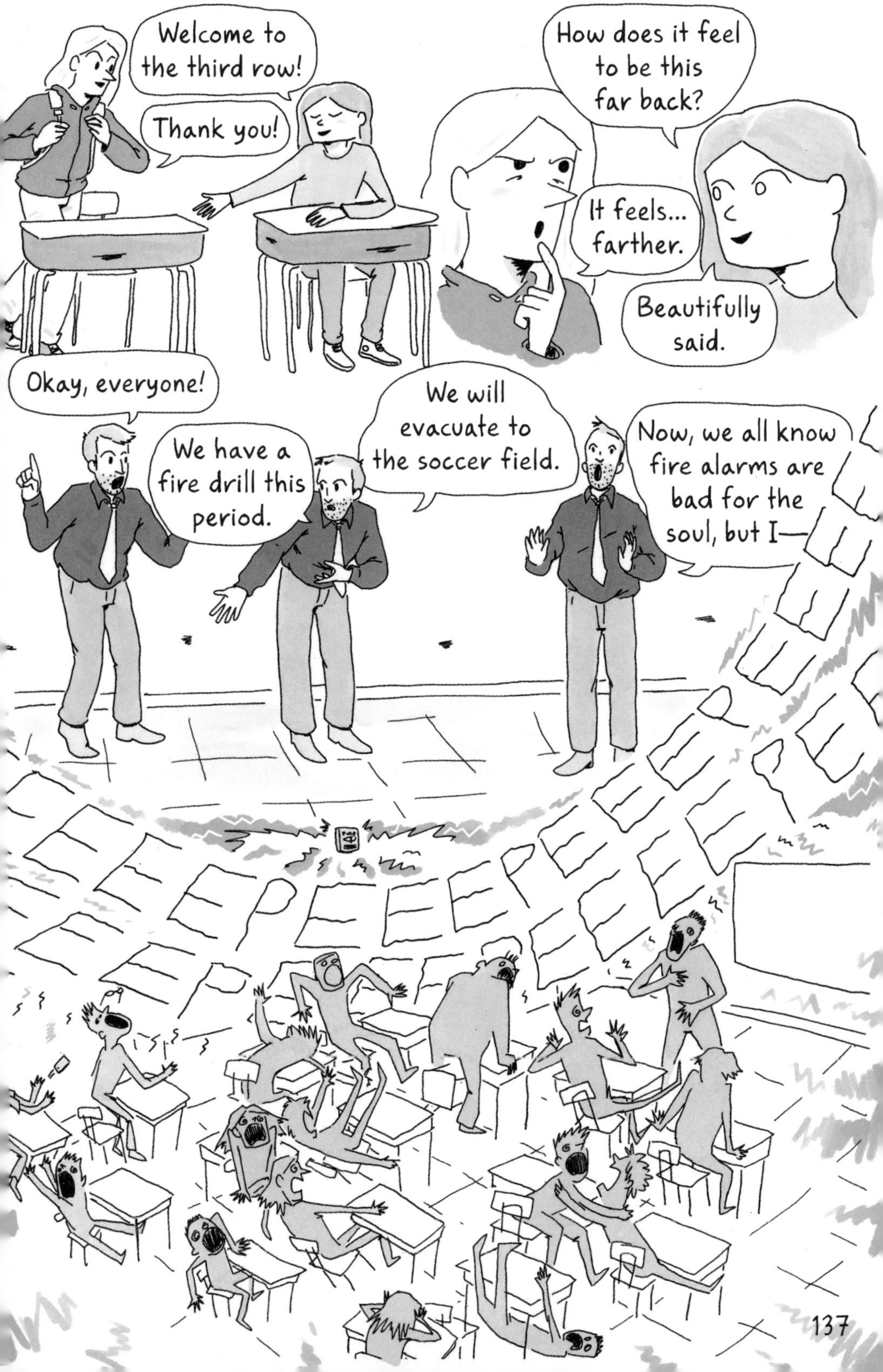
Welcome to the third row!
Thank you!
How does it feel to be this far back?
It feels... farther.
Beautifully said.
Okay, everyone!
We have a fire drill this period.
We will evacuate to the soccer field.
Now, we all know fire alarms are bad for the soul, but I—

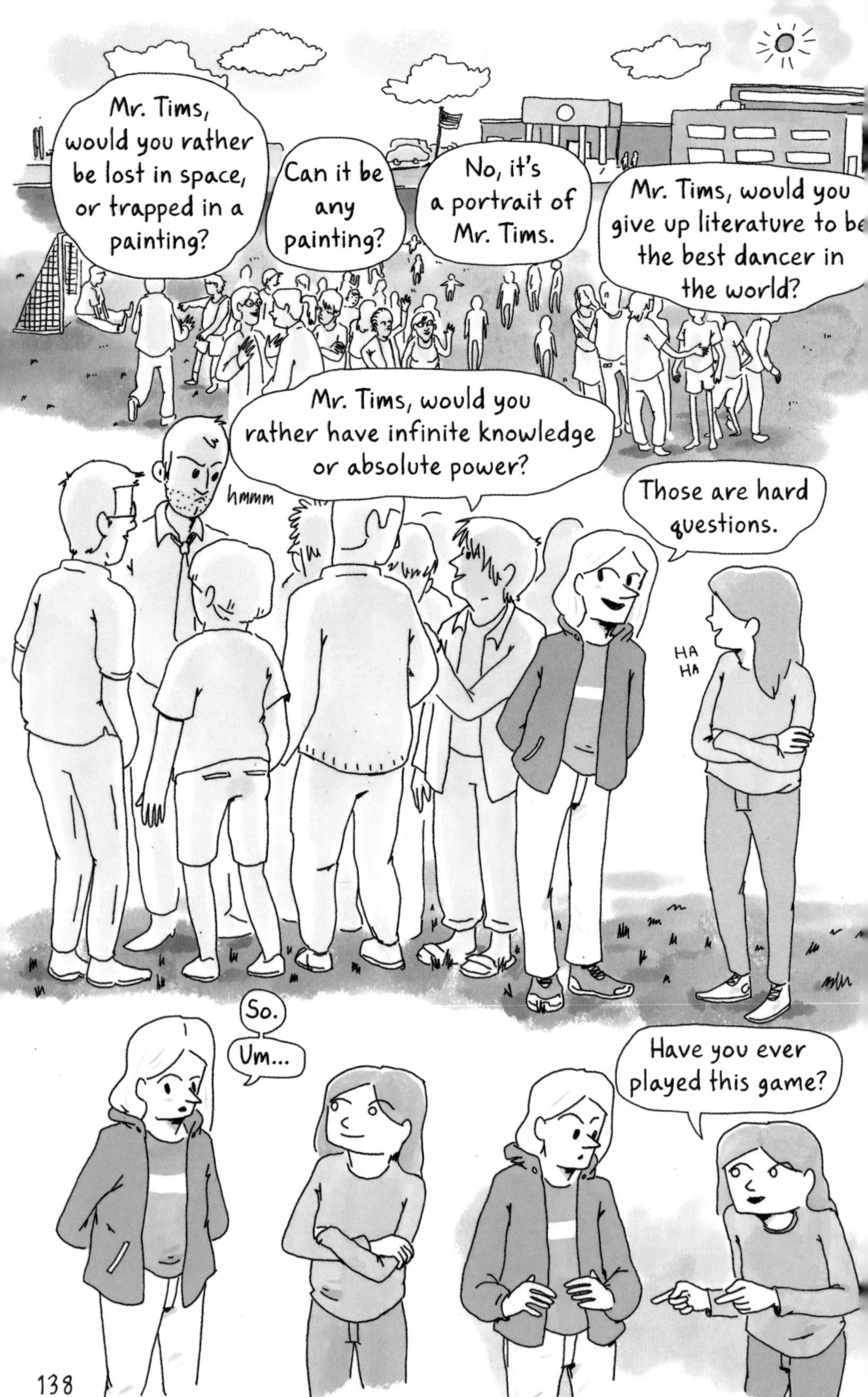
Mr. Tims, would you rather be lost in space, or trapped in a painting?
Can it be any painting?
No, it's a portrait of Mr. Tims.
Mr. Tims, would you give up literature to be the best dancer in the world?
Mr. Tims, would you rather have infinite knowledge or absolute power?
hmmm
Those are hard questions.
HA HA
So.
Um...
Have you ever played this game?

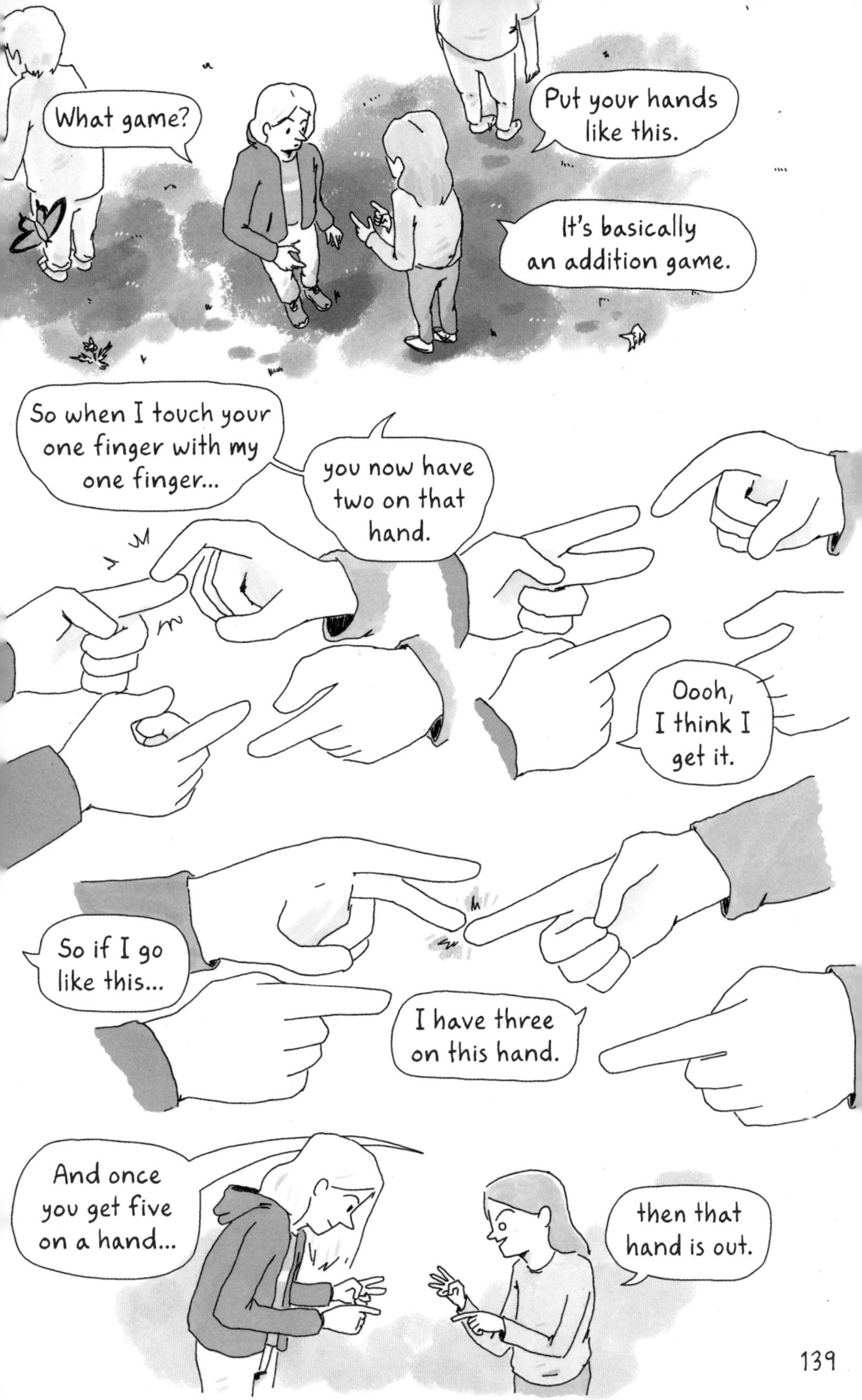
What game?
Put your hands like this.
It's basically an addition game.
So when I touch your one finger with my one finger...
you now have two on that hand.
Oooh, I think I get it.
So if I go like this...
I have three on this hand.
And once you get five on a hand...
then that hand is out.

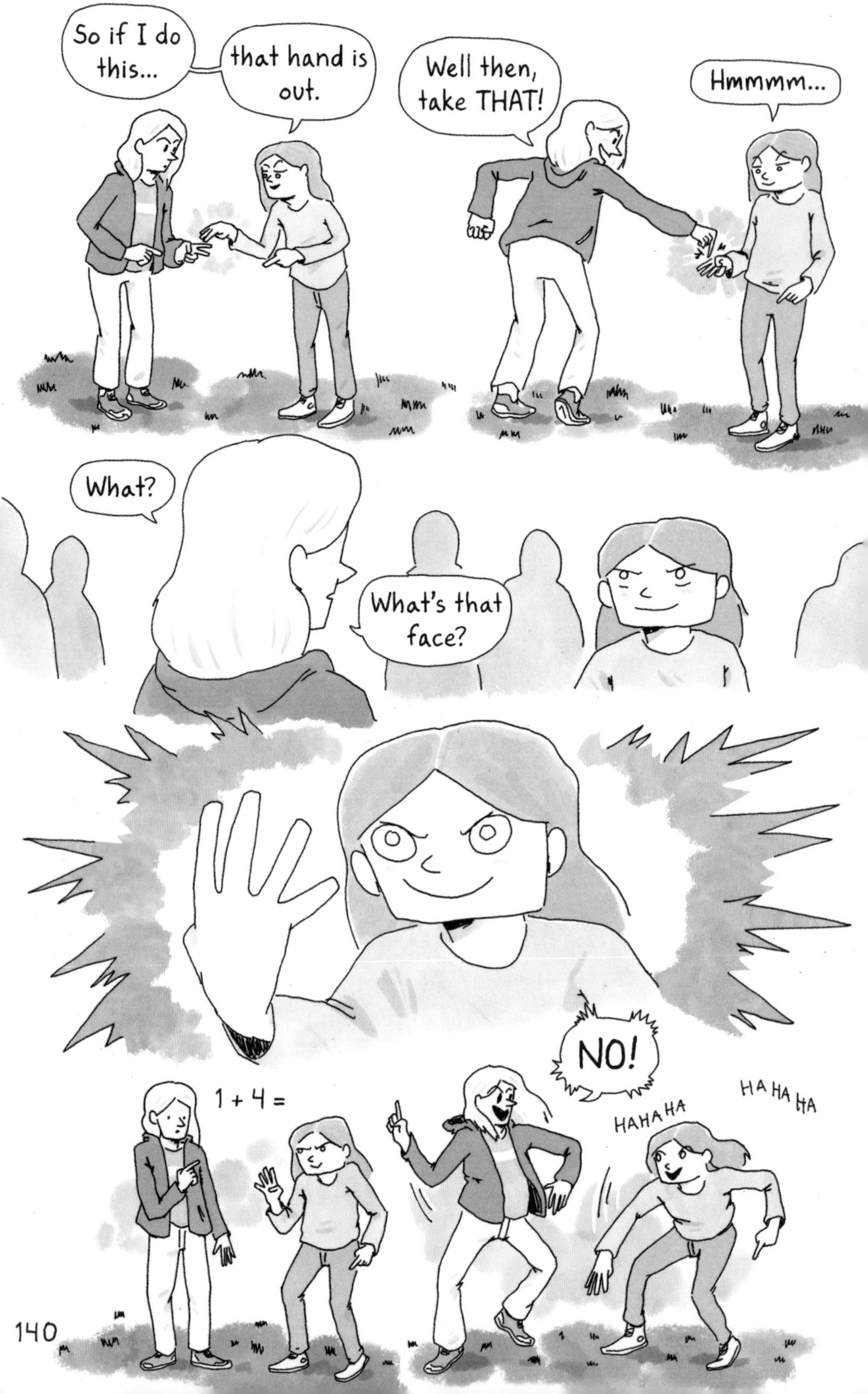
So if I do this...
that hand is out.
Well then, take THAT!
Hmmmm...
What?
What's that face?
1 + 4 =
NO!
HAHAHA
HA HA HA

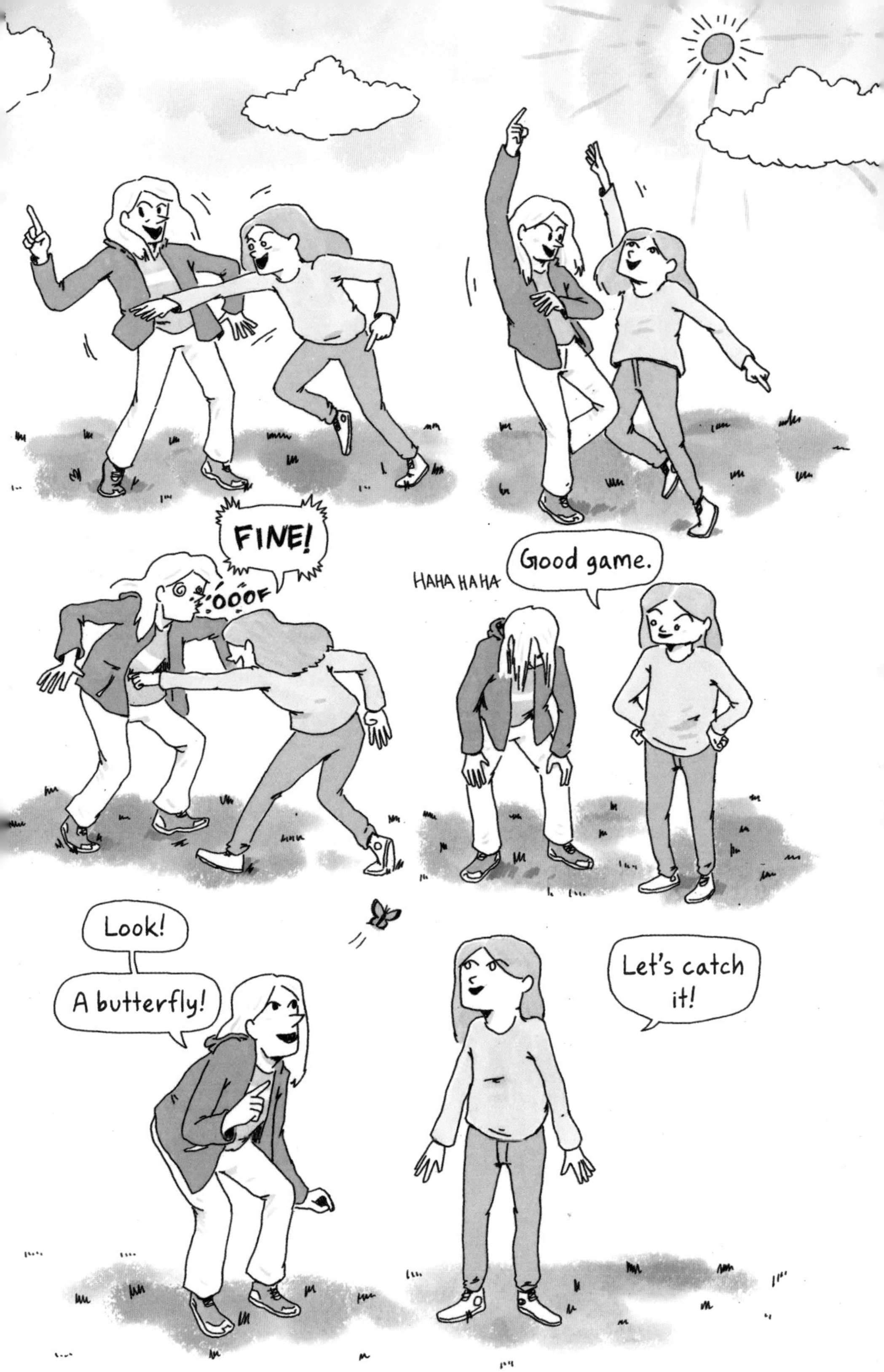
FINE!
OOOF
HAHA HAHA
Good game.
Look!
A butterfly!
Let's catch it!

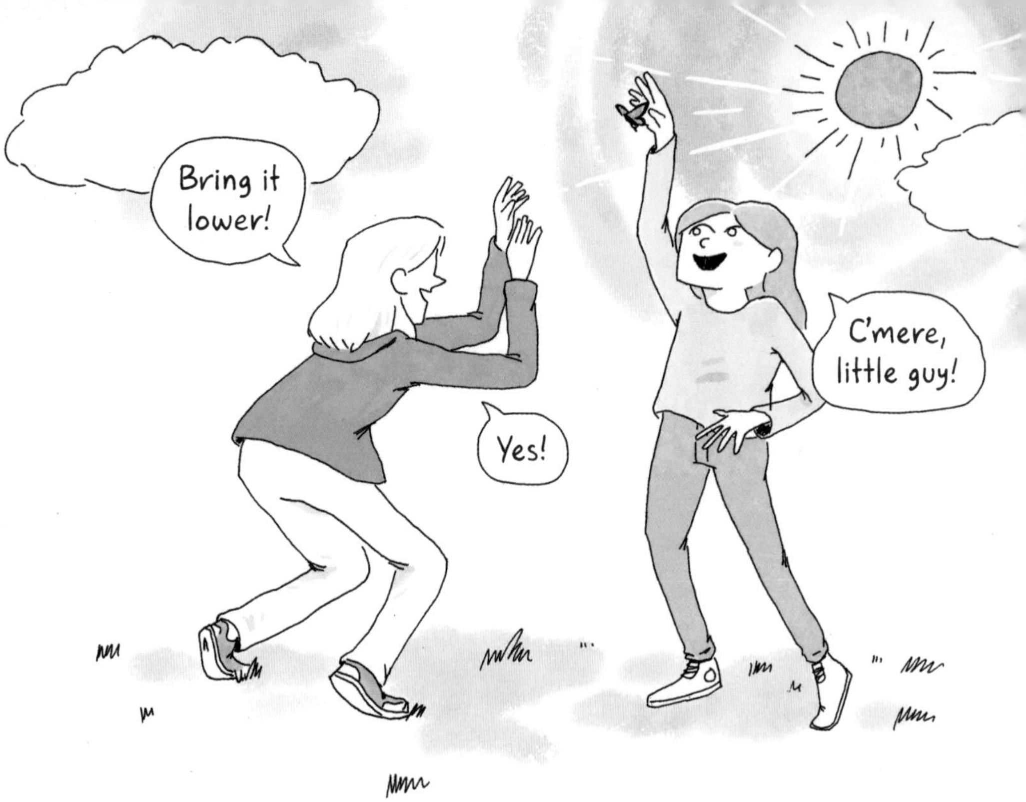
Bring it lower!
C'mere, little guy!
Yes!

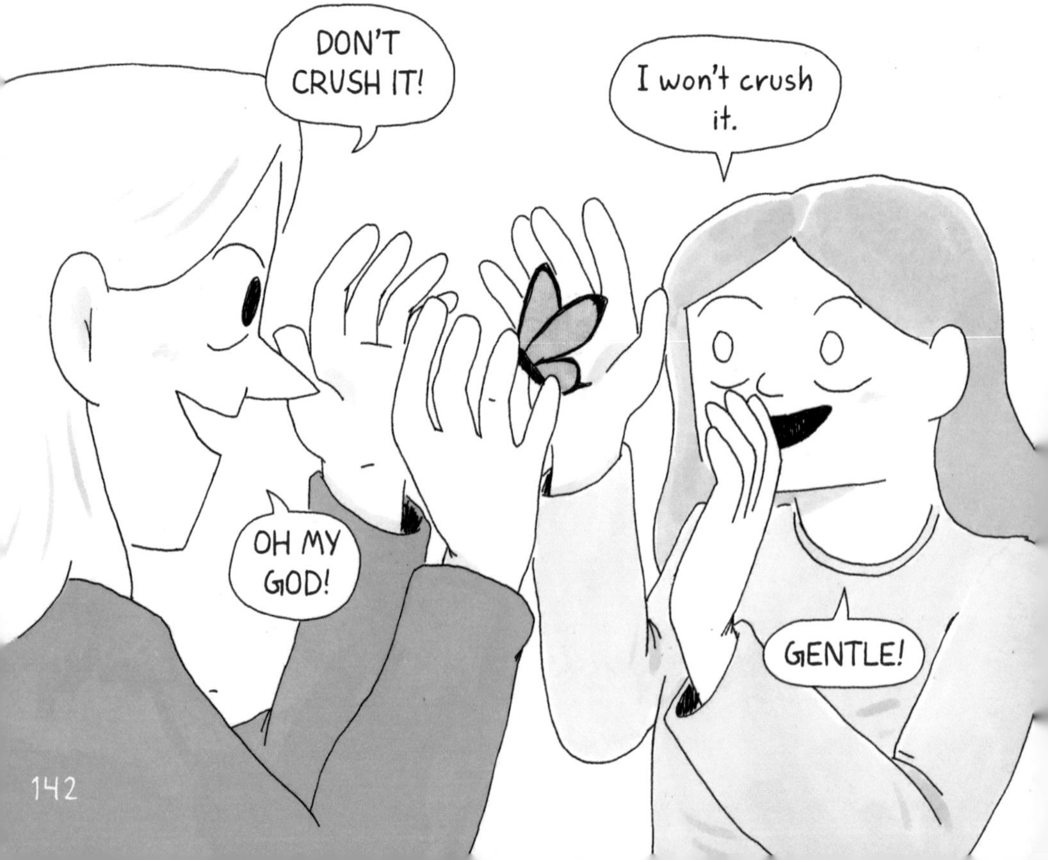
DON'T CRUSH IT!
I won't crush it.
OH MY GOD!
GENTLE!

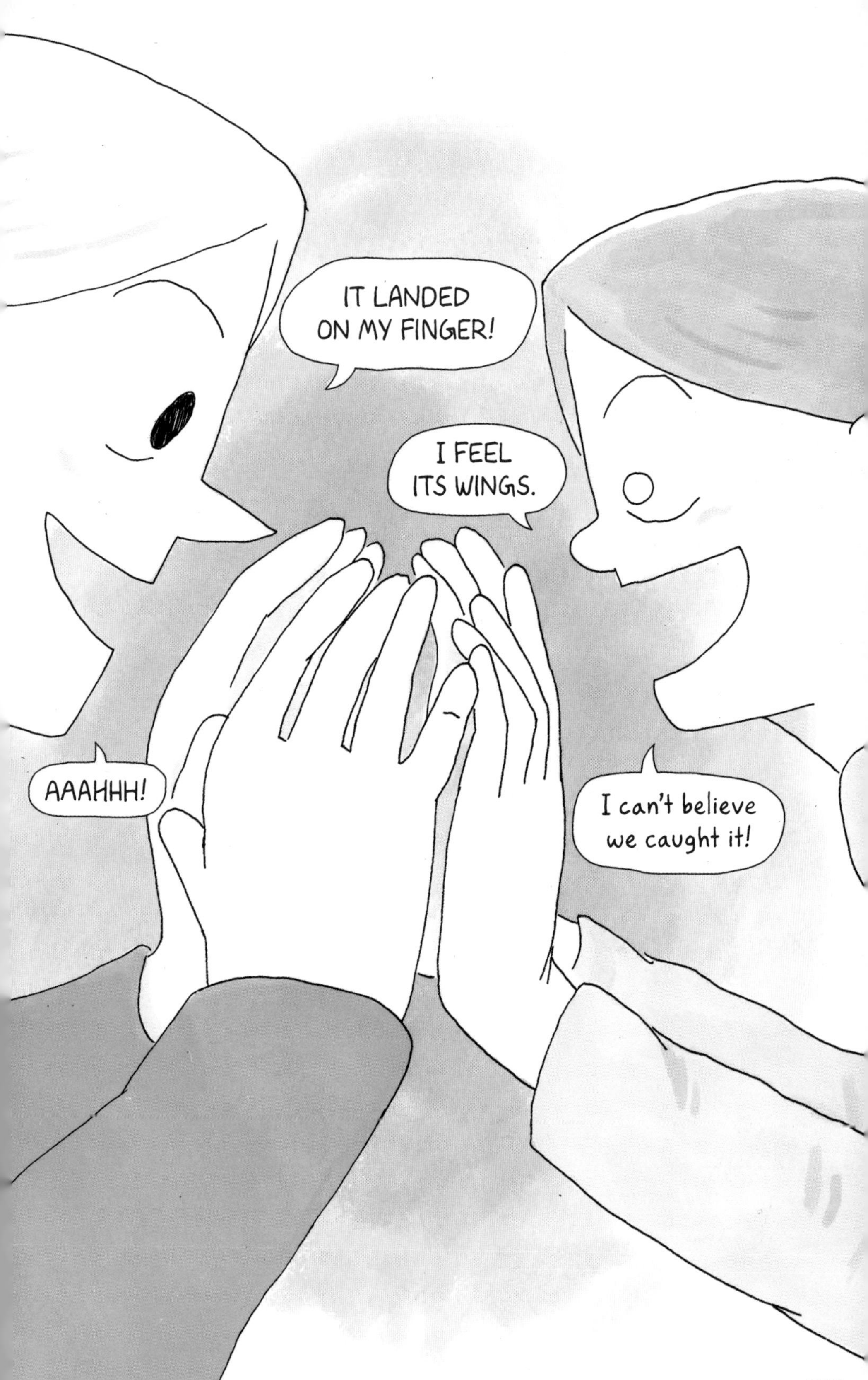
IT LANDED ON MY FINGER!
I FEEL ITS WINGS.
AAAHHH!
I can't believe we caught it!

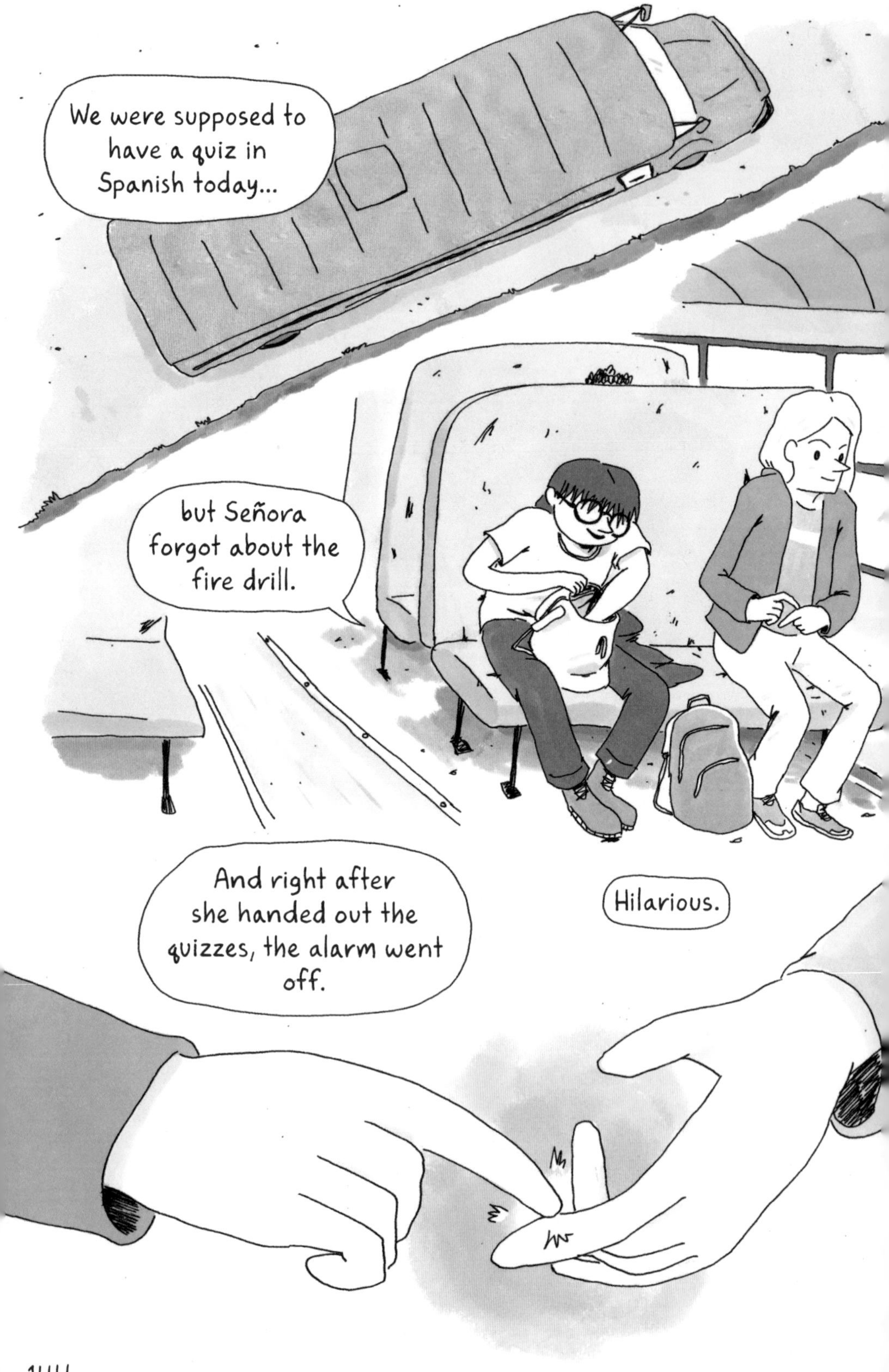
We were supposed to have a quiz in Spanish today...
but Señora forgot about the fire drill.
And right after she handed out the quizzes, the alarm went off.
Hilarious.

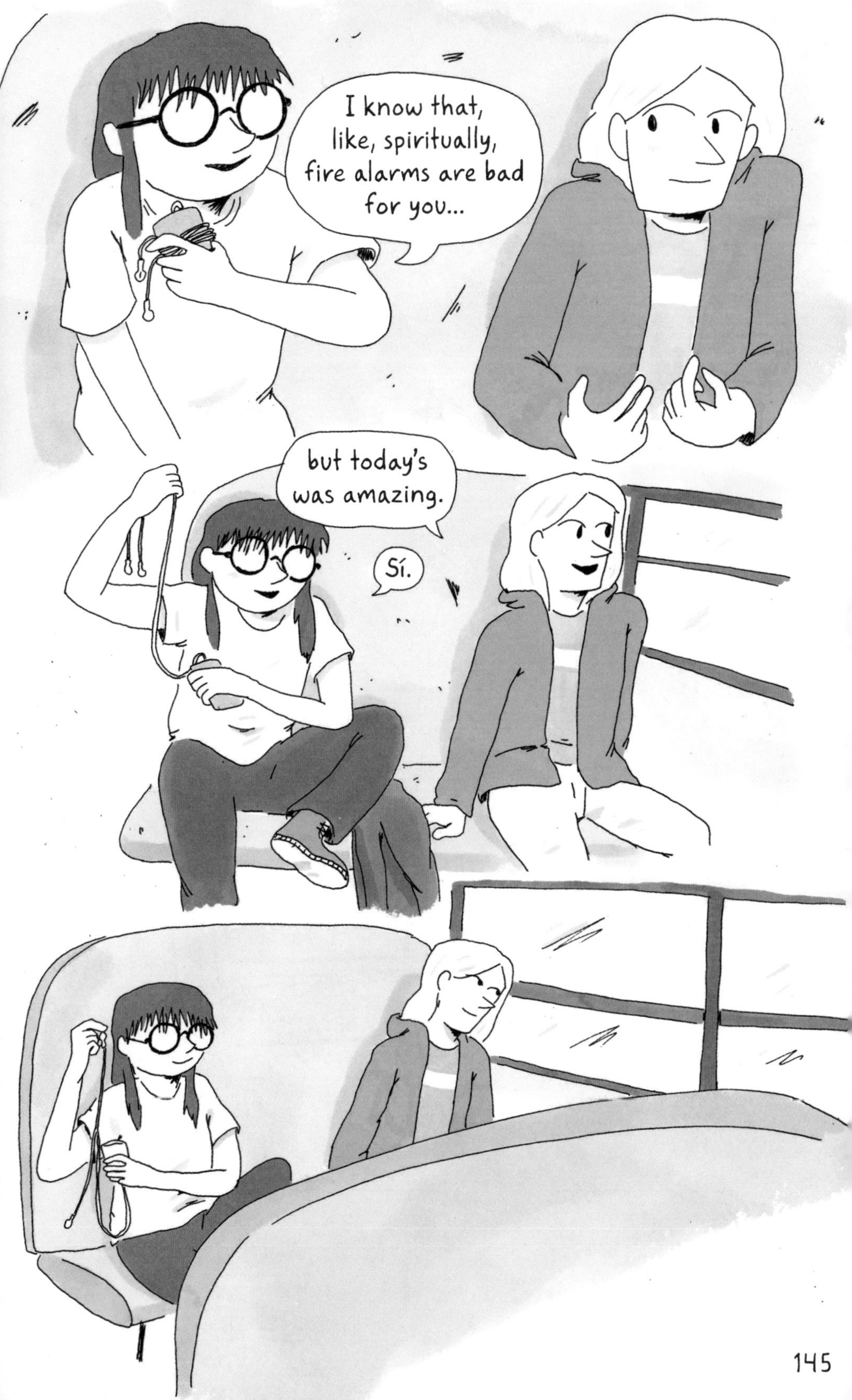
I know that, like, spiritually, fire alarms are bad for you...
but today's was amazing.
Sí.

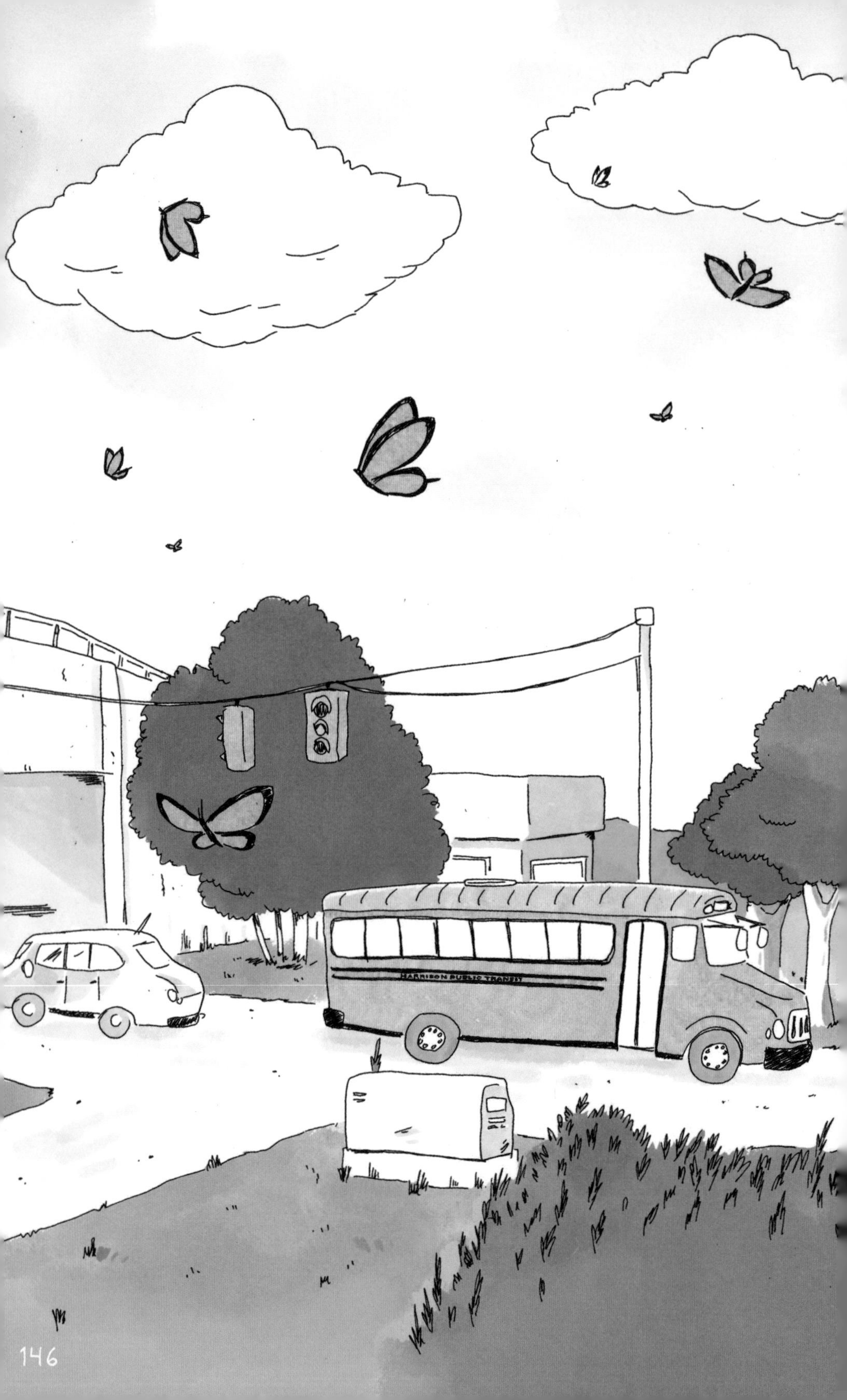
HARRISON PUBLIC TRANSIT

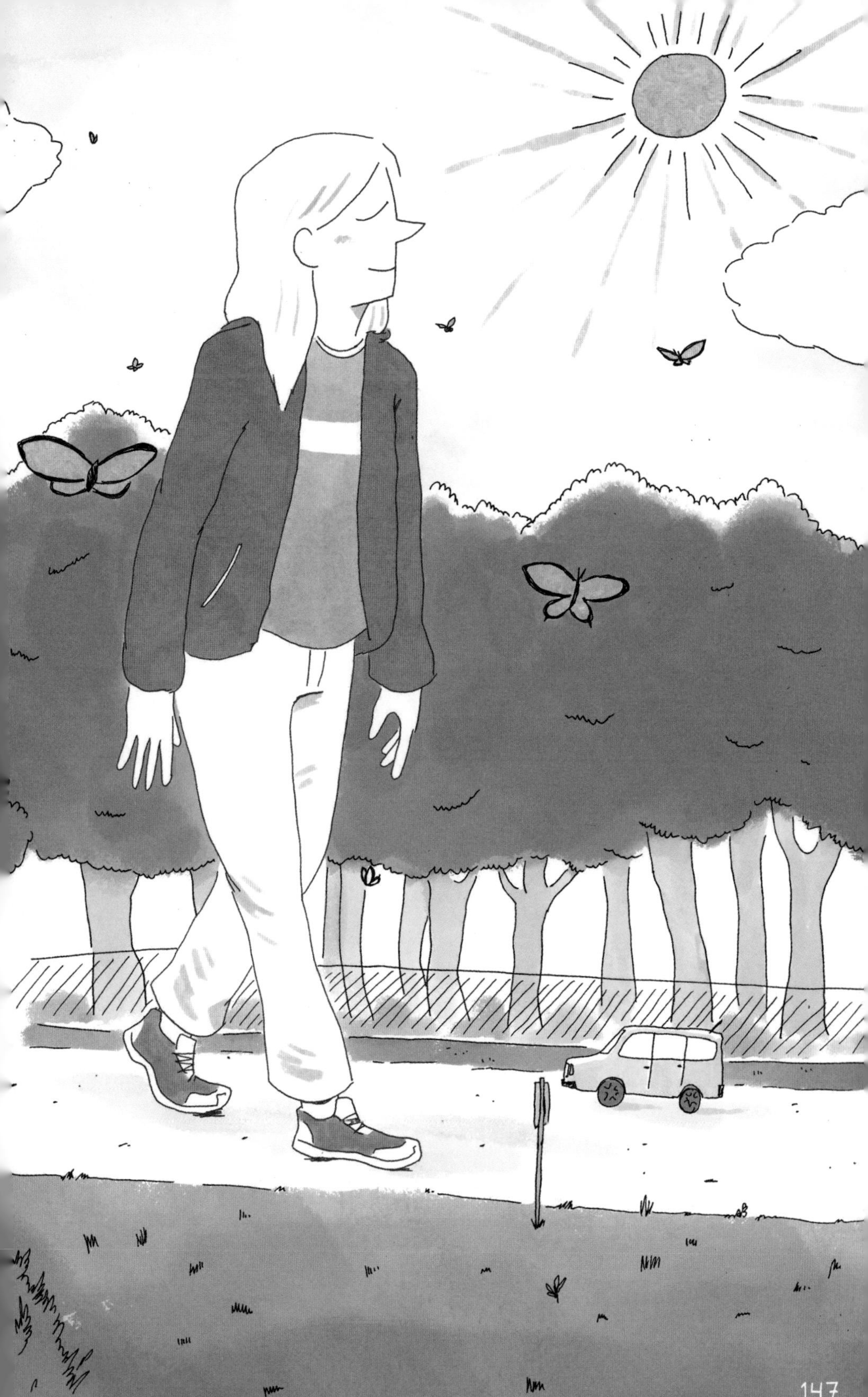

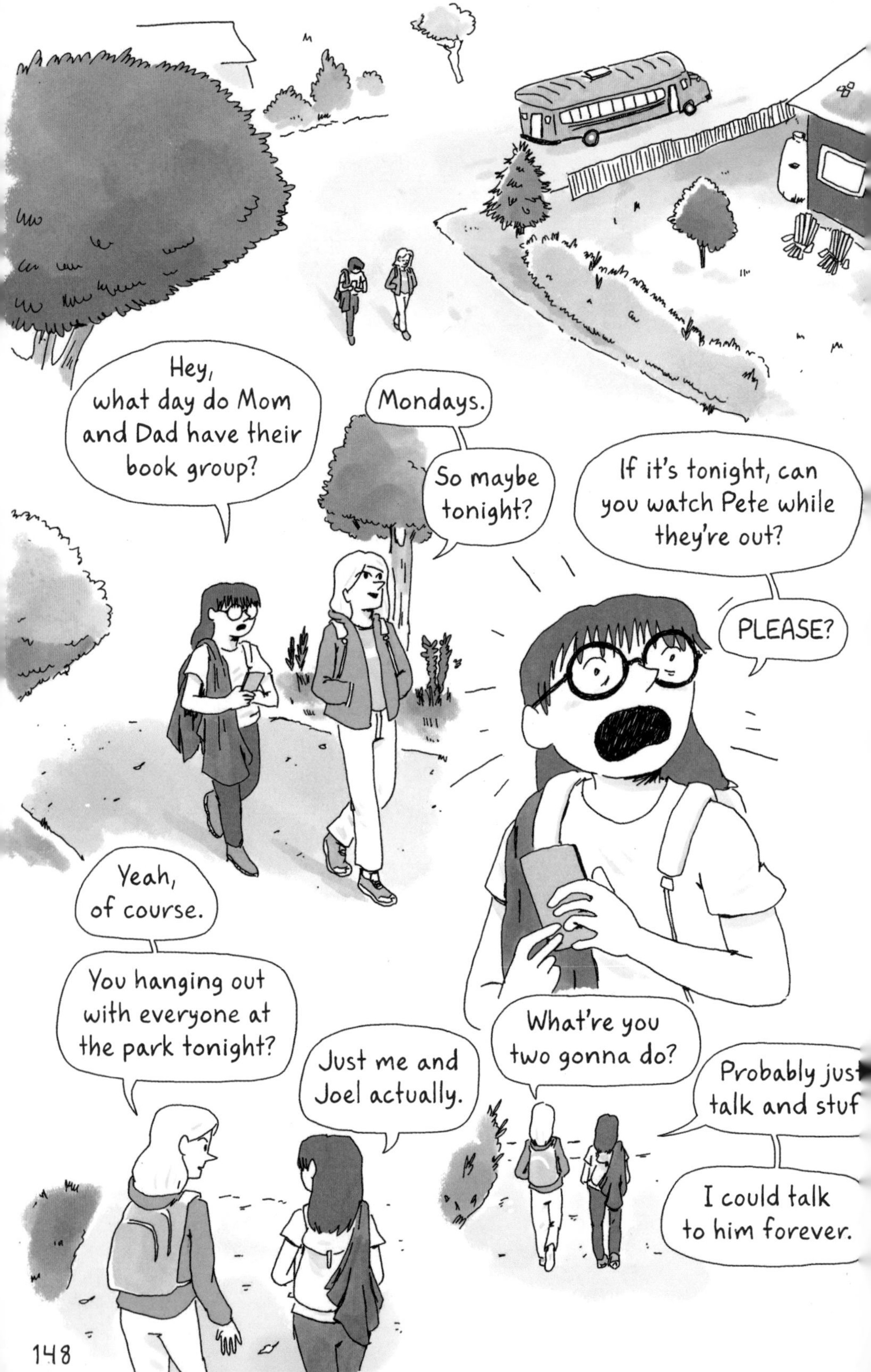
Hey, what day do Mom and Dad have their book group?
Mondays.
So maybe tonight?
If it's tonight, can you watch Pete while they're out?
PLEASE?
Yeah, of course.
You hanging out with everyone at the park tonight?
Just me and Joel actually.
What're you two gonna do?
Probably jus talk and stuf
I could talk to him forever.

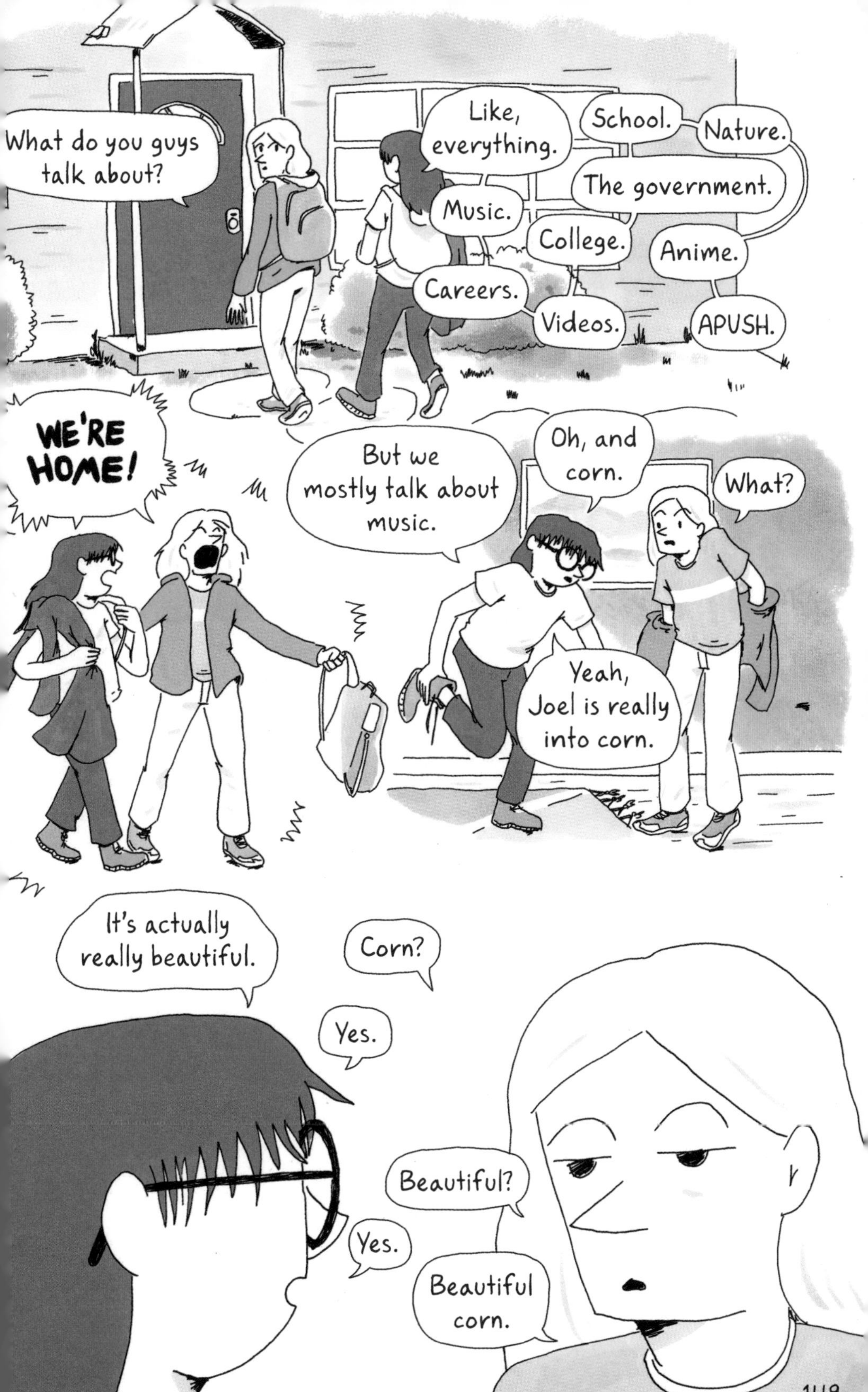
What do you guys talk about?
Like, everything.
School.
Nature.
The government.
Music.
College.
Anime.
Careers.
Videos.
APUSH.
WE'RE HOME!
But we mostly talk about music.
Oh, and corn.
What?
Yeah, Joel is really into corn.
It's actually really beautiful.
Corn?
Yes.
Beautiful?
Yes.
Beautiful corn.

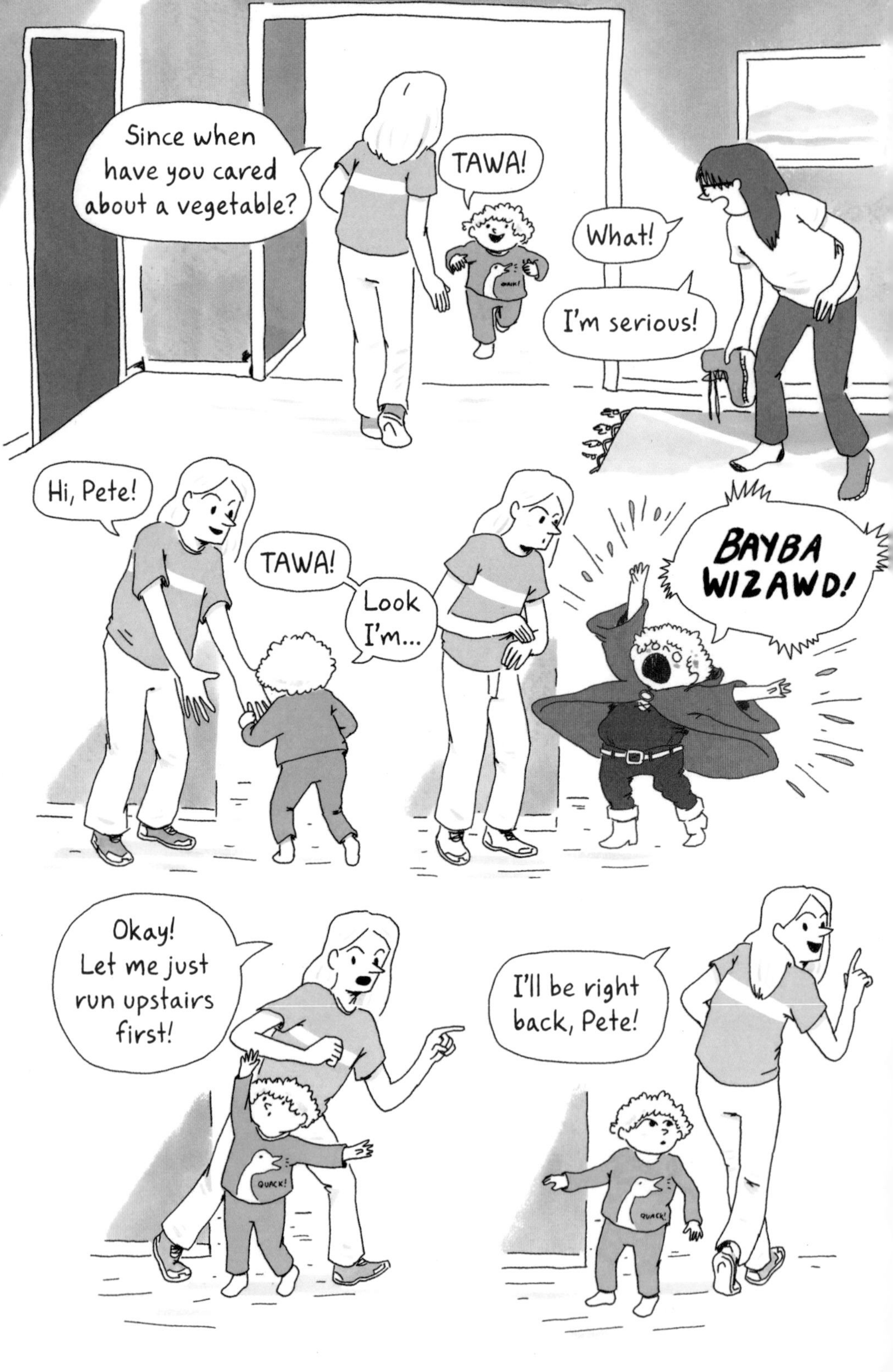
Since when have you cared about a vegetable?
TAWA!
What!
I'm serious!
Hi, Pete!
TAWA!
Look I'm...
BAYBA WIZAWD!
Okay! Let me just run upstairs first!
I'll be right back, Pete!

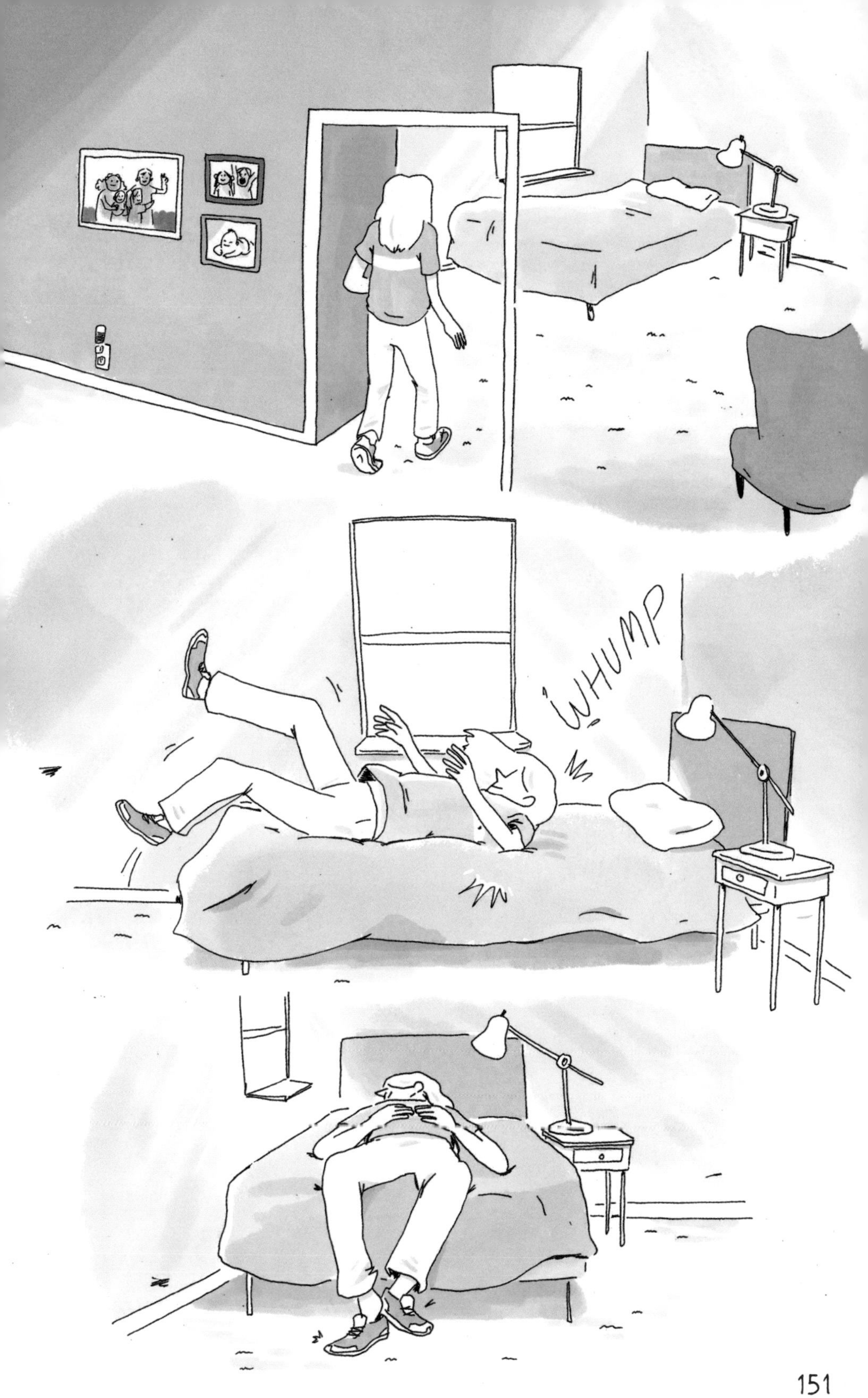
WHUMP

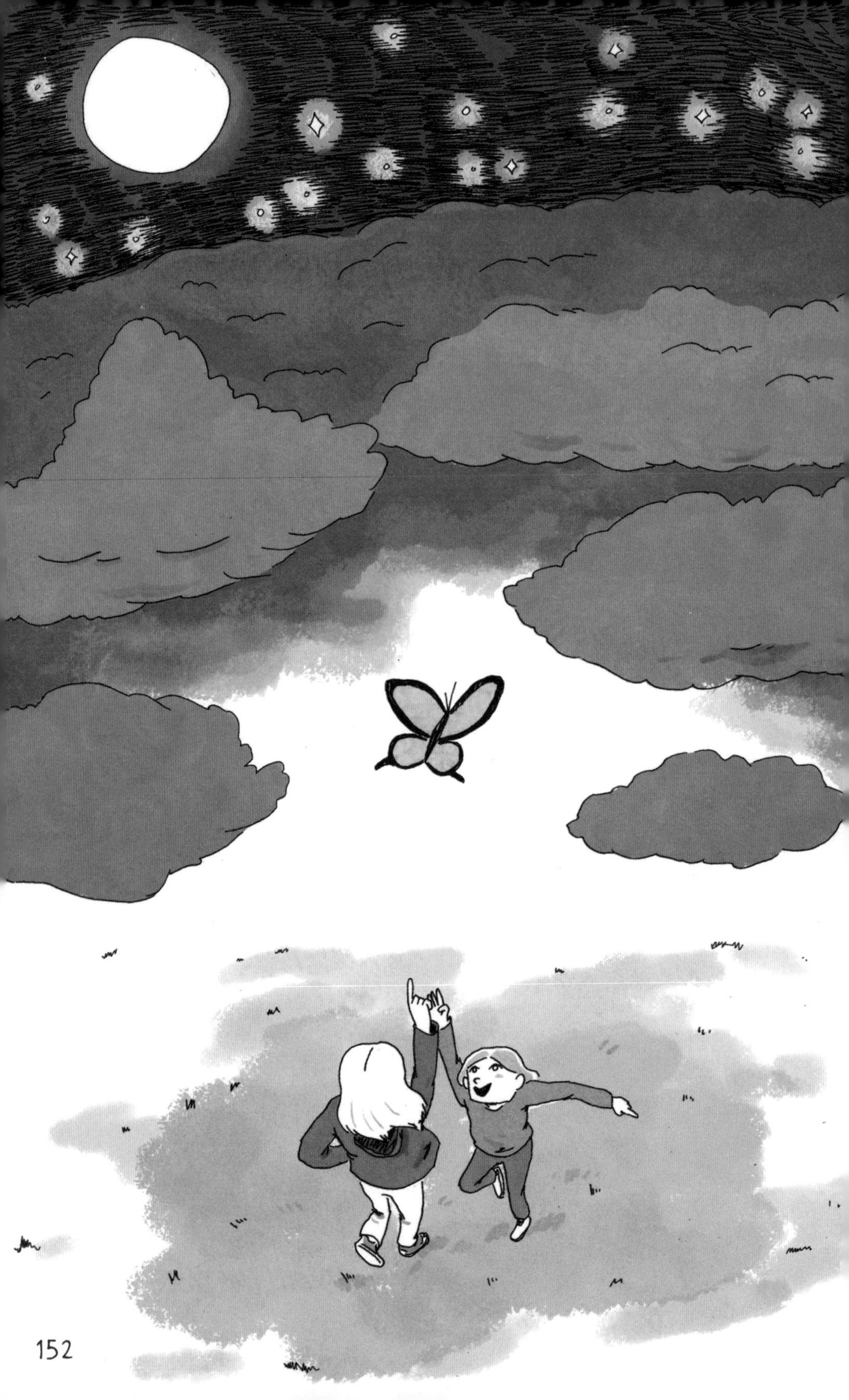

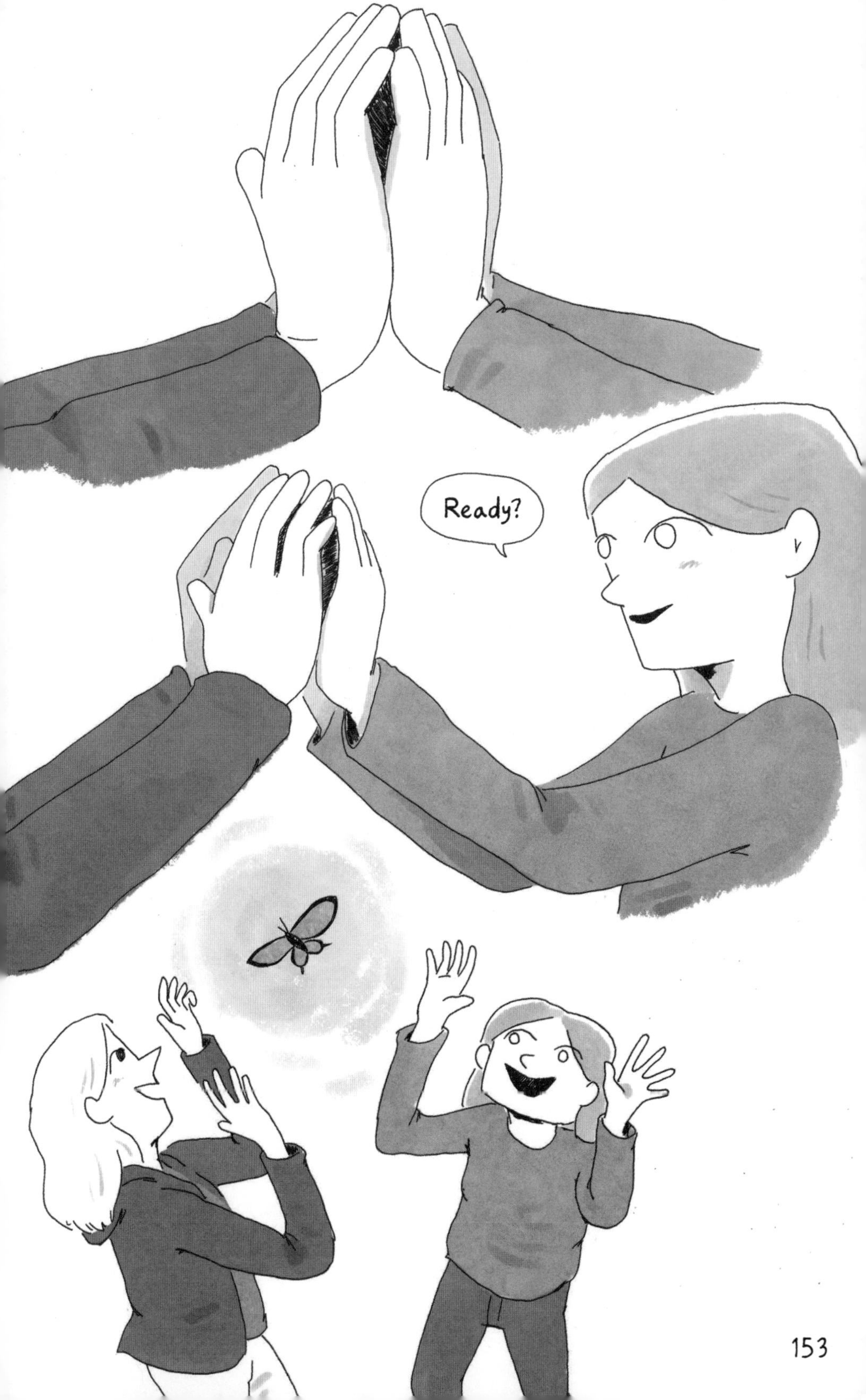
Ready?

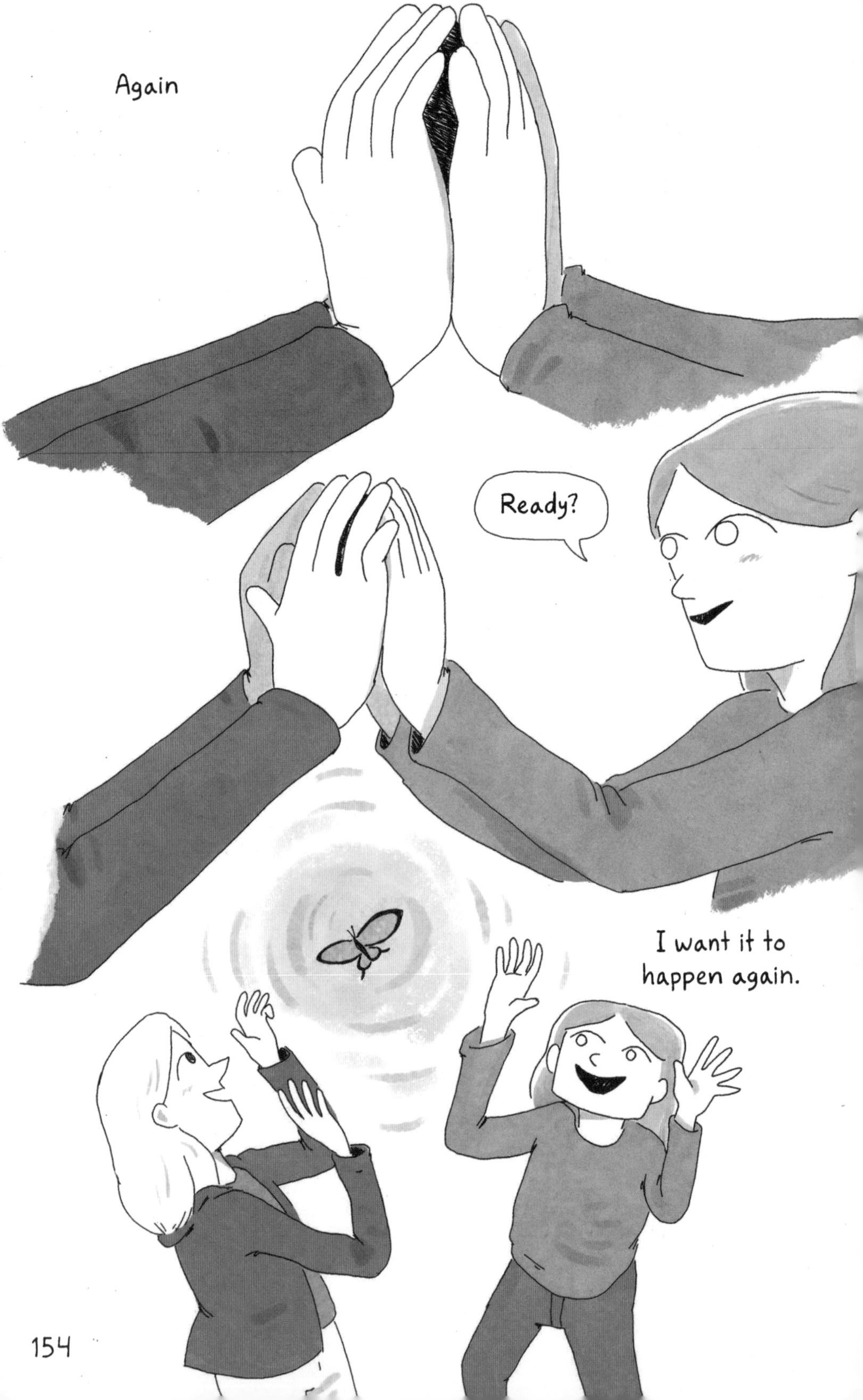
Again
Ready?
I want it to happen again.

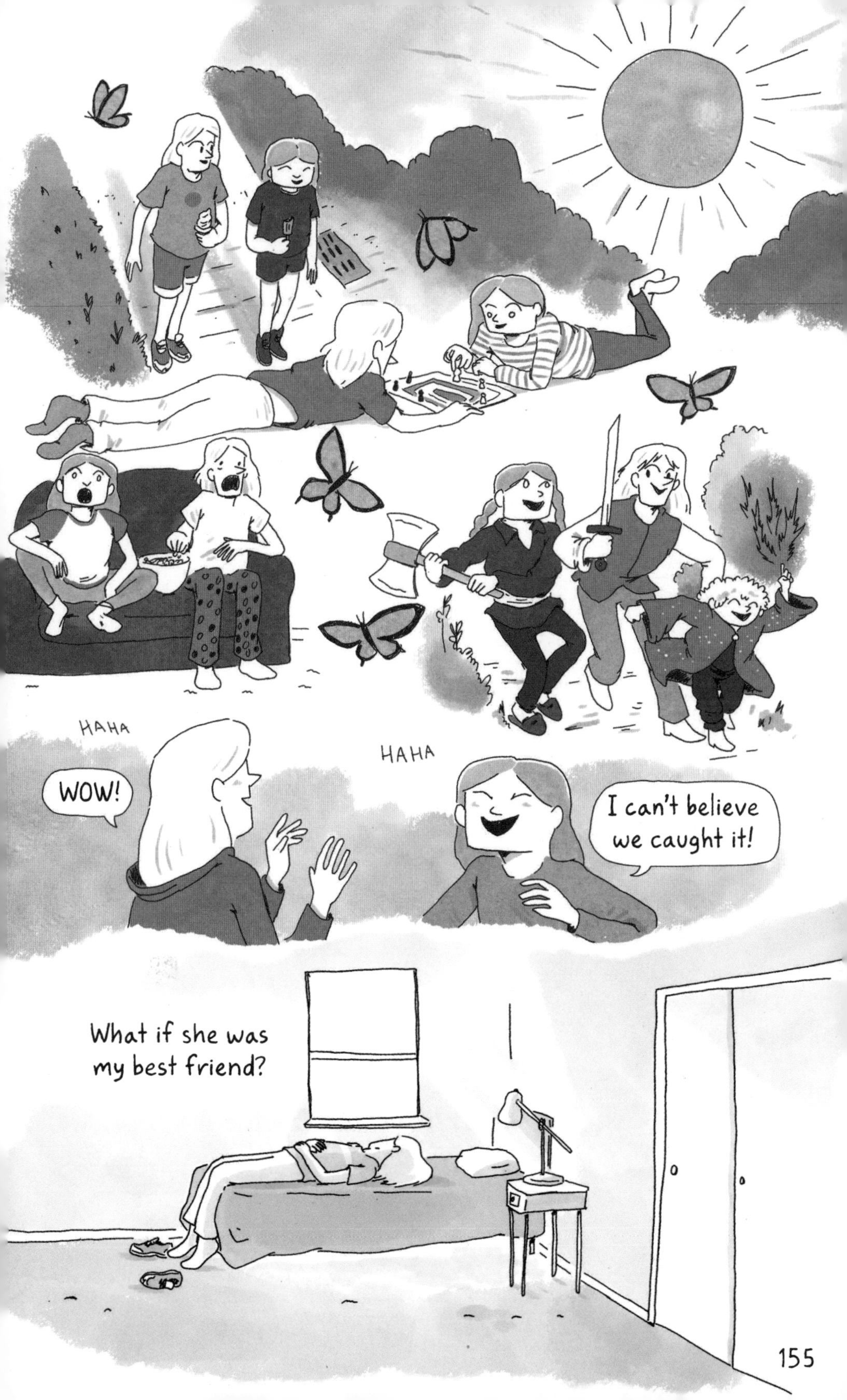
HAHA
HAHA
WOW!
I can't believe we caught it!
What if she was my best friend?

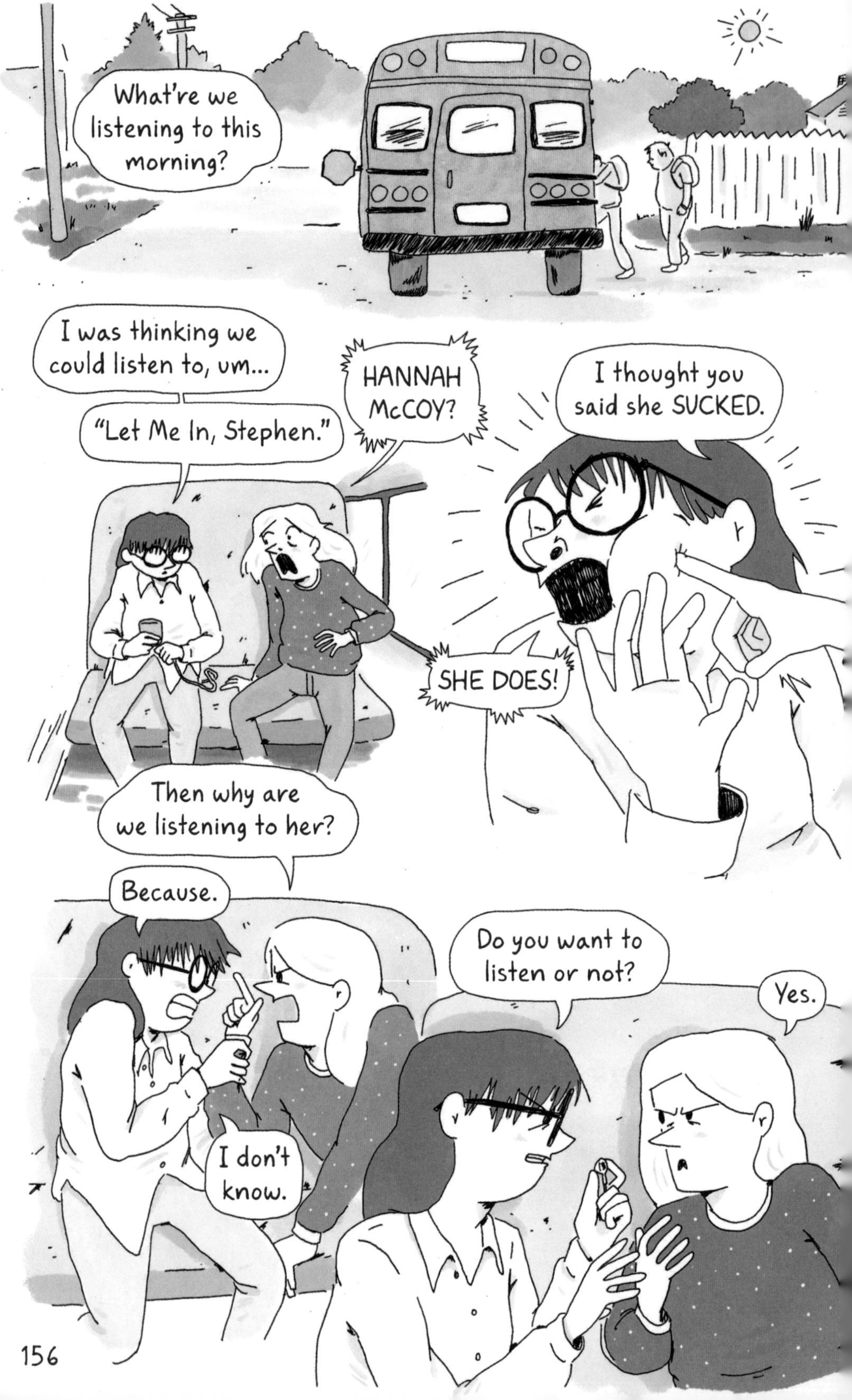
What're we listening to this morning?
I was thinking we could listen to, um...
"Let Me In, Stephen."
HANNAH McCOY?
I thought you said she SUCKED.
SHE DOES!
Then why are we listening to her?
Because.
I don't know.
Do you want to listen or not?
Yes.

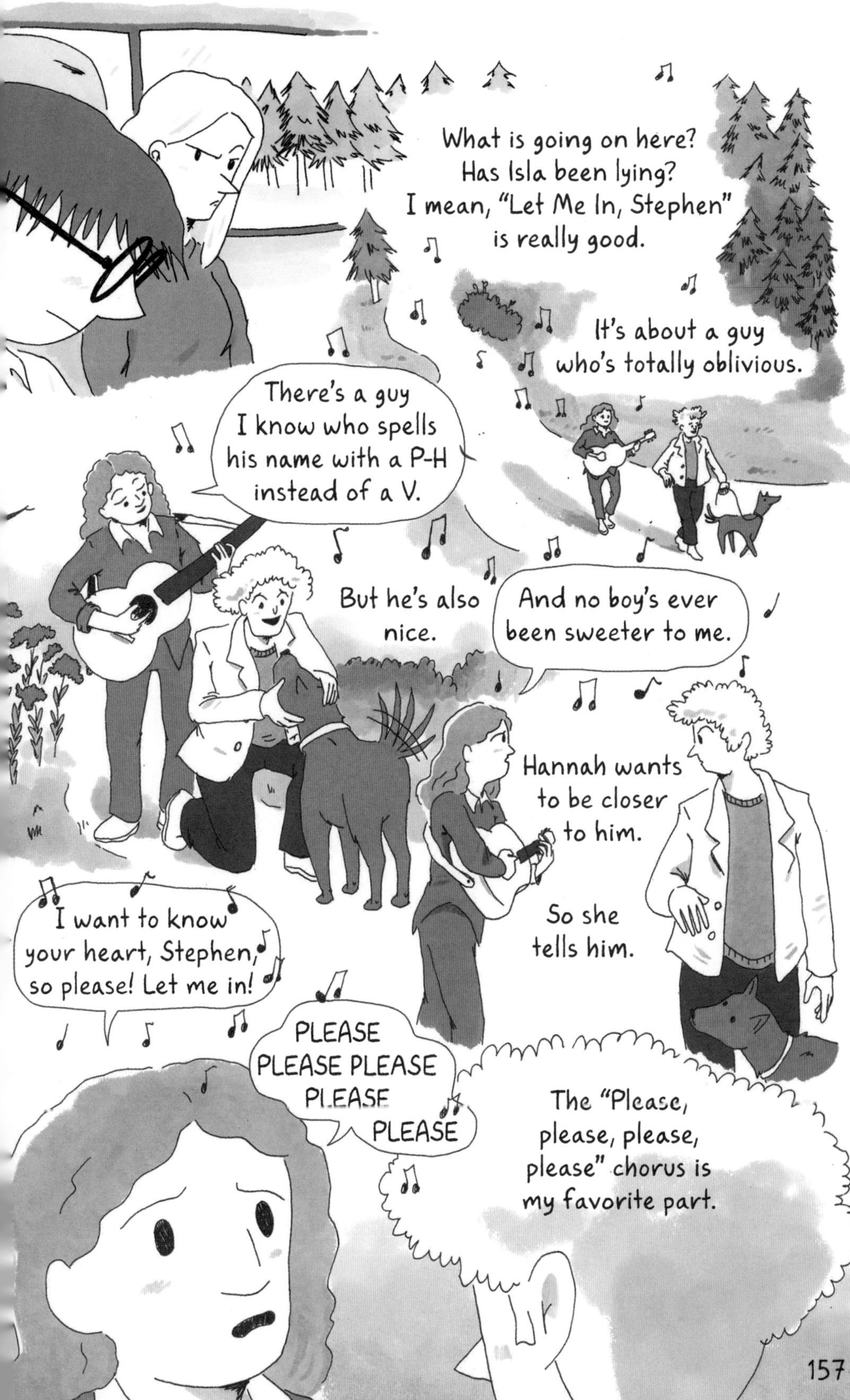
What is going on here? Has Isla been lying? I mean, "Let Me In, Stephen" is really good.
It's about a guy who's totally oblivious.
There's a guy I know who spells his name with a P-H instead of a V.
But he's also nice.
And no boy's ever been sweeter to me.
Hannah wants to be closer to him.
So she tells him.
I want to know your heart, Stephen, so please! Let me in!
PLEASE PLEASE PLEASE PLEASE PLEASE
The "Please, please, please, please" chorus is my favorite part.

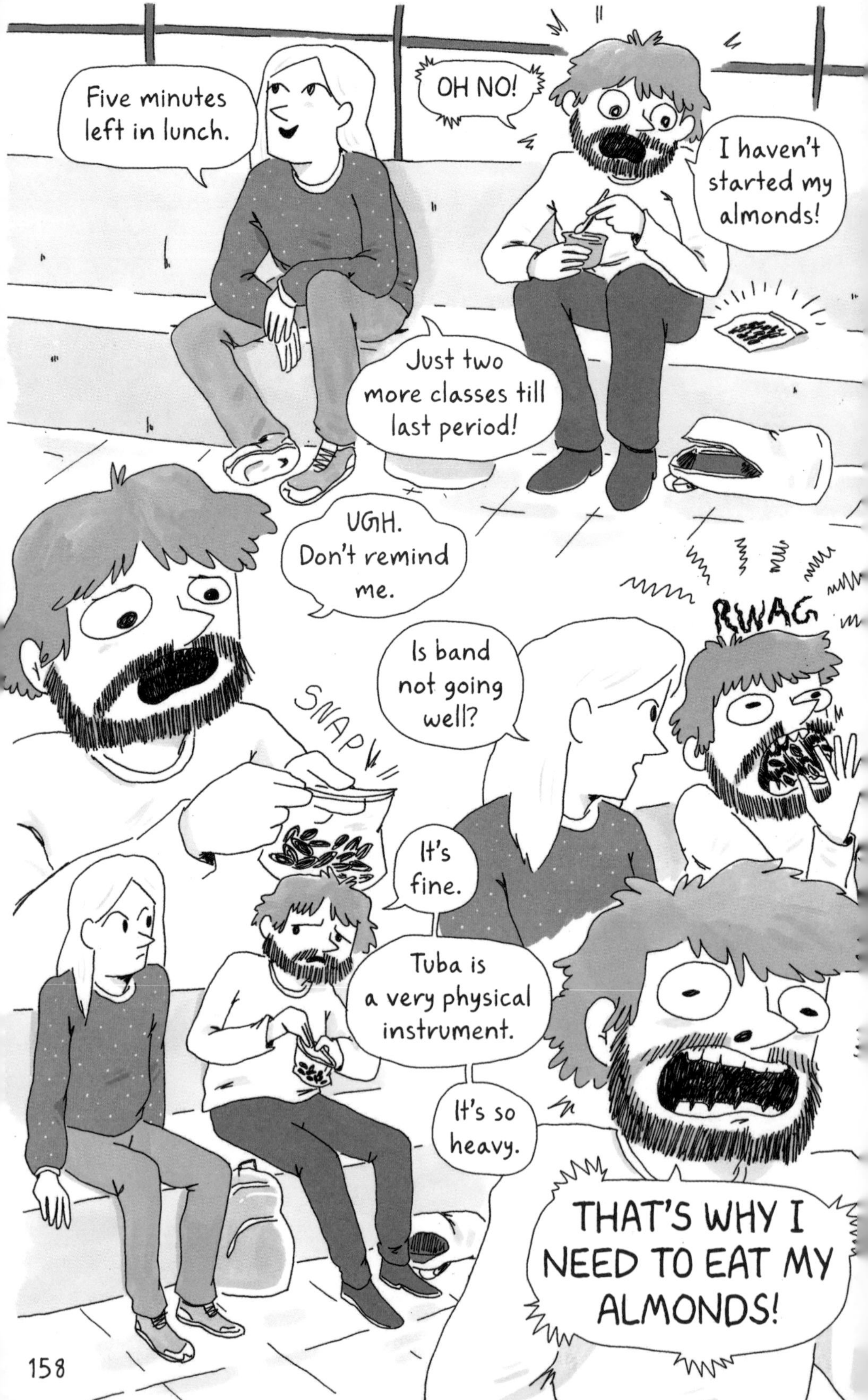
Five minutes left in lunch.
OH NO!
I haven't started my almonds!
Just two more classes till last period!
UGH. Don't remind me.
SNAP
Is band not going well?
RWAG
It's fine.
Tuba is a very physical instrument.
It's so heavy.
THAT'S WHY I NEED TO EAT MY ALMONDS!

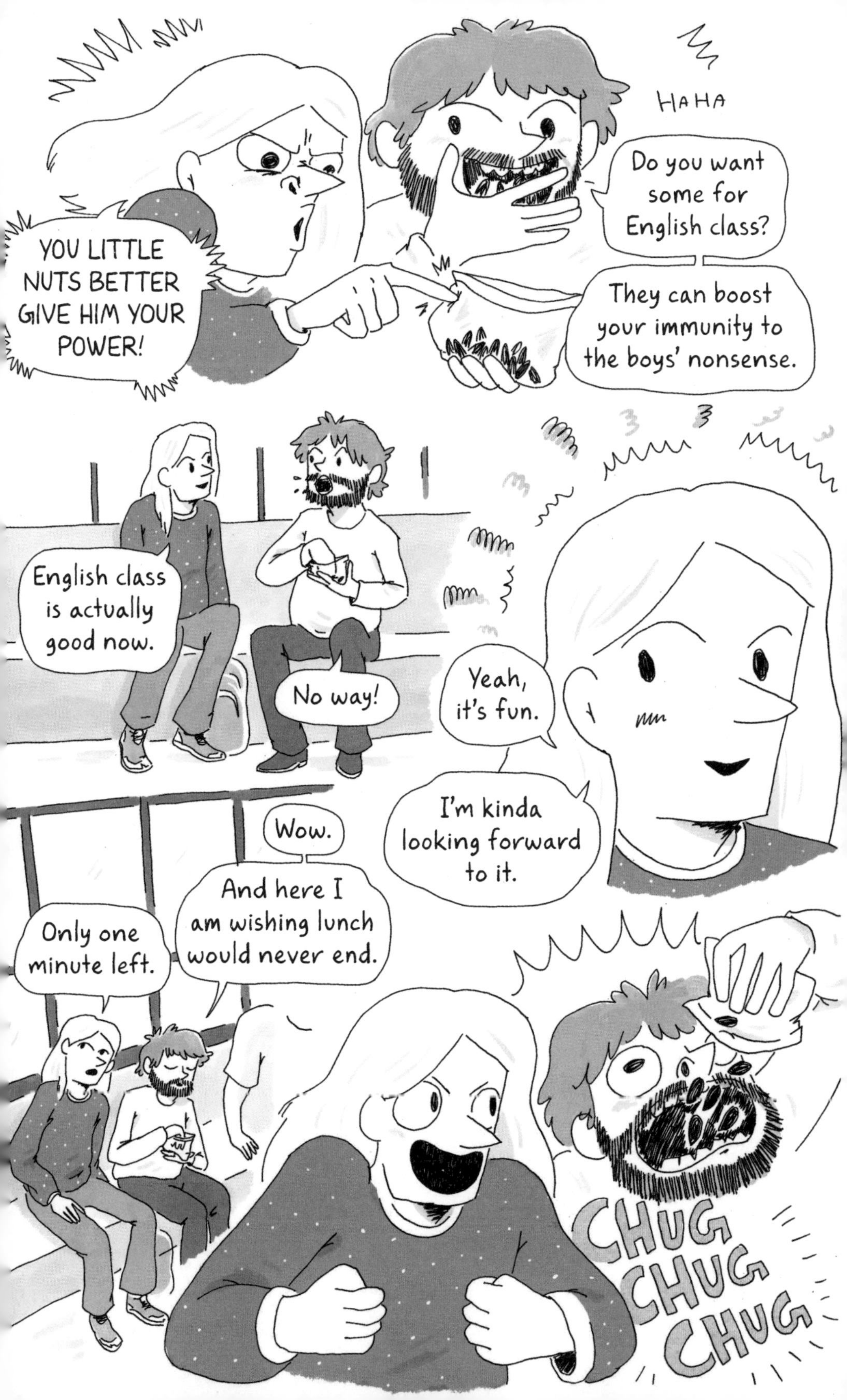

HAHA
YOU LITTLE NUTS BETTER GIVE HIM YOUR POWER!
Do you want some for English class?
They can boost your immunity to the boys' nonsense.
English class is actually good now.
No way!
Yeah, it's fun.
I'm kinda looking forward to it.
Wow.
And here I am wishing lunch would never end.
Only one minute left.
CHUG CHUG CHUG

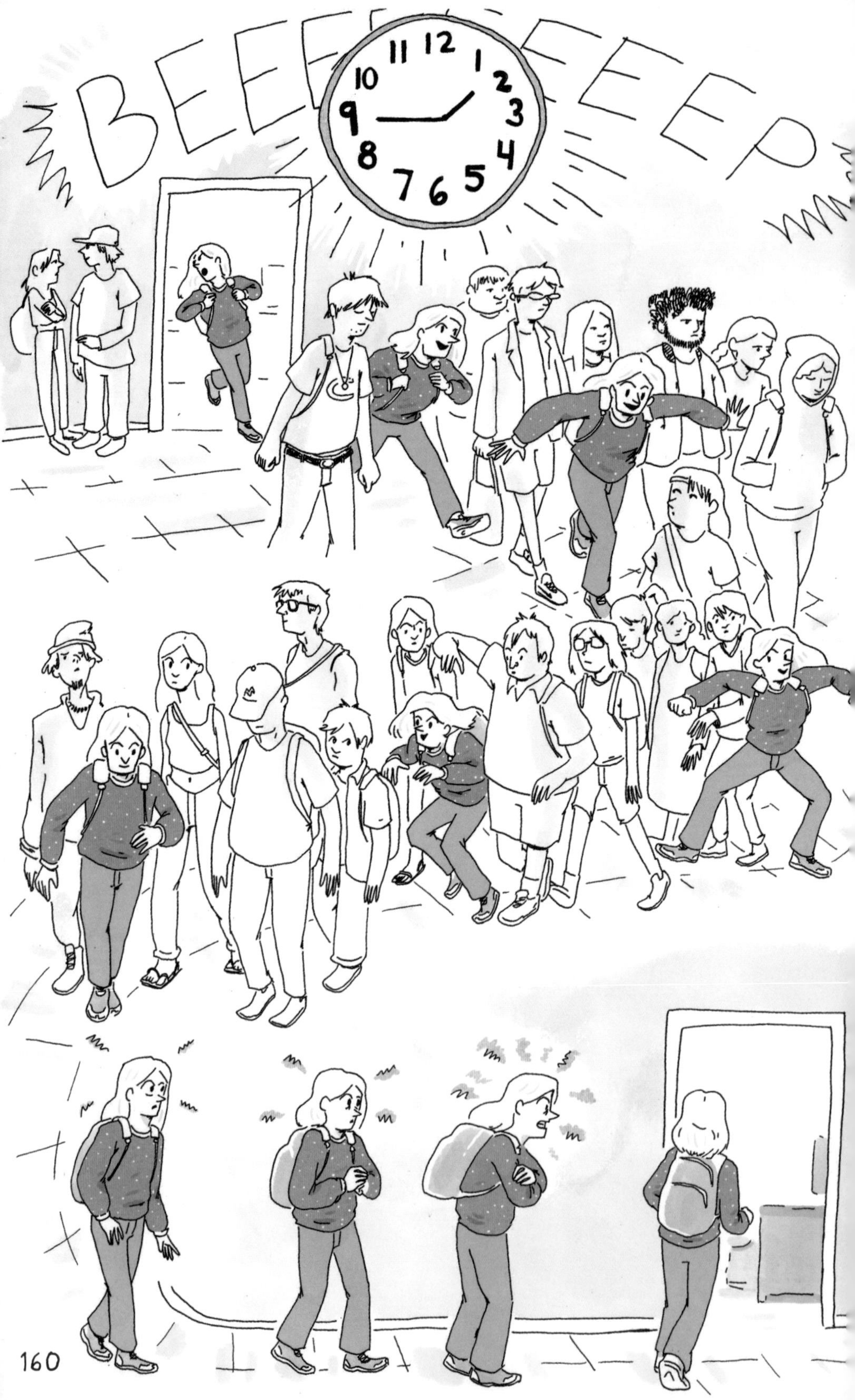
BEEEEEEEEEP

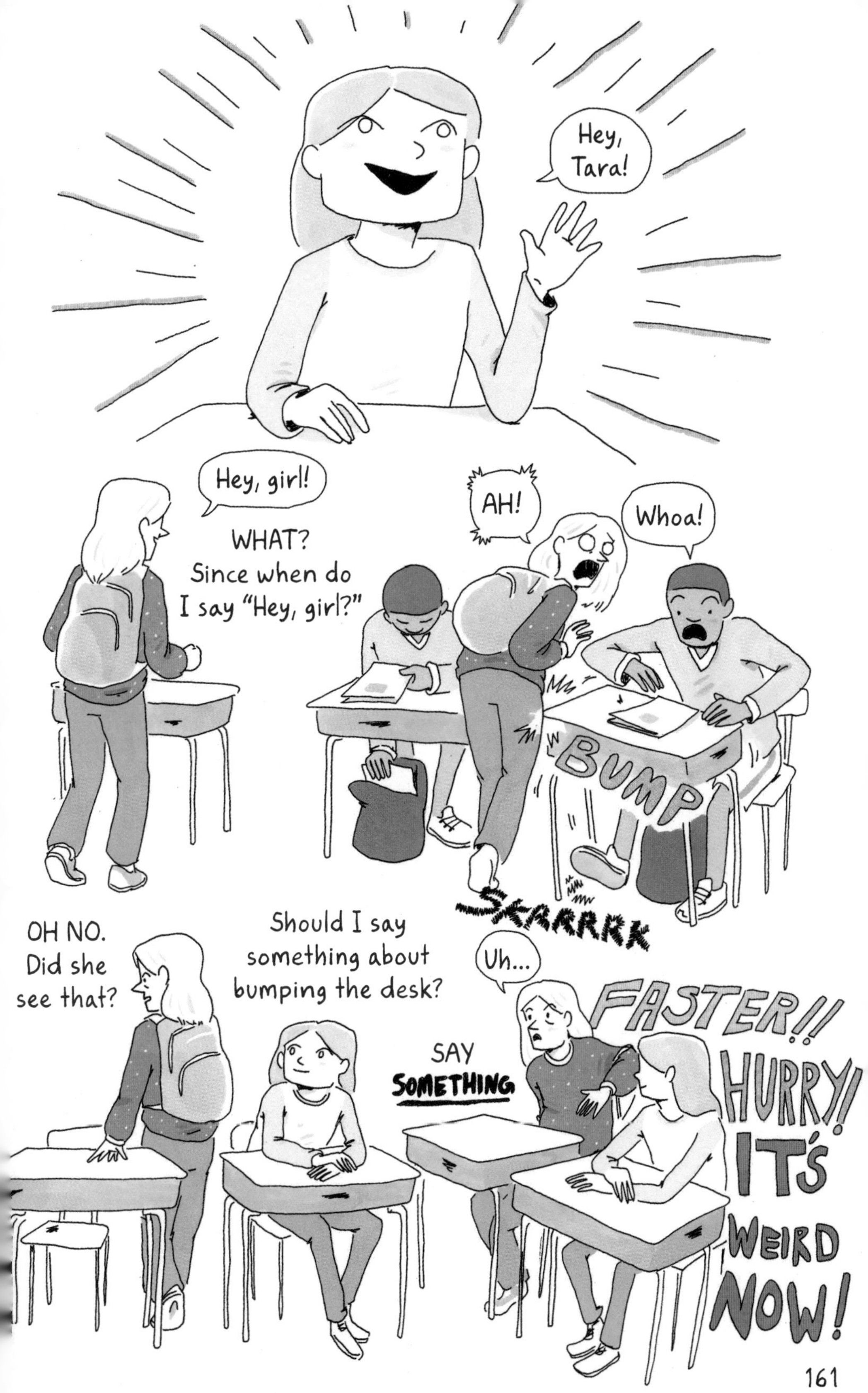

Hey, Tara!
Hey, girl!
WHAT? Since when do I say "Hey, girl?"
AH!
Whoa!
BUMP
SKRRRRK
OH NO. Did she see that?
Should I say something about bumping the desk?
SAY SOMETHING
Uh...
FASTER!!
HURRY! IT'S WEIRD NOW!

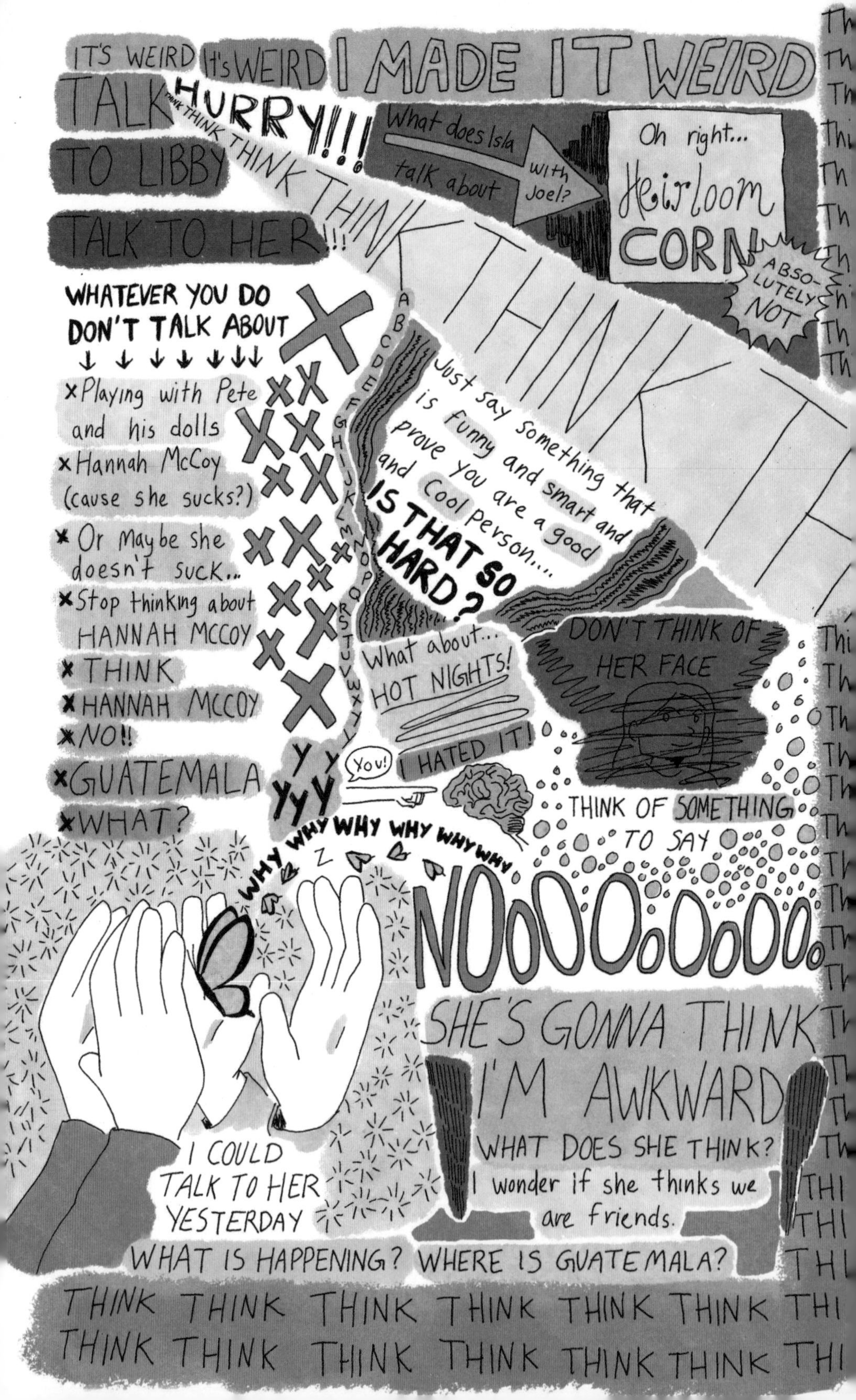
IT'S WEIRD
It's WEIRD
I MADE IT WEIRD
TALK
TO LIBBY
TALK TO HER!!!
HURRY!!!
THINK THINK THINK THINK THINK THINK
What does Isla talk about with Joel?
Oh right... Heirloom CORN
ABSOLUTELY NOT
WHATEVER YOU DO DON'T TALK ABOUT
×Playing with Pete and his dolls
×Hannah McCoy (cause she sucks?)
×Or maybe she doesn't suck...
×Stop thinking about HANNAH MCCOY
×THINK
×HANNAH MCCOY
×NO!!
×GUATEMALA
×WHAT?
A B C D E F G H I J K L M N O P Q R S T U V W X Y
Y Y
YYY
Just say something that is funny and smart and prove you are a good and cool person....
IS THAT SO HARD?
What about... HOT NIGHTS!
I HATED IT!
You!
DON'T THINK OF HER FACE
THINK OF SOMETHING TO SAY
WHY WHY WHY WHY WHY WHY
NOOOOOOOOOOO
SHE'S GONNA THINK I'M AWKWARD
WHAT DOES SHE THINK?
I wonder if she thinks we are friends.
I COULD TALK TO HER YESTERDAY
WHAT IS HAPPENING? WHERE IS GUATEMALA?
THINK THINK THINK THINK THINK THINK THI
THINK THINK THINK THINK THINK THINK THI

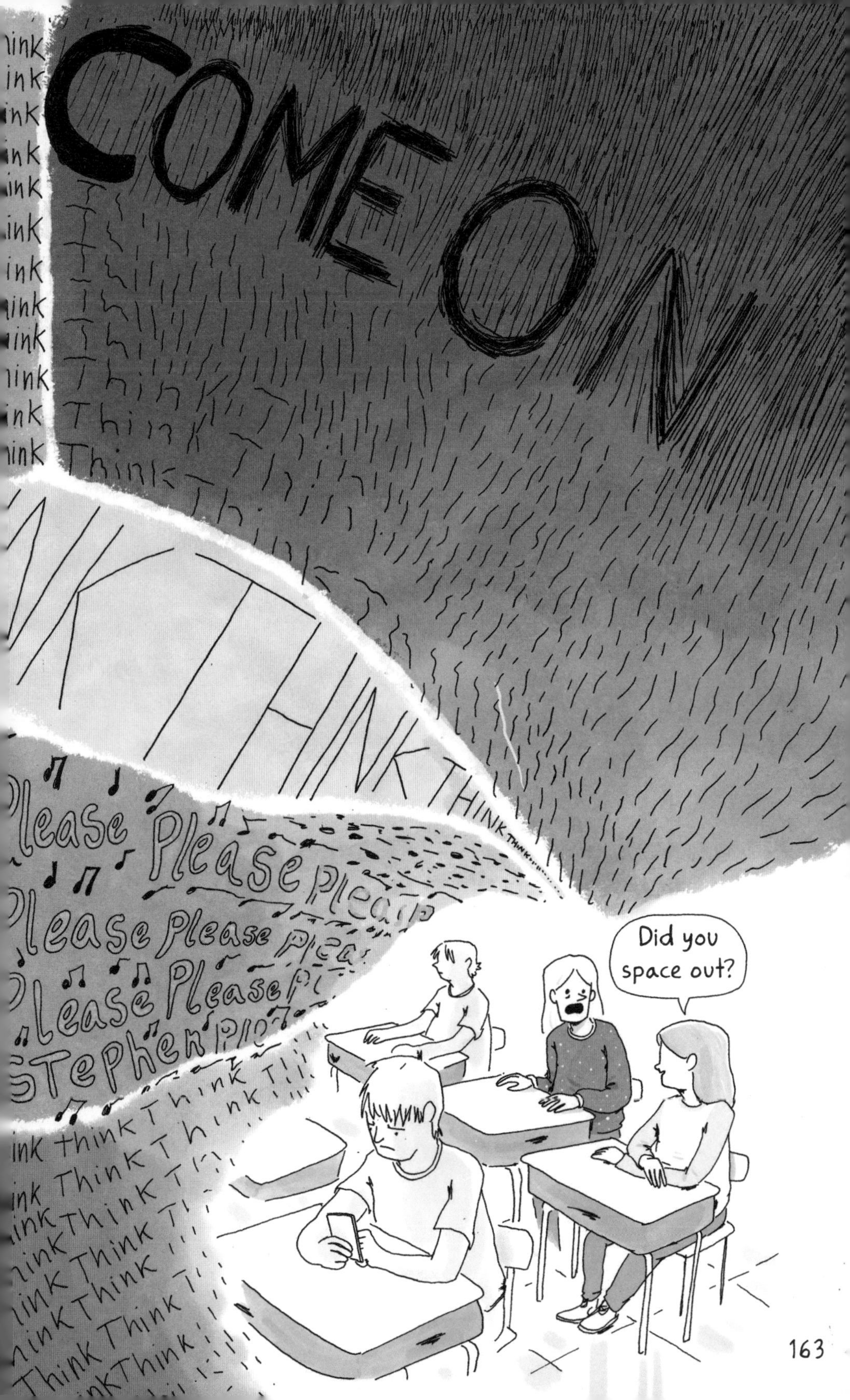
COME ON
THINK THINK
Please Please Please
Please Please
Please Please
Stephen
Think Think Think
Did you space out?

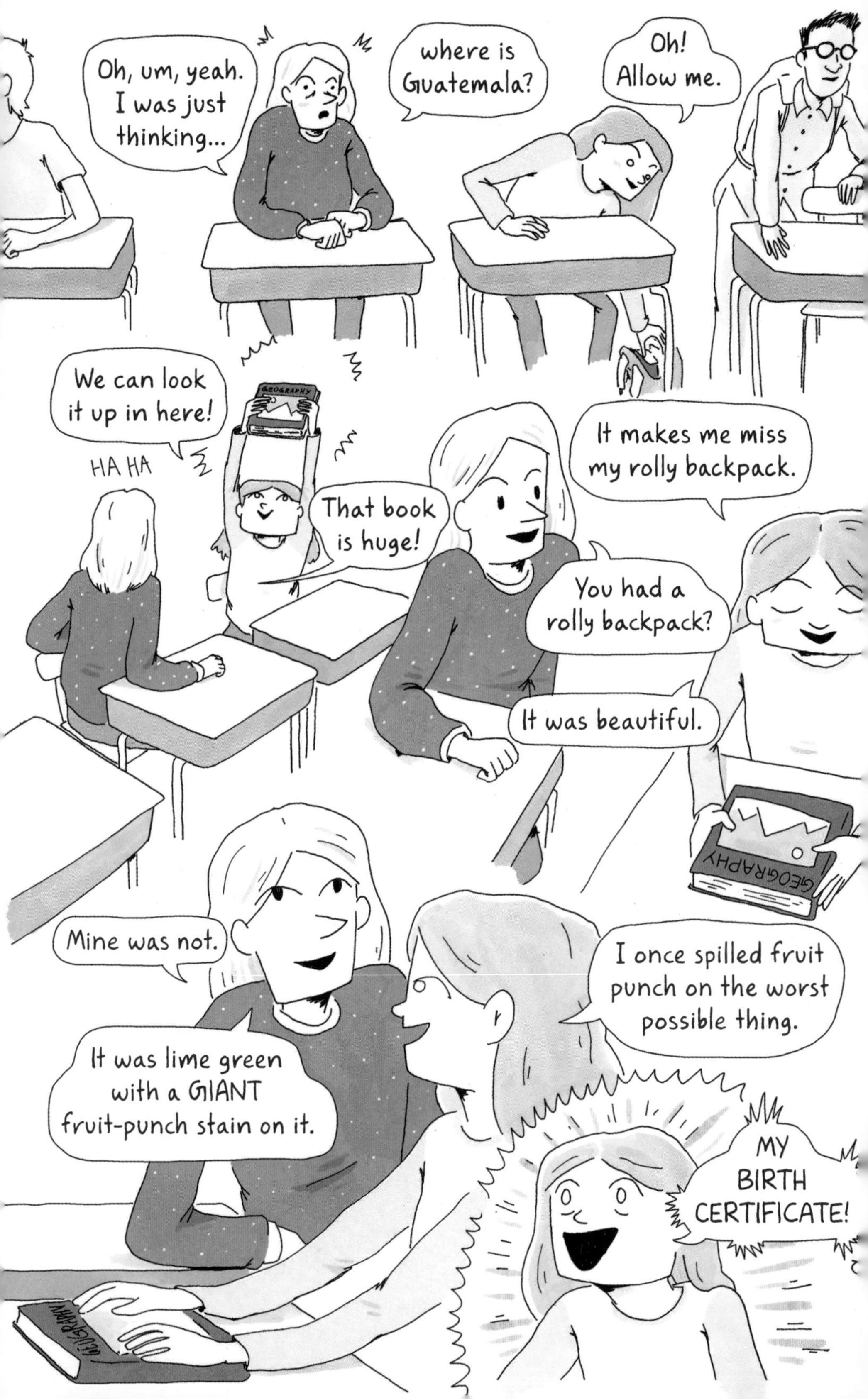

Oh, um, yeah. I was just thinking...
where is Guatemala?
Oh! Allow me.
We can look it up in here!
GEOGRAPHY
HA HA
That book is huge!
It makes me miss my rolly backpack.
You had a rolly backpack?
It was beautiful.
GEOGRAPHY
Mine was not.
I once spilled fruit punch on the worst possible thing.
It was lime green with a GIANT fruit-punch stain on it.
MY BIRTH CERTIFICATE!
GEOGRAPHY

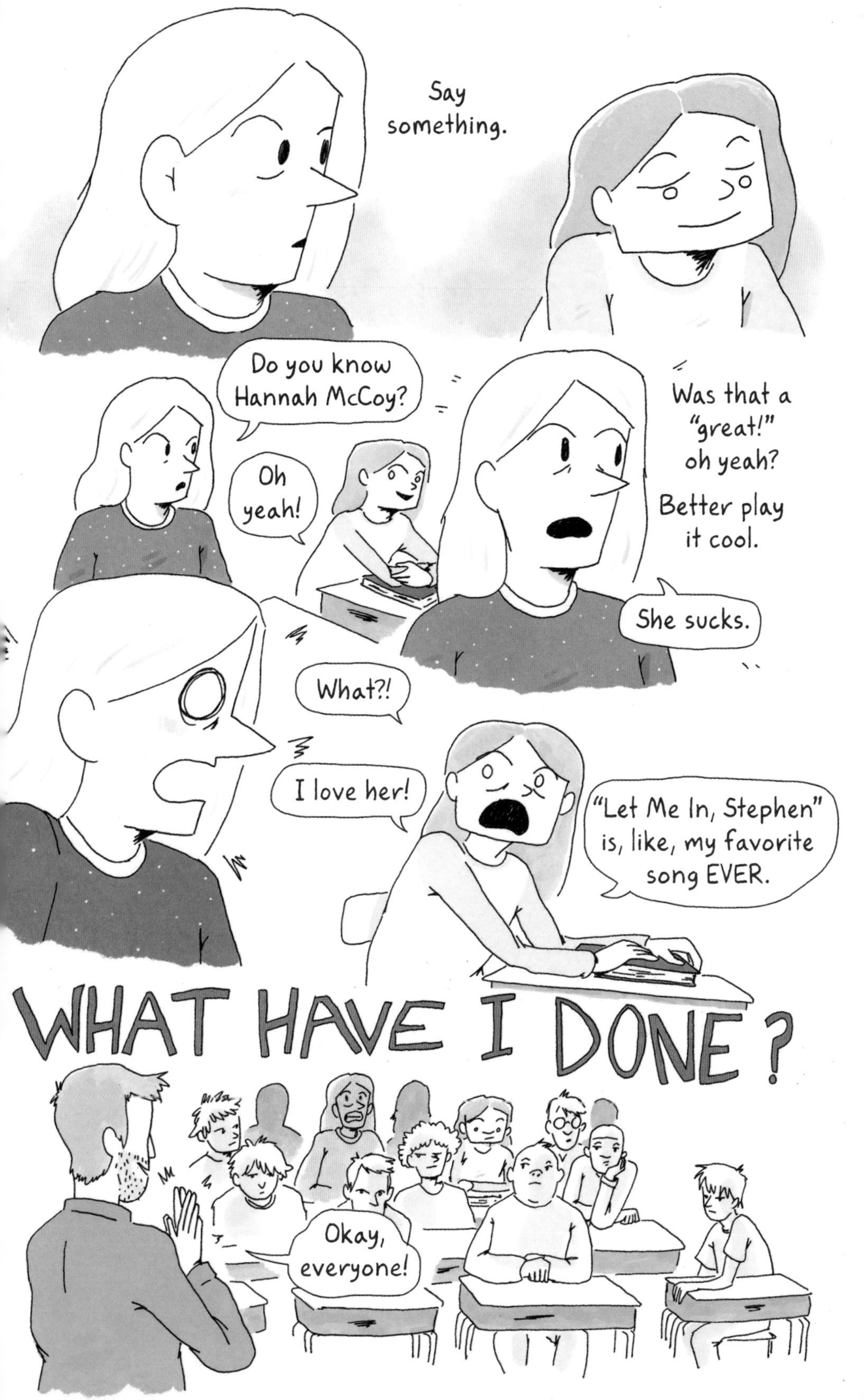
Say something.
Do you know Hannah McCoy?
Oh yeah!
Was that a "great!" oh yeah?
Better play it cool.
She sucks.
What?!
I love her!
"Let Me In, Stephen" is, like, my favorite song EVER.
WHAT HAVE I DONE?
Okay, everyone!

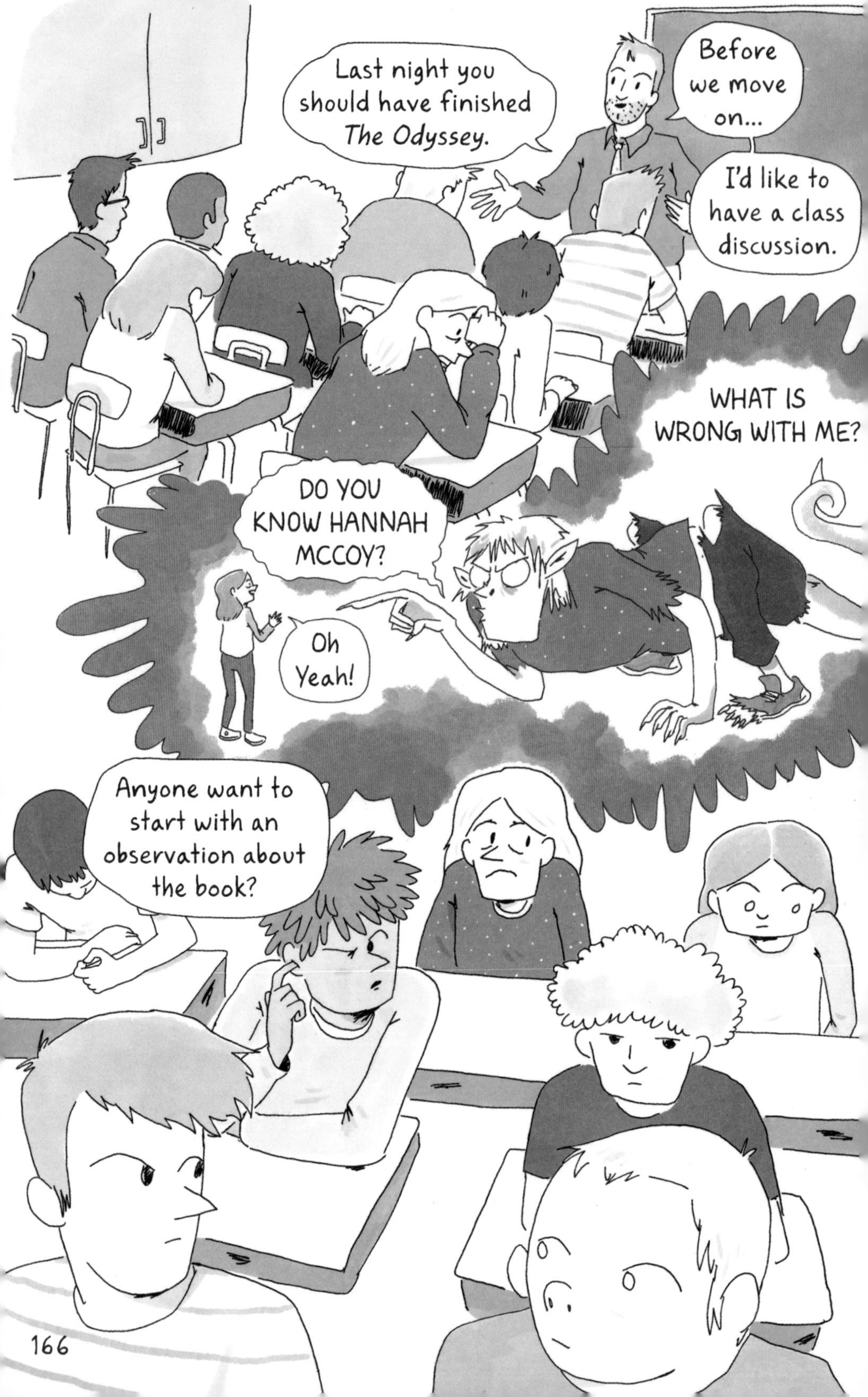
Last night you should have finished The Odyssey.
Before we move on...
I'd like to have a class discussion.
WHAT IS WRONG WITH ME?
DO YOU KNOW HANNAH MCCOY?
Oh Yeah!
Anyone want to start with an observation about the book?

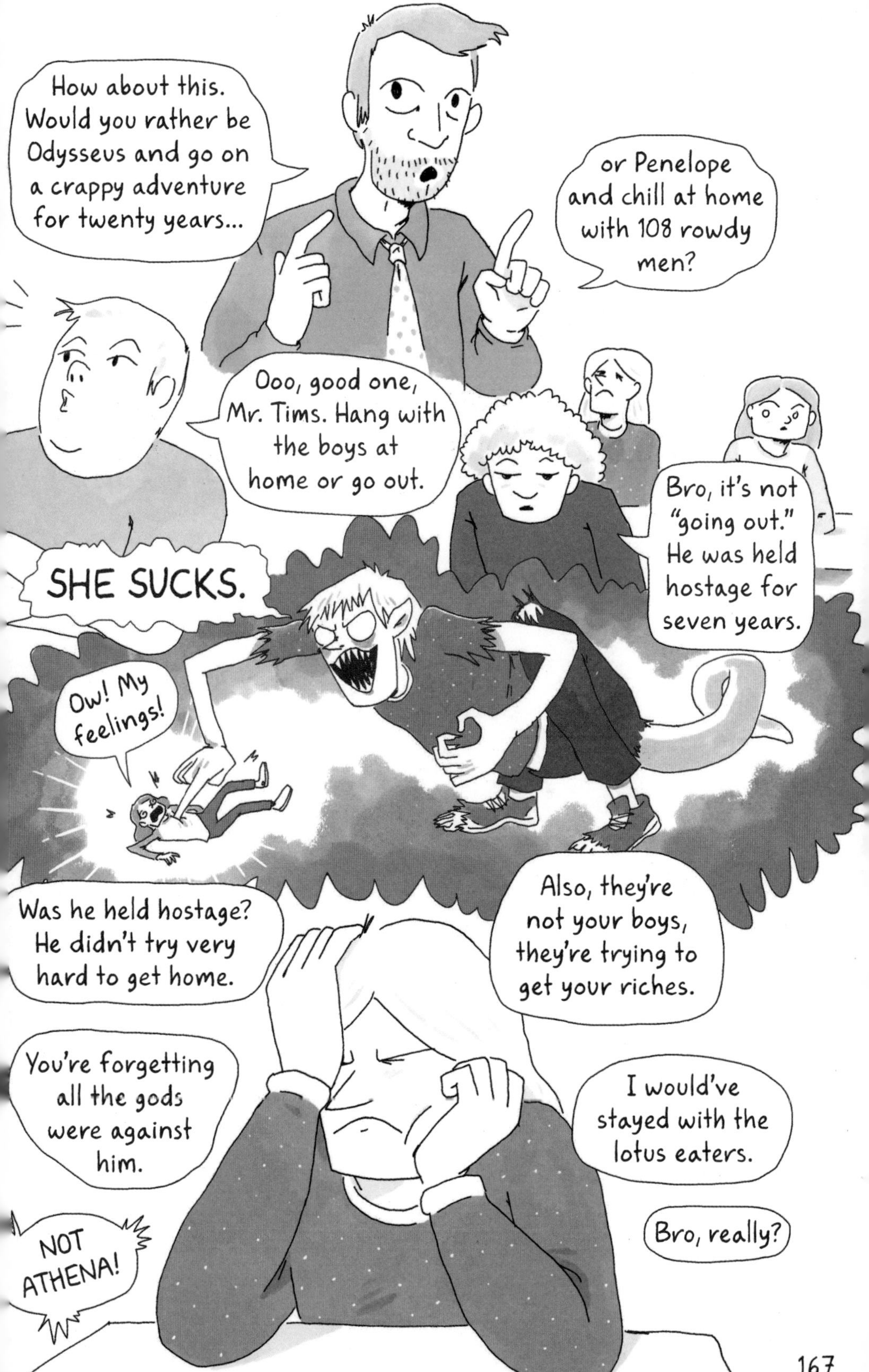
How about this. Would you rather be Odysseus and go on a crappy adventure for twenty years...
or Penelope and chill at home with 108 rowdy men?
Ooo, good one, Mr. Tims. Hang with the boys at home or go out.
Bro, it's not "going out." He was held hostage for seven years.
SHE SUCKS.
Ow! My feelings!
Was he held hostage? He didn't try very hard to get home.
Also, they're not your boys, they're trying to get your riches.
You're forgetting all the gods were against him.
I would've stayed with the lotus eaters.
NOT ATHENA!
Bro, really?

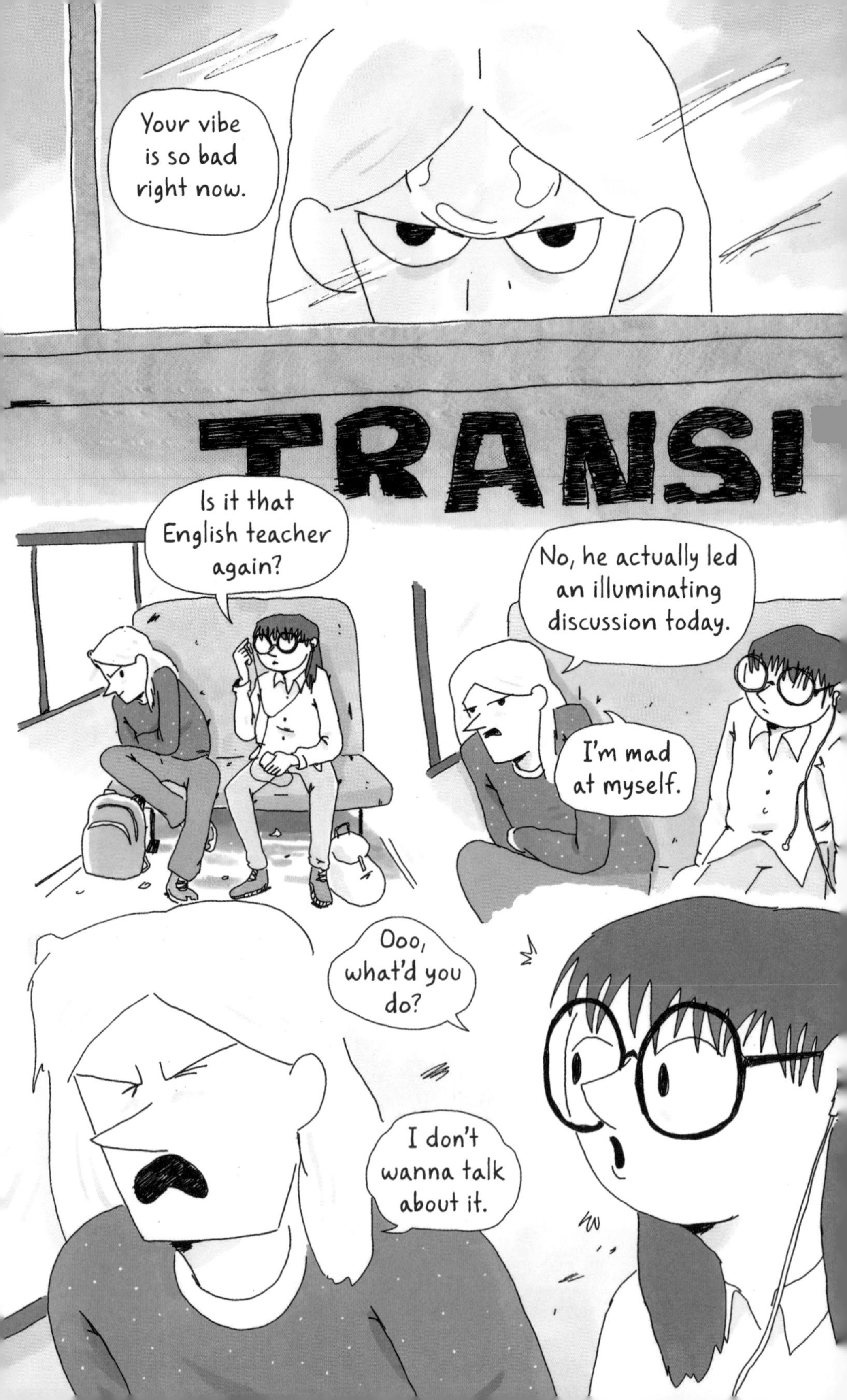
Your vibe is so bad right now.
TRANSI
Is it that English teacher again?
No, he actually led an illuminating discussion today.
I'm mad at myself.
Ooo, what'd you do?
I don't wanna talk about it.

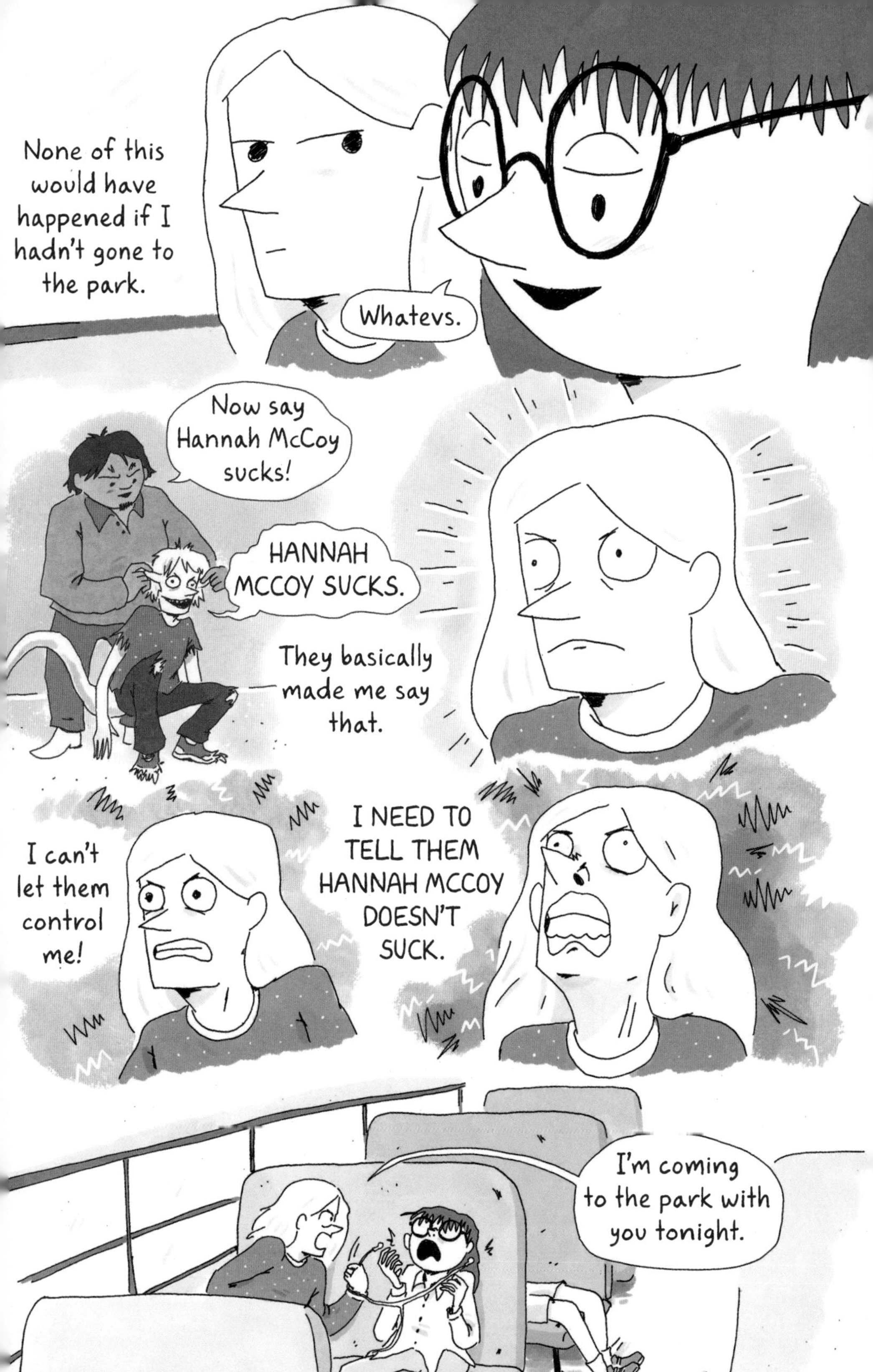
None of this would have happened if I hadn't gone to the park.
Whatevs.
Now say Hannah McCoy sucks!
HANNAH MCCOY SUCKS.
They basically made me say that.
I can't let them control me!
I NEED TO TELL THEM HANNAH MCCOY DOESN'T SUCK.
I'm coming to the park with you tonight.

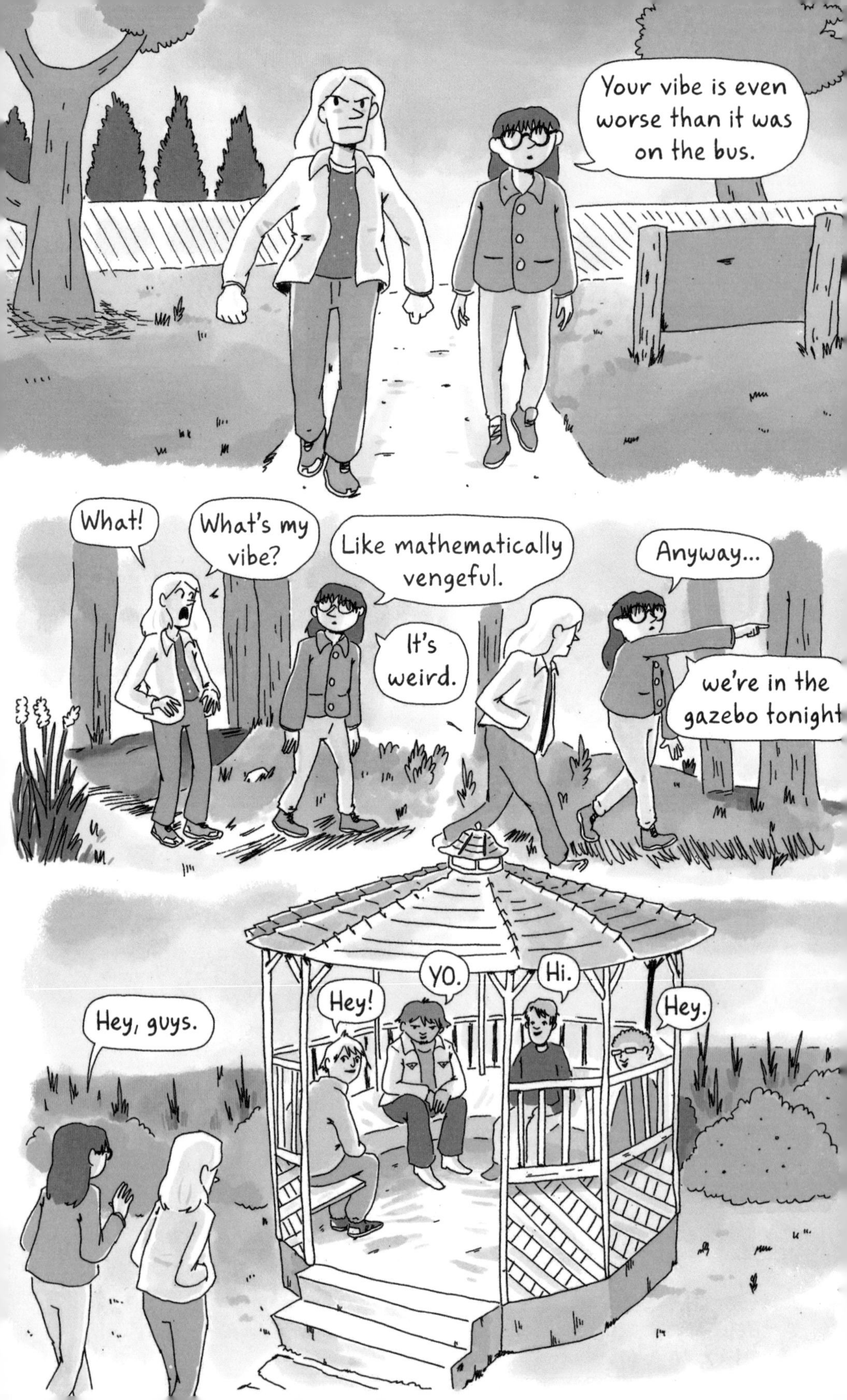
Your vibe is even worse than it was on the bus.
What!
What's my vibe?
Like mathematically vengeful.
It's weird.
Anyway...
we're in the gazebo tonight
Hey, guys.
Hey!
YO.
Hi.
Hey.

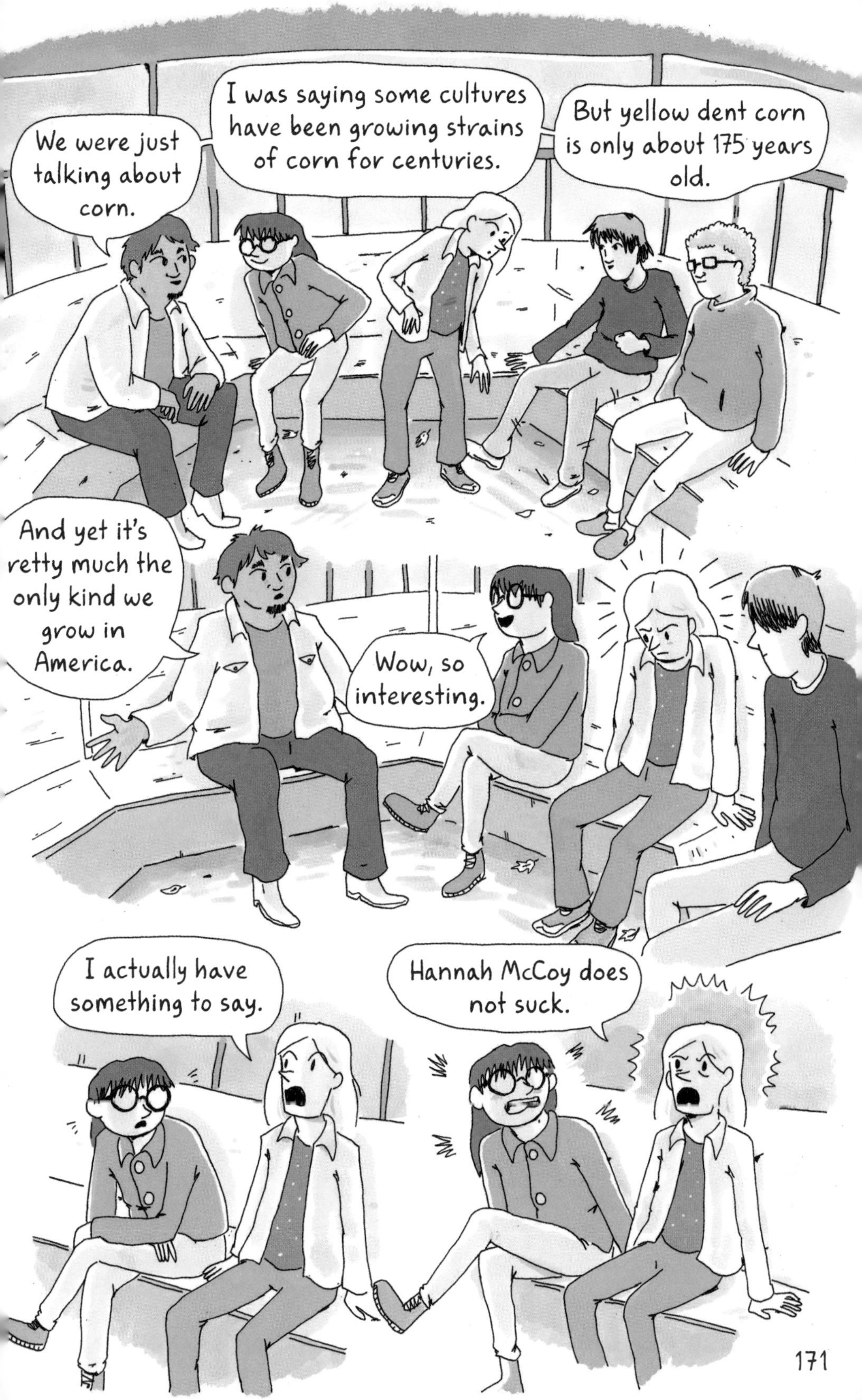
We were just talking about corn.
I was saying some cultures have been growing strains of corn for centuries.
But yellow dent corn is only about 175 years old.
And yet it's retty much the only kind we grow in America.
Wow, so interesting.
I actually have something to say.
Hannah McCoy does not suck.

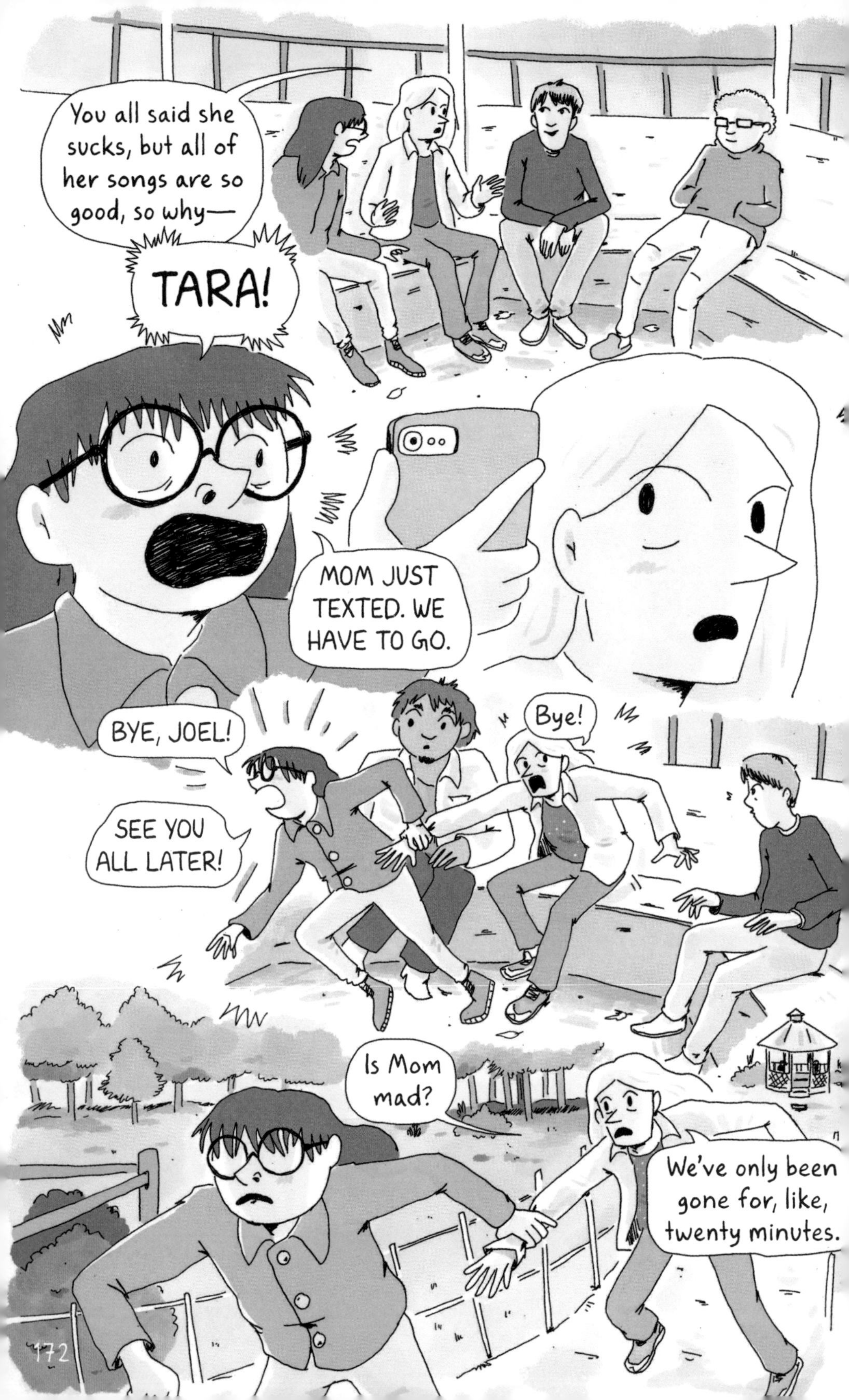
You all said she sucks, but all of her songs are so good, so why—
TARA!
MOM JUST TEXTED. WE HAVE TO GO.
BYE, JOEL!
SEE YOU ALL LATER!
Bye!
Is Mom mad?
We've only been gone for, like, twenty minutes.

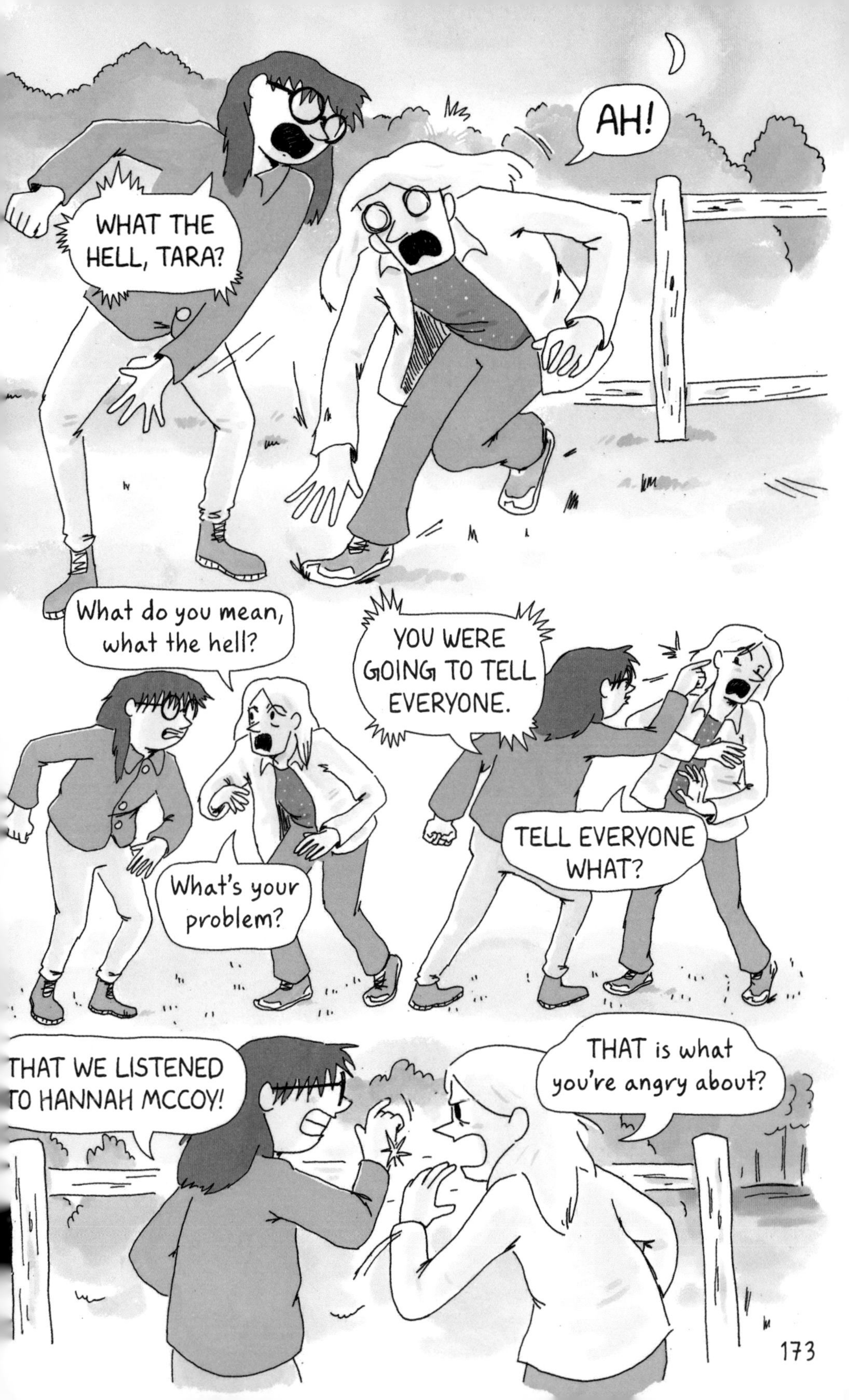
WHAT THE HELL, TARA?
AH!
What do you mean, what the hell?
What's your problem?
YOU WERE GOING TO TELL EVERYONE.
TELL EVERYONE WHAT?
THAT WE LISTENED TO HANNAH MCCOY!
THAT is what you're angry about?

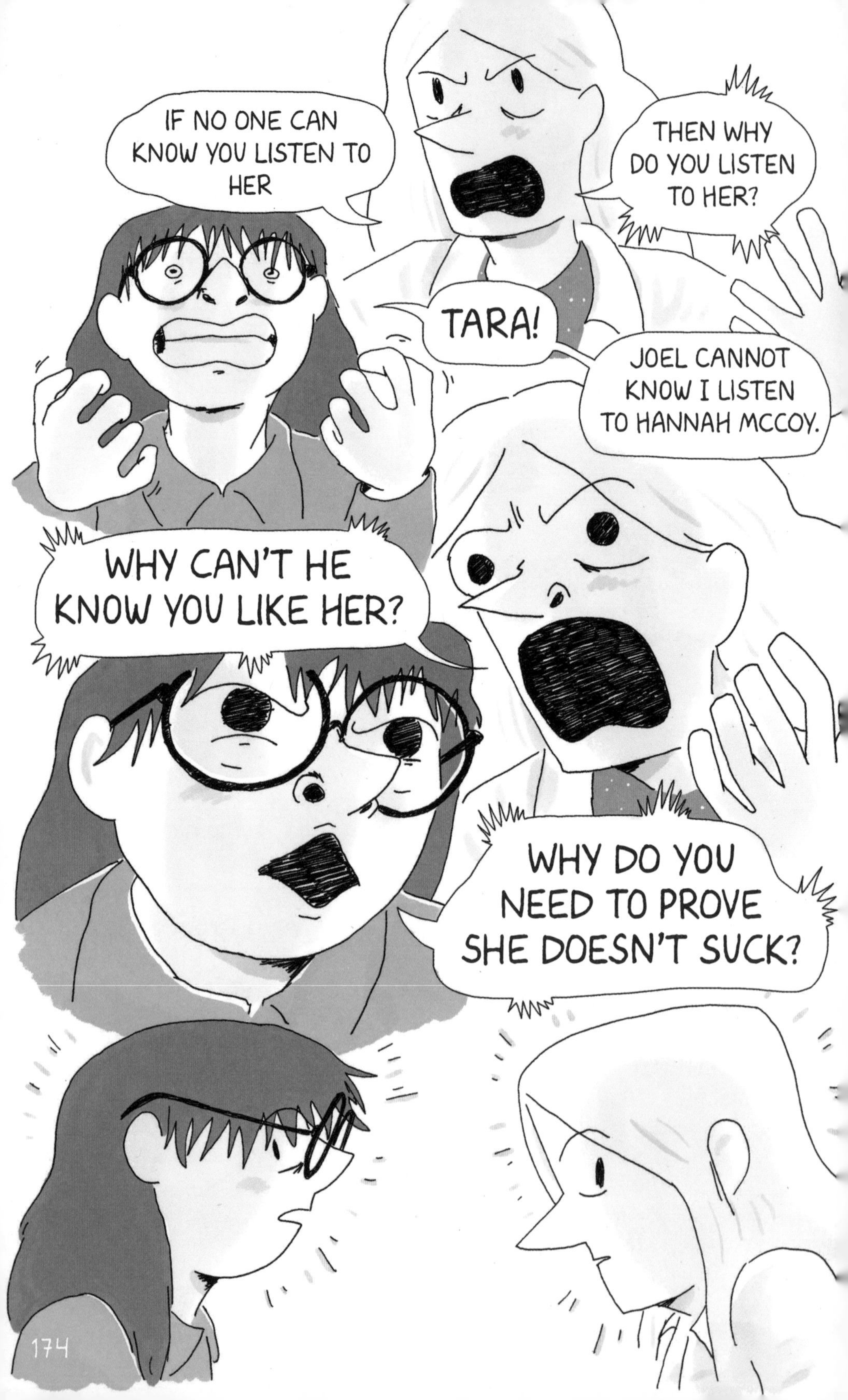
IF NO ONE CAN KNOW YOU LISTEN TO HER
THEN WHY DO YOU LISTEN TO HER?
TARA!
JOEL CANNOT KNOW I LISTEN TO HANNAH MCCOY.
WHY CAN'T HE KNOW YOU LIKE HER?
WHY DO YOU NEED TO PROVE SHE DOESN'T SUCK?

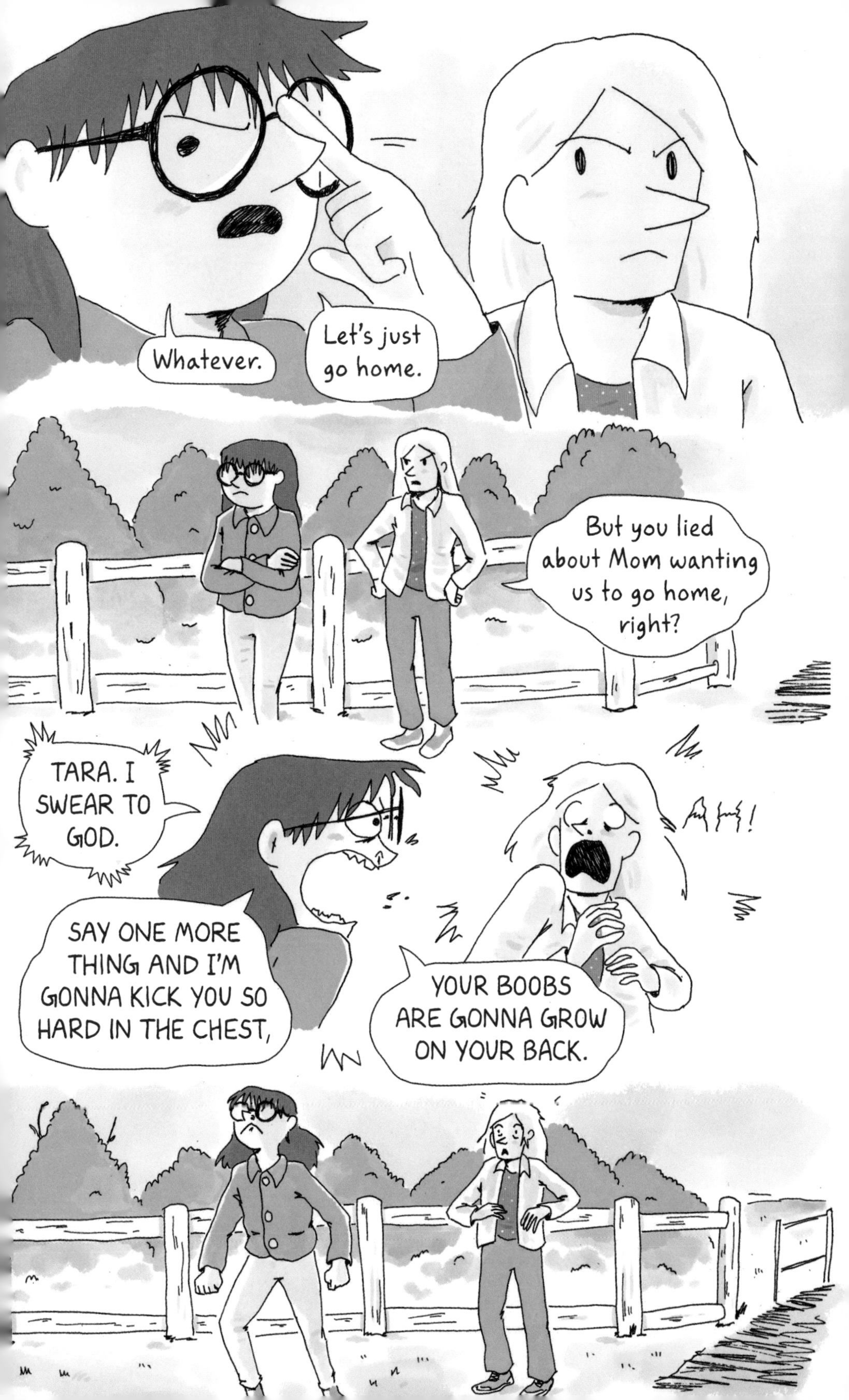
Whatever.
Let's just go home.
But you lied about Mom wanting us to go home, right?
TARA. I SWEAR TO GOD.
SAY ONE MORE THING AND I'M GONNA KICK YOU SO HARD IN THE CHEST,
YOUR BOOBS ARE GONNA GROW ON YOUR BACK.

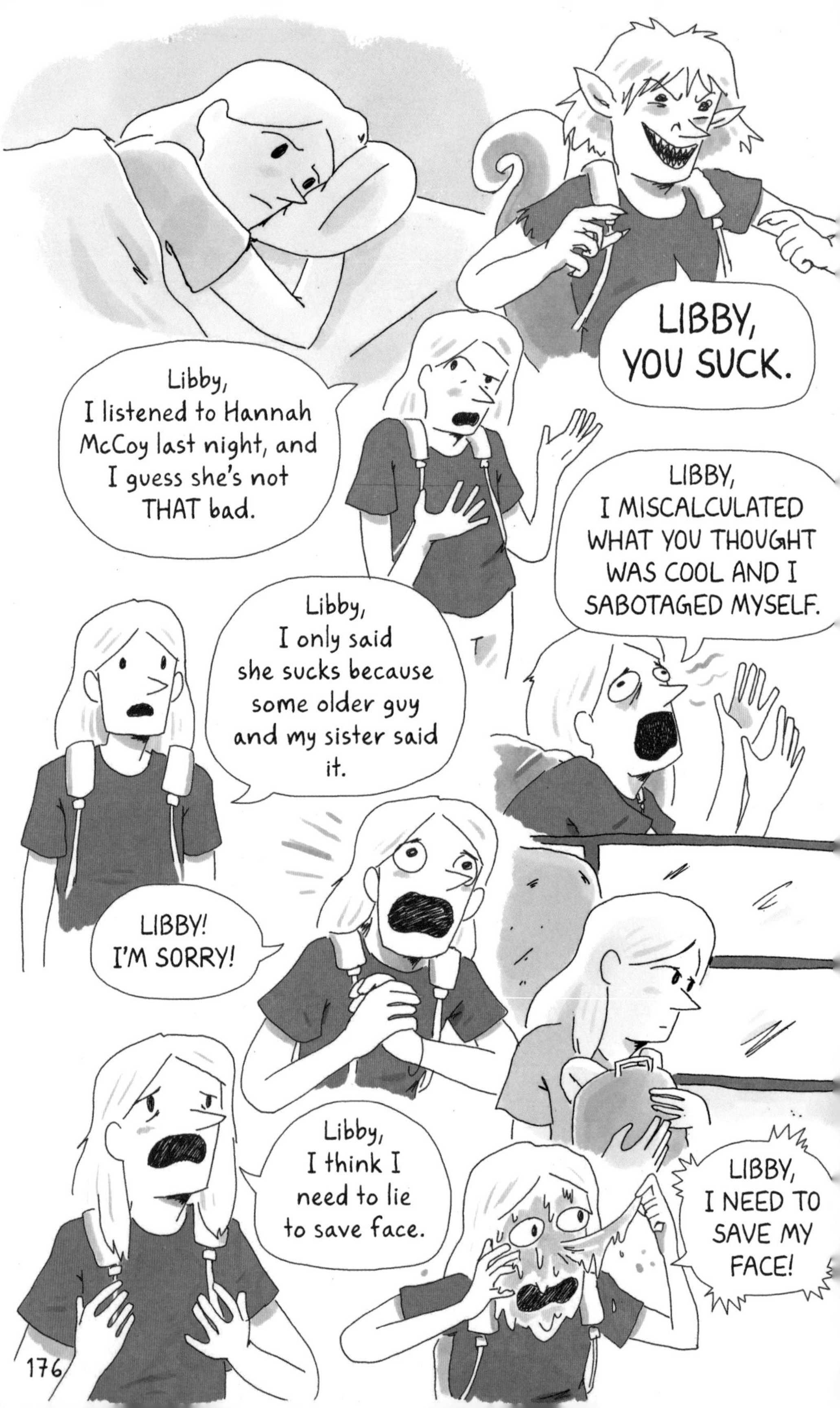
LIBBY, YOU SUCK.
Libby, I listened to Hannah McCoy last night, and I guess she's not THAT bad.
LIBBY, I MISCALCULATED WHAT YOU THOUGHT WAS COOL AND I SABOTAGED MYSELF.
Libby, I only said she sucks because some older guy and my sister said it.
LIBBY! I'M SORRY!
Libby, I think I need to lie to save face.
LIBBY, I NEED TO SAVE MY FACE!

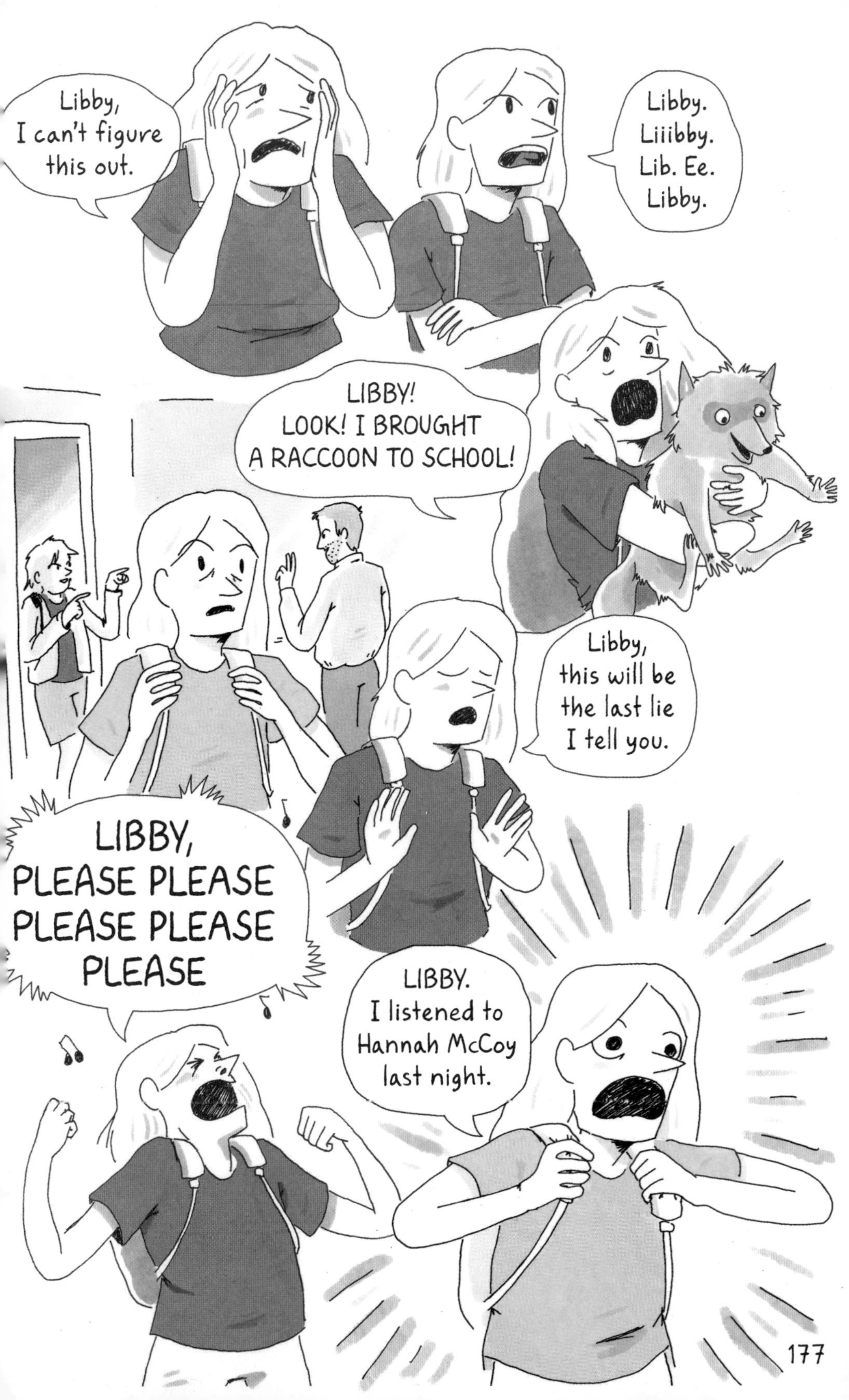
Libby,
I can't figure
this out.
Libby.
Liiibby.
Lib. Ee.
Libby.
LIBBY!
LOOK! I BROUGHT
A RACCOON TO SCHOOL!
Libby,
this will be
the last lie
I tell you.
LIBBY,
PLEASE PLEASE
PLEASE PLEASE
PLEASE
LIBBY.
I listened to
Hannah McCoy
last night.

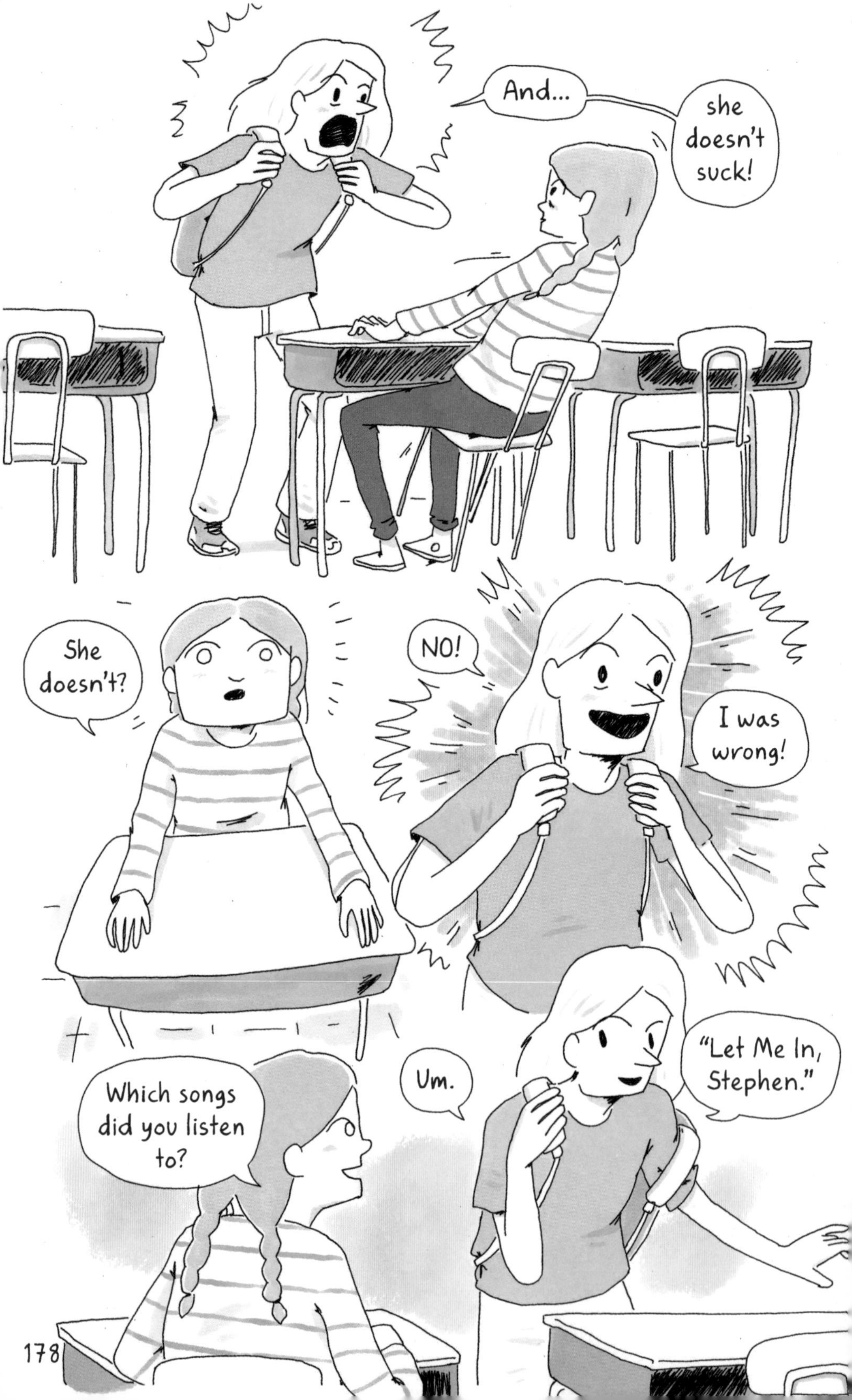
And...
she doesn't suck!
She doesn't?
NO!
I was wrong!
Which songs did you listen to?
Um.
"Let Me In, Stephen."

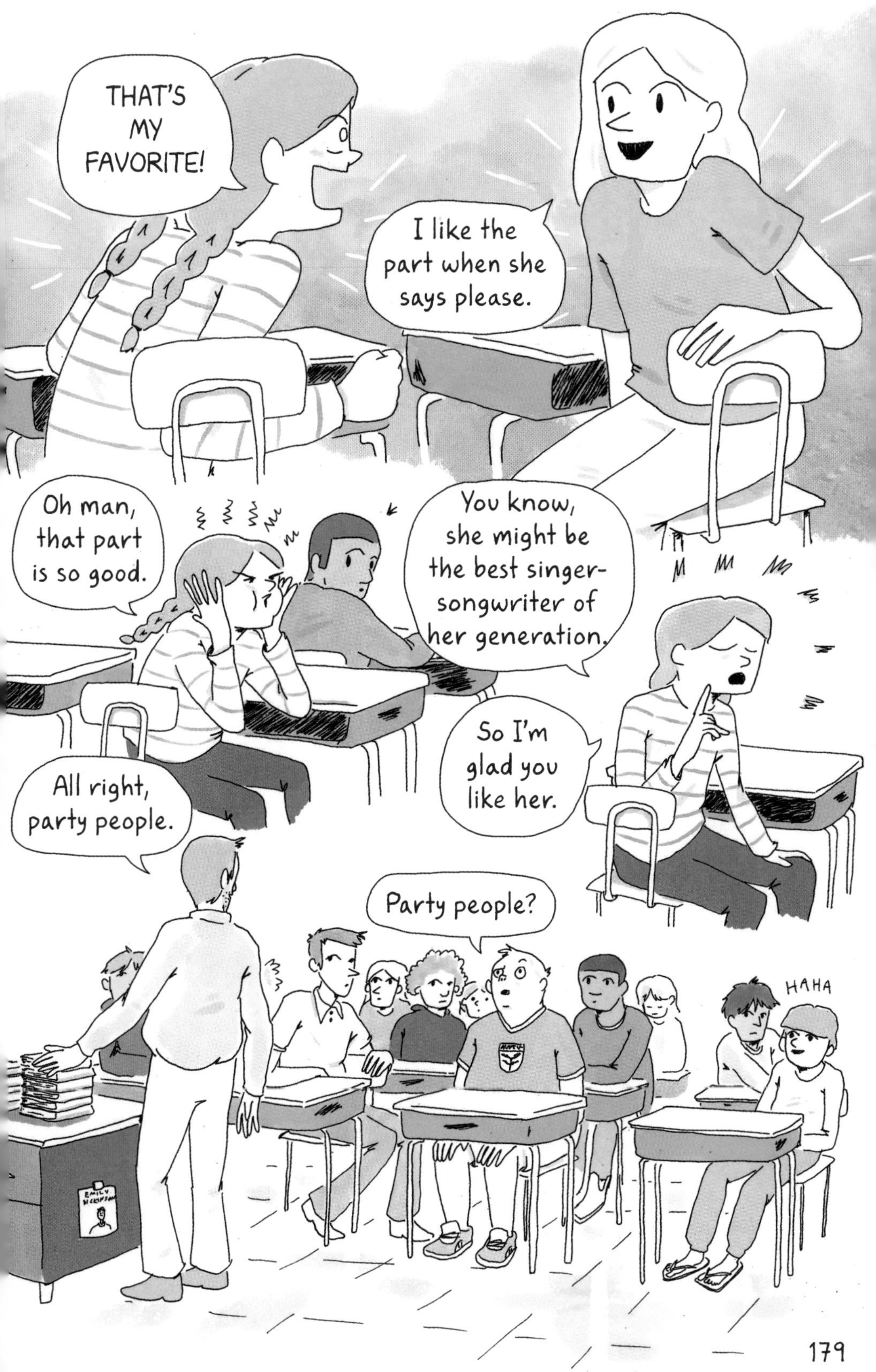
THAT'S MY FAVORITE!
I like the part when she says please.
Oh man, that part is so good.
You know, she might be the best singer-songwriter of her generation.
So I'm glad you like her.
All right, party people.
Party people?
HAHA

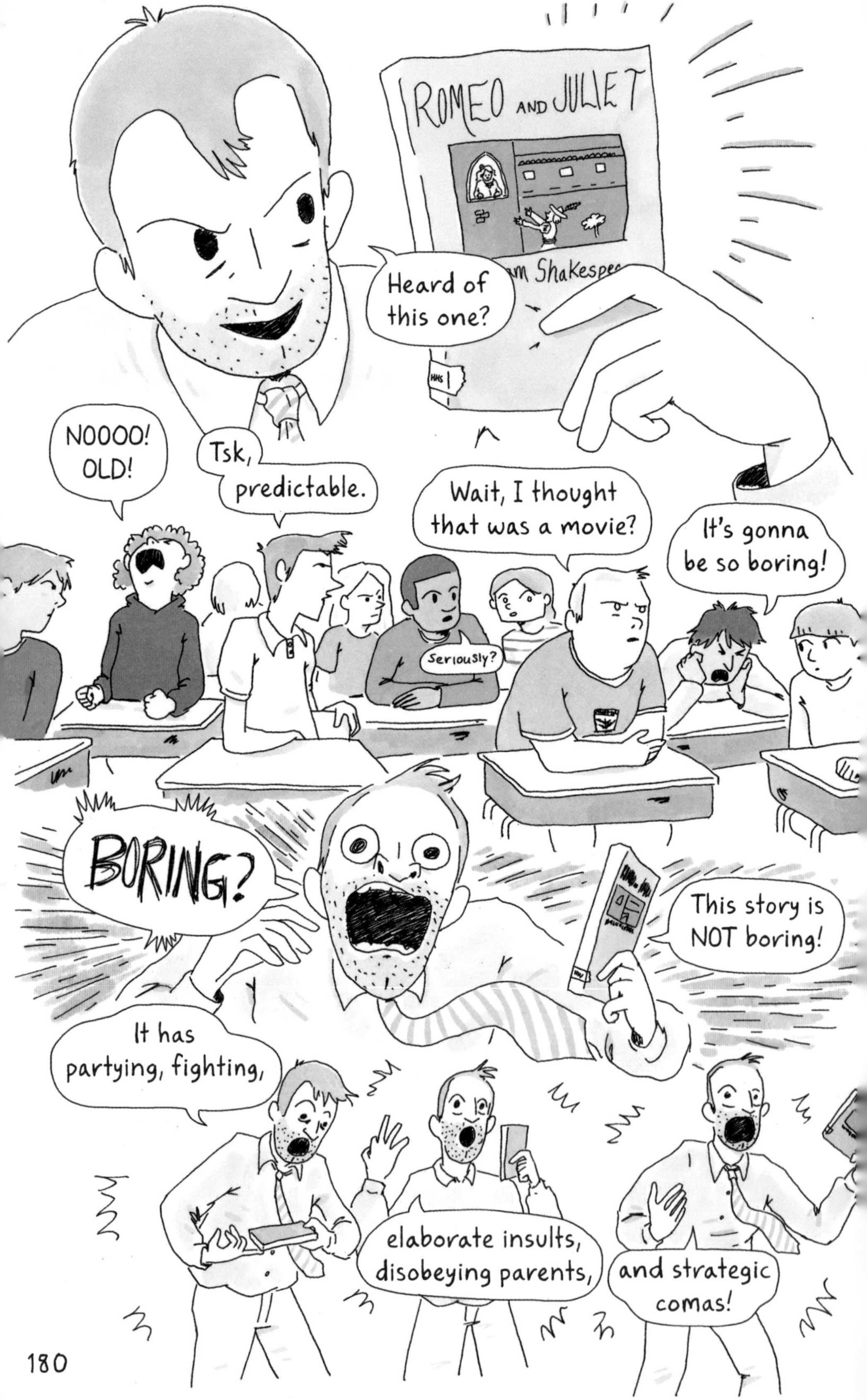
ROMEO AND JULIET
...am Shakespe...
Heard of this one?
HHS
NOOOO! OLD!
Tsk, predictable.
Wait, I thought that was a movie?
It's gonna be so boring!
Seriously?
BORING?
This story is NOT boring!
It has partying, fighting,
elaborate insults, disobeying parents,
and strategic comas!

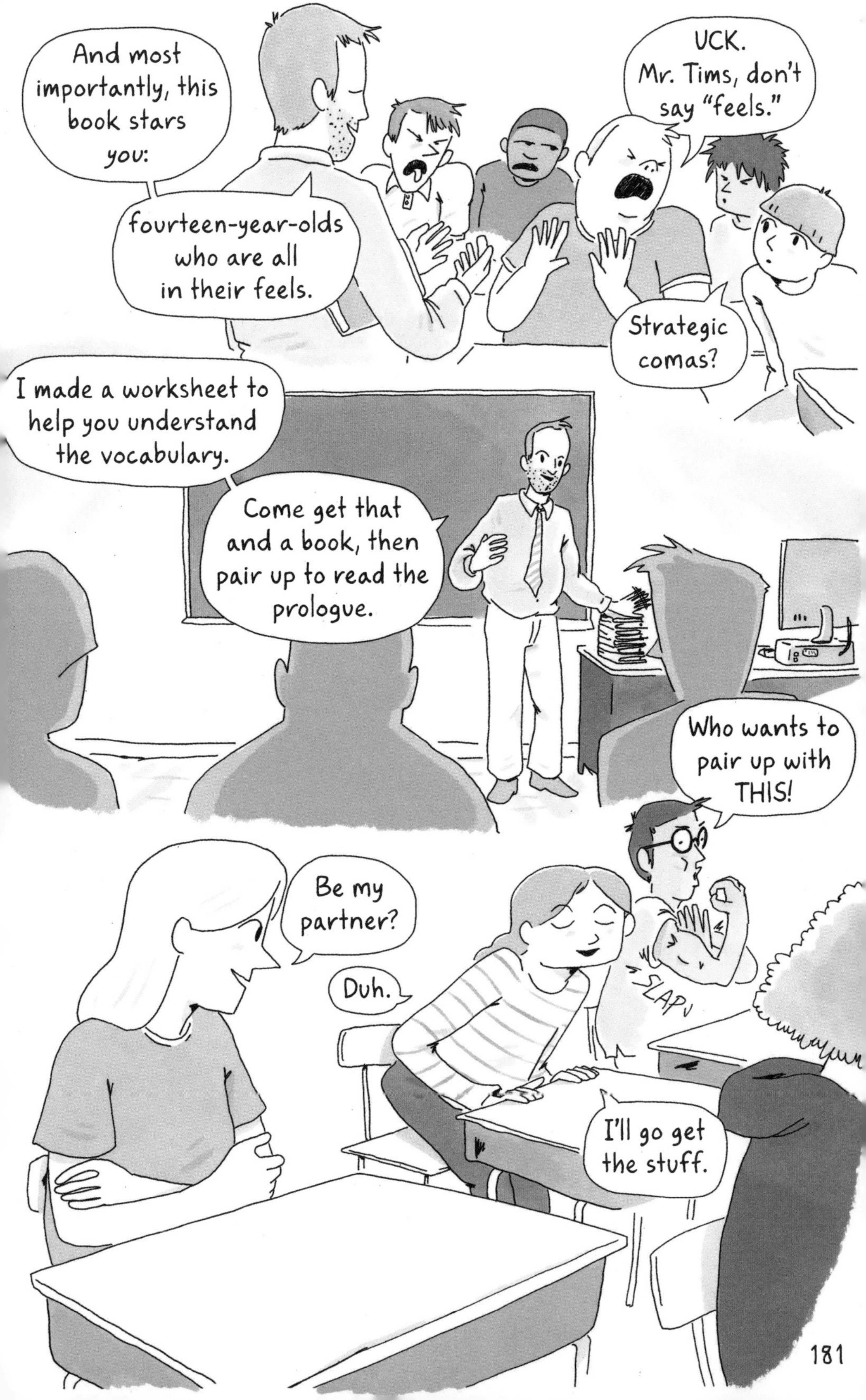
And most importantly, this book stars you:
fourteen-year-olds who are all in their feels.
UCK. Mr. Tims, don't say "feels."
Strategic comas?
I made a worksheet to help you understand the vocabulary.
Come get that and a book, then pair up to read the prologue.
Who wants to pair up with THIS!
Be my partner?
Duh.
SLAP
I'll go get the stuff.

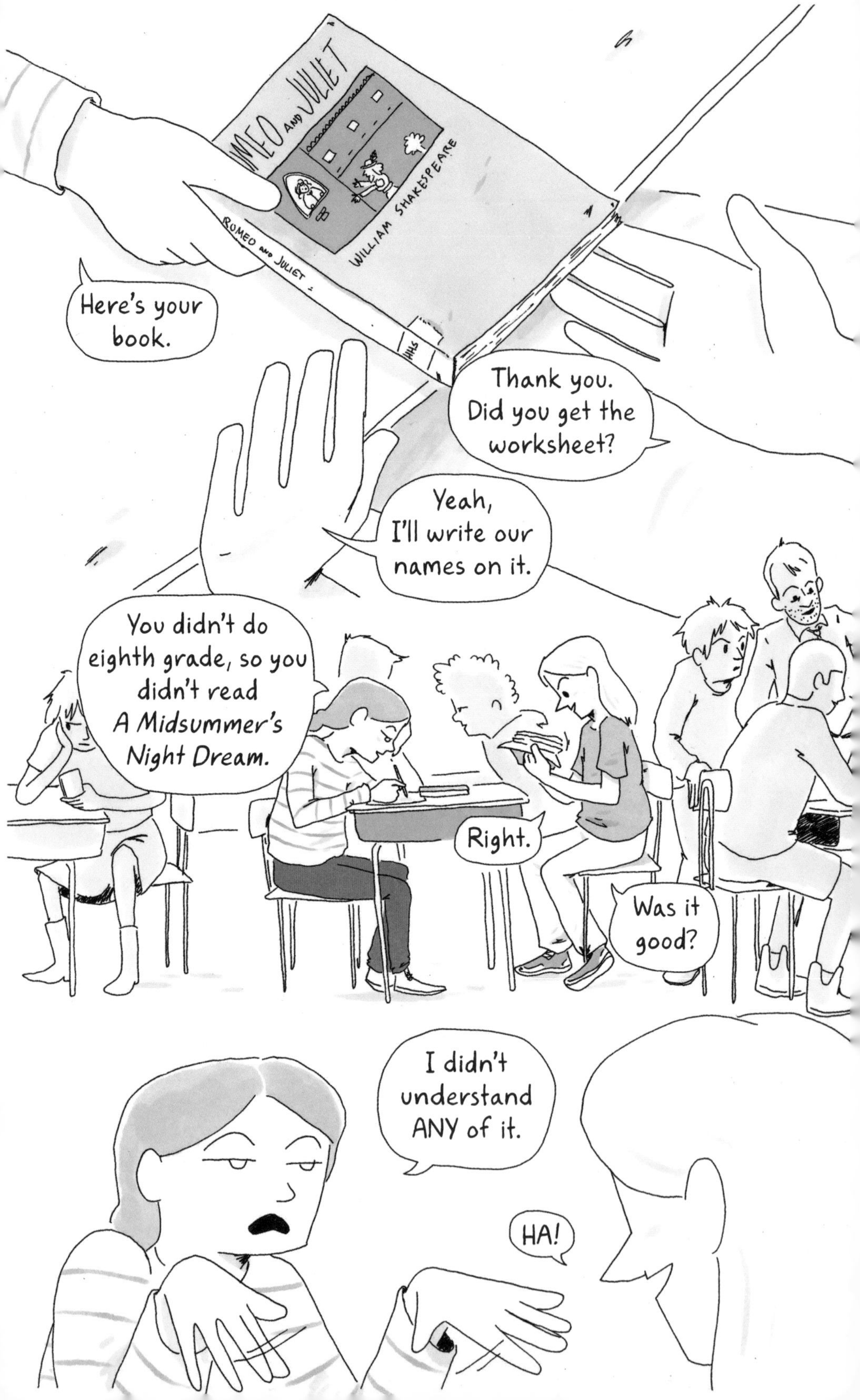
ROMEO AND JULIET
WILLIAM SHAKESPEARE
Here's your book.
Thank you. Did you get the worksheet?
Yeah, I'll write our names on it.
You didn't do eighth grade, so you didn't read *A Midsummer's Night Dream.*
Right.
Was it good?
I didn't understand ANY of it.
HA!

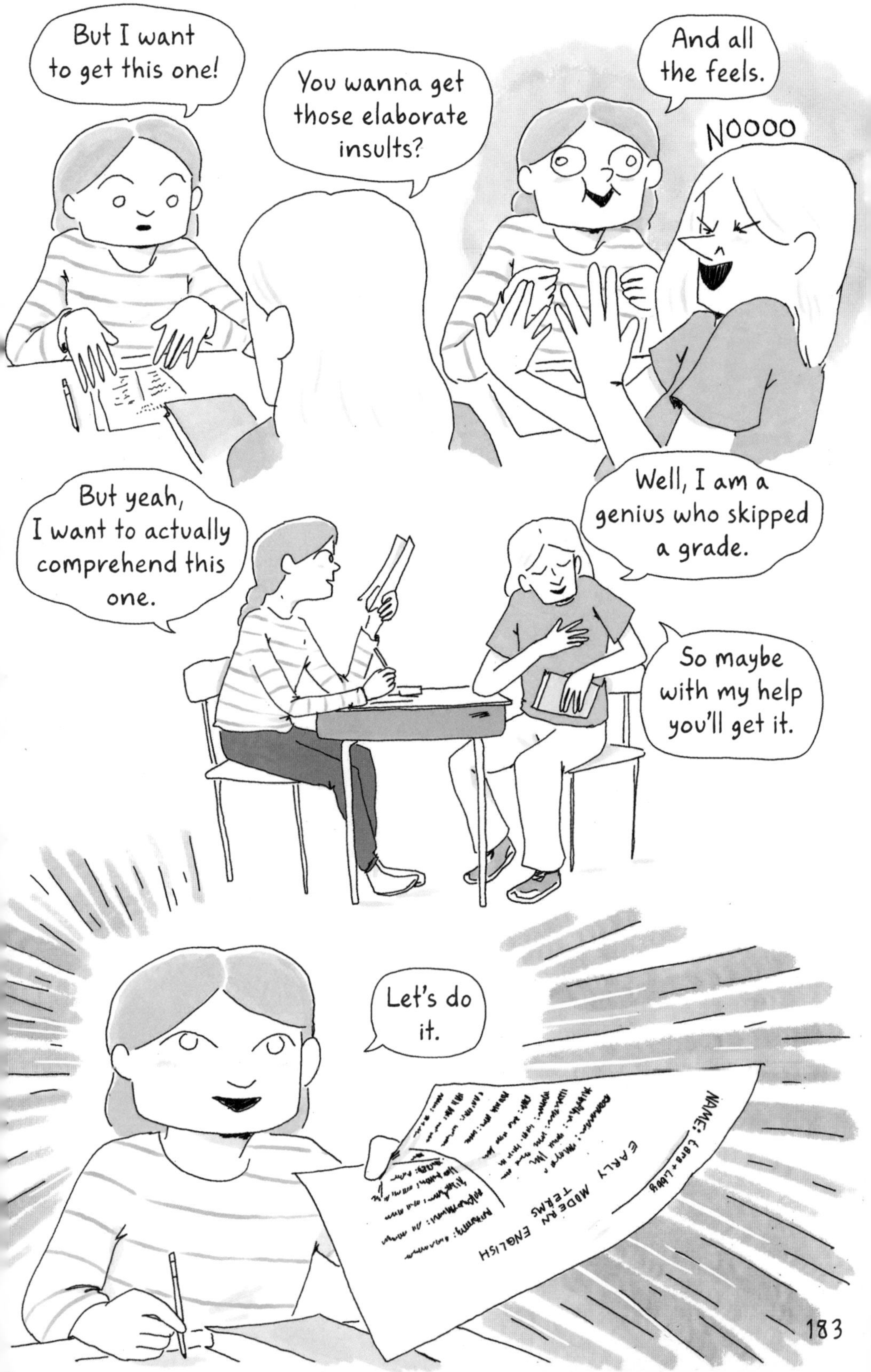
But I want to get this one!
You wanna get those elaborate insults?
And all the feels.
NOOOO
But yeah, I want to actually comprehend this one.
Well, I am a genius who skipped a grade.
So maybe with my help you'll get it.
Let's do it.

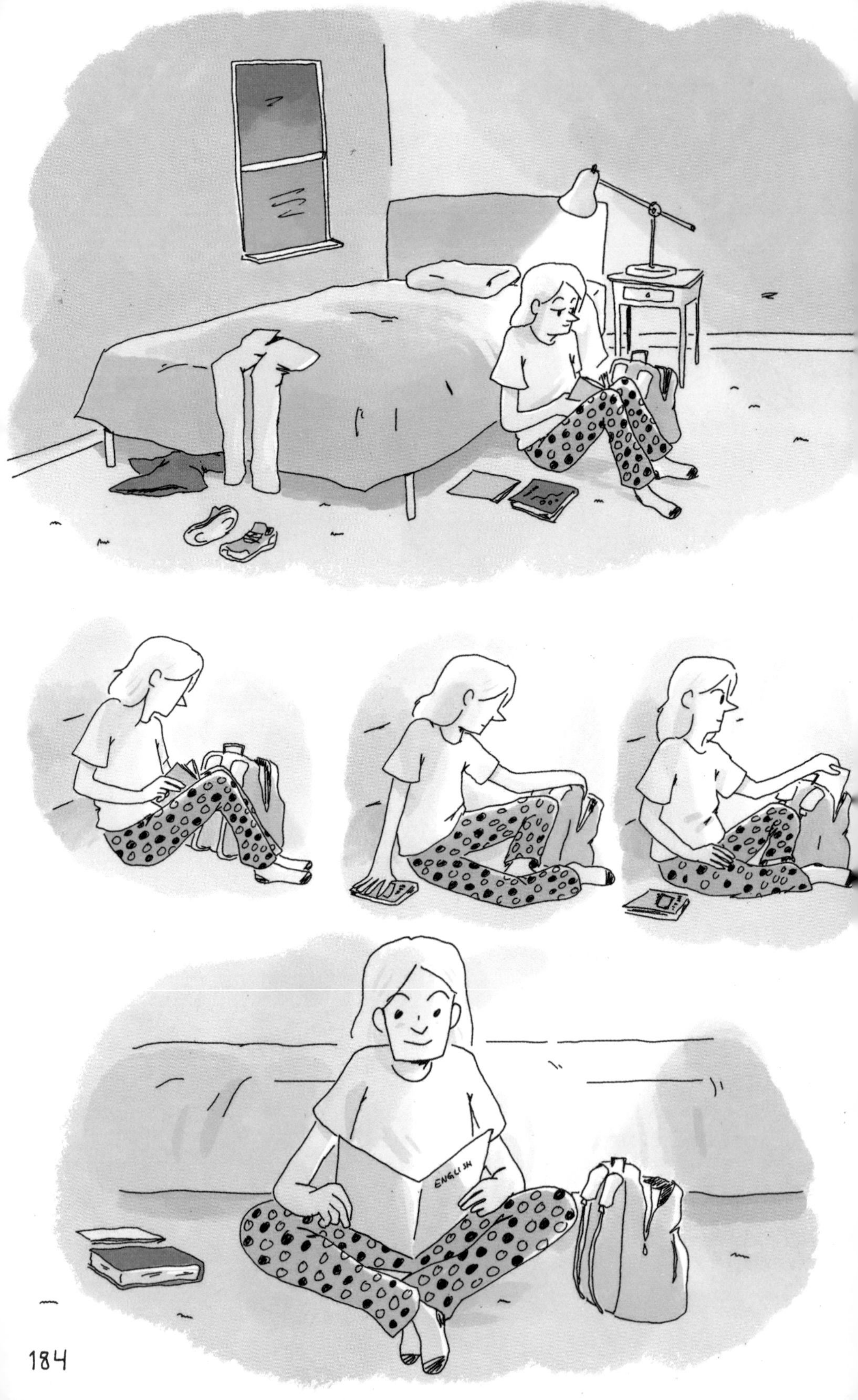
ENGLISH

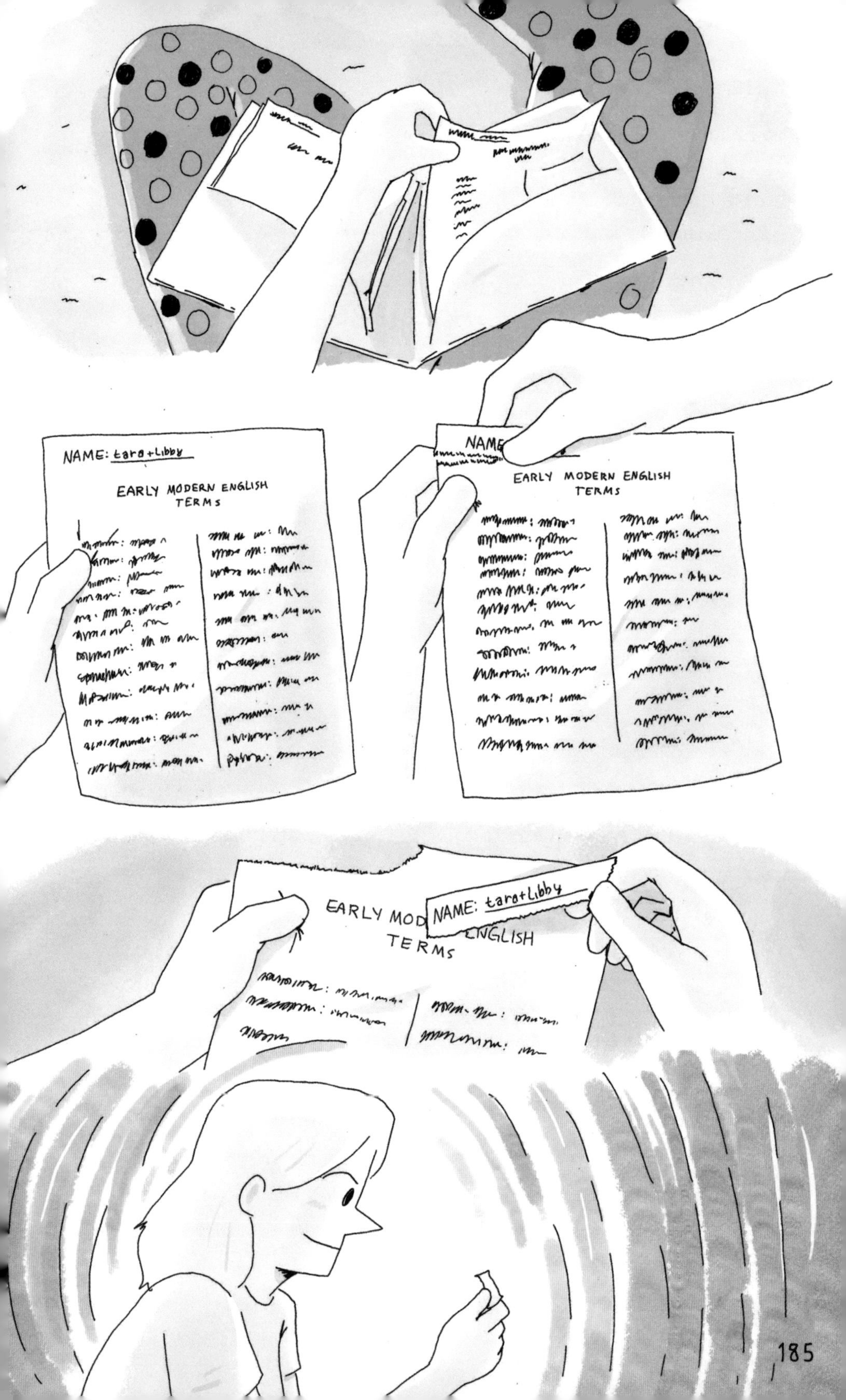
NAME: tara+Libby
EARLY MODERN ENGLISH TERMS
NAME
EARLY MODERN ENGLISH TERMS
EARLY MODERN ENGLISH TERMS
NAME: tara+Libby

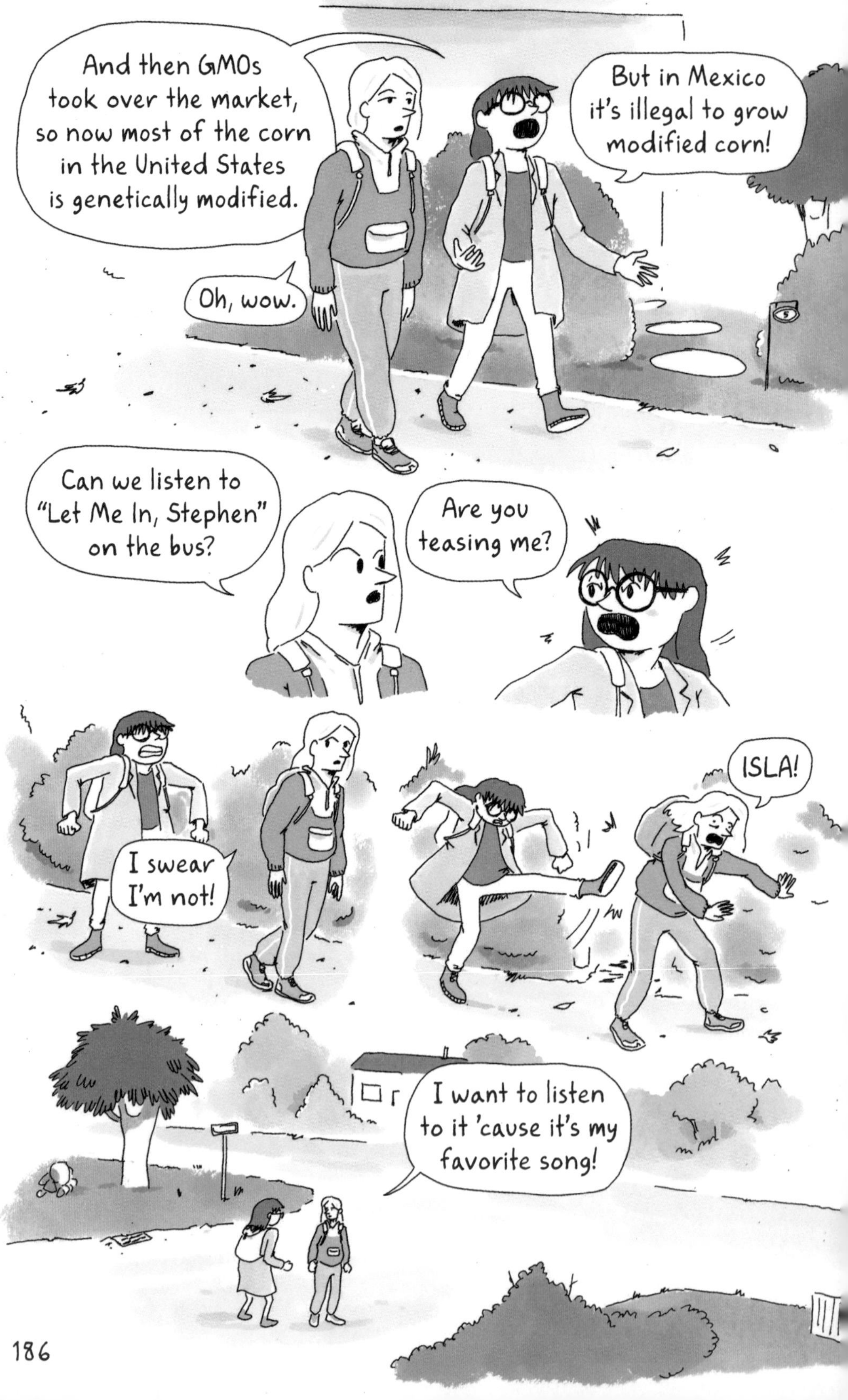
And then GMOs took over the market, so now most of the corn in the United States is genetically modified.
But in Mexico it's illegal to grow modified corn!
Oh, wow.
Can we listen to "Let Me In, Stephen" on the bus?
Are you teasing me?
I swear I'm not!
ISLA!
I want to listen to it 'cause it's my favorite song!

Now school is like listening to
a song on repeat.

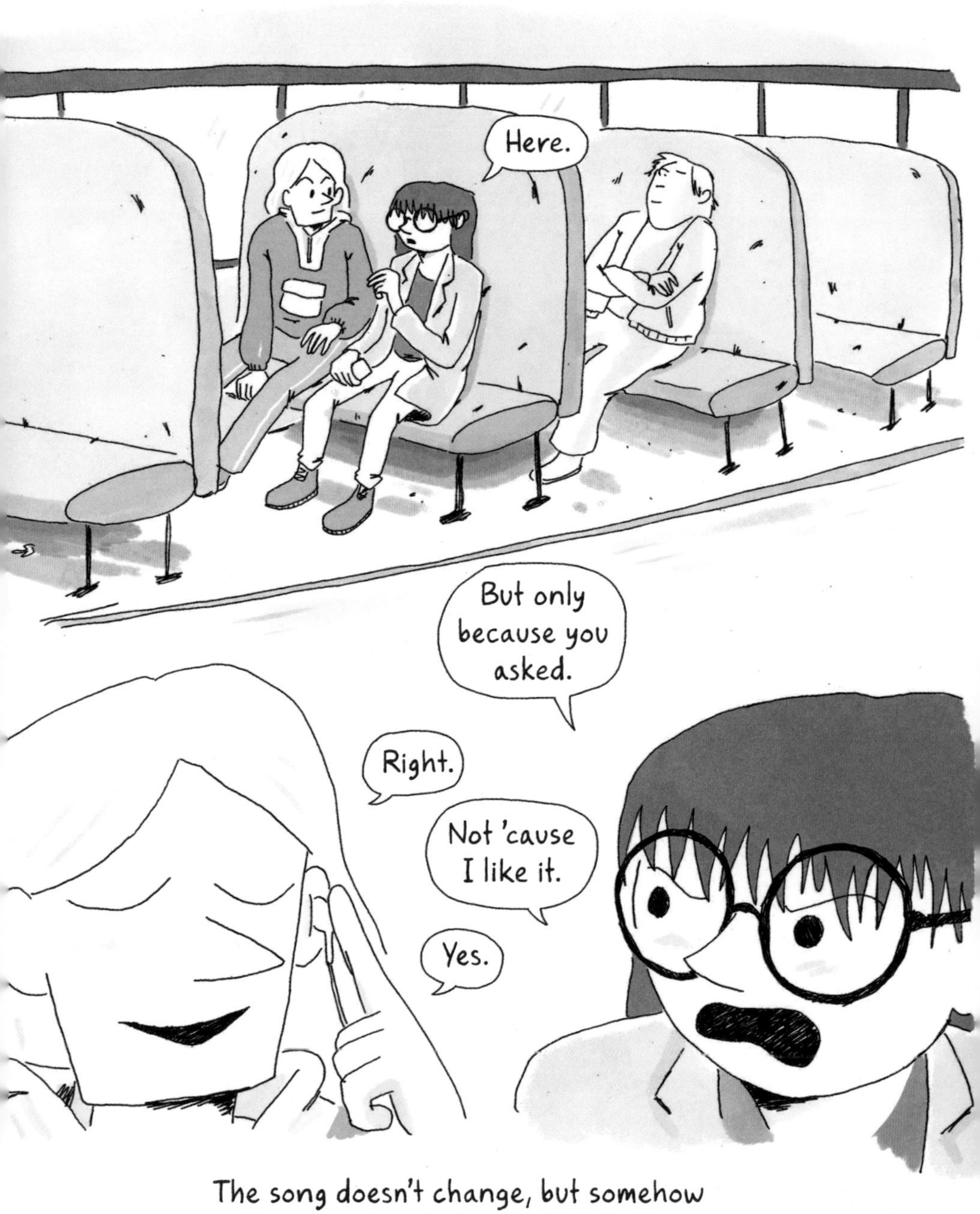
Here.
But only because you asked.
Right.
Not 'cause I like it.
Yes.

The song doesn't change, but somehow
every time you listen to it, it feels a
little different.

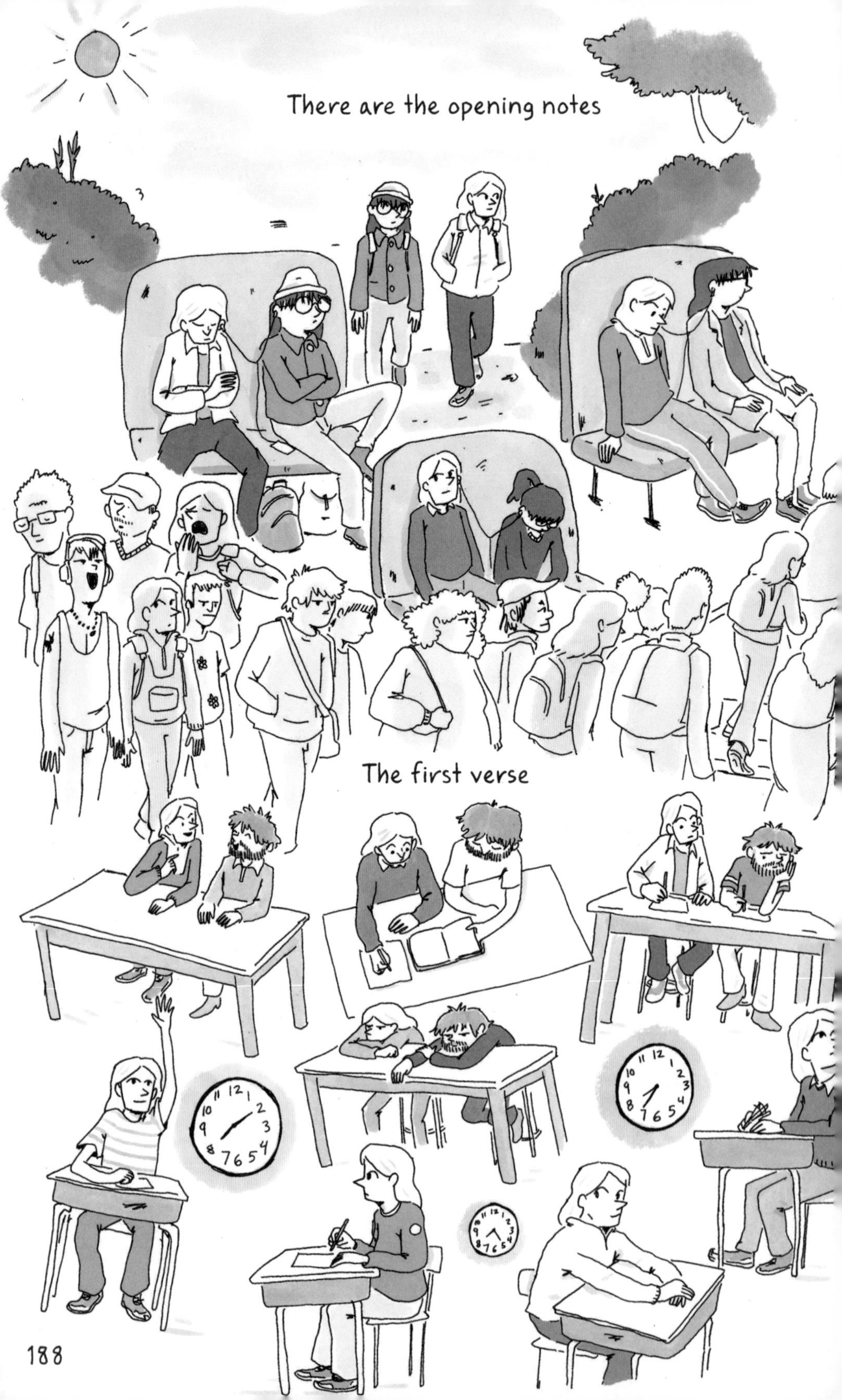
There are the opening notes
The first verse

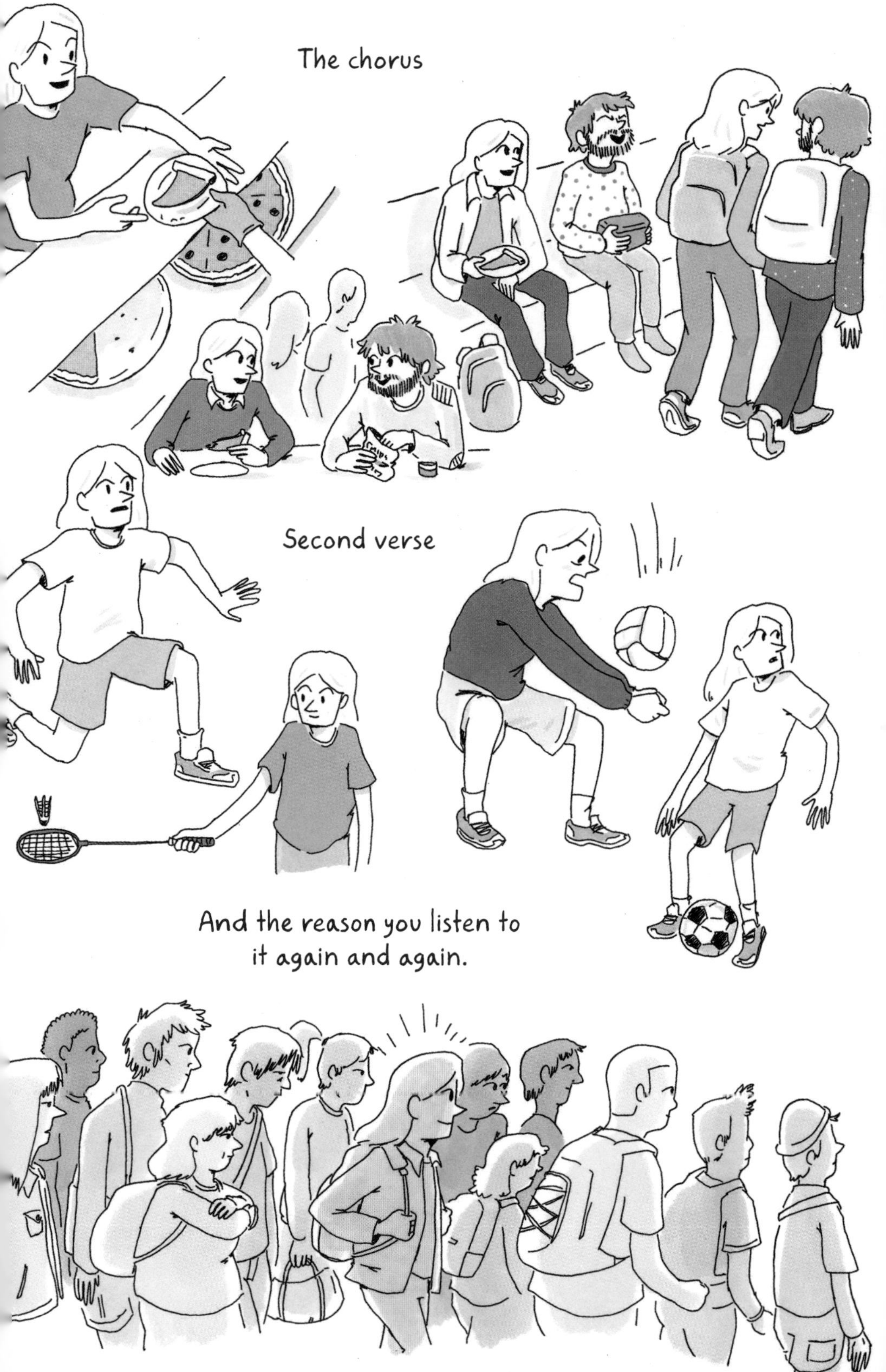
The chorus
Second verse
And the reason you listen to
it again and again.

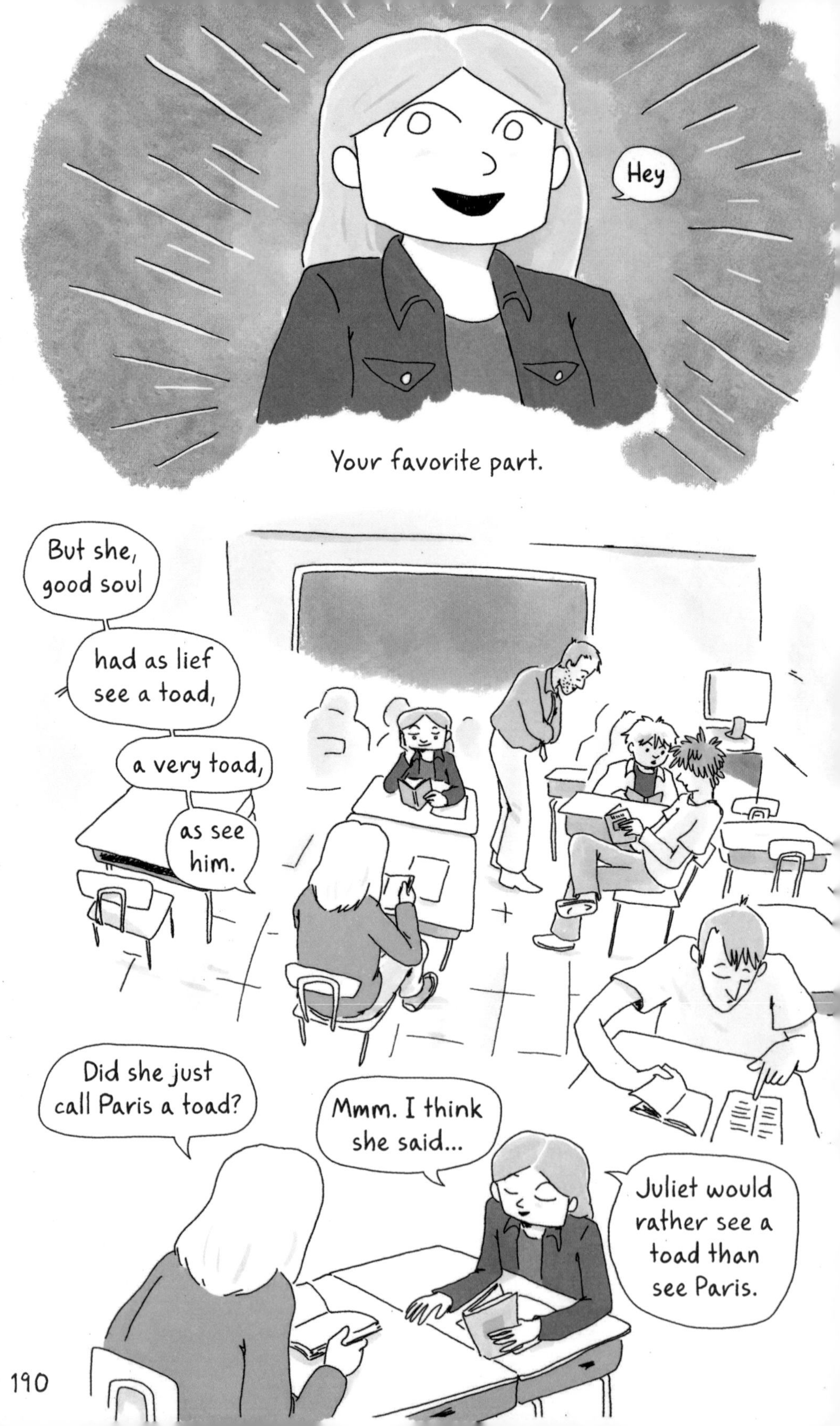
Hey
Your favorite part.
But she, good soul
had as lief see a toad,
a very toad,
as see him.
Did she just call Paris a toad?
Mmm. I think she said...
Juliet would rather see a toad than see Paris.

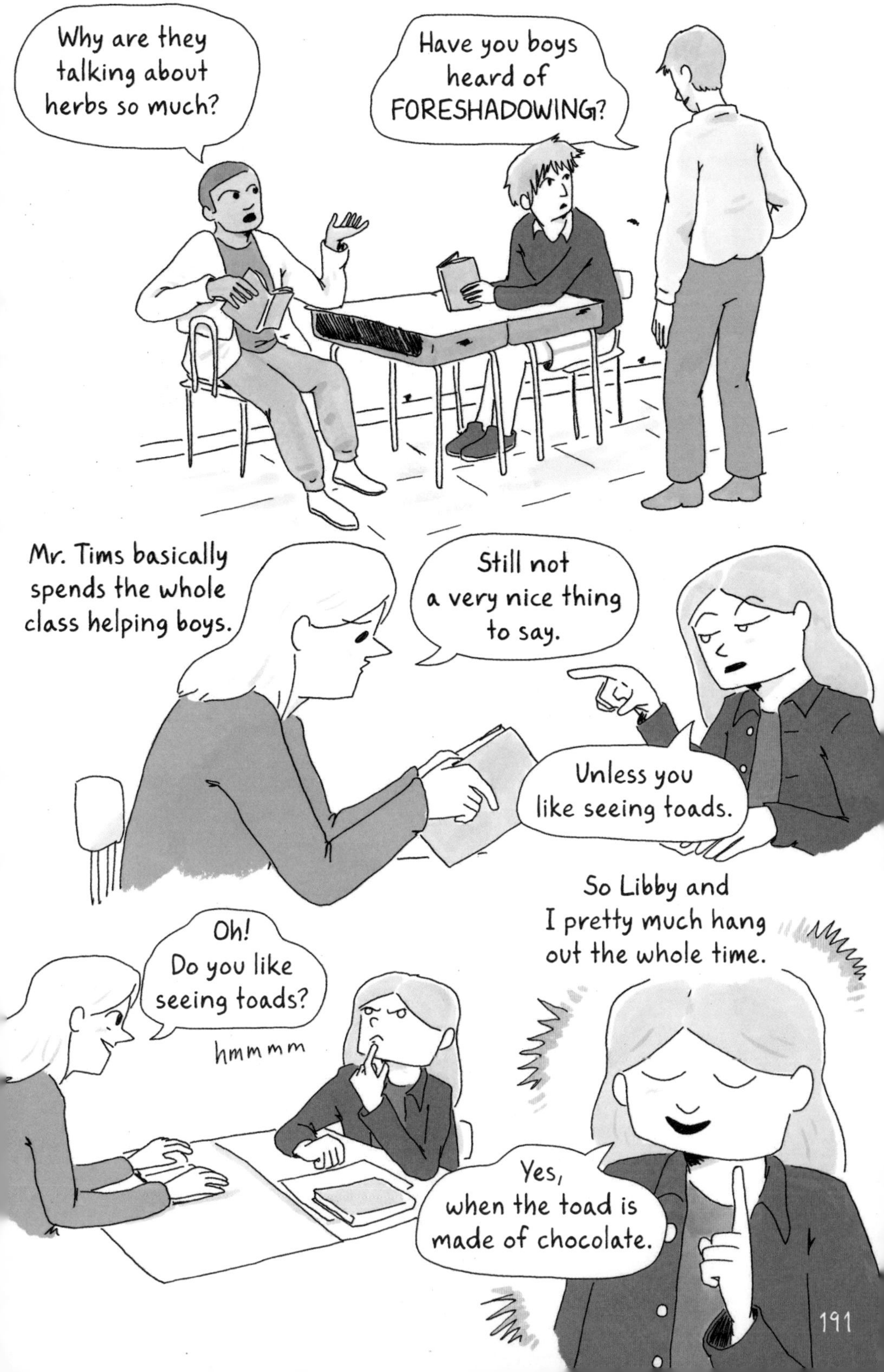
Why are they talking about herbs so much?
Have you boys heard of FORESHADOWING?
Mr. Tims basically spends the whole class helping boys.
Still not a very nice thing to say.
Unless you like seeing toads.
Oh! Do you like seeing toads?
hmmmm
So Libby and I pretty much hang out the whole time.
Yes, when the toad is made of chocolate.

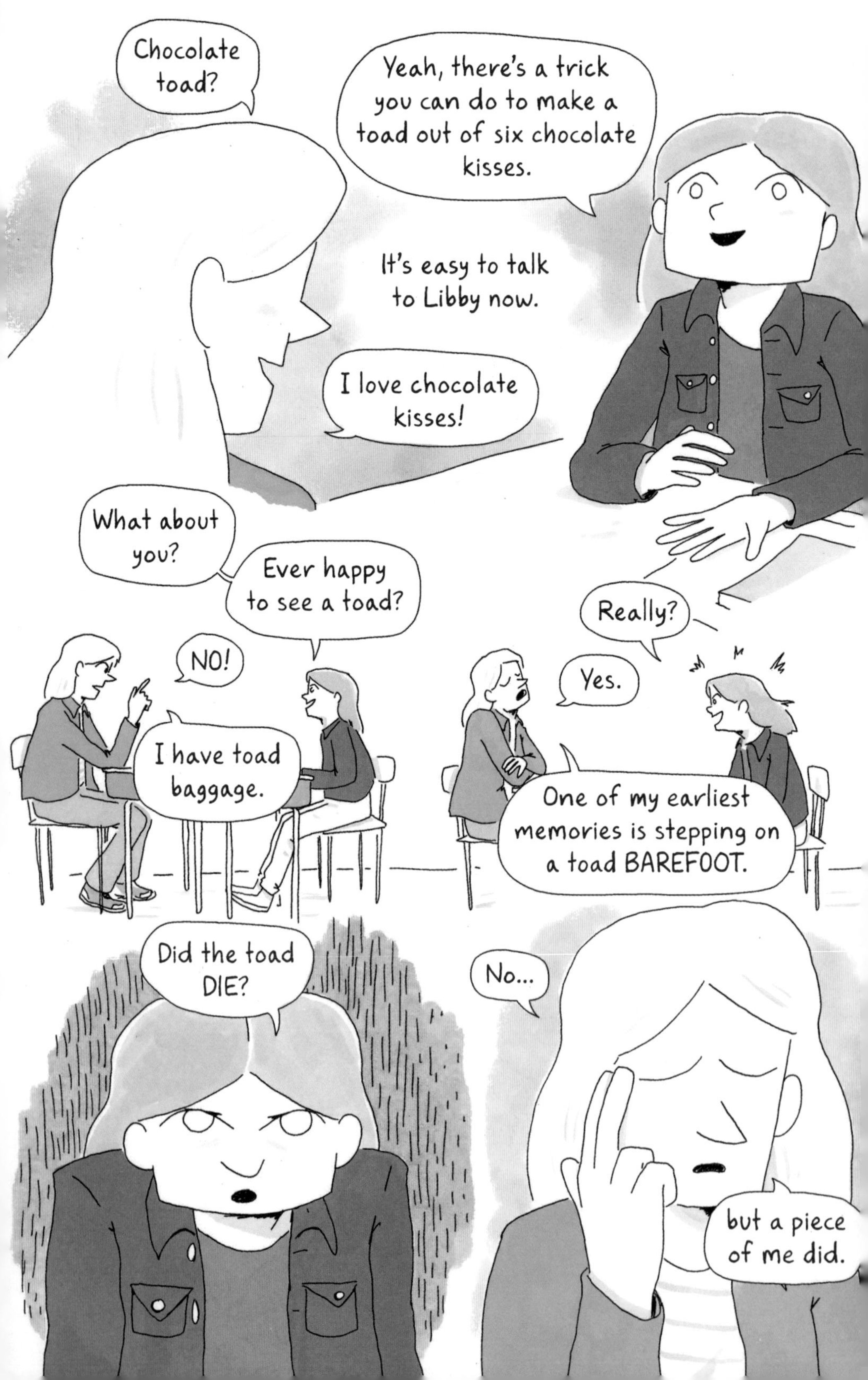
Chocolate toad?
Yeah, there's a trick you can do to make a toad out of six chocolate kisses.
It's easy to talk to Libby now.
I love chocolate kisses!
What about you?
Ever happy to see a toad?
NO!
I have toad baggage.
Really?
Yes.
One of my earliest memories is stepping on a toad BAREFOOT.
Did the toad DIE?
No...
but a piece of me did.

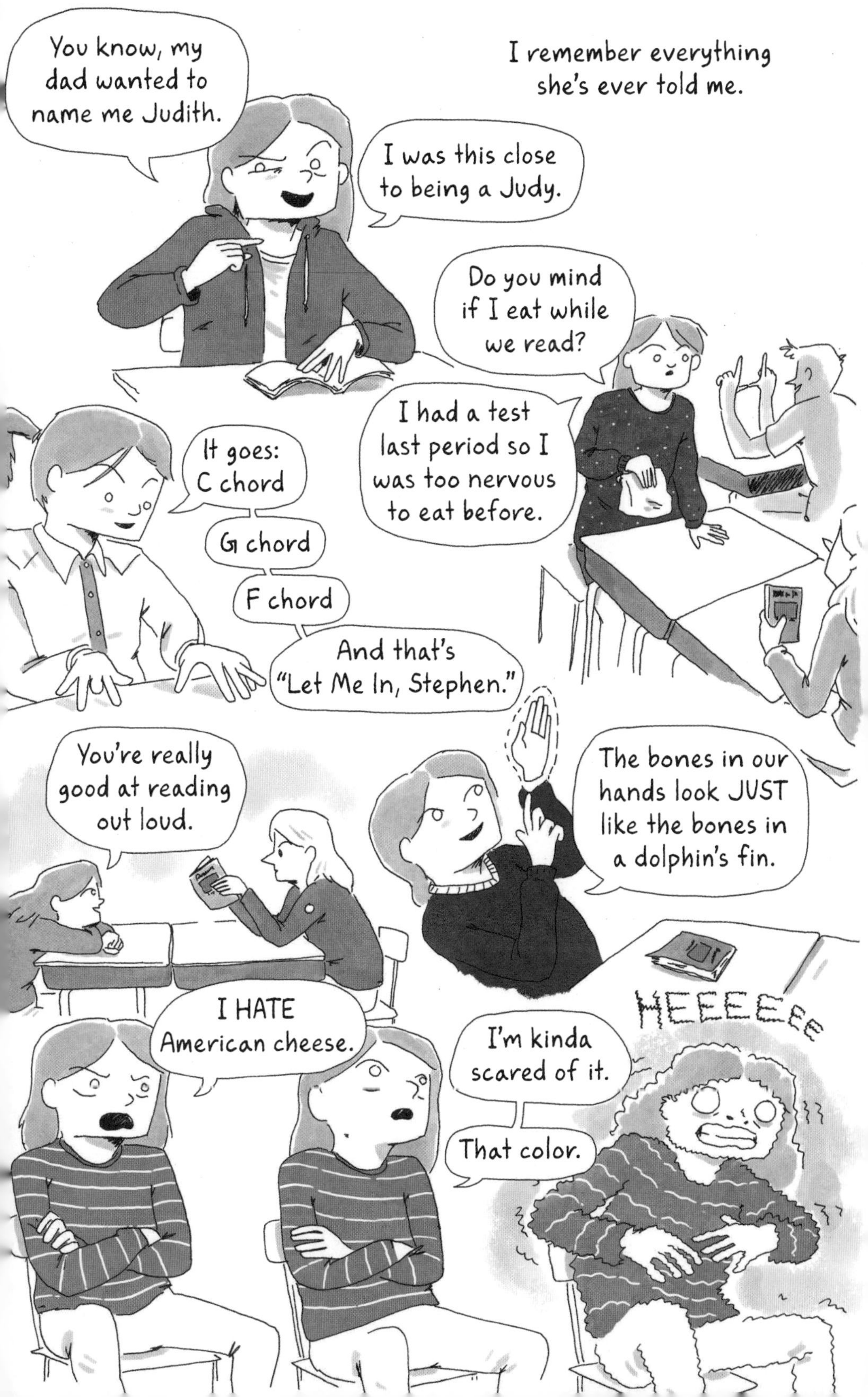
You know, my dad wanted to name me Judith.
I remember everything she's ever told me.
I was this close to being a Judy.
Do you mind if I eat while we read?
I had a test last period so I was too nervous to eat before.
It goes: C chord
G chord
F chord
And that's "Let Me In, Stephen."
You're really good at reading out loud.
The bones in our hands look JUST like the bones in a dolphin's fin.
I HATE American cheese.
I'm kinda scared of it.
That color.
HEEEEEE

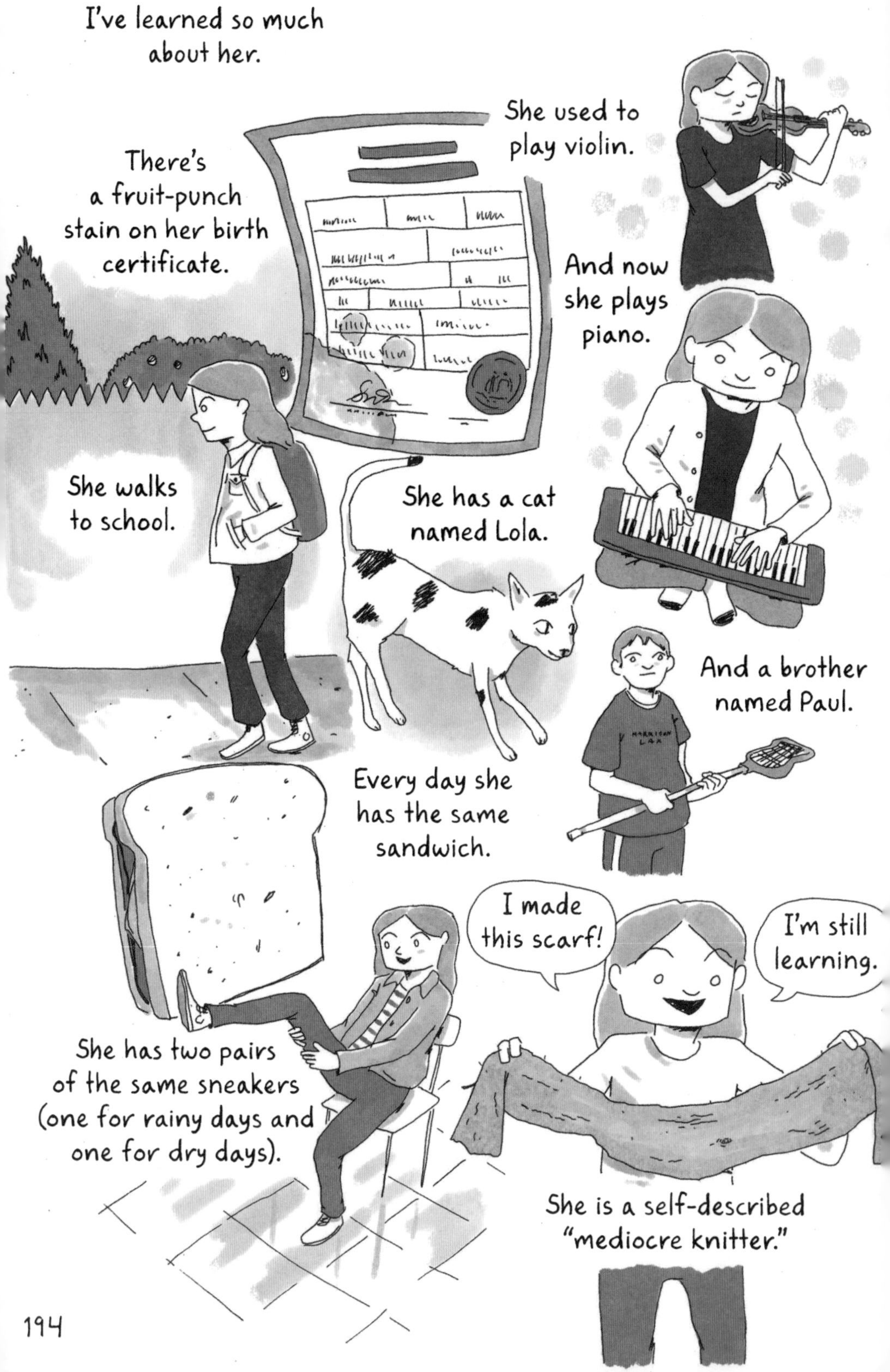
I've learned so much about her.
There's a fruit-punch stain on her birth certificate.
She used to play violin.
And now she plays piano.
She walks to school.
She has a cat named Lola.
And a brother named Paul.
Every day she has the same sandwich.
She has two pairs of the same sneakers (one for rainy days and one for dry days).
I made this scarf!
I'm still learning.
She is a self-described "mediocre knitter."

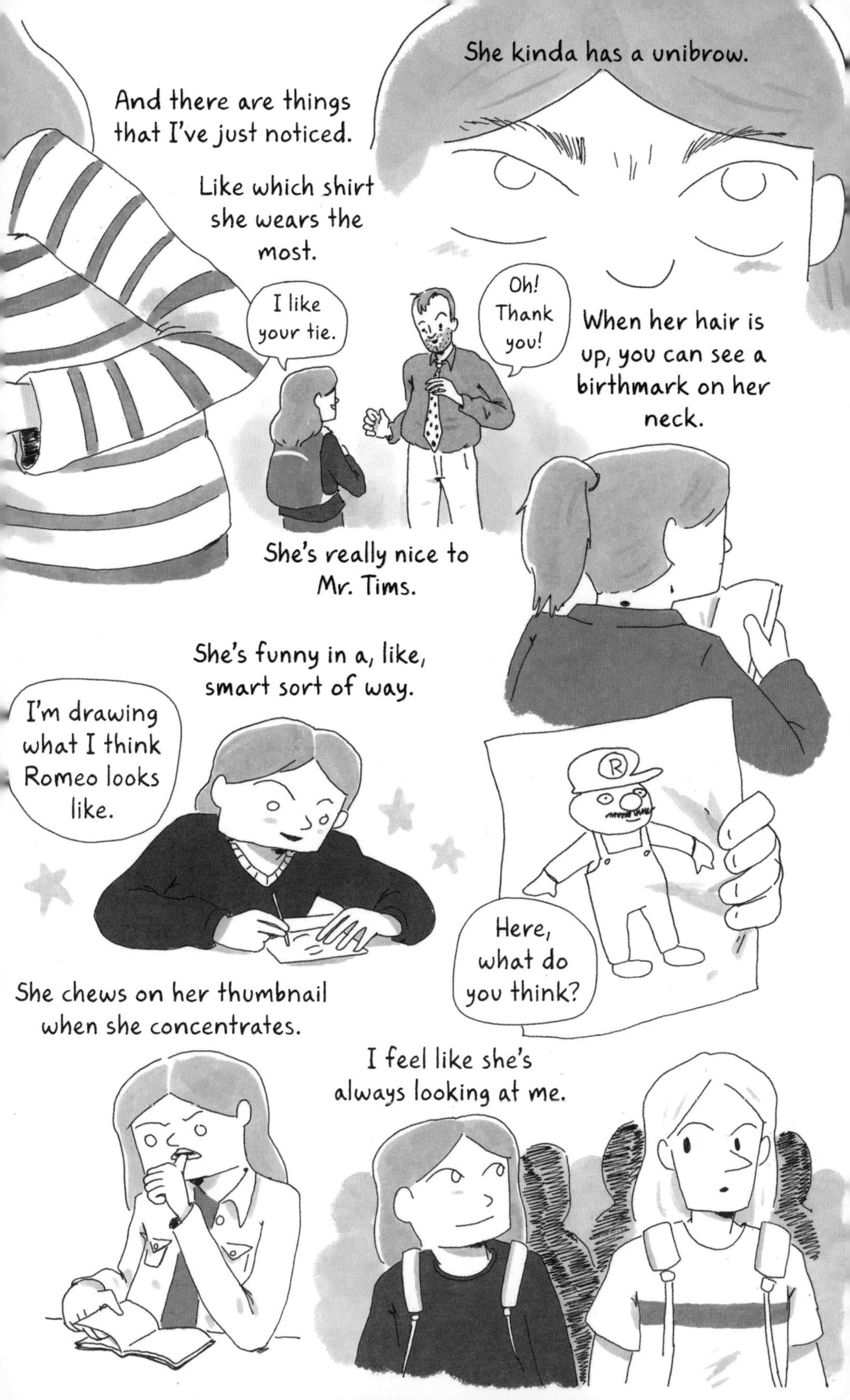
She kinda has a unibrow.
And there are things that I've just noticed.
Like which shirt she wears the most.
I like your tie.
Oh! Thank you!
When her hair is up, you can see a birthmark on her neck.
She's really nice to Mr. Tims.
She's funny in a, like, smart sort of way.
I'm drawing what I think Romeo looks like.
Here, what do you think?
She chews on her thumbnail when she concentrates.
I feel like she's always looking at me.

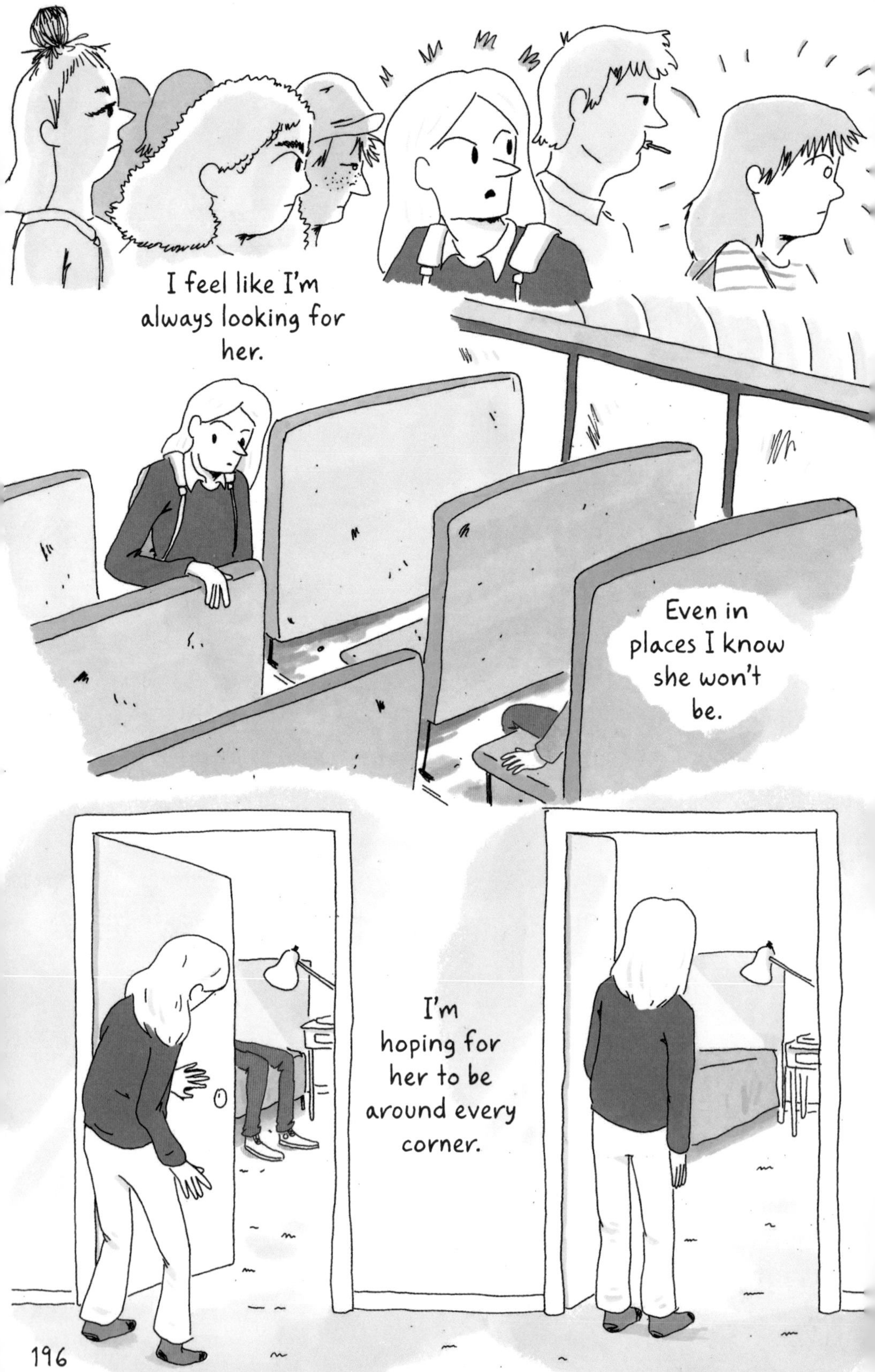
I feel like I'm always looking for her.
Even in places I know she won't be.
I'm hoping for her to be around every corner.

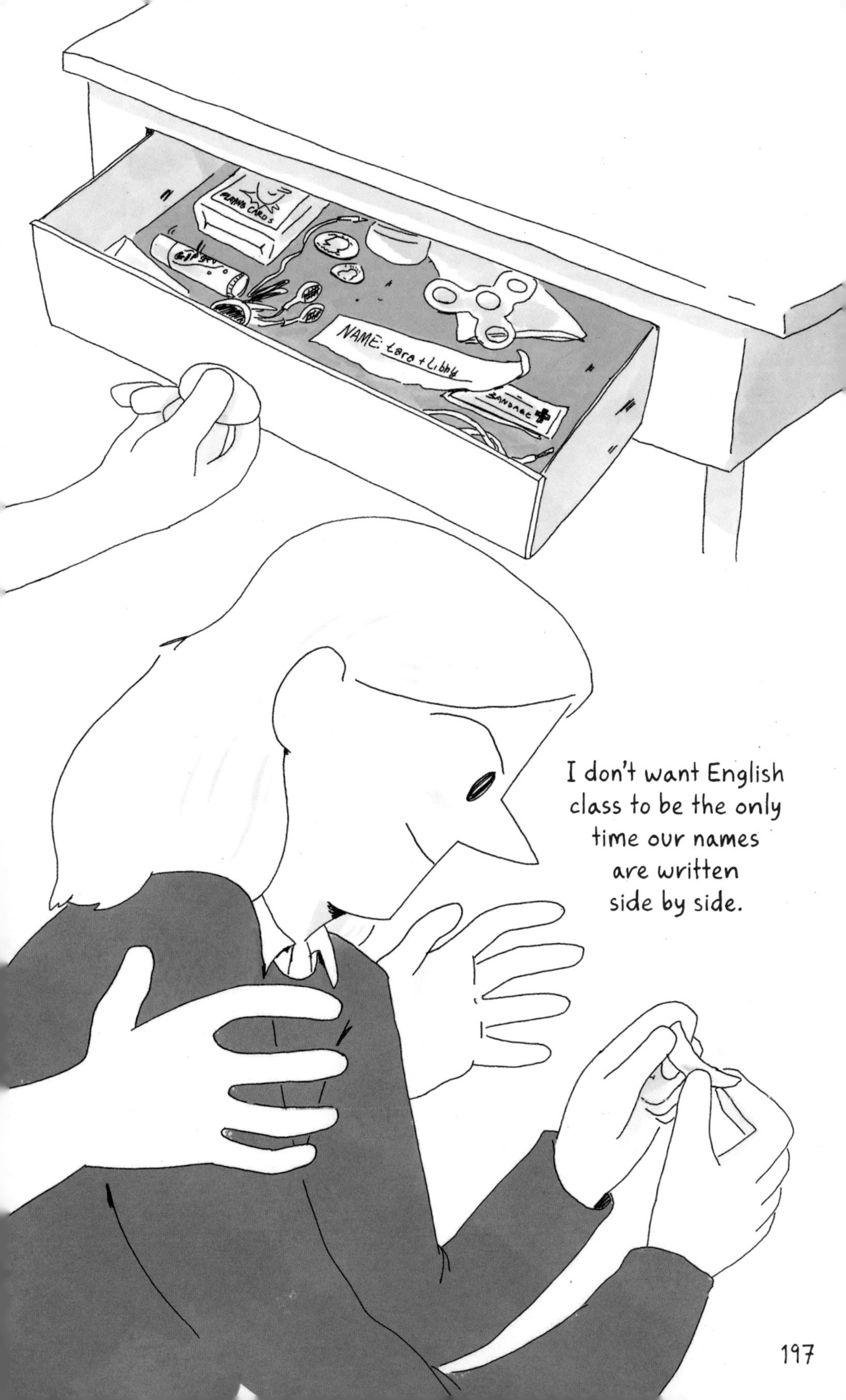
CARDS
NAME: Lara + Libby
BANDAGE
I don't want English class to be the only time our names are written side by side.

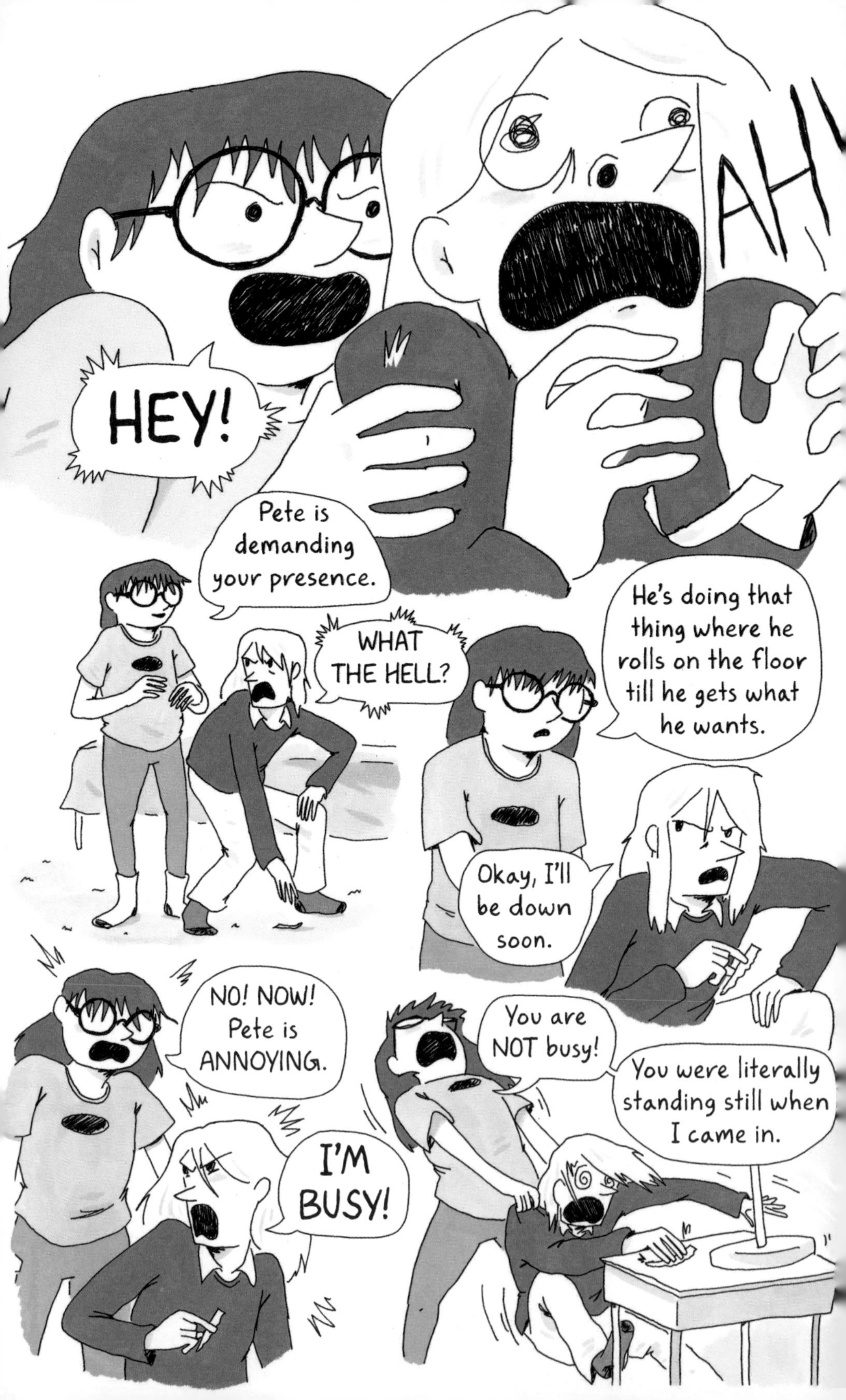
HEY!
AH
Pete is demanding your presence.
WHAT THE HELL?
He's doing that thing where he rolls on the floor till he gets what he wants.
Okay, I'll be down soon.
NO! NOW! Pete is ANNOYING.
I'M BUSY!
You are NOT busy!
You were literally standing still when I came in.

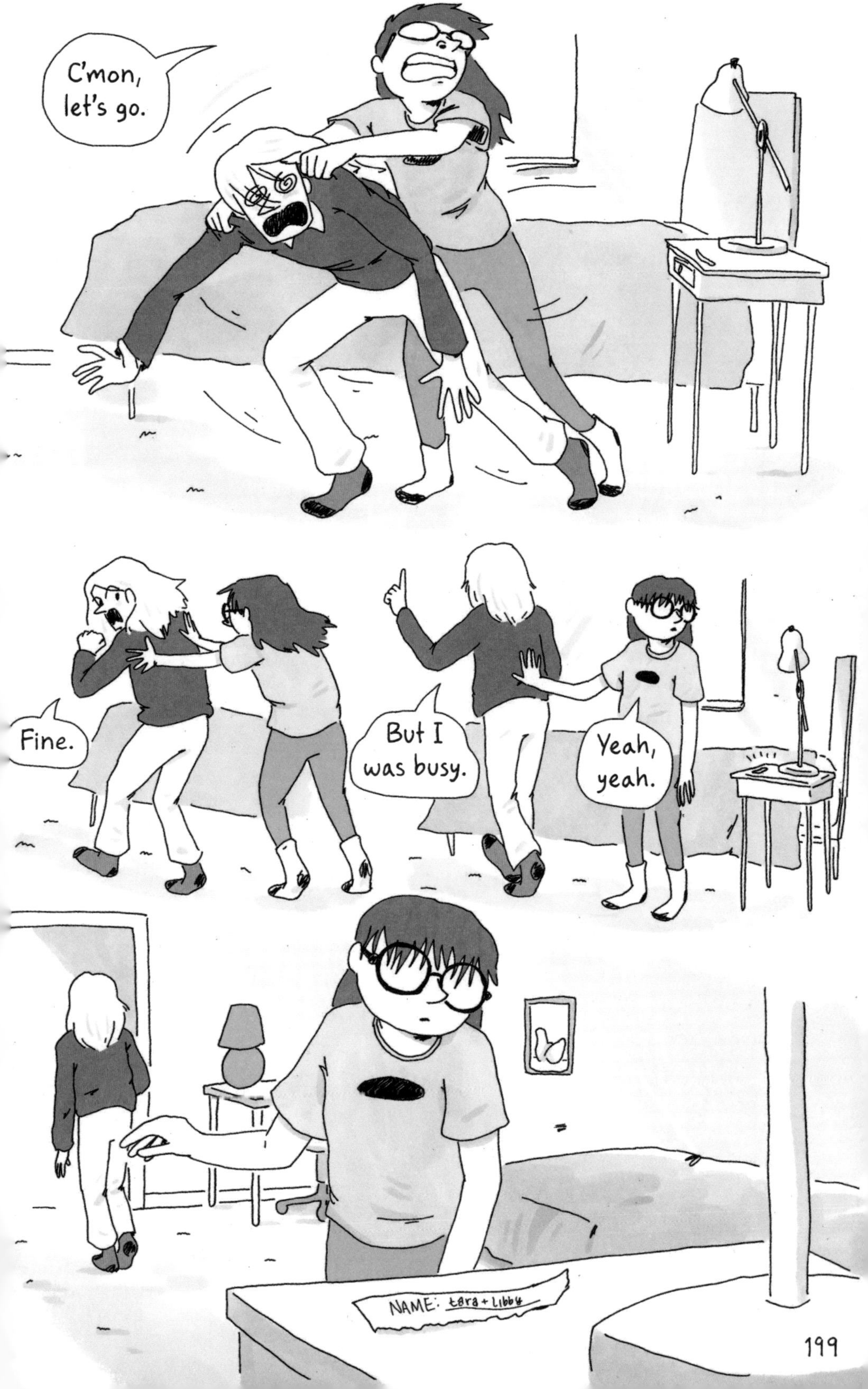
C'mon, let's go.
Fine.
But I was busy.
Yeah, yeah.
NAME: tara + Libby

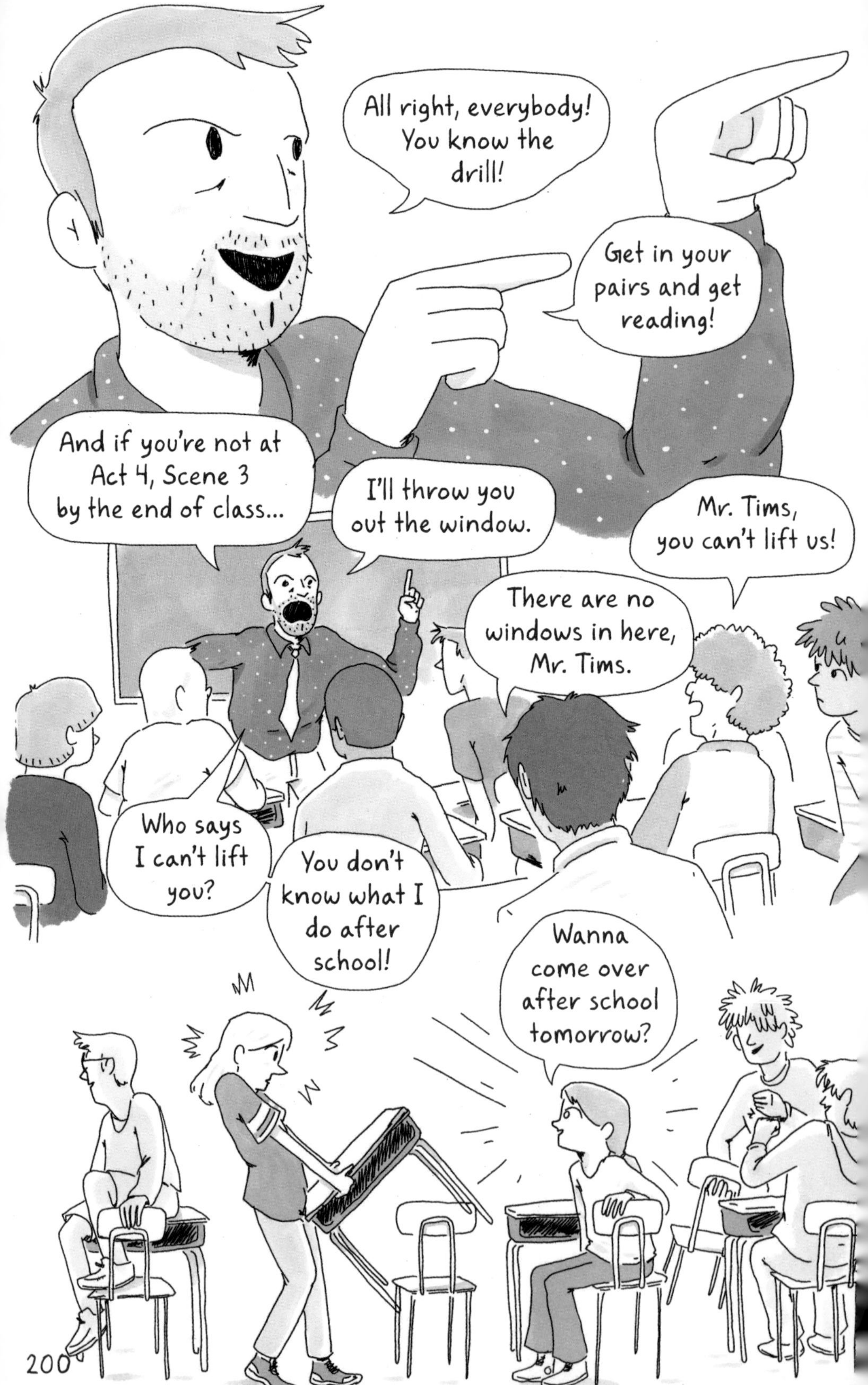

All right, everybody! You know the drill!
Get in your pairs and get reading!
And if you're not at Act 4, Scene 3 by the end of class...
I'll throw you out the window.
Mr. Tims, you can't lift us!
There are no windows in here, Mr. Tims.
Who says I can't lift you?
You don't know what I do after school!
Wanna come over after school tomorrow?

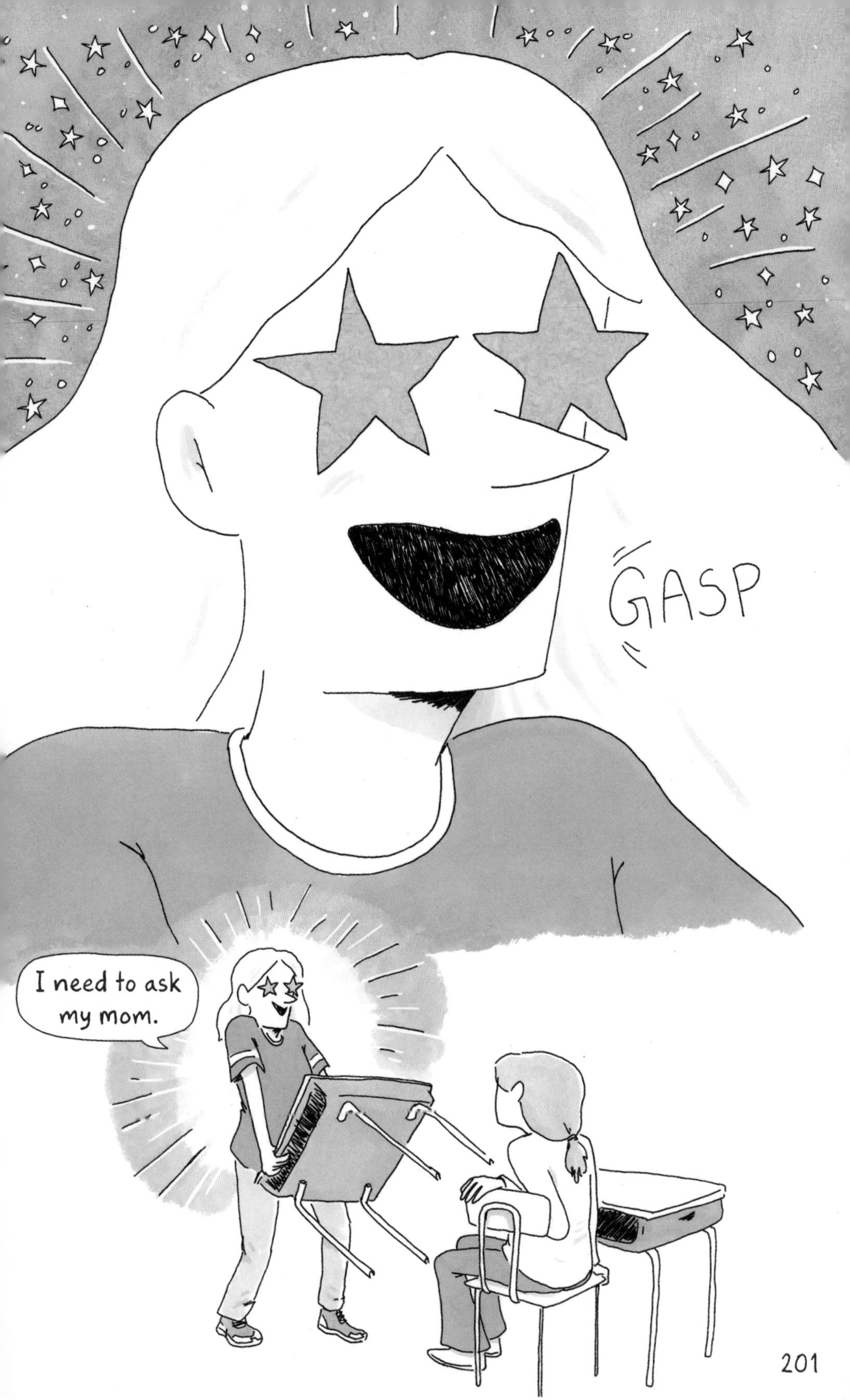
GASP
I need to ask my mom.

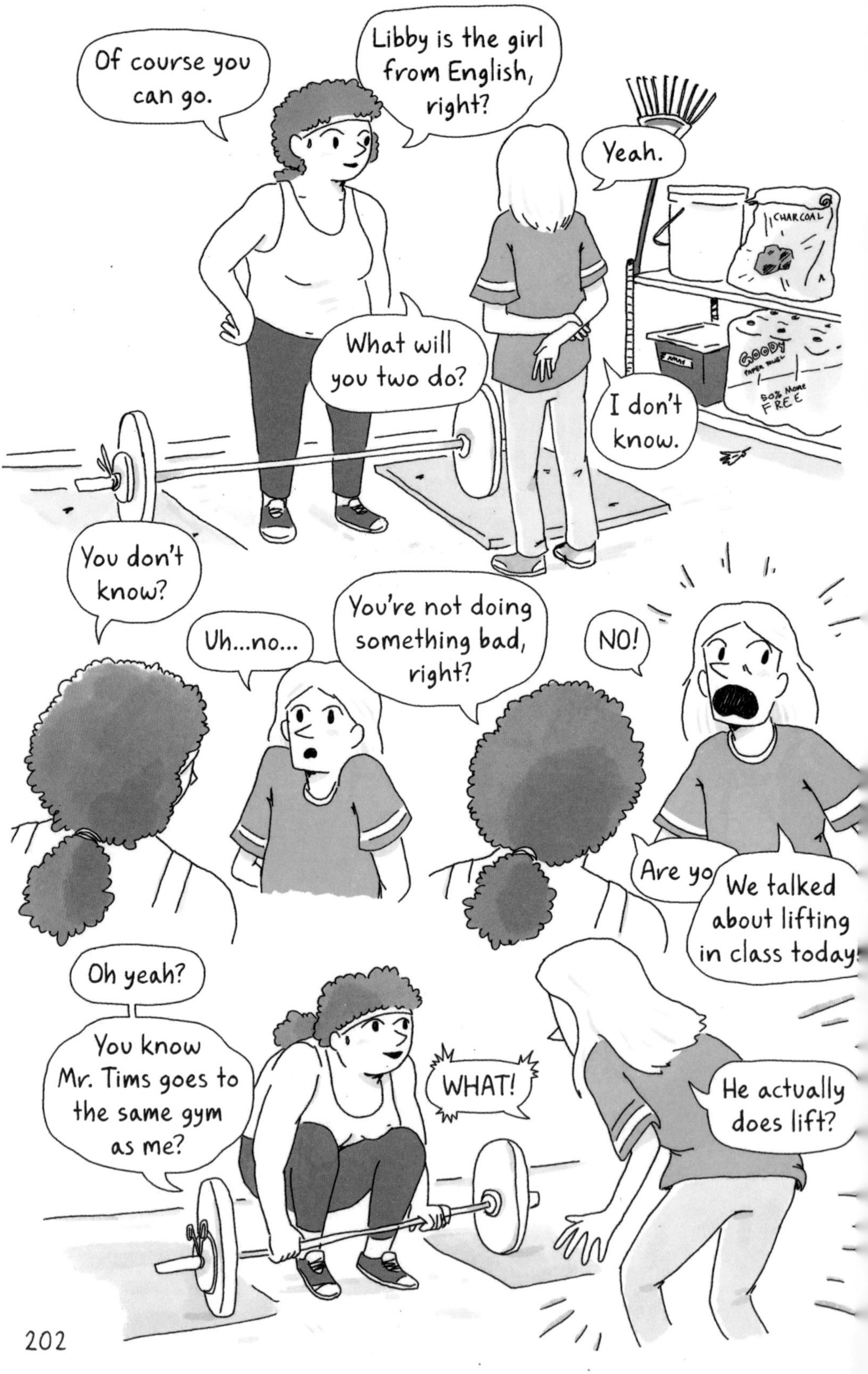
Of course you can go.
Libby is the girl from English, right?
Yeah.
What will you two do?
I don't know.
CHARCOAL
GOODY PAPER TOWEL
50% MORE FREE
You don't know?
Uh...no...
You're not doing something bad, right?
NO!
Are yo
We talked about lifting in class today!
Oh yeah?
You know Mr. Tims goes to the same gym as me?
WHAT!
He actually does lift?

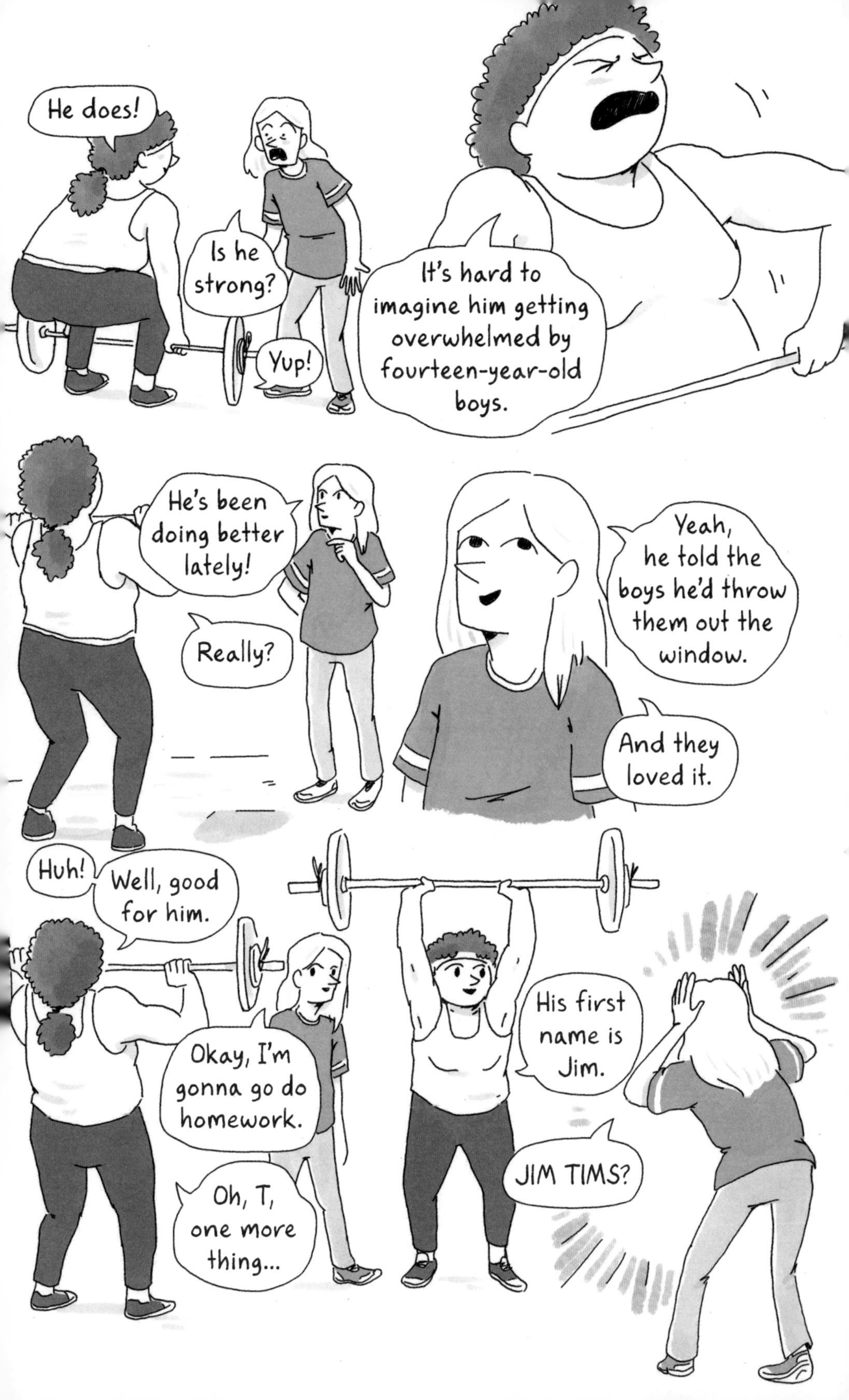

He does!
Is he strong?
Yup!
It's hard to imagine him getting overwhelmed by fourteen-year-old boys.
He's been doing better lately!
Really?
Yeah, he told the boys he'd throw them out the window.
And they loved it.
Huh!
Well, good for him.
Okay, I'm gonna go do homework.
Oh, T, one more thing...
His first name is Jim.
JIM TIMS?

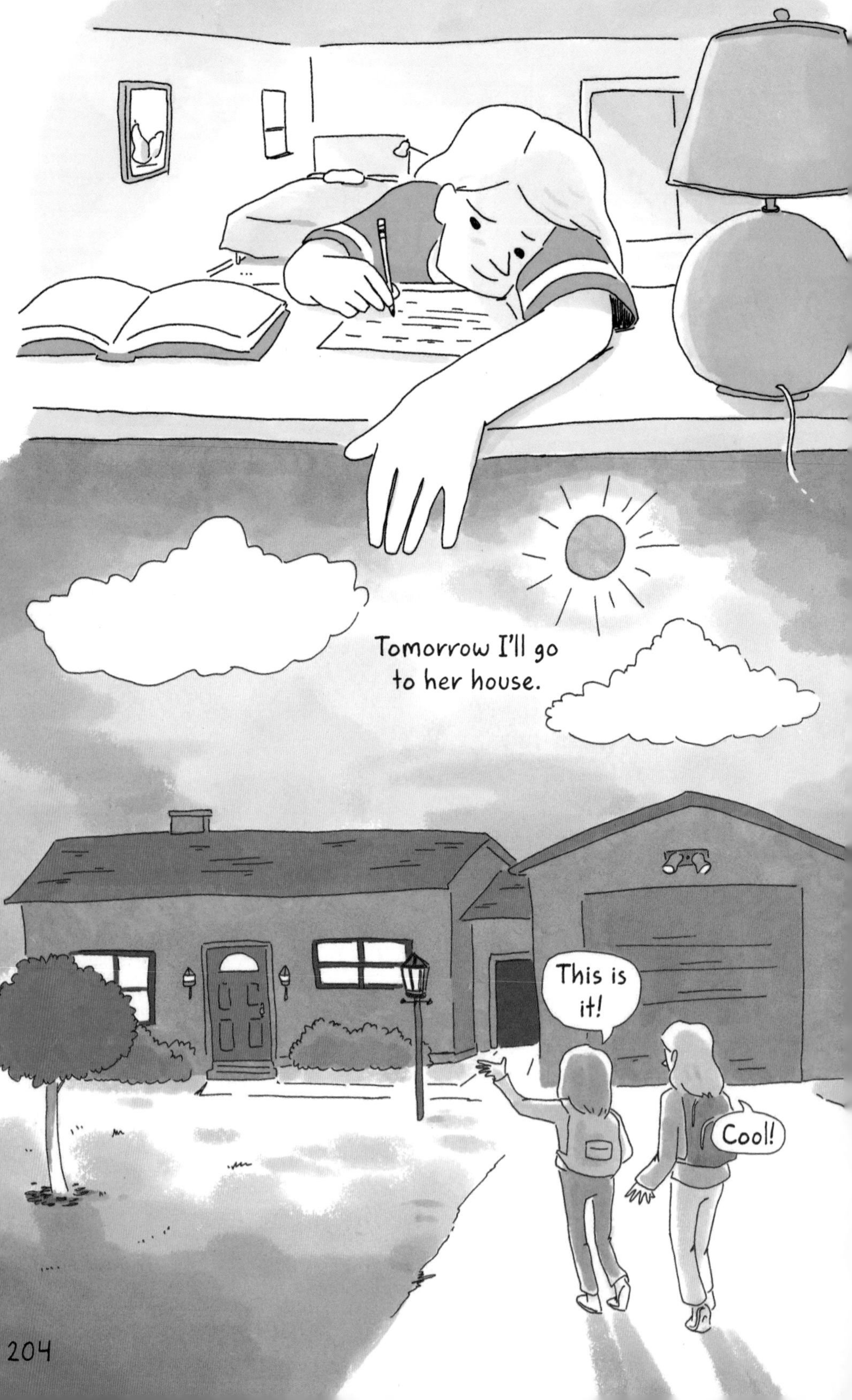

Tomorrow I'll go to her house.
This is it!
Cool!

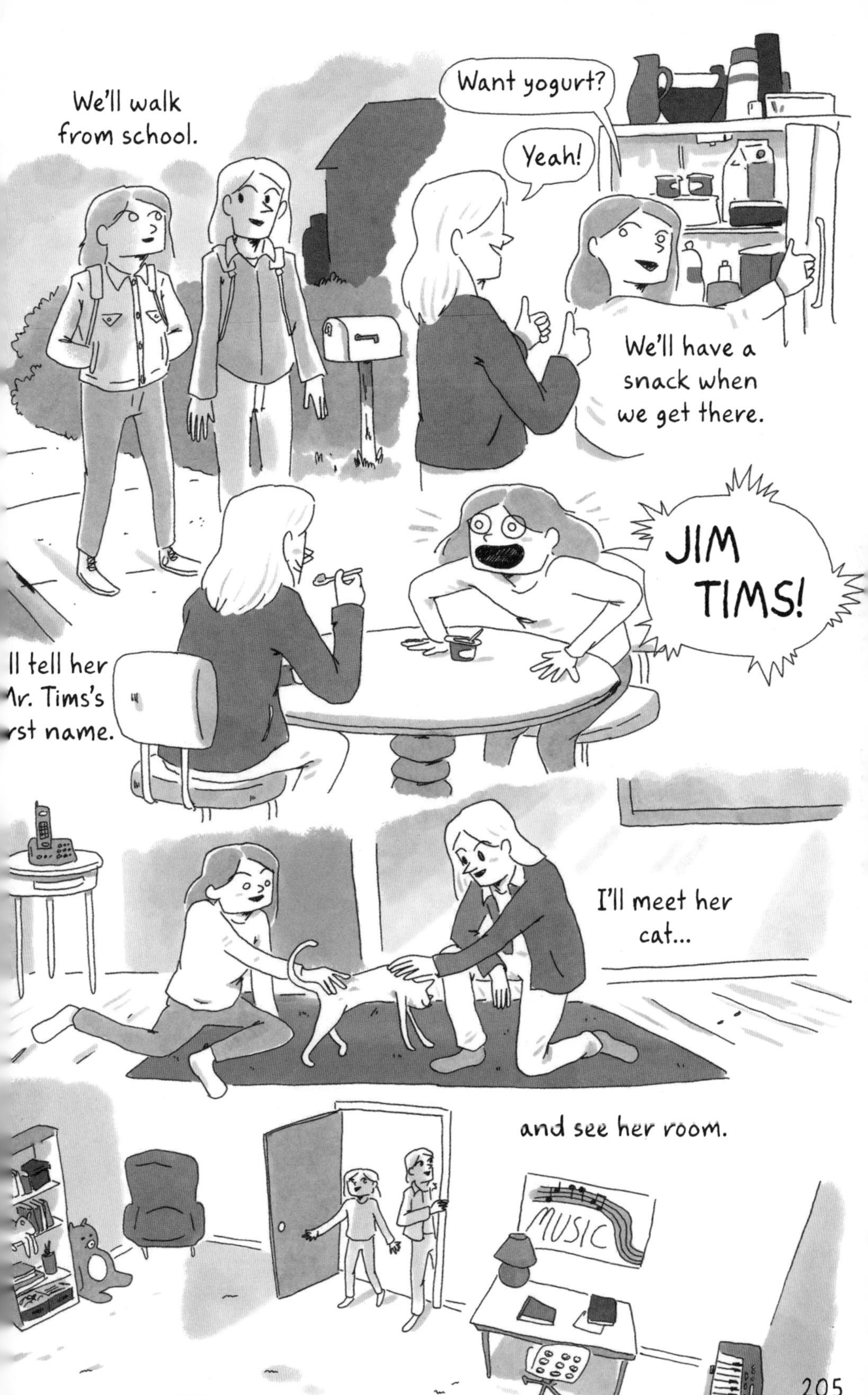
We'll walk from school.
Want yogurt?
Yeah!
We'll have a snack when we get there.
JIM TIMS!
ll tell her
Ar. Tims's
rst name.
I'll meet her cat...
and see her room.
MUSIC

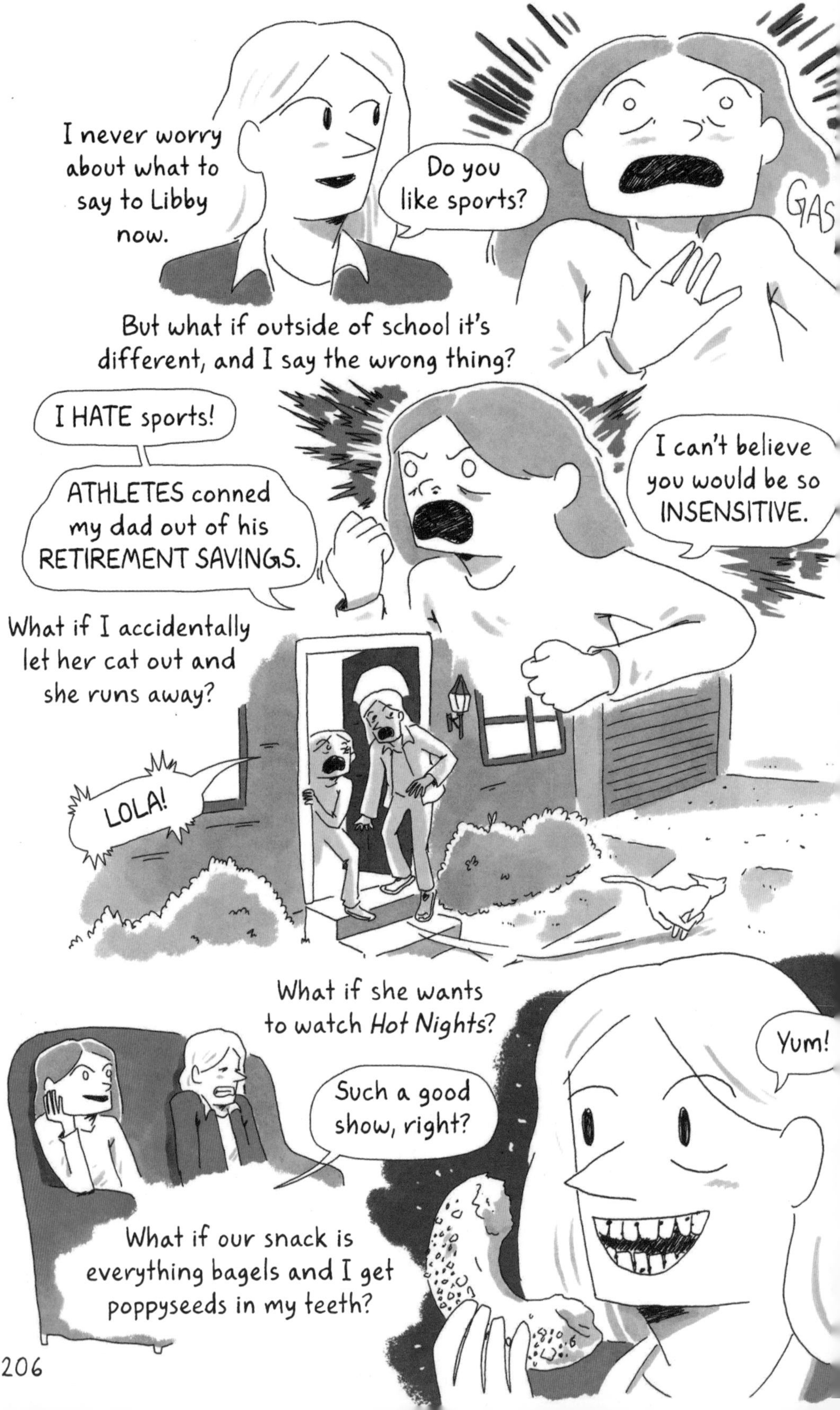
I never worry about what to say to Libby now.
Do you like sports?
GAS
But what if outside of school it's different, and I say the wrong thing?
I HATE sports!
ATHLETES conned my dad out of his RETIREMENT SAVINGS.
I can't believe you would be so INSENSITIVE.
What if I accidentally let her cat out and she runs away?
LOLA!
What if she wants to watch *Hot Nights*?
Such a good show, right?
Yum!
What if our snack is everything bagels and I get poppyseeds in my teeth?

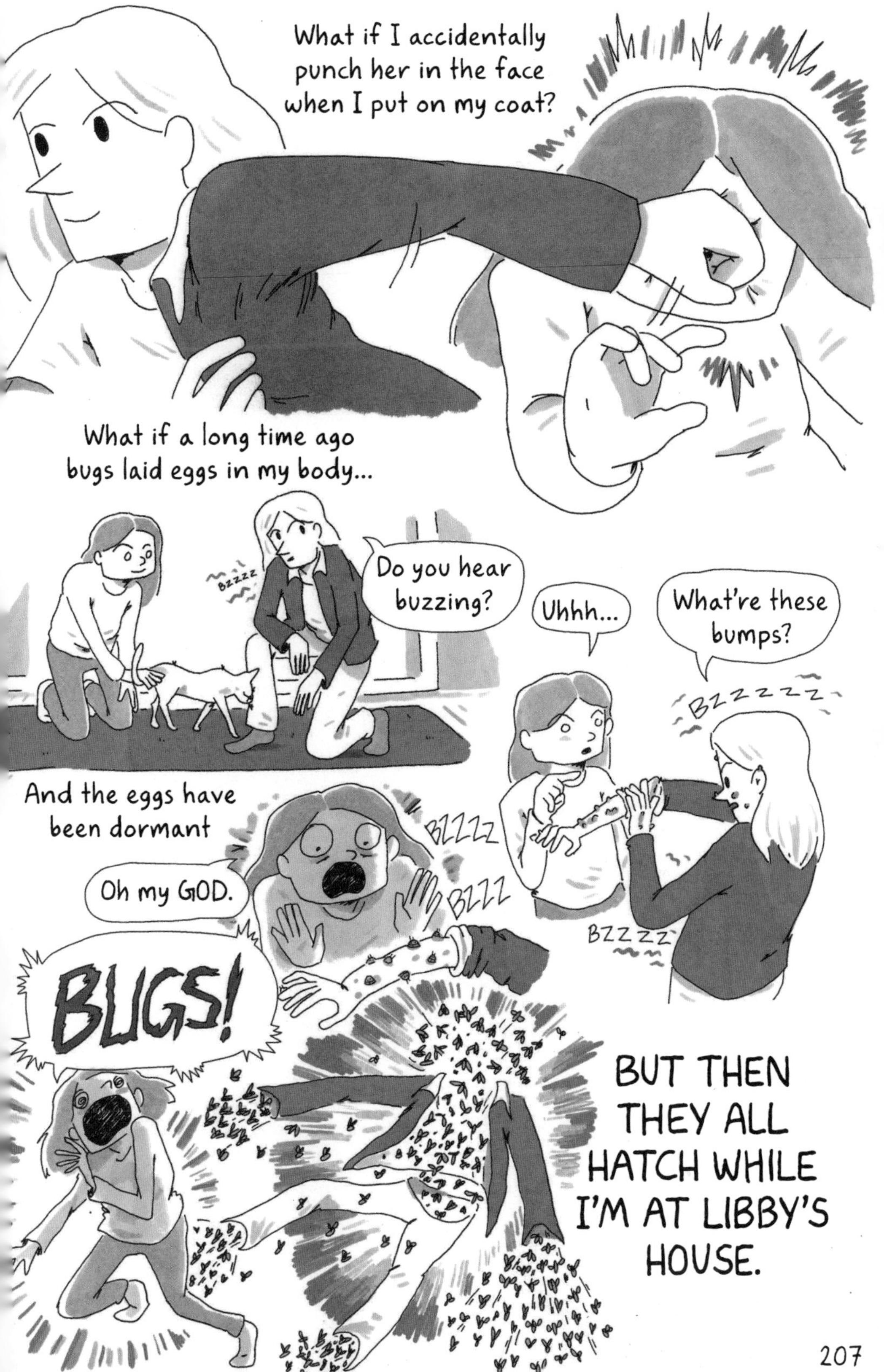
What if I accidentally punch her in the face when I put on my coat?
What if a long time ago bugs laid eggs in my body...
BZZZZ
Do you hear buzzing?
Uhhh...
What're these bumps?
BZZZZZZ
And the eggs have been dormant
BZZZZ
Oh my GOD.
BZZZ
BZZZZ
BUGS!
BUT THEN THEY ALL HATCH WHILE I'M AT LIBBY'S HOUSE.

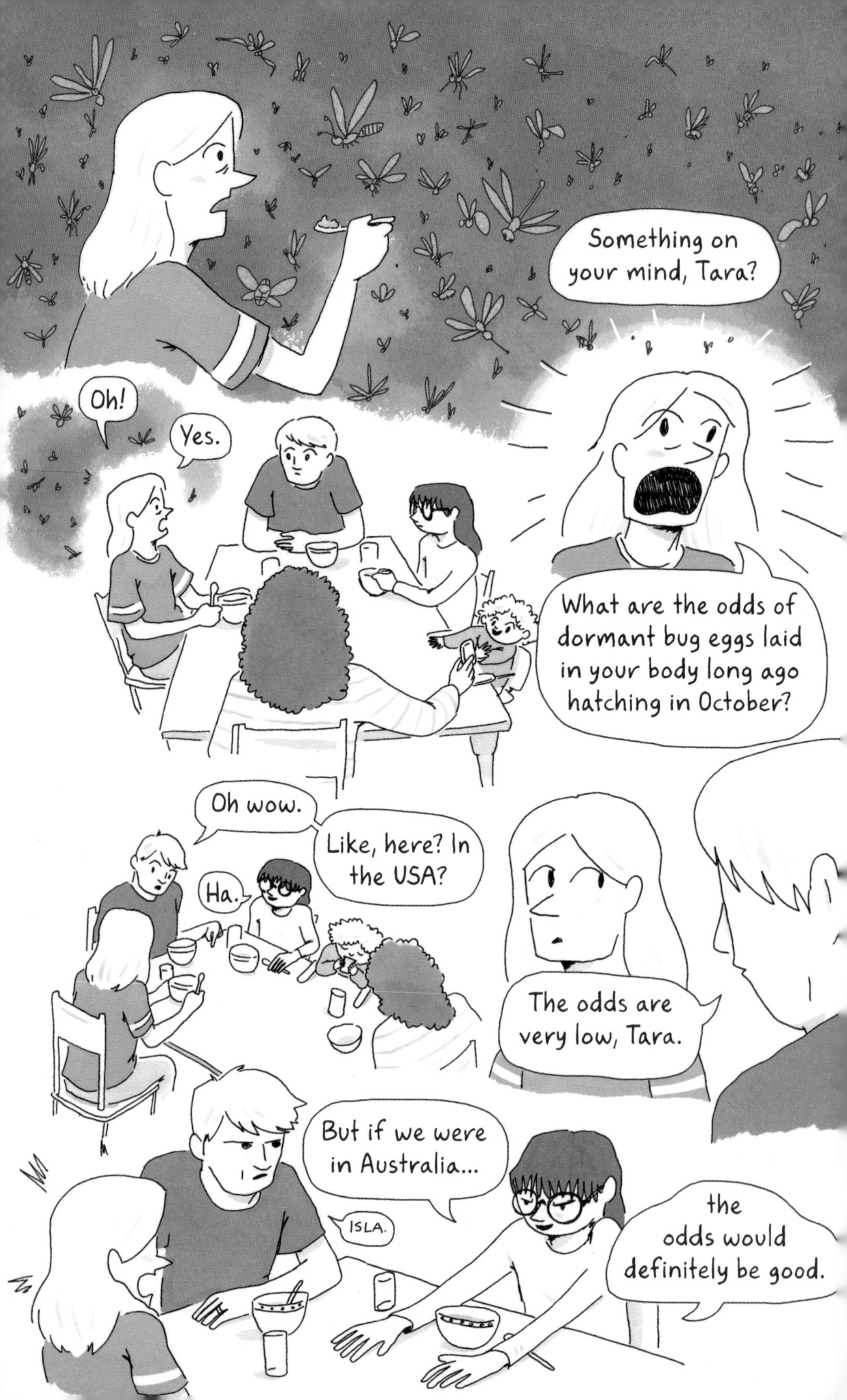

Something on your mind, Tara?
Oh!
Yes.
What are the odds of dormant bug eggs laid in your body long ago hatching in October?
Oh wow.
Like, here? In the USA?
Ha.
The odds are very low, Tara.
But if we were in Australia...
ISLA.
the odds would definitely be good.

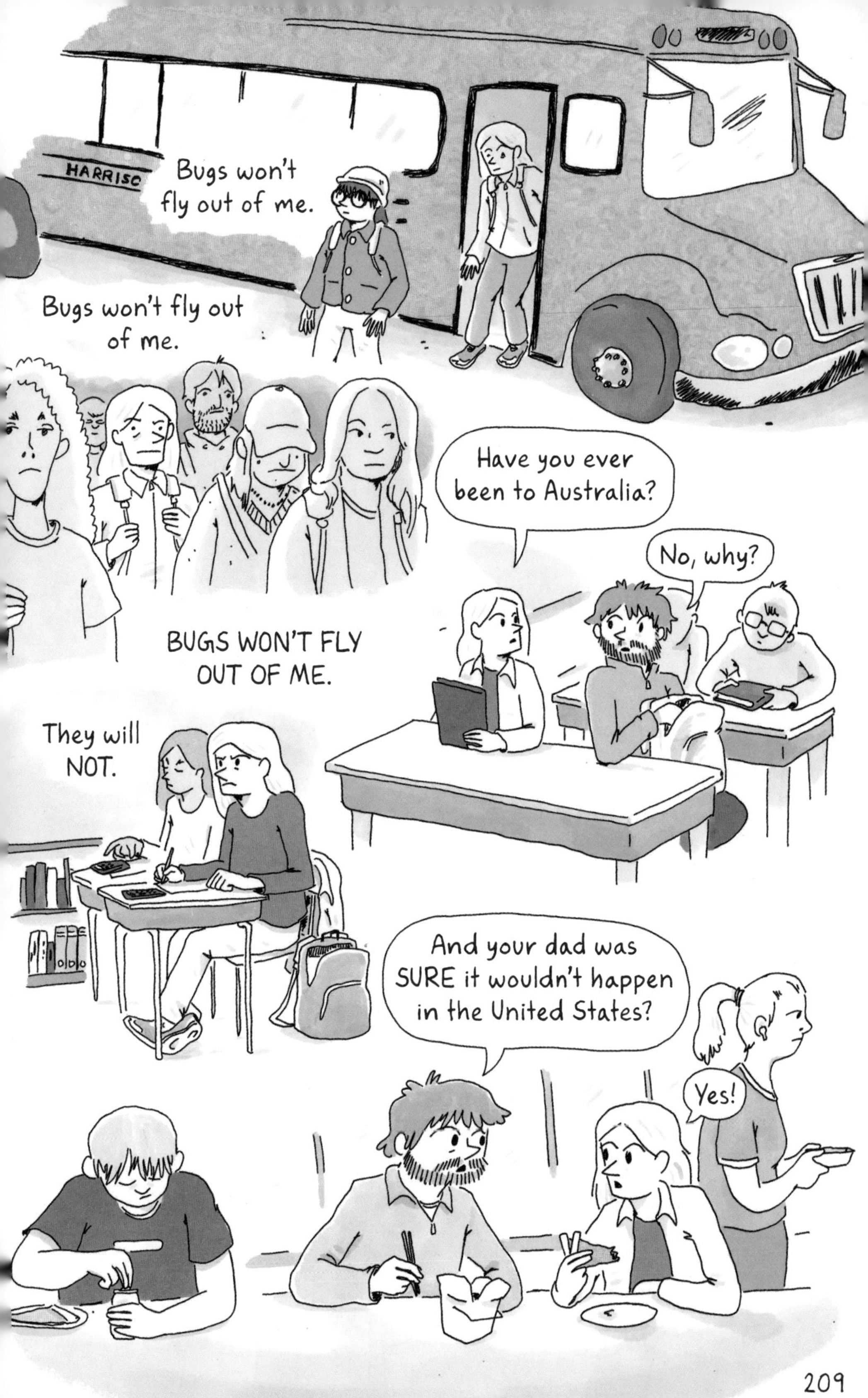

HARRISO
Bugs won't fly out of me.
Bugs won't fly out of me.
Have you ever been to Australia?
No, why?
BUGS WON'T FLY OUT OF ME.
They will NOT.
And your dad was SURE it wouldn't happen in the United States?
Yes!

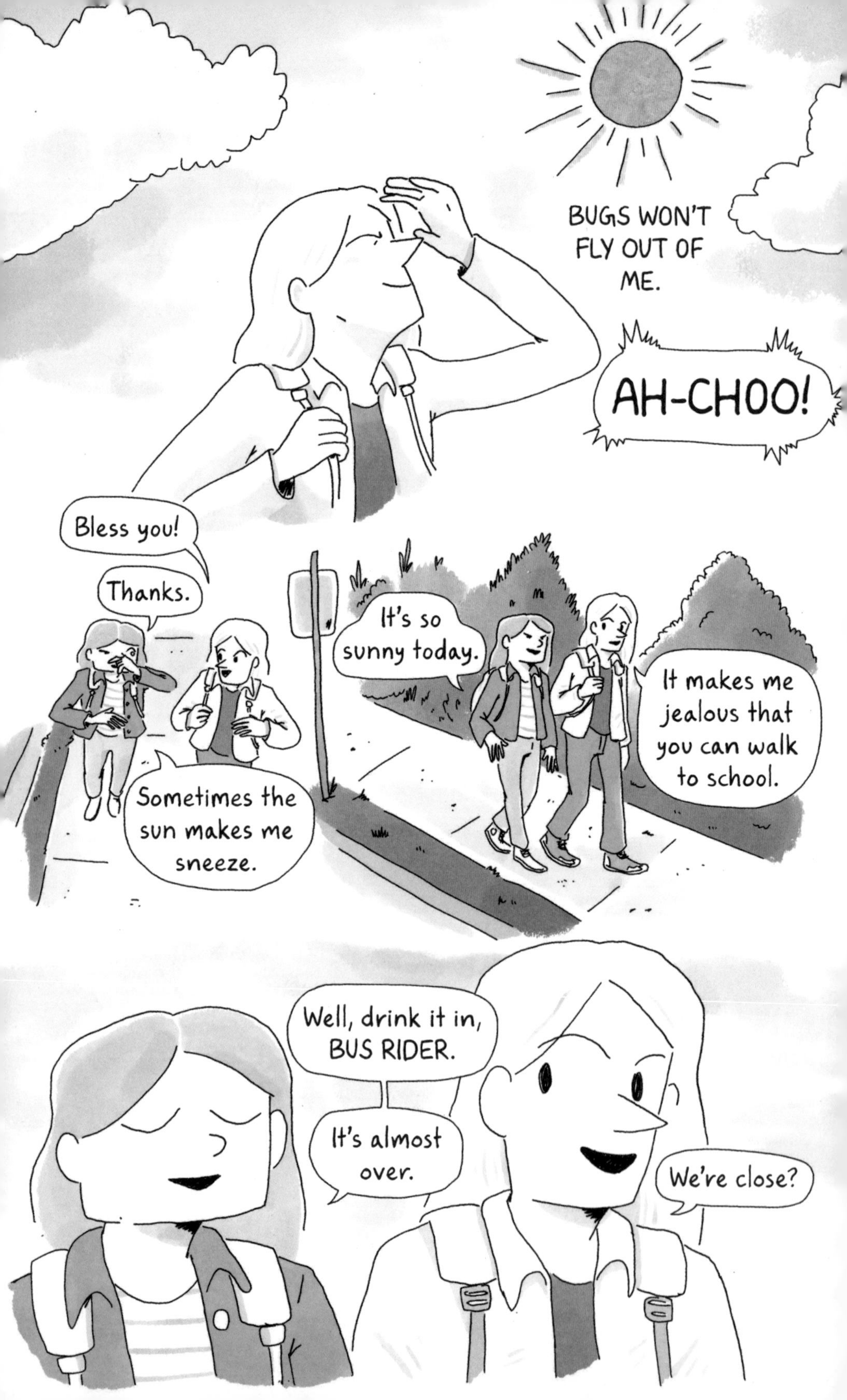
BUGS WON'T FLY OUT OF ME.
AH-CHOO!
Bless you!
Thanks.
Sometimes the sun makes me sneeze.
It's so sunny today.
It makes me jealous that you can walk to school.
Well, drink it in, BUS RIDER.
It's almost over.
We're close?

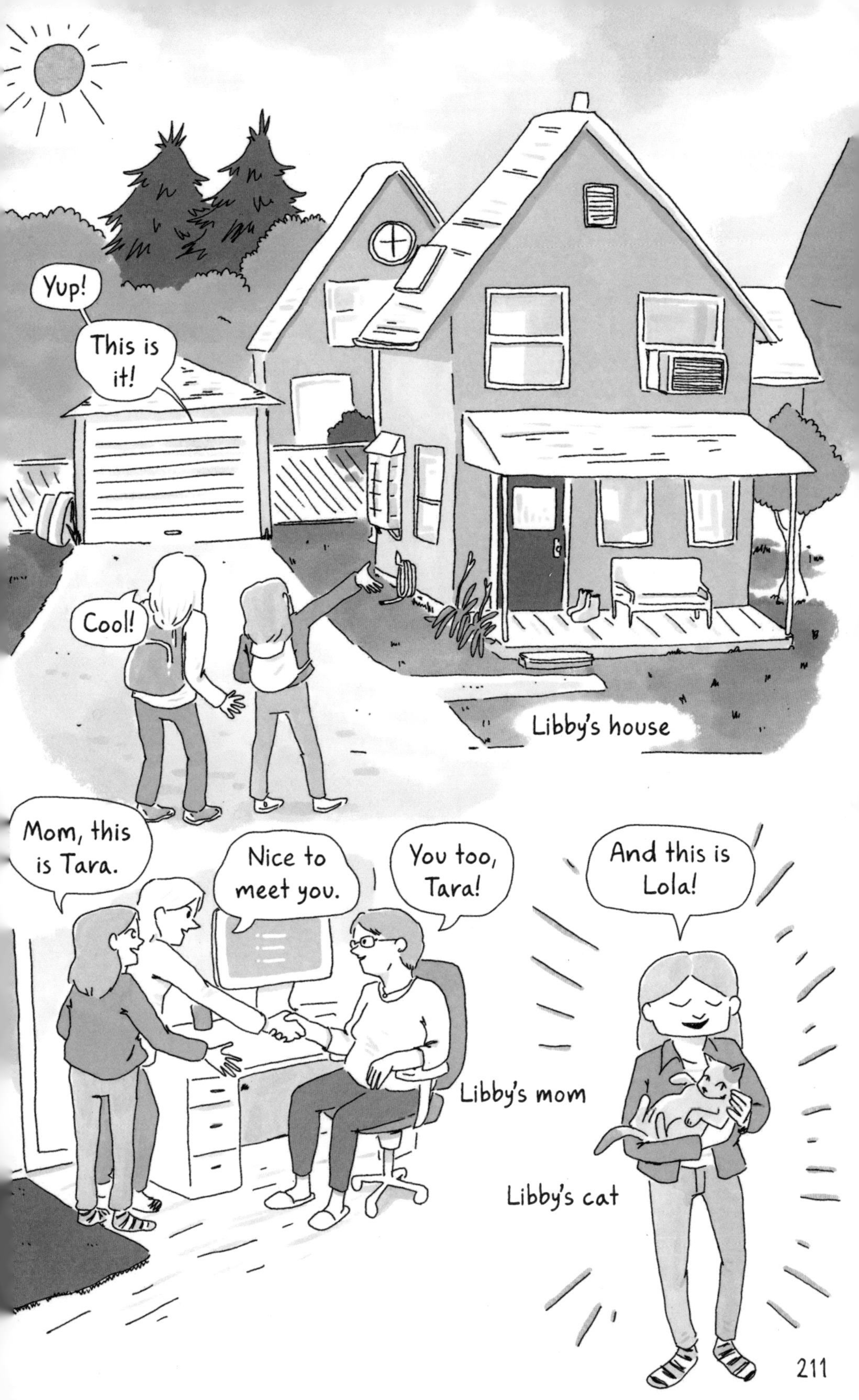
Yup!
This is it!
Cool!
Libby's house
Mom, this is Tara.
Nice to meet you.
You too, Tara!
Libby's mom
And this is Lola!
Libby's cat

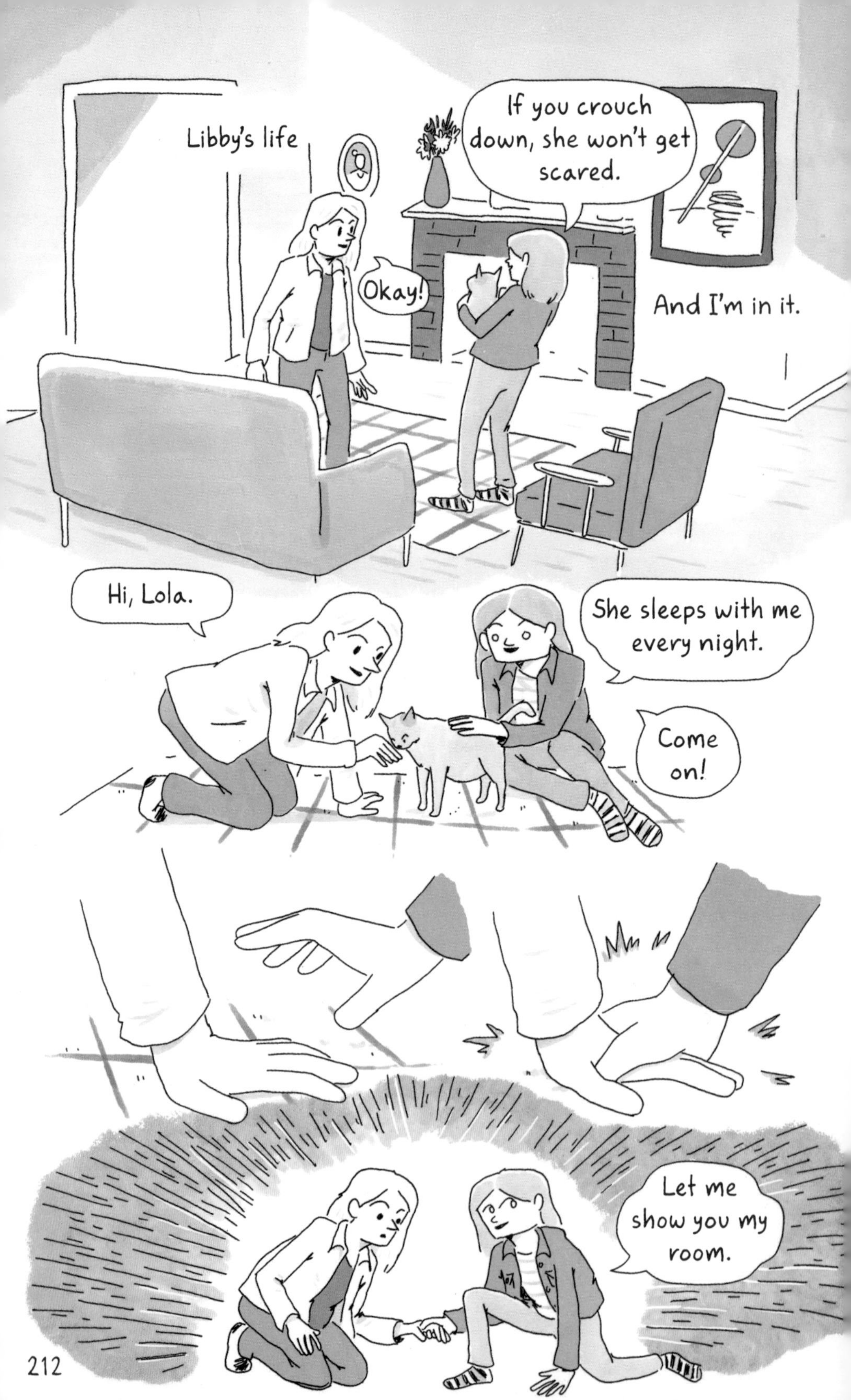
Libby's life
If you crouch down, she won't get scared.
Okay!
And I'm in it.
Hi, Lola.
She sleeps with me every night.
Come on!
Let me show you my room.

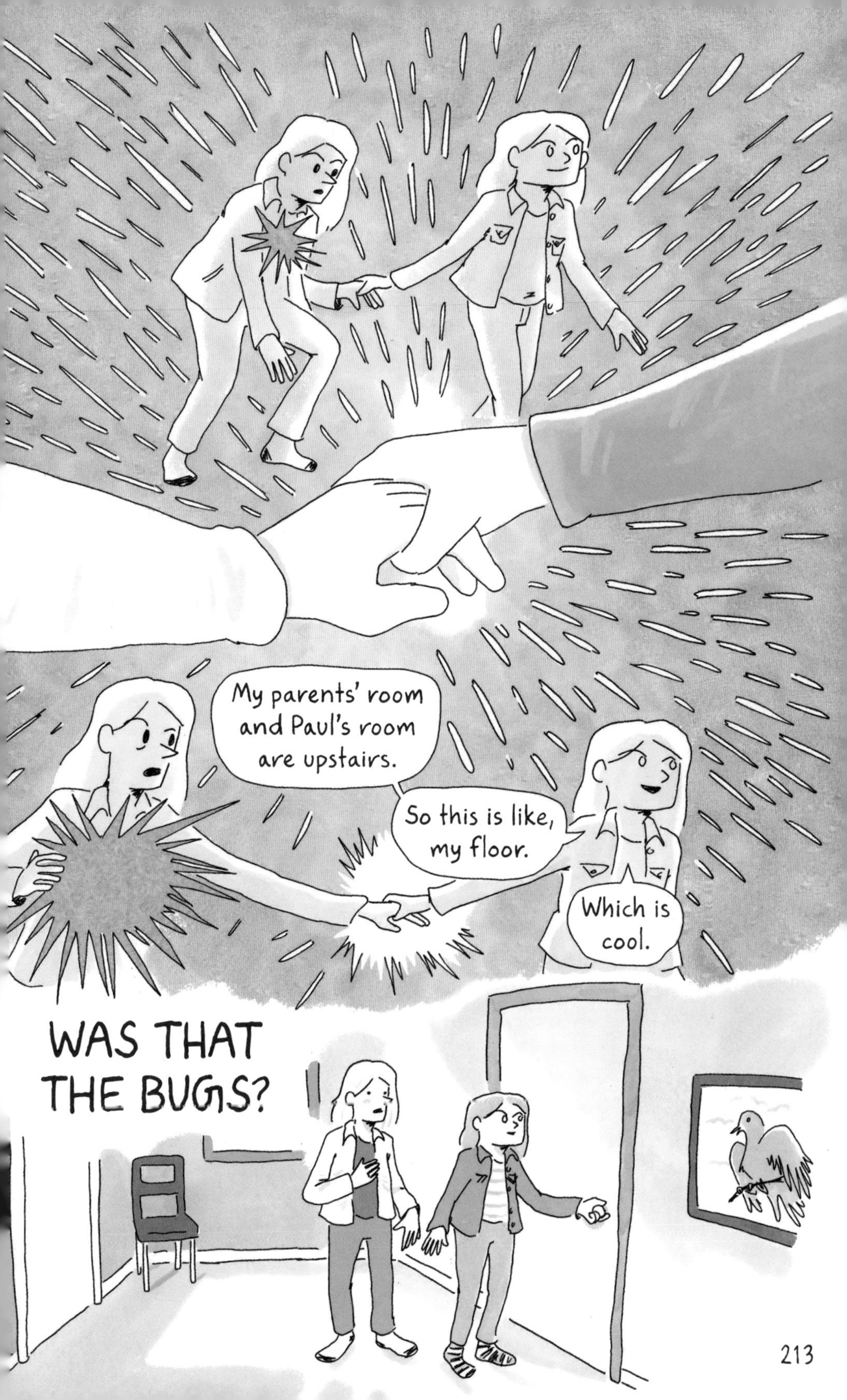
My parents' room and Paul's room are upstairs.
So this is like, my floor.
Which is cool.
WAS THAT THE BUGS?

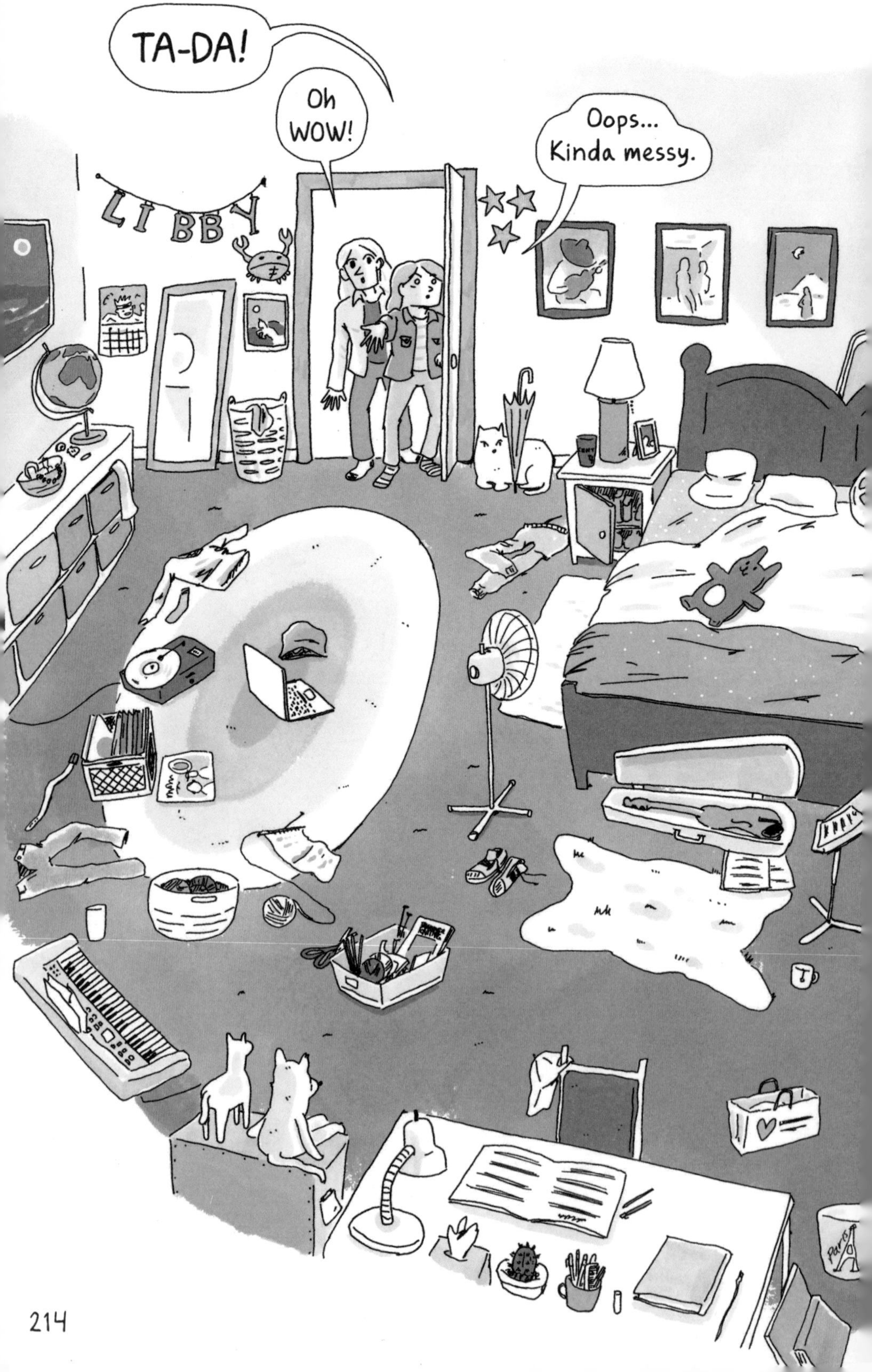
TA-DA!
Oh WOW!
Oops... Kinda messy.
LIBBY

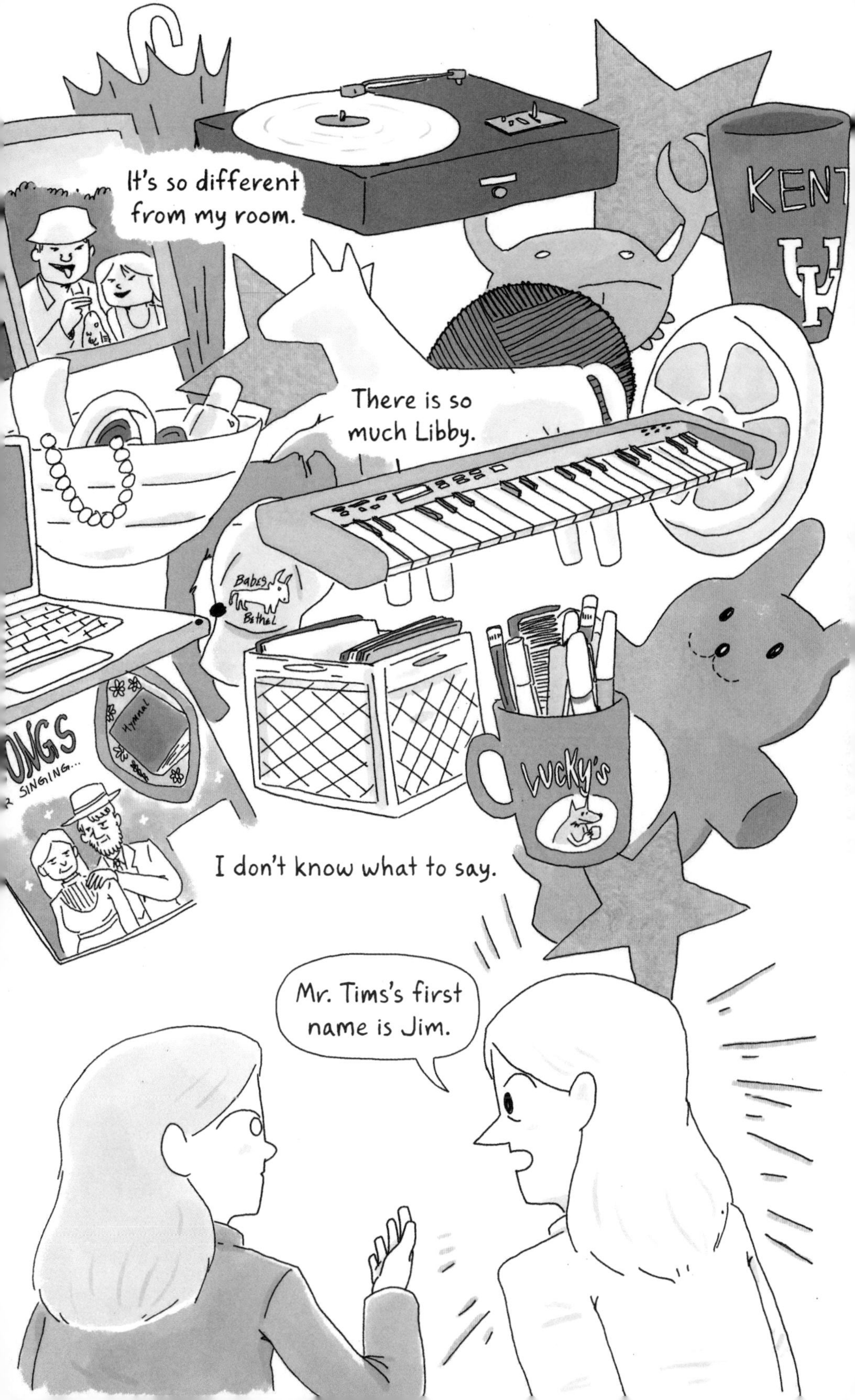
It's so different from my room.
KENT
There is so much Libby.
Babes Bethel
Hymnal
Lucky's
I don't know what to say.
Mr. Tims's first name is Jim.

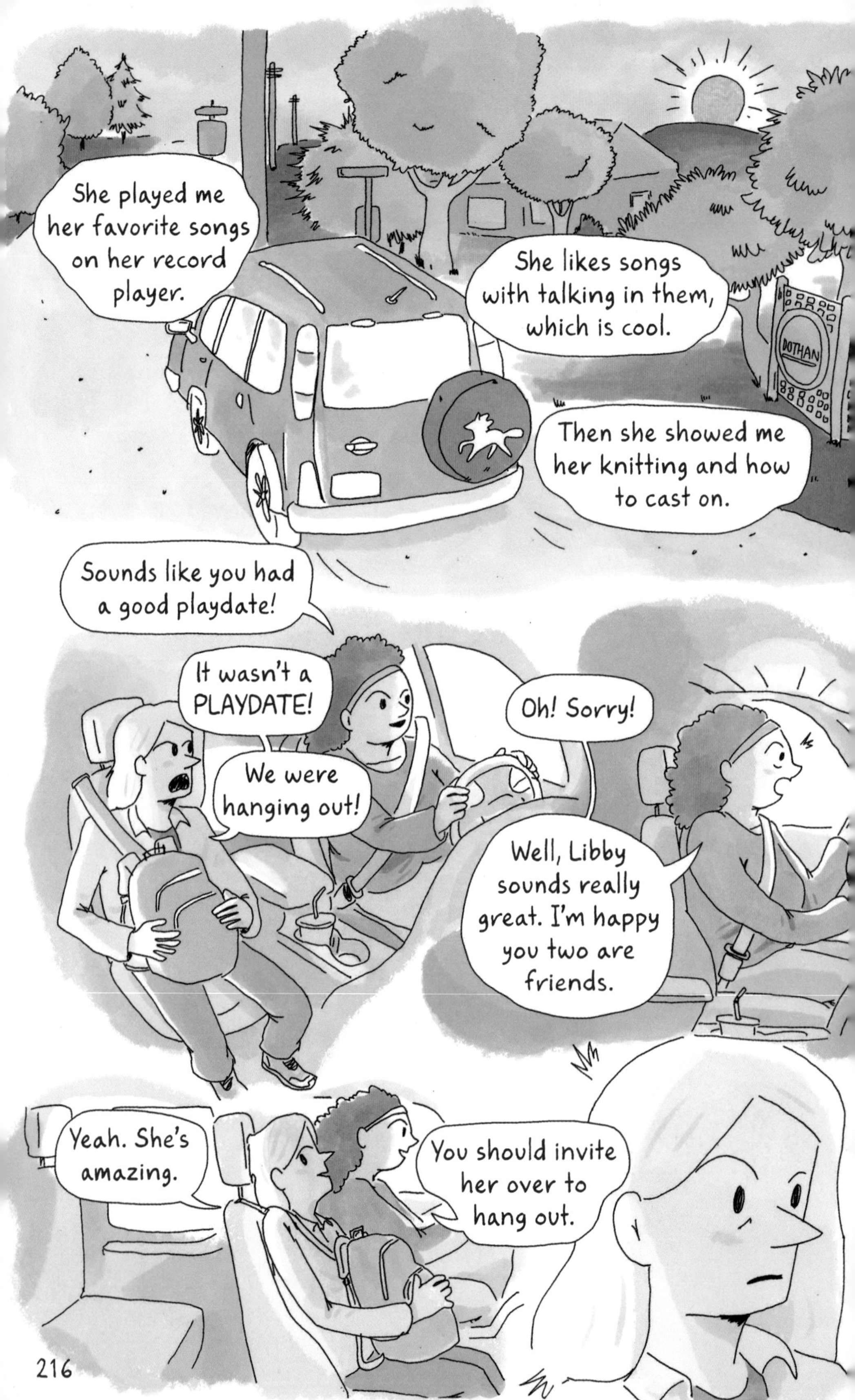

She played me her favorite songs on her record player.
She likes songs with talking in them, which is cool.
DOTHAN
Then she showed me her knitting and how to cast on.
Sounds like you had a good playdate!
It wasn't a PLAYDATE!
We were hanging out!
Oh! Sorry!
Well, Libby sounds really great. I'm happy you two are friends.
Yeah. She's amazing.
You should invite her over to hang out.

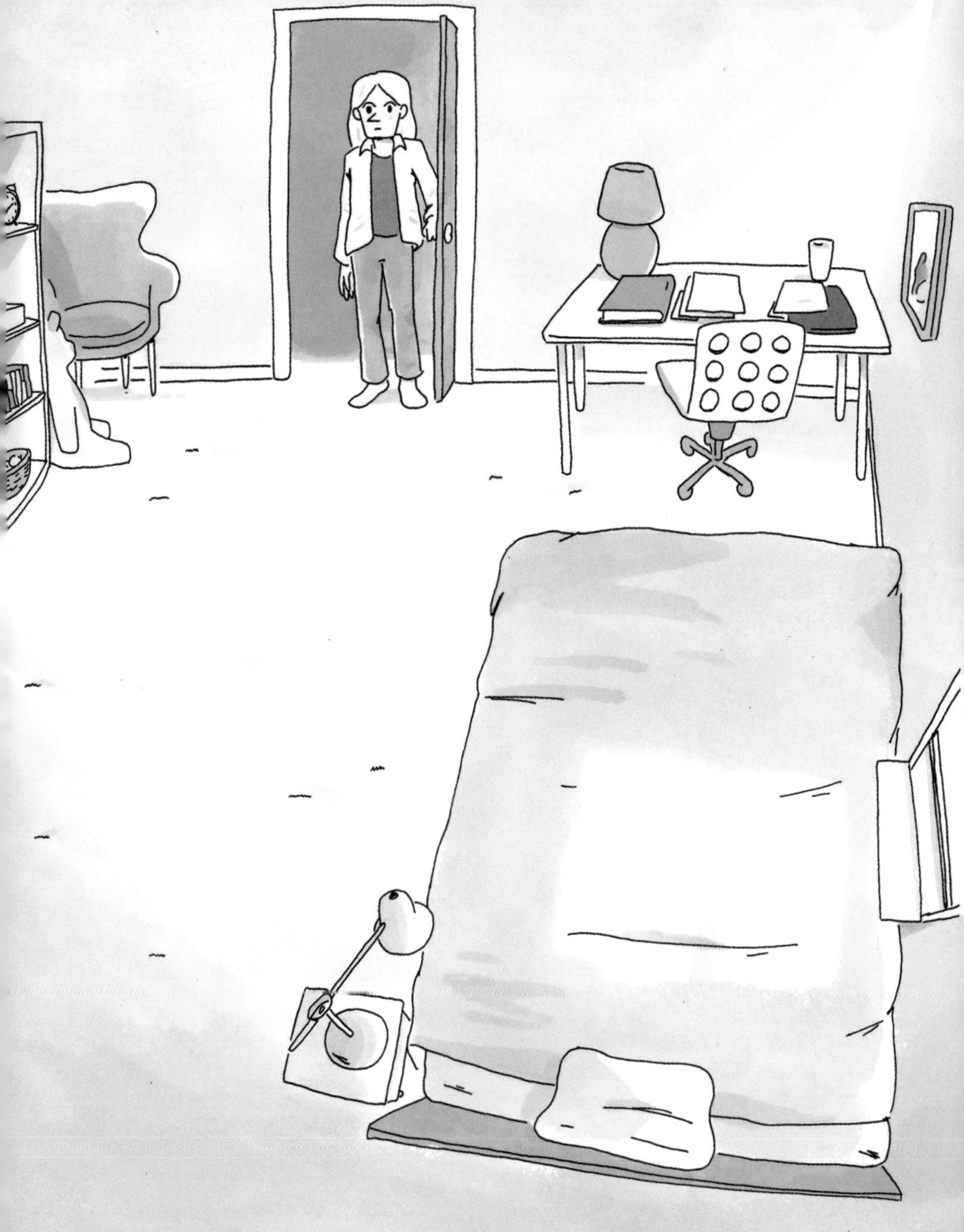

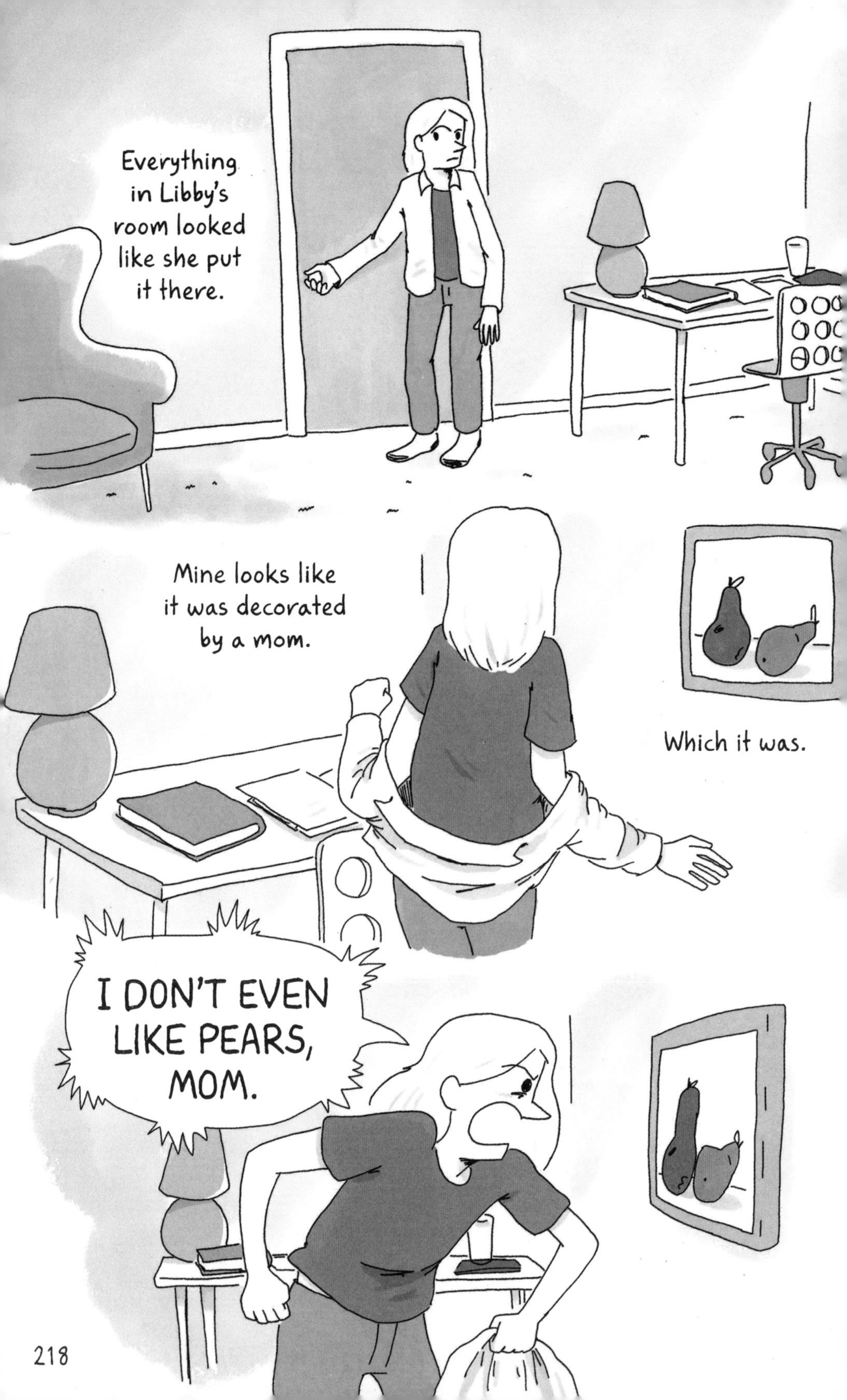

Everything in Libby's room looked like she put it there.
Mine looks like it was decorated by a mom.
Which it was.
I DON'T EVEN LIKE PEARS, MOM.

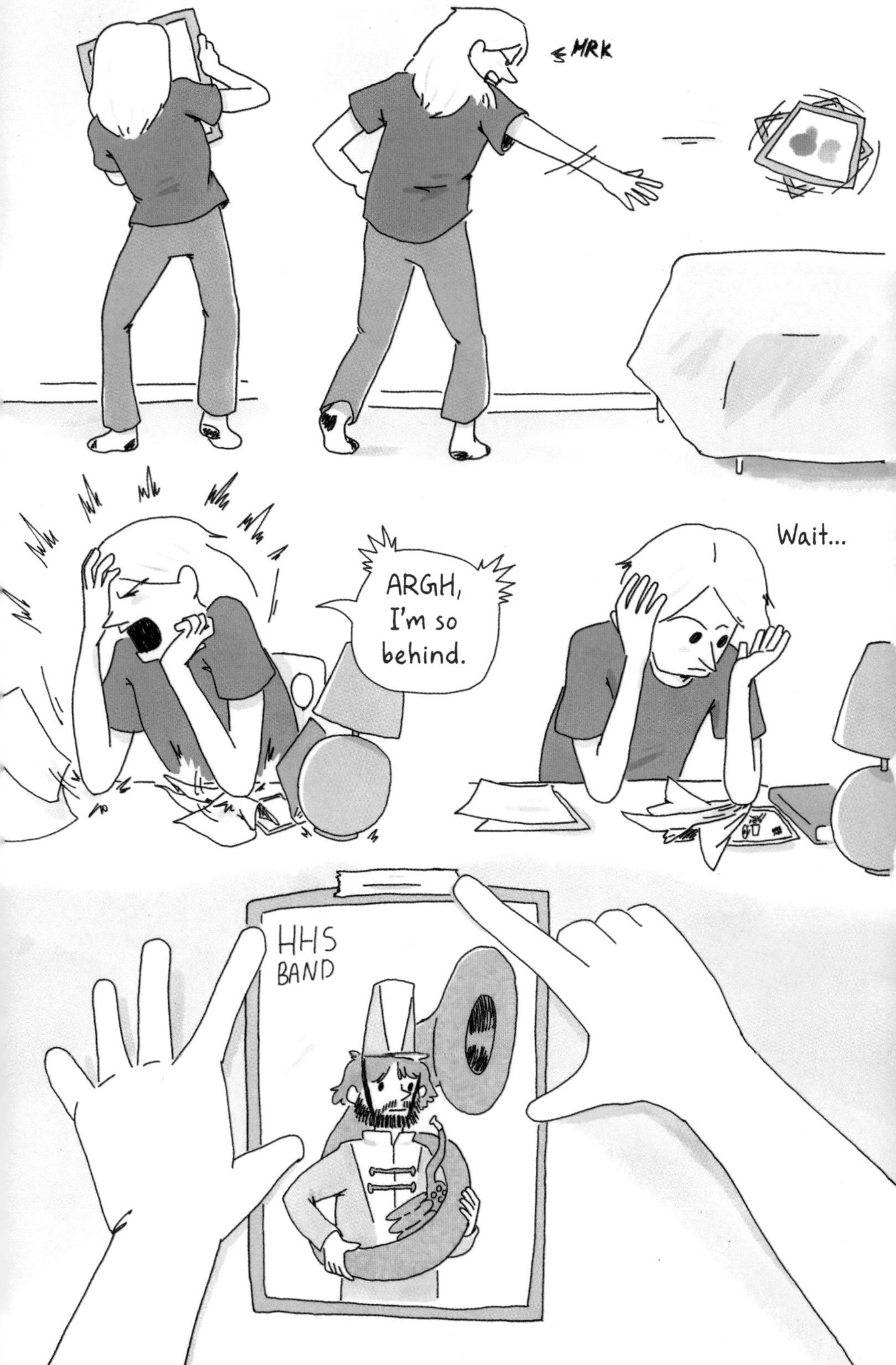
MRK
ARGH, I'm so behind.
Wait...
HHS BAND

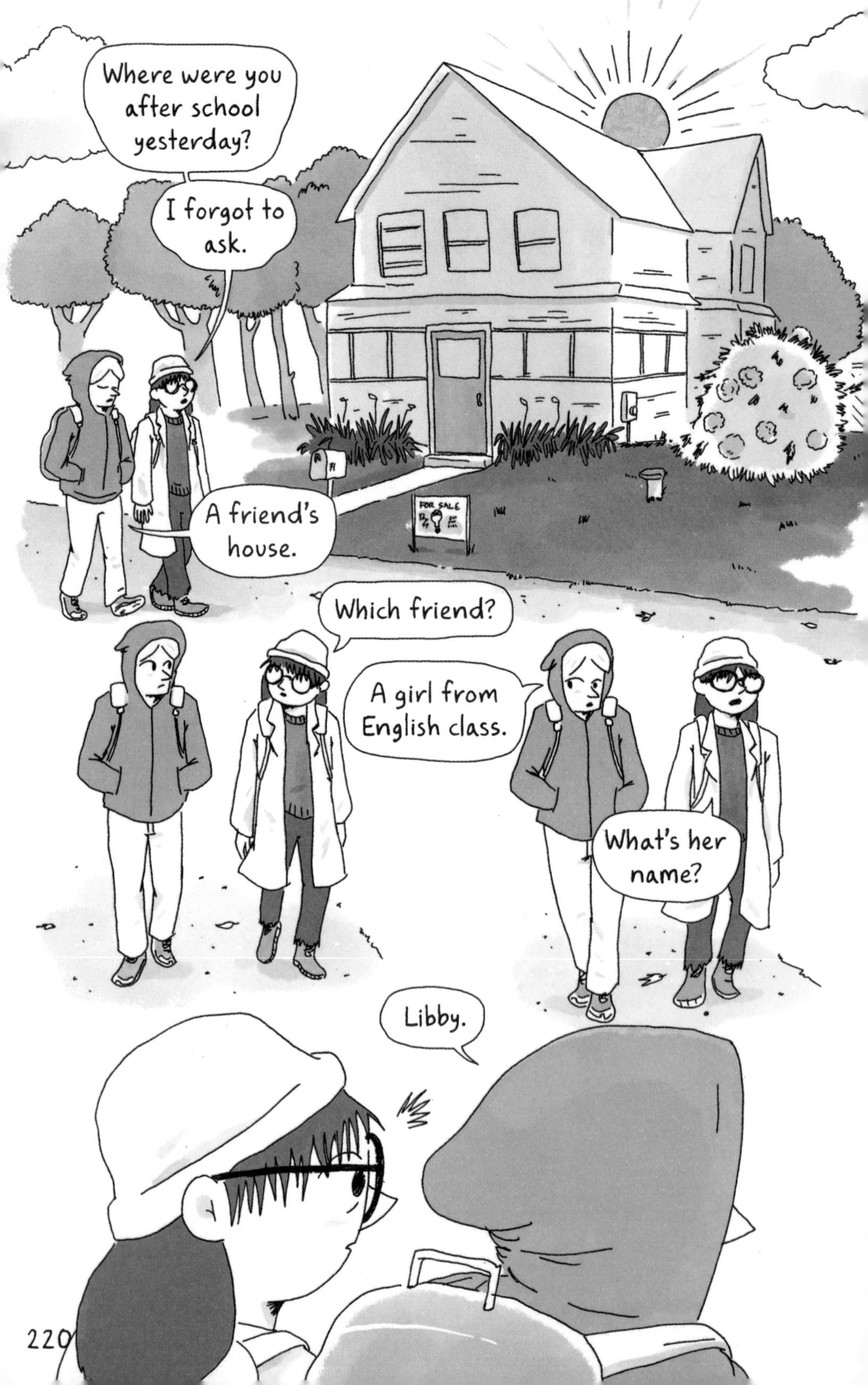
Where were you after school yesterday?
I forgot to ask.
A friend's house.
FOR SALE
Which friend?
A girl from English class.
What's her name?
Libby.

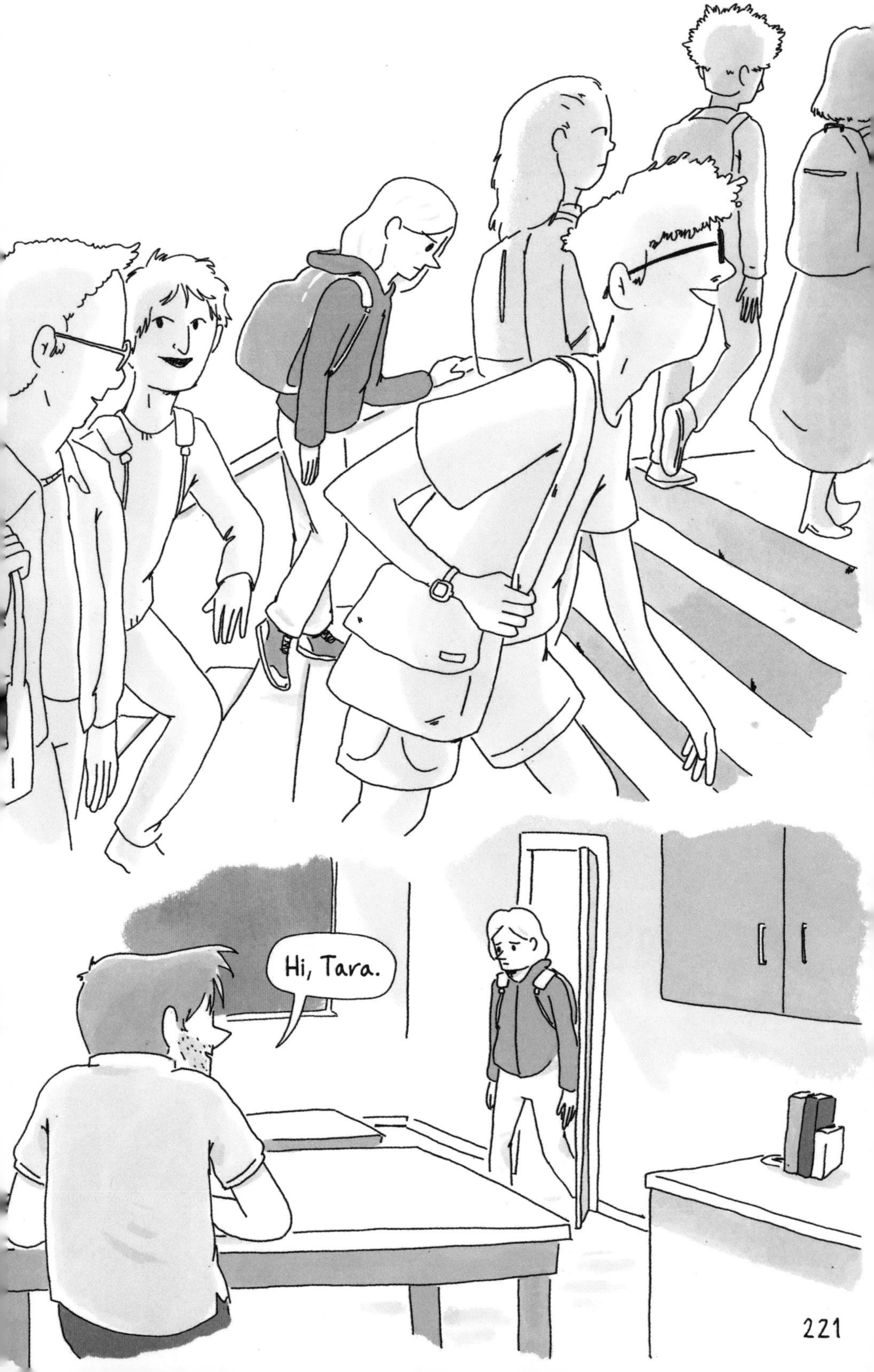
Hi, Tara.

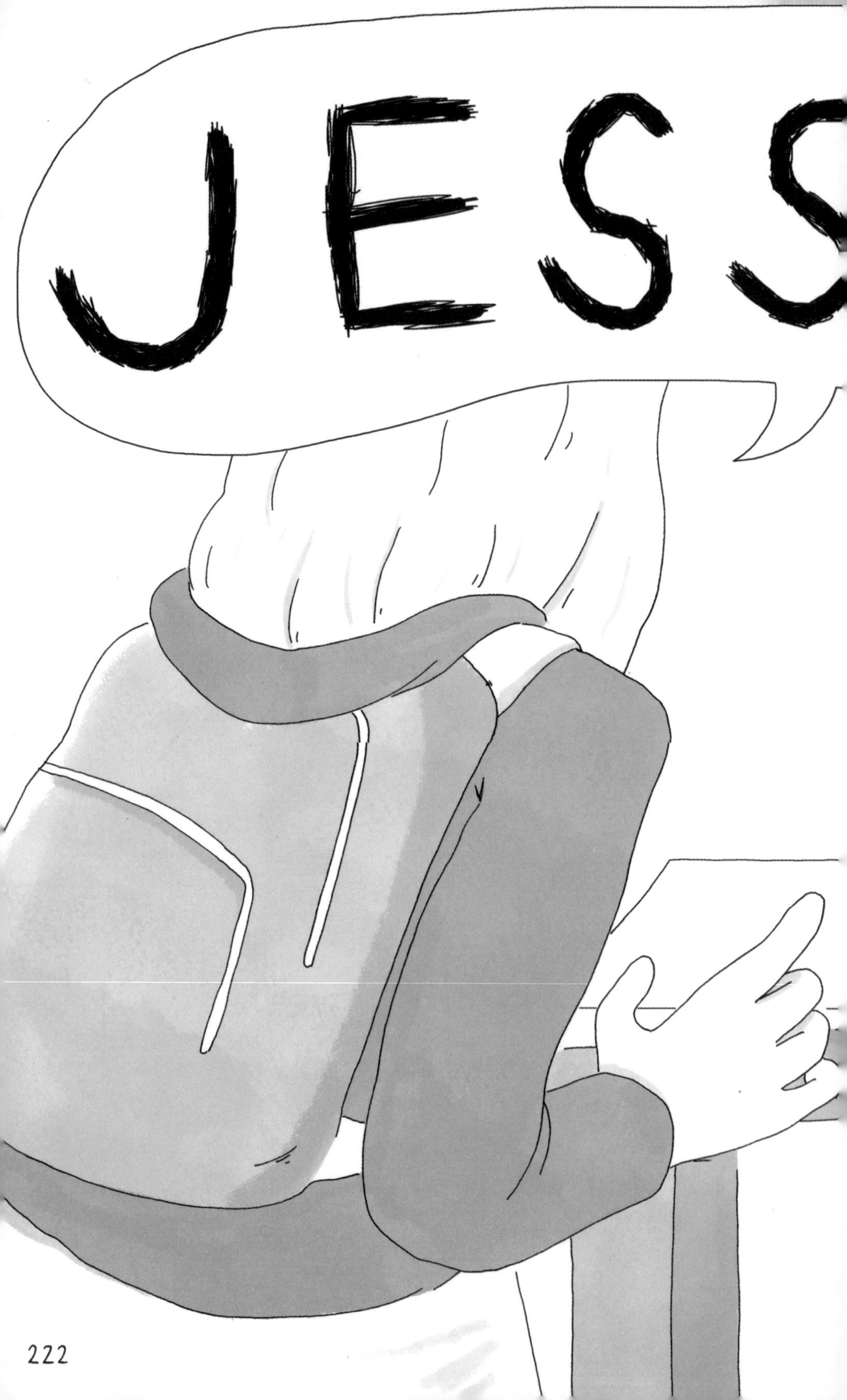
JESS

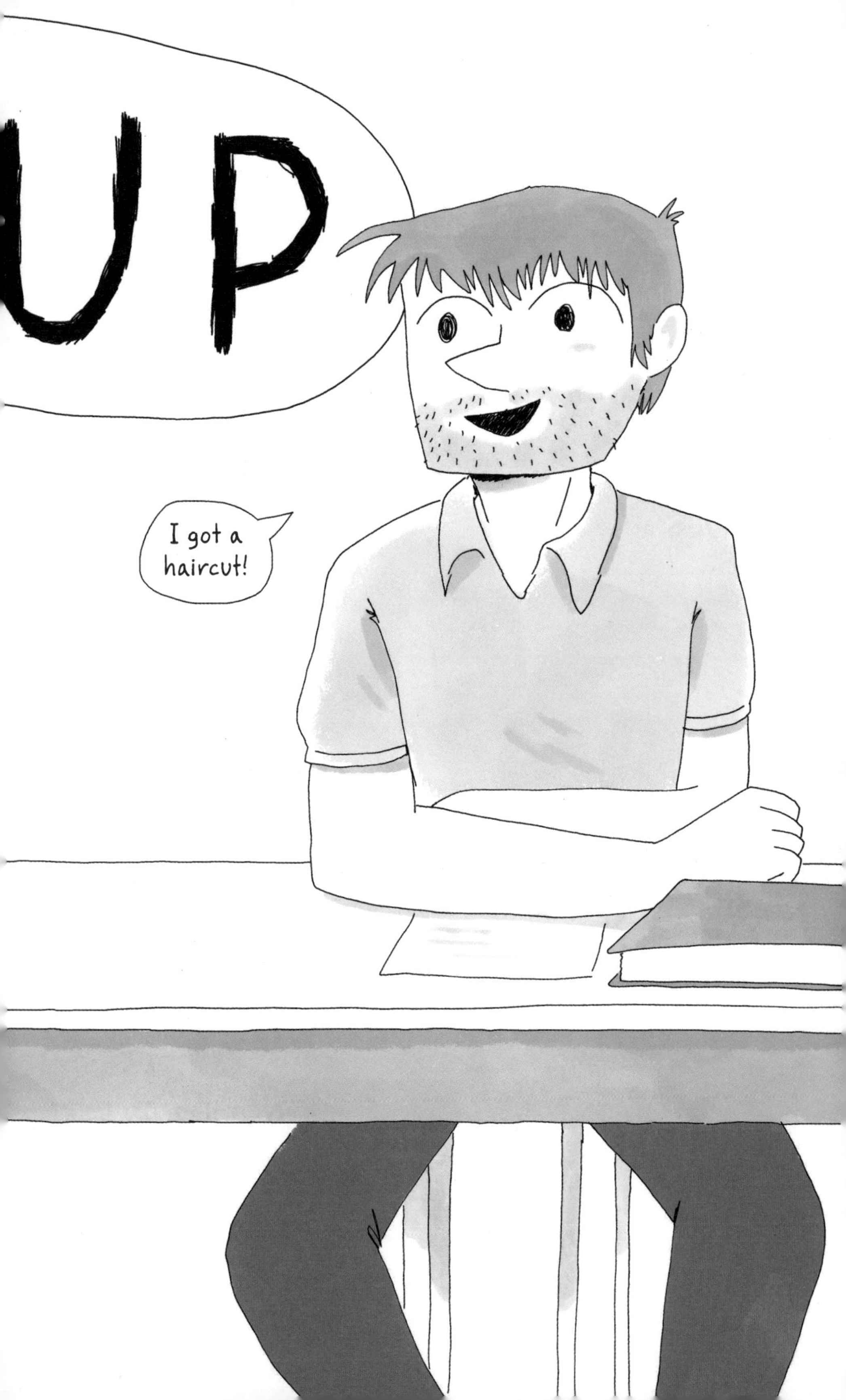
UP
I got a haircut!

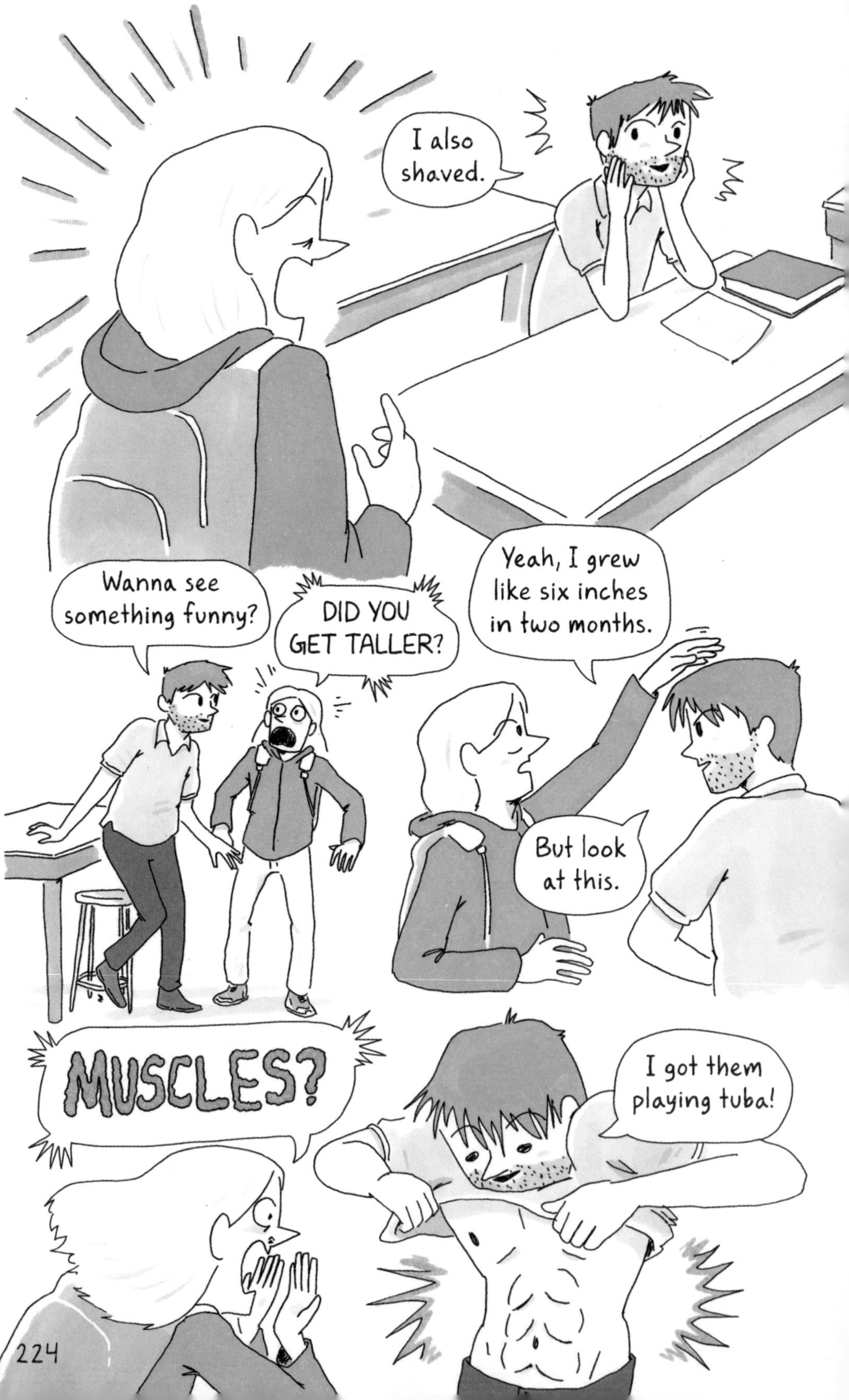
I also shaved.
Wanna see something funny?
DID YOU GET TALLER?
Yeah, I grew like six inches in two months.
But look at this.
MUSCLES?
I got them playing tuba!

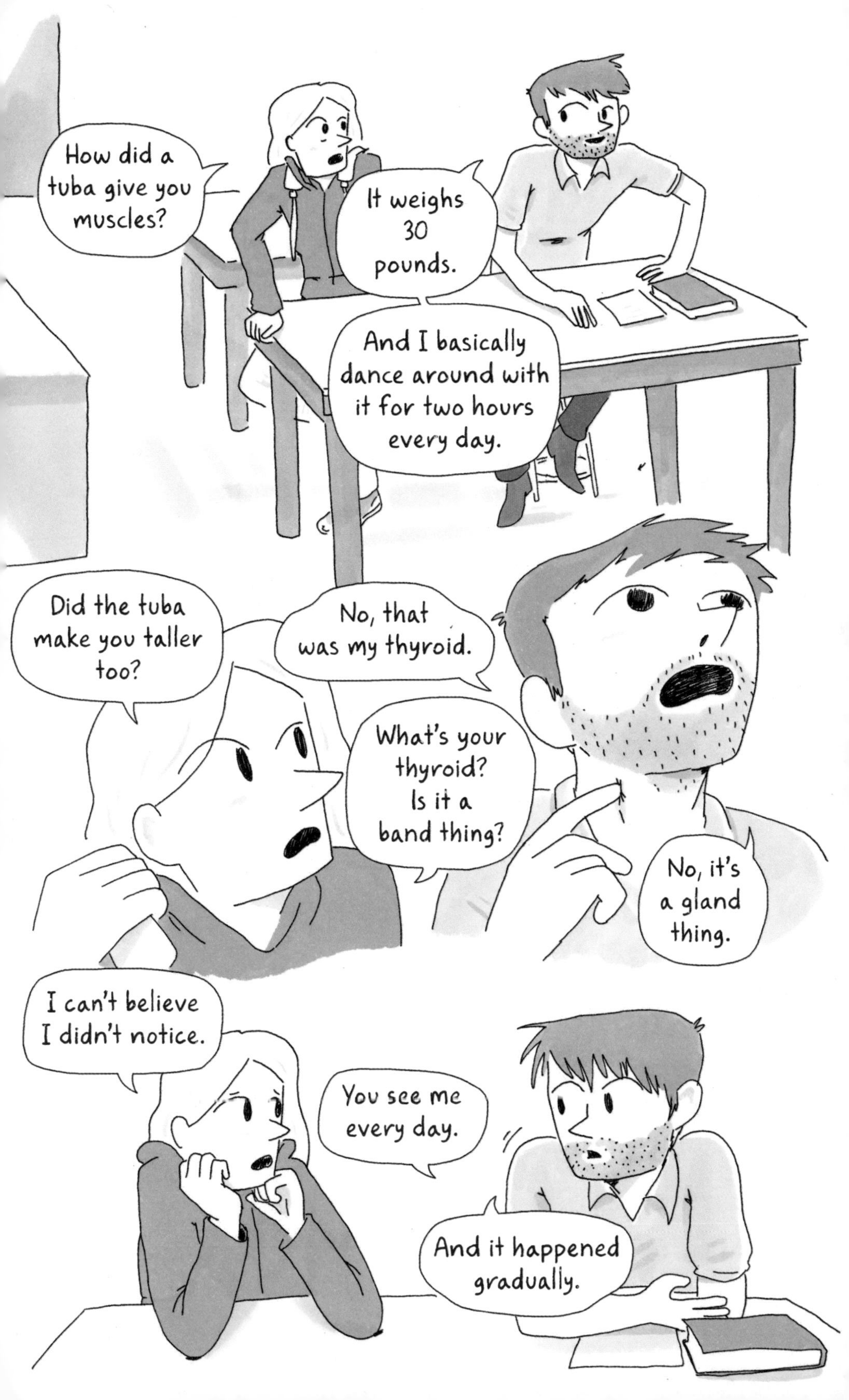
How did a tuba give you muscles?
It weighs 30 pounds.
And I basically dance around with it for two hours every day.
Did the tuba make you taller too?
No, that was my thyroid.
What's your thyroid? Is it a band thing?
No, it's a gland thing.
I can't believe I didn't notice.
You see me every day.
And it happened gradually.

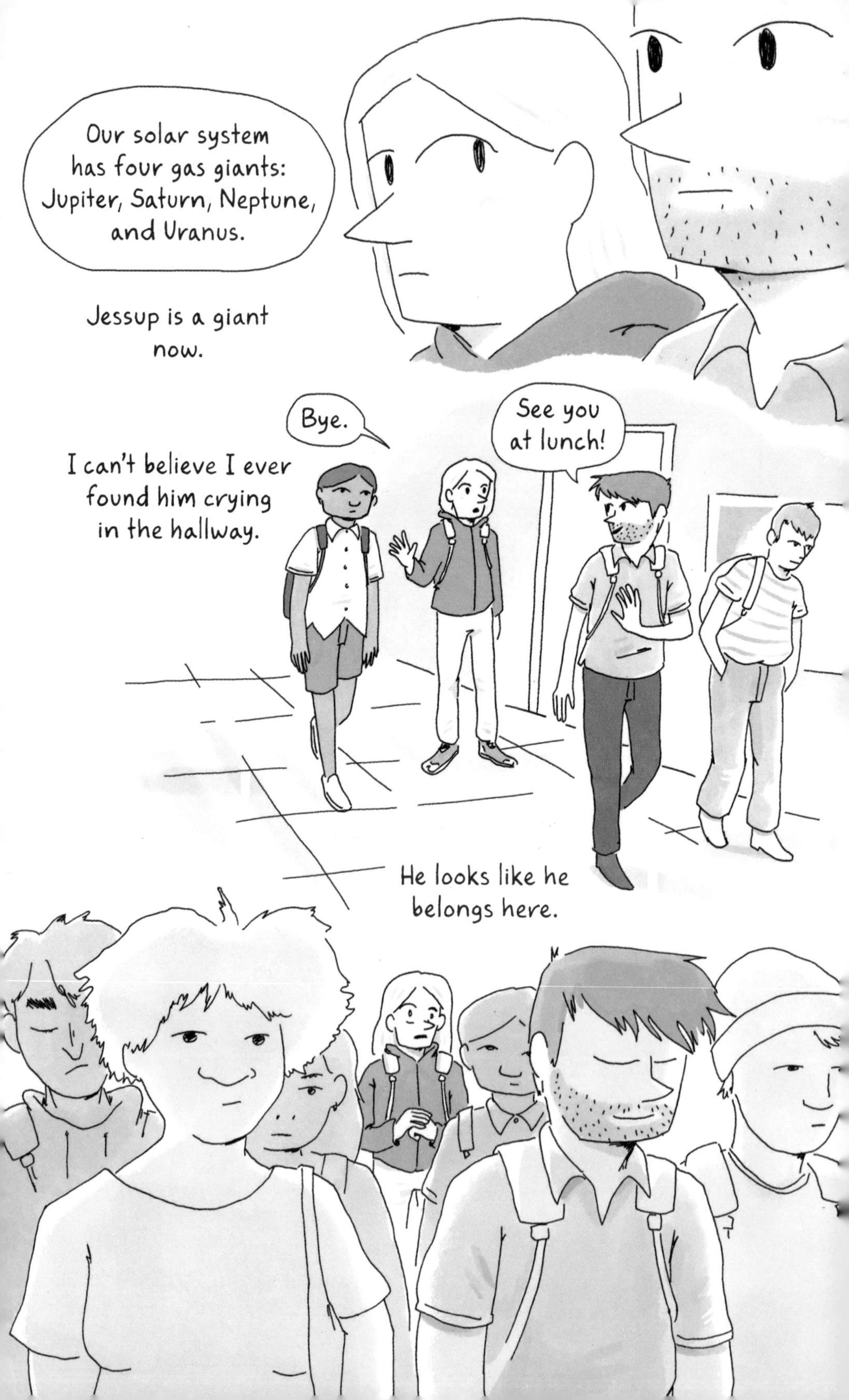
Our solar system has four gas giants: Jupiter, Saturn, Neptune, and Uranus.
Jessup is a giant now.
Bye.
See you at lunch!
I can't believe I ever found him crying in the hallway.
He looks like he belongs here.

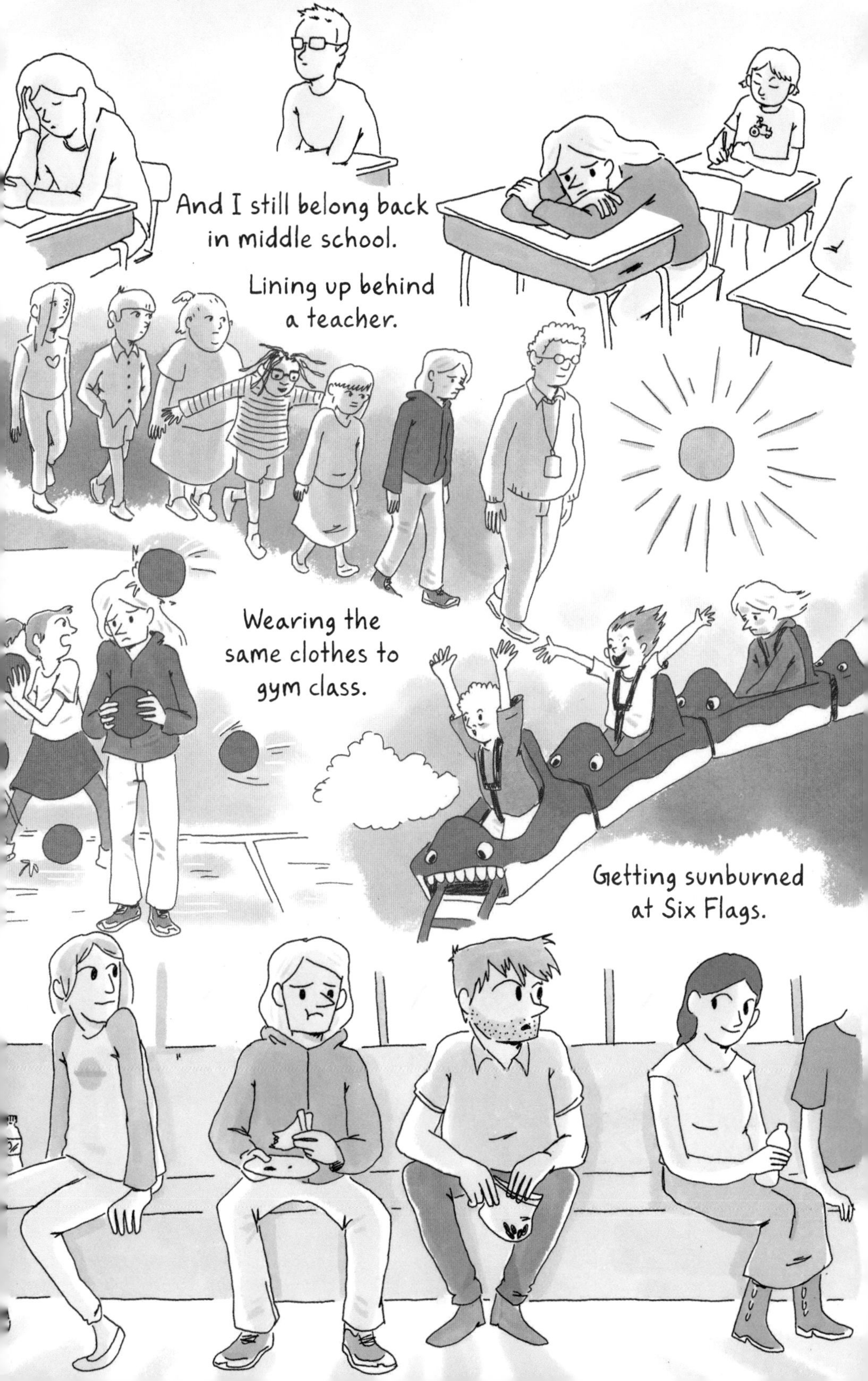
And I still belong back in middle school.
Lining up behind a teacher.
Wearing the same clothes to gym class.
Getting sunburned at Six Flags.

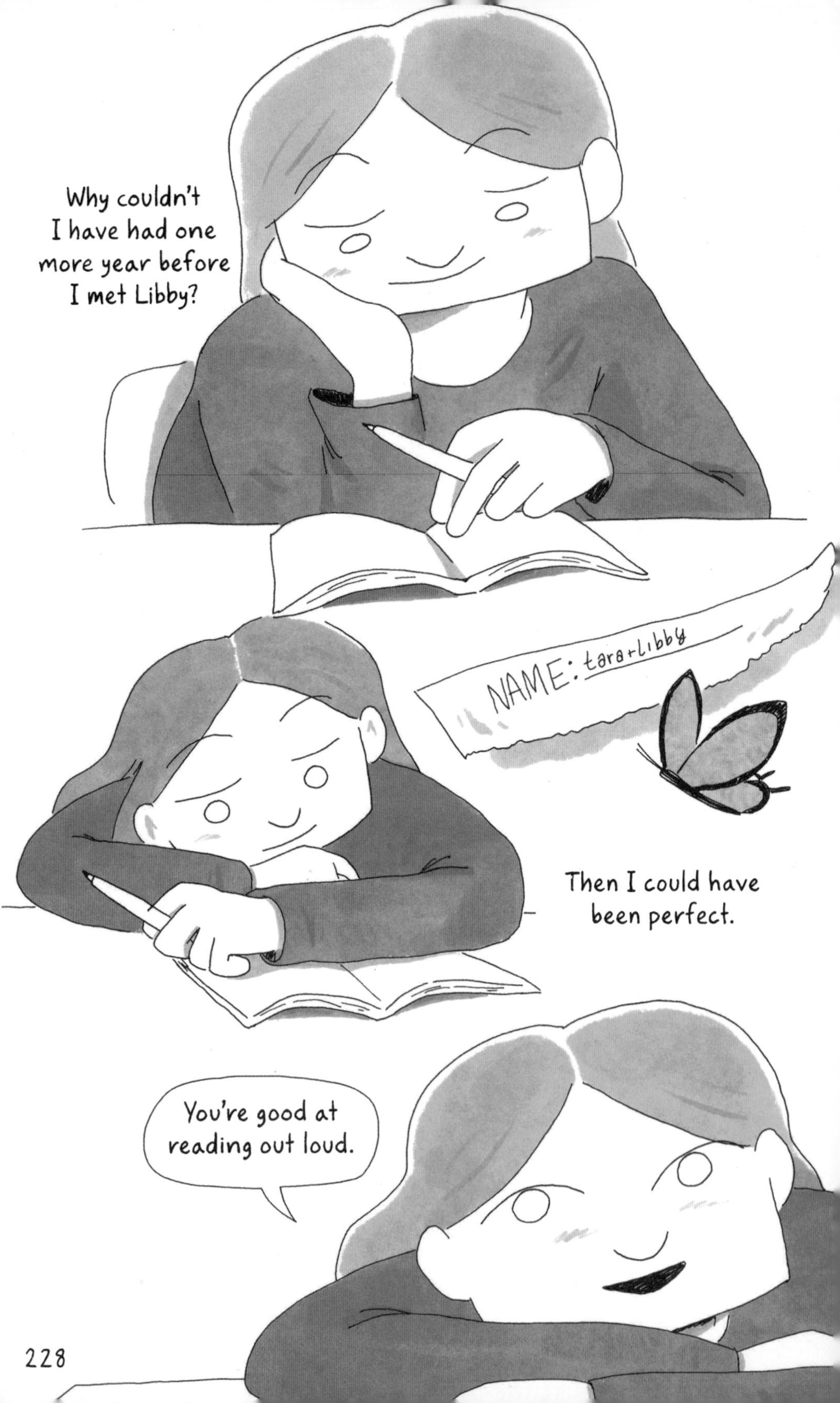
Why couldn't I have had one more year before I met Libby?
NAME: tara+Libby
Then I could have been perfect.
You're good at reading out loud.

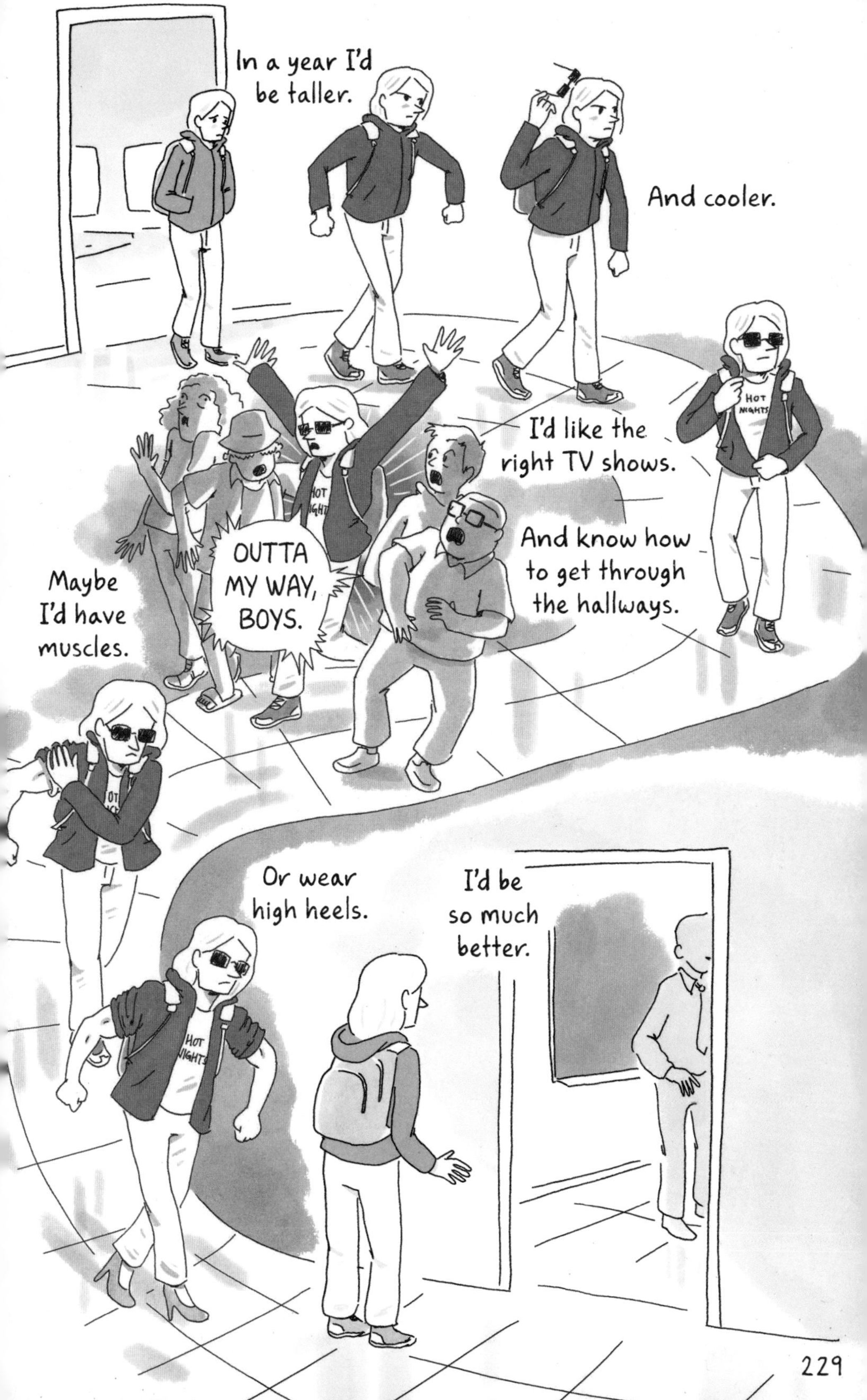
In a year I'd be taller.
And cooler.
I'd like the right TV shows.
And know how to get through the hallways.
OUTTA MY WAY, BOYS.
Maybe I'd have muscles.
Or wear high heels.
I'd be so much better.
HOT NIGHTS

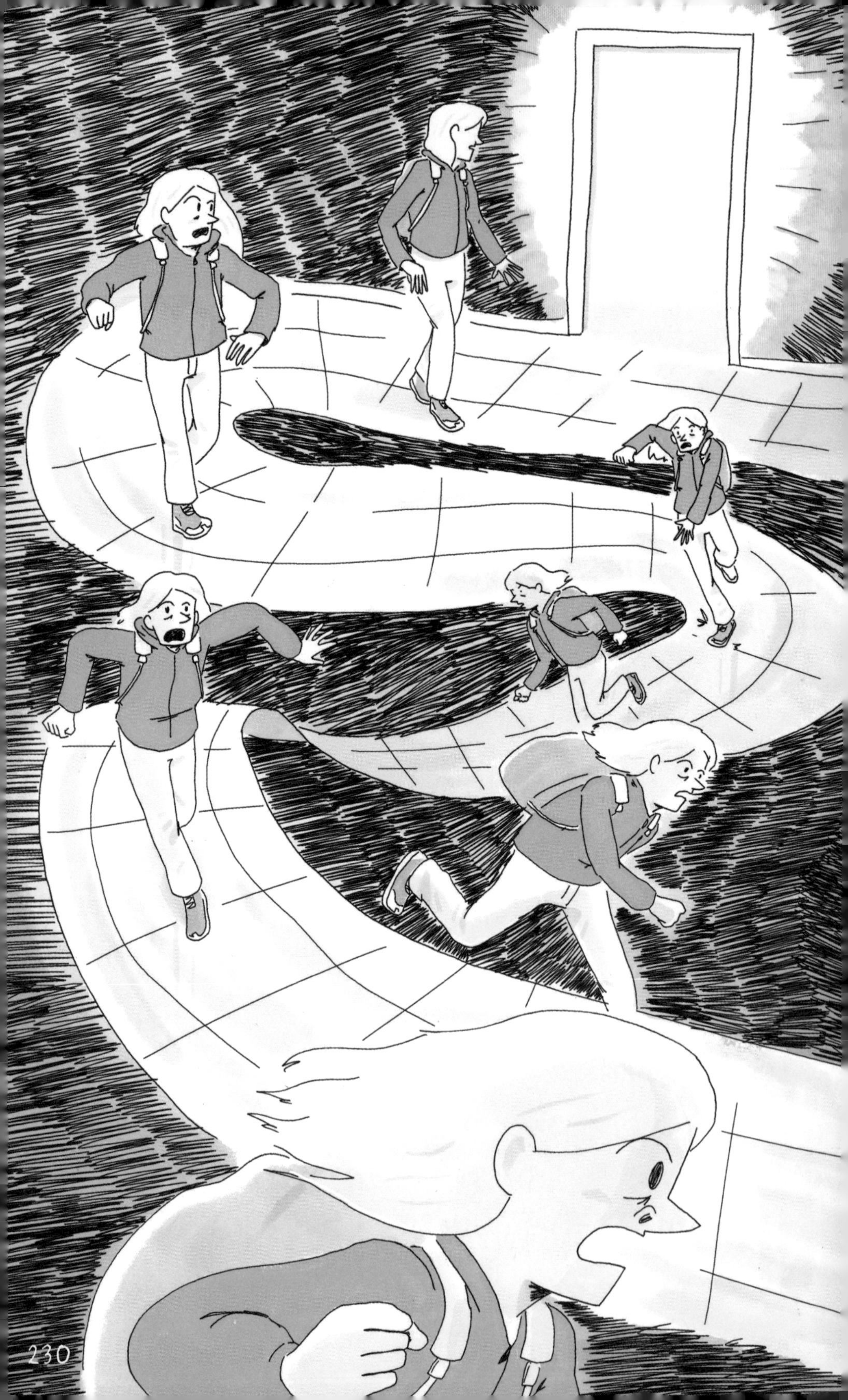

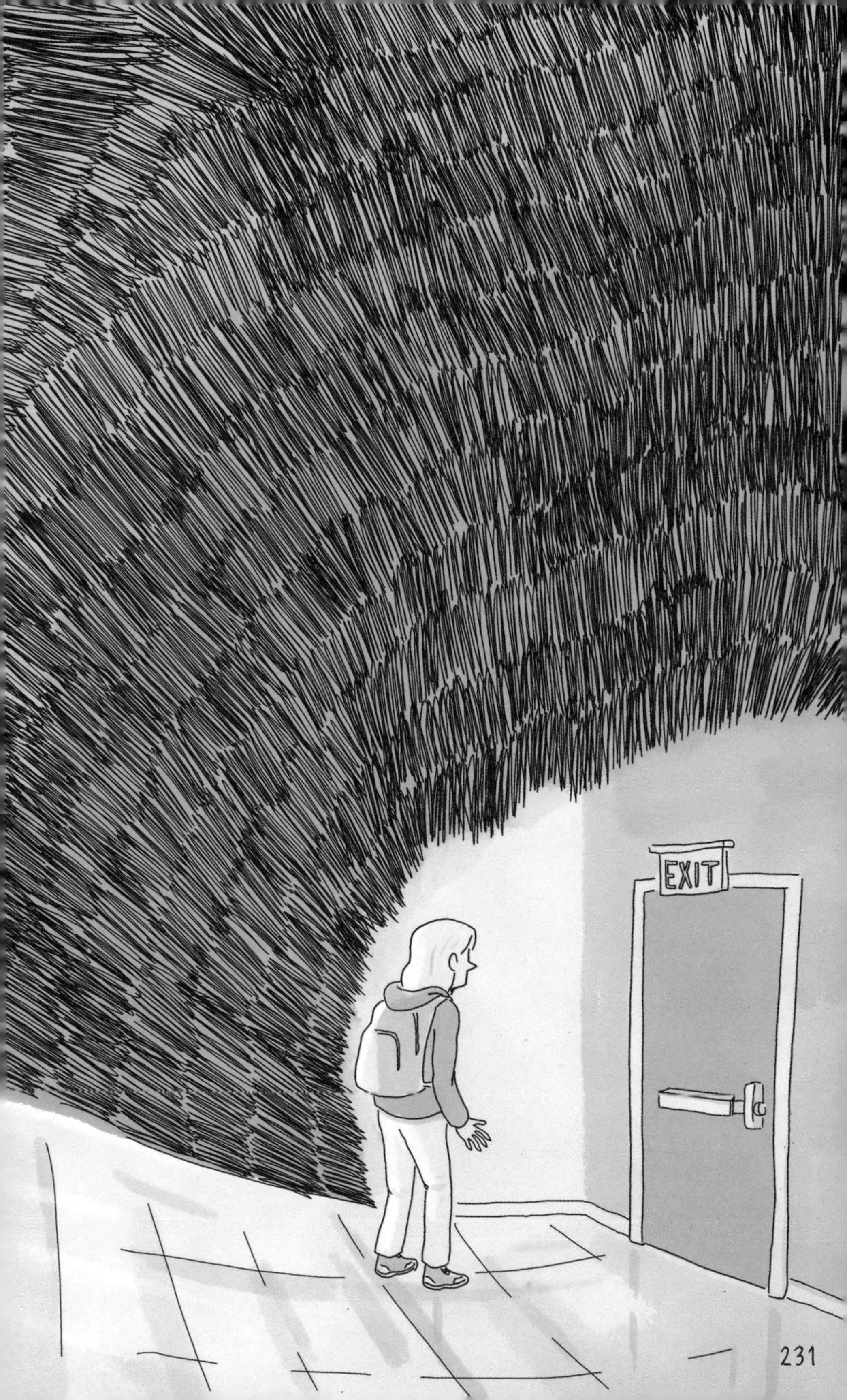
EXIT

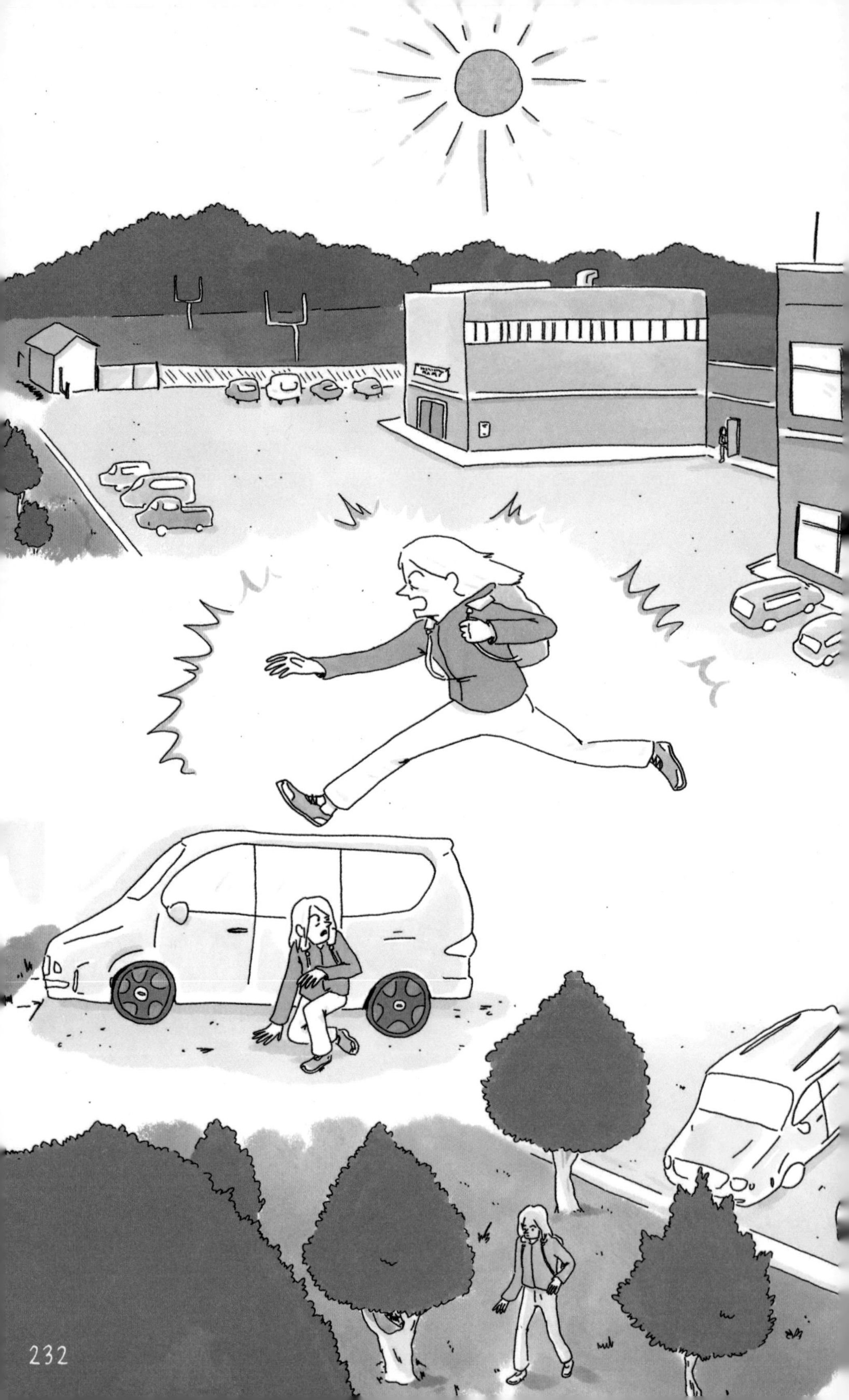

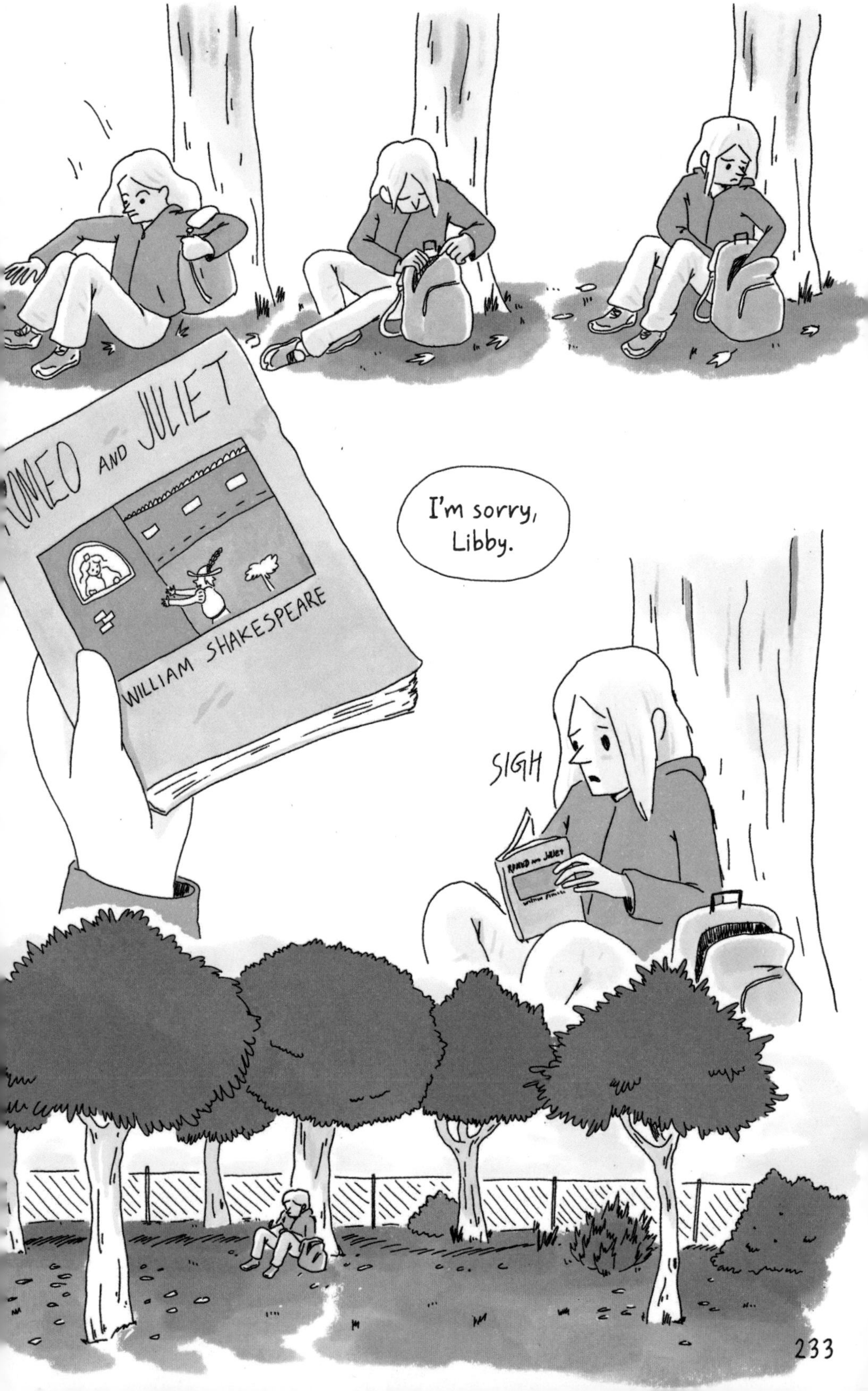
ROMEO AND JULIET
WILLIAM SHAKESPEARE
I'm sorry, Libby.
SIGH

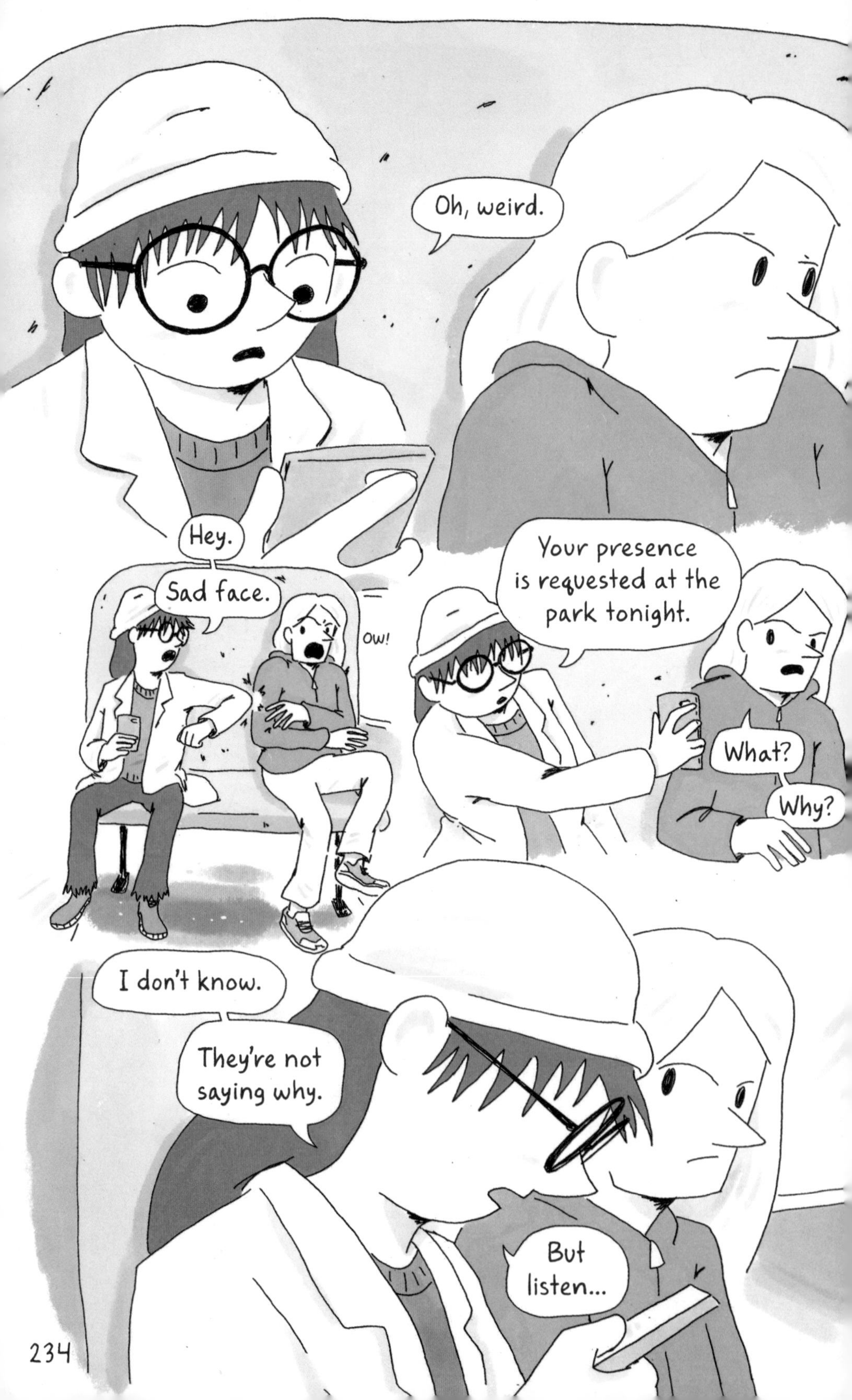
Oh, weird.
Hey.
Sad face.
OW!
Your presence is requested at the park tonight.
What?
Why?
I don't know.
They're not saying why.
But listen...

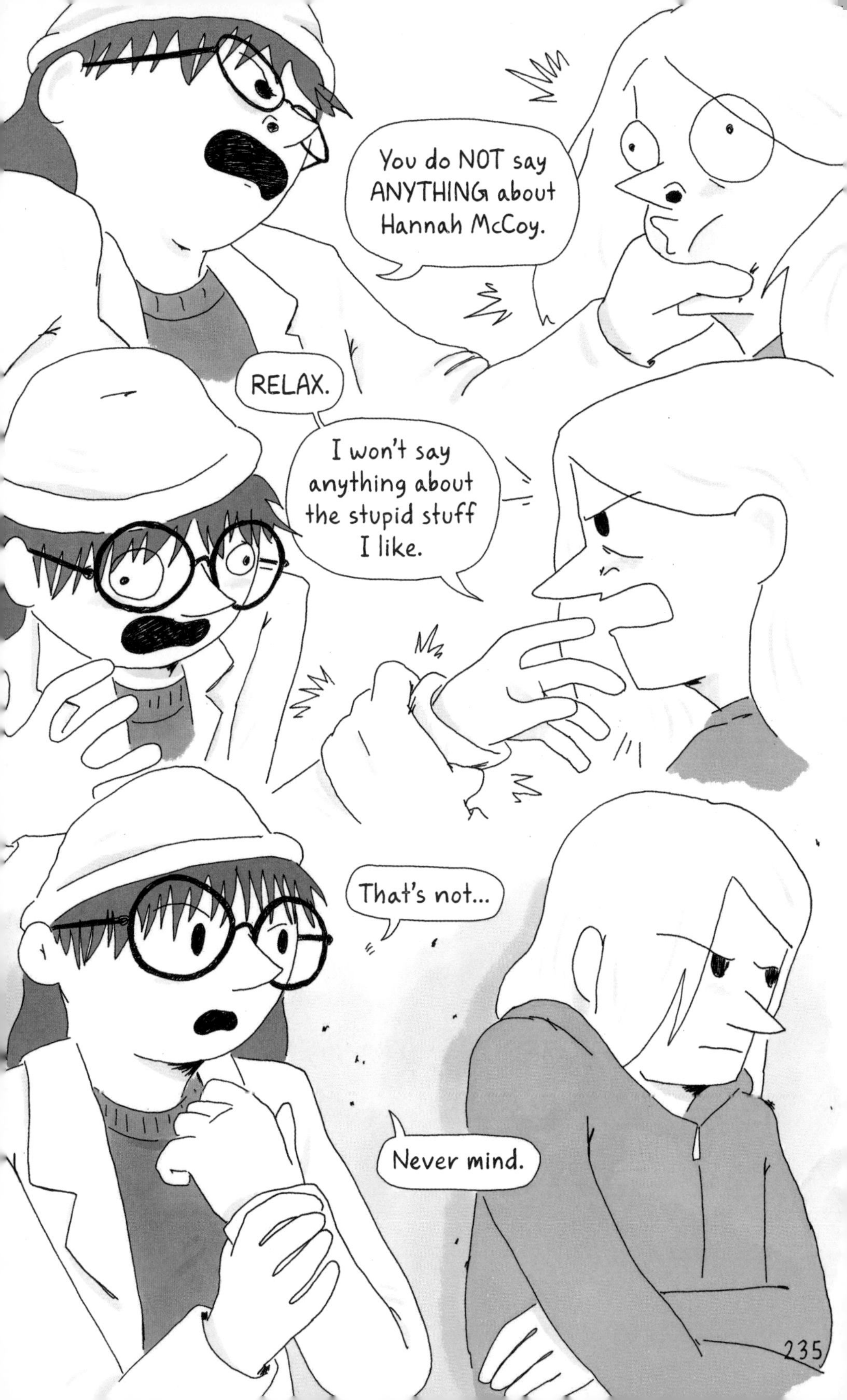
You do NOT say ANYTHING about Hannah McCoy.
RELAX.
I won't say anything about the stupid stuff I like.
That's not...
Never mind.

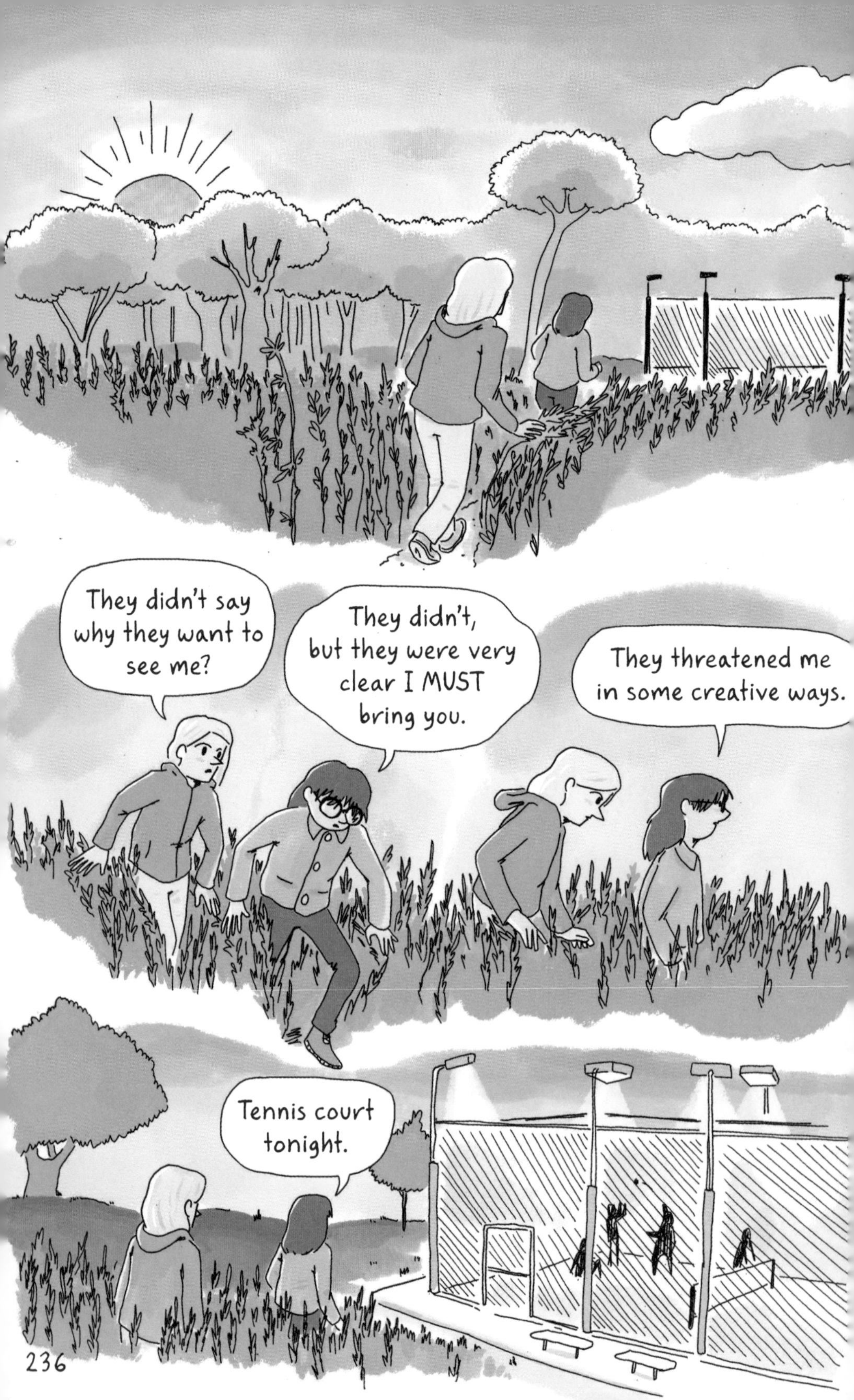
They didn't say why they want to see me?
They didn't, but they were very clear I MUST bring you.
They threatened me in some creative ways.
Tennis court tonight.

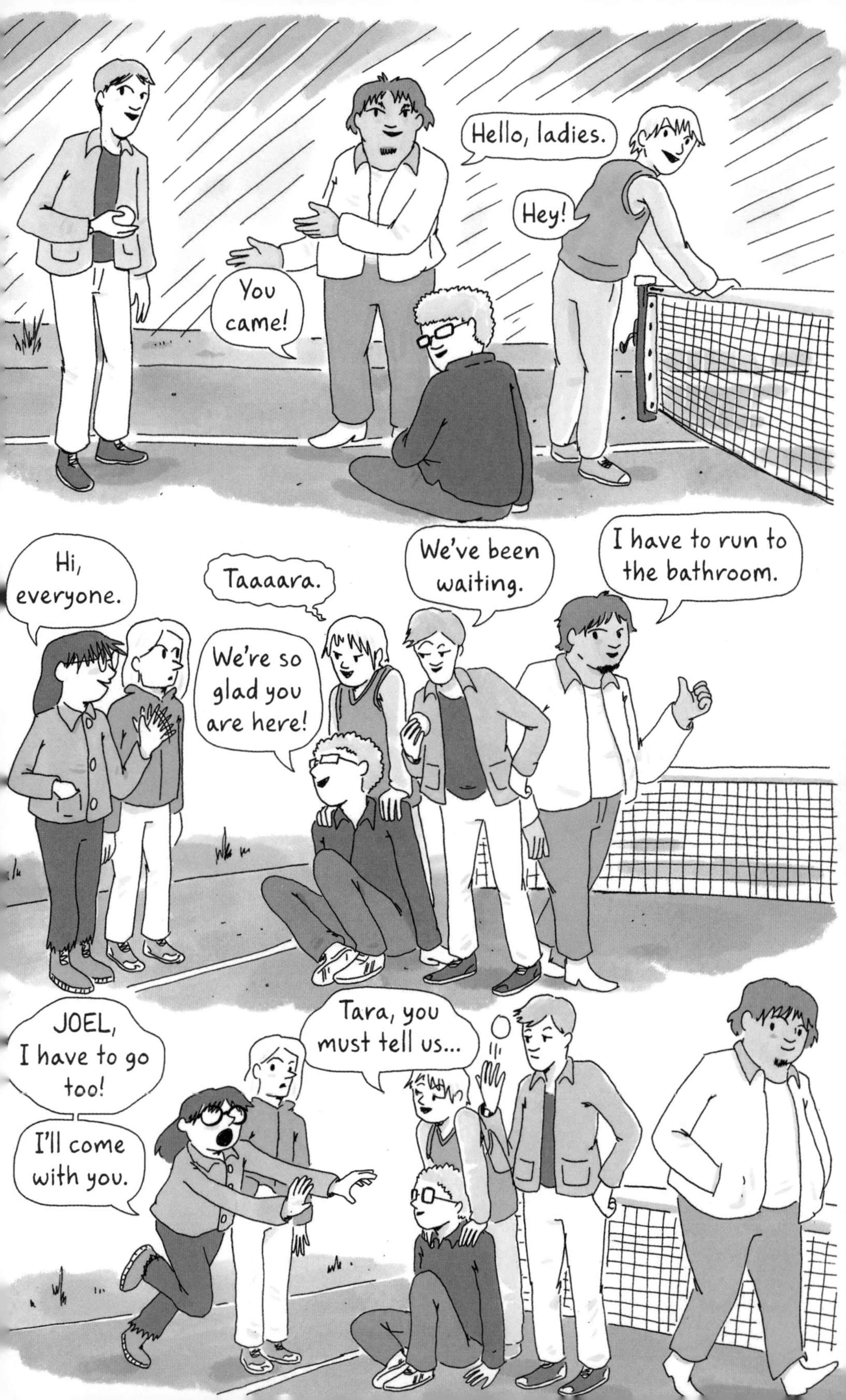
Hello, ladies.
Hey!
You came!
Hi, everyone.
Taaaara.
We're so glad you are here!
We've been waiting.
I have to run to the bathroom.
JOEL, I have to go too!
I'll come with you.
Tara, you must tell us...

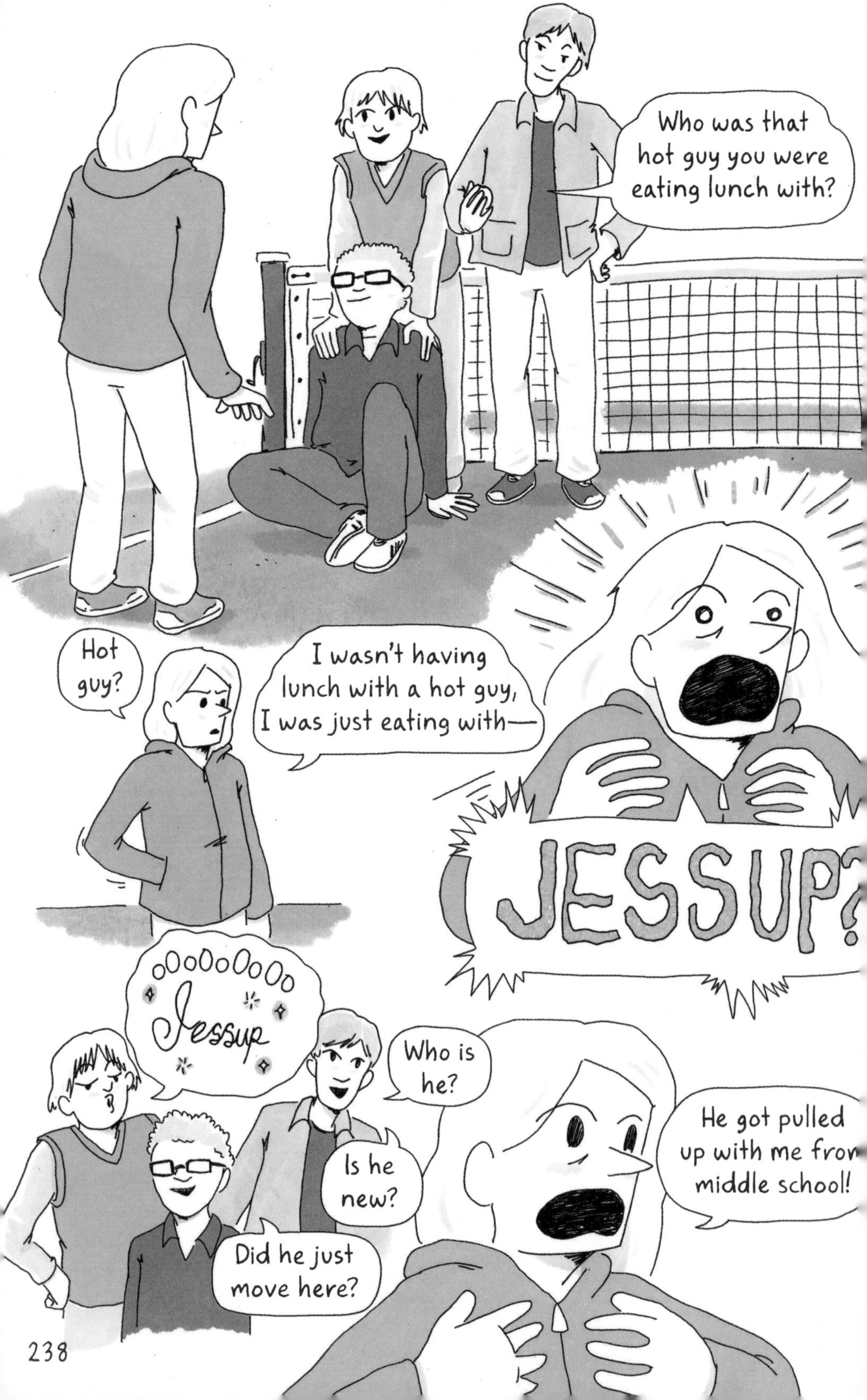
Who was that hot guy you were eating lunch with?
Hot guy?
I wasn't having lunch with a hot guy, I was just eating with—
JESSUP?
oOoOoOoOo Jessup
Who is he?
Is he new?
Did he just move here?
He got pulled up with me from middle school!

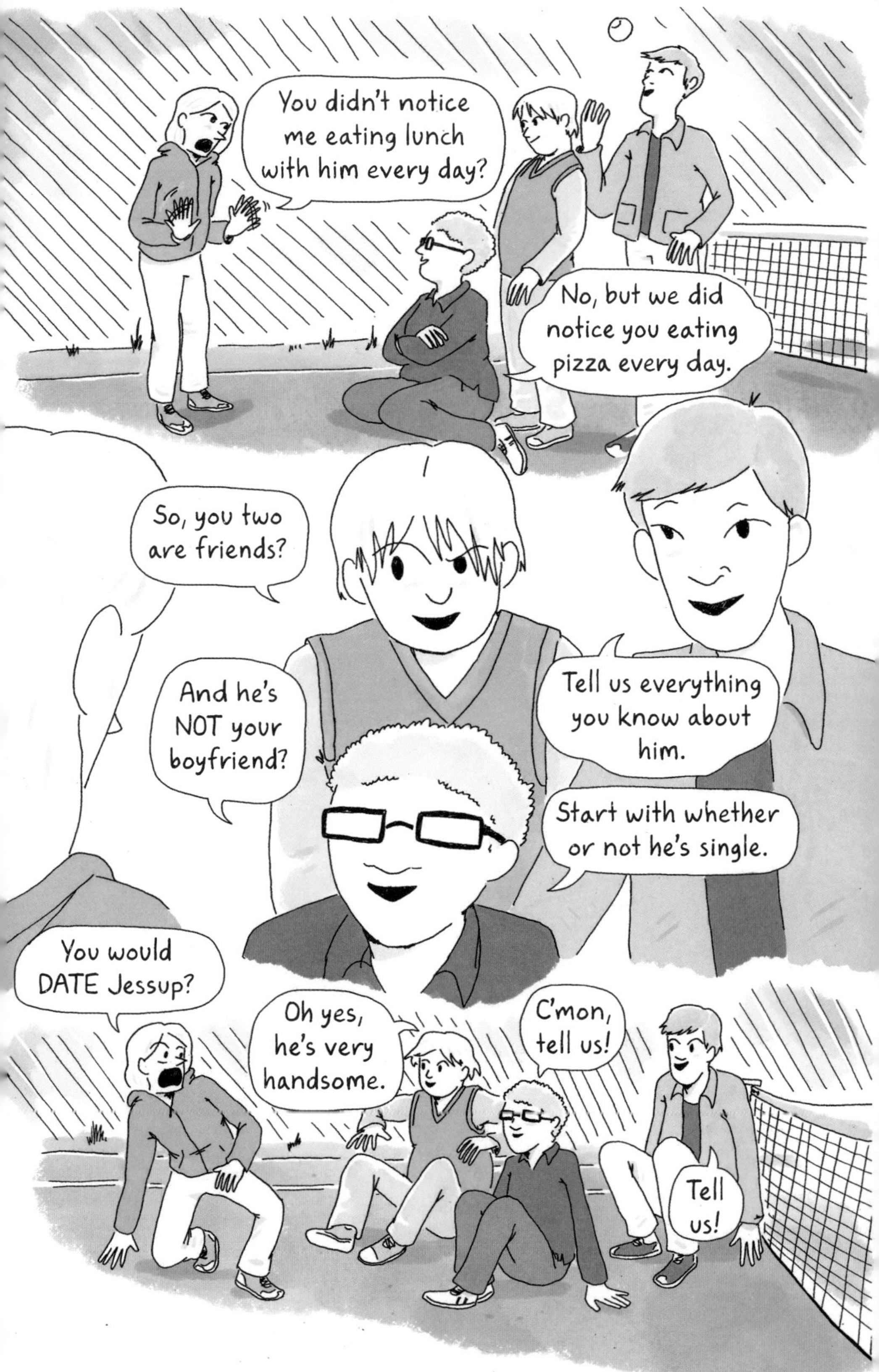
You didn't notice me eating lunch with him every day?
No, but we did notice you eating pizza every day.
So, you two are friends?
And he's NOT your boyfriend?
Tell us everything you know about him.
Start with whether or not he's single.
You would DATE Jessup?
Oh yes, he's very handsome.
C'mon, tell us!
Tell us!

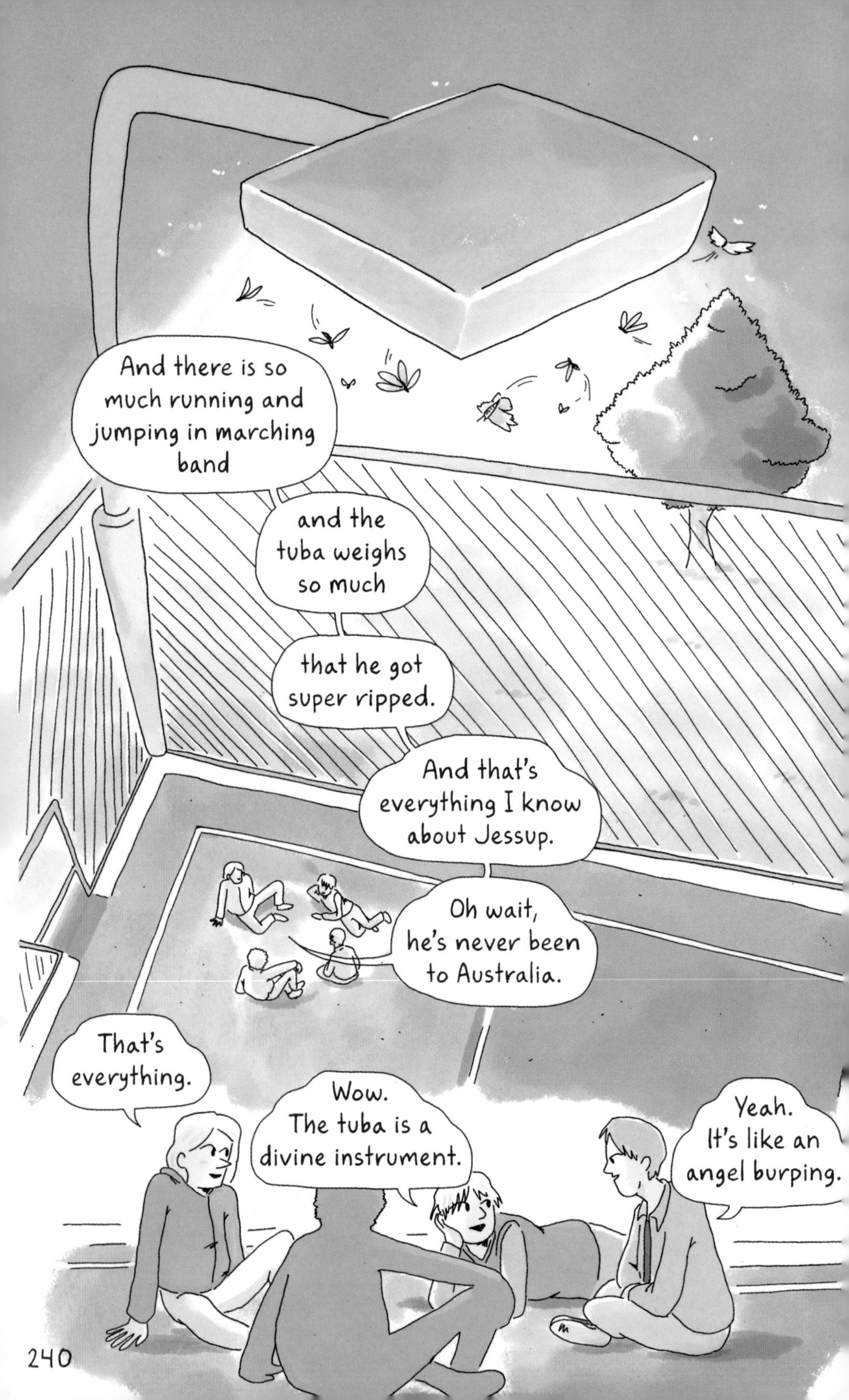
And there is so much running and jumping in marching band
and the tuba weighs so much
that he got super ripped.
And that's everything I know about Jessup.
Oh wait, he's never been to Australia.
That's everything.
Wow. The tuba is a divine instrument.
Yeah. It's like an angel burping.

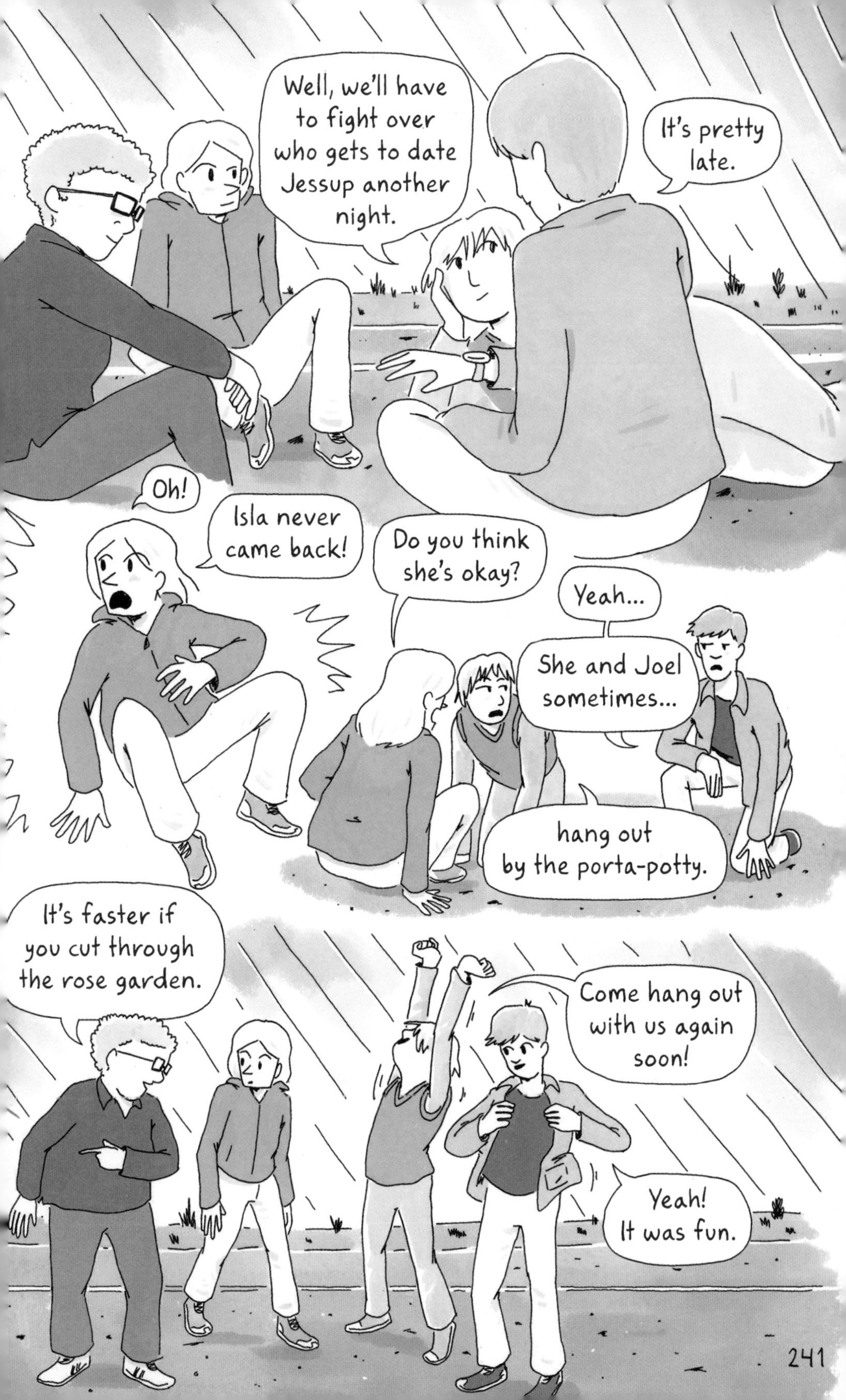
Well, we'll have to fight over who gets to date Jessup another night.
It's pretty late.
Oh!
Isla never came back!
Do you think she's okay?
Yeah...
She and Joel sometimes...
hang out by the porta-potty.
It's faster if you cut through the rose garden.
Come hang out with us again soon!
Yeah! It was fun.

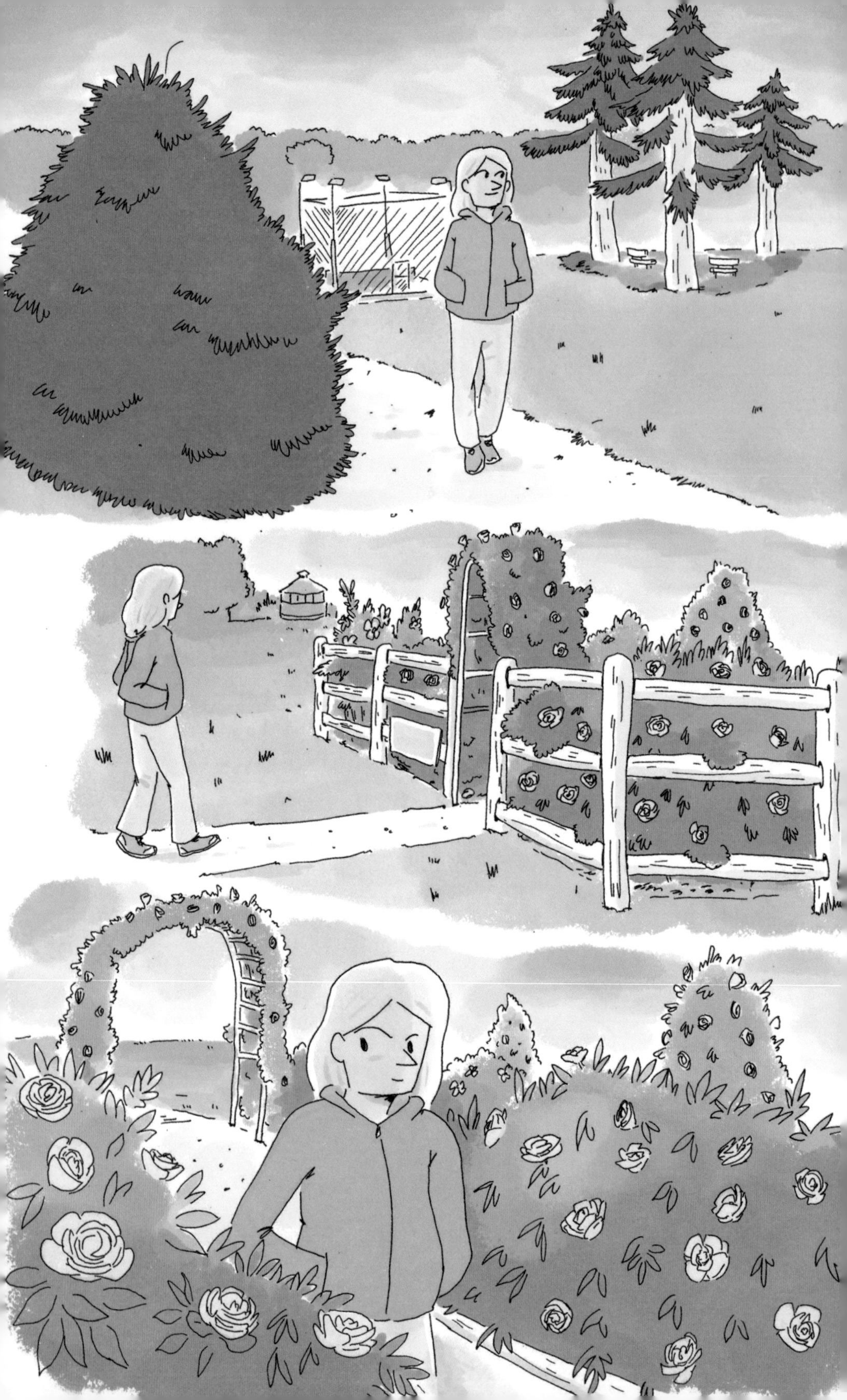

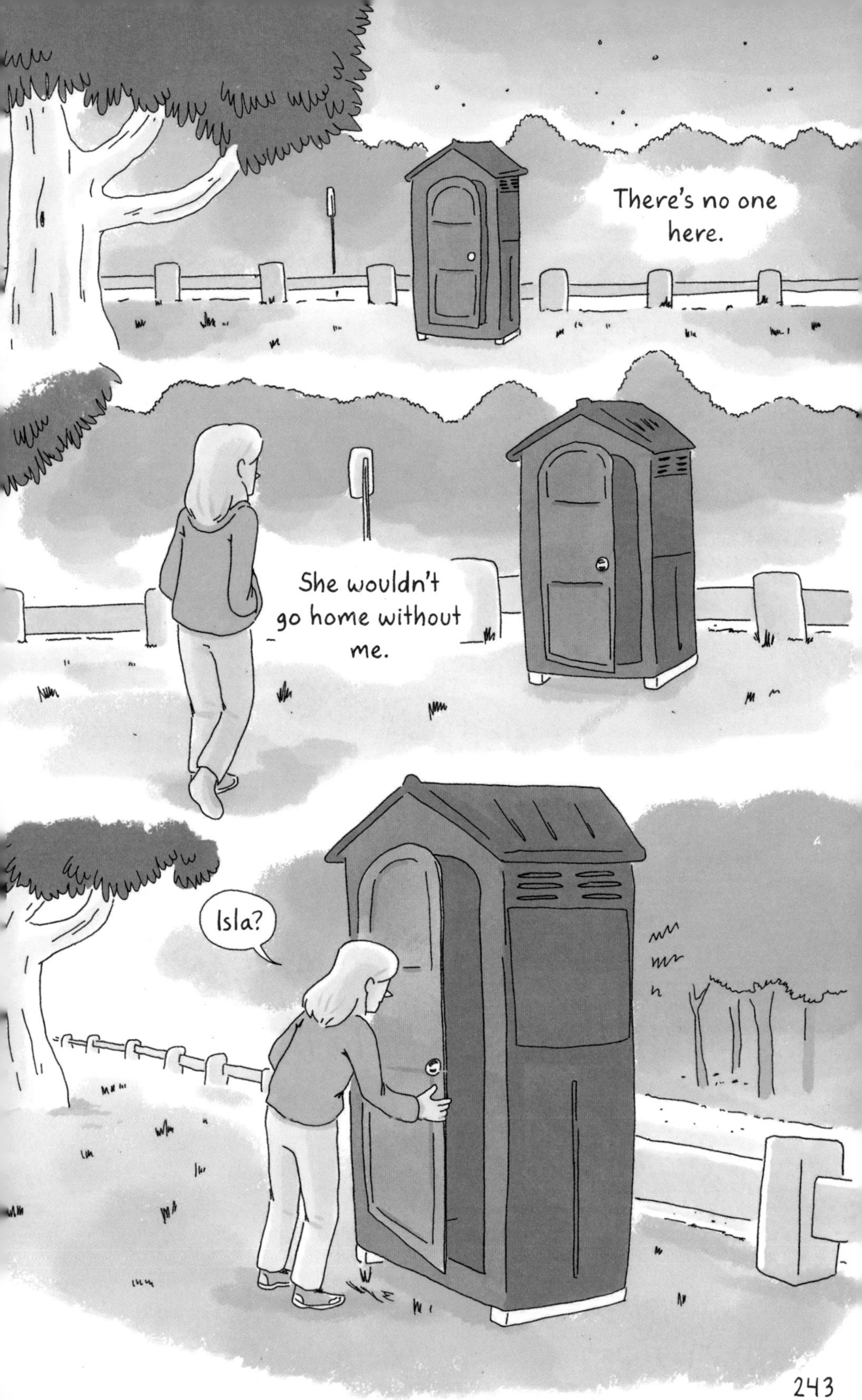
There's no one here.
She wouldn't go home without me.
Isla?

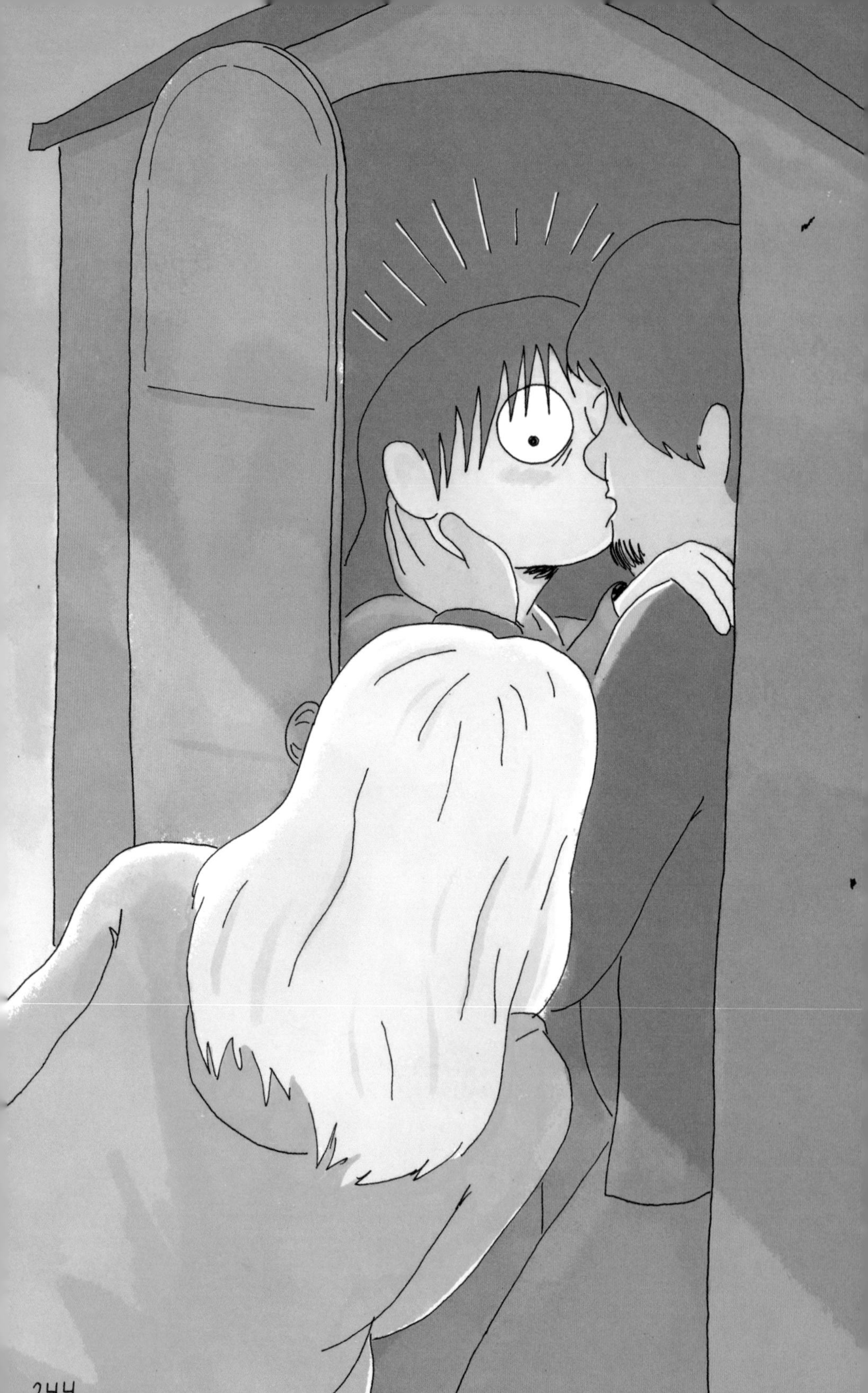

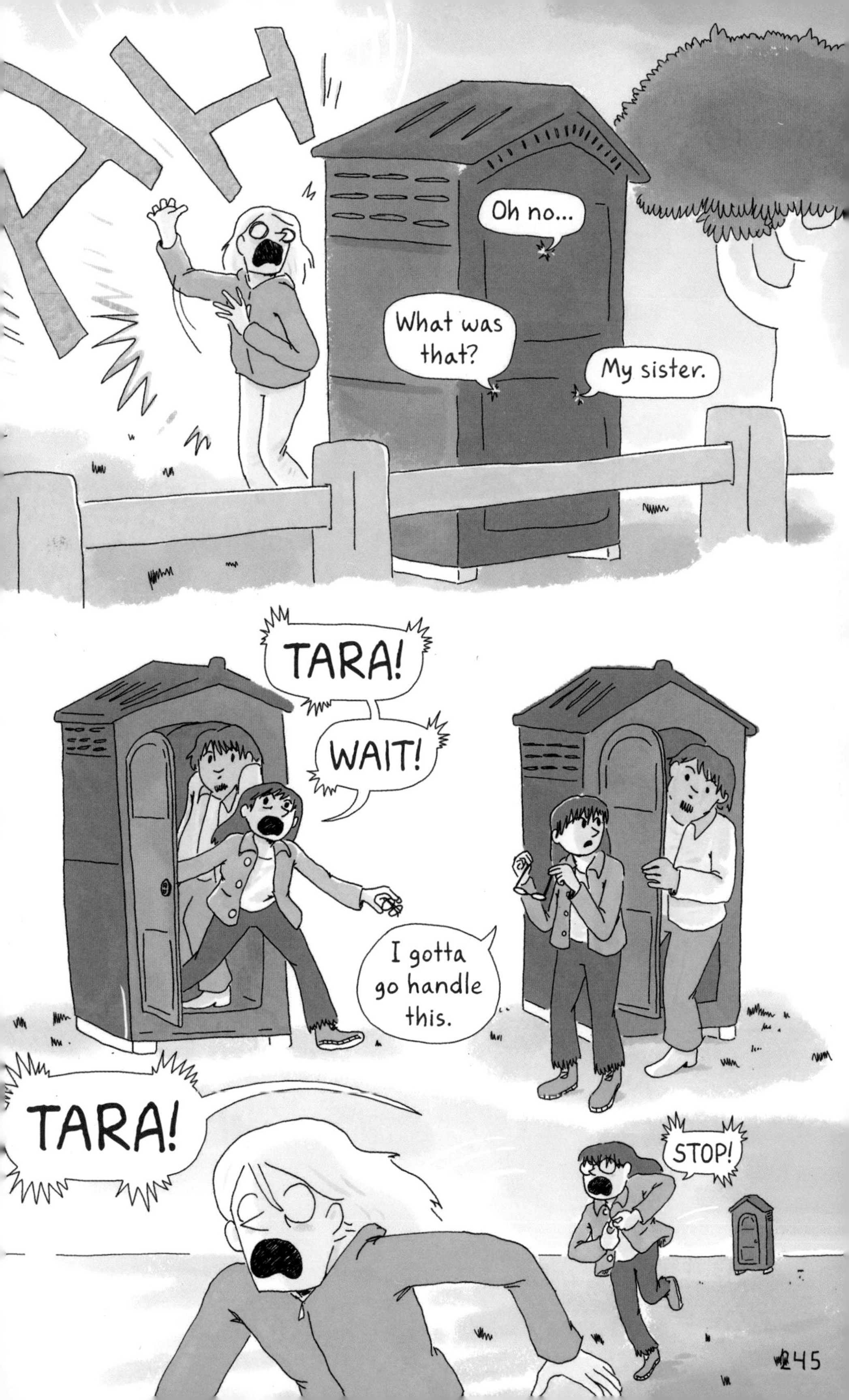
Oh no...
What was that?
My sister.
TARA!
WAIT!
I gotta go handle this.
TARA!
STOP!

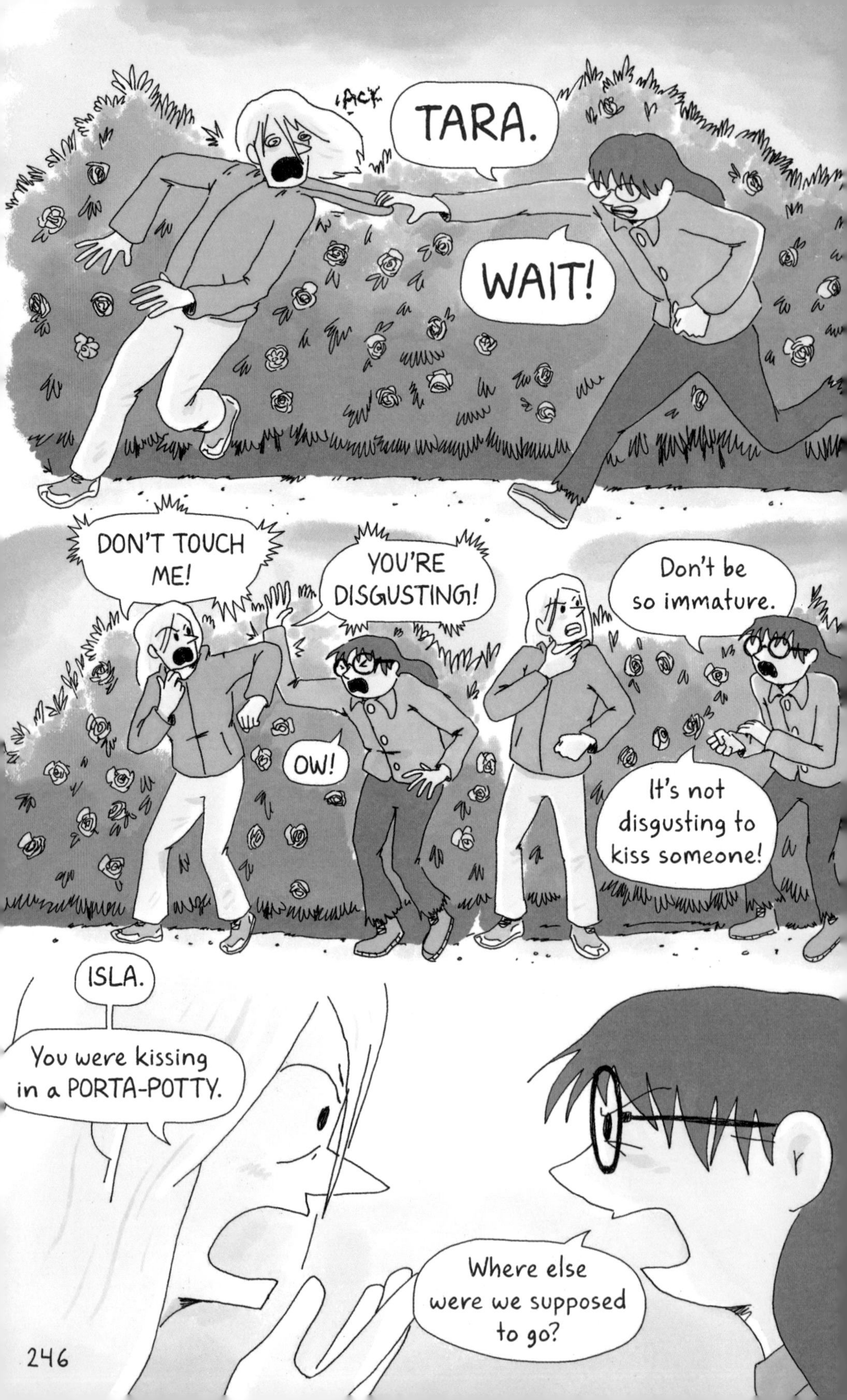
ACK
TARA.
WAIT!
DON'T TOUCH ME!
YOU'RE DISGUSTING!
OW!
Don't be so immature.
It's not disgusting to kiss someone!
ISLA.
You were kissing in a PORTA-POTTY.
Where else were we supposed to go?

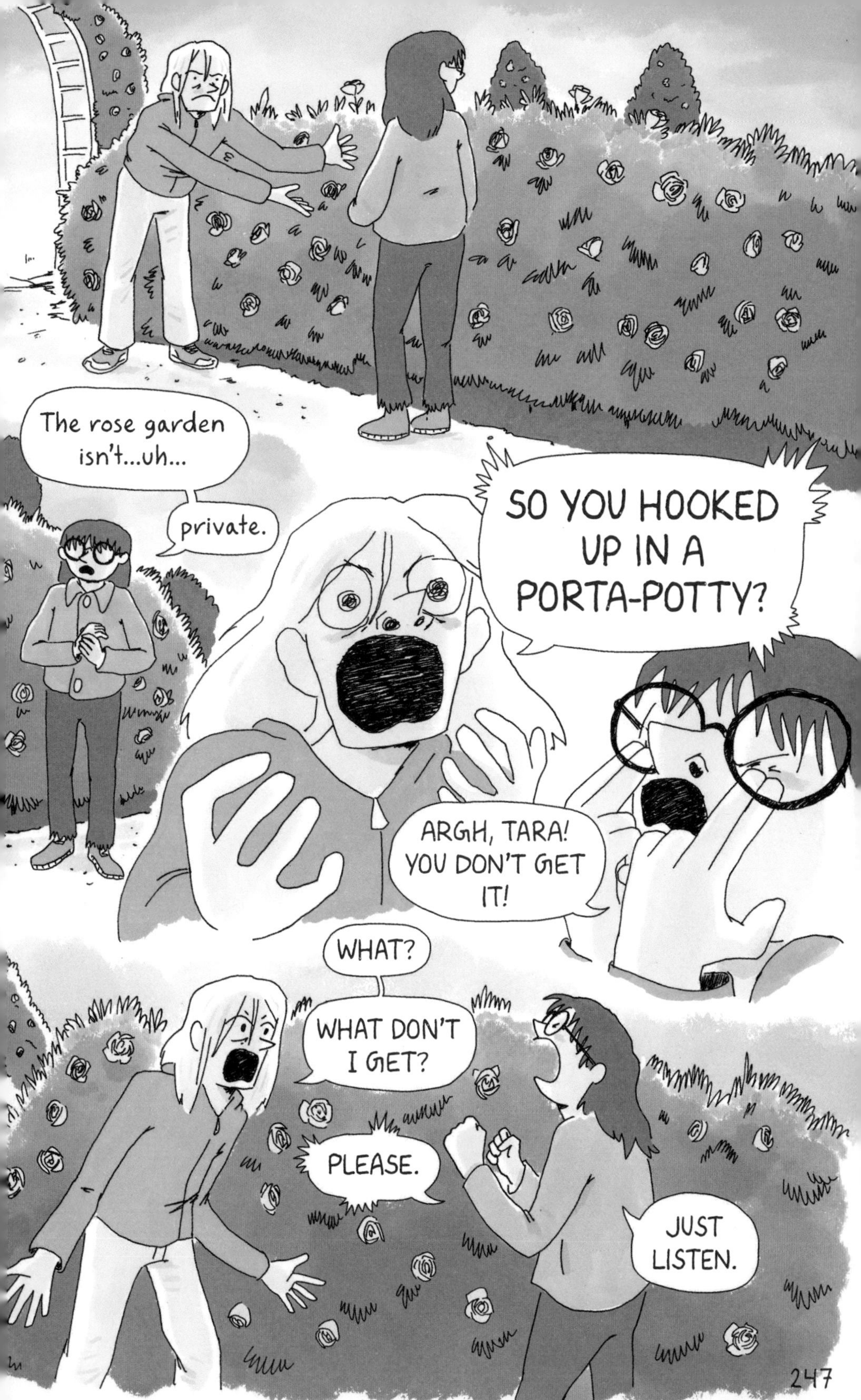
The rose garden isn't...uh...
private.
SO YOU HOOKED UP IN A PORTA-POTTY?
ARGH, TARA! YOU DON'T GET IT!
WHAT?
WHAT DON'T I GET?
PLEASE.
JUST LISTEN.

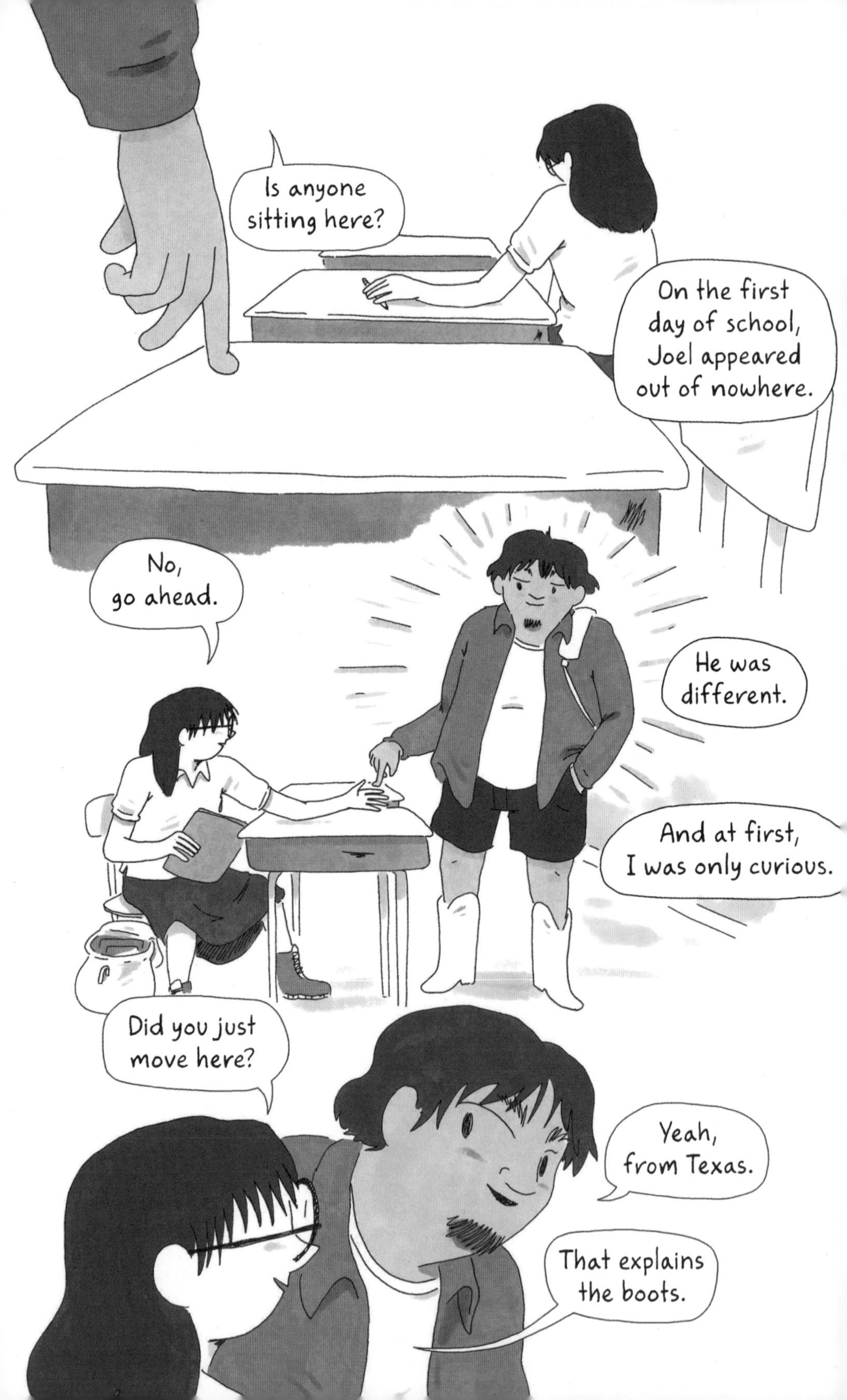
Is anyone sitting here?
On the first day of school, Joel appeared out of nowhere.
No, go ahead.
He was different.
And at first, I was only curious.
Did you just move here?
Yeah, from Texas.
That explains the boots.

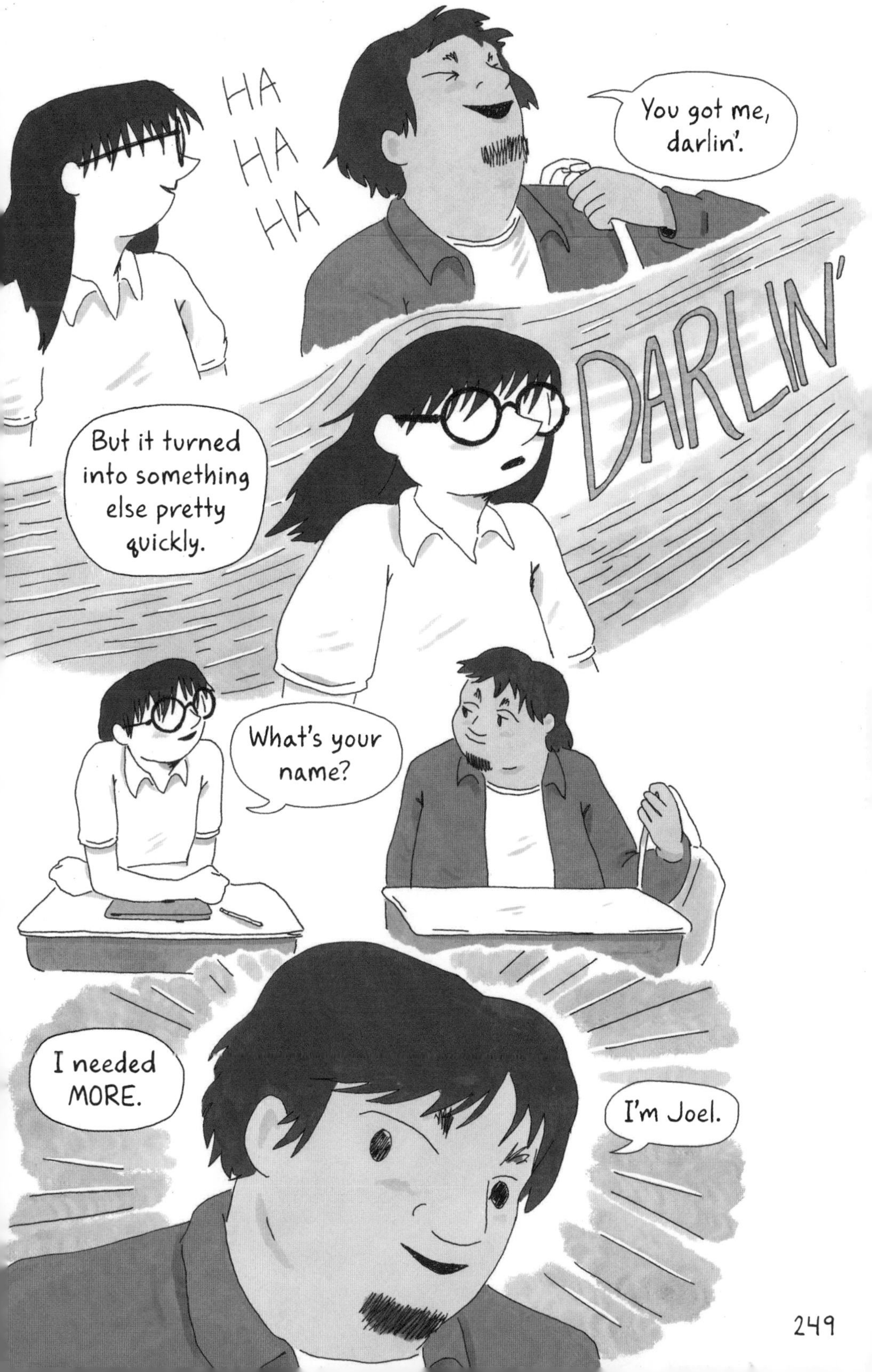
HA HA HA
You got me, darlin'.
DARLIN'
But it turned into something else pretty quickly.
What's your name?
I needed MORE.
I'm Joel.

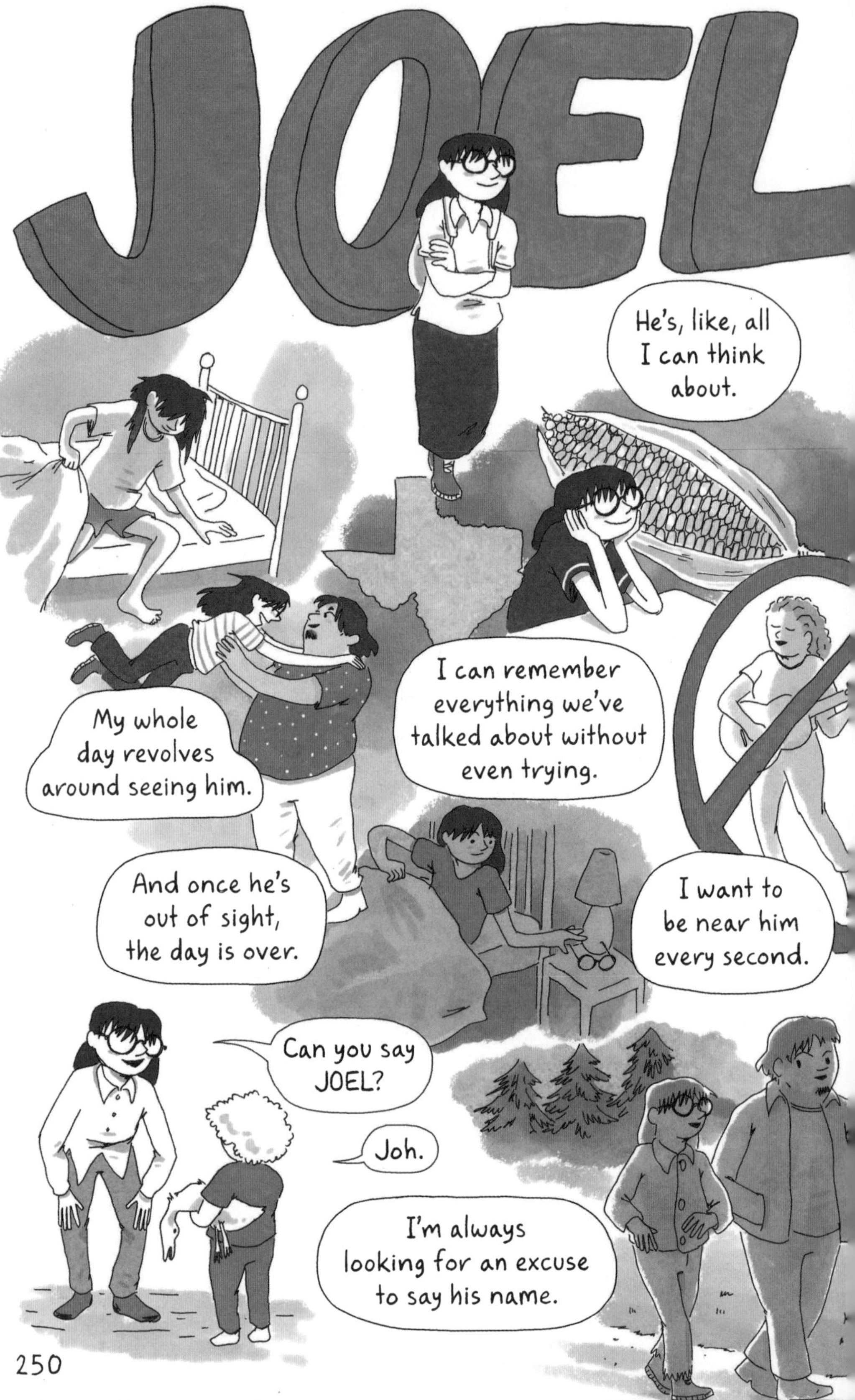
JOEL
He's, like, all I can think about.
My whole day revolves around seeing him.
I can remember everything we've talked about without even trying.
And once he's out of sight, the day is over.
I want to be near him every second.
Can you say JOEL?
Joh.
I'm always looking for an excuse to say his name.

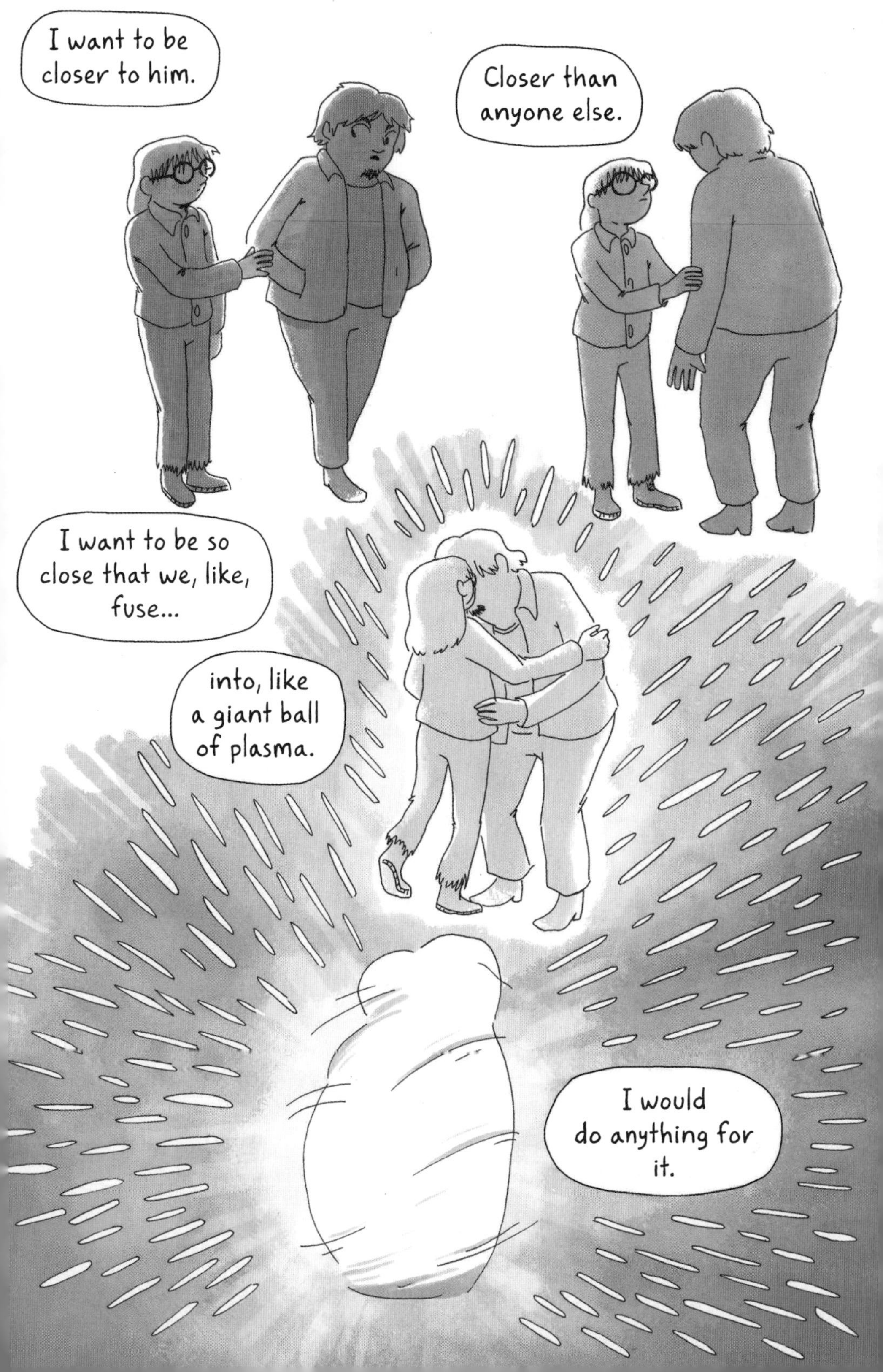
I want to be closer to him.
Closer than anyone else.
I want to be so close that we, like, fuse...
into, like a giant ball of plasma.
I would do anything for it.

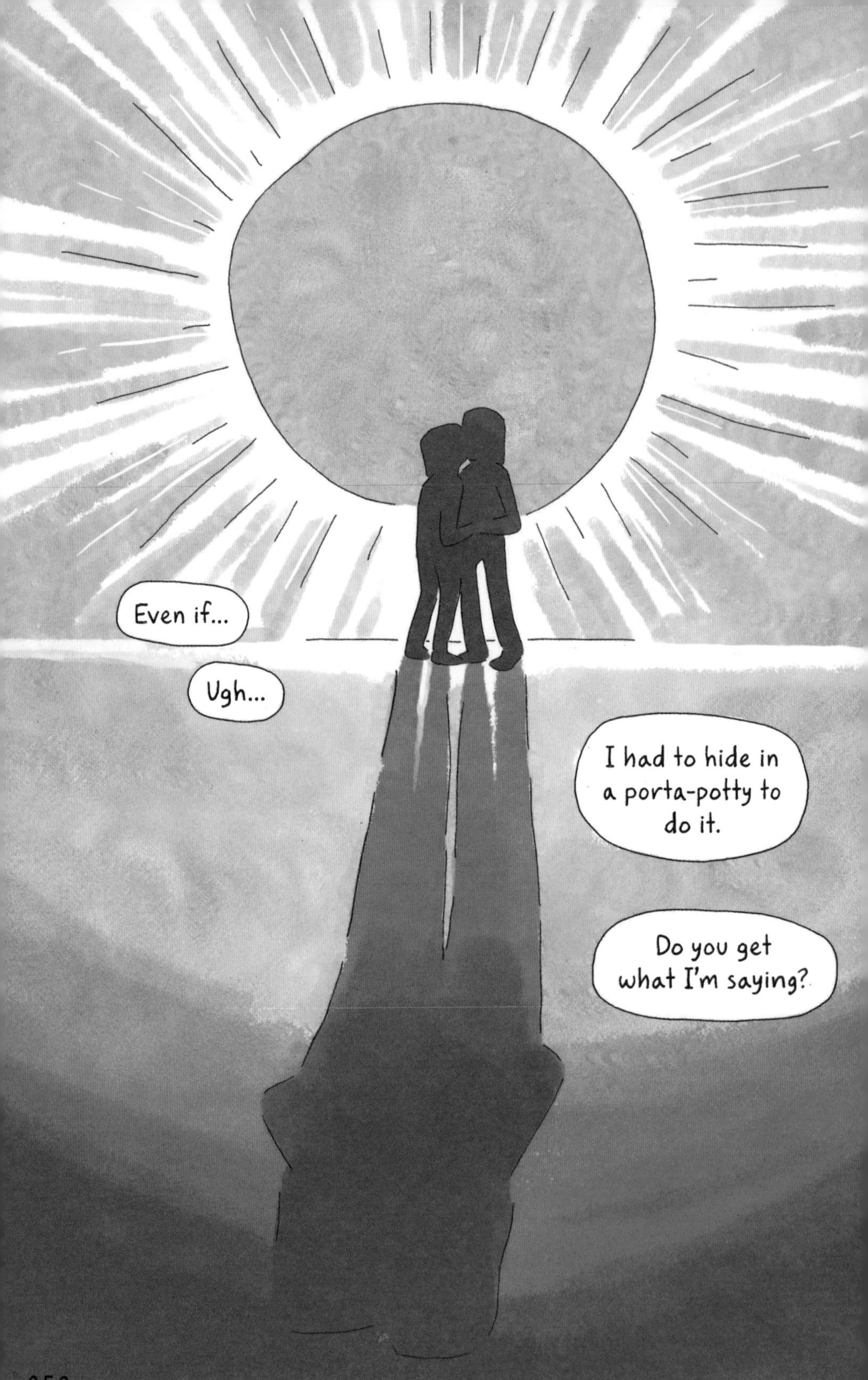
Even if...
Ugh...
I had to hide in a porta-potty to do it.
Do you get what I'm saying?

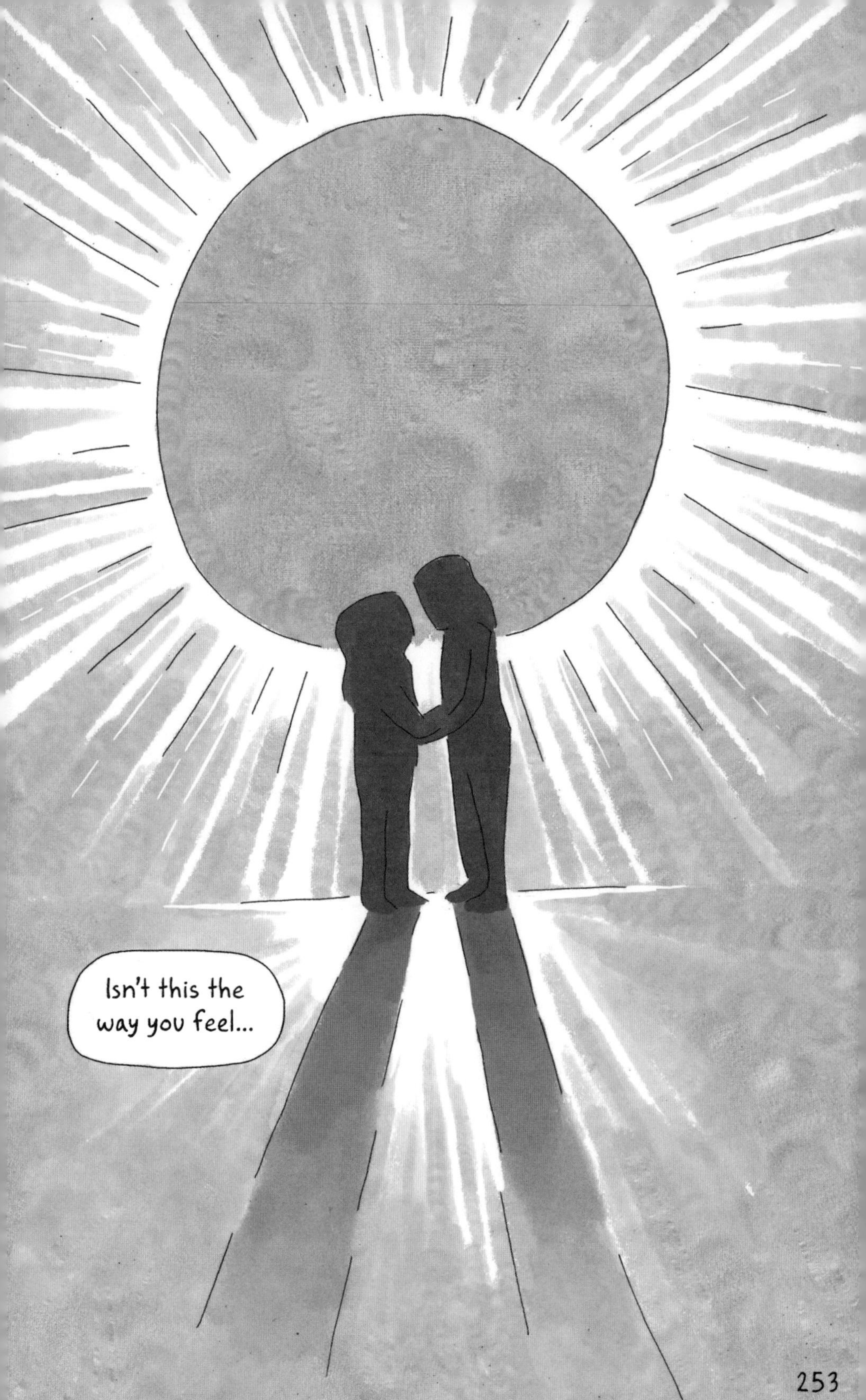
Isn't this the way you feel...

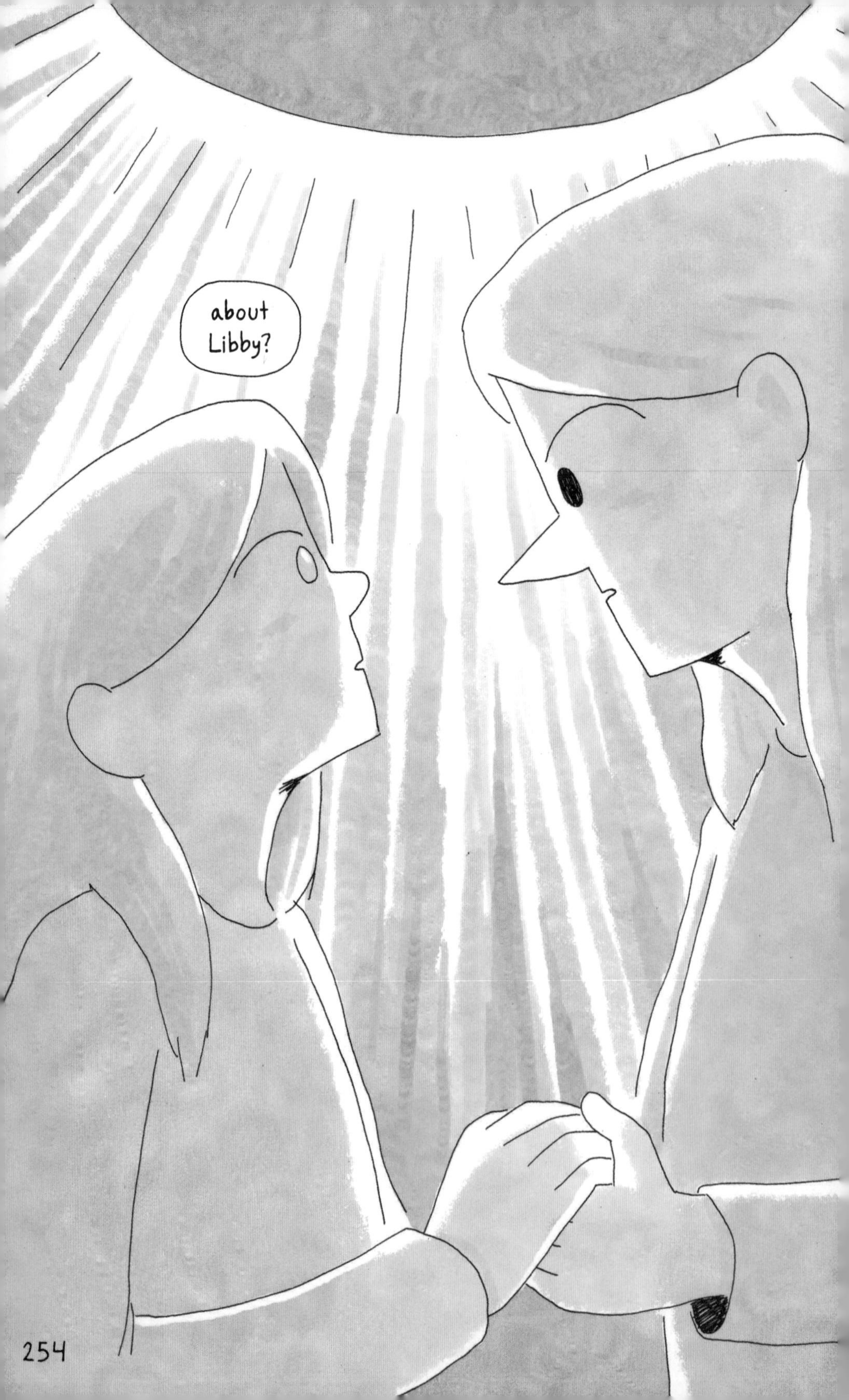
about Libby?

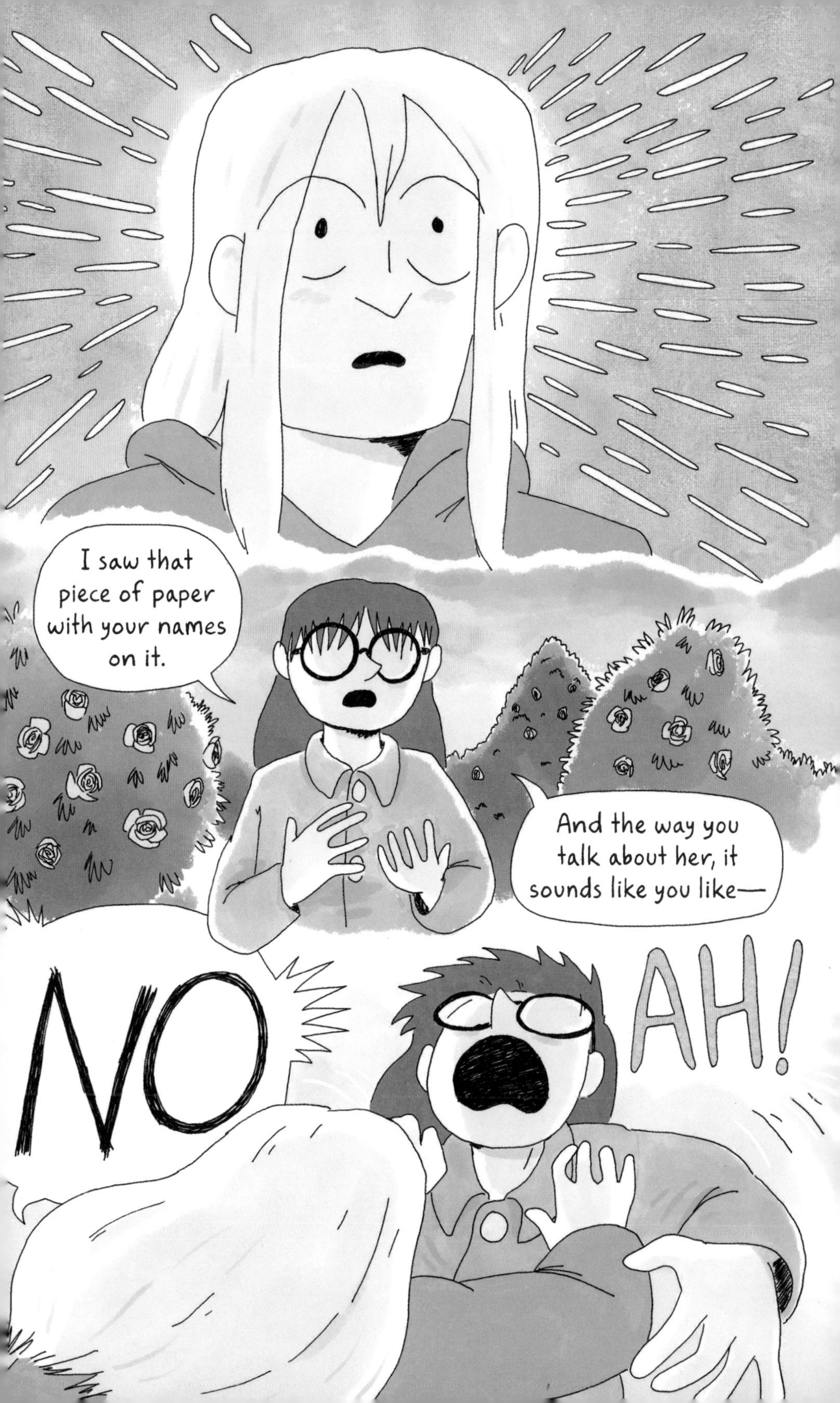
I saw that piece of paper with your names on it.
And the way you talk about her, it sounds like you like—
NO
AH!

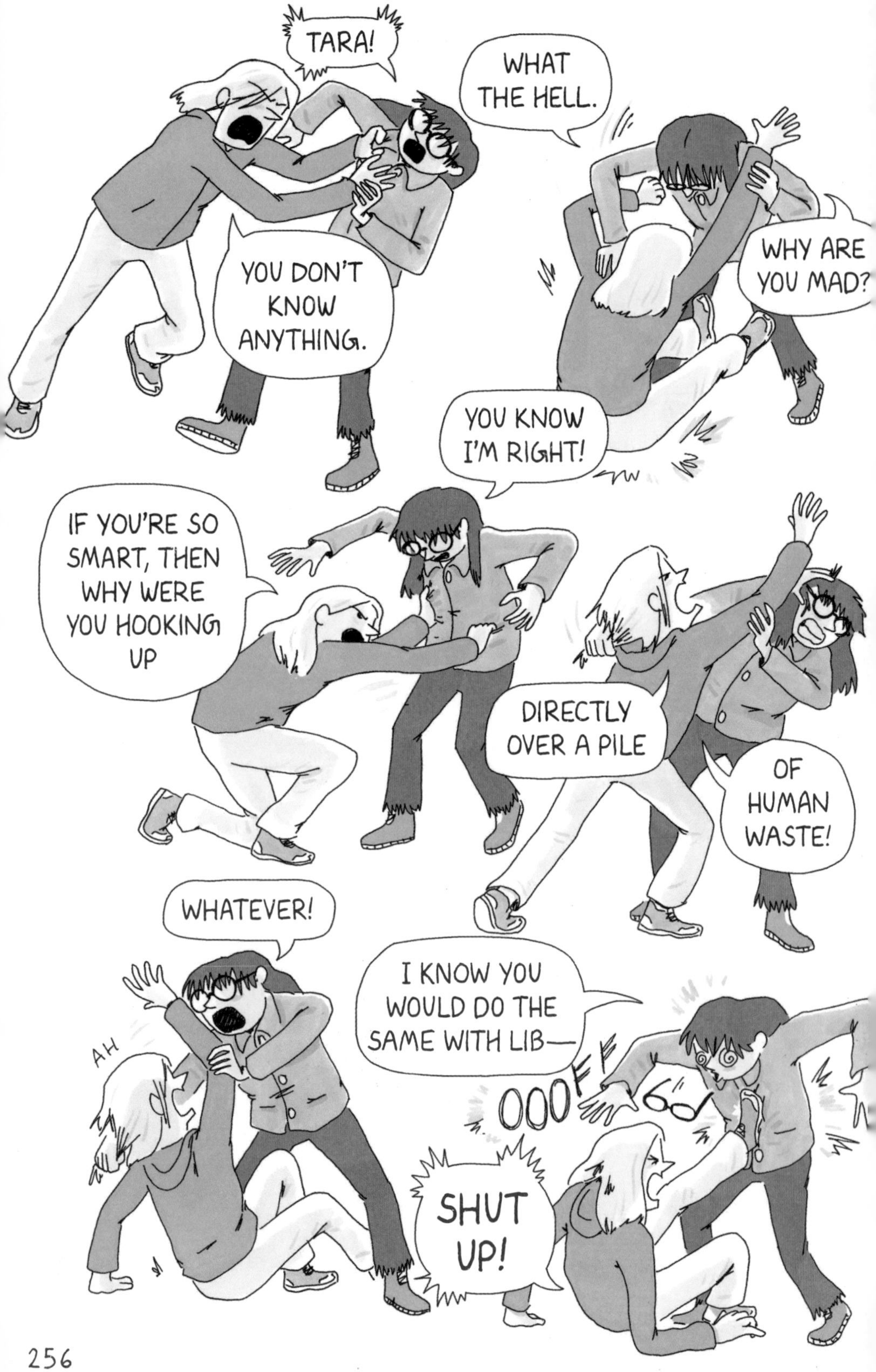
TARA!
YOU DON'T KNOW ANYTHING.
WHAT THE HELL.
WHY ARE YOU MAD?
YOU KNOW I'M RIGHT!
IF YOU'RE SO SMART, THEN WHY WERE YOU HOOKING UP
DIRECTLY OVER A PILE
OF HUMAN WASTE!
WHATEVER!
I KNOW YOU WOULD DO THE SAME WITH LIB—
AH
SHUT UP!
OOOFF

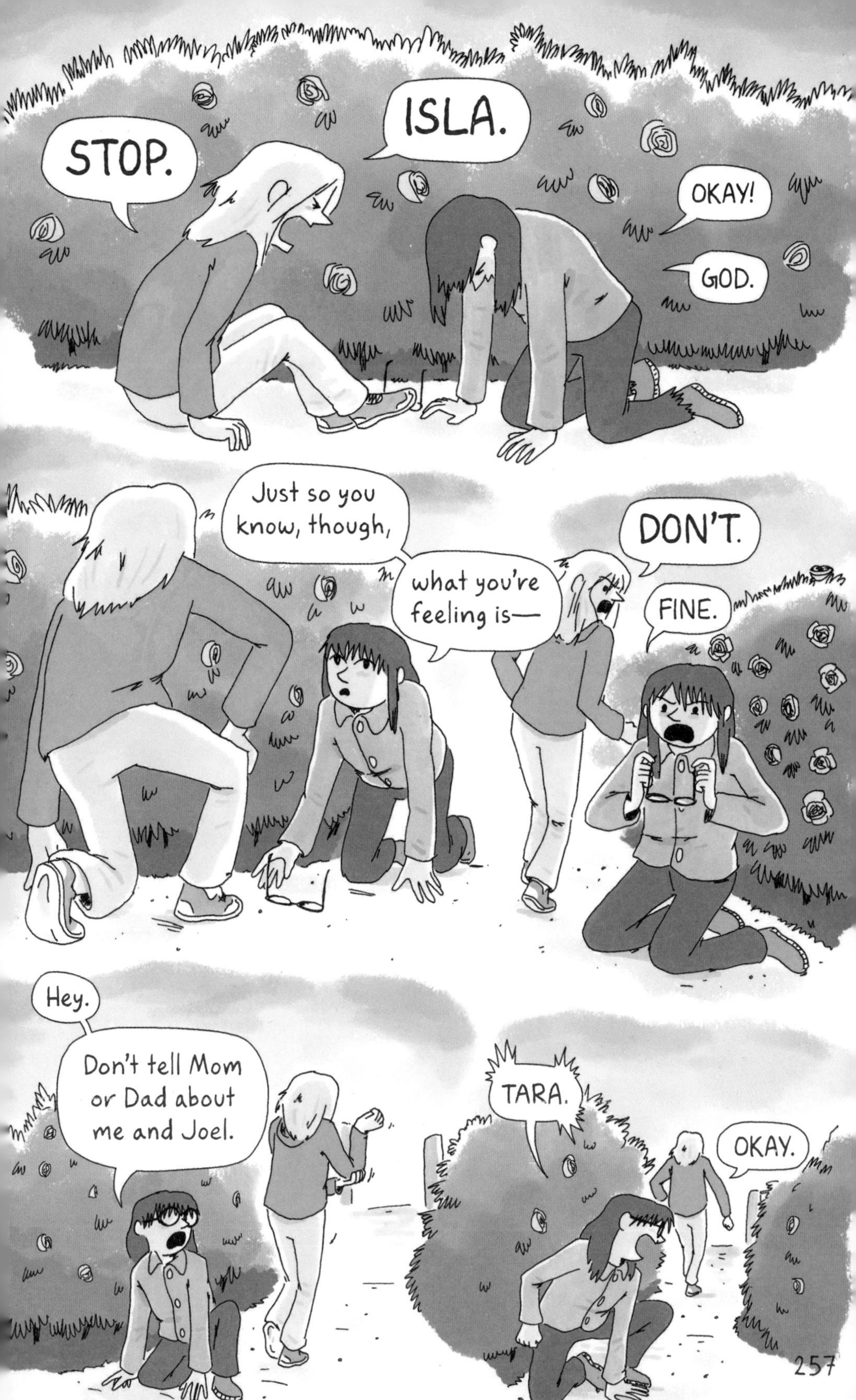
STOP.
ISLA.
OKAY!
GOD.
Just so you know, though,
what you're feeling is—
DON'T.
FINE.
Hey.
Don't tell Mom or Dad about me and Joel.
TARA.
OKAY.

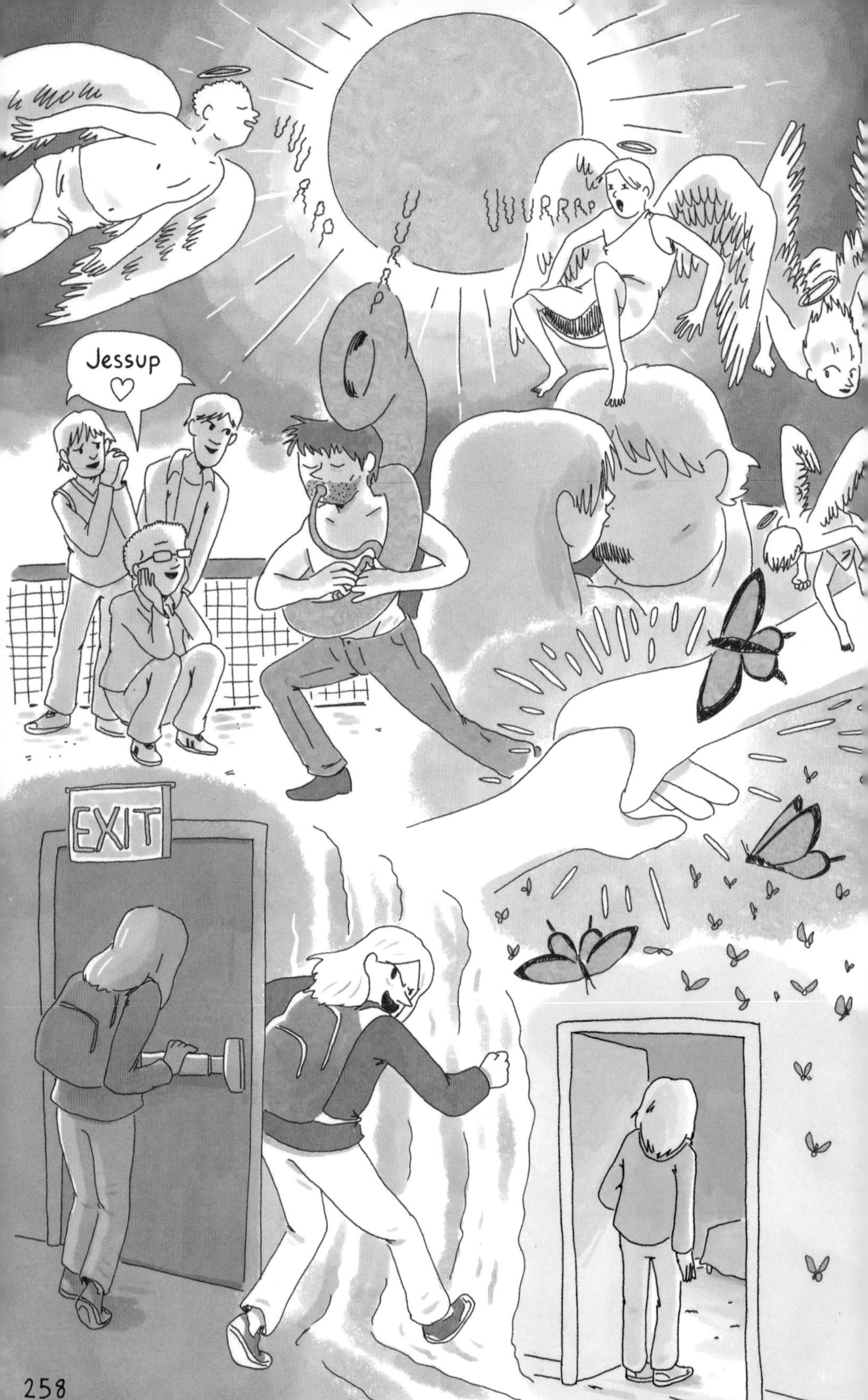
UUURRP
UUURRRP
Jessup ♡
EXIT

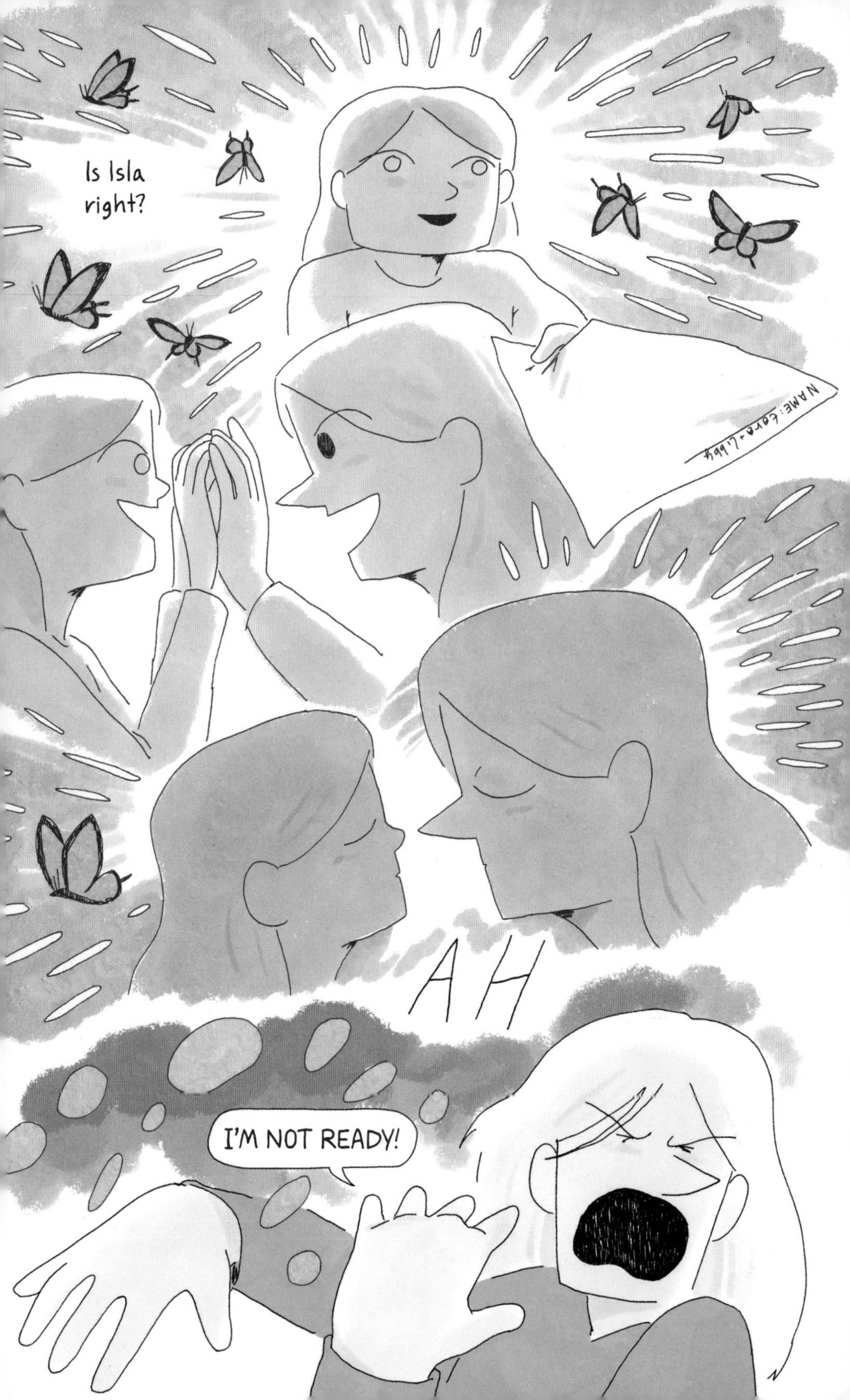
Is Isla right?
NAME: Lara+Libby
AH
I'M NOT READY!

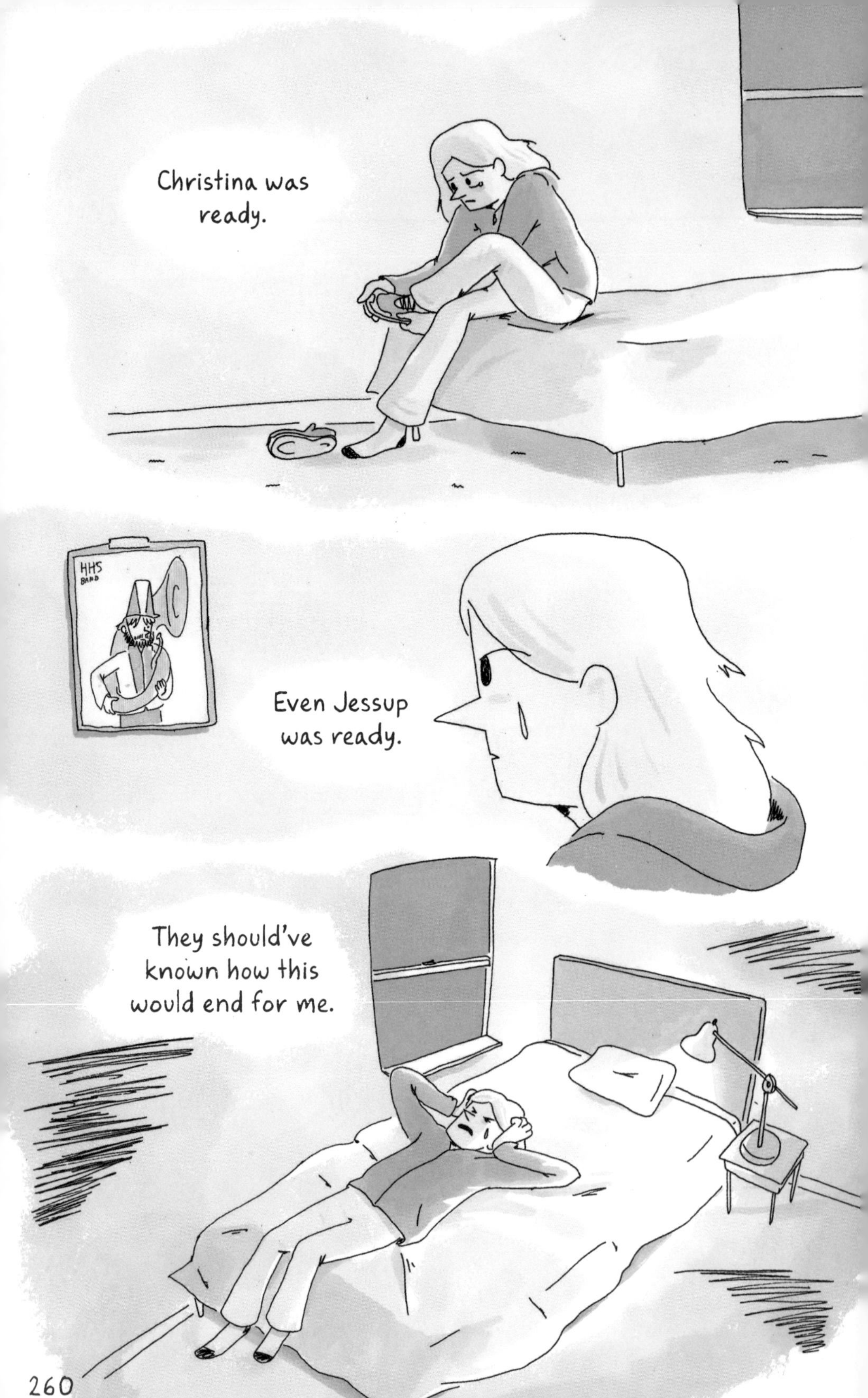
Christina was ready.
HHS BAND
Even Jessup was ready.
They should've known how this would end for me.

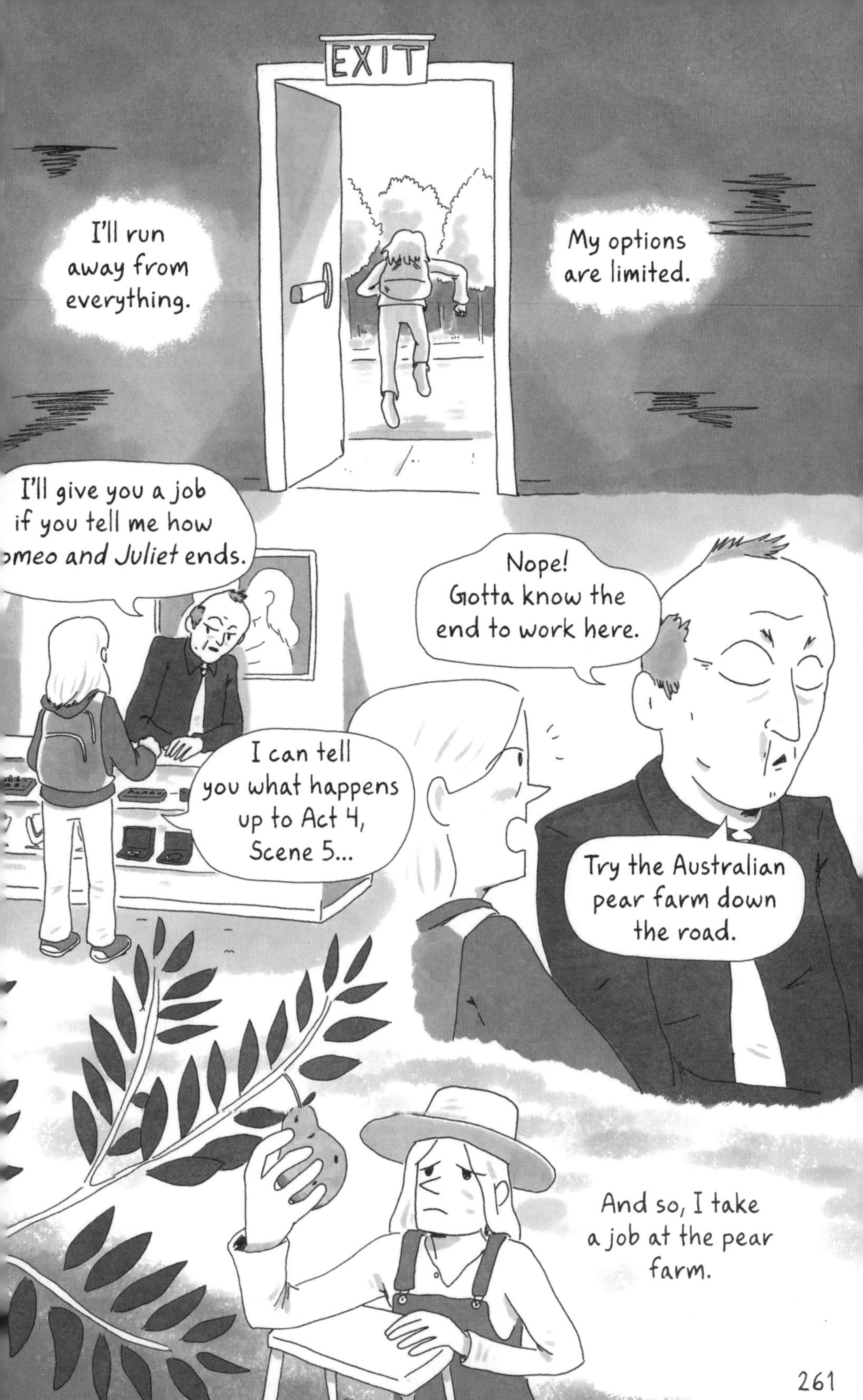
EXIT
I'll run away from everything.
My options are limited.
I'll give you a job if you tell me how omeo and Juliet ends.
I can tell you what happens up to Act 4, Scene 5...
Nope! Gotta know the end to work here.
Try the Australian pear farm down the road.
And so, I take a job at the pear farm.

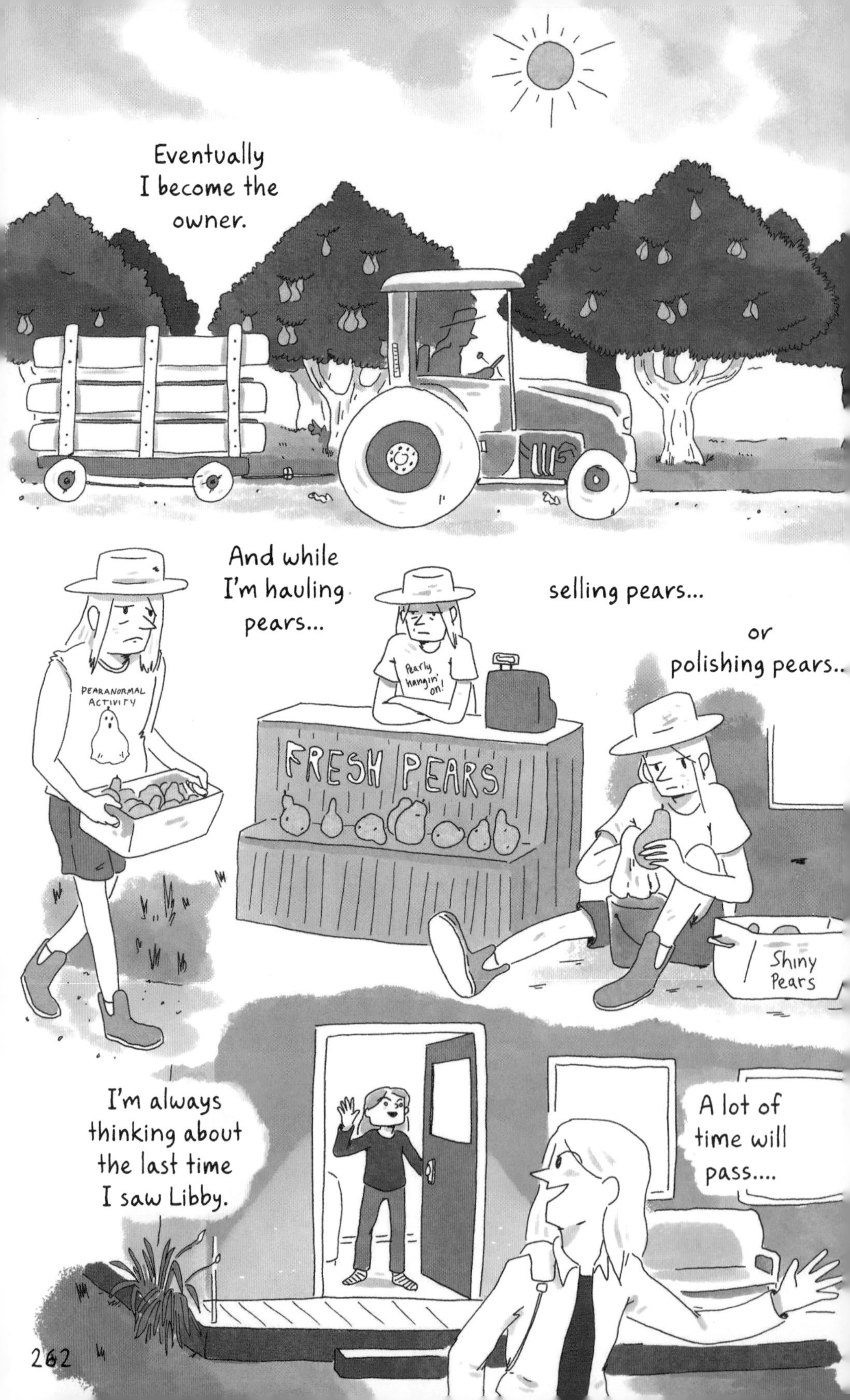
Eventually I become the owner.
And while I'm hauling pears...
PEARANORMAL ACTIVITY
Pearly hangin' on!
FRESH PEARS
selling pears...
or polishing pears..
Shiny Pears
I'm always thinking about the last time I saw Libby.
A lot of time will pass....

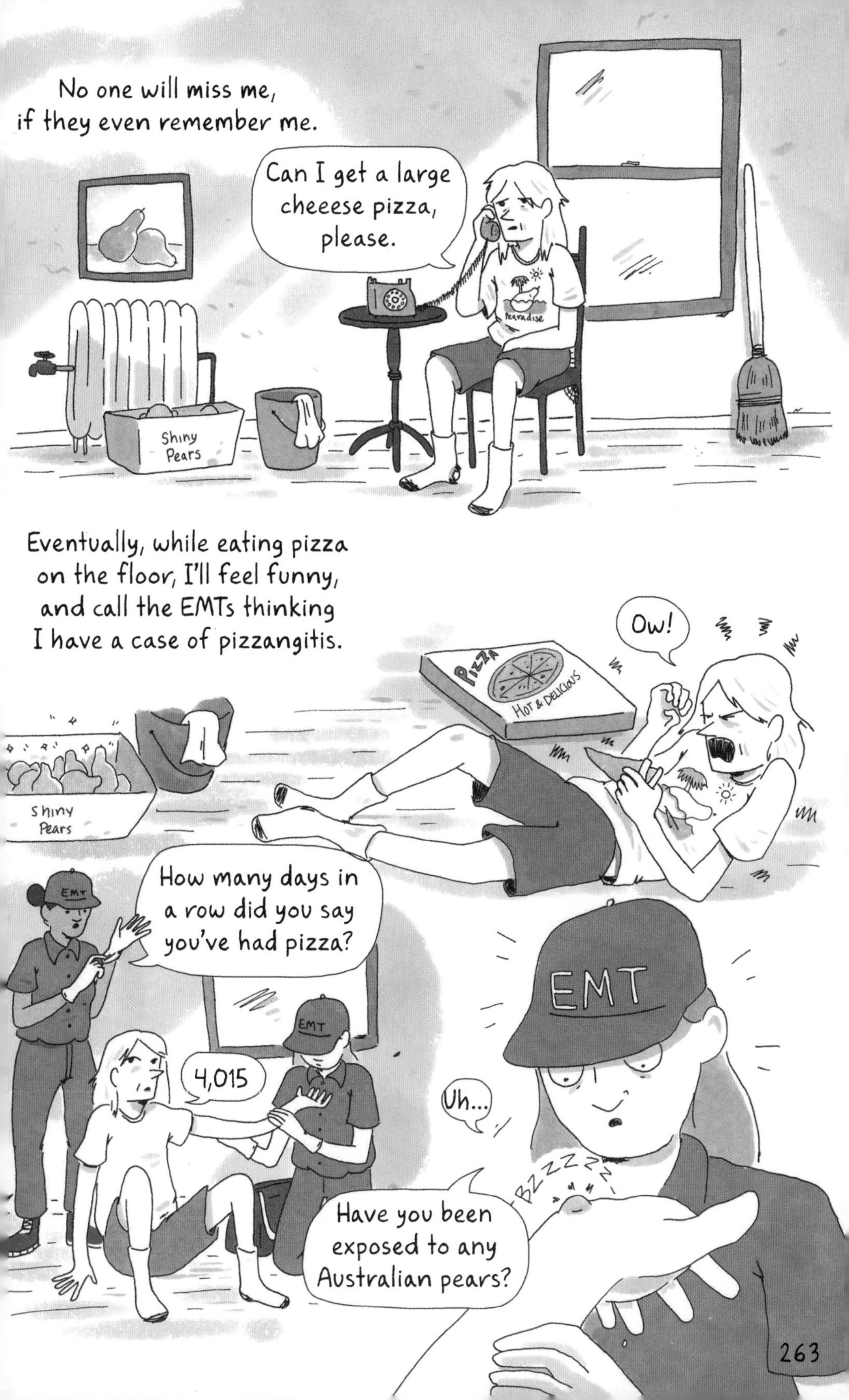
No one will miss me, if they even remember me.
Can I get a large cheeese pizza, please.
Shiny Pears
Pearadise
Eventually, while eating pizza on the floor, I'll feel funny, and call the EMTs thinking I have a case of pizzangitis.
Ow!
PIZZA
HOT & DELICIOUS
Shiny Pears
EMT
How many days in a row did you say you've had pizza?
EMT
4,015
Uh...
EMT
BZZZZZ
Have you been exposed to any Australian pears?

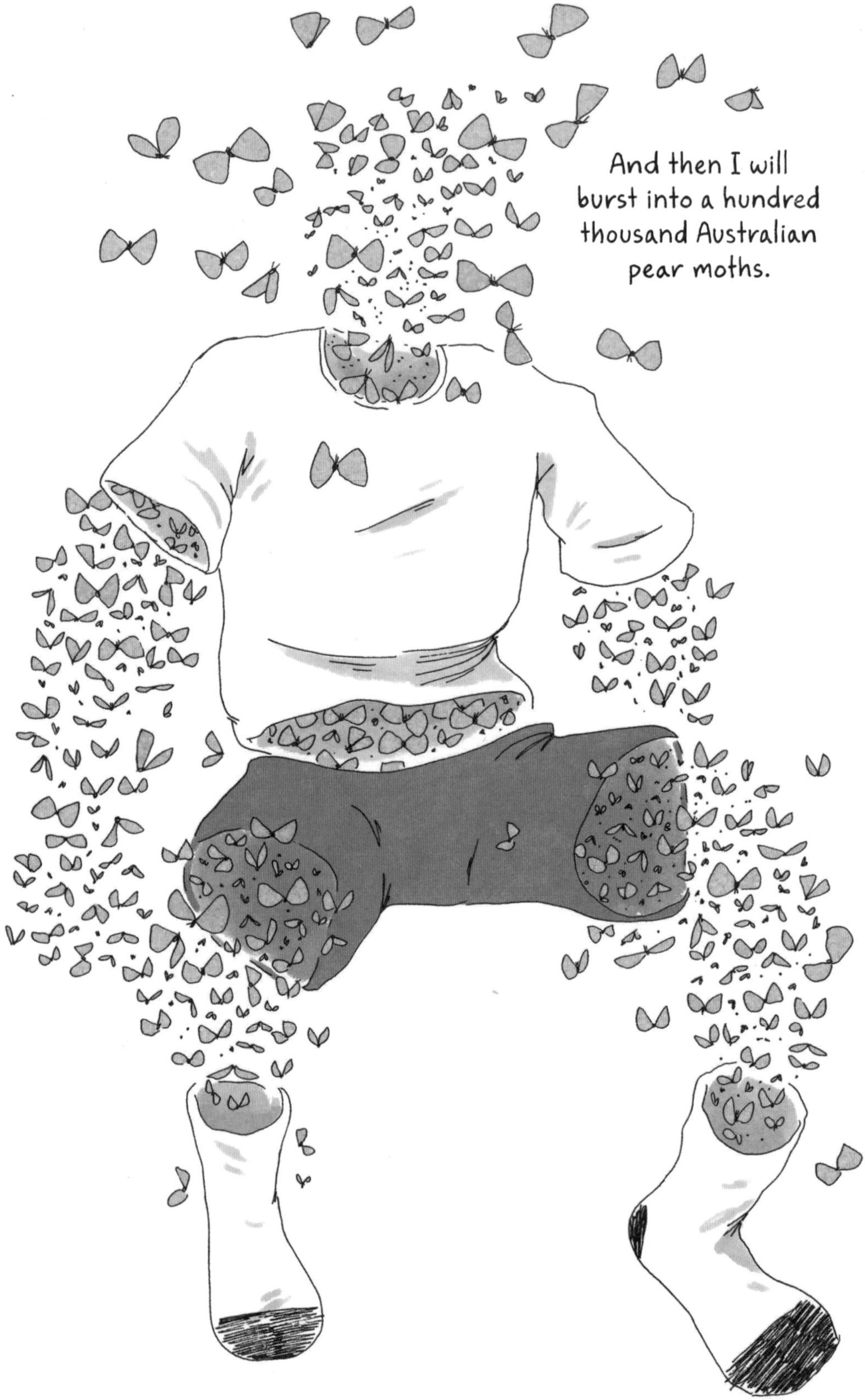
And then I will burst into a hundred thousand Australian pear moths.

THE
END

Tawa!

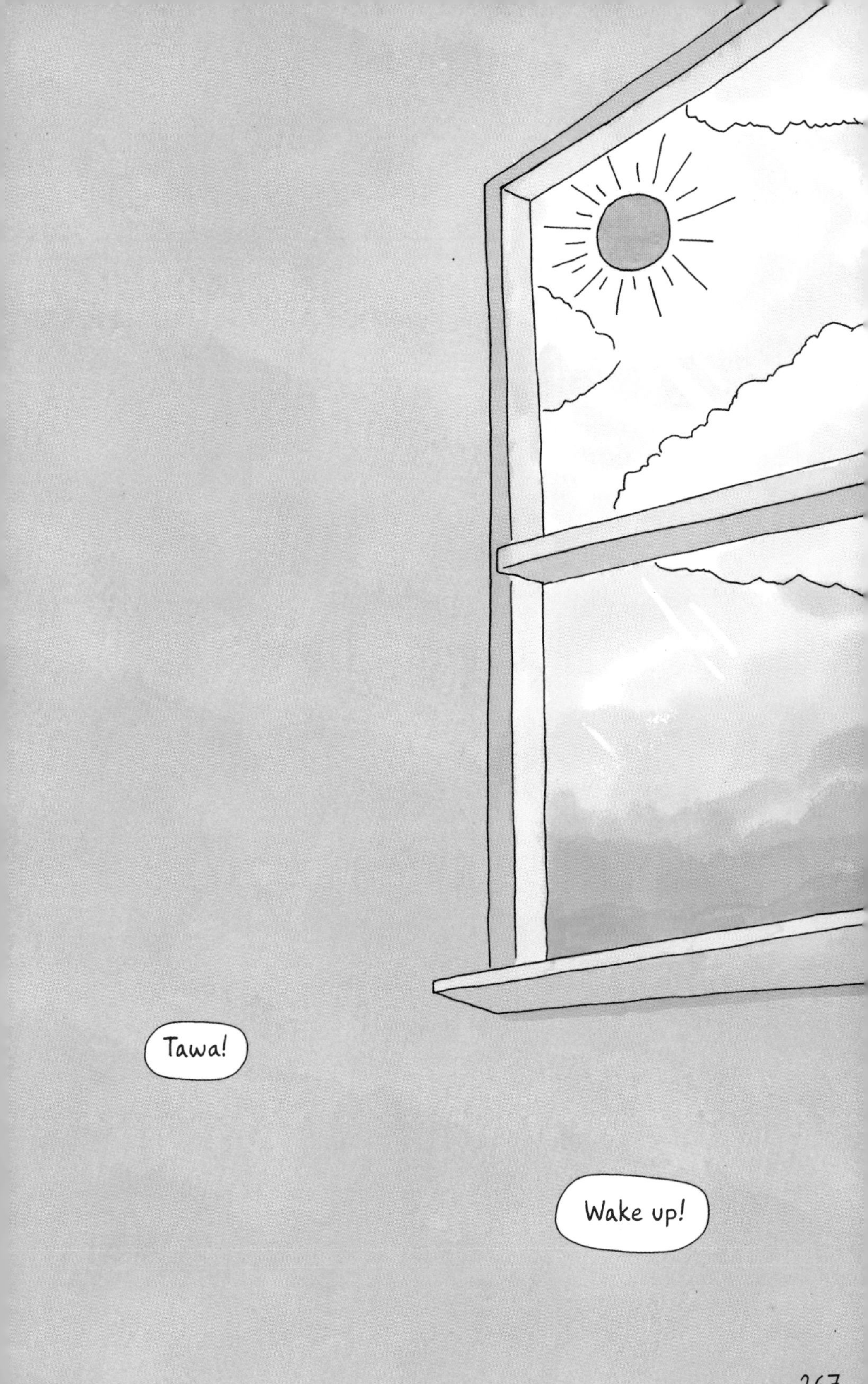
Tawa!
Wake up!

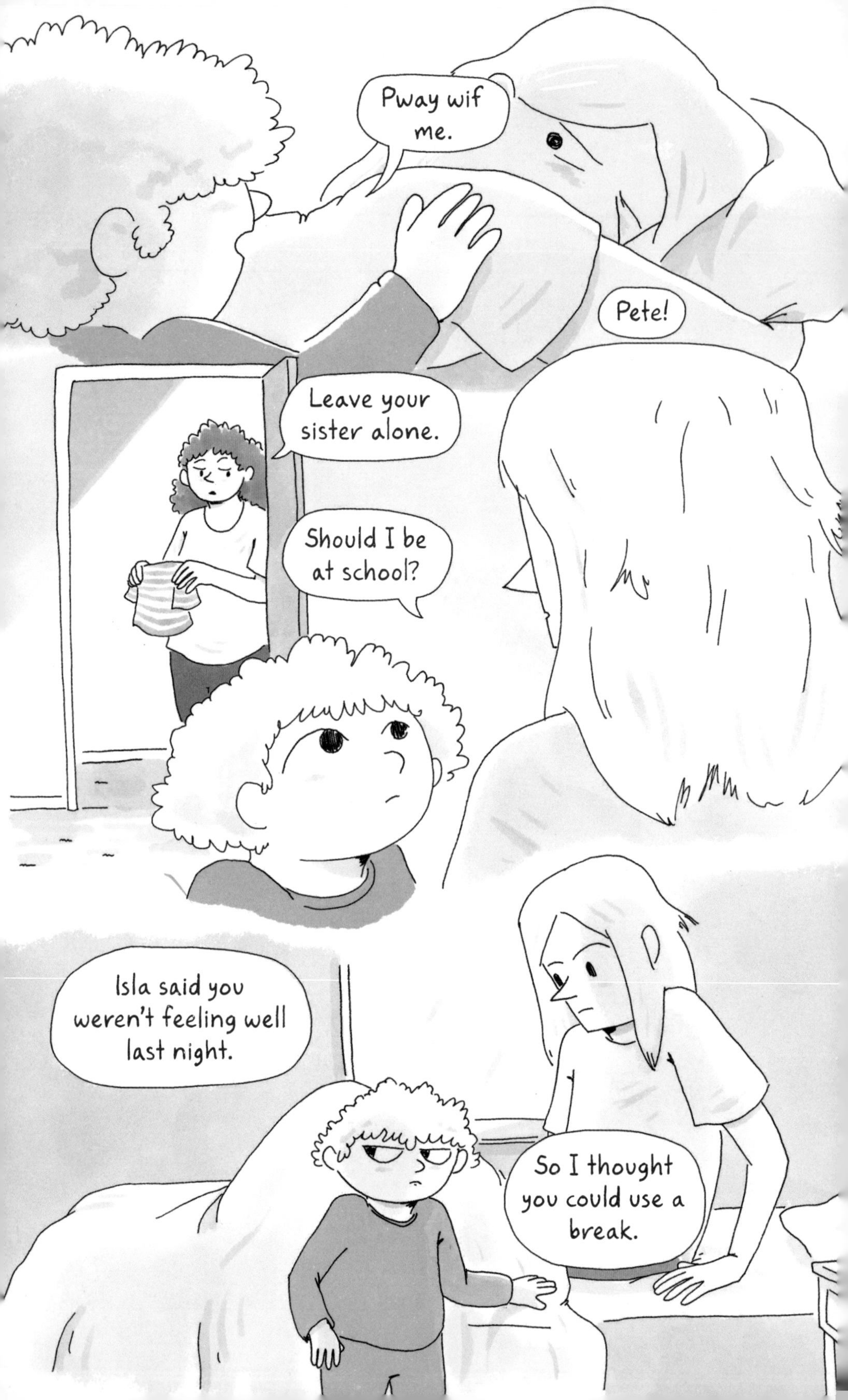
Pway wif
me.
Pete!
Leave your
sister alone.
Should I be
at school?
Isla said you
weren't feeling well
last night.
So I thought
you could use a
break.

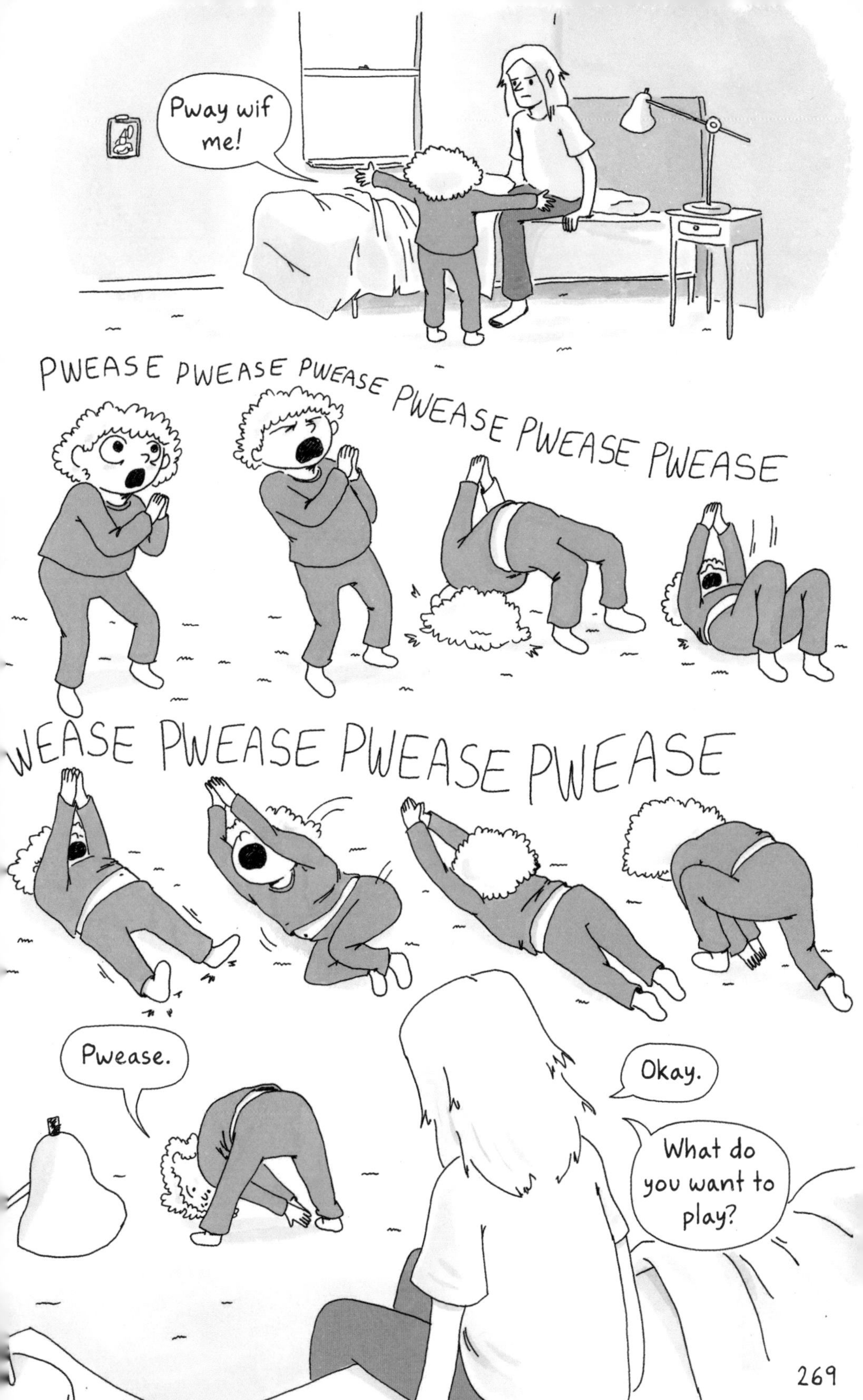

Pway wif me!
PWEASE PWEASE PWEASE PWEASE PWEASE PWEASE
WEASE PWEASE PWEASE PWEASE
Pwease.
Okay.
What do you want to play?

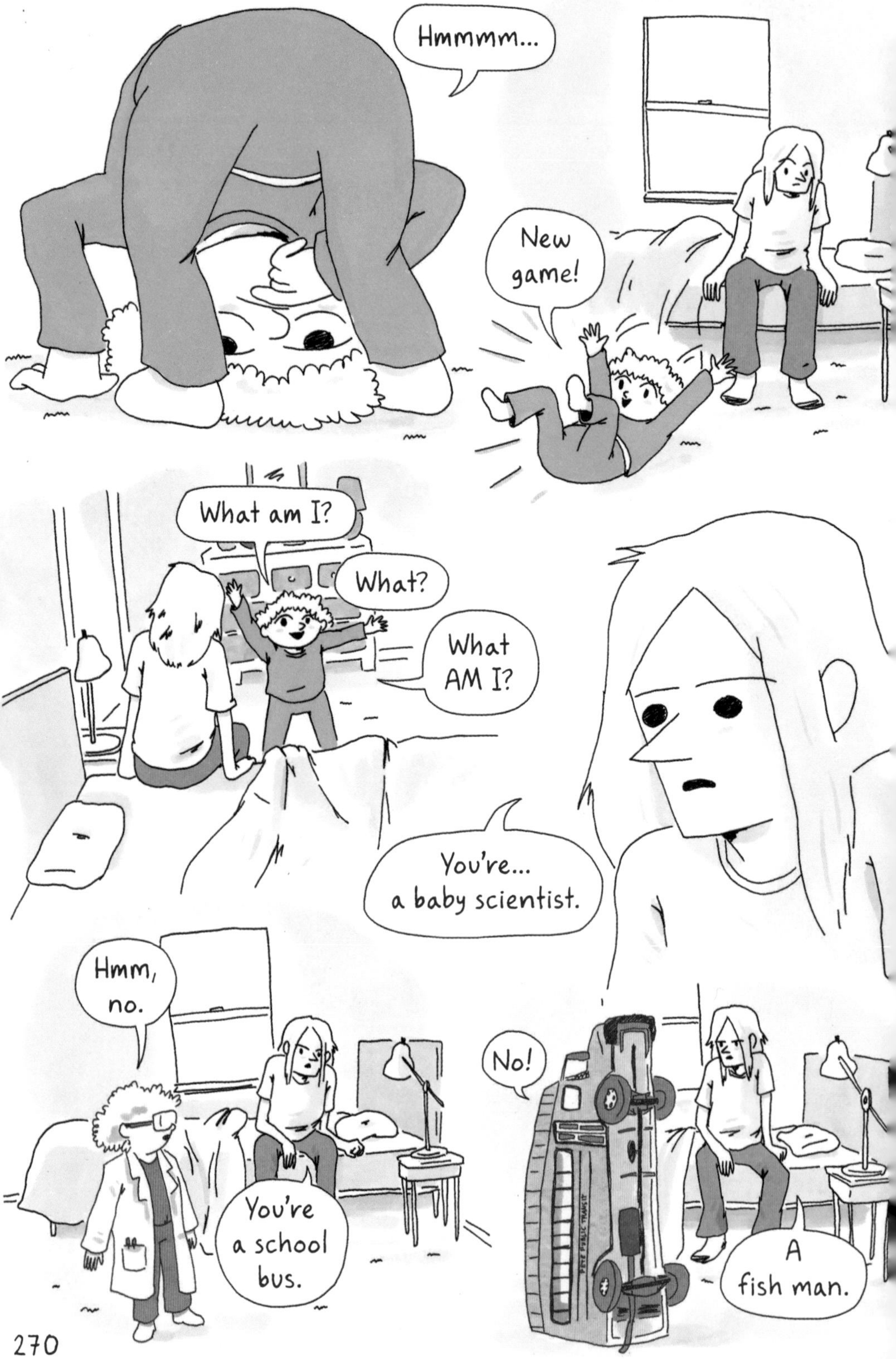
Hmmmm...
New game!
What am I?
What?
What AM I?
You're... a baby scientist.
Hmm, no.
You're a school bus.
No!
A fish man.

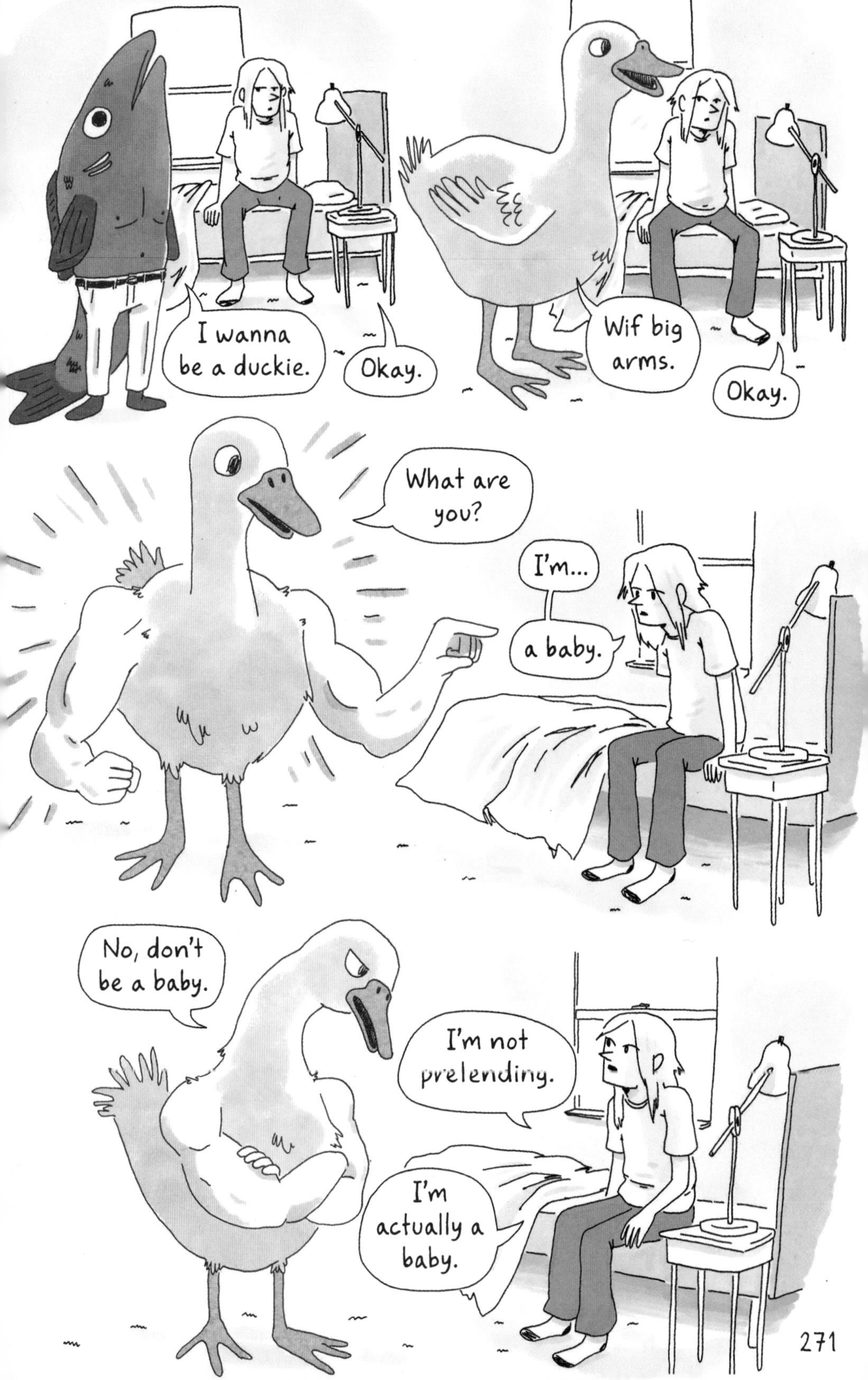
I wanna be a duckie.
Okay.
Wif big arms.
Okay.
What are you?
I'm...
a baby.
No, don't be a baby.
I'm not pretending.
I'm actually a baby.

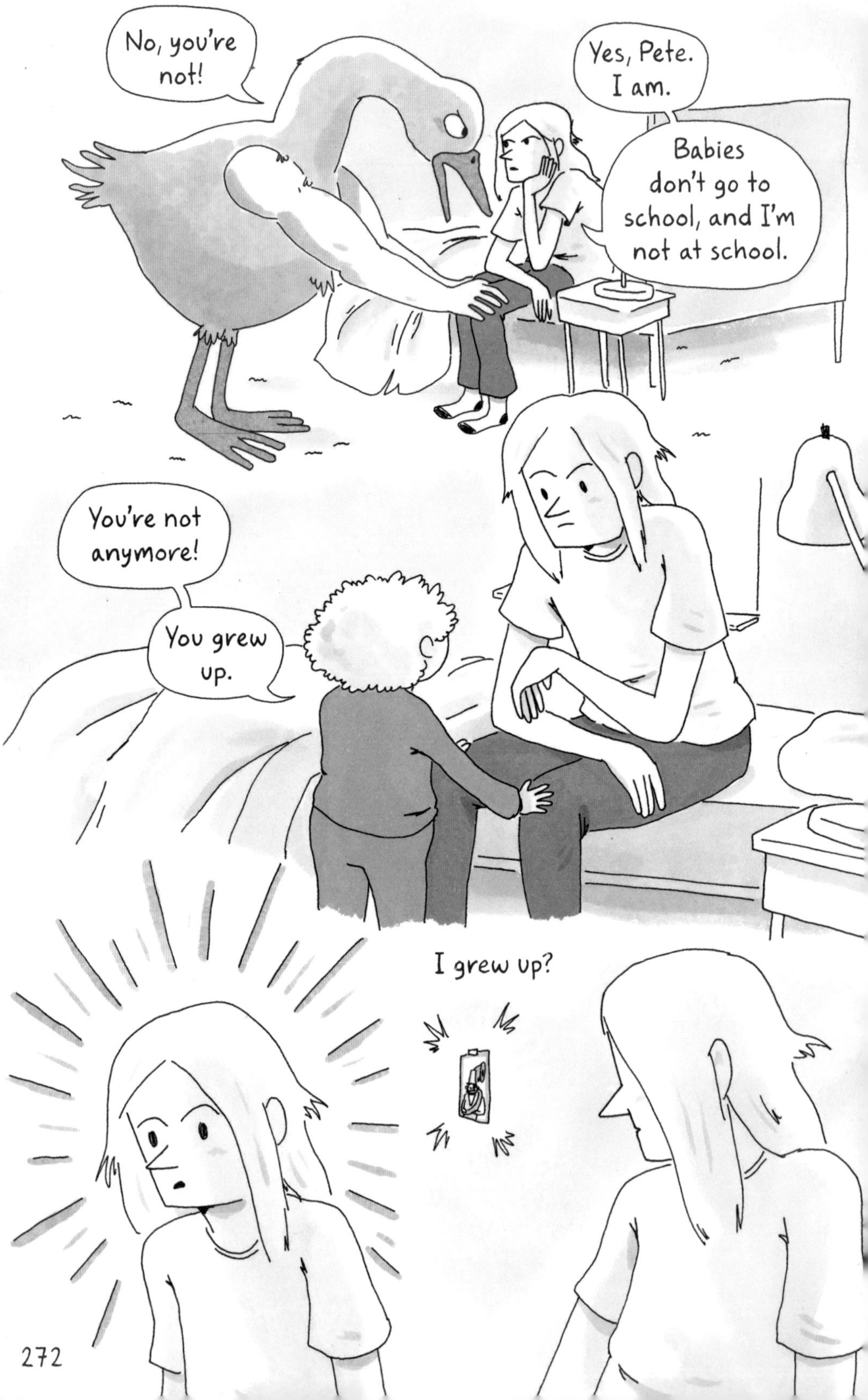
No, you're not!
Yes, Pete. I am.
Babies don't go to school, and I'm not at school.
You're not anymore!
You grew up.
I grew up?

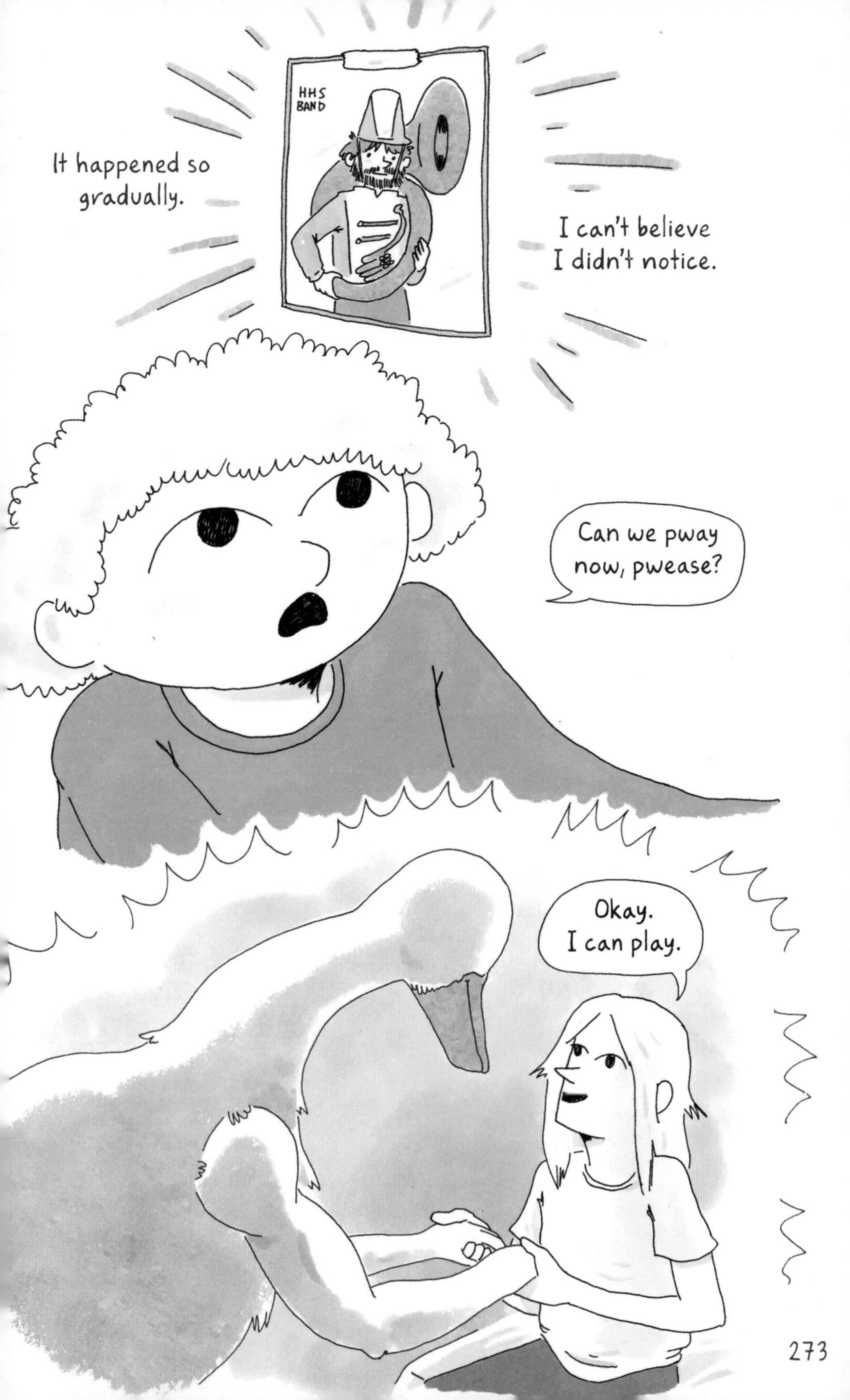
HHS BAND
It happened so gradually.
I can't believe I didn't notice.
Can we pway now, pwease?
Okay. I can play.

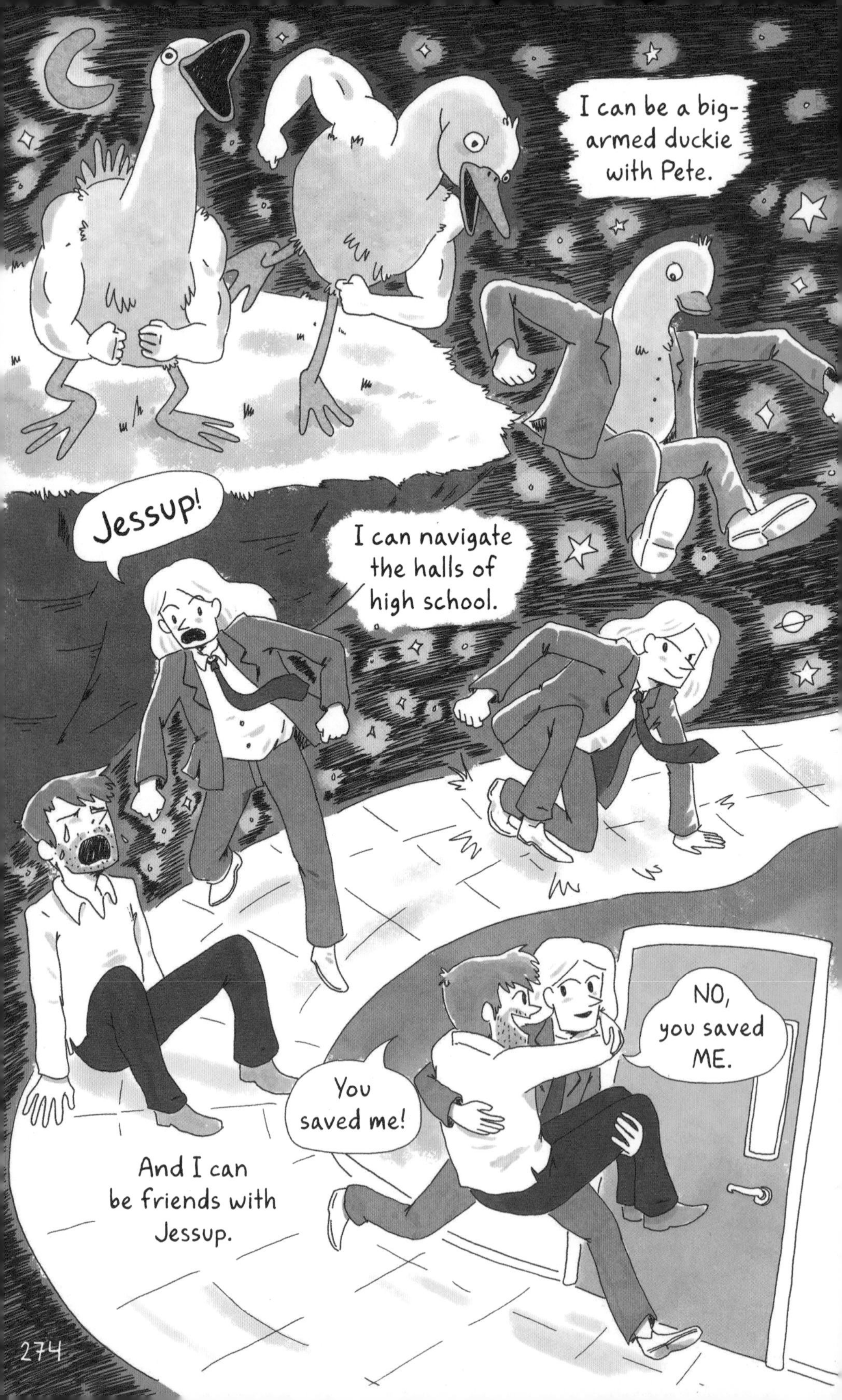
I can be a big-armed duckie with Pete.
Jessup!
I can navigate the halls of high school.
NO, you saved ME.
You saved me!
And I can be friends with Jessup.

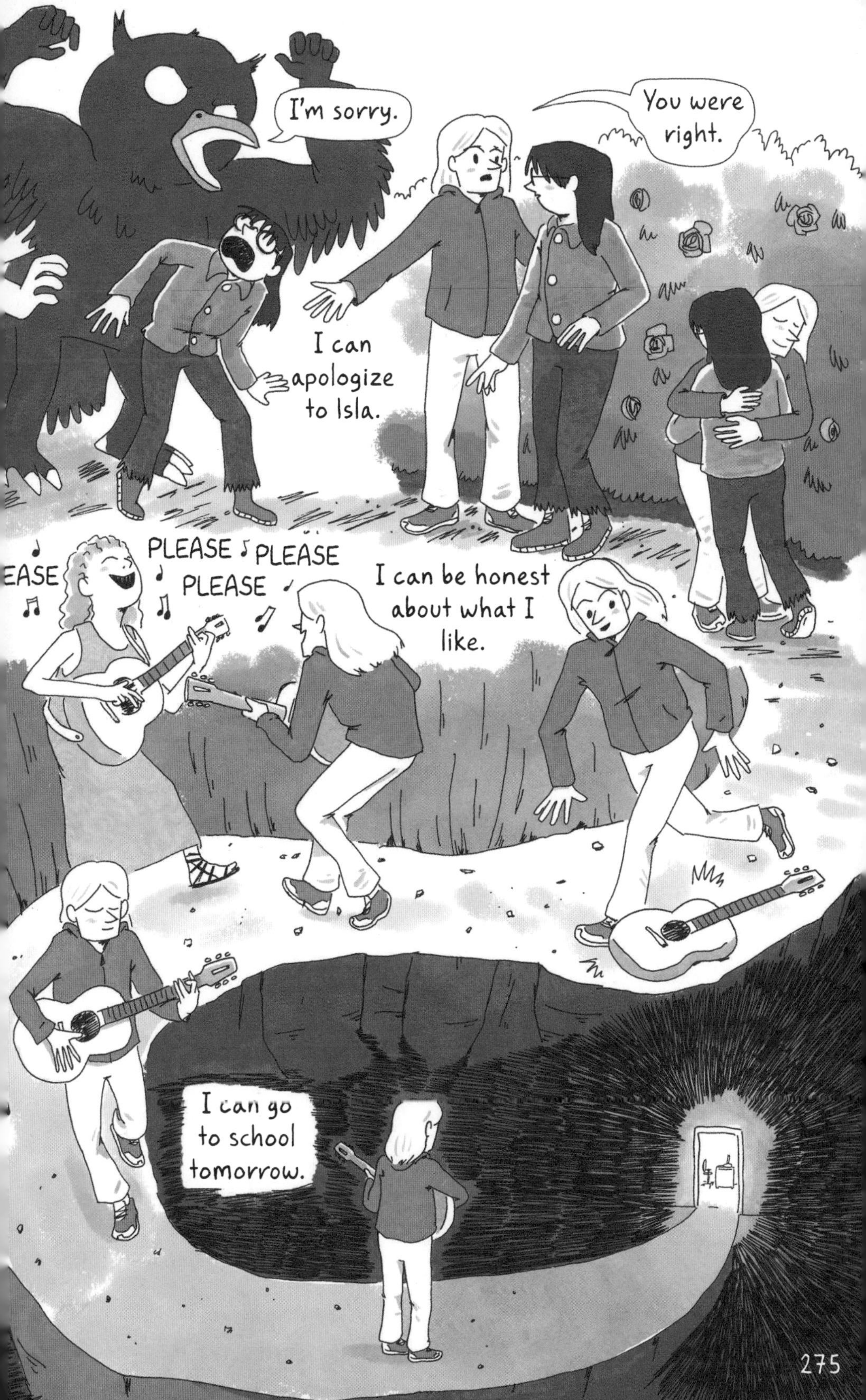
I'm sorry.
You were right.
I can apologize to Isla.
EASE
PLEASE PLEASE
PLEASE
I can be honest about what I like.
I can go to school tomorrow.

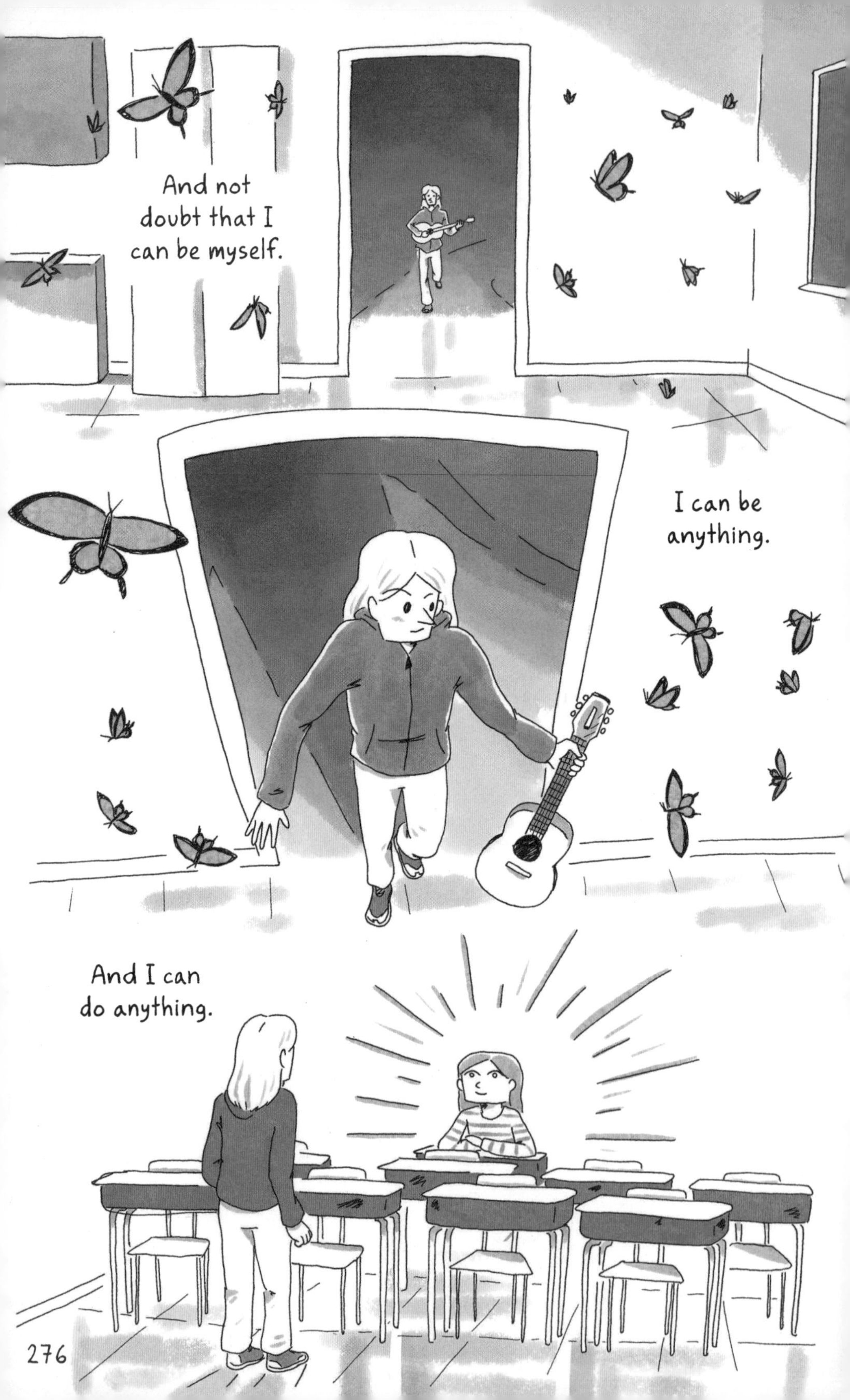
And not doubt that I can be myself.
I can be anything.
And I can do anything.

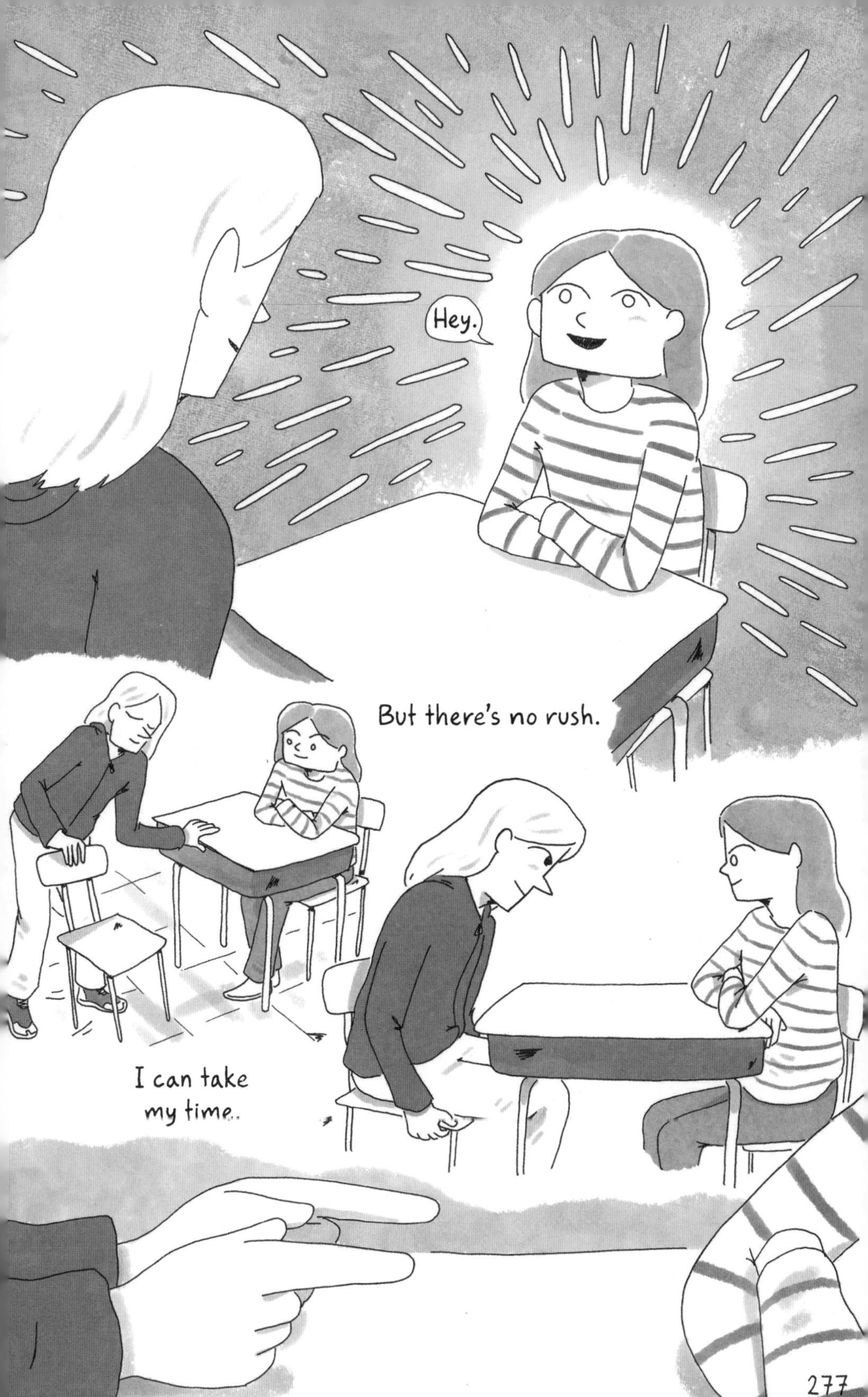
Hey.
But there's no rush.
I can take my time..

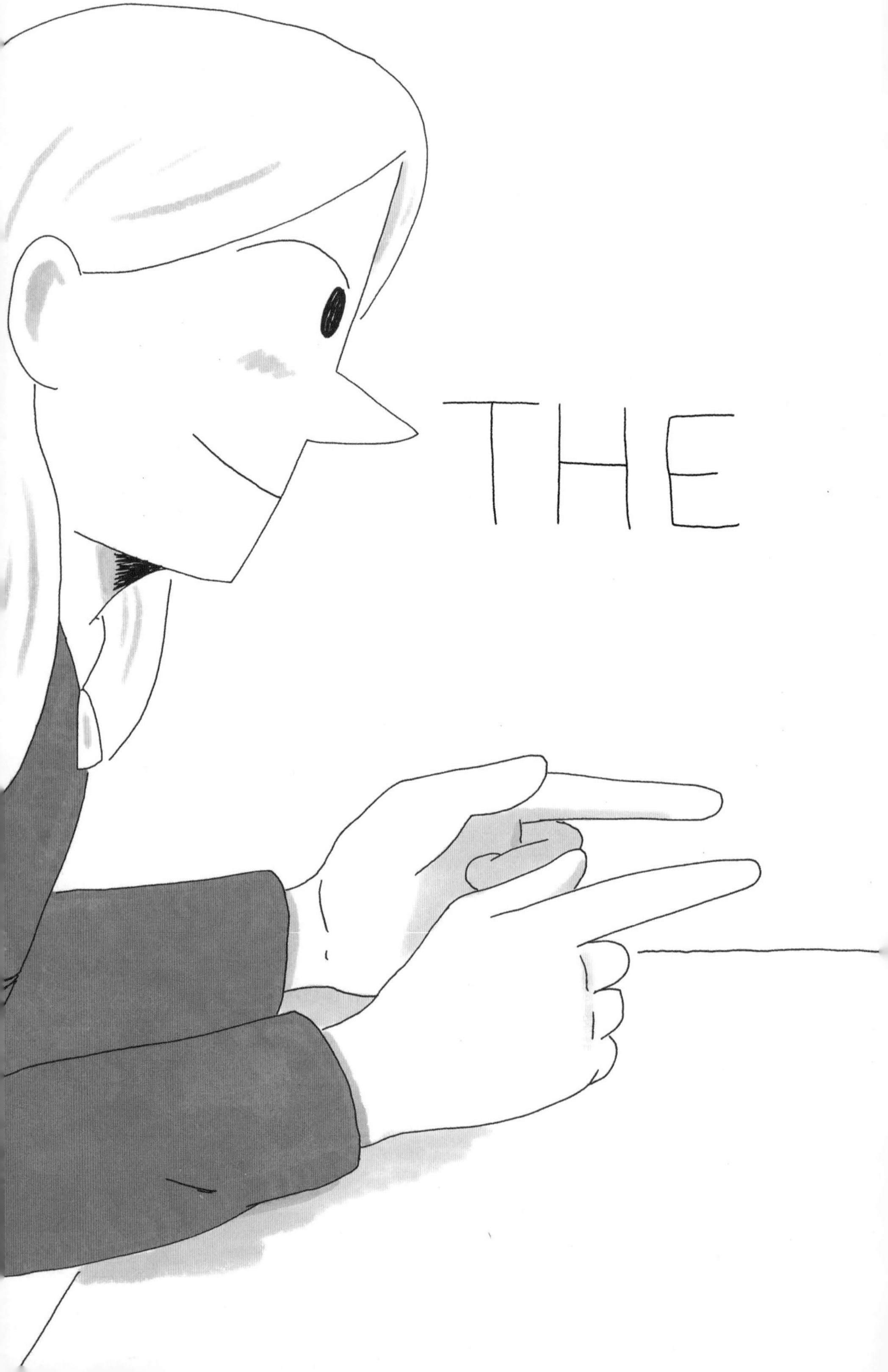
THE

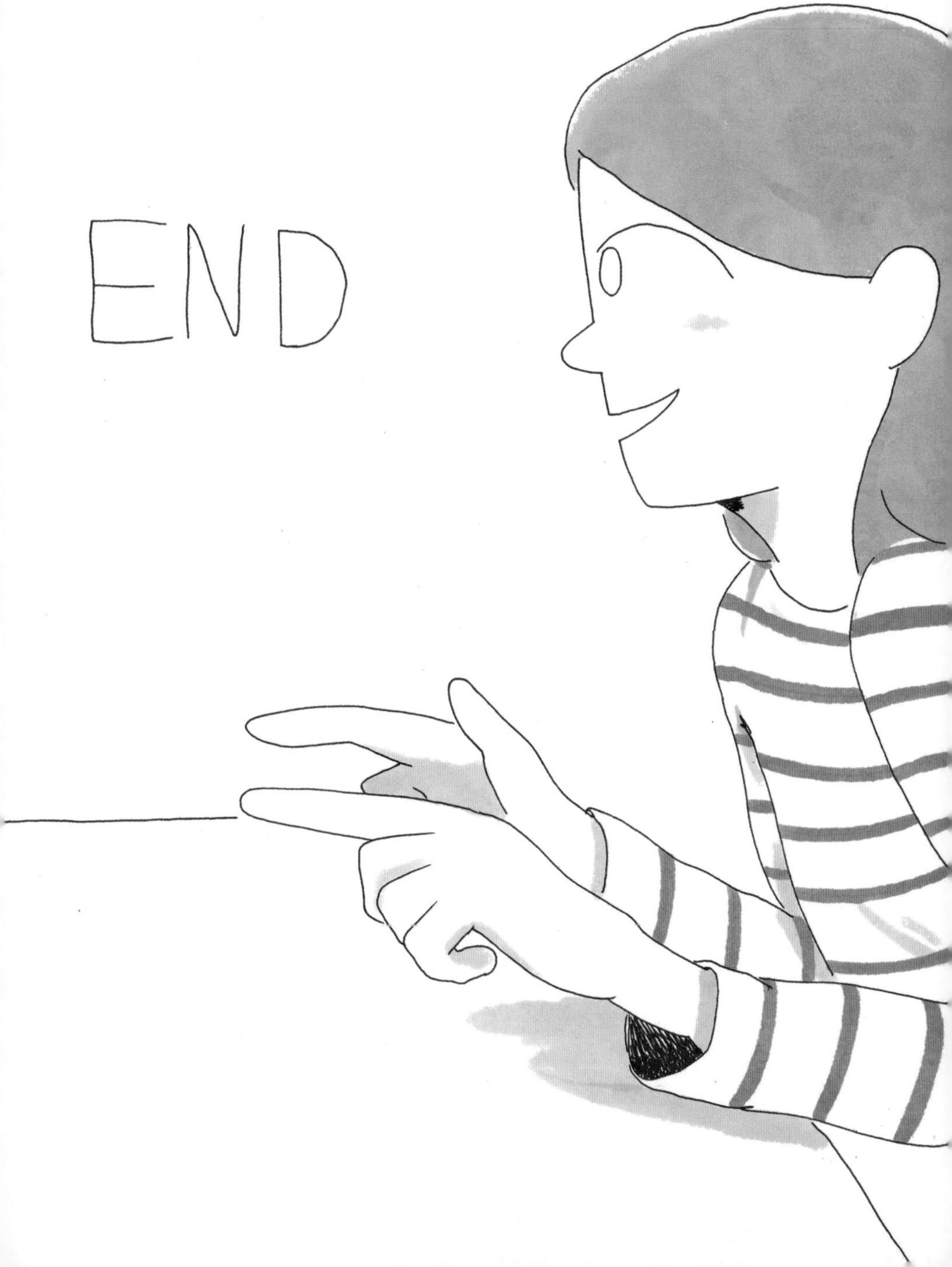
END

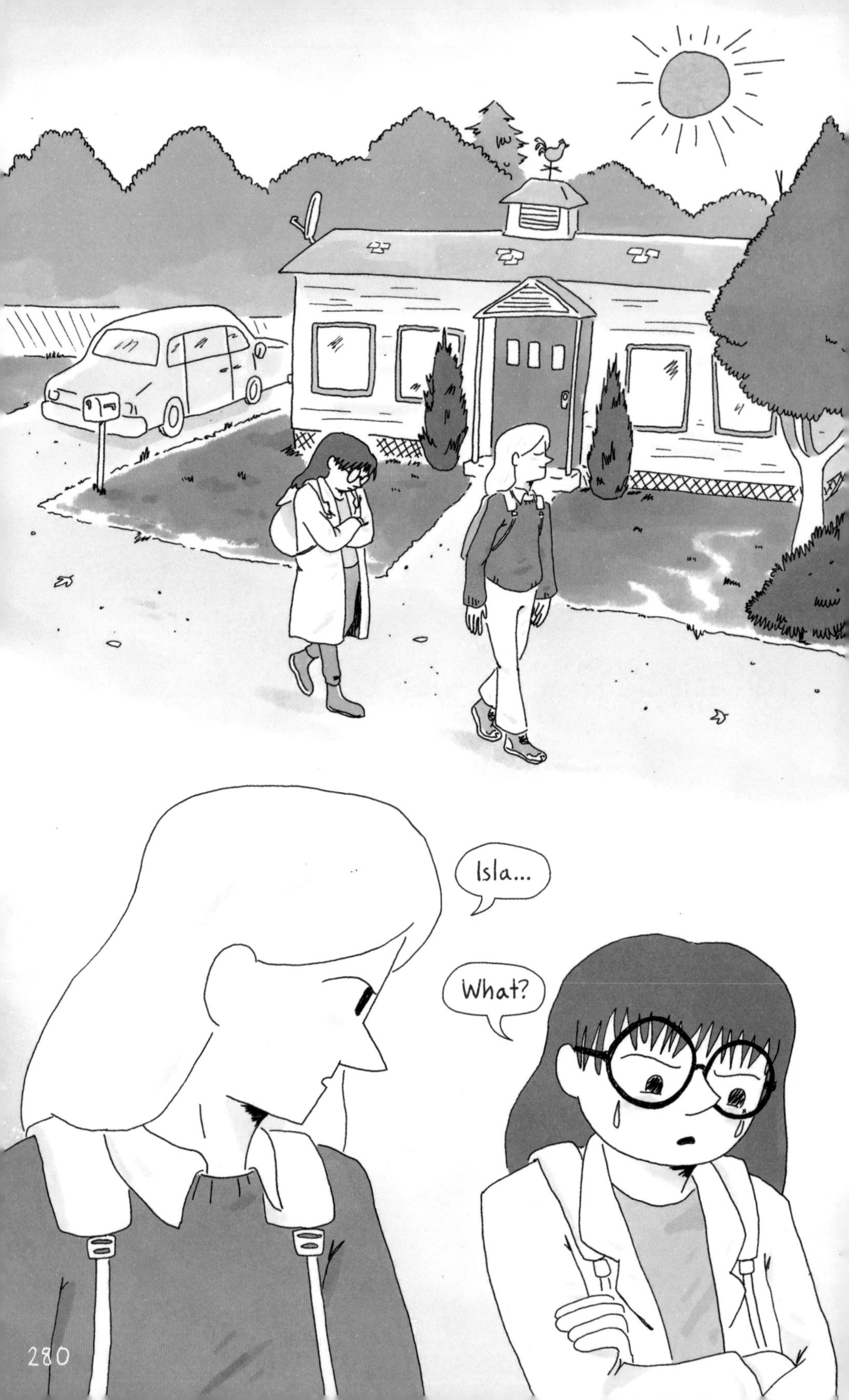
Isla...
What?

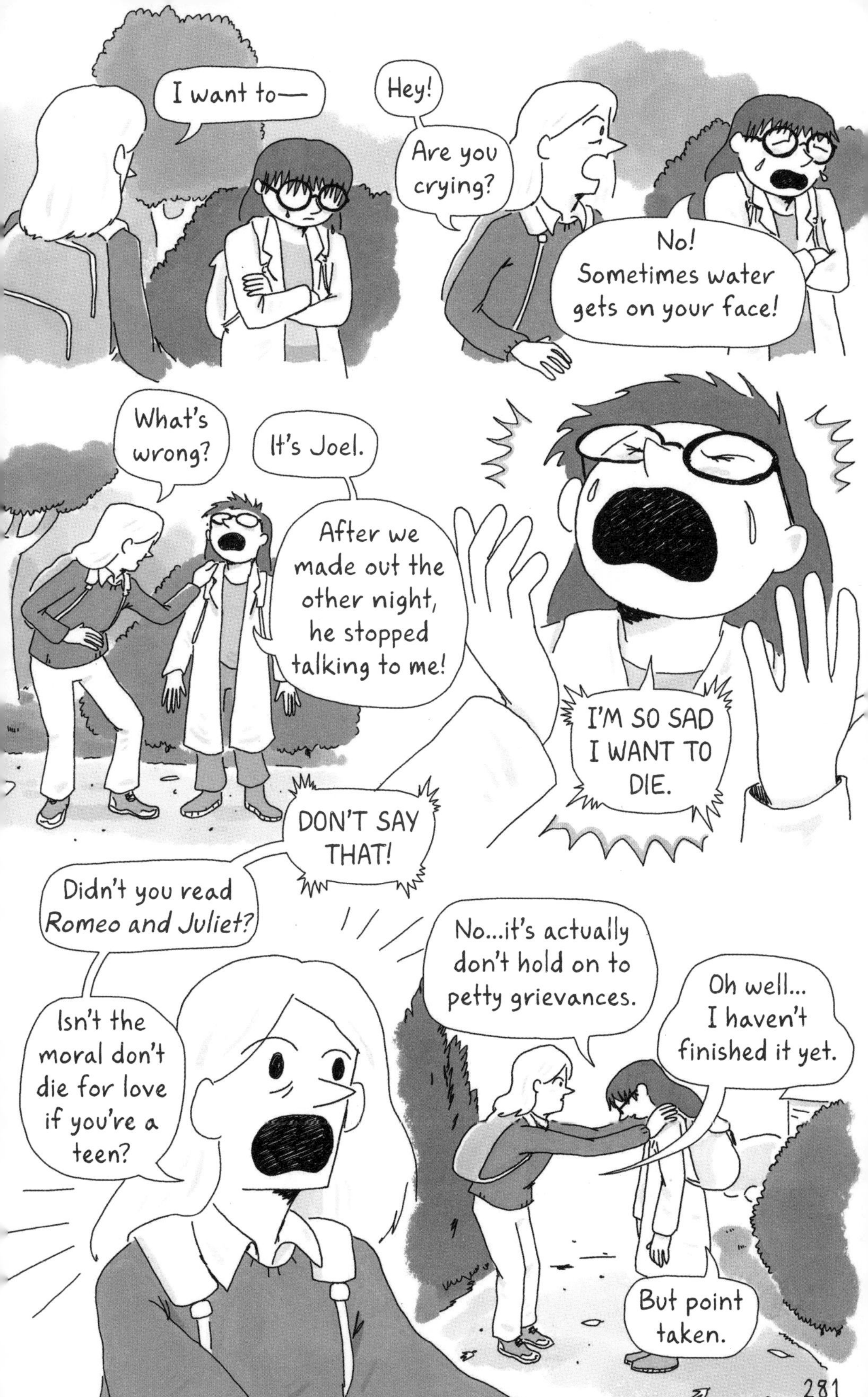
I want to—
Hey!
Are you crying?
No! Sometimes water gets on your face!
What's wrong?
It's Joel.
After we made out the other night, he stopped talking to me!
I'M SO SAD I WANT TO DIE.
DON'T SAY THAT!
Didn't you read *Romeo and Juliet*?
Isn't the moral don't die for love if you're a teen?
No...it's actually don't hold on to petty grievances.
Oh well... I haven't finished it yet.
But point taken.

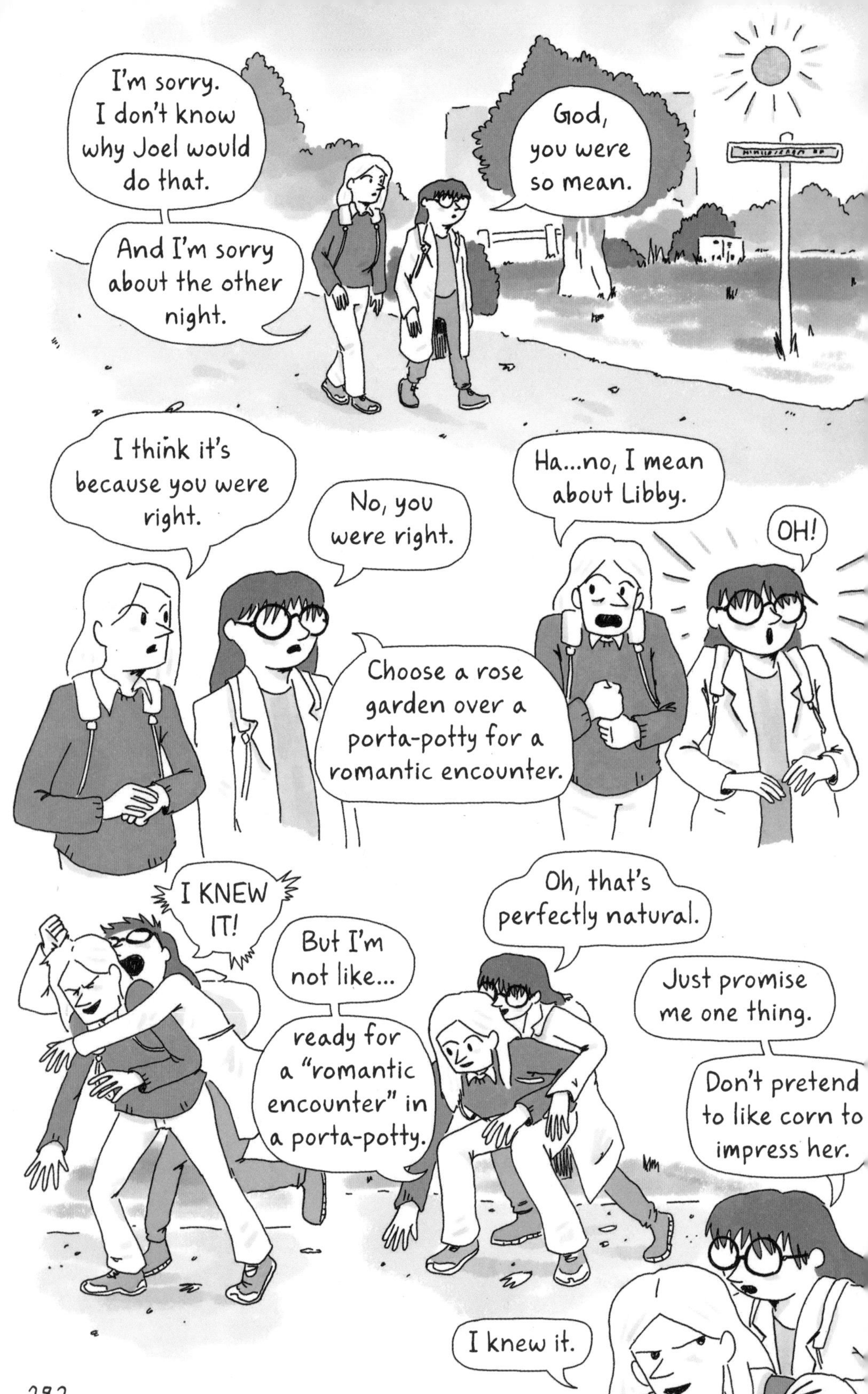
I'm sorry. I don't know why Joel would do that.
And I'm sorry about the other night.
God, you were so mean.
I think it's because you were right.
No, you were right.
Ha...no, I mean about Libby.
OH!
Choose a rose garden over a porta-potty for a romantic encounter.
I KNEW IT!
But I'm not like...
ready for a "romantic encounter" in a porta-potty.
Oh, that's perfectly natural.
Just promise me one thing.
Don't pretend to like corn to impress her.
I knew it.

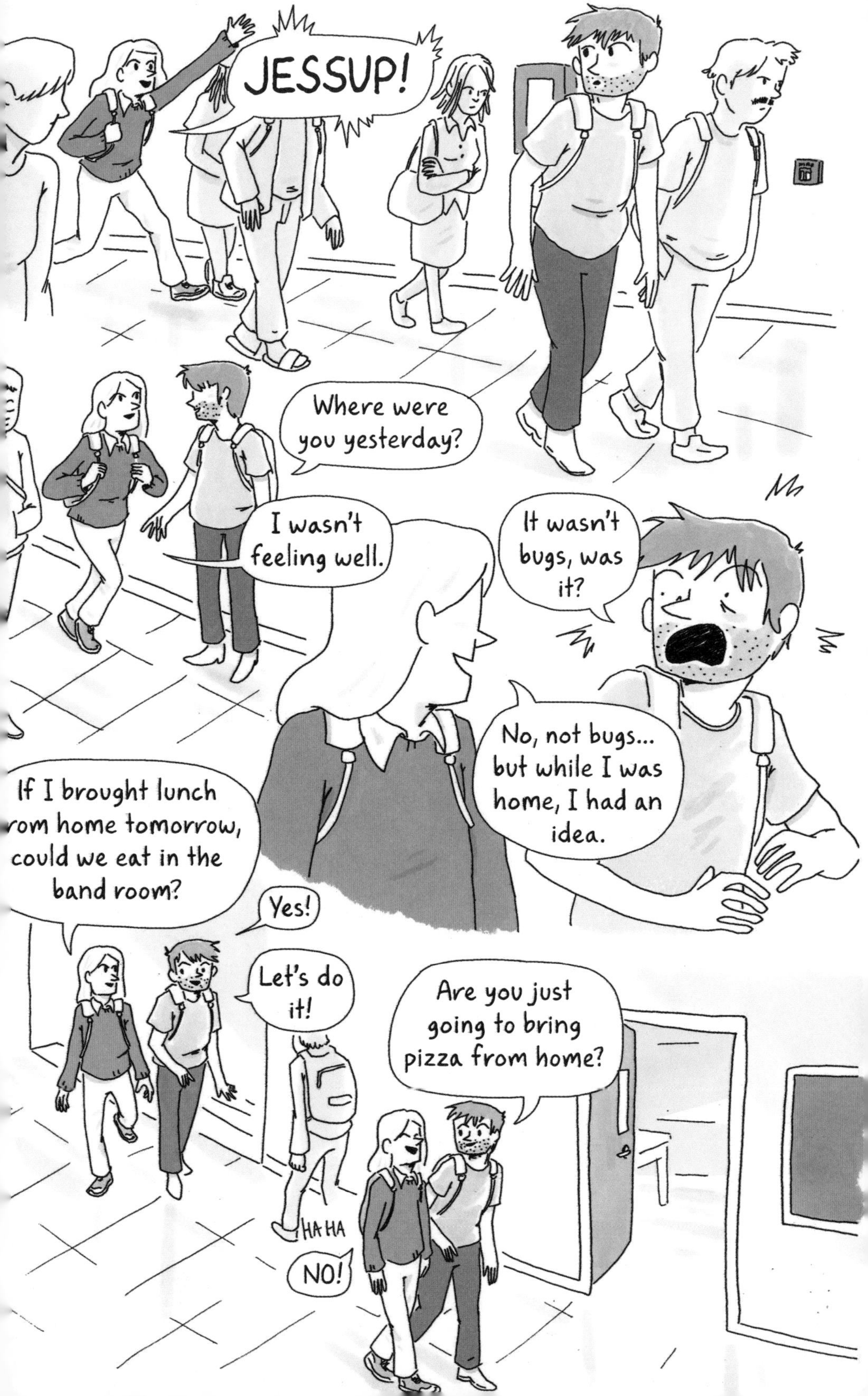
JESSUP!
Where were you yesterday?
I wasn't feeling well.
It wasn't bugs, was it?
No, not bugs... but while I was home, I had an idea.
If I brought lunch rom home tomorrow, could we eat in the band room?
Yes!
Let's do it!
Are you just going to bring pizza from home?
HA HA
NO!

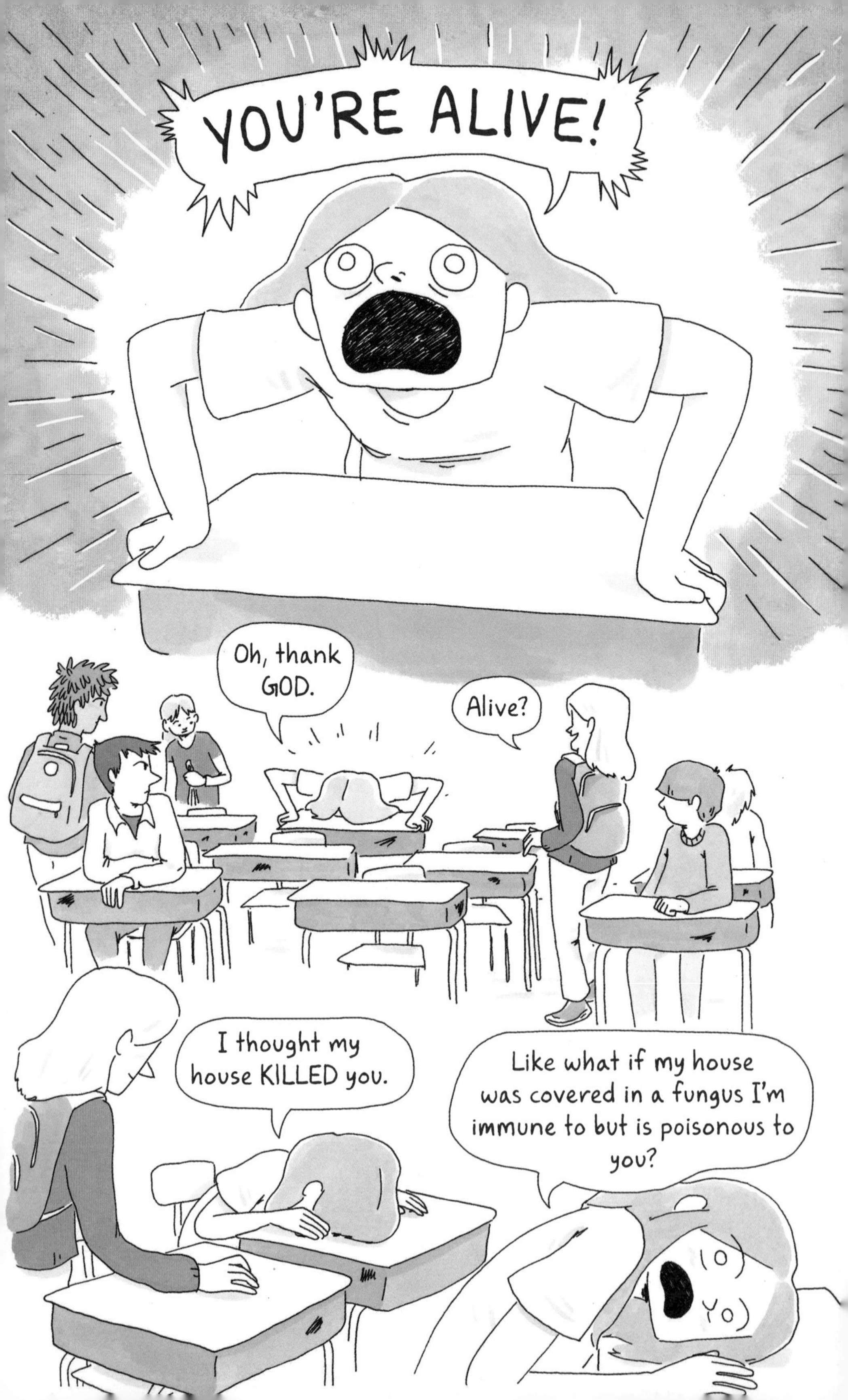
YOU'RE ALIVE!
Oh, thank GOD.
Alive?
I thought my house KILLED you.
Like what if my house was covered in a fungus I'm immune to but is poisonous to you?

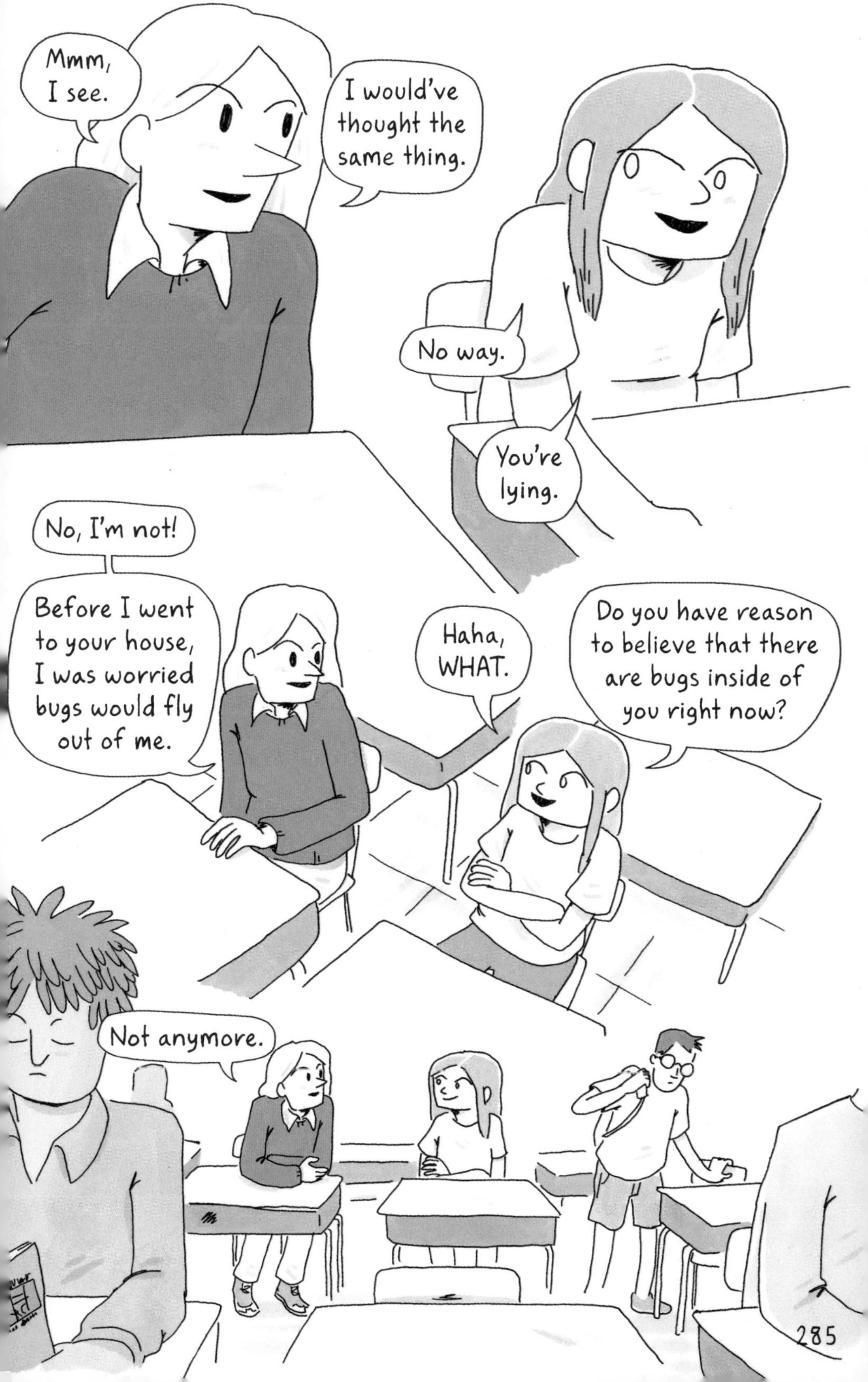
Mmm, I see.
I would've thought the same thing.
No way.
You're lying.
No, I'm not!
Before I went to your house, I was worried bugs would fly out of me.
Haha, WHAT.
Do you have reason to believe that there are bugs inside of you right now?
Not anymore.

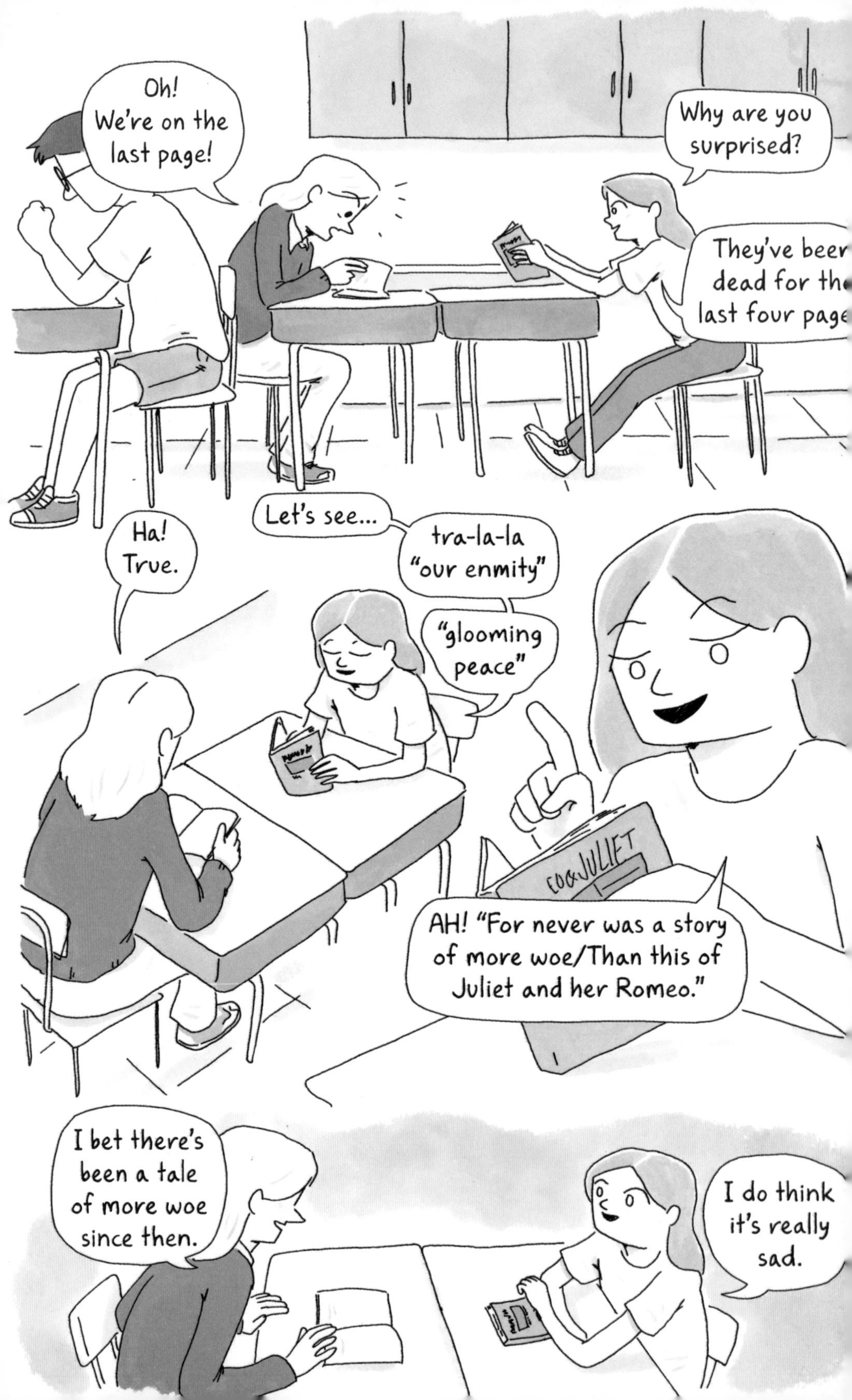
Oh! We're on the last page!
Why are you surprised?
They've bee dead for th last four page
Ha! True.
Let's see...
tra-la-la "our enmity"
"glooming peace"
AH! "For never was a story of more woe/Than this of Juliet and her Romeo."
I bet there's been a tale of more woe since then.
I do think it's really sad.

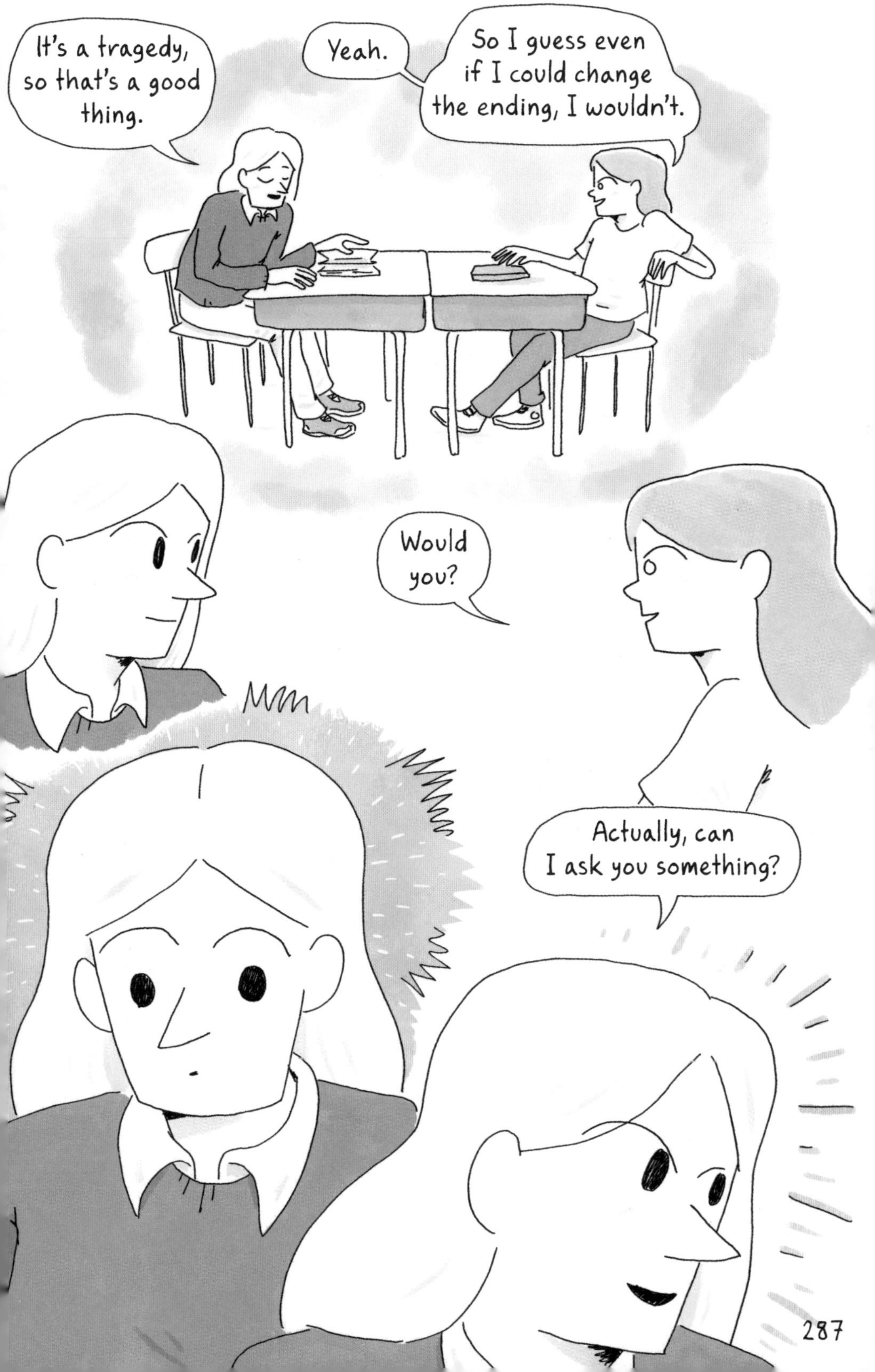
It's a tragedy, so that's a good thing.
Yeah.
So I guess even if I could change the ending, I wouldn't.
Would you?
MM
Actually, can I ask you something?

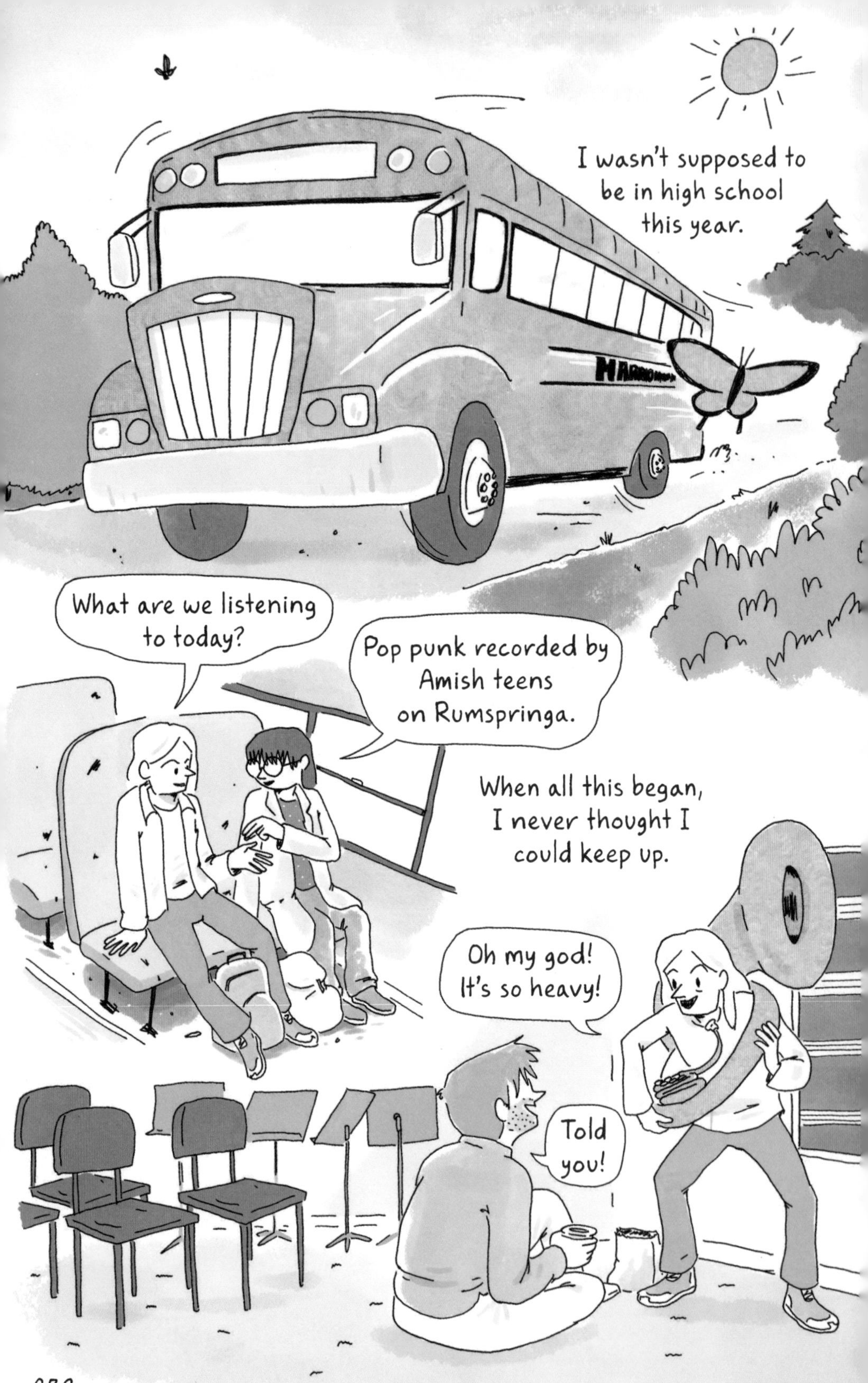

I wasn't supposed to be in high school this year.
What are we listening to today?
Pop punk recorded by Amish teens on Rumspringa.
When all this began, I never thought I could keep up.
Oh my god! It's so heavy!
Told you!

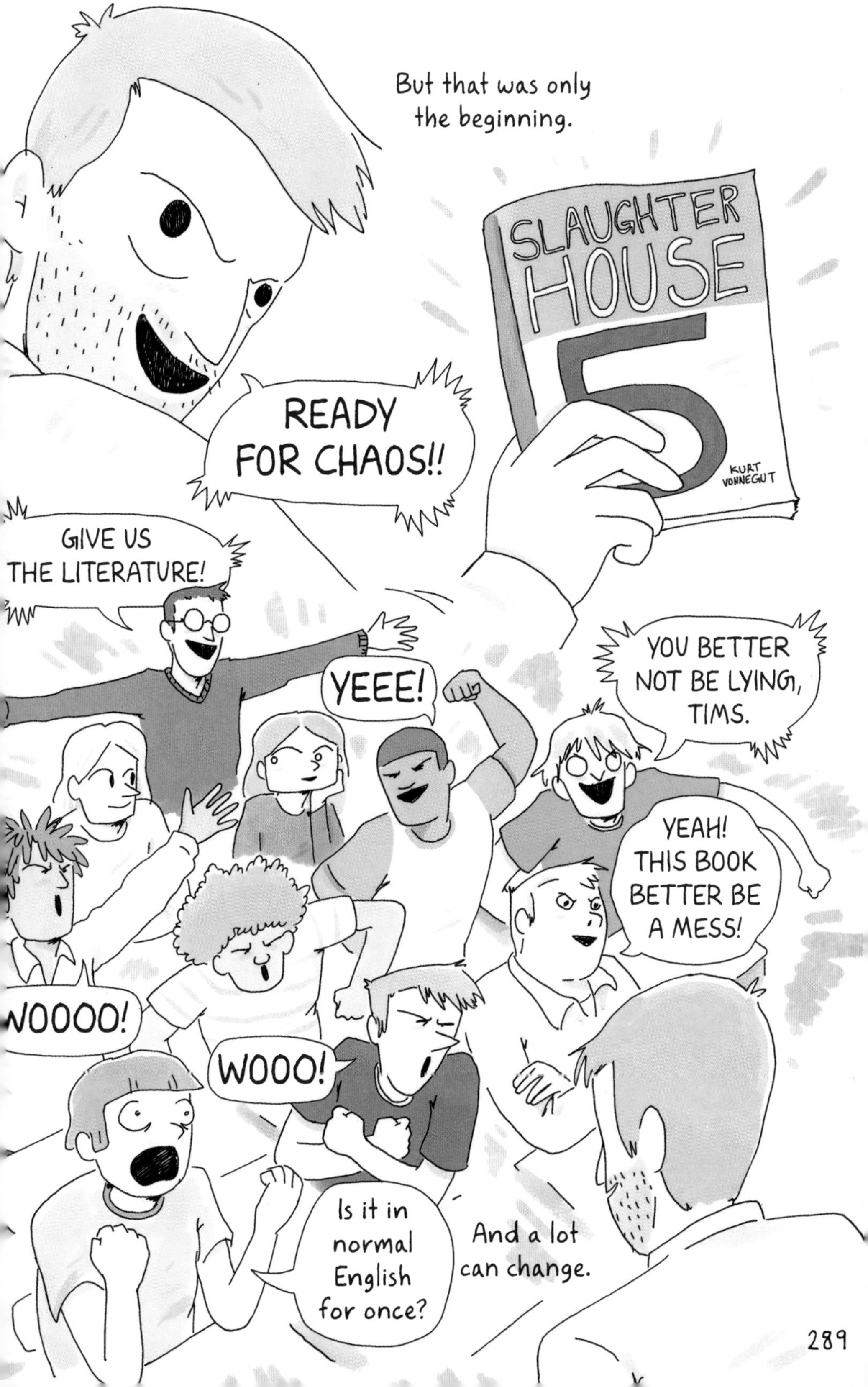

But that was only the beginning.
READY FOR CHAOS!!
SLAUGHTER HOUSE 5
KURT VONNEGUT
GIVE US THE LITERATURE!
YEEE!
YOU BETTER NOT BE LYING, TIMS.
YEAH! THIS BOOK BETTER BE A MESS!
WOOOO!
WOOO!
Is it in normal English for once?
And a lot can change.

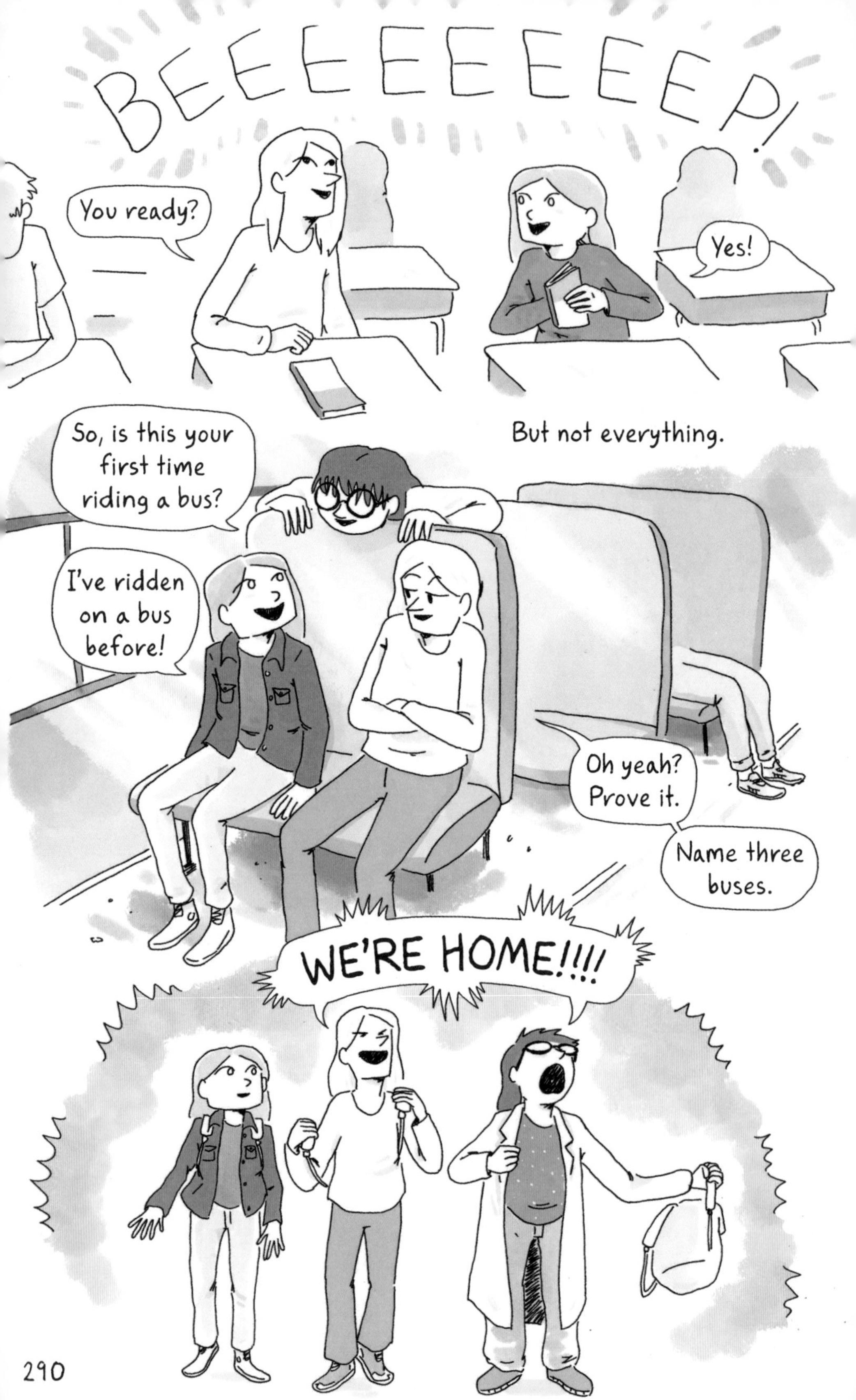
BEEEEEEEEEEP!
You ready?
Yes!
So, is this your first time riding a bus?
But not everything.
I've ridden on a bus before!
Oh yeah? Prove it.
Name three buses.
WE'RE HOME!!!!

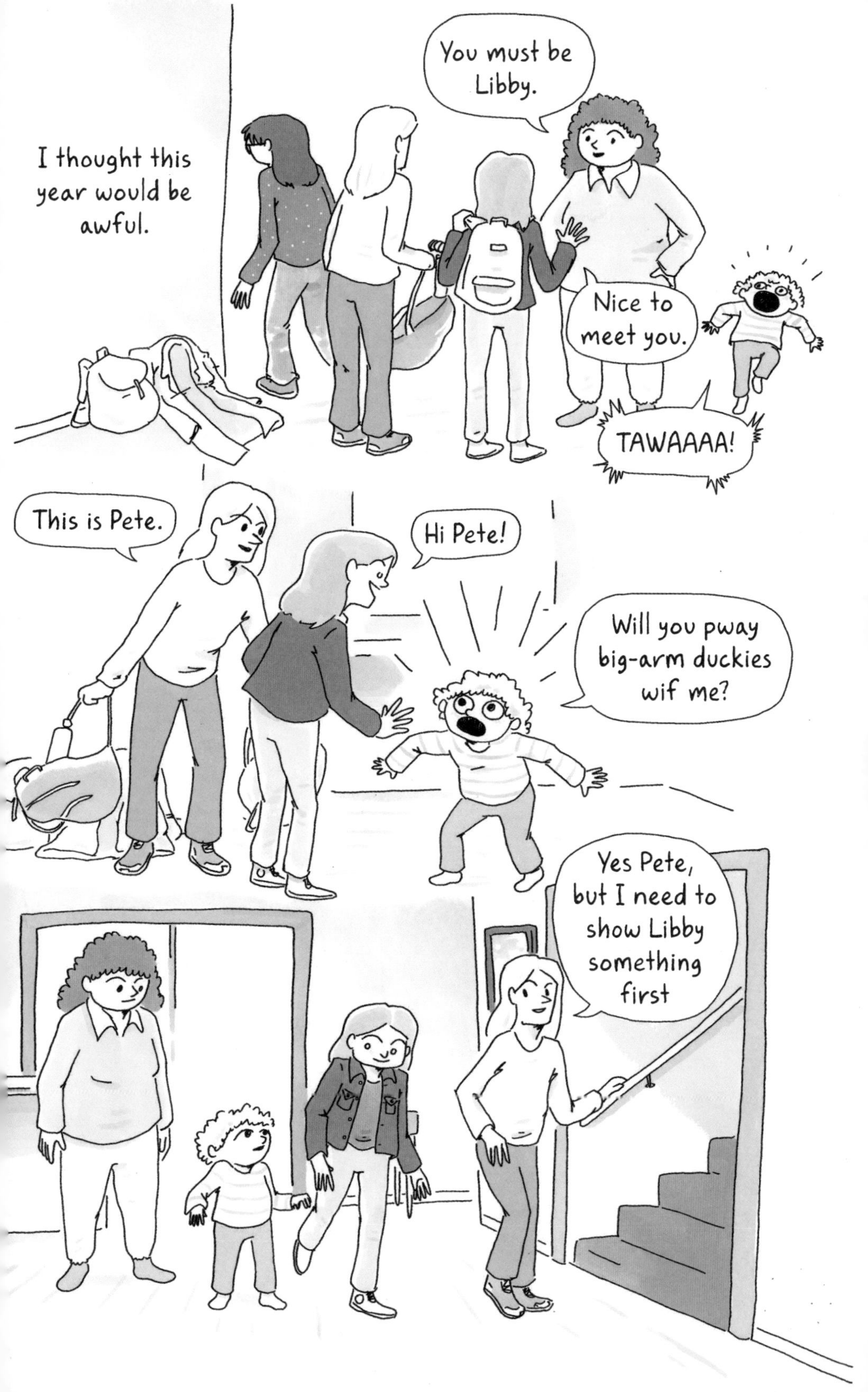
I thought this year would be awful.
You must be Libby.
Nice to meet you.
TAWAAAA!
This is Pete.
Hi Pete!
Will you pway big-arm duckies wif me?
Yes Pete, but I need to show Libby something first

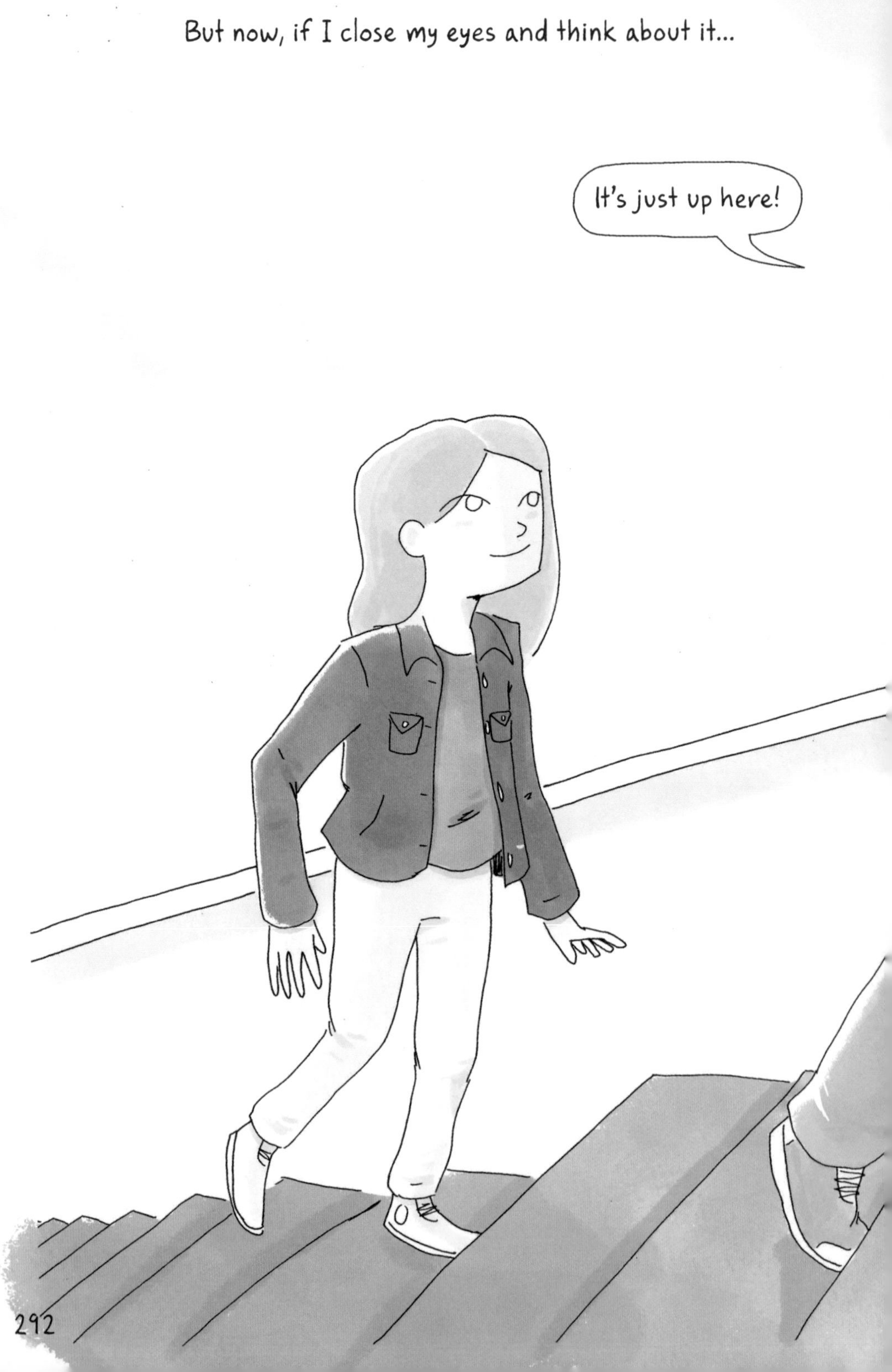
But now, if I close my eyes and think about it...
It's just up here!

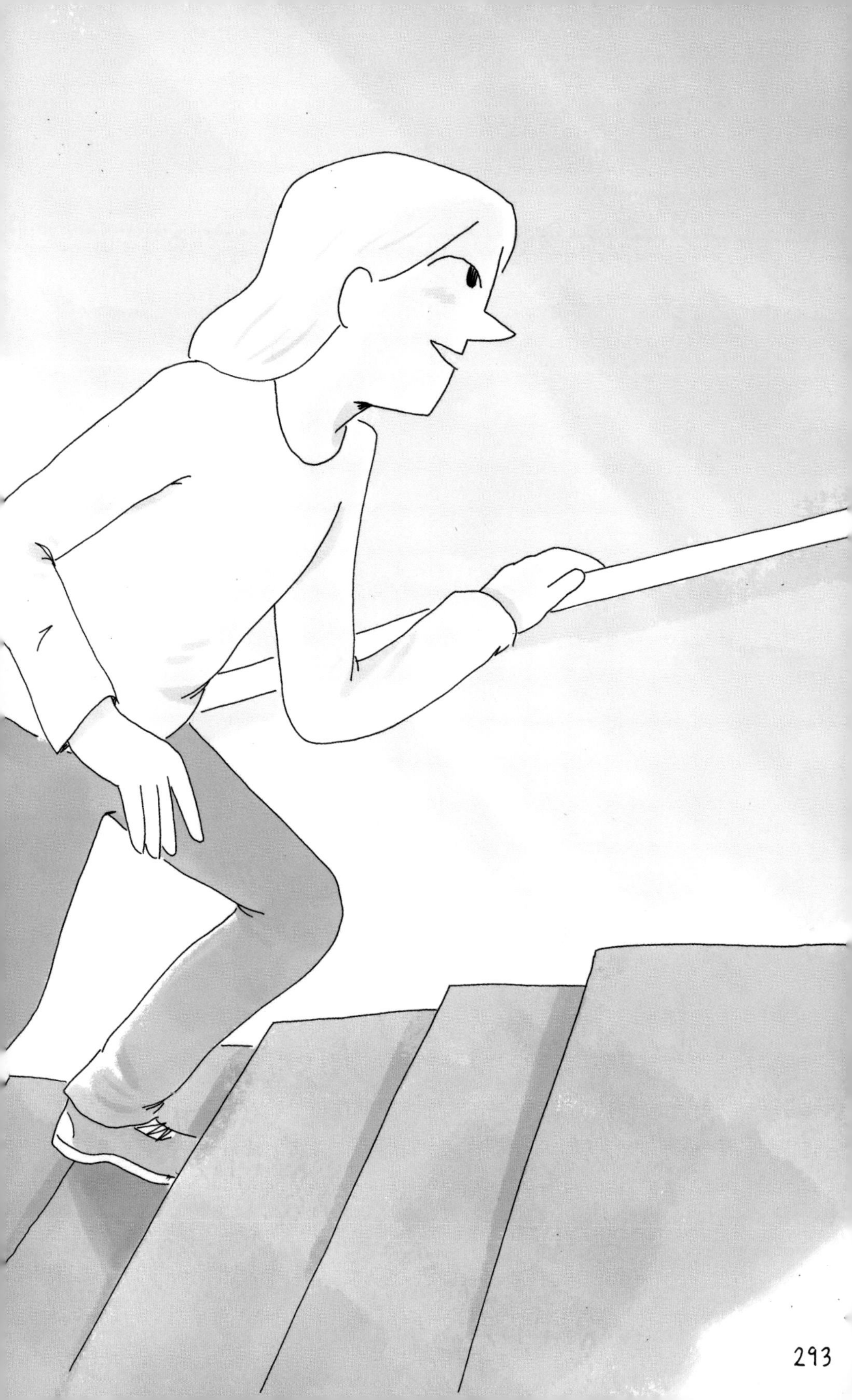

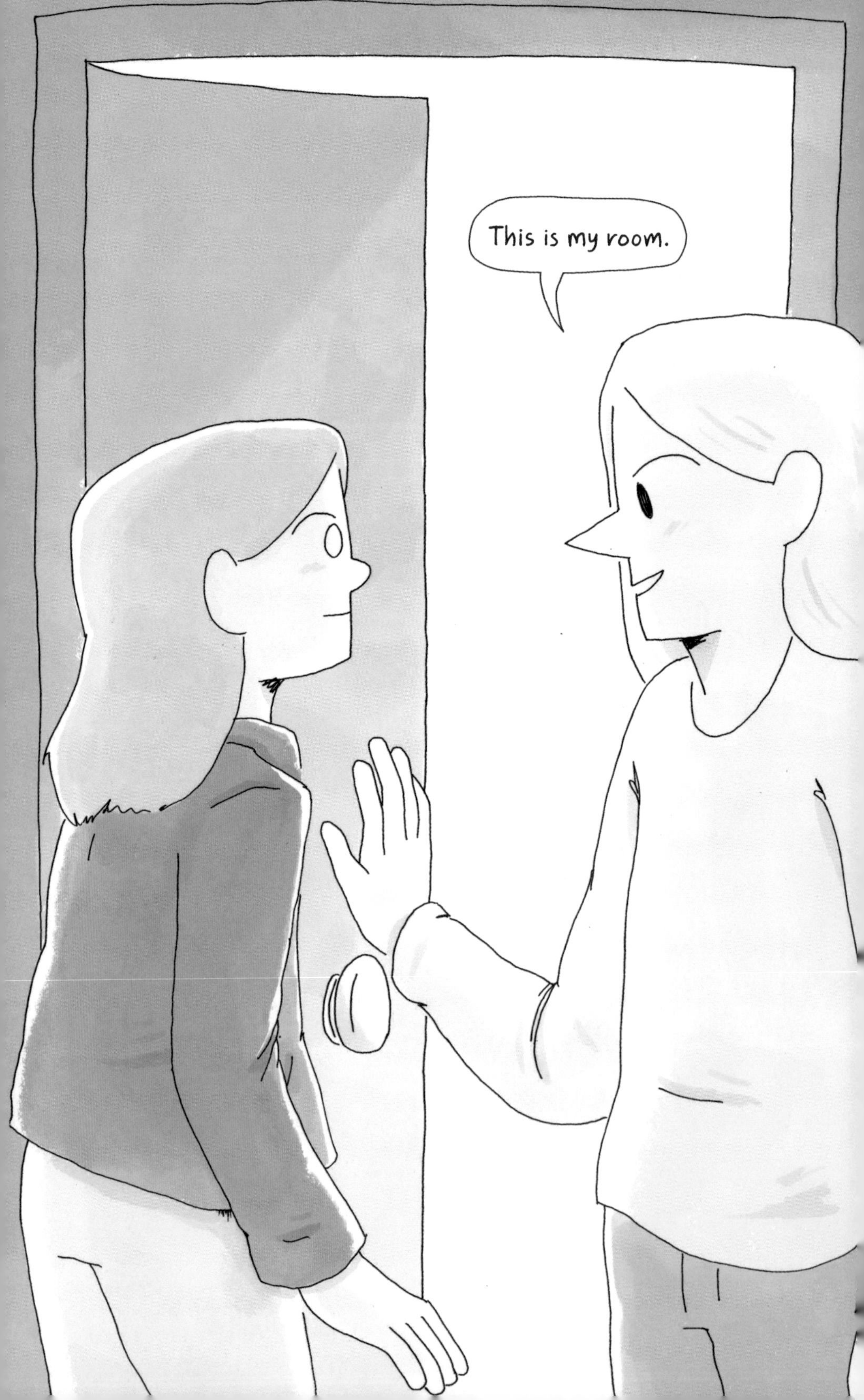
This is my room.

I can't imagine anything better.

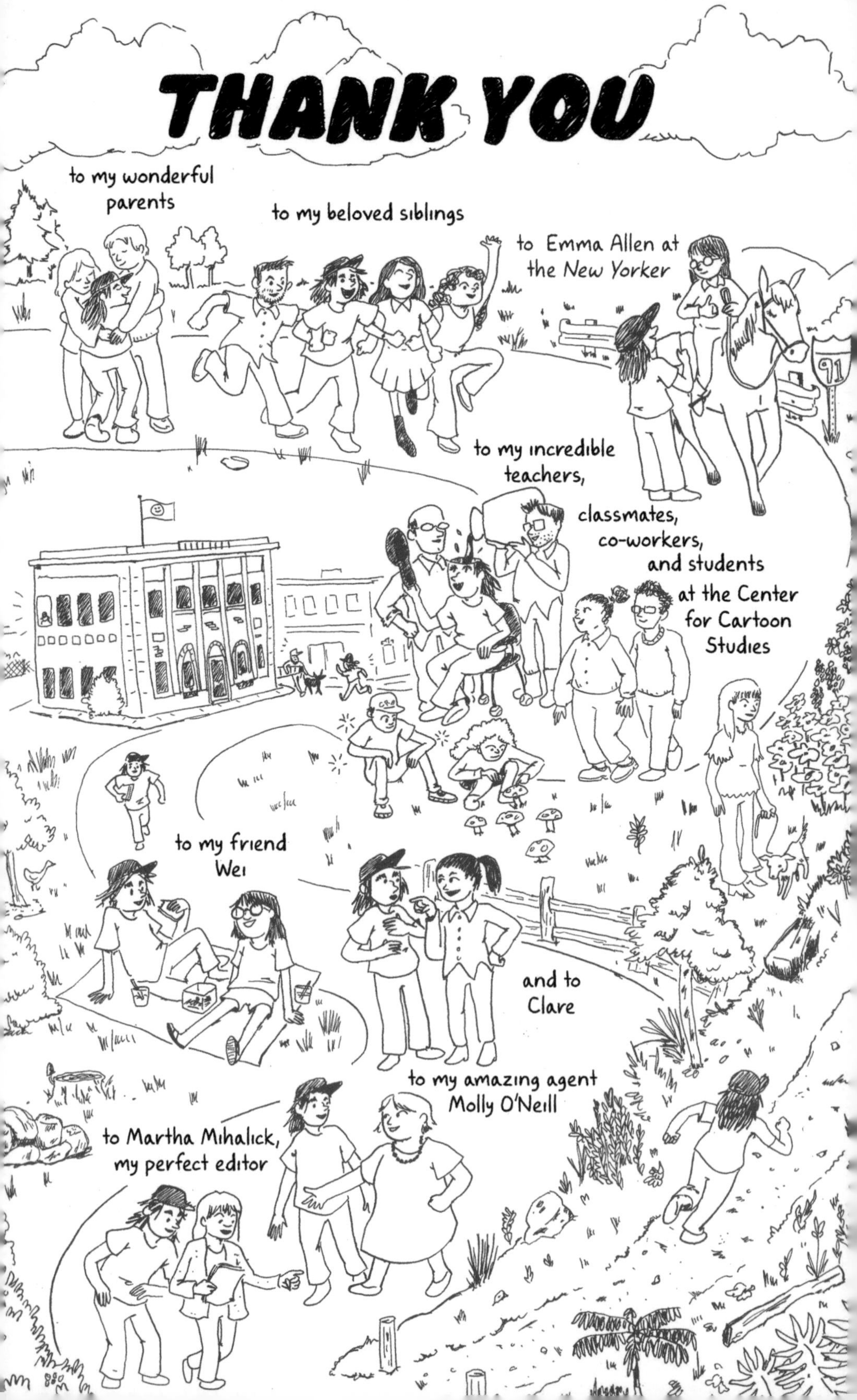

THANK YOU
to my wonderful parents
to my beloved siblings
to Emma Allen at the New Yorker
91
to my incredible teachers,
classmates, co-workers, and students
at the Center for Cartoon Studies
to my friend Wei
and to Clare
to my amazing agent Molly O'Neill
to Martha Mihalick, my perfect editor

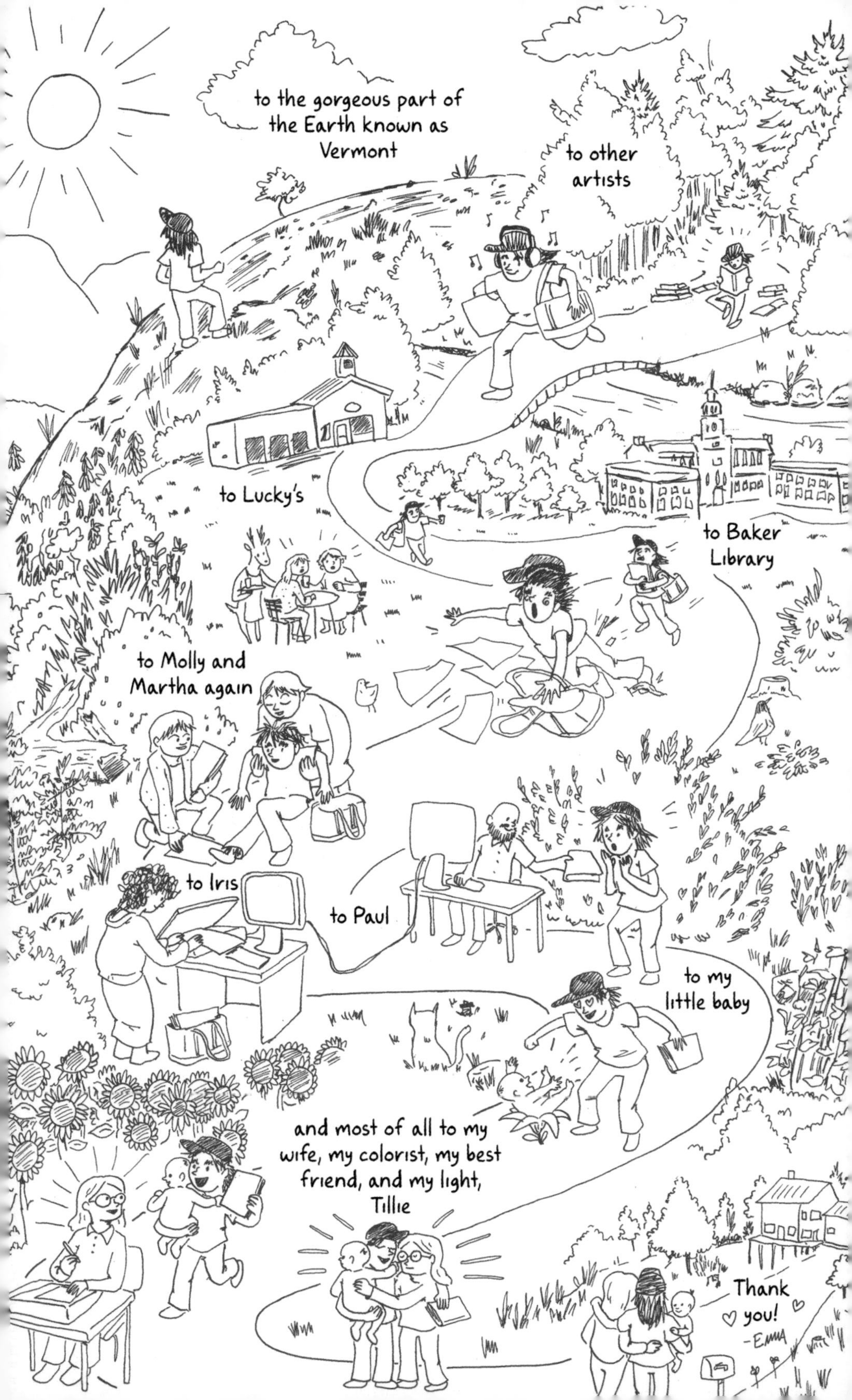
to the gorgeous part of the Earth known as Vermont
to other artists
to Lucky's
to Baker Library
to Molly and Martha again
to Iris
to Paul
to my little baby
and most of all to my wife, my colorist, my best friend, and my light, Tillie
Thank you!
-EMMA